DARK STARS

COMPLETE TRILOGY

A K DUBOFF

Published by Dawnrunner Press
Cover Copyright © 2020 A.K. Duboff

ISBN-10: 1954344155
ISBN-13: 978-1954344150

0 9 8 7 6 5 4 3 2

Produced in the United States of America

TABLE OF CONTENTS

CRYSTALLINE SPACE

DARK STARS: BOOK 1

1

FLIRTING WITH DEATH was the perfect way to spend an afternoon.

My slim shadow stretched behind me as I paced along the brink of the cliff, squinting into the setting sun.

Next to me, Adrianne prepared to leap. She grinned from her perch at the edge.

"Just jump already," I urged while securing my pink hair into a braid past my shoulders.

"Relax, Elle. I'm getting in the zone." She stretched her arms wide and leaned forward, surrendering to the wind.

I peeked over the lip as she plummeted toward the depths of the sandstone canyon.

Adrianne's gleeful cheer echoed through the chasm as she fell. She kicked off an outcropping, launching herself into a cartwheel through the air, which she transitioned into a somersault. Every movement was fluid, reaching and twisting in ways I'd never be able to achieve myself.

While I watched her aerial acrobatics, I gripped my left shoulder in my right hand with subconscious envy—my reminder that showing off sometimes came with a price.

"Reset!" I called out to our friend Jiro when Adrianne was almost to the canyon floor.

"Loading," he confirmed behind me.

The air electrified, tingling my skin and pulsing in my ears. White light crept into the corners of my vision, accompanied by an intensifying hum. With a flash, my vision went black.

For a moment, I floated in nothingness. Then, the physical world resolved around me once more. The blackness receded into sunlight and my feet were again solidly on the rocky ground.

I was now standing in the same position I'd been minutes before when I made the reset point at the access terminal. Suspended inside the monument was a two-meter-tall crystal that glowed with a swirling blue inner light.

It was one of four monuments in the vicinity of our community, each connected to a larger crystalline network woven throughout the planet and surrounding worlds. The remarkable properties of the crystals made our play possible.

Every time someone touched one of the crystals, it would record the precise physical state within its zone at that moment—including the kinesthetic abilities, clothing, and hair style of each person, along with the general environmental configuration. The access panel on the monument could then be used to reset the surrounding landscape and our physical forms into one of the previously recorded states with our cognition intact. Out in the remote canyon where it was just us, we could reset as many times as we wanted since the action was restricted to each crystal monument's specific zone.

Adrianne beamed, exhilarated by her recent fall that now only existed in memory. "I needed that."

I let my good arm drop to my side and stepped back from the terminal. "Showoff."

"Let's see your moves." She smirked.

Despite being an unfair competition, I took the bait. "Watch and learn."

"Be quick," Jiro instructed, sweeping aside a lock of dark hair that had fallen in front of his almond eyes. "We need to get back."

He was right; it was almost dinnertime. As much as I dreamed about ways to prolong our last summer of freedom, even resetting the physical world didn't alter the underlying flow of time, only the physical state within the crystal's zone.

"Last one for the night." I jogged to the edge of the cliff and peered into the familiar canyon. It was at least one hundred meters to the bottom, but the shadows made the depth difficult to gauge. I beckoned Adrianne over. "Spot me."

We had learned the hard way to reset before hitting the bottom. Since we retained all of our memories after each physical reset, the splat at the end kind of put a damper on the thrill of freefall.

"I'm watching," she assured me.

I took a deep breath and raised my arms—my left only making it forty-five degrees from my side due to the permanent effects of a childhood injury. Even though I couldn't put on an aerial show as well as Adrianne, I could still fly.

A gust of wind crested the canyon and I leaned forward.

"Wait!" Jiro shouted.

Adrianne yanked me back by my braid.

"What's wrong?" I asked, regaining my balance. No sooner had I spoken than I saw the reason for his concern.

The crystal that normally exuded pleasant blue light now contained a dark cloud.

Jiro took a step away from the monument. "What's wrong with it?"

Adrianne and I cautiously approached. As I neared, the cloud took on more definition, as though individual black particulates were floating inside the prism.

"I have no idea," I murmured.

Nothing had ever disrupted the crystal before. Its existence was a given—as much as the sun rising and having chores.

"We should go," Adrianne stated as she backed toward the path leading to our town.

"Maybe it needs to recharge or something," Jiro suggested, following her.

"Yeah," I agreed, though I didn't believe it, and followed my longtime friends away from the canyon.

"Should we tell someone?" Adrianne asked. "I've never seen anything like that in one of the crystals."

"That would require explaining why we were out here," Jiro pointed out.

"That's *definitely* not going to happen." There was no way my mother would approve of me repeatedly jumping off a cliff in the adjacent zone while she prepared dinner back home. Especially after what had happened six years ago, this was the last place I wanted her to know I hung out. What she didn't know wouldn't worry her.

"If we're going to keep this to ourselves, then we should monitor it," Adrianne said.

"We could come back to check on the crystal tonight," I proposed. "If it looks good, maybe we could get in a night jump."

Adrianne beamed. "I *do* enjoy falling under the stars."

"Well, it's not like I have anywhere to be first thing in the morning," Jiro said with a devious sparkle in his eyes.

"Sneaking out for a night jump… it's like we're fourteen again." I chuckled.

"Only now we're better at not getting caught." Adrianne winked at me.

I smiled back. "22:00?"

"Works for me," Jiro agreed.

Adrianne nodded. "You know I'm in."

We picked our way through a field of boulders along our standard path. The rough terrain would be difficult for the uninitiated to navigate, but vaulting over rocks and sidestepping sticker bushes was second-nature to me.

I kept my gaze straight ahead as we crossed the border from the canyon crystal's zone to the domain of the town's crystal, trying to ignore the rock formation that had changed my life when I was twelve. My fall from the four-meter-tall boulder in the town's zone had dislocated my shoulder and broken my arm—a seemingly minor injury at first—but deeper tissue damage that knitted into scar tissue forever impaired my arm's mobility. By the time the doctors realized what had happened, it was too late to repair and the window for a town reset had long since passed.

As I'd come to grips with the injury and what it might mean for my future, I'd often fantasized about a universal-scale reset that wasn't limited by the rules governing our town. If everything everywhere could be reset, I could go back to how I was before the accident, just like everyone else would get a second chance. We could make things how they should be. Of course, that was impossible; one girl's minor injury wasn't worth disrupting our community, let alone the dozens of planets in the Hegemony's purview.

My mom always told me what was in the past was done; the only way was forward. I'd heard it so many times that part of me believed it, but deep down there was still lingering bitterness. Thanks to that one stupid mistake as a kid, I feared I'd never be able to have the kind of future I'd dreamed about in the space force.

I suppressed the resentment welling in my chest. There was nothing I could do about it now.

Eventually, the trail became more defined, and we broke into a light jog. The sun was low in the sky by the time we reached pavement. I might be late for dinner, but not terribly.

The final path segment traced the upper ridge of the hills surrounding our town, Ochre. Stucco homes topped with solar panels were situated along meandering streets in the southern portion of the valley, and the administrative, commercial, and educational buildings occupied the north. A social square at the center of town was landscaped with mature trees, their sturdy branches distinct even from my distant vantage. The main crystal for our town at the center of the square cast a faint blue glow through the trees' shadows.

My family's house was toward the southeastern edge of town, so I'd made a shortcut trail down one of the slopes to facilitate easier access to the surrounding hills. "I'll see you tonight!" I called to Adrianne and Jiro as I dashed down my personal corridor toward home.

When I reached the bottom of the hill, I took a moment to dust myself off and smooth my hair. No need to call attention to the fact that I'd been running through bushes rather than focusing on preparations for my future.

I walked the rest of the way to the back entrance of my house. Light shone through the rear kitchen window, illuminating my path along the pavers bisecting my father's vegetable garden in the backyard.

The welcoming sight erased my apprehension about the strange cloud in the canyon crystal, but I tensed with the knowledge that these homeward treks were now numbered. Without the adrenaline rush of a good cliff jump to clear my mind, my impending departure for the vocational academy crept into my thoughts. In a few weeks, playing in the canyon with my friends would be a distant memory. No more resets for fun—only the pressure of trying to get it right the first time.

Heart heavy, I opened the back door and braced for a berating about my tardy arrival.

"There you are!" my mother exclaimed from the kitchen when the screen door to the mud room clicked shut.

Scents of apple pie and steamed potatoes wafted toward me as I slipped off my shoes. "Sorry I'm late!"

I padded into the kitchen, my stomach letting out a low growl. Seated at the wooden table in the center of the room, my younger brother, Ben, was absorbed in a puzzle game on his tablet. At the counter along the back wall overlooking the garden, my mother was in the process of spooning freshly whipped potatoes into a blue serving bowl.

With the hope of stealing a taste, I headed for the counter, ruffling Ben's blond mop of hair as I passed by.

He batted away my hand with more force than normal; I guess at fourteen he was getting a little old for me to mess with him. "Mom said it's your turn to take out the trash," he mumbled without shifting his gaze from his tablet.

"The fish from last night is… lingering," my mother said, wrinkling her petite nose beneath evergreen eyes like my own.

"I'm on it." I pivoted on my heel and went back to the receptacle in the mud room.

As soon as the lid was cracked open, I understood the urgency of the request. Holding my breath, I slipped out the bag while jamming my feet back into my shoes, then sprinted around the side of the house to deposit the garbage into the central collector. When the bin was safely re-sealed, I took a deep breath. "I won't miss this—"

The chime in the town square pierced the quiet evening.

My pulse spiked as I ran back inside. "There isn't a town meeting tonight, is there?" I asked the moment I was through the kitchen door, shoes still on.

Ben had set down his tablet, and my father now stood in the archway between the kitchen and living room with his own tablet in hand. The worried glances passing between my parents confirmed my suspicion that the alarm wasn't for a scheduled event.

"Dinner can wait," my mother stated, wiping her hands on a dish towel. "Let's go."

"Any changes to log?" my father asked as the four of us headed through the living room toward the front door.

I shook my head since I hadn't made any purchases in the last three days that had yet to be recorded in the Hegemony's central database.

Ben groaned. "My game is new. Lemme back it up real quick." He darted back into the kitchen to his tablet.

The lines of worry on my father's forehead deepened as we waited. Unscheduled meetings were a rarity, and they almost never brought good news.

However, I tried to remain positive. After all, if something terrible had happened, we could fall back on the town's archive in the event of an accident more serious than a broken arm. Any inanimate objects would reset, too, so long as the raw materials were still within the crystal's zone and the object had been inside the zone during the previous check-in. Occasionally, handmade trinkets may be lost in our local resets, but it was worth the wellbeing of our town's inhabitants—especially since digital content was always secure on the Hegemony's offworld servers.

When Ben was finished backing up his game, we stepped out into the street along with the dozen other families on our block. The group of us hurried past the row of stucco houses as we headed toward the central square.

"Have you heard anything about the meeting?" my father asked one of our neighbors.

"No," he replied. "Interrupting dinner like this—must be important."

As we merged onto the main street into the heart of town, I kept an eye out for Adrianne and Jiro. In the back of my mind, I couldn't help but wonder if the unscheduled meeting had anything to do with the dark cloud we'd witnessed up in the canyon crystal.

My mother's hand brushed my back. "There's no need to be nervous."

"I'm not." But part of me *was* concerned. I could only remember three unscheduled meetings in my eighteen years of life; something must be seriously wrong.

"Not just about tonight," my mother continued in the tone she slipped into when she was channeling her day job as a therapist. "I've seen you reading over the course offerings at the Academy. You'll find something that's a good fit."

I stared down at my feet as I walked. "It all seems so…"

"Boring?" she completed for me.

"I was going to say 'mundane', but yeah."

She smiled and squeezed my right shoulder. "Knowing you, you'll find a way to make it interesting."

Maybe she was right, but nothing in the course catalog had piqued my interest in the slightest. The only path that sounded remotely appealing was becoming a Ranger in the Hegemony's space force, but I wasn't ready to tell my parents I was interested in applying to Tactical School. Even though I knew the Rangers would probably reject me because of my bum shoulder, I couldn't help dreaming about it. But, I needed to be realistic. And have options. To satisfy my parents and keep multiple paths open, I figured I'd try the vocational academy for one semester and then take it from there.

We arrived at the town square and found that most of Ochre's two thousand other residents had already congregated in the open plaza facing the crystal and its surrounding access terminal. Members of the crowd were shifting on their feet, eyes darting. Parents clutched their children tightly as urgent conversations buzzed throughout the square, speculating about the reason for the alarm.

The atmosphere was a stark contrast to our standard weekly assemblies, a special service where we would watch Mayor Therman touch the crystal to initiate a backup record for our community. Though he performed the task every day, watching the task was a weekly tradition; it gave us assurance that there was always a backup, specifically to ease our minds in situations such as this.

However, assurances only went so far.

"Dad, what's going on?" Ben asked with a quaver in his voice.

"Here's Mayor Therman," my father replied, his gaze fixed on the platform surrounding the crystal. "I'm sure he'll explain everything."

The elderly mayor approached the railing at the edge of the platform a meter above the paved square. He held up a frail hand, and the din of conversation faded to silence. "Thank you all for coming so quickly. We received a message from the Capital this evening about reports from the outer colonies related to a crystalline network malfunction."

Conversations reignited in the crowd, overpowering the mayor's raspy voice.

"Quiet, please!" the city manager, Dilon, cut in. He held up his hands and waited for the townspeople to settle.

"As a precaution," the mayor continued, "the Hegemony has issued an order for us to perform a global reset. We will go back one month."

My parents each placed a reassuring hand on Ben's and my shoulders.

Local resets were common enough, but I'd only ever experienced one coordinated planet-scale reset before, when a transport shuttle exploded in a freak accident several years prior. We'd gone back three days to the previous check-in point that time. To go a whole month meant that something major must be going on.

"Just so long as I don't have to retake my final exams," I muttered in an attempt to break the tension.

"I'm sure the records have already been sent to the Academy, don't worry," my mother replied, missing my intended humor.

"Man, that's going to be a pain to reset all of the clocks," Ben added.

I wasn't sure if it was his own attempt at levity or genuine annoyance. Keeping track of *when* we were was always a challenge with any reset, by virtue of it being a rollback to a previous physical state rather than actual time travel. Anything outside the reset zone stayed the same, so we relied on the master clocks in the Capital for us to resync with the rest of society. We always made the town reset points for the same time of day to minimize confusion, but I couldn't remember where I may have been a month ago at the time of the reset point they intended to use.

Regardless of the logistic headache surrounding the reset, my chest tightened as I thought about why the order was given in the first place. I feared the reset must have to do with the darkness in the canyon crystal—it was too big of a coincidence. That meant it was on other worlds, too.

With a renewed wave of alarm, I realized that I had touched the infected crystal moments before the darkness appeared. "Dad, I should have said something sooner, but—"

"Resetting," the mayor announced as he reached for the access terminal.

Before I could finish my warning, an electrical charge surged through the air and my ears buzzed. The world distorted around me into white light. Everything vanished into nothingness.

I floated in the darkness, drifting with no sense of self. I waited. And waited.

The reset was taking far too long—reality should be reforming by now. My consciousness wanted to panic, but I had no corporeal form to react.

Then, a physical world finally began to solidify at the edges of my vision. Except rather than the town square, I appeared to be in some sort of glass enclosure too brightly lit for me to see beyond its boundaries.

My eyes struggled to adjust to the dazzling light above me. A dark-haired man in a black uniform came into focus on the other side of the glass half a meter from my face.

"Are you a boy or a girl?" he asked me.

I blinked with confusion. At least, I think I blinked. Somehow I still didn't feel fully connected to myself. "A girl…" I said.

"What is your name?"

"Elle," I replied, more certain in my response this time. "Elle Hartmut."

A warm tingle ran through my limbs. As it passed, I was left with a renewed sense of my physical form.

Before I could look around to get my bearings, the man activated a holographic projection in front of me, depicting a sword, a shield, and a wand with a star on the end. "What is your strength?" he asked.

I evaluated the symbols. Was it a test?

The shield called to me initially, given my defensive attitude toward the whole situation. However, the wand was a much more alluring choice, almost certainly indicating magic. I was about to respond with that selection, but I caught myself. I'd always wanted to be strong—to regain the physical prowess I'd lost when I was injured. "The sword," I stated.

"Are you sure?" the man asked.

"Yes." Another tingling wave passed through my limbs and torso. My senses sharpened and I felt physically charged, ready to push myself to my limits.

"You are a fighter. Use your strength well," the man stated as he stepped back. The front half of the glass cylinder, which had a frosted band in the middle, swung open. "You're lucky you survived."

"What do you mean?" I stepped out of the chamber, unsteady on my feet. Looking down at myself, I realized I was wearing a white, form-fitting jumpsuit that was nothing like anything in my wardrobe. My pulse spiked. "Where am I? Where's my family?"

The middle-aged man strode across the sterile room to the side wall and touched a panel. With a mechanical whir, a section of the wall rolled down behind the smooth interior surface.

My breath caught as I stared out the newly exposed viewport. A planet—*my* planet—loomed before me, luminescent blue and brown set against a starscape. Dark tendrils were snaking through the atmosphere.

Panic constricted my chest. "What's going on?"

"Elle, I'm Commander Alastair Colren and you are aboard the *Evangiel*," he replied. "I represent the Hegemony. We have a mission for you."

"HUH?" I WANTED to say something more articulate, but that was the best I had at the moment.

"Forgive me, this all must come as quite a shock." Commander Colren took a seat at a metal table near the viewport. He gestured to an acrylic chair across from him.

"You could say that." Dumbfounded, I stumbled toward the empty seat. I couldn't stop staring out the viewport at my home planet of Erusan. Was I really in space? I'd seen images and tried to imagine the view from a spaceship, but this... It didn't seem possible.

I took a shaky breath. "How did I get here?"

"I'll explain everything, don't worry," Colren replied.

"None of this makes any sense. What do you mean you have a mission for me? I'm no one."

Colren examined me with his piercing hazel eyes. "Had you recently come into contact with a crystal that exhibited a dark cloud?"

I struggled to think back to the events from a few hours before. "Yeah, I was hanging out with my friends outside of town, doing localized resets. We were just about to do another reset when we noticed it."

"In that moment, you were... altered," he explained.

I gaped at him. "What? How?"

"It's something like an immunity. You had a brief touch with the Darkness during the reset just prior, so when you encountered it again during the global reset, you were prepared to hang onto your sense of self."

My heart sank. "What about my friends? They touched the infected crystal, too."

"Unfortunately, we can only perform the extraction on one person at a time. You were the fortunate one," Colren replied.

"What about my family? My world?" Fear and worry clouded my mind. My parents, my brother, everyone who meant anything to me was still down there. They couldn't be gone.

The commander took a slow breath. "The world is suspended and its records are preserved in the Master Archive."

"Suspended? What in the stars does *that* mean?"

"It's a way of locking the records so they don't become corrupted. It's the best we can do once the Darkness infects a planet," he continued. "But you can help us do more."

I barked a nervous laugh. "Yeah. Right!" Either the last reset had messed with my head, or the man across from me was insane. I was leaning toward the former option; people didn't randomly wake up on spaceships. I had to be dreaming.

"Elle, I know this might seem like an elaborate prank, but I assure you it's not. You're special and we need you." The commander looked me square in the eyes—dead serious, as far as I could tell.

I inched back in my chair. "Whatever you think I am, I'm not. I can't help you." The Hegemony needed scientists or heroic soldiers. Not me. As much as I aspired to be a Ranger, I knew it wouldn't happen. I was physically broken—and I certainly wasn't a genius.

The commander folded his hands on the table. "You're *exactly* who we need."

"I'm a kid."

He nodded. "The young do seem to be the most drawn during the extraction; there's a fearlessness in youth. I'd never discount someone because of age alone."

I still didn't believe any of it was real, but he certainly did. I figured if I heard him out, maybe that would end the insanity; all I wanted was to go back home and finish my summer vacation. I crossed my arms and leaned back in my seat, studying his expression for any tells that might reveal his true intentions. "What is it you want me to do?"

"We are assembling a team of others that have been extracted like you. Together, we hope that you'll be able to help us track down the cause for the spreading Darkness, and stop it. With your immunity, you'll be able to go places others can't."

Articulate speech failed me again. Me, stop the Darkness? Now he was *really* talking crazy. I laughed and shook my head with disbelief.

"It first appeared three months ago," Colren continued, undeterred. "Initially, we thought it was an isolated anomaly, but when it started to spread, we had to take action. We developed the extraction procedure to give us a means to fight back."

I wanted to dismiss his statements, but I was struck by the gravity of his tone. Maybe this wasn't a nightmare after all. If I really was on a Hegemony spaceship, and if my world was now uninhabitable, as he indicated, I had no idea where I could go.

My heart pounded in my chest. "I still don't understand how I got here. It doesn't seem possible."

"We have certain technology that's not exactly public knowledge," the commander replied. "Frankly, we don't know how it works, but it does."

I raised an eyebrow. "Magic?"

He chuckled. "You joke, but it may as well be."

Crazy or not, the thought of legitimate magic use caught my attention. I leaned forward with my elbows on the table. "What was that test you gave me when I first woke up?"

"The extraction procedure is for consciousness, but your physical manifestation is more fluid based on fragmented data stored in the crystalline network. Those questions were to bring your new body into focus and solidify your innate traits."

It was then that I noticed the long hair hanging down around my shoulders—not the faded pink dye job from minutes before on my homeworld, but bright fuchsia. And it didn't look like dye. "What the—?" I nearly leaped out of my chair.

As I tensed, I noticed that my left shoulder didn't feel tight in the way I was used to. I rolled it and then raised my arm, finding that I had full range of motion.

"Stars, I—" My chest constricted.

"This is you," Colren said. "The real you that you wanted to be."

"How did you…?"

Colren smiled with compassion. "Think of it like this: pretend your mind is like a digital file that we would back up on one of the central servers. The original computer used to create that file became corrupted. That file has now been downloaded into a new, better computer that was optimized to run that file. Likewise, your new body was bioprinted in that chamber to fit the ideals contained within your consciousness—built to your own specifications."

It still sounded like madness. I ran my fingers through the soft, fuchsia strands. "I guess I did have a few changes in mind."

"Whoever you were before, you still are. Now, you're just a different version of yourself."

I could barely breathe. Losing my world, my family, my friends. But gaining a whole, new body? It was too much to process. I wasn't broken anymore, yet I was separated from my loved ones and had no idea if I'd ever see them again. As much as I wanted to be healed, it wasn't a worthwhile trade.

I swallowed the lump in my throat. "And now I'm alone."

"Not alone," he hastily replied. "The others we've extracted have also found themselves to be faster and stronger than they were before."

"Others?" My heart skipped a beat, relief washing over me with the revelation that I wasn't the only one who'd been unexpectedly yanked from my home. If nothing else, we'd have that in common.

He nodded. "You have two companions so far, but we hope to be able to extract others. They have each manifested certain… abilities."

"Like what?"

Before he could answer, a thud sounded through the interior bulkhead, followed by a series of scuffles and another bang.

The commander sighed. "It would seem that one of your companions is experimenting again."

"That doesn't sound good."

"Oh, he's only getting used to his new body." Colren glanced at the wall. "Some of the transformations have been more substantial than others."

Not that I'd had a choice, but I was wondering more and more what I'd been pulled into. I cautiously eyed the side wall where the sound had come from. "May I meet them?"

"No sense in waiting." Colren rose from his chair and headed for the door on the wall opposite the viewport. "Try not to stare."

"At what?" I asked as I followed him.

"You'll see."

The door automatically slid to the side when we approached, revealing a steel-lined corridor. Struck with a blast of cooler air, I folded my arms to augment the insulation offered by the ruched white jumpsuit and followed Colren through the doorway. Holopanels and information displays integrated with the corridor walls hinted at a level of technological utilization that was far beyond anything in my day-to-day life back home, and I found myself awestruck by features that were probably commonplace for everyone else on the ship. The corridor curved gradually to the side in both directions, so it was impossible to see the ends. Doors lined both sides of the hall at irregular intervals, and we headed for one six meters to the right, adjacent to the room where I woke up.

Colren pressed his palm against a panel on the smooth wall. Following a beep, the door next to it slid open with a low hiss.

Scuffling sounds echoed out into the corridor, accompanied by the shout of a youthful male voice, "Relax, Toran! It's just the commander."

"And I have a new member for your group," Colren said as he stepped through the threshold.

Steeling myself, I peeked into the room.

Inside, Colren had stopped half a meter inside the door with his back to me, partially obstructing my view. To his left, I could make out the refined profile of a man in his early-twenties. His medium-brown hair was styled into a faux hawk and well-muscled arms flexed the fabric of his white jumpsuit.

The young man turned to face the door, training his captivating sky-blue eyes on me. "Why, hello there." He cracked a smile, brushing his index finger over a translucent crystal pendant hanging around his neck.

"Hi." I smiled back, hating that my cheeks suddenly felt flushed.

"This is Kaiden," Colren said, swiveling to face me. "He was the first we were able to retrieve."

Kaiden mimed tipping an invisible hat to me. "Pleasure to make your acquaintance."

"I'm Elle," I replied.

"Nice hair," a deep voice said from beyond the commander.

Then, I noticed the behemoth of a man who had been obscured from view when I first entered. Standing two meters tall and with the broadest shoulders I'd ever seen, the other man was a solid wall of muscle. The tattered top half of his white jumpsuit was tied around his waist.

"I rather like the new color," I responded to his flippant comment while I tried not to gawk at his exaggerated proportions.

"And this is Toran," Colren continued. "It's only been two days since we retrieved him."

"I've been hitting the gym pretty hard since then," Toran said with a grin.

I relaxed, seeing his good nature beneath the chiseled exterior. "I bet I could still beat you in a footrace."

"If there's anything left to run over," Kaiden interjected.

The dented floor and walls near Toran illustrated his point, which was underscored by a pile of twisted metal that appeared to be chair remains and perhaps a handful of shelving units.

Toran shrugged. "Don't knock it until you try it. Folding a chair or two is surprisingly empowering."

"I'll bet," Kaiden muttered under his breath.

I examined Toran. "Let me guess—you chose the shield, in the test when you were waking up."

Toran nodded.

"What about you?" I asked Kaiden.

"The wand, of course," he responded with a matter-of-fact tone like it was the most obvious choice in the world. "Didn't you?"

I shook my head. "No, the sword."

"Shame. You're missing out." A ball of sparkling white light appeared over the palm of Kaiden's outstretched right hand.

"Not in here!" Colren cut in.

The orb faded from his palm. "The demonstrations will have to wait for another time, I suppose."

"Like when you can't accidently vent us into space by hurling a rogue fireball at the viewport." The commander smoothed his black uniform.

"I've gained a lot of control since then," Kaiden countered.

"All the same," Colren continued, "now that there are three of you— one from each discipline—we need to seal the Master Archive."

I glanced at the men's faces as they each nodded gravely. "Sorry, did I miss something?"

"The Darkness is advancing," Colren replied. "If we don't seal the

Master Archive, it will be consumed and we'll have no means to reset the worlds after we stop the Darkness."

"Right, I figured out that much from context. But what was that about 'one from each discipline', and why us?"

"Oh, we're the divinely gifted almighty ones," Kaiden quipped. "They do like to skip over that part of the initiation briefing."

Colren groaned. "It's hardly that dramatic. You see, when the part of your consciousness that exists outside of spacetime was re-knitting with your new body, you were tapping into your most ancient genetic history—drawing on fragments scattered throughout the crystal backups from back in the time when the crystalline network was still forming. We know of a place that is believed to be the origin of the crystals, and there's a sanctuary around it to protect the Archive if ever there was a threat in the future. That sanctuary needs to be activated by three individuals embodying the tenets of ancient culture—strength, protection, and higher-self. By aligning with one of those tenets, you were imbued with the skills and predisposition to embody its ideals. Together, you can activate the safeguards around the Master Archive and buy us time while we figure out how to stop the Darkness for good."

I pursed my lips. "Nope, that does sound pretty dramatic."

Kaiden made a flourish of vindication with his hands.

"Regardless," Colren pressed on, "we need you. Sealing the Archive will be your first mission as a team, and it's imperative that you're successful."

Toran grunted. "No pressure."

I took a deep breath, my nerves fraying. "Okay, so we have some sort of ancient abilities now. But how does the sealing work? Are there any instructions?"

"No. That is for you to figure out," Colren replied. "I'm sure it will become clear when you arrive."

"Yeah... not buying it," I said. "This all still sounds crazy to me."

Kaiden laughed. "See, Toran? It's not just us saying so."

Our eyes locked for a moment, and the apprehension I'd been feeling since I woke up started to melt away. As bizarre as the situation was, others were facing the same set of impossible circumstances. I don't know if it was a byproduct of the extraction procedure or something else, but I felt at ease with Kaiden and Toran. I'd always been one to know within a few seconds of meeting someone if we'd get along or not, and I could tell that my two teammates were my kind of people.

"We can talk more once we reach our destination." Colren pulled out a communicator from his front pocket and made an entry. "There's no reason for us to linger here."

A moment later, a woman's voice came over the comm, "Jump in T-minus five minutes."

"Not again…" Kaiden murmured.

"Get strapped in," Colren instructed. " I need to get to my pod in Central Command." He rushed out of the room.

"We're about to do a spatial jump?" I asked, apprehension pitching my voice. Interstellar travel was common enough between the dozens of Hegemony systems, but I'd never left my home planet. I hadn't yet wrapped my head around being on a spaceship, let alone the notion of traveling through hyperspace to another system.

"Don't worry. It's every bit as disorienting as it sounds," Kaiden flashed me another grin and jogged toward the hallway door. "The pods are this way."

Hesitantly, I followed him with Toran close behind.

Kaiden led us down the corridor to one of the interior doors a dozen meters past the previous room. The chamber contained six oval pods arranged around a circular center console. An open transparent cover on each pod exposed an ergonomic couch within.

Without hesitation, Kaiden hurdled into the pod furthest from the door and began securing a harness. "Make sure the straps are tight."

"Very funny," Toran growled as he squeezed himself through the opening of a pod to the left of the door.

I jogged around to the pod on Kaiden's right so I could examine how he had buckled his harness. After making a quick mental note of the configuration, I reclined in my pod and began clipping the belts across myself. "Is all of this really necessary?"

"See what you think after the jump," Kaiden replied.

Just as I cinched up the last strap, the same announcer came over the comm again. "Jump in T-minus one minute."

"Good luck!" Kaiden called from next to me as the lids to our pods slid shut.

In the enclosed space, my heartbeat and breathing were almost deafening.

"Jump in T-minus thirty seconds," the announcer informed through a speaker inside the pod.

A static charge hummed in the pod, and I felt heavier—like I was being sucked against the seat.

At the ten-second mark, the announcer began a final countdown. "… Two… One."

Next thing I knew, my stomach was in my ears and my heart was at my feet. Reality elongated around me, then everything went black.

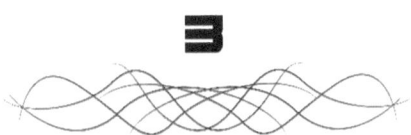

"ELLE. ELLE!" A voice roused me from the blackness.

My eyes shot open.

Kaiden was leaning over me, releasing my harness. "You passed out."

I groaned as I propped myself up on my elbows, realizing I was no longer strapped down. My head ached. "What just...?"

"Congratulations! You just completed your first spatial jump." Kaiden smiled down at me.

"I felt like I was being turned inside out."

"Yeah, good times."

I pressed the heel of my right hand to my temple. "I guess being strapped into the pods is a good idea, after all."

"I thought your opinion would come around," Kaiden replied, pushing back from my pod to give me some space.

"You'll get used to it," Toran's voice boomed from across the room. "Come on. We're being paged."

Still feeling like my stomach was lodged in my throat, I lurched out of the jump pod. "Where are we now?"

"That's a very good question," Kaiden replied as we exited the room. "They haven't exactly been forthcoming with the logistics about our mission."

"I feel like I'm in a dream." The throbbing in my head was beginning to fade, but the physical sensation enforced that what I'd just been through was real.

Kaiden offered a sympathetic smile. "I'm still trying to get over that feeling myself."

"None of this makes sense," Toran said. "Colren's account of why we were chosen doesn't really explain it."

I scrunched up my nose. "Yeah, that whole thing about getting an 'immunity' from the Darkness? What is the Darkness, anyway?"

"The cloud appeared after an emergency reset where I was," Kaiden said. "I'd never seen anything like it—freaked everyone out."

"Yeah, same with me. My friends and I weren't sure if we should tell anyone."

"No one else saw it?" he asked. "I thought planets like yours had a crystal in the town square or something."

"We do, but that wasn't where it appeared. We were out by one in a canyon."

"A localized reset, then?"

I nodded. "We'd go up there to play around."

He raised an eyebrow. "Doing what, rock climbing?"

"We'd jump off a cliff."

His eyes widened. "I was not expecting you to say that."

I smiled coyly. "I have an adventurous side."

"I used to collect rocks!" Toran looked down at his hands and sighed. "There wasn't a lot to do on Dunlore."

I awkwardly patted his huge shoulder. "Something tells me we're going to have plenty of adventure coming up."

We took the corridor to a nearby lift, passing by two groups of soldiers and a handful of solitary officers who cast us sidelong glances. I suspected that everyone on the ship knew who we were, at least in a general sense, and I found it odd that given our apparent importance we were expected to show ourselves around. Granted, it seemed like Kaiden had been given a proper tour and knew his way to the various locations of note; maybe they considered him our guide.

We entered the lift and rode it up two decks. I barely perceived any movement, unlike the elevators I was used to back home.

Kaiden must have noticed my awed expression, because he looked me over and chuckled. "It's just a lift, Elle."

"To you, maybe! I still can't get over the fact that I'm on a spaceship."

The door opened, and he smiled. "You haven't seen anything yet."

We stepped out and took a corridor to the left past a pod room and a weapons vault until it terminated at a door. Kaiden placed his hand on an adjacent panel. Rather than the door opening, a blue light blinked and a chime sounded.

"What's with the security?" I asked.

"This is the entry to Central Command," Kaiden replied. "I suspect they don't want people barging in right in the middle of a sensitive maneuver."

"I guess that makes sense. It just struck me as strange after they've left us to wander around on our own."

"They run the ship how they want it run," Toran said. "You know how boss people can be."

The door slid open, revealing Colren standing on the other side. "That's how us boss people are, huh?"

Toran turned bright red. "Sorry, sir, I didn't mean—"

The corners of Colren's lips curled up with amusement. "All things considered, that's an appropriate title. You're not officially military soldiers, so I'm not your superior officer beyond my role as captain of this vessel."

I eyed him. "But we also don't have much of a choice about being here."

"That was one of the things I wanted to talk with you about," he replied. "Let's get settled in the conference room."

We followed him into the open area beyond the doorway. Central Command appeared to be a cross between an administrative operations center and the starships' bridges I'd seen depicted in media. I knew the technology existed, but I'd never witnessed it in person. Everyone around me seemed in their element, but I couldn't help doing numerous double-takes as I studied the room.

The area nearest the entry door was flanked by two crescent-shaped workstations equipped with monitors, a touch-surface desktop, and a number of holographic displays with complex readouts that may as well have been in another language. The four crew members working at the consoles glanced up at us as we passed by. Based on their tempered reactions, it seemed that they must have seen Toran in the past; if anything, my bright fuchsia hair drew more attention. Even as the workstations drew my eye, I was awestruck by the attention to detail in the blue and gray crew members' uniforms and their effortless use of the complex systems around them. I'd never thought of Erusan as being a backwater world, yet seeing the Hegemony ship, I realized just how much I'd missed out on.

Further into the bridge, a single command chair was surrounded by four additional consoles, all facing toward an expansive viewscreen spanning the curved forward wall. The domed ceiling above was inlaid with a ring of lights, and additional lighting around the baseboard of the perimeter illuminated the space to almost daylight levels. The starboard wall contained a row of a dozen pods like the one I'd used for the jump, though these were arranged vertically.

My eye was drawn to the front viewscreen by the glow of a purple-hued planet below. Despite the strange color, the cloud cover looked similar to my homeworld… except it was in another star system.

I was about to visit another planet.

Excitement welled in my chest despite the confusion and uncertainty swirling in my mind. Though the circumstances were far from ideal, this was the kind of adventure I'd fantasized about for as long as I could remember. I could be scared, or I could embrace it for what it was. This was my chance to prove myself. I didn't want to mess it up.

Colren led us to the left toward a separate conference room with seating for twelve. A transparent wall separated the room from the main bridge. As the commander passed through the entry door, he passed his hand over the wall and it altered to opaque off-white.

"Please, take a seat." He gestured to the near side of the table while walking around to sit in the center across from us.

I grabbed a chair to Kaiden's right while Toran sat to his left.

"So, the mission…" Kaiden said on our behalf.

"Right." Colren folded his hands on the tabletop. "This planet, Crystallis, holds the Master Archive. Only a handful of people in the upper echelon of the Hegemony know its location. It's imperative that this site be protected at any cost."

"And all we have to do is 'seal it'?" I asked, trying to get myself in the right frame of mind to embrace the bizarre scenario.

He nodded. "Yes, but I suspect that will be more complicated than it sounds. As we understand it, regular people aren't allowed to access the Archive. We know it's there, in the sense that we can see how everything around it behaves, but we can't get to the thing itself."

Toran tilted his head. "Like dark matter, only... not?"

"The technology behind the crystals predates our civilization by millennia. Though we don't understand how they operate, exactly, we do know that this world is the hub of their power. What little we have been able to glean from the world has spurred all our scientific advances—from our jump drives to the device that harnessed your hyperdimensional consciousness and the bioprinter that created these new bodies for you. If we have any hope of finding a solution to this Darkness infecting our worlds, the clues will be down there."

I crossed my arms. "And only we can access that tech, because we're the only ones who have been modified by it. I'm not sure if that makes sense or if it's insane."

"Convenient, if nothing else," Kaiden responded.

"Sounds like a safeguard to make sure outsiders can't get too much, too fast. Need to master one development in order to advance enough to get the next," Toran hypothesized.

Colren inclined his head. "Quite possibly."

"Okay, say we seal the Archive. Then what?" I asked.

The commander looked each of us in the eyes. "Then we figure out how to fight back."

"Not to be too self-deprecating here," Kaiden said, "but are we really the right people to take that on? Three untrained strangers, and you're pretty much tasking us with saving all of known civilization. I mean, c'mon."

"Yeah, I just graduated secondary school a month ago," I interjected. Opportunity or not, the realist in me recognized that I was in way over my head.

"It's not an ideal scenario, I know," Colren said. "We won't force you to do anything, but I'll lay out the case in as compelling a manner as I can. As of right now, we don't know what this Darkness is or where it came from. All that we *do* know is that you are the only three people to have encountered it on your worlds and made it out."

I raised my hand, and Colren inclined his head for me to speak. "I still don't understand the technology behind our bodies materializing here on the ship, but I'll ignore that for now. What I really want to know is how you knew to be at our worlds to have us 'download' at that time?"

He nodded and took a slow breath. "We're still getting our bearings, as well. The short version is that we have information regarding the Darkness' advance, and we have been waiting near the impacted worlds with the hope that we might be able to extract a few people."

Kaiden folded his hands on the desktop. "You keep glossing over a lot of details. I've been here for more than a week now, and you still won't explain anything about the Darkness or how you knew our abilities would manifest."

"There's not a simple answer to that besides all of the pieces falling into place," Colren stated.

"Well, we're listening." Kaiden tilted his head.

The Hedgeman representative leaned back in his chair. "Okay, well, for starters, there's more to the Master Archive than we typically discuss on public forums," he began. "We talk about the records being a documentation of what's already happened... but there are also records of events that haven't happened yet."

My heart skipped a beat. "Pardon?"

Next to me, Kaiden froze. "Do you mean...?"

Colren nodded. "We think that at some point there must have been a universal reset."

"Stars..." My stomach clenched. Some people had suggested a reset on that scale might be possible, but I never imagined that it may have already happened. "Is there any way to know for sure?"

"Unlike the interface consoles with the colonies, there aren't dates attached to the Master Archive—at least not using a code we yet understand," Colren continued. "The only reason we began to suspect the Archive records extend beyond real-time is because we noticed that certain branches of the records have blank spots corresponding with worlds getting consumed by the Darkness, and those blanks continue for some undetermined amount of time before resuming again."

"So, we beat this thing?" Toran asked.

The commander nodded. "We hope so."

Kaiden squinted. "Wait, you said that no regular people could go into the Archives, and we're the first modified people to have a chance of entering. How have you seen any of that?"

"Like I said, it's not straightforward. We can't get into the vault, but we can still observe parts of it."

"How?" Kaiden pressed.

"There are certain… relays, which enable us to access parts of the data contained within the crystals. We only know of four such devices—one of which is on this ship."

"And that's how you first got the tech for jump drives and the rest?" I asked.

Colren inclined his head. "That was almost two hundred years ago. The Hegemony uncovered the first device on one of the moons in orbit of the Capital world, and we've been following the breadcrumbs ever since. Though use of the crystals dates back to our people's earliest records and we've had the rudimentary control mechanisms we use today, it wasn't until the discovery of the interface device that we started to understand how the crystals work and where they may have come from."

I leaned forward. "Which is…?"

"We don't know," the commander admitted. "Whoever made them did it a long time ago using tech far more advanced than we can comprehend."

"I always thought the crystals themselves were natural formations," I said.

"Yeah, same," Kaiden murmured.

Toran tilted his head. "Meaning, these new abilities come from some kind of tech rather than magic?"

"It's not a clear distinction," Colren replied.

Kaiden smiled. "Whatever makes it possible, I'll take it."

"Says Mister Fireball," Toran ribbed.

"Hey, we all got to choose our skills." Kaiden shrugged.

Toran folded his arms, causing his biceps to bulge. "I regret nothing."

"Me either," I said, but I wasn't convinced. The idea of having magic-like abilities still called to me, but a lot of that may be due to not having had the chance to test out the new skills I *did* have.

"The question remains, will you help us?" Colren pressed.

I met his gaze. "I will."

Kaiden nodded after a slight pause. "Yes, I'll never shy away from a challenge."

"I'm in," Toran agreed

"Thank you." The commander looked genuinely relieved.

"Probably best not to thank us yet," Kaiden said. "We have no idea how to do what you're asking."

Colren nodded. "Willingness to try is the first step."

"Do we, like, take a shuttle down there, or…?" I prompted.

"Yes, acquire your gear and arm yourselves, then proceed to the hangar," the commander instructed.

"Is there someone to walk us through that, or—" I started to ask.

"I trust that you don't require supervision. Kaiden knows where to go to get everything you need. Dismissed." Colren marched back to the bridge.

"For being the universe's last, best hope, isn't it a little weird that he's turning us loose on the ship to do our own thing?" I whispered. "Shouldn't we have escorts, or something?"

Kaiden shrugged. "I was a little thrown off by that when I first got here, too. What I've realized is that it's safe here, and all of the control rooms are staffed. If we can't be trusted to fend for ourselves on the ship, we'd be hopeless planetside."

"True."

We filed out of the conference room back through the bridge to the corridor.

When we were alone in the hallway, Toran let out a long breath. "Also, for getting answers, why do I have even more questions now?"

Kaiden chuckled. "The feeling is mutual."

I shook my head. "This entire thing feels ridiculous. I mean, the tech that they're talking about here…"

"Saying it's from ancient aliens?" Toran sighed. "What are they going to tell us next?"

"Honestly, I'm kind of relieved," Kaiden said. "I've always liked the idea of magic—"

"I know we just met, but that was pretty obvious by the fact that you picked the wand," I interjected.

He rolled his eyes. "Well, yeah. But even liking it, it was strange to think of something like a fireball materializing out of nothing. Though that explanation we got doesn't begin to explain how it's possible, it does at least indicate that someone at some time figured out how to make it work. That means there are rules, so it can be controlled."

I crossed my arms. "I hadn't thought about it that way."

"Yeah, I hadn't before, either," Kaiden admitted. "I got caught up in how fun it was to have the power at my fingertips, and then I realized that by not understanding it, I might eventually do something really bad. But if there's science behind it, there's also a pattern. If I can understand enough of the inner workings, I can maximize the abilities without losing control."

"I like the idea of you not accidently exploding a fireball on us," I said.

Toran nodded. "Yeah, start that studying ASAP… however you're supposed to go about doing that."

"Says the person who ruined all of the seating in what was supposed to be our lounge room." Kaiden raised an eyebrow at Toran.

"At least my practicing didn't involve lobbing balls of flaming energy at an exterior bulkhead."

I spread my hands flat at waist-level. "How about we just agree to no more magical attack spells on the spaceship?"

"Fine, so long as other practice doesn't involve destroying furniture we might not be able to replace," Kaiden replied.

"Okay," Toran agreed.

"Great." I smiled at them. "Now that we have some ground rules, I guess we should get down to that planet and figure out what we're supposed to do."

"You're forgetting something," Kaiden said.

"What's that?"

"You."

I tilted my head, brow furrowed. "What do you mean?"

"Seems like we should establish some guideline for using your abilities, too," he stated.

"Yeah, well, I don't actually know what those abilities *are* yet."

"You're supposed to have strength and fighting abilities, right?" Toran asked.

I eyed him. "Maybe, but you seem to have the strength thing covered."

"I think we're *all* stronger," Kaiden pointed out. "Toran was doing the chair-bending, but it looks like we'll also be able to take a beating."

I crossed my arms. "What other stuff?"

"Move fast, jump, strike, I dunno." Kaiden shrugged. "The only way to find out is to try."

"We already agreed no chair-bending, so Elle doesn't get to, either," Toran said.

"Fine, we'll figure out some other strength and agility tests when we get planetside," the other man agreed. "Really, I didn't start to figure out what I could do until I played around. The first few things just kind of came to me."

I grinned. "All right, then, I guess we should gear up."

GETTING EQUIPMENT FOR a planetside mission wasn't as straightforward as it sounded in my head.

Following Kaiden's directions, the three of us took a lift down four decks to an area that was presented as 'the place where you get stuff'. Despite that description aligning with our present needs, I was immediately skeptical of us being able to get anything useful when Kaiden led us into an empty room.

"Take a wrong turn?" I asked.

He flashed a knowing smile. "This is it."

I looked around the plain space—approximately five meters square. "What am I missing?"

Toran sighed. "Don't we have enough to worry about without you messing with us?"

"There's nothing in here," I said. "I was hoping for a sword and some stylish armor, or something."

"Step onto the scanner," a female synthesized voice stated over hidden speakers.

I jumped with surprise as a ring of white lights a meter in diameter appeared in the center of the floor.

"Step into the scanner for equipment fitting," the voice said.

"Huh." Toran nodded. "I stand corrected."

"Colren mentioned the 3D printer when I first got here, but I haven't tried it out yet myself," Kaiden explained. "I guess it'll scan us and adapt any of its built-in patterns to our size."

Toran glared at him—a terrifying look from someone of his proportions. "You mean I could have had a shirt this whole time?"

Kaiden took a step backward. "I kind of thought you didn't want one."

"Nah, man, it's *cold*! The jumpsuit just didn't fit well."

I rolled my eyes. "Let's note this as an example of why open communication is important."

"My, you're a sage advisor for someone your age," Kaiden commented with a smirk.

"Hah!" I laughed. "No, my mom's a therapist. It rubs off."

He smiled. "I know how that goes… the moment you realize you're starting to become your parents."

"Oh, stars, don't remind me," Toran moaned. "Just wait until you get a little older and see it really start to come out."

I looked him over, realizing that it was impossible to get an accurate reading of his age—not to mention the fact that all of us were in different bodies than the ones we were born into. "How old are you?" I asked.

"Forty-two next month," Toran replied.

Kaiden tilted his head. "Really? I guess the transformation took off a few years."

Toran nodded. "I was also skinny and thirty centimeters shorter, so there's that." He laughed.

"And, Elle, you said you just graduated secondary school, right? So, you're… eighteen?" Kaiden asked.

I nodded. "A teenager with no life experience—I know, *exactly* who you want on the team tasked with saving the universe."

"Stars, I'm only twenty-two and I won't graduate from the Academy for another semester," Kaiden revealed. "Not exactly the image of experience over here, either."

"What were you studying?" I asked.

"Agriculture." He laughed. "How's that for useful in what we're doing?"

I raised an eyebrow. "Wouldn't have guessed that."

He shrugged. "My family hauled grain for a living, so I decided I'd rather be on the production end and get to stay put."

"I understand the appeal," Toran replied. "You traveled a lot as a kid?"

Kaiden nodded. "I was on Falstan II for an internship when all this went down, but I spent most of my childhood on a freighter."

My eyes widened. "Wow, that's…" I couldn't help but feel envious. The notion of being mobile all the time and getting to live in space was something I'd dreamed about since I was a kid.

He smiled. "Whatever you're thinking, it wasn't. A lot of crowded living quarters, bland food, and not nearly as dramatic a view as you'd imagine."

Annoyance over his nonchalantness lodged in my chest, but I let his words sink in for a few moments. He was being sincere, and I shouldn't fault him for that. Maybe traveling on a freighter *wasn't* everything I'd dreamed about. "I guess living in a small town isn't all bad," I said after a pause. "Having an orchard in the backyard is nice."

Kaiden got a wistful look in his eyes. "There were times I would have done anything to have that."

"Same with me getting to travel around in space. I always wanted to go to Tactical School."

"Ah, the age-old desire to want what you don't have," Toran chimed in.

I swirled a length of my fuchsia hair around my index finger while looking over Toran's exaggerated physique. "I guess we're kind of walking personifications of that now, aren't we?"

Kaiden held up his hands as electricity crackled between his fingertips. "I have no complaints about the upgrades."

"What about you, Toran?" I questioned the other man. "Did you have a career and family before you were pulled here?"

He took a deep breath and looked down. "Yes, a wife and five-year-old daughter. I've been trying not to think about where they are right now."

A sharp pang struck my heart as emotion flitted across his face. I was worried about my own family, but they weren't reliant on me to keep them safe in a way a child needed parents. Toran couldn't do anything more to help his wife and daughter if he was frozen in suspended animation with them, but it was clear from his expression that he felt responsible for them all the same.

"They'll be fine," I tried to assure him.

"I was an engineer by trade, so I'm not one to sugarcoat facts," he replied. "I know we're in deep here. We can't measure what we don't know, and I haven't heard anything about our enemy that tells me what we're up against. Whatever happens, I'll be fighting for the well-being of my family. They're my universe."

I swallowed hard, wishing I had a more tangible person or thing to fight for. I wanted my world back—my family, my friends, my last summer of being carefree. But, even after defeating the Darkness, I *still* wouldn't have those things; I'd be leaving home. However, just because my life would change regardless, that didn't mean others' lives were in transition. People like Toran deserved to be reunited with their loved ones, and if I could help make that happen, I needed to do everything I could to make it a reality. After all, I'd wanted to be a Ranger. Now that my body was healed, all I had to do was prove I was ready to put others before myself.

"We'll get them back, Toran," I said, more confident this time.

He softened, cracking a smile. "I don't think they'll recognize me."

I smiled back. "There's more to a person than how they look."

"That's assuming these new bodies are permanent," Kaiden pointed out.

"You also half your size back home?" I ribbed.

He smirked. "No, aside from the new magic, this is pretty much me. And you?"

I pointed at my fuchsia hair. "Not my natural shade."

Kaiden laughed. "Right."

"Aside from that, though," I looked myself over, "pretty close."

But I did *feel* different, even if my appearance only had minor cosmetic changes. I was energized in the way I always was right after a cliff jump—filled with a sense that I could tackle any challenge. My injury hadn't held me back from trying most things, but now that it wasn't pestering the back of my mind, it was like a weight had been lifted that I hadn't even realized was there.

I didn't want to admit it to the others, but I was actually excited to face off against an unknown enemy and to have the chance to use abilities that normally were fanciful dreams. I'd been given the opportunity to be a new version of myself unburdened by my past. It would be a genuine adventure.

"Whoever we were before, we have strangers counting on us now," Kaiden said, echoing my private thoughts.

"I'll give it my all," I said.

"Me too," Toran agreed.

Kaiden nodded. "Same. I don't know what that commitment means exactly, but the three of us are in this together."

I was silent for several seconds. "We're all kinda screwed, aren't we?"

"Probably, but *magic*." Kaiden waggled his fingers.

"I can't wait to get back home and loom over the guys who made fun of me in Physical Ed at school back in the day," Toran said.

"Just a touch petty," I commented.

Kaiden cast me a sidelong glance. "Don't pretend you're not thinking of all the ways you could show off now."

My thoughts flashed to Adrianne and her aerial acrobatics—such a frivolous activity under present circumstances, but more than a little part of me wanted to see how much I could out-maneuver her now. "Okay, maybe there are a few things I'd do myself. Not that I even rightly know what I *can* do now."

"Right! The equipment, and the mission." Kaiden pointed at the illuminated ring on the floor.

The computer had remained silent during our conversation, and I'd gotten so wrapped up in talking with my new associates that I'd almost forgotten why we had entered the room in the first place.

"Who goes first?" I asked.

"Congratulations for volunteering. Go on ahead." Kaiden flourished his hand.

I eyed the illuminated ring. "Any idea how this thing works?"

"Haven't a clue," Kaiden replied. "But it's unlikely to vaporize you."

"That makes me feel *way* better, thanks."

"Only way to test out the interface is to do it," Toran said. "We'll be right here."

Knowing now he was a parent back home, I could hear the measured patience and assurance in his tone. That little girl of his had a good dad, even if she wasn't old enough to know it yet.

"All right," I agreed, stepping into the ring.

The moment I was stationary inside, a pleasant chime sounded and a downlight bathed me in a white glow. A moment later, a holographic projection popped up at torso height, wrapping one hundred eighty degrees around me. The screen had multiple menu items, ranging from weapons to armor and other accessories.

"Welcome. Do you have a saved loadout profile?" the computer voice asked.

"No," I replied.

"Commencing new configuration."

A ring dropped down from a hidden recess in the ceiling, waving a light over me as it descended to the floor. It repeated the activity on the way up. When it returned to the ceiling, the holographic image around me changed to have a fine wireframe wrapping my body. I lifted one arm a few centimeters and found the wireframe moved with me.

"Make item selection," the computer prompted.

For lack of any other instruction, I reached out to interact with the holographic menu, first selecting the 'Armor' icon, since that seemed like the logical place to start; I figured I'd build up from there.

The icons for the other elements shifted upward and shrunk into a mini-ring while the primary menu area altered to display various submenus for armor. Ranging from street clothes to powered suits, it looked like I could pretty much have anything imaginable.

"Powered armor, guys?" I glanced over my shoulder at my two companions.

Kaiden shrugged. "Might be a little overkill, but may as well be prepared for anything."

I swiped my hand over the powered armor submenu.

The screen flashed red, accompanied by a harsh tone. "Insufficient privileges. Prerequisite training required," the computer stated.

I frowned. "Guess that's a no-go."

"Then why give the option in the first place?" Kaiden sighed.

Toran, who I was quickly discovering was the more pragmatic of the two, stroked his chin pensively. "I wonder what kind of training is required to qualify?"

"What are the prerequisites?" I asked the computer on his behalf.

"Melee weapon proficiency, light armor proficiency, medium armor proficiency, fifty recorded combat hours—"

"Stop." I held up my hand. "Okay, yeah, no powered armor for us."

"Yet," Kaiden said.

"Fifty hours of combat? Not happening anytime soon," I pointed out.

He nodded. "Maybe we'll get there eventually."

That was kind of crazy to think about, but as shocking as the concept was, part of me was drawn to the idea. Essentially, it was beginning to look like I'd stumbled into being a Ranger without having to go through Tactical School.

I turned back to the holographic display, which had returned to its normal pale blue color. "Only display items that match my current clearance," I requested.

The screen reconfigured to show one-quarter of the previous options. At first glance, it looked like anything super fancy was out.

I flipped through the items, bringing up a preview image of each. "Street clothes, an awful onesie, hazsuits." I shook my head. "Once you see powered armor, it all seems kind of lame."

"Go back to those street clothes," Kaiden suggested. "I think I saw a note about ballistic ratings."

"Oh, really?" I scrolled back. Sure enough, the fabric was reinforced with ballistic-grade fibers to deflect projectiles, and a secondary treatment was designed to diffuse energy weapons fire or, presumably, magical attacks. "Okay, that's more intriguing than I initially thought," I admitted.

I narrowed the available designs to cuts most suited for a female figure. Though most of the outfits struck me as rather plain and boring, one coat jumped out at me. It was ankle-length, which would offer maximum protection, and a belt would allow it to be sealed in the front when needed. The garment came in a variety of colors, and I was initially drawn to the red. However, when I thought through the potential need to be stealthy while we were on our mission, I decided that plain black was the smarter option.

"I think I can work with this." I selected the coat, and the wireframe around me morphed to show the garment.

"Stylish," Kaiden commented.

"It suits you," Toran agreed.

I shrugged, and the coat moved with me. "Time to accessorize, I guess."

Next, I browsed through pants and selected a pair of black leggings to fit over my white base layer. I paired that with a pair of black knee-high combat boots with a purple accent trim that complemented my hair—no need to compromise on style while saving the universe—and a tactical belt from the same design group.

"That should cover it." I looked over my holographic outfit, pleased with how it had come together.

"Weapon," Kaiden prompted.

"Am I qualified to use anything?" I asked.

In response, the holographic display shifted to the weapons menu, which consisted of various swords and clubs. "No projectiles, then," I said. "Are the disciplines we picked literal, or...?"

"I think the icons for our disciplines are more symbolic," Kaiden said. "I draw power from my pendant, and a wand sounds really impractical. I'm thinking maybe a staff or something like that for myself."

The clubs struck me as a little too primitive, which left the bladed options. I looked over the menu. "Maybe a sabre? That's in the sword family."

Kaiden shrugged. "Get whatever you feel comfortable with. I doubt we'll need anything, anyway. I mean, we're just sealing the Archive, right?"

"Yeah, good point." I selected a sabre model with an electrified edge to enhance the sharpened metal. A representation of the weapon appeared in my hand and a scabbard for it at my waist. I waved the blade around. "This seems like it would be fun to use."

"Careful where you swing that when you get the real thing," Toran said with a smile.

"Confirm selections?" the computer prompted.

"Can you think of anything else I might need for now?" I asked my companions.

"Shirt?" Toran questioned.

"I don't know, I kind of like the look of the white suit under the black coat," I replied.

"Yeah, it works." Kaiden waved his hand. "Go for it."

"Confirm," I told the computer.

"Selection acknowledged. Processing." The main downlight in the ceiling and the lighted ring on the floor cut out. A moment later, a whirring sound started in the back wall of the room.

I stepped back toward the two men. "What's it doing?"

"Printing out the custom items, I imagine," Toran said.

"Step onto the scanner," the computer prompted.

"I guess we can get going on someone else while the first set prints," Kaiden said. "Go ahead, Toran."

The large man shook his head. "I don't believe that system is going to have many options for me. I'll watch over your shoulder while you go."

"All right." Kaiden stepped onto the platform and began going through the selection process.

After a few different configurations, Kaiden settled on an outfit consisting of a blue long-sleeve shirt, black pants, boots, and a black hooded cloak.

"A cloak? Really?" I razzed.

His sky-blue eyes seemed especially vibrant when contrast against the dark holographic hood framing his face. "You're envious, I can tell."

"It does offer better protection than your coat, Elle, with the hood up," Toran pointed out.

"Plus," Kaiden used one hand to draw the holographic representation of the cloak around his front, "stylish."

I rolled my eyes. "I really don't believe you were an agriculture major. You're way too dramatic."

"Never said I wasn't in theater."

"Now *that* I would believe."

A chime resonated through the chamber as the back wall slid open. My new garments were arranged on a rack, ready to wear.

I smiled. "That's service."

"Try it on," Kaiden encouraged.

I stepped around the scanner in the center of the room to access the rack. The pants fit well over the white suit I'd awoken in, and I slid on the boots and looped the tactical belt through the top of the pants. The belted coat fit almost like a cloak with sleeves, which seemed better suited for precise movements.

Finally, there was the sabre. I lifted it from its rack and slid it in its scabbard at my hip.

"I apologize in advance if I accidentally slice off one of your arms." I grinned at the two men while I walked back across the room.

"I can only hope sword fighting abilities come to you as naturally as magic spells did to Kaiden," Toran replied while Kaiden locked in his own selections.

"Well, if nothing else, the ensemble looks good," Kaiden commented while his gaze passed over me, lingering more than when we first met. "You've got a little…" He gently extracted some of my hair that was tucked inside my coat's collar and released it to fall down my back.

I tugged on some of the fuchsia hair hanging in front of me. "Thanks. It's a little longer than I'm used to."

"I like it." He met my gaze.

"Well," Toran cleared his throat, "time to get geared up myself." He lumbered into the center of the room.

Kaiden took a step back from me. "Yeah, mine should be ready any minute."

I crossed my arms and leaned against the wall while I waited for them to finish. While there was no denying Kaiden was my type, if I had to declare one, this was neither the time nor place to consider getting involved—or even to think about considering a possibility of something.

At least, not *yet*.

I caught myself. Things could get awkward and weird way too fast if I didn't divert from that line of thinking straight away. I wasn't in school anymore. I had more sense than that.

Setting aside the uninvited thoughts, I watched Toran try out clothing and armor options. He eventually settled on a new base layer and a set of lightweight, black scale armor that would accommodate his large frame, paired with a matching helmet and boots.

"If we ever have a chance to visit a city dressed like this, there is zero chance of anyone messing with us," I joked.

Toran confirmed his final selections then turned toward me. "I feel like we need a catchy team name."

"As cheesy as it sounds, I'm inclined to agree," Kaiden said.

"Yeah, I mean, if they want us to save the day, they better know who to thank," I agreed.

I evaluated our chosen outfits. "We're all wearing black. So, maybe something like 'Black Knights'?"

Kaiden scrunched up his nose. "The whole 'knights' thing might be a bit much."

"And 'black' feels a little... ominous," Toran said.

I ran through some synonyms in my head. "Something with 'defenders', maybe?"

"That's not bad. Or 'protectors' could work. How about a play on 'Space' or 'Void'?" Kaiden suggested.

"Or the Darkness," I added.

Toran thought for a moment. "How about 'Dark Protectors'?"

I shook my head. "That sounds like we're protecting the Darkness."

"Then, maybe 'Dark Sentinels'?" Toran suggested.

Kaiden lit up. "Yes."

I rolled the term around in my mind and mouthed it. It had a good ring to it, and the double meaning was a perfect bonus. "That will do very nicely."

5

KAIDEN HEFTED THE staff he'd selected to go with his new outfit. "I guess we should head down to the surface now?"

I raised an eyebrow. "I can't say I love the plan of running in there with no training or experience."

"What better way to *get* experience?"

"There's a lot wrong with that logic."

"I share Colren's concern about testing our abilities on this ship. Spacecraft are fragile," Toran jumped in. He was still adjusting the straps on his new black scale armor, which managed to make him look even more intimidating than he did walking around shirtless. Even though his gloved fists were his only weapon, I had no doubt that he'd be able to take out any opponent foolish enough to attack him.

"Fine," I agreed. "But I think we should experiment with our skills before we go into the Archive. There's no knowing what we may find in there."

"That works for me," Kaiden agreed. "Let's get ourselves a shuttle."

The hangar was on the same level as the room where we'd gotten our equipment from the impressive 3D printer. We followed signage in the corridors to a set of double doors, which opened automatically as we approached.

The cavernous bay beyond contained several dozen fighters as well as four shuttle craft approximately twelve meters long, which appeared to have thick plating suitable for atmospheric entry. Gathered near the shuttles, a group of six workers dressed in blue coveralls were performing an inspection and making notes on tablets.

"Ah, hello!" a red-headed woman in the group called out. She jogged toward our approaching party.

"Hi," Kaiden replied. "Colren sent us. We're supposed to go down to the planet."

She nodded, bobbing her ponytail. "Commander Colren informed me about the mission. We have a shuttle prepped for you." The woman headed back toward the craft being inspected, then glanced over her shoulder at us. "I'm Chief Taminoret, by the way, but you can call me Tami—everyone does. I'm the lead technical specialist and run the maintenance team around here. If you need anything, just ask."

"Thanks," I replied. "What have you heard about us?"

Tami stopped and turned around. "We know we're up against something that has the leadership scared, and you're somehow connected to the solution. That's all we need to know."

"And it doesn't worry you that it's, you know, *us*?" I gestured at our clothes and primitive weapons.

She shrugged. "Heroes come from all backgrounds. If the commander trusts you, I do, too."

I wished I had as much faith in myself as she seemed to. "Thanks."

Tami resumed walking to the shuttle. "These craft have an autopilot, so you won't need to do anything other than enter your destination."

"Good. I'm a little rusty," Kaiden said.

"You have piloting experience?" I asked him.

He smiled. "Can't grow up in the shipping business and not pick up a few skills."

"You'll be happy to know that the compensators in these are much more sophisticated than what you find in civilian tech," Tami told him. "You'll barely even feel the *g*s."

"That's a relief."

I frowned. "I wasn't thinking about space travel when I picked these clothes."

"You'll be fine," Tami said. "It looks like you have on a shipsuit underneath, so that will protect you."

"Oh, is that what these are?" I placed one hand on the white cloth covering my chest, which was one of the only parts of me where I hadn't added a second layer of clothing.

"They look thin, but they'll compress if the pressure changes and thermoregulate well," she explained. "It's a good thing to have on at all times."

I nodded. "Noted."

"So, your mission." Tami patted the shuttle's hull. "The nav computer is loaded with the coordinates for the Archive. No one else has been down there, so we can't say with any certainty how well the comms will work. Speaking of which…"

She motioned to one of the nearby workers, and he handed her a case containing three earpieces.

"Here are some comms for you," Tami said while distributing the earpieces to us. "Fair warning, there will be a—"

"Ow!" Kaiden exclaimed, gripped his right ear.

"—pinch when it implants," Tami finished. "It embeds next to your ear canal and jawbone so it can pick up barely audible statements. Tap behind your ear for controls: one tap to open a general channel, double-tap to mute, hold to disconnect, slide to cycle to private channels."

Taking a deep breath, I placed the device in my left ear. As soon as it was inside, the entire left side of my face started to burn, radiating from a single point near my jaw that felt like a molten bug was burrowing inside.

The pain receded after fifteen seconds, and I rubbed the side of my face to massage the rest of the burning away. "Please tell me that was a one-time thing."

"Yes, you're all set now," Tami said. "The comms will also serve as a combat recorder, of sorts, to passively log your activities."

"Is that what connects to the equipment system and the prerequisites?" I asked.

She nodded. "The system will sync with the comm's log when you go in for an upgrade."

"Sounds straightforward enough," Kaiden commented.

Tami smiled. "We try to keep it simple. Any more questions?"

I looked at my companions. "Aside from what we're supposed to do when we get down there, and pretty much everything else about what's going on? Nope, I guess that covers it."

The mechanic frowned. "Sorry, I'm afraid I can't offer any additional insights."

"Rhetorical question," I replied.

"We'll figure it out," Kaiden told her.

Toran nodded. "Thank you for the comm. Who will the general channel connect to?"

"Central Command," Tami said, "but you'll find a private channel for each of your team members, Commander Colren, and me here with the mechanical team."

I tapped behind my ear and then glided my hand downward. A synthesized voice similar to the computer in the equipment room stated names as I scrolled. I pressed the same place behind my ear and a low tone sounded, which I took to mean I'd closed out of the menu.

"All right, I guess we'll talk to you on the other side," Kaiden told her.

"Good luck." Tami placed her hand on a panel next to the shuttle's side hatch, and a door dropped open to form an entry ramp.

I followed Kaiden inside, with Toran close behind.

The opening led into a cozy common area with seating around a table and a galley. To the aft, a corridor had doors to either side and terminated in an airlock. Toward the nose of the craft, a corridor extended on the starboard side through the seating area, and next to the galley was a closed off room labeled as a lavatory.

"Homey," I said. The craft seemed entirely too small and vulnerable to travel on its own to a planet, extra hull plating or not.

"Are those bunk rooms?" Kaiden wondered aloud. He headed for the aft, seeming at home aboard the small vessel. He popped open the door on the port side, revealing a tiny room with a bunkbed. "Yep." He closed the door and checked the one across from it, which I couldn't see into from my vantage. "Same."

"I hope we don't have to spend the night in here," Toran said.

"Better than out in the open on an alien world," I countered. Another wave of nerves surged through me as it sunk in that I was on my way to another planet for the first time.

Toran nodded. "That's true."

With nervous anticipation, I wandered down the corridor toward the nose. Past the lavatory, the corridor opened into a compact bridge with two seats at the front and four additional seats at workstations around the back, each equipped with a flight harness. A broad viewport wrapped around the front of the bridge, offering a panoramic view of the hangar.

"No reason to delay," Kaiden said, coming up behind me. He took one of the front seats. "Want to co-pilot?" he asked me.

My heart skipped a beat. My first time on a shuttle and I'd get to co-pilot? "I'd love to, but I have no idea what to do."

"Don't worry. Just sit back and enjoy the ride." Kaiden's calm tone set me at ease.

"This is probably a bad time to tell you I hate flying," Toran grumbled as he entered the bridge through the corridor. His broad shoulders nearly brushed the side walls.

"Not ideal timing, no." Kaiden smiled back at him. "But if what Tami said is true, this won't be like any craft you've been on before." He pressed some physical controls on a front console, and a holographic overlay appeared on the console and over the front viewport.

Kaiden opened a navigation menu and located an entry for 'Master Archive'. "Ready to do this thing?" he asked us.

"Better go now before I change my mind," I replied.

"Let's get this over with," Toran moaned. He strapped into one of the chairs at the back, then closed his eyes.

I secured my own harness. "This will be the first planet I've been to other than my homeworld."

Kaiden glanced at me. "Really? Not even a trip offworld for vacation?"

"No, my family was more the camping sort."

"I must have stopped by dozens of worlds at one point or another, but only set foot on a few. I guess after all of that travel growing up, that's why I wanted to settle down somewhere."

"Literally *put down roots*, eh?" I smirked.

He shook his head. "Ugh, I walked right into that one."

Behind me, Toran groaned. "Elle, that was terrible."

"Better get used to my wit and charm. I can do this all day!"

"So it begins…" Kaiden made a final entry on the front console, and the shuttle began gliding across the hangar toward an opening covered in an electrostatic shield.

Despite knowing it was ridiculous, I couldn't help holding my breath as we passed through. A wave of yellow, crackling light passed over the front viewport, and then we were in complete blackness. Pinpoints of light shone in the distance, but from my vantage, we may as well have been completely alone in the void.

The shuttle arced to the port side on its programmed path, bringing the *Evangiel* into view. The ship was larger than I'd realized—close to half a kilometer long and at least fifteen decks tall. Based on my research in preparation for applying to Tactical School, the ship appeared to be of a cruiser class, designed more for speed than battle. However, energy weapons and rail guns were tucked away in recesses around the hull, so it could certainly put up a fight, if needed.

As the shuttle passed by the *Evangiel*, the front viewport tinted to block out the sudden light shining from the system's star behind the purple-hued planet. Cloud cover made it impossible to see anything on the surface, especially on the night side.

The approach path took us to the leading edge of dawn. I braced myself as the shuttle angled toward the atmosphere, causing a bright point of heat to appear at the nose of the vessel. I kept waiting for violent shaking or intense *g* forces to kick in, but there was barely any sensation of movement.

"What's taking so long to enter the atmosphere?" Toran asked behind me.

"We have." Kaiden stated. "We're at an elevation of eighty kilometers."

I peeked over my shoulder at the large man, and he had cracked an eye open. "Huh. I guess those compensators really *do* work."

"Nice ride, huh?" Kaiden kicked back in his seat with his hands behind his head. "I could almost take a nap."

"After we've done what we came here to do," I said. As much as I wanted to trust the autopilot, I really didn't like the idea of the only person on the craft with significant flying experience dozing off.

"I'm joking," he assured me. "I'm way too worried about what we're going to find down there to relax."

I was, too. The further we descended, the more my stomach tightened. I still couldn't make out anything of the landscape below, and my mind kept going to all of the ancient, mythical monsters that might be waiting for us.

A shudder wracked the shuttle. The console turned red and a warning claxon echoed in the bridge.

My heart leaped into my throat. "What happened?"

"I don't know." Kaiden's hands raced over the controls. "Shit! That's very bad."

"What?" Toran demanded from the back seat.

"The compensators are out and the guidance system lost its target. It's flying blind."

Concern added a quaver to Toran's deep voice, "Where are we going?"

"I don't know! I wasn't in control." Kaiden swept his hand over the front console and pushed a map overlay onto the front viewport. He pointed to a blinking point on the map. "This looks like where we're supposed to go."

"Okay, then let's go there," I said.

Kaiden motioned out the viewport. "Yeah, except I have no idea where *we* are *now*."

I knew next to nothing about ship controls, but even I could tell that the digital altimeter and GPS readouts were jumping all over the place.

"We should pull up," I suggested, trying to stay calm despite my racing heart. "If the positioning works from the upper atmosphere, we can eyeball it from above and take an approach."

"Won't help," he replied. "We're already on the entry path I would have taken when flying us in manually. If we're going to land this, we need to stay the course."

"Might get a signal again at a lower altitude," Toran said while gripping the armrests of his seat. "There's a blind spot like this when entering Dunlore."

"Let's hope," Kaiden murmured. "I think we're somewhere around ten kilometers up now. There could be mountains."

"Great." I tightened the straps on my harness and gripped the armrests. This really wasn't how or when I wanted to die. I pressed the comm activation point behind my ear, and it chirped. "Central Command, we've lost our nav lock."

Silence.

"Central Command," Toran said behind me. After a pause, he sighed. "Nothing. Whatever broke the lock and knocked out the compensators must be messing with the comms, too."

"At least we were headed in the right direction," Kaiden said. He pulled the manual yoke toward him, which had been locked at the base of the control console. The shuddering subsided a little as he leveled off.

"I wish these clouds would break," he muttered.

"Try the docking guidance system," Toran suggested. "The sensors use lasers to verify distances."

"Not sure what kind of range that will get us, but better than being blind." Kaiden located the appropriate system and activated it. "See if you can pull up the readings, Elle."

I grabbed the holographic of the data and dragged it toward me. It presently showed a schematic of the shuttle with a green border around it, but there were no other indicators. The menu offered no clues, but then I spotted a 'Settings' option. Flipping through that, I noticed an option for 'Show actual distances'; that sounded promising.

As soon as I selected the setting, numbers appeared around the edges of the shuttle schematic. Behind and above only showed an infinity symbol, but to the forward starboard corner one number was counting down fast.

"Turn to port!" I shouted.

A rock face parted through the clouds two hundred meters ahead. The shuttle banked hard to port, and my harness dug into my shoulders.

Kaiden swore under his breath as he fought to get a new trajectory that would take us around the slope. "That was way too close."

"This isn't detailed, but it's something." I moved the schematic showing the distances back to the center display so Kaiden could see it while flying.

He glanced between the distances on the schematic and the map of the original course, which was floating at the top of the view. "We need to set down and get our bearings. I have no idea where we are."

"Any option that involves not dying is good with me," I said.

Kaiden kept an eye on the proximity readings until he found a path where the front and sides were clear and only the distance below was counting down.

Finally, at an altitude of one kilometer, the cloud cover thinned and we got our first look at the planet's landscape. There was almost no vegetation or signs of water, with bizarre dark rock formations stretching as far as I could see. A mountain range towered in the distance, and the land dropped away other places into what I assumed were canyons. The path in front of us appeared to be fairly flat and free of potential hazards, but the shuttle bucked against strong winds.

"That lighter patch up ahead looks like a good landing spot?" he asked no one in particular while fighting to keep the shuttle level as the winds swirled around us.

"Sure," I said, willing to agree to anything just to be back on solid ground.

The shuttle descended the remaining distance. As we neared the ground, I saw that the topography was more varied than I'd initially thought, with some of the seemingly smooth areas actually being boulder fields that reminded me of my home.

Kaiden selected a patch of gravel and set the shuttle down. With a relieved sigh, he shut off the engine, and the holographic overlay faded from the controls. "Yay! We didn't die."

"Good flying," I told him.

"I do what I can."

"Well, this mission is off to a *great* start." I unbuckled my harness, my heartrate returning to normal. I pressed behind my ear to try the comms again. "Central Command?" Like before, there was no reply. "Okay, so we're on our own."

"Figured." Kaiden sighed. "Good thinking on the docking sensors, Toran. Do you have piloting experience, too?"

The large man shook his head. "A little, but control systems were a required course as an engineering student. Glad I was paying attention in class!"

"Thank the stars for that," I murmured. Even if we were out of communication with the main ship, I felt much better knowing my companions had experience to offer.

Toran smiled for a moment, then it faded. "So, how do we identify our position?"

"I was trying to figure that out," Kaiden said while he pushed back from the console. "We might need to take the shuttle up and circle around. I'm not crazy about hanging out at a low altitude beneath the clouds with those strong winds, though."

"What do we know about where we were going?" I asked.

Toran brought up the map from the original navigation plot using the console next to his seat. "It appears to be at the base of a valley between three peaks."

"That kind of formation should be easy to identify from the ground, provided the peaks aren't too hidden in the clouds," Kaiden said.

With a clear course of action at hand, I jumped up from my seat. "Let's head out!"

Toran frowned. "You might be a little too enthusiastic, given the situation."

"First time on another planet, what can I say?"

"All right, lead the way," Kaiden said.

"Have your weapon handy," Toran cautioned. "We don't know what may be out there."

I kept my hand on my sword hilt as we exited the bridge into the common room. "Wait, the air is safe, right?"

"Pretty sure they wouldn't have sent us down here without suits if we couldn't breathe," Kaiden pointed out.

"Clearly they don't know everything about this place," I countered.

Toran checked a panel next to the door. "Oxygen levels and temperature look okay."

"Good enough for me." Kaiden released the door lock.

THE SEAL RELEASED with a hiss, and the hatch swung outward to form a ramp down.

A gust of warm air ruffled my hair, carrying an aroma of dirt and iron. "Something doesn't feel right about this place."

"Definitely not the most hospitable." Kaiden motioned toward the hatch. "Do the honors, Elle."

I peeked outside. Everything in the monotone landscape had a matte appearance in the diffused light; only the gravel beneath us had the slightest degree of sparkle. I'd always pictured other worlds to be vibrant and filled with strange plants, but the landscape around me was closer to a barren wasteland. I cautiously walked down the ramp, my excitement turning to nerves at the prospect of venturing out into the unknown.

I finished my descent and took my first steps on an alien world. An exhilarating tingle passed through as the sparkly gravel crunched underfoot. I grinned up at my companions. "I'm officially an interstellar traveler."

Kaiden smiled back and descended the ramp. "Congratulations!"

I crouched to get a better look at the strange ground covering. "Is this crushed crystal?"

Kaiden bent down next to me and scooped up some of the gravel into his palm. "Huh. I think it is."

Toran joined us on the ground, surveying the area. "This formation looks like too perfect a circle to be natural. Do you think it may be the result of weapons fire?"

Kaiden frowned. "Anything is possible. Who knows the last time someone may have been around this planet. It could be from a battle a millennium ago."

"Kind of crazy to think about." I stood up and scanned the horizon for any sign of the three peaks we were looking for.

"Maybe that battle is what prompted the ancient civilization to make the sanctuary around the Master Archive, in case another conflict happened," Kaiden hypothesized.

"I could see that," I agreed. "And that would explain why the Master Archive is hidden in the first place."

"The power to control records of the past and potentially see the future. That seems very valuable," Toran murmured.

"Do you think it's true—about the Archive having a record of events that haven't happened yet?" I asked.

Kaiden shrugged. "It sounds a little crazy, but having my consciousness downloaded into a bioprinted body also sounds mad."

"I won't discount anything unless I see compelling evidence to disregard it," Toran stated. "The last few days have changed my views on what I previously thought were certainties."

"Yeah, I know what you mean." I nudged the gravel with the toe of my boot; now that I was on the world, it didn't seem very foreign at all. "Yesterday, the most important question on my mind was what classes I should take my first term at the Academy."

"A week ago, I was taking soil samples as part of a new fertilizer study." Kaiden laughed. "Stars, what happened to us?"

Toran shook his head. "I believe this is what's meant when it's said that someone's life has been turned upside down."

"It certainly feels that way," I muttered. The thrill of adventure I'd sensed on the shuttle was fading quickly now that I was on a barren world with little direction about how to complete our vague mission.

Kaiden straightened. "Hey, are those the peaks?" He pointed to the east.

I jogged over to him so I could follow the sightline of his arm. Just shy of the horizon, a collection of mountains rose from the surrounding landscape and disappeared into the cloud cover, with three peaks standing out as a slightly different shade of gray from the rest.

"That could be it," I said. "I wish we could see the top."

"Nothing we can do about that. These clouds aren't going anywhere," Kaiden replied.

"I can't tell from here if the shade is different," I continued. "If it is, it might indicate a different material and why those peaks were called out as landmarks on the map."

Kaiden nodded. "Maybe if we could get a different angle it would show up differently."

"My thoughts exactly."

Most of the area around us was flat, but to the south there was a low hill with several boulders near the top. "Maybe up there—" Before I'd finished my statement, Toran broke into a run toward the hill. "Where are you going?" I shouted after him.

"I want to see if I can lift that rock!" he called back.

"Is he serious?" I muttered.

Kaiden shrugged. "We *did* want to get in some practice with our abilities."

"Yeah, that was before we crash-landed and—"

"Elle, just go with it. Trust me, you'll go crazy if you try to control this situation. Consider yourself at the mercy of the universe's will, and you'll have a much better time."

I stared at him, blinking slowly.

Kaiden grinned. "Race you to the top!" He took off full-speed after Toran.

I bolted after him, despite my better judgment about running headlong into the unknown. Reckless or not, I wasn't about to let someone beat me in a footrace; running was one thing my shoulder injury hadn't taken from me.

It only took a dozen strides for me to overtake Kaiden and his brief head start. I surged ahead, amazed at how effortlessly my legs pumped across the ground. Even though I'd considered myself in good shape back home, it was clear that my new body was even more tuned for athletics. I wasn't winded in the slightest from the run up the hill, and my pulse was barely above normal. It was freeing in a way I'd never experienced before, like I'd found a calling I'd never known to look for.

At the top of the rise, Toran was sizing up a meter-tall boulder.

I slowed to a jog and came to rest next to him. "Moving on from chair-bending to rock-lifting, huh?" I asked.

He chuckled. "You're not the least bit curious if I can lift it?"

I smirked. "Didn't say that."

Kaiden made it to the summit. "Damn, you're speedy, Elle!"

"You challenged the wrong opponent if you expected to win," I gloated.

He bristled. "Well, can you do this?"

Flames licked the end of his staff, swelling into a spherical blaze. When the orb reached the size of his head, Kaiden discharged it toward a boulder forty meters from our location. The orb exploded on impact, enveloping the tan rock in flames before it died out. A charred circle marred the stone where it had born the blunt of the assault.

I pursed my lips. "Impressive."

Kaiden looked rather pleased with himself. "That's the biggest one yet."

"And *this* is why we agreed not to practice on the ship," Toran stated. He wrapped his arms around the boulder. "Now, let's see..." His fingertips found suitable grip points, and heaved the massive rock upward, releasing a cloud of dust.

"Hey, look at that!" Kaiden raised his eyebrows as Toran stood upright with the rock.

I smiled with excitement. "Stars!"

Toran beamed, though his face was red from the exertion. "Can't wait to see what else I—"

A growl behind me broke the quiet of the landscape.

Toran dropped the boulder, his expression changing from jovial to serious in an instant.

Every muscle in my body tensed, poised for action. As if driven by instinct, I drew my sabre. The electrified edge of the steel blade glowed blue in the soft purple light. I pivoted on the ball of my foot to face whatever had made the sound.

A four-legged creature crept from the shadow between two boulders ten meters from us. Standing ninety centimeters tall at the shoulder, it had a spiked ridge down its back, which transitioned into a barbed tail, and its talon-like feet sported fifteen-centimeter claws. Three yellow eyes were recessed in a thick skull, and its jaws parted to reveal jagged teeth.

Next to me, Kaiden had leveled his staff toward the creature, and

Toran's hands were now clenched into fists wrapped in his knuckle guards.

"How are we going to handle this?" I asked in a low voice. It didn't thrill me that my first brush with an alien creature might be a fight—especially considering that I hadn't yet had a chance to test my own abilities.

"It might just be guarding a nest," Toran said.

Kaiden shrugged. "Or it wants to eat us."

The stone lizard stepped forward and hissed. Two more creatures appeared in nearby crevasses, and then a fourth emerged to my right.

I swallowed. "I think we're on the menu."

"All right, so maybe backing away and leaving it alone isn't an option," Toran concluded.

"Kaiden, you want to magic these things away?" I questioned.

"I have no idea how much damage a blast will do against these things, but I'll try." He gripped the crystal around his neck in his left hand and pointed his staff at the stone lizard to my right. The staff began to glow with blue light, and then an energy orb shot from the end toward the creature.

Blue electricity danced across the stone lizard's skin as the blast connected. It shrieked and took a step back, but its three eyes narrowed with what appeared to be renewed focus.

The stone lizard in the middle right took the opportunity to rush forward, snapping at my leg.

I pulled my coat around me to block it, and it only got a mouth full of fabric. I kicked it as hard as I could.

The creature slid backward a meter from the force of the blow, then returned to the offensive line with the others.

"I already don't like these things." I raised my sword with both hands and charged for the same creature on the right that Kaiden had attacked. A meter from the target, I slashed at an angle to slice it at the base of the neck.

The blade carved through the armored flesh, spewing dark purple blood. With a sickening gurgle, it dropped to the ground, dead.

I stood in stunned silence. I'd never killed anything bigger than an insect before. But it had attacked me—a wild creature intent on killing. I buried the impulse to feel remorse for taking a life. I had a job to do, and that would mean cutting down anything that barred my way.

While I was frozen in reflection, Toran charged the second creature, which had attacked me moments before. He punched downward on the top of its head with his armored knuckled. A sharp *crack* echoed around the boulders as his fist impacted.

The creature staggered back but remained standing.

Toran jumped clear just in time for Kaiden to lob a fireball from his staff toward the wounded stone lizard. The flames enveloped the creature. It shrieked as it fell into a burned pile on the ground.

"Fire works better on these things, it seems," Kaiden commented.

"Yes, do more of that!" I shouted while running toward the third creature with my sword.

I mirrored my first attack, swiping downward at an angle toward the stone lizard's neck. However, it dodged my attack at the final moment and lunged for my ankle. The powerful jaws wrapped around my boot and it shook its head.

The thick material on the boot shaft managed to keep the fangs from breaking through, but the violent thrashing of the creature's head was enough to throw me off-balance. I hit the ground hard on my back, my limbs spread to my sides. Fortunately, I hadn't lost my grip on my sword, but I had no leverage from that angle.

The fourth creature lunged for my throat. I tried to swing my sword up, but the stone lizard was moving too fast. I braced for the bite.

A fireball flew past my head and struck the creature in the face a mere thirty centimeters away.

I squeezed my eyes closed against the light from the blast. Heat burned my face, like I'd just stuck my head into an oven.

The heat subsided after a second, leaving the creature stunned and blinded.

I took the opportunity to bolt upright, stabbing my sabre into the side of its neck. The blade pierced several centimeters in, and I twisted.

Dark purple blood oozed from the wound, and I withdrew the blade as the stone lizard collapsed into a lifeless pile on the ground.

Toran dashed toward the remaining stone lizard, a fist raised above his head. He struck the side of the creature's skull, crushing it between his fist and one of the boulders. The stone lizard fell to the ground, blood trickling from its smashed jaw.

Kaiden slowly released a breath. "Okay, so that just happened."

Toran took two deep, rapid breaths. "That felt weird, right?"

I scrambled to my feet. "If by 'weird' you mean way too natural for never having done those things before, then yeah. Very, very weird."

Kaiden examined the corpses of the creatures. "I can't decide if I should feel bad about killing them."

"I was wondering the same thing," I admitted. "I mean, they *did* attack us."

"We have a mission to complete, they got in the way," Toran said.

I nodded. "I imagine they won't be the last things to try to stop us."

"Almost certainly not." Kaiden rested his staff on the ground. "I think this staff amplifies my abilities somehow—or makes them easier to channel."

"Yeah, those fireballs are pretty awesome." I grinned.

He smiled back. "It was kind of nice to let loose against a specific target."

"And for not having a weapon, those fists did a lot of damage," I commented.

Toran inspected his knuckle guard. "I did what I had to do to keep us safe."

"Yeah, thanks for the help back there," I said to them. "I thought I was done for when that one took me down."

"We need to work as a team. For a first go-around, I think that went well," Kaiden replied.

"I think so, too," I agreed. "I guess now I have some sense of what I can do."

He nodded. "See? Hands-on learning is quite informative."

I raised an eyebrow. "Yeah, that was never up for debate. I just thought it might be nice to practice, you know, where things weren't trying to kill us."

"Weren't you the one who couldn't wait to get off the shuttle?"

"I… That's beside the point. *I* didn't go running off toward the rocks with the vicious lizard things."

"The possibility of their presence was not something I had considered," Toran admitted.

"Doesn't matter. It all worked out." I cleaned my blade on one of dead creature's hides and then sheathed the sabre.

Kaiden cast me a playful sidelong glance. "All part of going with the flow."

I took a deep breath. "*Anyway*, I believe we were about to get a look at those mountain peaks."

"Right." Kaiden walked over toward a boulder with a relatively flat top. "This looks like it would make a good vantage point."

There didn't appear to be a good way up around the smooth sides, and no lower rocks were close enough to climb. "Could I get a boost?" I asked Toran.

"Of course." He cupped his hands for me to step in, then easily hoisted my legs to his shoulder height while I used my hands to stabilize me on the rock. The boulder curved to a manageable angle at that level, and I was able to scramble the rest of the way to the top.

I stood up and surveyed the surrounding landscape from the new vantage. The fifty meter elevation gain from our shuttle's landing position didn't reveal any deep secrets, but the different angle did confirm that the three peaks in the distance were a distinctly different shade than the surrounding mountains, and the configuration was remarkably similar to the map we were working from.

"I think that those mountains *are* our target," I called down to my companions.

"Great, but how do we get there?" Kaiden replied. "We'll need to go over the pass, but we'll be flying blind through the clouds."

"I believe we have answered the great mystery about why no one ever comes here," Toran stated.

"Super welcoming place, isn't it?" I slid down the side of the boulder and Toran caught me, lowering me the rest of the way to the ground. I dusted myself off. "Back to the shuttle? Maybe a path through will reveal itself closer to the mountains."

"Guess we don't have another choice," Kaiden agreed.

We jogged down the hill back to the shuttle and returned to our seats on the bridge. The target mountain range was behind us based on our landing orientation, so Kaiden powered up the shuttle and rotated it to face the direction we needed to go. Strong winds wracked the craft as soon as we were a hundred meters off the ground.

Kaiden fought the controls to hold it steady. "We'll need to fly with the proximity sensors and naked eye."

"I'm on it," I said, getting the display configured for him like I had before. The overlay appeared on the front viewport.

I cinched my harness tighter as the shaking from the wind intensified closer to the mountains. The foothills sloped upward into the clouds, leaving no clue as to the best way into the valley we hoped was waiting for us on the other side.

"Maybe up through there?" I suggested, pointing toward one of the hill slopes that was slightly more gradual than the others.

"Worth a shot." Kaiden directed the craft toward it, keeping a distance of approximately two hundred meters from the ground as it angled upward.

The hillside eventually intersected with another, barely visible at the edge of what we could make out through the thick clouds. However, paired with the proximity readings, it was just enough to make our way through a pass between the mountain peaks.

As if a veil had been lifted, the clouds parted on the other side, revealing a valley dotted with crystal spires.

I sucked in a breath. "Wow."

"You can say that again." Kaiden's jaw slacked. "Some of those have to be a hundred meters tall."

"I had no idea crystals could get that big," I murmured.

"I suspect many of the things we'll find on this world don't exist elsewhere," Toran said.

"Good point."

I tore my gaze from the amazing formations beneath us to look upward. The clouds were as thick above us as elsewhere, but they stayed above the interior edge of the peaks almost like there was an invisible dome keeping them out.

The winds had also vanished as soon as we broke through the clouds, allowing Kaiden to relax at the controls. He followed my gaze upward. "There's something different about this place, that's for sure."

"A good sign we're where we're supposed to be," I said.

He nodded. "But where is the Archive entrance itself?"

I hadn't a clue what to suggest. The valley had to be at least two kilometers in diameter at its widest point, and there were so many formations around the landscape that there was no clear target.

"Might just have to walk around until we find it." I glanced over at

Kaiden to gauge his reaction to the statement, and I noticed the crystal pendant around his neck was glowing the way it did when he was casting a spell. "Uh, Kaiden… your necklace."

He looked down at his chest. "Stars! When did it start doing that?"

"I don't know. I just noticed it."

"What's going on?" Toran asked, unable to see from his vantage.

"My pendant is glowing," Kaiden explained.

"Curious," the large man mused.

I looked at him over my shoulder. "Have a theory, or…?"

"Where did that crystal shard come from?" Toran asked.

"It appeared with me in the bioprinter," Kaiden revealed. "It was strung around my neck, just like this."

"Well, you've indicated it's part of whatever gives you magical abilities. If that power is all connected, then maybe it's responding to this place," Toran conjectured.

"I guess that makes sense," Kaiden said. He looped the shuttle around as it approached the far edge of the valley.

At the furthest point in the arc, I noticed that the light in the crystal dimmed. "Hey, what if it grows brighter the closer it is to the power source?" I suggested.

"Keep an eye on it. I'll take us around to see what it does."

I watched the light intensity as Kaiden circled the shuttle through the valley. After completing a circuit, it was clear the light was brighter in one specific area near a particularly large crystal with two smaller crystals forming an irregular 'V' at its base. On the first pass, I'd thought the crystals had broken and fallen that way naturally, but I was starting to suspect that it marked an entrance.

"That's gotta be it," I said, pointing to the location.

"All right, let me set us down."

Kaiden found a relatively flat spot with enough clearance between the other formations to accommodate the shuttle, and he landed.

I unstrapped my harness as the holographic overlays deactivated. "What do you think we'll find inside?"

"Hopefully, a clearly labeled button for 'Seal Archive' and a pile of gold for our trouble," Kaiden said with a grin.

I laughed. "That would be pretty spectacular."

"As nice as that would be, I suspect there will be a trial," Toran said in a serious tone. "Colren said that someone from each of the three disciplines was required to seal the Archive, so we'll likely each have to do something."

"Yeah, I was worried that might be the case." I frowned.

Kaiden rose from his seat. "No sense worrying about it until we get inside and know exactly what to do."

"You're right. Only one way to find out." I followed him toward the common room.

"We just have to work together, like we did in the fight," Toran said while following me.

I smiled over my shoulder at him. "We're old pros now. We've got this."

They chuckled even though the statement was ridiculous. I had no clear sense for how long I had been unconscious during the jump earlier in the day, but I suspected that only a few hours had passed since I was in the canyon on Erusan with my friends. I was used to physical changes happening around me due to resets, but there was always consistency in what was happening. To be thrust into a new environment with people I didn't know was nothing short of disorienting. At least we were united by the experience of having no idea what was going on.

We exited the shuttle to find that the ground underfoot had a similar sparkle to the gravel near our previous landing site, but there were also distinct chunks of crystal here.

Kaiden's pendant was almost blindingly bright as he bent down to pick up a piece. Curiously, the fragments on the ground didn't seem to react to the presence of his crystal at all. "These feel different," he said.

I grabbed a crystal chunk from the ground myself. "What do you mean?"

"It's like there's a current running through mine, but these are just a plain piece of mineral," Kaiden explained. "Can you sense it?" He held out the pendant dangling from the chain around his neck.

I wrapped my hand around the crystal and tried to focus on it. There was a warmth to the stone—more than a product of being carried next to his chest. "Yeah, there is something."

"May I?" Toran asked.

I released the pendant, and Toran took it in his hand. "Hmm. Doesn't seem particularly different to me, but I'll take your word for it." He let it go.

Kaiden shrugged. "Maybe there are different types of crystals?"

I dropped the inert crystal I'd picked up, then looked over at the crystals framing the opening. "We won't get any answers standing around out here."

"All right, let's do it." Kaiden trudged toward what we hoped was the entrance to the Archive.

The terrain was broken up by clumps of crystal amid rocks and boulders of various sizes. Some of the formations towered twenty meters above us, and others barely cleared the top of my head. The dark stones were similar to those where we'd encountered the stone lizards, so I kept my hand on the hilt of my sheathed sabre just in case.

The final stretch of terrain was only a slight incline, but the gravel and crystal shards underfoot shifted with every step. I slid down almost as much ground as I gained with each stride. After several unsuccessful attempts, I took a running start and loped up the hill as quickly as I could. To my relief, the strategy worked. I found solid footing at the top of the slope.

I grinned down at my companions. "What's taking you guys so long?"

Kaiden sighed. "Very funny." He stepped back and then took a running start like I had, clearing the patch of scree in a dozen rapid strides.

Toran followed suit. "That shouldn't have been the most difficult thing we've done today."

I chuckled. "The day isn't over yet!"

The flat landing outside the entrance was only four meters deep, so I had to crane my neck to look at the top of the two crystals framing the entrance. Each was approximately ten meters tall, with flat faces near their pointed tops arranged so they held each other in place against the base of the one-hundred-meter-tall crystal behind them.

Standing at the entrance, I could now tell that the path inside hugged the outside edge of that mammoth vertical crystal, with the glass-like surface on the left and dark, rough rock on the right for as far as I could see into the dim cave mouth.

"I was expecting something more high-tech," I commented.

"Me too. 'Archive' sounds more like a datacenter, not a cave," Kaiden agreed.

Toran strode through the opening, undeterred. "No telling what's inside."

I followed him in. The temperature immediately dropped by five degrees.

"I don't suppose anyone brought a light?" Toran asked. "I didn't think to grab a flashlight from the ship."

"Me either," I realized. With the image of a datacenter in my head, illumination needs weren't even a consideration.

"No worries." Kaiden followed us in. The glow of his pendant cast a pool of soft blue light around him. He then extended his right hand, and a larger orb appeared in his palm.

I raised my eyebrows. "Neat trick."

"See? Not all fireballs and blasting stuff."

"Lead the way." Toran motioned for Kaiden to go ahead.

The light cast from the orb was just bright enough to illuminate the cave's ceiling eight meters overhead. Shadows seemed to absorb the light, but the crystal wall to the left shined with extra brilliance, though none of its glow extended beyond the crystal's face.

Past the entry archway, the cavern sloped downward as it spiraled around the massive central crystal, gradually narrowing until the tunnel was six meters wide and five tall. One hundred fifty meters in, the glow from Kaiden's hand hit what appeared to be a back stone wall. A single two-meter-tall crystal column stood at the center of a domed chamber at the terminus, with the wall of crystal still to our left.

"That's it?" I frowned.

Kaiden's brow knit. "No, there has to be more here."

The three of us approached the opaque, white column. As we neared, I discovered that the back wall wasn't as featureless as I'd assumed from the distance. There were three symbols carved into the stone wall, each inlaid with crystal: a sword, a wand, and a shield.

"Those look familiar." I pointed at the symbols.

"Sure do," Kaiden agreed.

Toran scrutinized the freestanding crystal column. "I believe there's writing carved on here."

I walked over next to him to take a look. There were definitely markings in the crystal, but the language didn't look familiar to me. "No clue what that says."

Kaiden joined us. "Huh. I think that's Laeric."

I'd never seen the ancient root language in print before, but I'd heard about it in my writing composition classes in school. "You know it?"

He winced. "Not *exactly*. A lot of the biology terms from my agro classes have Laeric roots. I took one semester of the language years ago as a foundation course, but that's…" He shook his head.

"It's a lot more than I can offer," I said.

Toran sighed. "I'm afraid my studies were more focused on numbers than words."

"What we need is a camera so we can run it through the translator in the shuttle's computer," I said.

"Didn't think to bring one of those, either," Toran said.

"Yeah, and I'm guessing it's not one of those things that's randomly in the emergency supplies." I sighed. "Okay, so this has been a good learning experience about *other* gear we should get."

"The little things you don't think about," Kaiden muttered. He pursed his lips as he examined the column. "Some of this *is* familiar. Like, this word here, comes up in plant genetics talking about the… original, or iconic, standard for a species. I believe the literal translation is something along the lines of 'artifact'."

I raised an eyebrow. "Any idea what that means?"

"No. But I also see mentions of 'three' and 'open'," he said. "Could be referencing us."

"Perhaps we each need to touch the symbol associated with our discipline?" Toran suggested.

"Makes sense to me." I returned to the back wall and touched the carved sword symbol with my right hand.

Kaiden and Toran each touched their respective symbols.

I waited. After ten seconds of nothing, I scowled. "Is there some sort of secret incantation, maybe?"

"If that's the case, it could be anything." Kaiden looked around the chamber. "Open Archive?"

We waited another five seconds with no avail.

Kaiden tried again, "Access Master Archi—"

"This is pointless," Toran interrupted. "No designer would make it so people had to guess random phrases. We're missing something."

Kaiden groaned. "You think?"

I thought for a moment. "That center monument might be instructions. What if the 'artifacts' it's talking about are actual *objects*?

Like, ancient relics or something."

Toran frowned. "Meaning we might need to gather those objects—whatever they may be—in order to access the Master Archive?"

Kaiden sighed. "Well, that's going to be a problem."

7

I WANDERED OVER to the column in the center of the chamber. "How do we figure out what and where the artifacts are, if that is what this is indicating?"

"There's more here, but I can't read it," Kaiden said returning to the monument. "Maybe it's instructions for how to find them."

"We need a copy of this." I ran my fingertips over the crystal's surface. The text was carved, leaving a recess for each stroke. "And it doesn't have to be a picture. What about a rubbing?"

Kaiden's face lit up. "Good thinking! We just need a sheet of something thin and smooth."

"What about a writing implement?" Toran asked. "I haven't seen anything non-digital since I arrived on the *Evangiel*."

"Charcoal?" I suggested.

Kaiden grinned. "All I hear is an excuse to burn something with a fireball."

"Let's go raid the shuttle and see what we can find." I jogged up the shallow incline of the tunnel.

Upon exiting the cave, Kaiden extinguished his light orb, and we skidded down the scree to get back to our shuttle.

Finding a suitable material for our needs was tricky. I'd hoped that maybe we *would* find a camera or something else to snap a shot of the carving, but the only devices capable of capturing an image were integrated with the ship and would be too difficult to remove. That left the alternative plan of a rubbing, but we needed a sheet of thin paper or something similar that would be able to pick up the fine lines of the carved text.

I considered the bed sheets on the bunk, but they were too thick. The only other thin-ish materials were sheets for emergency patching, but those had no give to get a relief imprint. Even the materials in the lavatory came up short.

"There *has* to be a way to duplicate that image aside from re-drawing it," I said, staring at the scavenged supplies strewn around the common room.

"Might just have to go back to the *Evangiel* to get a camera and come back," Kaiden said.

"No, we just need to get creative." My eye was drawn to the patching supplies. "Maybe we've been thinking about this the wrong way."

"What's the other option?" Toran asked.

I grabbed the sheet of patching material. "I was originally thinking we could take a relief rubbing, but what if we take a negative instead?"

"Ah, yes!" Toran nodded. "Paint something on the face of the column and use it like a stamp on the sheet."

"Exactly."

Kaiden drooped. "So, no more fireballs."

"Not right now."

He sighed. "Oh well." He eyed the items on the floor. "That black sealant could work for the paint."

I smiled. "I think we're back in business."

We grabbed the supplies, including a flashlight, and scrambled back up the hill to the cavern. I took the sealant so Kaiden could light our way, and Toran carried the piece of sheeting.

Once we were back at the crystal column, I had a pang of regret. "Is it wrong of us to deface monument like this?"

"There won't be anything left of it if we can't protect it, and we can't protect it if we can't get inside the Archive," Kaiden pointed out. He switched from the light orb in his hand to the flashlight; the new illumination didn't fill the cavern as well, but he'd need both hands free.

"Sealant can be removed," Toran said. "When we come back with the artifacts, we'll make it good as new."

I nodded. "Okay."

The sealant painted on easily using an applicator at the top of the can.

I coated the front of the column, careful not to get any of the material in the carved grooves of the letters. When the area containing text was completely coated, Toran and Kaiden lifted the sheet into place. Toran held it steady against the column's face while Kaiden carefully smoothed his hands over it to make sure it made consistent contact. They then pulled it straight back to avoid smudging the imprint.

I breathed a sigh of relief as soon as I saw the result. The characters had crisp lines at their edges surrounded by the black sealant. The contrast wasn't great with the black against dull gray, but a little digital manipulation of the scan and the computer on the *Evangiel* could sort out the translation for us.

Kaiden nodded with satisfaction as he looked over our handiwork. "For not planning any of this, that went surprisingly well."

"If the universe-saving doesn't go well, I think the Dark Sentinels have a future as archaeologists," I joked.

"Always smart to foster multiple career prospects." Kaiden smiled.

Toran seemed disinterested in the joking as he grabbed hold of the sheeting. "This will take time to set completely. We should get back to the shuttle."

I took one last look around the cavern. "All right. We'll be back."

Toran carried the sheet out while I took the sealant and Kaiden restored his light orb.

We set a brisk pace, anxious to get back to the *Evangiel* and learn what the engraving said. When we reached the shuttle, we secured the sheet on the floor in the common room and then took our seats on the bridge.

"Everyone is going to be really disappointed when they find out we haven't accomplished anything," I said while I strapped in.

Kaiden powered up the shuttle. "We did do *something*. I mean, we have more information than we did before."

"Even Colren admitted that this wouldn't be straightforward," Toran added. "I imagine they were prepared for us to return having not completed the task."

I nodded. "All the same, you always *hope* you're wrong and that everything will go smoothly."

"That's true."

"At least we're bringing back something with us," Kaiden said.

"That's true—it's something tangible," I agreed. "They won't be able to accuse us of flying around and not trying before we came back."

Kaiden laughed. "I'd really hope they wouldn't do that."

I shrugged. "These military guys, you never know. 'If you're still breathing, you didn't try hard enough!' "

Toran snorted behind me. "And you still wanted to go to Tactical School?"

"Well, yeah. Because… spaceships."

"I guess things are working out pretty well for you now, then," he replied, a touch of bitterness in his tone.

"Believe me, this is *not* how I expected my summer vacation to go." I looked over my shoulder at him. "I don't want you to think I'm taking this situation lightly. I may joke around, but that's how I deal with stress."

"I got that impression," he murmured.

I softened. "Hey, I get that you're worried about your family. I am, too."

"It's sinking in now," Toran continued. "Colren had been telling us all we had to do was wait until we extracted someone who picked Strength, and then we could seal the Archive and go back to our lives. Maybe we'd play a role in stopping the Darkness, whatever it is, but our only certain task was to protect the Master Archive. Now, we know that sealing it isn't an easy afternoon activity. And if *this* is complicated, you can bet the rest of it will be, too. I don't know when I'll be able to see my family again, or if we'll even be able to seal the Archive while there's anything left to save."

"Thinking about the worst case scenario isn't going to help us," Kaiden said while he lifted the shuttle off the ground. "We can freak out if the text from the column doesn't give us any clues, but I'm going to count today as forward progress until I know otherwise."

I nodded. "Yes, we need to stay positive. Everyone will be safe in suspended animation until this gets sorted out." I needed to believe it was true for my own sake—for my loved ones back home.

Then it struck me, too. I had no idea where my home was relative to our present location. Down on this alien world, for all I knew, we could be the only three people left in existence.

I shook off the feeling and buried the thoughts in the back of my mind. The here and now is what mattered. Worrying about things that were beyond my control would only distract me. Even if it came off as aloof to Toran, we all had to cope with the situation in our own ways.

The shuttle rose up in the center of the valley until it was enveloped in clouds. Turbulent winds shook the craft as soon the valley was out of sight.

"Enough of this." Kaiden angled the craft upward and initiated the control sequence to launch it into space.

The initial acceleration without the compensators pinned me against the back of my seat. After a minute of feeling too heavy to lift my hand, the pressure began to subside.

The control console chirped.

Kaiden chuckled. "Sure, *now* we have a navigation lock." He changed the destination to the *Evangiel*, and the autopilot took over. The shuttle glided toward the larger ship in orbit of the purple planet. He tapped behind his ear. "*Evangiel*, this is Shuttle 1 returning from the surface."

"We read you, Shuttle 1. This is Central Command," a woman said on the shuttle's central comm. "Proceed to debrief with Commander Colren upon arrival."

The docking assist display that had saved us appeared on the front screen as we made the final approach. With barely more than a bump, the shuttle touched down on the landing platform and then passed through the golden electrostatic field. Workers ran over to receive the craft as it returned to its parking space inside the hanger, and the engine wound down.

"We probably shouldn't say anything about what we found down there until we've talked with Colren," I suggested.

"Agreed," Toran said.

"Should be an interesting debrief." Kaiden unstrapped his harness and stood up.

I rose from my own seat. "On the bright side of things, we got in a fight and are now two minutes closer to meeting the prerequisites for powered armor."

Kaiden laughed. "Seriously, that's what you're thinking around right now?"

"Hey, it's related to the mission!"

Toran groaned. "I'll get the sheet with the inscription."

Kaiden released the side hatch to drop the exit ramp, and I followed him down while Toran brought up the rear with the piece of sheeting.

"Sorry it's kind of a mess in there," I said to Tami when she approached. "We, uh, needed to improvise. And, the inertial compensators are out."

"Also, a portable camera would be super helpful," Kaiden added.

She squinted at us and tilted her head. "What in the stars did you do down there?"

"Impromptu archaeology," I replied, then followed Kaiden toward the exit.

"We're starting out with such a good impression with the maintenance team." Toran shook his head.

"I don't remember where anything in there goes. Better they put it back how it's supposed to be," Kaiden replied.

"I think we should make ourselves a travel bag with all the random stuff we might need," I suggested.

Kaiden raised his staff. "Yes."

"It may be difficult to anticipate everything, but I think that's a very good idea," Toran concurred.

We exited the hangar and took the lift up to the level with Central Command. We were buzzed in at the main door.

Colren greeted us from the center of the bridge. "We weren't expecting you so soon." His eyes narrowed when he saw Toran carrying the piece of sheeting. "What's that?"

"That requires some explanation," Kaiden said.

The four of us got situated in the conference room.

Kaiden folded his hands on the tabletop. "First off, I saw nothing on Crystallis that would prevent a regular person from setting foot on it. The cloud cover is a hindrance, but once at a lower elevation, it's more or less like any other world."

The commander frowned. "I was told it was impossible."

"Well, either we missed something, or your information was inaccurate," Toran replied. "Lore and legend can have a way of twisting the truth."

"What *did* you find down there?" Colren prompted.

We took turns explaining the events that had occurred since our departure for the planet. The commander sat quietly while we recounted the details, and he became visibly more engaged when we got to the part about the valley and the cavern entrance.

"Now, it *does* appear that only people with specialized skills can access the Archive," Kaiden explained. "However, it might not be the people alone. My Laeric is rusty, but I think there's mention of three artifacts."

Toran placed the piece of sheeting, which had dried, on the table.

Colren's face paled. "I was afraid you were going to say that."

My eyes widened. "You knew about this?"

"Like you said, legend and lore... it's difficult to know what's accurate." The commander sighed. "Let's hope these are instructions."

He tapped on the tabletop and made an entry. A moment later, a beam of light projected from the ceiling passed over the piece of sheeting. To my right, a black rectangle two meters in diameter appeared in the center of the previously blank wall. The black was soon replaced by a scanned image of the sheet.

"Now to find out what it says..." Colren murmured, making additional entries.

The image of the screen flipped to its mirror image, and the contrast adjusted so the dark gray lettering stood out from the surrounding black sealant residue. White outlines appeared over the letters, and an overlay of blue text appeared above the original.

"It's indeed Laeric," Colren said.

The opening text read:

> *Those who seek knowledge must be willing to work as one. Three must come together with their artifacts of power. What was done is not fated to always be. Join as one to seize destiny.*

Beneath the cryptic phrase were three additional blocks of text containing a string of numbers. The first was labeled as *Valor*, the second as *Spirit*, and the third as *Protection*.

Colren tilted his head. "Hmm. Apparently, we didn't get the translation right before."

"Spirit doesn't sound as fun as Magic," Kaiden said.

Toran looked thoughtful. "I rather like Protection."

"Valor has more of a ring to it than Strength," I said.

"Regardless of the preferred translation of the discipline names," Colren continued, "there remains the matter of acquiring these artifacts and how they will be used."

"What are the numbers?" I asked.

"Need to run an analysis," the commander replied. He selected the three number blocks and instructed the computer to evaluate the sequences. After ten seconds, blue text appeared on the screen with the numbers arranged in a different format. "They're coordinates."

Kaiden nodded. "Makes sense, given the context."

"Coordinates to what?" Toran asked.

"We'll have to map them," Colren responded, his fingers already moving over the tabletop. He removed the imprinted sheet and leaned it against the side wall.

A hologram of a star map appeared above the table. Three red dots lit up.

"Looks like planets," Kaiden observed.

"They're far apart. We'll need to jump to get a closer look at each," Colren stated.

My stomach turned over. "Great."

"Which one would you like to investigate first?" he asked.

"I'd vote for going after the Spirit artifact, since Kaiden has a better handle on his abilities than us at the moment," I suggested.

Toran frowned. "I've been practicing, too."

Kaiden's gaze flitted between us. "Considering we have no idea what kind of challenge we'll face, a physical or defensive type engagement might be more straightforward than one involving magic."

I nodded. "That's a good point."

"So, me first?" Toran asked.

"Sounds good," I replied.

"Okay, I'll arrange the jump to those coordinates. Stand by." The commander rose from the table and gave us a parting nod.

My chest constricted. "Ugh, I'm not looking forward to more jumps."

"They get easier," Kaiden assured me. "You may even stay conscious long enough this time to experience the sensation of your heart being at your feet."

"I think that's right around the time I blacked out last time."

He smiled. "Ah, then you still have the joy of tasting blue and seeing the sound waves."

I crossed my arms. "That sounds more like a bad drug trip."

Kaiden shrugged. "They like to leave the synesthesia out of the travel brochures."

I scowled. "No wonder they always put civilians under while in transit."

Toran nodded. "But, *we* need to be alert the moment we arrive. Five minutes to get our bearings rather than two hours of grogginess while working off the sedatives."

"I dunno, I could go for a nap right around now," I said.

Kaiden grinned. "Nonsense! That's what stims are for."

"Ten minutes until jump," a woman announced over the intercom.

I sighed and followed my companions toward the door. "Fantastic."

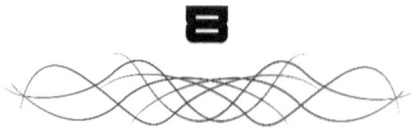

I WISHED I hadn't stayed conscious during the jump, but I did.

Kaiden's irreverent description didn't do the real thing justice. The initial transition into hyperspace was definitely the worst, when all sense of physical order evaporated, but the remaining duration of the jump warped what little remained of my sense of reality. As I heard colors and tasted sounds, the only constant was my heartbeat—though it was occasionally in my feet and other times in my chest where it should be. I focused on the rhythm and tried to relax.

I had no definitive sense of time passage while in hyperspace, but eventually the synesthesia subsided and the pressure holding me against the bottom of the pod lessened.

A chime sounded over the speaker in the pod, then the synthesized voice of the ship's computer stated, "Jump complete."

The seal on my pod released with a hiss.

Shaking slightly, I released my harness and pushed up the pod's lid.

Kaiden sat up in the pod next to me, wearing only his shipsuit base layer. "Hey! You made it."

I smiled back weakly. "I'm a quick study, I guess."

Toran squeezed out of his pod. "I'm with Elle: jumps are terrible."

"Better than spending years in transit." Kaiden exited his pod and started donning his outer clothes.

I hauled myself up, bracing on the edge of the pod while my senses settled. "It's still better than sitting through one of my old chemistry teacher's lectures."

Kaiden raised an eyebrow. "That bad a class, huh?"

"He liked to use the analogy that chemistry was the literature of molecules, and would proceed to explain chemical reactions as though it was a bizarre love triangle."

Toran and Kaiden blinked, then burst out laughing.

"I don't know what you're talking about. That class sounds *amazing*!" Kaiden exclaimed.

"Oh, it was, the *first* year. Yes, the joys of living in a small town when you get the same teacher multiple times. And it was all fine, until he was the teacher assigned to teach Sex Ed, and those analogies reversed."

The two guys completely lost it. Kaiden dropped his staff on the deck he was laughing so hard, and Toran had to lean against his pod, doubled over. Whether they genuinely found it that amusing or they just needed to release some of the tension from the events over the past few hours, I was happy to see them unwind.

I casually got dressed while I waited for them to regain some semblance of composure.

"So, anyway," I said when their faces were less red, "just remember that valence electrons are promiscuous temptresses."

The two men continued snickering while they finished getting dressed.

"Thanks, Elle, I needed that," Toran said while securing the final clasps on his armor.

I gave a little curtsy. "Happy to be of service."

"We should assemble our goodie bag of random helpful things," Kaiden suggested.

"Good call." I crossed my arms. "Where do we do that?"

"Tami?" Toran suggested.

I nodded. "She did say she'd help out with anything we need."

"That was *before* we trashed her shuttle," Kaiden pointed out.

"Well, we wouldn't have needed to rip everything apart if we had a bag like that in the first place, so…" I faded out.

Kaiden bowed his head. "Tami it is."

We returned to the hangar five decks below. Though we considered calling over the comms to make the request, it seemed more polite to go in person so we could apologize again for the mess.

Not surprisingly, Tami didn't look pleased to see us.

"You're back. What can I do for you?" she asked with the forced friendly tone of a disgruntled service worker.

"Hey, hope it wasn't too much trouble to clean up the mess on the shuttle. Sorry about that," I said, feeling it best to address the issue before asking for a favor. "We had a situation."

We explained the circumstances to Tami, and her demeanor softened as soon as she realized what we'd been up against.

"That was a creative solution," she said when we finished. "I'm glad you were able to work it out."

"Yeah, us too," I replied. "We were hoping to stock up so we don't find ourselves in a tough spot like that again."

"Camera, rope, tape, and paper, for starters," Kaiden said.

"Tactical accessory pack, basically." Tami nodded. "We can definitely set you up. Are you heading out again already?"

I looked to my companions. "Not sure, exactly."

"I guess we need to figure out where on the planet to go," Toran said.

"All right," the mechanic said. "If you'd like to finish planning, I'll gather some materials for you."

Kaiden nodded. "That would be great, thank you. We'll call down when we're getting ready to head out."

"Sounds good." Tami turned back to her work.

"Well, that went a lot better than I feared it might," I whispered while we walked out of the hangar.

"Nah, people in her position are used to picking up after people who make way bigger messes than we did—like getting ships blown up," Toran said.

"I guess that's true."

Kaiden glanced over his shoulder to make sure no one was nearby. "So, about the Protection artifact... how are we supposed to find it? Coordinates to a planet aren't specific enough to find an item."

"Colren didn't seem concerned," I said.

"Well, Colren also has a crew to manage and bosses to report to." Kaiden directed us to the side of the hallway and stopped. "As long as the ship is moving, it looks like we're making progress. And as soon as he sends us down to a planet, it's on *us* to deliver, not him."

I scowled. "You think he brought us here only to dump us off and hope for the best?"

"I wouldn't put it past him. You've seen how much he dodges direct questions."

"My hope was that he'd warm up after we produced something, which we did."

"A copy of some text off of a crystal column?" Kaiden scoffed. "Sure, it's not *nothing*, but the guy has been tasked with stopping the Darkness. Yeah, a thing they just called 'the Darkness' because no one knows what it is. I've been involved in this for a week, but the Hegemony has known about it for three months. If they've been working on a solution for that long and have turned to *us* for a solution, they're all kinds of desperate. You better bet he'd do something like turn us loose on a planet and hope for the best."

My stomach dropped. "Stars! You think it's really that bad?"

"I had my suspicions, but I thought maybe I was being paranoid. Based on how he reacted when we brought in that duplicate, though... I think I'd greatly underestimated the situation."

"All right, no more joking." I hugged myself.

"No, please do," Toran said. "I shouldn't have tried to stop you before. We need to stay sharp, and the best way to do that is by not getting wound too tightly."

Kaiden massaged between his eyes. "I really wanted this whole thing to be overblown theatrics—the Hegemony following some ancient lore because they thought it would play well in the ratings, while they actually have a real plan going and we're a distraction. Now, I'm starting to think we *are* the plan."

"Yeah, we said 'we should go here' and a jump was scheduled within minutes," Toran said. "People in Colren's position don't take orders from people like us under normal circumstances."

I sighed. "Guys, what have we gotten ourselves into?"

"We didn't get ourselves into anything. The trouble found us," Toran said.

"How'd you come in contact with an infected crystal, anyway?" I asked him.

"I was doing maintenance on a crystal interface console."

"Wait, you know how those things work?"

"The interface, yes," he confirmed. "Like I said, I'm an engineer by trade."

I turned to Kaiden. "What about you?"

"There was a crystal in one of the fields I was monitoring for my internship research. I used it for check-ins since it was the most convenient to get to."

"So, it was everyday life. It really *was* random," I said.

"Unless there's some validity to Colren's statement that the reality we're living in now was part of a universal reset no one remembers," Toran pointed out.

"Is that possible?"

"At this point, I'm willing to believe anything is possible," Kaiden replied. "But even if it is, it doesn't change what we're up against now and what we have to do. They're looking to us for answers."

"Our part isn't going to be finished when we seal the Archive, is it?" I asked.

Kaiden shook his head. "That's looking less likely the more I learn."

"I meant it when I said I'd do whatever it takes," Toran said.

"Me too," I murmured. "Even though it's on us to solve, we're the lucky ones. We're here—not trapped in a suspended state of nothingness."

Toran shook his head. "I hope they don't know where they are or what's happened."

I hoped so, too. The few seconds I was floating in nothingness before I materialized on the *Evangiel* were some of the most terrifying moments of my life. I can't imagine what it would do to a person to have that stretch on for hours, let alone months. "No sense worrying about things we can't control, as my mom always used to tell me," I said, trying to stay positive. "Let's just focus on getting them out of there."

He nodded. "Right."

"The question remains, how do we find the artifacts on these worlds?" questioned Kaiden.

"Well, we know your pendant reacts with the magical energy, right? Maybe we can use that somehow," I suggested.

He didn't look convinced. "That was within a couple hundred meters. Searching an entire planet is a completely different scale."

"There has to be some way, though, right? There must be a signal or something we could scan for," I insisted.

"You know, you might be on to something with that," Toran said slowly. "I had a bunch of equipment I'd carry with me for the interface console maintenance, of course, and some of the electronics would go haywire if they got too close to the crystal. I think it's safe to assume they do put off a measurable energy signature, but I can't say from how far away it could be detected."

I shrugged. "Sounds worth investigating."

Kaiden nodded. "I'll vote for anything that saves us from aimlessly wandering hostile continents looking for clues."

"I'll talk with the comm tech and see if we can figure something out," Toran offered.

"In the meantime, I don't suppose I could take a break? I really wasn't joking about that nap," I said. "It was dinnertime when I materialized up here—not that that has bearing on the new body, necessarily… I dunno."

"Yeah, now that you mention it, I'm starving," Kaiden said. "Why don't we grab a quick meal and then we'll get you some sleeping quarters?"

"Sounds good. Toran?"

He shook his head. "I'll eat while I work. I'll reach out when I have something."

"Okay, good luck," Kaiden bid as he led me toward the lift.

We walked several meters down the corridor in silence.

Kaiden glanced over this shoulder and stopped; we were alone. "How are you holding up?" he asked.

"Keeping the freak-outs at bay, so pretty good." I forced a smile.

"I can still barely wrap my head around any of this."

"You seem like you know what you're doing."

He chuckled. "Then I'm faking it well. This is so far beyond anything I would have done in my normal life."

"You seem pretty outgoing."

He shook his head. "I used to keep to myself—as soon as I wasn't trapped on a freighter forced to be around the same eight people all the time. Joking is your coping mechanism, trying to take everything in stride is mine."

There were moments when I'd thought Kaiden was maybe putting on an act, but I'd always assumed it was to show off in the way I'd seen people do in school when they were hoping to gain a measure of social notoriety. Talking with him now, however, I started to second-guess those impressions. "It's not a bad attitude to have," I replied after a pause. "I could have benefitted from that philosophy at other times in my life."

"It's weird," Kaiden mused. "When I woke up here, it was like a switch flipped. I'd always been the shy, nerdy guy who watched everyone else have all the fun, but I never knew how to get in on the action. I mean, have you ever known an agriculture major to be the life of a party? They called me 'plant guy', for stars' sake!"

I winced. "Not the best nickname."

"Other people had worse. But I was far from popular, and I was certainly never in a position to be the center of attention. To go from that to then suddenly have magical abilities and be *important*? I guess it went to my head. Now, though, seeing what deep shit we're in, I mostly just want to go back to being the anonymous guy collecting plant samples."

"Like it or not, we're no longer the people we used to be," I murmured.

"The more that sinks in, the more I'm not sure who I want to be going forward."

I was struck by the sincerity of Kaiden's statement. Any façade he may have put on before was gone. This was the real him, and he was just as scared and confused as me about our uncertain future. It was more than just our mission—we'd been reborn and offered the chance to become the people we'd always aspired to be. Our new selves were there for the taking. Except, it wasn't easy to let go of the parts of our pasts preventing us from completing that transition.

"I'm not sure who I want to be, either," I admitted.

His sky-blue eyes met mine, deep with a wisdom beyond his years. "I think you do. You just need to realize there's nothing holding you back now."

"Same for you."

Kaiden tore his gaze away. "Everything was so certain two weeks ago."

"Adapt and move forward, right?" I smiled.

He smiled back after a moment. "Yeah, I guess so."

We continued our stroll toward the lift and called it.

When we stepped inside, I leaned against the back wall. "I can understand why you adopted your new life philosophy. I can't imagine what it would have been like being the first to wake up here."

"Yeah, it was… disorienting, to say the least."

"You must have thought Colren was out of his mind when he told you what happened."

He laughed. "I did. It wasn't until Toran showed up that I started to think maybe there was some truth to it."

"Did you see the Darkness?" I asked him somberly. "In the crystal, I mean."

"Yes." He looked down. "That's the only reason I didn't take one of the shuttles and leave right away."

"What do you think it is?"

"Something unlike anything else we've seen before. My fear is that it's as ancient as the crystals themselves, and if we don't understand the tech we use, then how are we supposed to understand the alien tech attacking us?"

"Well, the Master Archive might have some answers."

"I hope so. And I hope Toran can come up with an artifact detector, or whatever might give us some direction."

I caught his gaze. "Hey, we'll figure this out."

He shook his head and laughed. "Elle, you are being *way* too calm about all of this."

"I may be young and inexperienced, but I've been through enough to know that losing my cool doesn't improve anything. I spent a lot of time being angry at the universe, and all it did was expend energy I could have spent working toward an actual solution."

"What were you angry about?" Kaiden asked as the lift doors opened.

I hadn't intended to bring up anything about my past, but I couldn't very well backpedal. "I used to do some reckless things with my friends," I explained while he led me toward the Mess. "We'd hang out in the hills above our town and do flips off of boulders and stuff. We were kids, so we thought the world revolved around us. If anything went wrong, there was always a reset to make it right.

"Then, one day, I fell and broke my arm, and I learned that the universe *didn't* revolve around me. I was twelve and should have known better by then. Anyway, it didn't heal right, so I could only raise my left arm up to here," I demonstrated the range of motion, "and there went my dreams of being a Ranger or anything else that would keep me away from a normal desk job."

He gave me a sympathetic nod. "For what it's worth, the central worlds have some pretty great medical tech these days. I bet they would have been able to fix you up."

"Maybe. But to a girl in a small town on an outer colony world, I didn't feel like I had options. I spent the better part of a year afterward moping that they didn't take the injury more seriously when it first happened, but really I was upset with myself for taking stupid risks."

"So, you started jumping off cliffs instead?"

I laughed. "I didn't say I was good at learning from my mistakes."

We reached the Mess entrance and Kaiden stopped outside the door. He was silent for several seconds. "I can understand how that injury on your homeworld changed a lot of things for you, but it doesn't define your future anymore."

"I know, and I'm grateful for that, despite the rather large caveat that the fate of our civilization is partially in my hands."

"Everything has a price."

"But, come on!" I held up my hands to mime a scale. "Shoulder injury. Interplanetary savior. The universe might be asking for a bit much here."

"In all fairness, you *did* get more than just your shoulder fixed. I mean, the pink hair had to cost at least two planets' worth of saving."

"I think I might also be a centimeter or two taller, so that's probably another four planets right there."

"It adds up fast. You might have gotten the Interplanetary Savior-level upgrade package after all."

"Damn! I'm locked in now." I snapped my fingers.

"Better make the most of it."

"I do have new friends to keep me company. It could be a lot worse."

"Admittedly, things got a lot better when you showed up—" Kaiden cut himself off and looked at the rubberized floor. "We should get food so you can have that nap."

I placed my hand on my stomach. "Yes! I'm starving. Fighting stone lizard-things apparently works up an appetite."

We stepped forward and the doors to the Mess parted, revealing a rectangular room with seating for seventy people at tables of various sizes. The starboard bulkhead sported broad viewports running the length of the room, and the port side had a buffet line and bar.

"Fancy," I commented.

"Don't let it fool you. They serve military gruel at its finest."

We grabbed trays and browsed the buffet line. I got an assortment of items to sample, most of which were more difficult to identify than I would have liked.

The tables were relatively empty, being an irregular hour for a meal, so we were able to get seats at a four-top by one of the viewports. Though the planet wasn't visible, there was a picturesque view of two moons.

I dug into my meal. After one bite, my shoulders slumped. "All right, I see what you mean."

"Yeah, even as an agro major, I have no idea what this green stuff is."

"I'm just going to pretend its arugula and call it good."

He nodded. "Can't argue with that plan."

We ate mostly in silence, only making the occasional comment about missing fresh produce from our respective homeworlds. It was nice to find we could be comfortable sitting together without saying anything; I'd found some people always had to keep a conversation going or they'd get nervous and weird. That was something I'd always valued in Adrianne and Jiro back home—hanging out at the cliff on a sunny afternoon quietly enjoying the view. I hoped the meal was a sign I'd be able to have a similar rapport with Kaiden as we got to know each other better.

My eyelids were heavy by the time we finished eating. After bussing our table, Kaiden showed me the residential area one deck below, near our jump pod room and the bioprinter.

"It's not much," Kaiden said as we approached, "but you do get your own room."

"That's good. I'm not used to sharing."

"Only child?" he asked.

"No, younger brother." A sharp twinge struck my heart as I thought about him and the rest of my family.

"I have two older brothers, myself. Fortunately, they took an interest in the family business so I wasn't forced in that direction, too."

I released a long breath. "Being the oldest does come with a lot of expectations."

"Just wait until you get to tell your parents this story."

"They'll flip—and that's only based on what's happened so far. I can't imagine what it'll be like by the end."

"We'll find out soon enough." Kaiden gestured to one of the doors. "This one will be you."

I placed my hand on the panel next to the door, and the door slid open. Inside, the chamber contained a single bed, wardrobe, and wash facilities behind a partition.

"Not bad," I said.

"I'll be next door if you need anything. Or, comms." He pointed to his ear.

I smiled. "Thanks."

He glanced at his own door. "All right, sleep well. See you in a few hours."

"See you then. I'm looking forward to seeing what Toran comes up with."

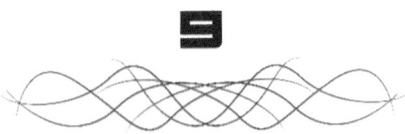

I DRUMMED MY fingers on the tabletop, regretting my agreement to get out of bed.

"You really think this will work?" I asked Toran.

"It's all guesstimated science. There's no way to be certain," he admitted.

"Only one way to find out." Kaiden removed the crystal pendant from around his neck and handed it to the other man, per the proposed plan.

While Kaiden and I had slept for the past five hours, Toran had been hard at work with one of Central Command's communication specialists in the same common room where I'd been introduced to my two companions, though it now contained replacement chairs and Toran's sculpture of twisted metal had been removed.

Toran had supposedly figured out a way to scan for the unique energy signature emitted by items with magical properties. His explanation for how the detection system worked sounded straightforward enough, but we hadn't had a great track record of things going according to plan. The result of his efforts with the communication tech was a device the size of a dinner plate, which has a cradle to serve as the interface with Kaiden's crystal. Based on what Toran had explained, the device would read the energy signature from the crystal and then amplify and broadcast it using the *Evangiel*'s communication and sensor suite.

Though Toran had explained the science behind it, I was more interested in the results.

"Here it goes…" Toran placed the crystal in the device on the table in front of us.

As soon as the crystal pendant was in the cradle, a soft hum filled the air. I was drawn to the tone, though I had no direct way to interact with it. I imagined a current of energy flowing through me, and the sense of it filled my mind.

On the table, the device emitted a soft blue glow, though the crystal itself remained unchanged.

"Hmm, interesting," Toran said.

"What's happening?" Kaiden asked. There was a hint of concern in his tone, which I attributed to his crystal being used in the experimental activity.

"The good news is that the device is working how I hoped," Toran explained. "The less good news is that we're getting multiple hits on the planet."

I frowned. "So, we still don't know where the artifact is?"

"No, but this narrows it down a lot," he said.

Kaiden pursed his lips in apparent thought. "What might also resonate with this tone?"

"Likely crystals."

"And how similar are those crystals to each other?" Kaiden asked.

"You know—they come in all sizes," Toran replied.

"But what about their resonance, or whatever? Is there a unique signature?"

Toran perked up. "I see where you're going with this."

He made some entries on the touch-surface tabletop, and a list of numeric values appeared. "Okay, these are all of the hits we got on the planet. Let's run an analysis to find their similarities and differences." He made another entry.

The items in the list shifted to the left and additional columns appeared—some numerals, and others showing a waveform. Segments of the waveforms and secondary lines within them were highlighted in different colors.

Toran pointed to one. "Okay, it looks like this green line is the common thread in all of them. The waveform depicted with the purple line appears in all but four of the samples, though its amplitude changes."

"Maybe that has something to do with the crystals of different sizes— larger the crystal, larger the amplitude?" I suggested, somewhat amazed that anything from my physics class had stuck with me.

"Could be," Toran agreed.

"Hasn't the Hegemony studied all of this?" Kaiden asked. "You'd think there'd be documentation of the crystals' properties."

"Yes, their research is why this analysis has taken seconds rather than days. I've cross-referenced our readings with the metadata," replied Toran. "This is different, though—none of those researchers had access to the kind of crystal that you have. I don't know what makes it different, exactly, but it's throwing off some weird readings that don't match anything on the record."

My brow knit. "Do any of the readings on the surface have those same weirdnesses?" Well, at least I'd been able to ask one question while sounding like I knew what I was talking about.

Toran continued to examine the data. "That's what I'm trying to figure out. It's difficult to gauge because the sensors aren't designed to measure this sort of thing. I think they're missing some of the nuances."

Kaiden leaned on the desktop. "You mentioned that the purple line is missing in four of the samples. That may be significant."

"Yes, I was thinking that, too." Toran's eyes narrowed as he scanned over the details about those four data points. "There's definitely something different about these. It's possible they're not recording crystals at all."

"One might be the artifact," I said.

Toran nodded. "Perhaps."

"Well, it's only four sites, right?" Kaiden said. "That's a whole lot less to search than an entire planet. Why don't we just do a fly-by and check it out?"

"Sounds good to me. They're all on the same continent, so we don't even have to circle the globe."

I smiled. "Even better."

Kaiden tapped behind his ear. "Commander, we have targets on the planet." He explained what we'd found and the plan to perform a visual assessment. Within a minute, we had confirmation to proceed.

I called down to Tami to give her a heads up about our imminent departure, and we proceeded to the hangar.

"I can't wait to see what the artifact is," I said.

"I'm not holding my breath for anything wondrous," Toran replied.

"It's gotta be ancient though, right?" I said. "These things probably date back to when the crystalline network was created."

"I'm certainly intrigued. I mean, as of a day ago, I didn't even know the crystals *were* created, so any items developed by those same designers must be pretty powerful."

"True. If nothing else, it will have unique properties—though that doesn't mean it will be useful."

"Hey, as long as it gets the Archive open, it doesn't matter what else it does or doesn't do," I pointed out.

Kaiden held up his index finger. "Excellent point."

We arrived at the hangar and found Tami waiting for us by the shuttle with a backpack resting on the deck.

"We have everything ready for you," she said. "Shuttle is put back together, and I have some extra supplies for you." She hoisted the backpack from her feet and held it outward.

Toran took it from her like it was a feather. "Thank you."

"I threw in a couple of extra things I thought might come in handy— med supplies, emergency rations, fire starter, thermal blankets. You never know."

"I've got the fire starting handled," Kaiden said with a grin, holding up his index finger with a flame on its tip.

"But if you're unconscious, we're screwed," I countered. "Thank you, Tami. We'll try not to tear it apart again this time around."

She flashed a weary smile. "If you do, we'll just put it back together again."

After an exchange of well wishes and reiterated thanks, we boarded the shuttle and assumed our seats on the bridge. Kaiden initiated the startup sequence, and we began taxiing toward the electrostatic shield.

"Fingers crossed that the weather on this planet cooperates," I said.

Our shuttle glided out of the hangar and followed its automated course to the first location Toran had identified on the planet.

Kaiden remained much more attentive than he had at the beginning of the previous voyage—not surprising, given what had happened last time. However, his concerns proved unwarranted as we descended through the atmosphere toward the target.

The cloud cover was light, especially in contrast to the last planet, and I took in the view of the landscape on the approach. All the land as far as I could see in every direction was green, broken only by the occasional body of water. The terrain was predominantly rolling hills, though several mountain ranges towered in the distance. At least three-quarters of the visible land was forested. I couldn't make out the type of trees at altitude, but the canopy was thick enough that I had no idea what secrets the forests may contain; a hidden tomb for an ancient artifact wasn't out of the question.

"We're coming up on the first location," Kaiden announced.

I followed the line displayed on the front viewport's holographic overlay. It appeared to lead to one of the green hills in a treeless area, indistinguishable from the others around it.

"I don't see anything there," I said.

"Yeah, I don't, either." Kaiden frowned.

"This was the strongest of the anomalous signals, so it seemed to be the most likely location," Toran reported from behind me.

"Should I set us down?" Kaiden asked. He checked his pendant and it was glowing, but only slightly.

"Circle us around. Let's see if any landmark jumps out," Toran suggested.

Kaiden took over manual control of the shuttle and performed three circles of the target area.

I kept an eye on the ground with each pass, looking for anything that might explain the energy readings. As far as I could tell, it was only hills, forest, and a field—no different from the landscape for kilometers in every direction.

"Another cave?" Kaiden proposed.

Toran shrugged. "Perhaps, but that could take a long time to identify. Let's see if the other locations have anything obvious, and we can circle back to here if we come up short."

"I like that plan," I said.

Kaiden switched back over to the automated flight path, setting the second location as the destination.

The landscape transitioned into mountains and then open grasslands as the hundreds of kilometers zoomed by beneath us. The greens yellowed the further northeast we went, and eventually turned to a warm golden hue.

"This reminds me of where I was doing my internship on Falstan II," Kaiden commented.

I scrunched my nose. "It's a little... plain."

"Flat, rock-hard soil, and little precipitation—the perfect environment for testing experimental strains of grain to support new colonies trying to become self-sustaining in the border worlds," he replied.

"Ah, yes. That makes sense."

After four hundred kilometers, the shuttle slowed and descended toward a crystal monolith rising from the flat landscape.

"Okay, now *that's* something worth investigating," Kaiden said after confirming that his pendant was glowing in its presence.

"Agreed, set it down," Toran said.

Kaiden piloted the shuttle to twenty meters from the crystal. It came to rest on the ground with a slight bump.

"Investigating time!" I jumped up from my seat. If I was going to be the 'new me' and commit myself to the mission at hand, I needed to get psyched up.

"I can't match that enthusiasm. Lead the way." Kaiden flourished his hand.

I smiled. "I figured I should compensate for the lack of scenery. I mean, the last place was in a hidden valley with giant crystals and stuff. This is... grass."

Toran followed me into the common room. "Not very riveting, is it?"

"It would be a *lot* more interesting if we found an artifact buried at the base of the crystal," I said.

The large man chuckled. "I appreciate your dedication to finding the redeeming qualities of the location."

I shrugged. "Hey, with the size of the task in front of us, I figure we should focus on the little things."

"And that includes, 'Ooo, we saw a pretty thing'?" Kaiden asked.

"Was that an objection?"

"No..."

I nodded. "Good, then there's no harm in appreciating the sights. After all, we're out to save these worlds—I think it's worth knowing exactly what it is we're fighting for."

"Protecting my home was already enough motivation," Toran said.

"For me, too, but Elle's right—this isn't just about us," Kaiden said.

Toran released the hatch seal, dropping the ramp. "I know."

We filed out of the shuttle and jogged the twenty meters to the crystal monument. The ground was firm underfoot, and the amber, knee-high grass crunched with each step.

The monument was different than what I was used to back on Erusan. Rather than an enclosure and a high-tech interface panel, this four-meter-tall crystal only had three stone columns placed around it.

"Okay… what do we do?" I placed my hands on my hips.

"Excellent question." Kaiden crossed his arms. "Toran? This is the Protection artifact, so I imagine you'll have to be the one to retrieve it."

Toran lumbered toward the central crystal and reached out toward it. The crystal's soft blue glow intensified as his hand neared, but there was no other change. He made contact.

An electric shock radiated from the crystal and arced to the three columns. The stones shuddered, then rotated ninety degrees to the right.

My eyes widened. "Okay, that was something."

Kaiden looked around. "Is there a door, or…?"

Toran frowned. "I don't understand."

I circled the crystal, looking for any clue. It was only unremarkable grass beside the monument. "I've got nothing, guys."

"Neither do I," Kaiden said.

Toran took a deep breath. "Why don't we inspect the other locations? This might not be the first one, or perhaps one of those has a clue."

Kaiden nodded. "All right."

We returned to the shuttle. As we took off, I kept an eye out the viewport to see if there was any change to the surrounding landscape, but nothing was visible from the air, either.

The next location was to the south. Grasslands became sub-tropical forests as we continued southward. The elevation increased, and eventually we arrived at a plateau surrounded by lush jungle. Like the previous site, there was a solitary crystal with three stone columns arranged in a triangle around it.

Kaiden set the shuttle down near the crystal at the center of the plateau.

"Any bets on if this one does the same thing?" I asked.

Kaiden shook his head. "I'm not taking that bet. The answer is too obvious."

Toran rose from his seat. "Let's find out if you're right."

We jogged down the shuttle's ramp and approached the monument. Kaiden and I kept our distance while Toran walked up to it with his hand outstretched. Again, the crystal's glow intensified as he approached, and then electricity arced out to the columns when he touched it. The columns each turned ninety degrees.

I titled my head while staring at the configuration. "Is it just me, or is the layout of those stone columns relative to the crystal remarkably similar to the placement of these monuments and that first site we checked out?"

"It is," Kaiden agreed.

"We should go to the fourth site and then return to the first," Toran said.

I pointed over my shoulder with my thumb. "Back to the shuttle."

We repeated the process of activating the crystal at the final site, which was in the mountains to the west.

As we flew back toward the first site in the rolling hills, I held my breath that there would be an obvious change to the landscape that would indicate we'd done the right thing. Unfortunately, it looked the same.

"Kaiden shook his head. "I don't get it."

"I never suspected it would be easy," Toran said. He caught himself. "Well, I *hoped* it would be, but I didn't figure that would be the case."

"And just think, after we do this, we get to do it two more times on different planets!" I threw up my hands with mock excitement.

Kaiden sighed. "Except, it will probably be something completely different, because it would be way too straightforward to, you know, let us just do the thing."

"We need to demonstrate worth," Toran said. "I believe the point is to show our commitment to the disciplines we chose."

"What might Protection embody?" I asked.

"I have no idea."

"Well, looks like we'll need to do some wandering, after all." Kaiden set down the shuttle in a relatively flat area in the dip between two hills. There were few trees in the surrounding kilometer, but a dense forest ringed the site in a crescent shape to the west and north.

"We're a little southeast of the signal's epicenter, but this looked like the best landing site in the vicinity," he stated.

"It will be fine." Toran grabbed our backpack of emergency supplies and led the way off the shuttle.

The ground was spongier here, almost like walking on padded carpet. Vibrant green grass grew to my knees in most places, with some patches nearly waist-height. The numerous hills made it impossible to see more than fifty meters in any direction while at the low points, so we stopped at each crest to survey our surroundings.

"Ugh, there could be something one ridge over and we'd never know," I groaned after we'd been wandering aimlessly for half an hour.

"Are you sure your discipline isn't 'patience', not 'protection'?" Kaiden joked.

"A solution will present itself," Toran stated, but anxiety added a quaver to his voice. More than any of us, he bore the self-imposed weight of responsibility to look after his family. His very transformation from a small-statured man to his present hulking proportions spoke to his commitment to care for them. To him, I imagined this search for the Protection artifact was more than just finding an item—it was a tangible representation of his duty to defend his loved ones.

"Yeah, just have to keep looking." I wanted to say something more flippant, but I could tell he was already on edge. I didn't envy what it must feel like to know my child was in danger.

I followed Toran down the hillside to one of the more open areas we'd encountered. The grassy plain transitioned into forest a hundred meters away, and a high ridge was ahead of us to the northeast. A gentle breeze rustled the grass as we walked. Aside from our own footprints and the wind, the world was eerily quiet. Eventually, though, a new sound was carried on the breeze—a series of low thuds.

I came to attention, not sure if it was only in my head. Listening intently, trying to identify the source of the sound. I determined it was coming from the direction we were headed—and it was getting louder. The ground rumbled underfoot.

I froze. "Uh, guys… What is that?"

10

THE HAIRS ON the back of my neck stood up. Whatever was on the other side of the ridge was closing fast on our position.

Tremors shook the ground—a steady rhythm I feared was footsteps.

My concerns were confirmed a moment later when a stone face appeared over the crest of the hill. It looked as though its features had been carved into a boulder, with deep eyes, a shallow nose, and cracked lips molded in an expressionless line. Flecks of moss provided green and brown contrast, creating the illusion of a patch beard and hair on top of its head. As it lumbered up the far side of the hill, broad shoulders with the same stone-like appearance came into view, followed by a deep chest.

I didn't wait to see the rest of it. "Run!"

Pivoting toward the tree line, I broke into a full-on sprint with Toran and Kaiden to my right.

"Where did it come from?" Kaiden shouted while we ran.

I kept my attention on the ground in front of me. "No idea. And I don't want to find out if it has friends!"

We were almost to the trees—just another dozen meters to go.

"Gah!"

Kaiden stumble at my side, apparently having tripped over something hidden in the knee-high grass. Toran caught his shoulder to keep him from falling.

"Thanks." Kaiden found his footing and continued moving forward.

Toran, however, stopped.

I slowed. "What are you doing?" I called back over my shoulder.

"I think this creature is what we're looking for." He pointed toward Kaiden's chest.

The crystal was glowing vibrant blue, like it had on Crystallis when we found the valley containing the Archive.

I stopped and turned around. "No way!"

"*That's* the thing emitting the signal?" Kaiden stared with a slack jaw at the rock titan pursuing us. "What are we supposed to do with it?"

"I believe that's for me to figure out." Toran clenched his fists and squared off against the approaching giant. "I'm here for the Protection artifact!" he bellowed.

The giant halted. It was even larger than I'd estimated, standing nine meters tall with rock forearms the size of Toran. "Prove your worth," it boomed.

"How?" I asked no one in particular.

The giant clapped its massive hands, then crouched down and pounded its palms against the ground. The force shook the land underfoot, and the rumbling continued to intensify. It was soon shaking so much I had difficulty keeping my footing. Just when I was wondering if it would ever stop, new forms emerged from the ground, swelling under the grass and soil.

I stumbled backward. "What the...?"

The first creature emerged—a stone golem reminiscent of the rock titan, only two meters tall. The others broke through with a spray of soil and the shaking stopped. Six of them surrounded us; all had their fists raised, ready for a fight.

I drew my sabre. "Do we have to take out all of those things?"

Kaiden conjured an orb of electrical energy on the end of his staff. "I think we're about to find out."

Toran made the first move. He ran toward the nearest golem five meters away, raising his right hand on the final approach. His fist connected with the side of the golem's head

The creature roared in a deep, raspy voice. It swung at Toran with its club-like arm, catching him in the center of his chest.

Toran groaned and staggered back but managed to stay on his feet. Without hesitation, he drove his left first upward to uppercut the golem.

Before I could see its reaction, the wind was knocked out of me and I found myself face-down in the grass. I quickly rolled onto my back, annoyed with myself that I'd been distracted by a single engagement while completely ignoring my own surroundings. I wasn't surprised to look up at two golems standing over me.

"Hey, guys!" I greeted the creatures while slicing my sword toward their heads.

The two golems blocked the slash with their forearms, then drove their other fists down as a counterattack.

I rolled free just in time, then leaped to my feet. "That's how you want to be, huh?"

I attacked and parried, the golems using their arms to swing and stab as they circled me.

My responses to their attacks came to me as a clear vision a moment before I acted. Without thinking, I spun and ducked, occasionally thrusting or slashing my sword when an opening presented itself. I hadn't ever trained in that type of combat, but it was a part of me now like I'd been practicing for my whole life. I was strong, precise, agile—the way I'd always dreamed of being. Through whatever process had re-formed me on the *Evangiel*, I had also been imbued with muscle memory to make the most of my new body. And I loved it.

Unfortunately, those skills weren't going to win the fight with my current foes. Despite repeatedly landing clean blows on the golems with the electrified edge of my sabre, I wasn't making a scratch. I needed a new strategy.

I risked a look around to locate my companions. Toran was out of my field of vision, but I spotted Kaiden seven meters away to my right front. He was engaged with one golem of his own, and a pile of mud rested on matted grass nearby.

"Did you take one out?" I shouted to him.

"Yeah, the energy orbs eventually did the trick," he replied, lobbing another crackling ball at the golem near him.

"My sword is useless." I kicked one of my golems away as it got too close, then blocked a swing from the other. "This is getting old."

"Almost... done... here..." Kaiden said in between rapid-fire orbs cast from his staff.

The golem lunged for him in what appeared to be a last-resort move, and Kaiden thrust his staff forward at the same moment another energy orb released. The staff entered the golem's chest. The creature disintegrated into a pile of mud.

I had no time to offer congratulations before the two golems attacking me decided to try a new move. One reached out to hug me, and the other dropped down and tried to curl itself around my legs.

It was a brilliant move, I had to admit. They must have realized that Kaiden's weapon was a genuine threat, so, by entwining themselves around me, they could gain some measure of safety, assuming he wouldn't be willing to fire on his comrade.

I wasn't about to go down without a fight.

I lifted my right leg in time to keep it out of the bottom golem's grasp, and then pinched my outside leg against the golem's back. The top golem had pinned my arms against my sides, but I hadn't lost my grip on my sword. I thrust the blade into the ground to use it as a pivot point, then kicked upward with my right leg as hard as I could. The force was enough to loosen the bottom golem's grip on my boot, and I got free.

The top golem still had me wrapped in a vise-like embrace, however, and it tightened its grip around my chest, forcing the air from my lungs.

An electrical shock coursed through me, and the golem's grip loosened. Without hesitation, I ducked from its grasp and leaped free. I ran five meters away.

In the corner of my vision, Kaiden was advancing with his staff leveled on the golem. Another orb blasted from the end of the weapon.

I took a deep breath, flexing my bruised ribs.

"You okay?" he asked while stepping sideways toward me.

"Yeah, thanks." I repositioned so we'd be standing abreast when he reached my position. While I'd normally not like the idea of someone hurtling magical attacks in my direction, it was clear Kaiden had banked on the fact that it took numerous blasts to bring down a golem, so the creature would absorb most of the attack and leave me unscathed. Fortunately, he had been right.

Despite the number of blasts required, those magical attacks *did* have a measurable impact on the golem, while my sword did nothing. "Hey, do you think you could charge my sword?" I questioned when he was by my side.

Kaiden kept firing toward the golems. "What?"

"I saw what happened when you took out the last one—the end of your staff was electrified and it pierced its chest," I explained. "My sword isn't breaking the surface, but maybe…"

"We can try," Kaiden said. He paused his assault for a moment, touching the end of the staff to my sabre's blade. Electric sparks danced across the metal. "Huh. I think that actually worked."

I grinned. "Nice!"

"Might not last long. Get swinging!"

While he focused on the golem that had grabbed my chest, I refocused on the bottom one that had gone after my feet. It had since stood up and appeared to be sizing up another attack.

I made my move, racing forward for a strike center mass. To distract it, I pretended to be swinging for its neck, but I brought my shoulder back at the last second and switched to a stabbing motion. My electrified blade plunged into the creature's chest. A roar turned to a gurgle as the golem dissolved into a muddy mound.

I wiped my forehead with the back of my hand. "That was ridiculous."

Kaiden lowered his staff. "Where's Toran?"

I spun around to search for our other companion. After three seconds, I spotted him engaged with a golem twenty meters away.

We ran in his direction. After going no more than five strides, one of Toran's fists struck the golem in its chest, and the creature disintegrated. He must have already taken care of the other one, as I didn't see any golems remaining.

"Was that it? Was that the test?" I asked.

Kaiden shook his head. "I don't know. There's still that." He gestured at the rock titan looming over us.

The massive creature stood motionless, watching us with its expressionless eyes.

I released a long breath. There was no way we could take on something that big, considering how much trouble the little golems had given us. We'd taken out its minions; that seemed like a reasonably rigorous challenge.

"Is that the proof you needed?" Toran shouted to the giant.

In response, the giant clapped its hands together, then pounded its palms against the ground. Following the tremble from the initial impact, the shaking intensified, and the ground once again swelled upward until half a dozen new golems burst through the soil.

My jaw dropped. "You *have* to be kidding!"

11

"I AM *NOT* doing all of that again," Kaiden groaned.

Toran stared up at the rock titan. "We've been going about this wrong. We need to go after the giant itself."

I pointed up at it. "That? How are we supposed to take on *that*? It's huge!"

"I don't know, but we'll figure out something." He ran toward its foot.

"He pretends to be rational, but he's out of his mind!" I objected.

"We can't let him go in alone," Kaiden said. "Don't get crushed."

Dumbstruck, I ran after them. "What kind of advice is that?"

"Sorry, it's all I've got."

I looked down at my sword; the electrical charge had dissipated. If the blade had been ineffective against the golems, it was laughable against the rock titan. "Do the thing to my sword again," I requested.

Kaiden touched his staff to my blade while we kept moving forward, slowing just enough to minimize the bounce in our strides. The blade lit up with electrical energy once again.

"Thanks. Be careful," I told him.

"You too."

We bolted in separate directions, with Kaiden heading to the giant's right while I joined Toran on the left to go after it with physical attacks. I knew the clock was ticking with the charge on my blade.

The giant was entirely stone, from what I could see, so there weren't vulnerable parts of it like there would be with flesh. Its proportions were alien to my eye, with arms that hung down to its knees, short legs, and a rounded torso. I didn't know how we could possibly disable or kill a stone creature, but I figured the best way to start was to knock it down.

So, I went for its foot. After all, I figure that stubbing my toe always made *me* want to sit down, so having a sword jammed into a heel probably wouldn't feel great, either... assuming the creature *could* feel anything.

The foot more closely resembled a flat-ish boulder than anything in my anatomical frame of reference. I ran up to it and slashed with my sword. The electrified blade sliced into the stone, but the giant seemed completely unfazed. I drew my weapon back and stabbed it at the point where an ankle bone would be on a person. Again, no effect.

"This isn't working!"

Next to me, Toran was pummeling his fists into the back of the giant's calf. "Persistence."

I didn't buy it. At the rate we were going, the giant might be injured enough to fall sometime in the next century—if it didn't get annoyed and step on us first.

We'd need a more aggressive approach. I only stood to approximately the middle of the giant's calf, and its ankle was close to the height of my waist. I'd need to get higher if I was going to access a part of the rock titan that might be more susceptible to real damage.

The giant lifting up its left foot to take a slow step. I took the opportunity, jumping onto the top of the foot.

"Elle!" Toran called, but I ignored him. This was my chance to prove to myself that I had what it took to be a part of the bigger fight unfolding around me.

I held out my hands to either side to keep myself steady as the giant raised its foot. The creature's forearm was angled at forty-five degrees above me to my left; it was the closest thing to a ramp I'd ever get to access its head. Keeping one arm outstretched for balance, I quickly sheathed my sword. The rock titan was about to complete its step, and I needed to make my move at apex of its stride.

I leaped, spreading my arms as I flew toward its wrist—the only point with a small enough circumference to give me a chance of hanging on. My chest slammed against the stone, almost knocking the wind out of me as I landed on an awkward angle half on top of the giant's hand. I searched with my fingertips for any semblance of a handhold. My left hand came up empty, but I was able to lock in my right hand. Fortunately, my left leg had hooked over the top of the wrist, so I was able to hold myself in place while I continued to search for a proper grip for my left fingers.

The giant raised its hand, blurring the world around me. My stomach lurched from the sudden motion, but I managed to lock in my grip.

A second later, the giant flicked its wrist in an attempt to shake me off. I held on with all my might, realizing that I hadn't thought through my plan very well—or, at all.

My fingertips burned as I clung to the stone. I started to slip.

The shaking subsided. I may only have a moment to act.

"Elle!" Toran called from below. I look down and saw him holding up a length of rope from the bag Tami had prepared for us.

I shifted my weight to straddle the giant's wrist, freeing my hands. Toran chucked the rope bundle up to me, keeping hold of one end in his hands. I caught the rope and then dashed up the top side of the giant's arm toward its shoulder.

I'd only made it as far as the creature's elbow when its other hand swooped in to brush me off. There was no doubt in my mind I'd be crushed between the two stone surfaces.

With no other option, I rolled off the far side of the arm, still gripping the rope with Toran holding the other end. The rope caught in the stone groove between the creature's forearm and elbow. I dangled five meters high in the air, not sure if I should climb back up or descend.

"We've got it, come on!" Toran shouted. He was waving for me to descend.

I slid down the rope. My palms burned, forcing me to loosen my grip. I couldn't control my fall at the end, and I landed hard, rolling to the side.

"Grab the rope!" Toran instructed.

I leaped to my feet and managed to get a hold on the rope before the giant yanked it away. I pulled down my coat sleeves to cover the raw palms of my hand, and then tightened my grip.

A sudden roar behind me almost made me drop it again. One of the six new golems was lumbering toward me.

"Ugh, those things are still here?" I backed away from it, wishing I could sprout another set of hands to hold my sword.

Toran ran toward me while keeping his end of the rope taut on the giant's arm. He circled his rope above me; the two lengths crossed behind the creature's arm and cinched tight, unlikely to slip off.

"This way," he said, dashing behind the rock titan to outpace the pursuing golem.

We kept the rope taut as we looped around the back side of the giant. I wasn't sure exactly what Toran had planned, but he had the look in his eyes of someone with a vision.

The plan started to become clear as we rounded the creature's right side. The rope was now angled across the giant's back from where it was wrapped around the left elbow. Unfortunately, there were also five golems waiting for us, who had encircled Kaiden.

"What are you doing?" he questioned us while blasting an electrical ball at one of the golems.

"Taking this thing down," Toran replied. He cut across the giant's front, jumping over its right foot and then the left.

I followed him as closely as I could, glancing to my side to see that Kaiden had halted his energy ball hurling and was backing away from the giant and the golems while keeping an eye on what we were doing.

We rounded the giant's left ankle, coming full circle with the loop.

"Kaiden!" Toran called.

The other man ran over to us, glancing over his shoulder to make sure the golems couldn't reach him.

"Hurry," Toran urged.

We bundled the two ends of the rope together and continued the circuit around the giant's back for a second pass, taking us dangerously close to the group of golems. At the giant's right side, the three of us lined up with Toran at the head of the group. Together, we leaned back and pulled as hard as we could.

The rope cinched tighter, keeping the giant from being able to lift its feet. We didn't have the strength to draw the creature's legs together and knock it off balance, but it was enough to distract it. The other golems didn't seem to like us getting the upper hand; they made a run for us.

"Stand clear! Going to rope one," Toran instructed.

I didn't know what he meant until I saw him duck one of the golems' attacks, then roll and loop it from behind with the rope. He deftly circled it, pinning the creature's hands against its sides.

The golem shrieked, then ran away as it tried to get free from the tie. However, this only drew the rope tighter around the giant. The remaining golems weren't fooled as easily, and they lunged for us.

"If there's another stage to the plan, we should do it now!" I shouted over the golems' roars, drawing my sword once more; the electric charge had long since worn off, but I could at least use it to block attacks.

"I'll handle them," Toran said in a calm, even tone.

His hands clenched into fists and he charged toward the golems. He barreled into the throng, landing a firm blow on each golem as he ran past. Something had changed in his offense, though there was no external alteration in appearance. The calm confidence he exhibited moments before had morphed into an aura of determination.

As he raced toward the enemies with his fists drawn back, his eyes narrowed and he set his jaw.

The blows connected two at a time, plowing through the golems and knocking them backward and to the side. Before the first two creatures had fallen halfway down, they had already begun disintegrating. He struck the next two, and they toppled aside, and in one motion he finished off the remaining golem nearby.

With its arms bound, the rock titan was unable to summon more. The one bound to the end of the rope continued to struggle, tightening the hold around the giant.

Toran rounded on the enormous rock beast. "What more must I do to prove myself?"

The rock titan made no verbal response. It looked down at me and nodded, the gaze of its dark eyes burrowing into me. Then, it fell forward—directly for us.

Kaiden and Toran ran to the side.

I was frozen; I knew I had to get out of the way, but it felt like my feet had been rooted to the ground.

"Elle, move!" Toran shouted.

A shadow passed over me as the giant tipped over toward where I was standing.

I willed myself to move, but my feet wouldn't obey. There wouldn't be time to escape.

Toran dash toward me in the final moments before the giant would crush me, towering over me to face the falling giant.

I braced for the impact.

A deafening crack of colliding rocks overwhelmed my senses. The light blocked out around me as the giant reached the ground. Only, I wasn't crushed. Toran and I were still standing, and we were surrounded by a mound of soil. A smaller mound to my left stood where I had last seen the final golem.

Heart pounding in my ears, I brushed the dirt off my hair and shoulders. "What happened?"

Toran shook his head. "I don't know. I held up my hands over you, and it fell apart the moment it touched me."

Kaiden ran over to us, gathering his cloak in his hands so it didn't drag in the wet soil. "Are you all right?"

"Yeah," I replied.

Toran frowned. "That wasn't how I expected that to go. I thought the giant would give us the artifact if we defeated it."

Kaiden was silent for several seconds. "Maybe defeating it wasn't the point. The discipline is Protection, right? You put yourself in harm's way in an attempt to save Elle, and that's when it dissolved."

"Hmm." Toran nodded. "Perhaps, but what about the artifact?"

"I don't know. Maybe it's not a literal 'thing' but rather achieving a certain state of mind?" Kaiden suggested.

I scrunched up my nose. "That doesn't seem right, given our experience on Crystallis."

"We assumed it must be an item when we looked at the translation, but there also wasn't anything in the chamber to indicate a place to insert a physical thing," he countered.

Toran brushed himself off. "We should look around. Perhaps something new has appeared in the landscape. That giant came from somewhere."

We hopped over the piles of soil in the battlefield and cleaned ourselves up as best we could. After checking the mound of the former giant to make sure it hadn't had an item inside it, we decided to go back toward the hills in the direction the rock titan had come from.

We crested two ridges on our trek northeast. The first was identical to the dozens of other rises we had traversed since leaving the shuttle, but at the brow of the second, the landscape changed. In the place that appeared to be a former hill, there was now an open maw of moist soil, presumably the place where the giant had been birthed. At its center was a crystal monument similar to the others we had visited on the planet, only twice the size.

Every crystal I had seen in my lifetime was opaque white that glowed with a soft blue inner light. Aside from the Darkness, there was never anything inside the crystals. This one, however, was different. Suspended within the crystal, three meters from the ground, was a dark object; I couldn't make out what it was, exactly, from this distance.

"Was this here before?" Kaiden asked.

I shook my head. "We flew right over this area with the shuttle. It must have been covered up until the giant was formed."

Toran's gaze was fixed on the object inside the crystal. "I imagine that must be the artifact."

"A reasonable guess," I concurred.

Without another word, Toran loped down the hillside toward the eight-meter-tall crystal. Unlike the other crystals on the world, this one didn't have any secondary stones ringing it. The base was more than two meters wide, placing the object inside deep in the crystal. As we approached, the object took on more definition, and I realized that it was actually two items placed next to each other—a set of gauntlets.

Toran surveyed the crystal. "If those gauntlets are the artifact, how am I supposed to get them out?"

"Try touching it," I suggested. "The others activated when you did."

Tentatively, Toran reached out to place his right palm on the crystal's smooth side.

The inner, blue glow intensified until I needed to close my eyes to slits. With a sudden burst, the crystal shattered into a fine dust. The gauntlets within floated gently to the ground.

Toran stood in stunned silence for a moment, then reached down to pick them up. As his fingers brushed the gauntlets, a golden wave of light radiated from them and enveloped him. It only lasted for a second, but when it faded, a contented smile was on Toran's lips and he had a brightness in his eyes where there had only been concern and sadness before.

"I think we found the magical item," I quipped.

"Indeed." Toran slipped the backpack off of his shoulders, setting it on the ground, and rested the gauntlets on top. He removed his knuckle guards and placed them inside the bag, then gently picked up the gauntlets.

The gloves didn't look large enough to accommodate his hands to my eye, yet they slid on with no trouble. Once in place, they moved and flexed more like a second skin than armor. Predominantly black, the gloves were adorned with golden accents and lines of ornate scripture, which appeared to be in the same Laeric language as the crystal monument on Crystallis.

"One down, two to go," Kaiden said.

"How do you feel?" I asked Toran.

He examined his hands as he rotated his wrists front to back. "Different, but I can't quite explain how." He thought for a moment. "You know that moment when you first woke up on the *Evangiel*, and you selected your discipline? It's like that—imbued with a new sense of power, only more intense."

Kaiden smiled. "I have a feeling you just became even more badass."

The other man shrugged. "I can't say I was anything special before."

"You one-hit those rock things. I think that counts for something," I said.

"I suppose I did."

"Plus, you saved me," I added. "Thank you. I should have said that earlier."

"Of course, Elle. We're a team. We're in this together." Toran smiled warmly.

"Well, I guess we got what we came for, right?" Kaiden asked.

"I believe so," Toran replied.

Kaiden nodded. "Then we should head back. We still have two more artifacts to pick up, and who knows what that will entail."

We turned to head up the hill toward the shuttle.

"Which one should we go after next?" I asked.

"I still think the Spirit artifact might be the most complicated," Kaiden said. "Yeah, I've *technically* practiced more than the two of you, but I've only had these powers for a week. I'm by no means an expert."

I nodded. "Mine then?"

"Are you okay with that?"

"Sure," I told him. "I mean, we all helped with this, even though Toran ended it. I know I won't be going into it alone."

"Of course, we'll have your back," he assured me.

"Okay, then Strength—er, Valor—artifact it is!" I grinned. I'd survived this engagement, so now it was time to prove myself as a capable leader in my own challenge.

We returned to the shuttle and Kaiden piloted it back to the *Evangiel.* When we had docked, Tami seemed pleased to see that we hadn't ripped apart the vessel's interior again, and she was especially happy to hear that the rope in our new supply kit had come in handy. Since we'd left the previous length on the planet, as it had been mostly buried in the soil when the giant disintegrated, she provided a new bundle to replace it.

With Toran sporting the new gauntlets, we took the lift to Central Command to give Colren our report.

"Good, you're back," the commander said as soon as we were buzzed through the door to the *Evangiel*'s bridge.

"We got the artifact," Toran announced, showing off his new gauntlets.

Colren barely glanced at them, much to my surprise. "I'm glad to hear it, but there's no time to revel. We need to head out right away; we just got word another world is about to be tainted by the Darkness."

My heart sank. "That's awful."

His expression was one of someone who'd already experienced loss too many times to feel it anymore. "It's another chance to extract someone," he said.

Toran's eyes widened. "Oh. I'd thought it would just be us."

"This is a large task for three people alone. The more we can add to your numbers, the greater your chance of success."

I didn't necessarily agree with the commander's logic. Sometimes, more people complicated a situation rather than helping it. "How does it work?" I asked.

"We need to jump to the world. You can watch the extraction procedure, if you like—assuming we are able to lock onto anyone."

I looked at my comrades. "I'm curious to see what happened to me from an observer's vantage."

"Yeah, I skipped the others, but I'm curious, too," Kaiden said.

Toran nodded.

"Very well," the commander said. "Get to your jump pods. I'll meet you when we arrive at the world."

12

AFTER ANOTHER STOMACH-CHURNING jump, we gathered in the room where I'd first woken up.

The bioprinter pod was situated near the interior bulkhead, next to a control workstation. On the opposite wall, the shade over the exterior viewport was drawn. Colren directed us to stand along the forward wall to observe the extraction, a position where we'd be out of sight of the newcomer when they first awoke. With the disorientation of waking up still fresh in my mind, I appreciated his concern.

"How does it work?" I asked Colren, who was seated at the workstation adjacent to the pod.

He glanced up from the monitor. "The technical specifications are beyond me. Suffice to say that the alien tech is able to isolate a single hyperdimensional consciousness. Someone who's been altered by exposure to the Darkness has a unique signature. The equipment tries to snare a candidate and draw them in. When it does, it reverse engineers a physical form based on the image in the candidate's thoughts."

Kaiden crossed his arms. "It's strange to think of a person in a way other than their body."

Colren smiled. "We could spend years debating the nature of existence. But right now, we need to try to get someone out of limbo."

"How do you pick which candidate to extract, or is there only one option?" Toran asked.

"We focus on whichever signal is the strongest," the commander replied. "But there isn't someone receptive on every planet."

"And now?" I asked.

He nodded. "We have three candidates, and hopefully we can coax one of them here."

We watched him work in silence, not wanting to compromise the procedure. I couldn't decide which discipline I hoped we got to add to the team. Maybe it was the immediacy effect from our recent mission, but Toran's toughness was coming in handy with our engagements.

"Okay, trying to draw the consciousness here now," Colren said. He pressed a control switch, and the lights turned off in the room. Only the faint glow from his monitor offered any illumination.

The bioprinting pod whirred to life. In the faint light, I saw it lay the foundation for a new form with long, slim limbs. Frosted glass around the torso obscured the details as it filled out the blank, but I could make out the general shape of curvy hips and breasts.

"I think we're getting another girl," I whispered to Kaiden next to me.

"I noticed that."

When most of the body was formed, Colren rose from his workstation and approached the pod to begin the syncing sequence. "Are you a boy or a girl?" he asked.

The young woman blinked, but her eyes stared blankly ahead. "A girl," she replied in a high, lilting voice.

"What is your name?"

"Maris."

The bioprinter added the final layer of details to her body, caramel skin, dark hair, and hazel eyes. She looked to be a year or two older than me—though, as we'd discovered with Toran, that didn't necessarily mean anything. When the physical features were complete, a white jumpsuit appeared around her.

Colren activated the holographic projector inside the pod, displaying the sword, shield, and wand icons. "What is your strength?" he asked.

"The wand," Maris answered after several seconds.

"Are you sure?" Colren asked.

"Yes."

The bioprinter had completed its work, but Maris arched her back like something had just been done to her. Then, a pendant just like Kaiden's appeared around her neck.

Thinking back to my own experience, I realized that I'd felt different after making the final selection, too. Maybe there *was* something to the alien tech being tantamount to magic.

"You are a caster. Use your power well," Colren stated as he stepped back. The door on the pod swung open. "Welcome."

The young woman took an unsteady step, smoothing her hands down her white jumpsuit. "Where am I?"

"You're on board the *Evangiel*, a Hegemony ship. I'm Commander Alastair Colren."

"Wha...?" She looked around. "I don't understand."

"I know this is disorienting," Colren soothed her. "Come, sit down." He beckoned to the table where I'd had my first conversation with him.

She noticed us standing along the wall and took a rapid step in the opposite direction. "What's going on? Who are you people?"

"It's okay, I went through this two days ago," I told her. "I'm Elle."

"Went through *what*?" Her tone was downright shrill now that she was agitated.

"Your world was infected by a Darkness. We extracted your consciousness to a new body designed to your specifications," the commander explained.

The look on Maris' face was probably just like the one I must have had when I was told the same thing. "This is insane," she said.

"I know it's a lot to process." Colren gave her an abbreviated overview of the details he'd shared with us over the past two days.

By the end of the explanation, Maris looked like she was about to cry. "I didn't ask for any of this."

"You have strength of spirit or you wouldn't be here," Colren said. "Now that you are, we need your help."

She tucked a length of her long dark, hair behind her right ear. "Can't you just send me back?"

"Doesn't work that way," Kaiden said. "But hey, at least you'll have people to show you the ropes."

"Heh, we did some great literal rope work earlier," I said.

Maris tilted her head. "Was that a euphemism?" She glanced between Kaiden and me.

"No!" Kaiden hastily replied. "We were fighting a rock titan."

"For an artifact," Toran added.

"Artifact?"

I sighed. "We have some more catching up to do."

"I'll leave you to get acquainted," Colren said. "The jump drive is recharging, but we'll jump in forty minutes to the planet with the next artifact."

"We agreed to go after the Valor item next," Kaiden said.

The commander frowned. "With a new caster on your team, I suggest you retrieve the Spirit artifact next."

Kaiden looked to us. "Do you care?"

"I'm fine waiting for mine," I replied. "I don't feel like I've really tapped into my latent skills yet."

Toran nodded. "If you're comfortable, Kaiden, I will support whatever decision."

He took a deep breath. "Okay, Spirit artifact next, I guess."

The commander inclined his head. "I'll arrange the jump. Prepare to depart as soon as we arrive." He left the room.

Maris stared at the three of us with a knit brow. "Does anything you just said actually make sense?"

I laughed. "It does sound like gibberish, doesn't it?"

The new woman looked all of us over from head to foot, and she took a step back when she evaluated Toran. "I don't know what kind of cult you're running—"

"Whoa! No." I held up my hands. "I know this all sounds crazy, but there's a perfectly reasonable explanation for everything. Well, *mostly* reasonable."

"Ninety percent sensical," Kaiden agreed.

Maris paled. "You're all completely out of your minds."

"We're not. It's the universe that has gone crazy," Toran said in as soft a tone as his bass voice allowed.

"I want to go home," Maris whined.

"Not an option." Kaiden walked over to the viewport and activated the shutter.

The covering opened, revealing a view of a blue planet. Except, there were dark tendrils weaving around the world, slowly consuming it.

"Stars! What *is* that?" Maris took a sharp breath, her face twisted with horror.

"That's the Darkness," Toran stated. "This world has been corrupted. You can't go back there."

She crossed her arms. "Colren said that we're immune. Are we or aren't we?"

I was all geared up for a defensive response against her constant objections, but I caught myself. She brought up a very good point. The commander had insisted that it had to be *us* to accomplish the tasks because we had a special immunity to the Darkness due to our partial exposure, yet all of his statements were about where we *couldn't* go.

Kaiden and Toran appeared to have the same revelation. We exchanged glances.

"I suppose we haven't actually tried," Kaiden admitted.

"Okay, so let's go," she said.

Toran shook his head. "It's not worth the risk."

"If anything you've been told is true, there shouldn't *be* a risk," Maris insisted.

"Fine, then what's the *benefit*?" I countered. "We were in the middle of something before this detour to come pick you up. Is there something valuable on the planet we should retrieve?"

Maris worked her mouth. "I don't know. I just... I want to go back to Yantu."

"Look at it." Kaiden pointed at the Darkness, which was continuing to spread around the world. "That's no place to be right now. Wouldn't you rather help find a solution to return your world to how it was?"

She nodded slowly. "But what can we do?"

Kaiden gave her a reassuring smile. "Let's go over some basics and get you geared up," he said. "You'll get to learn the rest in the field."

We started explaining the artifacts and what we'd learned about the clues to open the Master Archive while we walked Maris down to get prepped for our upcoming mission. We had just reached the equipment room door when we finished going over the most relevant details.

She shook her head. "I don't like it."

"What do you mean?" I asked.

"I dunno, just sounds like a lot of tedious work. I'll pass."

I glanced at Kaiden and Toran. "You're in this now, like it or not."

"This is the best way you can help your world," Toran said.

Maris threw up her hands. "But I'm no one! I can't imagine taking out a giant the way you did."

"You may surprise yourself," Kaiden told her. "You haven't even *tried* to use your new abilities."

She hesitated. "I don't know where to start."

"Not here," Toran cautioned. "We don't need any more close calls."

Maris tilted her head questioningly.

"I maybe accidently almost punched a hole through the hull with a fireball when I was trying to show off to Toran when we first met," Kaiden admitted.

I smirked. "Oh, *that's* what happened."

Kaiden flushed slightly. "Ancient history now. But, at any rate, we have a rule for no significant magic use on the ship."

"Why don't we get your equipment and you can come with us on this next mission?" I suggested. "You can play around with your new abilities and get to know us a little better. If you still don't want to participate, you don't have to come on the next one."

Maris searched my face. "Why are you being so nice to me?"

"Why wouldn't we be?" I asked.

"I called you crazy."

The three of us laughed.

"We'd think *you* were if you didn't," Kaiden said. "I mean, we can cast magic now. That's wild."

"I won't believe it until I see it," she replied.

"Soon enough," I told her. "Let's get you some proper clothes and a weapon in the meantime."

She wrinkled her nose. "I don't like weapons."

I stepped toward the door to the equipment room and it opened automatically. "Believe me, you'll want something if a rock lizard comes after you, or a golem."

"They aren't friendly," Kaiden agreed. "I hope we don't get into a lot of fights, but you need to be prepared just in case." He followed me inside.

Toran beckoned for Maris to enter the room. "You'll find you have new skills. Actions will come naturally for things you never would have thought you could do."

She stepped inside the equipment room. "If you say so."

"Step onto the scanner," the synthesized female voice stated.

Maris jumped. "Wha—"

The illuminated ring appeared on the floor.

"Oh." Cautiously, Maris stepped forward.

The scanning ring took its readings of her, and then the holographic mesh appeared around her body and the menu popped up.

"Whoa," she murmured.

"Starting with the armor seems like it's easiest," I suggested.

Maris selected that option from the menu, and the different clothing options appeared. "What do I pick?"

"Our white onesies make a good protective base layer, we were told," I replied. "Beyond that, it looks like we're locked out of the cool stuff like powered armor. You should be able to find something in the civilian catalog with ballistic fabric."

She turned around, her face draining. "Ballistic-rated clothing? What are we going up against?"

"These textiles are a trifecta of awesome," Kaiden jumped in. "Projectile, magic, and slash resistance. Just take our word for it—it will come in handy."

She eyed his cape. "Is that so?"

"You're living in adventure-land now, Maris. Embrace it," I advised.

She returned her attention to the holographic menu and began making selections. In the end, she picked out an armored corset that accented her chest way more than seemed appropriate for proper armor, tight pants, and a knee-length hooded cape in a deep maroon shade. The accompanying heeled boots seemed entirely impractical, but clearly we had different definitions of 'battle gear' given her other choices.

"You've come around to the pro-cape camp, I see," Kaiden commented.

She smiled at him. "Looks good on you."

I fought the impulse to roll my eyes. "Still need to pick out a weapon."

"Do I need a wand for casting?" she asked.

"No, I think these crystals focus our power," Kaiden replied, touching the pendant on his neck.

"Why the staff, then?"

He held it horizontal and thrust it forward. "Makes a good stabby and blocky thing."

Maris flipped through the options in the weapons menu, pausing on a set of throwing daggers. "I still don't like the idea of having to attack anything."

"Then go with something like that where you can keep your distance,"

Toran said.

She nodded. "All right, I'll give it a try. You're right, it's better to have something and not need it than the other way around."

She locked in the selections, and the 3D printer got to work preparing her specified items.

While we waited, we found out that she was twenty years old and had been working as a bartender. I wanted to ask if the skimpy outfits or the work gig came first, but I thought better of it.

"I like taking care of people," she explained. "I never intended to make it a career, but I enjoy it."

"Don't think we'll have much chance for mixology, I'm afraid," Kaiden said. "But you can clearly multitask and are coordinated, so that will come in handy."

A chime sounded when Maris' items were finished printing, and she crossed the room to retrieve them. The items layered nicely, following a color scheme of black and maroon with the occasional silver accent.

When the corset was in place, it was even more accentuating than it had appeared in the holographic preview. Kaiden and Toran, to a lesser extent, had clearly noticed, as well.

"Looks good," Kaiden commented, his gaze lingering on certain parts of her more than I wished it had.

After reminding myself that I wasn't in high school anymore and she could wear whatever she wanted, I forced a smile. "All right, ready for your first mission?"

13

AS IT TURNED out, Maris didn't seem ready at all. I couldn't blame her. The process of waking up on a spaceship with no sense of grounding would throw off even the most level-headed person. Unfortunately, my first impression of her was that she was on the opposite end of the spectrum.

"What is it we're supposed to do, exactly?" she asked while we walked up to the room containing our jump pods.

"We go to the planet and wander around until we find the thing that we need—but we won't know what that is until we find it. Then we come back here and go for the next thing," I replied.

She scrunched up her nose. "How do you know that you got the right thing if you don't know what you're looking for?"

"It just kinda makes sense when we find it," Kaiden replied.

"But, you had to fight that giant before you even knew you were going after the gauntlets. What if you'd gone through the fight but it wasn't actually connected to the artifact?" Maris pressed.

"But it *was*," Toran said.

She shook her head. "I don't know. It seems like a lot of work for not knowing if you're doing the right thing."

"We never said this would be easy," Toran responded. "In fact, I believe we have only indicated quite the opposite."

"I still don't understand why you were all so willing to go along with what the Hegemony is asking. They should have specialists to take care of this, not rely on recruiting random people."

"They don't understand the enemy," I said. "I think they tried other things first, but we're a Plan B that was launched when nothing else worked."

Maris sighed. "They should just do a master reset and purge the Darkness from the worlds."

"Is that even possible?" I asked. I'd heard about resets happening on multiple worlds simultaneously, but my understanding was that those were independent, coordinated resets. If it was possible to do a universal reset, it had certainly never happened in my lifetime.

"I heard rumors from some of the engineers at work," Toran revealed. "Opinions were very divided about whether or not it could be done."

Kaiden shook his head. "I don't see how it could, personally. When talking about an interplanetary reset or something on a universal scale, what would be the locus of the event? A reset needs a point to serve as the constant from which everything else is synced."

"That's the biggest argument against it," Toran replied. "Plus, the slew issues concerning the capacity of the crystalline network."

"It *would* be pretty handy if we could reset to four months ago, or so," I mused.

"The problem is, even if the crystalline network could reconcile that much data through the hyperdimensional links—which I don't think it can, based on what I know—none of our society's backup systems are designed to handle that scale of reset," Toran continued. "The servers in the Capitol don't have an external backup point."

"Not to mention, the Darkness came from *somewhere*," Kaiden added. "Even if we reset to four months ago, it would still come a month later. We'd need to locate where it's coming from and eliminate the root cause."

"Which we'll probably have to do anyway," I pointed out.

Maris sighed. "This just keeps getting better and better."

I cast her a sidelong glance. "I, for one, would rather be taking action rather than sitting at home helpless while my world falls apart around me."

"As much as I never thought of myself as having a hero complex, I have to agree," Kaiden said.

Maris thought a moment. "Yeah, I guess you do have a point."

"And the universe is far from falling apart yet," Toran stated. "We already have one of the artifacts, and soon we'll have a second."

"That's the spirit." I pumped my arm with exaggerated enthusiasm I wasn't feeling at the moment, especially since we'd reached the room containing the jump pods.

"Like I said, we can see how things go on the next planet," Kaiden reiterated while entering the chamber.

Maris nodded. "Okay."

"Jump in T-minus five minutes," the announcer stated over the comms.

I headed to what had become my usual pod and started stripping down.

"Where are our sedatives?" Maris asked.

"We don't use them here," Toran replied.

"But—"

"Better get in the pod. We don't have a lot of time," Kaiden interrupted. He'd already stripped down to his white base layer and was climbing into his pod.

Maris frowned at the restraint system. "How do you strap in?"

Kaiden stepped back out of his pod. "Get in." He motioned to her pod.

Maris hopped inside and reclined.

"This goes up here and this down here." Kaiden arranged the harnesses. "Buckle in and cinch it tight."

"Okay, thanks."

While I lay down in my own, I saw her smiling up at him as he leaned over her pod.

"T-minus two minutes," the announcer stated.

There were several rapid footsteps followed by clips and fabric rustling as Kaiden got situated in his pod.

The final countdown sounded, and then I was once again in the uncomfortable altered reality of hyperspace.

I listened to my heartbeat and breathing throughout the duration of the jump, just like I'd found was helpful on the last two legs. Now that I knew what to expect, it was much more tolerable than it had been the first time around.

The jump didn't seem to last as long as the others, so I was surprised when my sense of weight diminished and my internal organs felt like they were in their proper places again.

I sat up and stretched as soon as I'd unbuckled my restraints after the pod opened.

Not surprisingly, Maris had yet to emerge.

I exchanged glances with Kaiden as he sat up in his own, and he vaulted out of his pod to go check on her.

"Maris?" He crouched over her.

I came up behind him.

Maris was unconscious and looked pale despite her naturally tanned skin. I reached down to touch the back of my hand to her forehead. It was cold and clammy. "I think she might be in shock."

"Let's get her up." Kaiden reached in and hoisted her torso, I grabbed her feet to keep them from hitting the lip of the pod's lid.

"Should we bring her to Medical?" Toran asked.

"Maybe. Let's give her a minute. Grab my cloak." Kaiden nodded toward his bundle of clothes in the locker behind his pod.

Toran gathered the cloak and spread it on the deck.

I gently set down Maris' legs and Kaiden lowered her the rest of the way.

Her face scrunched up and she moaned.

"Maris, wake up," Kaiden urged. "We're here. The jump is over."

He brushed Maris' hair back from her face. The color began to return to her cheeks. Slowly, her eyes fluttered open.

"Wha— What happened?" she stammered.

"You decided to implement your own sedative," I said from her other side.

She frowned. "Huh?"

"You passed out," Toran clarified. "Do you feel okay?"

Maris placed a hand on her stomach. "A little queasy. Feels like a bad hangover."

"That'll pass." Kaiden held out his hand to help her to her feet.

She wobbled as she found her footing, and Kaiden supported her with one arm.

"How long was I out?" she asked, her voice faint.

"We just got here. Do you remember any of the jump?" he replied.

Maris shook her head. "Just the sensation of being slammed against the bottom of the pod."

"Yeah, that initial acceleration is really disorienting." He loosened his grip on her as she stabilized. "Doing okay?"

"Yes, thank you." She took a deep breath. "Getting better every second."

Kaiden stepped away. "Get dressed. We need to figure out where to go on the planet."

We each donned our outerwear and sheathed our weapons. By the time we were dressed, the color had fully returned to Maris' face and she was looking more confident.

We went down the hall to the room where Toran had set up his device for our ongoing magic locating needs.

Kaiden removed his pendant and placed it in the cradle. "Let's see what this planet's deal is."

The device hummed as it activated, and the crystal glowed soft blue. The touch-surface desktop displayed the waveform of a single contact point.

"Hmm," Toran mused. "That seems surprisingly straightforward."

Kaiden frowned. "I don't believe it."

"What's wrong?" Maris asked.

"Last time, we had four contact points—those three crystals we needed to activate," I explained. "After that complication, this just seems way too easy."

She tilted her head. "But easy is good, right?"

"I suspect the complicating factor will come in a different form," Kaiden said with a sigh. "Let's check it out."

We headed down to the hangar. Workers were huddled around our shuttle when we arrived, as usual. There were also four backpacks waiting by the entrance ramp.

Tami stepped forward to greet us. "You must be the newest member of the team. Welcome." She smiled. "I'm Tami, the lead tech specialist around here."

"Hi," Maris replied with a faint smile.

"Here's a comm for you." Tami held out a case containing a single micro earpiece.

"Fair warning, it's not going to feel great going in, but it doesn't last long," Kaiden warned.

"I'm sure I can handle it." She took the earpiece and placed it in her left ear. She winced as the comm embedded but otherwise made no indication of the discomfort. Maybe she had a tough streak in her, after all.

"I took the liberty of preparing packs for each of you," Tami continued. "This world appears to have some challenging terrain, so it seemed prudent to offer provisions for a longer stay planetside."

"Thanks." I grabbed one of the packs—heavy, but manageable with my new augmented strength and functioning shoulder. I'd never done well with heavy packs after my injury, so it was liberating to no longer have weight be a concern.

I scaled the ramp and dropped the pack in the far corner of the common room, with the others following suit close behind me.

As soon as we were all inside, I was penned on the far side of the common room and needed to wait for the others to go down the corridor to the bridge. As they filed in, Maris made a direct line for the seat at the front where I'd been sitting in the shuttle.

Not wanting to seem petty, I kept my mouth shut and headed for one of the passenger chairs in the back across from Toran.

"Actually, that's Elle's spot," Kaiden said on my behalf.

Maris looked between him and me, then shrugged. "Sorry, I didn't realize there was assigned seating."

"It's not, exactly, but we've kind of got our groove going," he said.

She held up her hands and stepped back. "Don't let me intrude."

While I really didn't like judging people before I got to know them, Maris wasn't making a great first impression. I was sympathetic to the situation—being thrown into unknowns with a ton of pressure to deliver—but the mixture of self-centeredness and sense of entitlement was getting to me.

As I took my usual seat in the shuttle, I snuck a glance toward Kaiden. He took a slow, deep breath and gave me a subtle nod.

Okay, so it wasn't just me.

At least, I hoped that's what he was indicating. It was possible he was just telling me to chillax because I was clearly on edge. I decided to just strap in, cross my arms, and stay quiet. However, even that simple plan proved to be overly optimistic in Maris' presence.

"Is this going to take long?" she asked. "What did that Tami woman mean about a longer stay?"

"It will take as long as it takes," Toran replied.

She frowned. "What will we have to do?"

"We'll figure that out when we get down there have a lay of the land," Kaiden said while activating the autopilot to take the shuttle out of the hangar.

"Will we need to fight another rock titan?"

"I imagine this will be a different challenge fitting of the Spirit discipline," Toran told her.

The shuttle glided through the electrostatic shield into the void. It arced and glided the length of the *Evangiel* before beginning the descent to the brown planet.

Following the automated flight path toward the target Toran had identified, we descended through the cloud cover—nowhere near as thick as on Crystallis, but enough to hamper visibility—until we reached an elevation of three kilometers. The clouds cleared, revealing a flat expanse of marshland. According to the map, the target was right up ahead.

The marshes gave way to a lake of murky blue-green water. In the middle was a tiny island with a crystal monument at its center.

"Is that it?" I asked.

Kaiden took manual control of the shuttle and looped it around, making multiple passes over the island.

The crystal hanging around his neck glowed more intensely the closer we got to the crystal monument.

"Yeah, looks like it," Kaiden concluded. "Well, there's that complication we knew was coming."

I frowned. "Everywhere around it is marsh. We have to be at least ten kilometers from solid land."

"Not to mention, how are we supposed to get to the island once we make it to the edge of the lake?" Kaiden sighed.

I scanned the area around the island. "Wait, is that a pathway?" I pointed to the northeast.

He directed the shuttle toward where I was pointing. Almost invisible against the dark water was a stone pathway—only, it appeared to be below the water's surface.

"Hmm, maybe there's a way to raise it up?" Kaiden suggested.

"Likely. Either way, it looks like we should try to land in a place with access to this side of the lake."

He sighed. "This is going to be a long day."

"Looks like we might need to break out those bedrolls," Toran said.

Maris gasped. "You never said anything about camping!"

"We do what the mission dictates," I responded. "If that's where we need to go, then we'll need to hike in."

"This isn't what I agreed to."

I glanced at her. "You're here now. Best make the most of it."

"Can't you bring me back to the ship?" she asked.

"And explain to the commander why we wasted valuable time and fuel? No." I knew the statement was terse, but a person could only listen to so much complaining before it got to be too much.

Maris scoffed and crossed her arms. "Way to show a little compassion."

That was officially all I could handle. I turned around in my seat as much as I could with my harness secured. "Maris, *all* of us were pulled away from our lives and thrown together. Whatever sense of entitlement you think you have, you don't. We're all trying to save our homes. We can either work together and get that done, or complain and moan about not getting our way. So, what do you say that you buck up and try rather than playing the victim card?"

Kaiden cast me an appreciative glance and nodded slightly.

Maris gaped at me. "You want me to pretend everything is okay? I was just ripped from my world and told that everything I took for granted about my reality may be because of some crazy alien tech no one understands. And you think I'm playing a *victim* card?"

"Hey," Toran soothed, "let's just—"

"We're not each other's enemies here," Kaiden cut in. "What we're up against is bigger than all of us. We need to work together, not be divided."

"Well, way to make me feel part of the team," Maris snapped.

Kaiden scoffed. "Because I won't take you back? No, the only way we're ever going to learn to work together is by going through the motions. If you want to quit after this, fine, but you promised to make a genuine attempt to learn about your abilities before you decide whether to help us or not."

She slouched in her seat. "Fine."

I turned to face forward, drawing a slow, deep breath. Kaiden's and my eyes met for a moment, setting me at ease. I appreciated him having my back.

Given Maris' reaction, it seemed like maybe the criteria for who to extract needed a little refining. Thinking along those lines made me question my own selection, however, so I dismissed the idea. If I was worthy, so was Maris—she just needed to find the part of herself where she could come into her power. Getting upset with her didn't help either of us. Maybe I could use an attitude adjustment of my own.

With our spat resolved, Kaiden consulted the map overlaid on the front viewport.

"I think this is as close as we'll be able to get." He pointed to a patch of solid land just over ten kilometers from the lake.

"We'll make it work," I said.

He nodded. "We don't have another choice."

14

"LET'S START WALKING," I said, hoisting the backpack containing extra supplies onto my shoulders.

We'd loaded a map of our destination onto a handheld device—one of the new additions in the packs Tami prepared for us—and we were facing a challenging journey across narrow strips of land through ten kilometers of bogs. The path reminded me of the kind of circuitous route we'd take through the boulder fields in the hills back home, only this was much longer and had a lot more opportunity for dead ends.

Fortunately, we'd recorded aerial footage on the fly over to our landing site. The image was loaded onto the handheld along with an optimized path through to the edge of the lake where the underwater path led.

Kaiden lifted his own pack. "Everyone have everything? Double check."

I nodded. "I'm good."

Maris groaned as she picked up her pack. "Do I really need all of this?"

"We don't know what we may find out there, and we'll be a long way from resources," Toran stated. "Unless you want to potentially find yourself hungry and sleeping on the bare ground, having the contents of that pack on hand is in your best interest."

"Or, you can stay here in the shuttle by yourself for however long we're gone," I muttered.

Maris only flipped her hair out of her face in response.

"I'm ready," Toran said in response to Kaiden's original question.

"Okay, then let's head out." Kaiden set off along the specified path.

After a quarter of a kilometer, the first signs of the marshlands appeared. The ground softened underfoot, and the air took on a faint aroma of decay. Shallow puddles of water popped up in our path. As we went deeper, the puddles multiplied and merged into waterways.

The solid ground on the path we were following was, in reality, only firm when compared to the standing water around it. Covered in short reedy grass, my boots sunk in at least three centimeters with each step, making for an exhausting slog through the maze of relatively dry pathways. Some areas were six or seven meters wide and the four of us could comfortably walk abreast, but in the other places, the pathway narrowed to a meter and we'd have to hop over to another landmass.

After an hour of walking and jumping, my pack was digging into my shoulders. To distract myself, I kept an eye on the water for any signs of life.

The water was still in most areas, but as we got deeper into the marsh, I started to see the occasional flutter of water out of the corner of my eye. Whenever I turned toward the movement, there was only a telltale ripple on the surface, which could easily have been caused by a gust of wind. The appearances were too random and numerous, though, for me to believe that was the only explanation. Something was out there.

"Hey, have you noticed anything in the water?" I asked when I was certain the sightings weren't in my imagination.

"Yeah, I've been watching that, too," Kaiden replied. "I can't tell what it is."

"Wait, is there something stalking us?" Panic pitched Maris' tone even higher than normal.

"It's probably just fish or frogs or something," I said.

Kaiden nodded. "This water isn't very deep. It can't be a large creature."

I hoped that was true. Frankly, it was impossible to tell how deep the water went. It *looked* like it would be shallow, given the pattern of dry land, but for each of the larger areas of land, there were twice as many broad patches of open water. It was possible a creature of substantial size was lurking in the depths. My hope was that we were seeing evidence of multiple, smaller animals rather than one, large creature tailing us for the last kilometer.

Given Maris' predisposition to theatrics, I thought it best to keep that thought to myself. Based on how Toran was keeping a watchful eye on our surroundings, though, I suspected he may have had similar thoughts.

We continued forward in silence.

While traversing one of the narrower land segments, only two meters wide, a distinctive splash sounded to my left. My hand instinctively went to my sword hilt.

"Did you see it?" Kaiden asked.

I shook my head. "No."

Another splash sounded on my other side and I spun around. This time, I caught the back of a creature with dark, green-brown skin slipping beneath the water. It had to be at least a meter long, based on what little I saw.

I swallowed. "We're not alone."

We pivoted to stand back-to-back, with Kaiden and Maris facing one direction and Toran and me the other.

"Looks like you'll get your first chance to use magic," Kaiden said to Maris.

"What do I do?"

"My first time, I just thought about what I wanted to happen, and then it did."

"I don't want to accidently blow you guys up."

He chuckled. "That's not going to happen."

I drew my sabre from its scabbard. With any luck, we wouldn't have any more rock-creatures and the blade would do its job.

Something dark broke the surface of the water and lunged for me. I brought up my sword to block the creature from striking my neck, seeing no more than a dark blur hurtling toward me.

My blade sliced into tough flesh, and the creature shrieked. It flopped to the ground at my feet.

Just over a meter long, it had six stubby legs with webbed feet, and the oblong body tapered into a flat tail. Its head was as broad as its shoulders, with jaws the entire width. Dark eyes positioned near the top of its head were covered in an iridescent film. It was gazing up at me with what I took to be a mixture of confusion and bloodlust. The gash from my sword ran for five centimeters along its left shoulder, and it was favoring the nearest leg.

I held my attack, waiting for it to make the next move. If it went on its way, I saw no reason to harm it further.

The marsh monster shrieked again and wrapped its jaws around my right ankle before I even saw it move.

I felt pressure around my leg, but my boots did their job to halt its bite. The marsh monster thrashed and tried to roll.

"You had your chance." I stabbed my sword into the base of its neck.

The creature gurgled as viscous, dark blood oozed from the wound and trickled from its mouth.

"Good job, Elle," Toran said next to me.

After twitching for five seconds, the creature fell still.

Two shrieks sounded behind me, and another to my right. Then, a deeper roar chimed in.

My heartrate spiked. "Stars! How many are there?"

"Watch each other's backs!" Kaiden said. "All right, Maris, stay focused. Anything comes near you, think about what you want to do and do it."

"Okay," she acknowledged, a quaver in her voice.

Toran clenched his fists while scanning the dark water for signs of the enemy creatures. "Maybe you scared them off?"

I shook my head. "They're here. I can feel it."

No sooner had I spoken than a black form leaped from the water toward Toran. He batted it to the side with one of his powerful fists.

From behind, the crackle of electrical energy filled the air as Kaiden launched his initial assault. "Attack them!" he urged Maris

"I'm trying!" she cried. "I'm thinking about fire, but nothing is happening."

Another marsh monster leaped from the water toward me, somehow rocketing from the water high enough to snap at my neck. The scent of rotten fish and decaying vegetation assaulted my nose. I elbowed the creature as it approached my face. It flopped to the ground and slipped back into the water before I could attack.

"These things are so quick!" I groaned.

Next to me, Toran tried to smash a creature mid-leap as it charged for his knee, but it recoiled mid-lunged and disappeared into the water in a split second.

Splashes sounded on the other side of the land as Kaiden's energy balls struck the water.

"They're dodging," he said with obvious frustration. "How did you get that first one?"

"I don't know. Maybe I caught it by surprise?" I replied.

A different marsh monster leaped for me, and I slashed at it with my sword. Like Toran's experience, the creature somehow pivoted midair and evaded my swing.

"We need to move faster somehow," Maris said.

A foreign tingling sensation washed over me, and the world took on an orange hue.

The surface of the water broke. One of the creatures emerged, leaping toward me—but, somehow, in slow motion.

I assessed how to make the best intercept strike. When the creature was in range, I plunged my sword into its abdomen and ripped the blade sideways. My movements felt fluid and natural even though my surroundings had slowed to a crawl. The creature slowly dropped to the ground.

Toran was watching the engagement with wide eyes next to me. His own movements appeared to be normal, like mine.

"What ha—" I cut off as a wave of the creatures leaped from the water—seven of them, all charging the two of us.

"Shit! There's too many of them!" Kaiden exclaimed behind me.

We were surrounded.

I slashed and stabbed my way through the mass of marsh monsters. Their bodies dropped to the ground, dark blood hardly distinguishable from the mud.

Toran punched at the creatures nearest him, while blasts from Kaiden sounded behind me. When all of the creatures had fallen, everything was still. The orange glow faded as quickly as it had emerged.

"What was that?" I asked.

"That was incredible!" Maris exclaimed. "You were moving at super-speed."

"Really?" Kaiden asked.

"Yeah, your movements were a blur, then everything dropped dead. It must have only been three seconds."

My mouth fell open. "That last attack only lasted for *three seconds*?"

Maris shrugged. "Or something. I wasn't timing it."

"Did you do this?" Kaiden asked her.

She scoffed. "I was just standing here. All I said was that we needed to move faster."

The tingling sensation washed over me again as the world tinted orange.

Toran rolled his eyes, and Kaiden's lips parted with surprise. Maris, however, was shrugging in slow motion.

"Huh." I nodded with satisfaction.

"So she can speed up our movements," Kaiden commented. "Haste magic will come in handy."

"Indeed it will." Toran looked out over the water. His heavy brow lowered. "Sooner than later."

I shifted my attention in the direction he was looking and saw a new creature emerge from the water. This one was four times the size of the others, and it looked pissed.

THE GIANT MARSH monster lumbered toward us—movements that would be a blur in real-time, but were now a slow plod thanks to Maris' haste magic.

"Is this the thing we need to fight for the artifact?" Toran questioned, his fists raised and poised for a fight.

Kaiden turned around to join our line. He glanced down at his crystal pendant; it wasn't emitting any light. "No, we're still too far from the lake island. This is something else."

"Great." I adjusted my grip on my sword.

The new marsh monster was nearly four meters long and stood two meters tall at its shoulder. Its broad head and jaws were a meter wide, and tusks poked up from its inky lower lips. As it loped forward, the front two of its six legs cleared the water, revealing sharp nails at the end of its webbed toes.

While it wasn't a rock titan, the thing was still a formidable foe.

Kaiden made the first move, blasting a ball of electrical energy toward its face. The creature bucked and snorted, but it continued its forward charge.

Toran and I exchanged nods. When the marsh monster was within striking distance, Toran and I simultaneously struck it—my blade stabbing into the side of its neck at the base of the skull and Toran punching it beneath its eyes.

It roared in response, tossing its head back. The creature shifted its weight sideways, aiming its tusks for Toran.

One of the boney points struck him in his left shoulder beneath the pauldron. Toran winced as it made contact, but he took another swing with his right fist.

The punch spurred the creature to buck its head, driving the tusk deeper into Toran's shoulder. When it dropped its head, the bloodied tusk pulled out from the wound. The creature started to align its head for another gore.

I gripped my sword with both hands and drove it into the underside of the marsh monster's throat, twisting as I thrust.

It gasped, opening its jaws wide.

I gagged on the stench of rotten fish, holding my breath as I dragged the blade sideways to open the wound. The creature stumbled, and I ripped the blade out, staggering backward.

As soon as I was clear, Kaiden blasted the monster with an electrified orb, followed by a column of flames cast from the end of his staff.

With a shriek and gurgle, the creature collapsed to the ground and was still.

I took a deep breath, laughing a little. "All right, then."

Toran grunted. "I hope we don't meet more of those." He examined his injured left shoulder; blood trickled from the wound.

I quickly flicked my blade clean and then wiped the creature's remaining blood off my blade using its hide, then sheathed the sword. "Are you okay, Toran?"

"Yeah, it's minor," he replied, wincing as he moved.

"We should clean it out and patch you up," I said.

"This place might not be safe," Kaiden cautioned.

I looked around at the corpses. "I dunno. If I was one of those things, I think I'd steer clear."

"Fair point," he conceded.

The world shifted back to standard color, motion returning to normal.

"Stars, not again!" Maris exclaimed.

Kaiden smiled. "We'll need to work on your casting for yourself, too."

She frowned, seeing that Toran was injured. "What happened?"

I gestured to the slain creature. "Battle wound."

Maris stepped forward. "Maybe I can help."

Kaiden nodded. "Not sure if healing magic is a thing, but I didn't think haste magic was, either."

"I'll try," she said. She approached Toran and placed her right hand over his wound while gripping her crystal pendant in her left. Closing her eyes, she continued to take slow, steady breaths.

A soft green glow appeared beneath her hand, glowing and sparkling as ribbons of light traced around Toran's shoulder. He jumped with surprise when he saw it, then remained still—though his gaze kept darting to the side.

After thirty seconds, the glow faded and Maris opened her eyes. "How was that?"

Toran rotated his shoulder. "The pain is gone." He dropped his backpack to the ground, then unclipped the front of his armor and the shoulder pauldron to inspect the injury. When he bared his flesh, there was only a faint pink mark of new skin. "Amazing," he murmured.

Maris beamed. "I did that?"

Kaiden patted her on the back. "Well done."

"Have any other neat tricks?" I asked.

"Let me see if I can do something for the rest of you." She closed her eyes again.

A wave of renewing energy washed over me—like I'd just slept for six hours and then downed a packet of pure sugar. "All right, yep. That'll do it!"

Okay, so she'd found her niche on our team.

"Why do I suddenly feel like I could climb a mountain?" Kaiden commented.

Toran nodded. "I could get used to this restorative magic."

Maris grinned. "I didn't know this kind of magic existed."

"I'm not sure it did before us," Kaiden replied. "Well, at least not since the ancient times when the crystals were created. The magic of the crystals was always a given in our lives, but nothing like casting."

"The mythology of it has always been there," I pointed out. "There was never a doubt in my mind when I saw the wand icon that is denoted magic."

Kaiden nodded. "I guess now we know that those cultural cues came from the ancients—and that magic is very much a real thing."

"And that the power is more mysterious than we initially realized—the ability to injure but also to heal," Toran added.

"When you described everything to me before, it was all about fireballs and stuff," Maris said. "While that's impressive, and all, it's not really *me*. I enjoy helping people, like I said."

"Hey, I'm all for having a medic on our team," I said.

She smiled. "You know, I was actually planning to go to school to be a nurse."

Kaiden chuckled. "Congratulations! You just got fast-tracked to a degree at Magic University. The curriculum is entirely self-taught, but you're guaranteed to graduate in record time."

Maris laughed. "I'll try to be a model student." She tucked her hair behind her ear while looking him over.

"Well, we should get going!" I said resuming my trek along the path.

"Yeah." Kaiden cleared his throat. "We're almost halfway there."

We picked our way through the narrow strips of land snaking through the swamp. Following the adrenaline rush of the fight, it was nice to walk in relative silence with only the squish of our footsteps.

A kilometer from where the creatures attacked us, I started to see signs of movement in the water again. "Guys, I think more of them have come to say hello."

"Ugh, I really don't want to deal with more of those things," Maris groaned.

"Maybe this is a good opportunity to get in some additional practicing before we go for the artifact," Kaiden suggested.

Maris glanced at Toran and me, then she focused on Kaiden. "What kind of practice?"

"I know you don't want to use offensive magic, but it would be good to get a handle on some basic spells, if you can manage," he explained. "You need to be able to protect yourself."

"Yeah, I guess," she admitted. "I just couldn't get it to work when I tried before."

"Well, there was a lot of pressure then. You can give it a shot now while there isn't something threatening to eat you."

Maris nodded. "Okay, I'll try." She took a deep breath and held out her right hand while gripping her crystal pendant in her left.

I kept an eye on the water and my hand on my sword hilt in case something else decided to attack us.

Toran was equally vigilant. While it wasn't necessarily best for the two people keeping watch to not have any longer-distance attack abilities like Kaiden with his magic, at least we wouldn't be caught off-guard.

After an awkward minute, nothing had happened with Maris' attempted casting.

"This isn't working," she grumbled.

"You're overthinking it." Kaiden placed a hand on her shoulder. "Picture the result like it's already happening."

"I don't know if I can."

"*That's* your problem—you doubt yourself. You control the abilities, not the other way around."

She sighed. "I guess."

"Think about when you were casting haste before, or when you healed us. You just did it without thinking."

"Maybe that's the only kind of magic I *can* cast." Maris shrugged.

Kaiden gave her a stern look. "Not everything will be easy. You'll have to dig deeper and find it."

She tilted her head. "Then why don't *you* learn the curative and support casting, too?"

The question appeared to catch him off-guard. "Well, offensive magic comes easily to me, and the other to you, so—"

"But you want *me* to learn the other kind. Shouldn't that go both ways?"

I had to admit, she did bring up a valid point. "You know, if we had *two* casters giving us extra bonus skills…"

"Okay, I'll work on it," Kaiden conceded. "But my bigger concern right now is making sure you can defend yourse—"

A dark creature burst from beneath the water, heading straight for Kaiden.

Maris yelped, her hand still outstretched for the practice. As soon as the creature's shoulders cleared the water, a column of flames shot from her hand and enveloped the marsh monster.

Its shriek pierced the silence, only lasting a moment before fading out. It dropped back into the water and lie still at the shore, its rubbery flesh charred.

I let out a relieved chuckle, my eyes wide with surprise. "That's one way to take care of things."

Kaiden grinned at Maris. "See? You're a natural."

"Still nowhere as good as you." She giggled.

I tried to suppress an eye-roll. I don't think I was successful, but she didn't seem to be paying attention.

"All right, so now we know Maris can get badass with the offensive magic in a pinch. But shouldn't we keep moving? You can practice more while we walk," I said.

"I concur. We still have a ways to go," Toran added.

"Right, yeah. We'll keep working on it," Kaiden acknowledged.

We set out again at our same brisk pace. A fireball or electrical blast occasionally shot out behind me while Kaiden and Maris practiced casting. It would have been annoying were it not for Maris' restorative spells thrown into the mix, which helped mitigate my weariness from slogging through the mud for hours.

Our path was true for most of the trek, with the exception of two times we needed to backtrack when we discovered that what had looked like land on the aerial image was actually exceptionally murky water. On the second backtrack, two of the smaller marsh monsters attempted an ambush, but we quickly dealt with them using quick reflexes and Kaiden's casting skills.

After two and a half hours, the putrid water began to clear. According to our tracking on the downloaded map, we were almost to the lake.

"Nearing the artifact site," Kaiden reported in over the comm to Central Command.

"We've been tracking your progress," Colren said in my ear comm. "It looks like you've logged some combat time. Is everything okay?"

"Yes, nothing we can't handle," I replied.

"All right, keep us updated on your progress. Sunset is coming up on you quickly, so it looks like you won't be able to make it back to the shuttle before nightfall."

I frowned; the notion of trying to traverse the marsh after dark didn't appeal to me, but spending the night on the alien world with hostile creatures didn't have a great ring to it, either.

"We'll be in touch," Kaiden assured him.

A low double-beep sounded as the commlink disconnected.

"Staying here overnight?" Maris moaned.

"I suspected that would be the case as soon as we saw the island, but I'd hoped we at least wouldn't have any predators to deal with," I said.

Kaiden nodded. "It isn't ideal, but we have everything we need to make it through the night."

"We should find a campsite and set up before we lose daylight," Toran suggested.

"Yeah," I agreed. "Let's find that stone bridge. Maybe there's something paved around there."

"Good thinking." Toran took the lead.

"This will be my first night sleeping outside," Maris said while we walked.

"Total 'city girl', huh?" I asked.

She chuckled. "Yeah, I guess you could say that. Yantu, my homeworld, was pretty focused on interplanetary business. Most of my customers at the bar either worked for the Hegemony as administrators or were in middle management or executives for private industry."

I cocked my head and glanced back at her. "Ever overhear any juicy gossip?"

She smiled. "All the time! You know that you can convert pericol into tridarium holdings then cash it out and avoid the import taxes?"

"I have no idea what you just said."

"Ugh, commodities trading," Kaiden groaned. "I spent way too much time dealing with that for my parents' grain transport business."

"That's way more important than anything I heard about," Maris said. "You were helping to feed people; all of my customers just wanted to make money so they could retire somewhere on a beach far away."

"Can't say that's a bad aspiration," I admitted.

"No, but a little *too* aspirational, given our present circumstances. I'm more focused on *not dying* right now than my future earnings prospects," she replied.

I looped my thumbs behind the shoulder straps of my backpack. "You know, that's a good point. What's going to happen after this is over?"

"We are operating on behalf of the Hegemony. I'd hope they would compensate us as independent contractors," Toran chimed in.

"Seriously, guys?" Kaiden raised an eyebrow. "We're tromping through a bog on an alien world and you're wondering if we're going to get paid for saving known civilization?"

I smiled at him. "Well, when you put it that way, it would be ridiculous for them *not* to give us all the money for being the bestest heroes ever."

He narrowed his eyes. "I can't quite tell if you're joking or not."

"Probably because you recognize I bring up a valid point."

"It *does* seem like we should get something for going to all of this trouble," Maris interjected.

"I could see getting an endorsement deal," Toran said. "Pretty sure there's a fitness company that would want to get in on this." He flexed his arms to model his sculpted torso.

"You've all lost your minds," Kaiden muttered.

"Probably swamp gas," I quipped.

He sighed. "And here I thought I'd get to finish out my last term of school in solitude charting the growth patterns of new hybrid alfalfa strains."

I turned back toward him. "Kaiden, I'm not gonna lie, that sounds really lonely."

"Okay, granted, it wasn't the best. I was attracted to the agro angle because I thought I could be part of a community. Turns out it wasn't quite what I thought."

"Do you regret it?" I asked.

"No." He paused. "Maybe. I don't know. I just wanted to have a sense of grounding that I never got growing up."

"You know, sometimes it's about the people you're around more than the place," I said.

"Yeah, I've heard that, too." He sighed. "I have a feeling that this whole experience is going to upend my plans. I'll see how it shakes out in the end."

"I'm never going to be able to look at things the same way again," Toran murmured.

"Wow, that conversation took a turn for the deep and introspective." Maris chuckled.

"I guess being faced with mortality and the fate of one's world can do that to a person," I said.

She took a deep breath. "Yeah, I have a lot to think about, too."

"Like, I mean, the whole *magic* thing is a game-changer," Kaiden said.

"That is very true. It complements being a nurse, but this would be different," replied Maris.

I nodded. "Tough to know how the established medical community will respond to the notion of magical healing."

"Can't argue with the results, though." Kaiden pointed out.

"The very confirmation of magic will change many perceptions," Toran mused. "I could see us becoming the subject of many studies."

"No, there have to be others, right?" Maris asked. "We're not the only casters."

"Have you ever heard of a genuine magic user?" I questioned. "I haven't. I was familiar with the idea, and I was taught that magic was commonplace during the time the crystals were created, but those were the last known instances of true magic, as far as I know."

"That's what I learned growing up, too," Kaiden said. "When I saw the wand, it called to the fanciful dreams I had as a kid. I never imagined… this." He cupped a flame in his palm.

"There's a lot to worry about before we think about returning to our normal lives," Toran stated. "Let's focus on the Spirit artifact."

"To that end, I suspect it's somewhere over there." Kaiden pointed to the west.

A shimmering expanse of blue-green water was now distinct from the surrounding marshy landscape. At its center, the small island rose a few meters above the water's surface and measured approximately ten meters in diameter. The crystal at the summit of the island's rise shone with soft blue light, beckoning us to approach.

However, the sun was getting low in the sky, and nighttime would be upon us within the hour. We'd have to wait to tackle the island in the morning.

We continued toward the lake, the last half-kilometer going faster as the ground transitioned from sticky mud to drier, plant-covered clay.

As we approached the lakefront, I kept an eye out for any signs of a road or bridge, which might connect to the underwater pathway to the island.

"I wonder if there's a magical switch," I mused aloud.

"What, now?" Kaiden asked.

"You know, the bridge," I clarified.

"Oh that, yeah." He nodded. "I'm hesitant to try anything tonight, since it may trigger another battle like that one with the giant. I *really* don't want to attempt a magic fight in the dark."

"Might actually be easier than a physical fight in the dark, though," I pointed out.

He took a deep breath. "The intent of that statement was *any* nighttime battle equals bad."

"I can't argue with that."

Toran squinted. "Is that the entry to the bridge up ahead?"

I diverted my attention from Kaiden to where Toran was pointing at two horizontal stones along the water's edge.

"That does look promising," I agreed.

"Let's get a closer look." Kaiden picked up his pace.

We slowed on the final approach, instinct taking over to warn us that we might be walking into a trap.

"I don't feel any active magical presence," Kaiden said.

"Me either," Maris agreed. "Not that I know what that is, exactly, but nothing stands out as this being different than any other stone."

"Assuming this is the trigger for the bridge, let's not wake it up just yet," Kaiden cautioned.

"Yeah, no." Maris shook her head.

Toran gazed thoughtfully at the strip of land to which the bridge connected. "I believe this will make a suitable campsite."

The low, horizontal stones formed walls along a sloped ramp leading into the lake. The walls would make for reasonable seating, and a flat, paved area between them would serve for a relatively dry campsite to lie down with our blankets and tend a fire.

"I like it," I said. "We should get a fire going. That tends to deter most creatures."

Toran nodded. "I had a similar thought."

"What are we going to burn?" Maris asked.

"No trees, no wood," I realized.

"Those reeds and bushes?" Maris suggested.

Kaiden shook his head. "Good tinder, but there's no staying power to the burn on something like that."

She frowned. "Then what?"

"Peat," I said. "We used to bring bricks of it camping with us."

"Uh, Elle, if you haven't noticed, everything is wet here," Kaiden countered. "We can't burn anything from the ground here."

"All that you need to prepare it is pressure and heat." I gestured to Toran and Kaiden. "This ground is packed biomass. It'll make the perfect long-burn fuel with a little preparation."

Toran nodded slowly. "You may be onto something there. Don't know until we try it." He shrugged.

"How do we get it out of the ground?" Kaiden asked.

Maris scowled. "What are you even talking about?"

"You know, peat." I stamped my foot on the ground.

She tilted her head. "Who's Pete?"

I sighed. "Just watch." I dropped my pack on the stone ledge and rooted around inside. We weren't lucky enough to have a shovel in our collection of random useful things, but I did have my sword, a plate, and a bunch of tape; I always loved improvising.

My makeshift 'shovel' was slightly horrifying to behold, but when I gave it a test-scoop in the ground, it worked surprisingly well. While Maris watched with crossed arms and a bemused expression, I scooped out a dozen chunks of the ground from near the water's edge where the reeds grew. It had the right kind of fibrous look I recognized from untreated peat back home, so I was hopeful it would fulfill our needs.

"All right, let's make this into something that will burn," I said.

With Kaiden and Toran's help—Maris didn't want to get her hands dirty—we relocated the chunks of wet biomass to the paved stone area and stomped on it as a first pass to get out the moisture. Then, I removed the plate from my sword and Toran also got out his. He pressed the chunks between the plates until they were relatively dry pucks. We then set the pucks on the stone pathway, and Kaiden held a flame in his hand—enough to heat the pucks without igniting them.

As the last of the sun dipped below the horizon, the pucks appeared to be about as dry as they'd get.

"Let's see how this burns," I said.

Kaiden nodded. "All right."

We located a suitable spot in the center of the stone ramp to use as a fire pit, and Kaiden focused a low-intensity flame on the puck. It sputtered at first, then ignited in a warm, golden glow.

We laughed with relief and glee; our efforts had paid off.

"Now *that's* how you improvise a fire," I said.

"Huh." Maris nodded. "So, did Pete invent this, or—"

"Different spelling," I cut in, holding up one of the pucks. "P-e-*a*-t. Apparently, they don't teach you *everything* in the city."

She crossed her arms, accentuating her figure even more in the firelight. "Yeah, we didn't burn a lot—not even candles."

"I barely knew about the material, myself," Toran admitted.

"Fire can be fun," Kaiden interjected.

I smiled. "You were a total pyro as a kid, weren't you?"

He looked off to the side. "Well, let's just say it's not surprising that a fireball was the first thing I cast."

With the immediate needs of warmth and animal deterrent tended to, we got settled into our campsite for the night. We had thin sleeping pads and thermal blankets in our inventory, along with half a week's rations, a water filter, and various other gadgets.

The horizontal walls to either side weren't ideal for sitting on, but at least it would be a dry place to sit off of the ground. I selected a spot on one of the mossier sections to get some extra insulation from the stone. Across the campsite, Kaiden noticed me getting settled and started to head over. Before he could sit next to me, however, Toran plopped down.

"I bet it gets cold at night," the large man commented.

"Yeah, we'll need to get cozy." Maris grabbed Kaiden's arm and tugged him to toward the wall across from me.

He sat down next to her, seeming a little reluctant, but I wasn't sure if that was only in my head.

As the temperature dropped, we found ourselves scooting closer together and leaning in toward the fire to gather as much warmth as we could. True to Tami's statement, the base layer of our clothing *did* regulate temperature well, but even with that, the chill crept in.

We ate a simple meal around the fire, admiring the starry sky as the last of the light faded. To my relief, there was no sound of animal activity around us.

"You know, maybe spending a night outside won't be so bad, after all," Maris said, breaking the intervening silence. "It's peaceful out here."

"See? Told you." Kaiden nudged her gently with his shoulder as they sat side by side.

An unwanted wave of jealously rose in my chest. He wasn't actually warming up to her, was he?

Like I was one to talk—even I wasn't finding her as annoying now that her unique magic skills were coming into play. And, aside from the 'Pete' incident and occasional whining, I was probably overreacting to her attitude. I could see how anyone could be drawn in by her perfect figure and desire to nurture.

Meanwhile, I had never considered myself anything special to look at, I had a tendency to slash things with my sword when they upset me, and snark was my go-to mode of communication. When evaluating girlfriend potential, I may as well admit defeat in a competition I didn't want to have in the first place.

I did my best to suppress the thoughts. Petty distractions. But, seeing Kaiden sitting next to Maris, I knew ignoring my feelings wasn't going to be that easy.

I rose from the wall and plopped down on my bedroll. The ground was hard, even with the pad, but I'd have to tough it out. "We should get some rest."

Kaiden drew away from Maris to head for his own sleeping pad. "Yeah, sleep well. We'll cross to the island at daybreak."

16

I HAD A restless night on the cold ground under the stars. I'd always enjoyed camping as a kid, but being on an alien world knowing that creatures who wanted to eat me might only be a dozen meters away didn't make for restful sleep.

As the first golden light peeked over the horizon, I sat up and stretched.

The last of our peat bricks were now smoking ash, but they'd served their purpose and gotten us through the night.

Maris, surprisingly, was the next to stir. Somehow, her hair was still perfectly styled despite spending a night on the ground with no pillow.

I ran my fingers through my own tangled mess of fuchsia hair, making a mental note to pack a comb for our next outing.

Kaiden stretched on his pad, then cracked open an eye. "Morning already?" He rubbed his eyes.

Toran startled awake. "Toast?" He looked around. "Oh, right."

I chuckled. "Everything okay over there?"

"Yes, just thinking about my family," he replied. "Breakfast, anyone?"

My heart dropped as I thought about my own family and how nice it had always been to wake up to the scent of baking muffins on the weekends. "Yeah, sounds great."

We ate more of the bland rations identical to our meal the night before, then packed up our simple camp.

When everything was stowed in our backpacks, Kaiden took a deep breath and turned toward the island. "Now we need to figure out how to get over *there*."

I had no idea what to suggest. The previous locations we'd visited to access the artifacts had columns or some other indicator to mark what we were supposed to do. This, however, was a flooded bridge, a crystal on an island, and a whole lot of nothing everywhere around us.

"Do we have to swim over?" Toran asked.

Kaiden approached the water's edge. "That doesn't seem right. But this water is definitely too deep for us to wade across the bridge."

"Maybe the landscape has changed over time," I suggested. "It's possible everything flooded. Who knows when all of this was built—a lot can change in a few hundred or thousand years."

"That's a good point." Kaiden turned around and looked at the paved area we were standing on. "What do you think this was?"

I took a step back and examined the area more objectively in proper lighting. At first glance, it reminded me of a boat ramp, though I knew that was unlikely.

Then, it hit me. "What if all of the ground settled and the columns fell over?"

"These walls we were sitting on?" Kaiden returned to our campsite and rubbed the layer of sediment and moss off of a top segment to expose the stone underneath. "This *does* look like the stone that was around the crystals on the other planet."

"I touched the crystal to activate the stones on the other world," Toran pointed out.

"Doesn't mean it will work the same way here." Kaiden nodded toward the other stone wall. "Maris, try touching that one. Maybe they need to be activated by casters at the same time."

"Wouldn't the system be designed to work with one person?" I asked.

Kaiden stretched out his hands toward each column, falling a meter short to either side. "Definitely can't reach both of these at the same time. I guess it's possible that someone is supposed to cast magic at them from a distance—or maybe they fell down farther apart than they were when standing."

Maris glanced at the column and then at Kaiden. "So, do you want me to touch it or not?"

Kaiden looked to me and Toran.

I shrugged. "This is your discipline. Follow your instincts."

He nodded. "You're right—this is different from the other one, but that could be done by one person so this should be, too. Must be related to casting."

"Makes sense," Toran concurred.

"Stand back." Kaiden raised his hands.

I cleared the vicinity and stood with Toran and Maris four meters to the side of the stones.

Kaiden took a deep breath and extended his hands, holding his staff in his right. A warm glow danced across his fingertips and to the end of the staff, and then a dazzling tendril of yellow light snaked through the air toward the stones.

The stones emitted a blue glow in response to the magic, which radiated through the ground toward the water. Blue light traced all the way to the island at the center of the lake. The light intensified as the ground began to tremble.

I broadened my stance to keep my balance in the shaking. "That seems to be doing *something*."

The water above the path through the lake churned as the stones beneath began to rise. The ramp leading down to the water leveled out to meet with the newly raised path, and when the stones were on the same plane, the trembling ceased.

Kaiden lowered his hands and the magical ribbons dissipated. "Well, that wasn't so hard."

"Neither was activating the other columns," Toran replied. "There is likely still a trial ahead."

"Walking through that bog wasn't enough of a trial?" Maris sighed.

"Tolerance for wet feet isn't the test." Kaiden looked at the puddles on the stones along the path to the island. "Despite all evidence to the contrary."

"Well, my feet are toasty and dry in these boots," I said, heading for the path. "Are we going to do this or what?"

Kaiden pointed his staff ahead. "Let's go."

I followed him onto the stone walkway with Toran and Maris close behind. The rock was slick from algae growth, so I had to keep my hands outstretched for balance, since my weight was thrown off by the heavy pack.

It was just over two hundred meters to the island. The crystal at its center gleamed in the early morning sun, and for a minute, I could almost convince myself that it would be a straightforward task to retrieve whatever artifact awaited us.

As we approached the island, I focused on the crystal with the hope of seeing what kind of artifact it may be; nothing obvious was placed inside the crystal, as with Toran's gauntlets. By the time we were almost to the land, however, I could discern a faint shape within the four-meter-tall crystal.

"Is that the artifact?" I asked.

"I think so," Kaiden replied, "but I can't make out what it is."

We reached the land and walked up the gradual incline to the crest of the hill. Standing in front of the crystal, I realized that the object embedded inside it was a silver circlet, which explained why its delicate shape hadn't been visible from a distance.

"You get to be king?" I joked.

Kaiden grinned back at me. "Only a prince."

I drew my sword.

"And you're… staging a revolt?" Kaiden questioned me.

I laughed. "No. Just have a feeling that the moment you touch that crystal, this is going to turn into a battle zone."

He nodded. "Well, it started out as a nice, quiet morning."

"Those never last." I turned so I could see both the crystal and the lake, taking a defensive stance.

Maris and Toran took up mirror positions on Kaiden's other side.

"Okay, here it goes." Kaiden extended his hand toward the crystal.

A singular chime sounded, as though a bell had been struck. But, rather than fading, the sound intensified. The ground began to tremble underfoot again, this time agitating the entire lake. Water surged toward the island, a solid wave moving as one from all directions around the island.

Panic set in. I dropped my backpack, bracing for the water to hit. I wondered if I should ditch my coat, too, to have a better chance at swimming. But, when the mini tsunami reached the island's shoreline, the water shot straight up for ten meters and then arched overhead to form an aquatic dome.

I looked at my comrades with confusion. "Wasn't expecting that."

"We're trapped in here," Toran stated the obvious.

"What do we do?" Maris asked, more than a hint of concern in her tone.

Kaiden glanced down at his pendant; it was glowing brightly. "There's something here."

Maris' pendant was glowing, as well. "I feel it," she murmured.

My spine tingled and a pressure filled the back of my mind. I hadn't sensed anything like that around the rock giant, but this was a different artifact guardian with its own unique properties—that is, assuming it was its presence I was feeling. I couldn't see anything in the water beyond faint light shining through the thin dome overhead.

"Where are you?" Kaiden called out. "I'm here to claim the artifact."

The water swirled in response, a distinct wave rippling around the circumference of the island. When it had completed the circuit, the wall of water swelled in front of us, taking on a lighter iridescent sheen compared to the darker water surrounding it.

"You think you are worthy?" a musical voice spoke all around us, as though coming from the water itself.

I swallowed and tightened the grip on my sword—like that would do any good against a wall of water.

"I hope to prove that I am," Kaiden replied.

"Your companions are driven by might, but that will not win you your prize."

"I will meet any challenge you present me."

In response, an arm of water reached out from the wall and knocked Kaiden to the side. His staff flew from his hand and clattered to the stones at the shore.

"And you call yourself worthy!" the voice taunted. "This lake will become your grave."

The wall swelled inward to envelop Kaiden where he stood.

"No!" he bellowed. "I am here to prove myself." He raised his hands. In the direction he pointed, the water froze to ice. The ice crystals shattered and dropped to the rock like chimes.

I'd only seen fire and lightening before, but if there was any time for him to add a new spell to his arsenal, this was it.

"How can we help?" I asked.

"I don't know," Kaiden shook his head. "I haven't figured out what it wants me to do yet."

A blob of water launched from the wall and landed two meters from Kaiden, standing as an oblong column on the ground.

"Uh... what?" I scowled at it.

Kaiden shook his head. "I have no idea."

The blob shuffled toward him.

"Ideas?" Kaiden asked.

"Smash it," Toran suggested.

Kaiden frowned. "Pretty sure that's *not* it."

"Casting. This whole challenge is about Spirit, right?" Maris said.

"But casting *what*?" Kaiden stared down the blob. "What do you want me to do?"

The blob leaped forward and dropped down onto Kaiden's shoulders, completely enveloping his head.

His eyes widened with obvious panic. He clawed at the water, but it flexed around his fingers and it couldn't get any purchase.

"Maris, do something!" I shouted.

"I can't fight *that*!" she exclaimed.

Kaiden gasped, a flurry of air bubbles escaping his mouth.

"He's going to drown." I dropped my sword and ran to him, not sure what relief I could offer, but I needed to try *something*.

His eyes pleaded to me.

"This is a test," I told him. "There's a way out using your magic. You can do this."

He shoved me back from him and brought his hands to his face once more. This time, they glowed red and the water vaporized where he touched it.

The blob around his head burst, drenching him.

Kaiden took a gasping breath, coughing and sputtering.

"Are you okay?" I asked while bending down to pick up my sword.

He nodded, though he was still coughing. "What was that?"

"You were just attacked by a blob of water," I replied.

"Yeah, I got that. But... *what* was it?"

I shrugged. "Angry water?"

He rolled his eyes. "I have no clue what we're supposed to do here."

"I liked the rock giant," Toran interjected. "We just had to smash it."

"That was a lot more straightforward," I agreed. "But only after we found it. There was a lot of sciencing to locate the correct location."

"That's true," Toran replied. "We wouldn't have been able to find it so quickly if I didn't have my engineering background."

I nodded. "Maybe there's more to these challenges than the main engagement itself."

"Either way, I feel like I'm missing something really obvious here," Kaiden said.

Another blob emerged from the wall and landed near Kaiden. It scooched toward him.

"Oh, no. You're not going to try to drown me again!" Kaiden blasted the blob with a fireball. The water vaporized.

"Progress, maybe?" I shrugged again.

A moment later, another blob appeared.

"This is going to get old really fast," Kaiden muttered.

"Maybe a different spell?" Maris suggested.

Kaiden conjured an orb of electrical energy in his palm and lobbed it at the new blob. The pillar of water burst apart, leaving only a puddle behind.

I placed my sword tip-down on the ground and crossed my hands on the butt of the hilt. "Okay... Not sure where this is going, exactly."

"That makes two of us," Kaiden huffed.

Another blob leaped from the wall and formed a column of water near Kaiden.

He rolled his eyes. "You have to be kidding!"

"Have any other spells you've been meaning to share?" I asked.

Kaiden took a deep breath. "It doesn't work like that. Things just... come to me sometimes."

"Like the ice earlier?"

"Yeah." He examined the blob. "I guess I could try that one again." He held up his hand, and the water column turned to ice crystals. It shattered.

"Well, looks like you have that one down now," I commented.

"It's toying with you," Toran said. "Maybe we need to try to break down the wall."

In response, the walls and domed roof began swirling and crashing as the enclosure turned into a turbulent whirlpool.

"I don't think it likes that idea," I observed.

Three water blobs launched from the frenzy and landed as glistening columns in front of Kaiden.

"Okay, that's new." Kaiden launched three fireballs in rapid succession.

The columns vaporized, but the water became more frenzied.

Another three blobs emerged from the wall.

Kaiden shook his head. "Was that the wrong spell?" He tried freezing them instead.

The swirling water rose to a roar.

The three blobs appeared again.

"The three appeared after you'd cast three different types of magic," I observed. "Maybe you need to hit each of these with something different?"

Kaiden stared at the blobs. "I think you're onto something." He frozen the first, cast a bolt of electrical energy at the second, and vaporized the third with a fireball. Then, a new, solitary blob appeared.

"What do I do with this one?" Kaiden asked.

"Does the pattern start over?" I wondered.

He shook his head. "No, that doesn't feel right."

"The other side of yourself," Maris suggested. "You have destroyed, now you must heal."

Understanding passed over Kaiden's face. "Yes, that's it. But I've never used that kind of magic."

He stepped closer to the blob. Though featureless, I couldn't help but get the impression it was looking up at him with a kind of helpless innocence, wondering if it was about to be helped or destroyed.

Kaiden placed his hands to either side of it ten centimeters from the water's surface. He closed his eyes.

A soft green glow appeared between his palms, passing through the water and radiating within it until the entire blob glowed with the green light.

Then, without warning, the blob collapsed into a puddle.

The deafening roar of the waves stopped, and the water stilled.

"You have mastered the challenge," the voice said. "You have shown a balanced spirit worthy of wielding the power bestowed upon you. Use it well."

The wall of water encircling the island dropped back into the lake with a splash, and then all was still.

I took a deep breath, wiping my damp hair back from my eyes. "I think we're getting the hang of this."

Kaiden cracked a smile. "Couldn't have done it without all of you."

The glow of the crystal behind us intensified, and I turned to face it. The light appeared to pulse, beckoning.

Kaiden approached it, transferring his staff to his left hand. With his right, he reached out to place his palm on the smooth crystal.

The light intensified, and with a blinding flash, the crystal shattered into fragments no larger than a grain of sand. The silver circlet within floated to the ground along with the fragments, coming to rest atop the shimmering pile.

As Kaiden reached out toward it, a purple gem affixed in the front of the circlet began to glow. Indigo light flowed from the gem and momentarily wove around Kaiden before it absorbed into him. He picked up the circlet and placed it on his head, the gem resting at his hairline. "Do I look ridiculous?"

I smiled. "Well, you might draw a few strange looks in a bar, but it goes with the whole cloak vibe thing you have going on."

Kaiden beamed. "It's doing something. I feel... stronger."

Toran nodded. "I had a similar experience when I got my own artifact."

"I can't wait to—" I cut off when the ground started to tremble.

Water lapped at the edge of the stone path leading to the island. The stones were sinking.

"Run, hurry!" I shouted. I swung my backpack over my shoulders and dashed toward the mainland.

The stones seemed even slipperier underfoot than the way out, but I did my best to run at top speed. If the path sank before we made it back, it might be impossible to swim the rest of our way with our gear; I didn't want to try to navigate the swamp without a map or weapon.

The water level was up to my ankles by the time I reached the halfway point of my run to safety. I glanced over my shoulder to check on my companions, and I saw Maris struggling on the slick stones while Kaiden tried to help her along using his staff. I ran back.

Toran turned back, as well. I motioned for him to keep going, and he complied after a moment's hesitation.

"Go, Elle!" Kaiden urged. "We'll catch up."

"No, we need to balance together," I insisted, wrapping my hand around Maris' other side.

The three of us splashed down the path as the water reached our knees. It was as cold as it was dark, chilling me. With water sloshing over the top of my boots and pooling inside, each step was heavier and more difficult than the last.

Only a dozen meters to go. The water eddied around my thighs, and I was soaked past my waist from the splashing.

"We might have to swim it," I said.

"No." Kaiden stopped suddenly, gripping his staff.

My skin tingled as a strange energy surrounded me. The crashing water crystalized to either side of the path, and I quickly jumped up on it before my feet were frozen in position. Maris scampered up next to me, and we steadied each other on the slick ground.

The purple gem on Kaiden's circlet was glowing brightly as he joined us on the strip of ice. "Hurry!" he shouted.

Taking each other's hands for balance, we ran toward the shore as the frozen water slowly turned to mush underfoot. With a final surge of speed, we made it to the ramp's upward incline just as the final ice remnants melted away.

I released Maris' and Kaiden's hands then leaned against the fallen column. "That's a neat new skill."

"I like this new circlet," Kaiden said with a weary smile. The glow in the purple stone had faded; it looked like the more powerful magic had taken a lot out of him.

"Glad you're okay," Toran said. "That was quite a feat freezing part of the lake."

"I'll need to play around to figure out what other new abilities I have thanks to the artifact," Kaiden replied. He brushed his fingertips along the silver circlet.

Maris took several panting breaths. "Lesson learned. As soon as we get back to the *Evangiel*, I'm getting some shoes with better traction."

I laughed. "The things you don't think about, right?"

Toran gazed out at the island slowly sinking into the lake. "What caused the path to fall apart?"

"I think whatever magic allowed us to raise the stones vanished as soon as the Spirit artifact was claimed," I said. "Without that magic to hold it in place, everything returned to how it would naturally be."

"Pretty incredible to think about," Kaiden said, taking one final look at the lake.

Maris nodded. "We get to control a piece of that ancient power."

"And we have a lot we need to do with it." Kaiden tore his gaze away from the water. "Come on. We should get back to the ship."

17

WE MADE GOOD time on our slog back to the shuttle, now that we had a better sense of how to navigate the waterways with minimal backtracking. Plus, since we were already wet, we waded through some channels that we would have otherwise found a way around.

I felt grimy and sensed that I probably smelled like rotten fish by the time we made it to the shuttle. The craft was one of the most welcome sights I could imagine after the miserable ten kilometer hike.

"First order of business when we get back is a shower," I announced as we approached the shuttle.

"Definitely," Kaiden agreed.

We tried to clean off our mucky boots as best we could before boarding, but we tracked muddy footprints up the ramp despite our efforts.

I sighed. "So much for Tami warming up to us."

"In all fairness, it's probably *more* unusual that we brought it back last time clean and intact," Kaiden said.

"May as well set reasonable expectations," Toran agreed.

We climbed aboard the shuttle and dropped our dirty bags in the common room. As I feared, as soon as we were in the enclosed space, a decidedly fishy smell filled the cabin.

Kaiden wrinkled his nose. "I'm really glad it's not a long flight."

"Please, let's get out of here." I rushed to the bridge.

We went through pre-flight checks as quickly as possible, then strapped in and were on our way. By the time the *Evangiel* came into view,

I no longer noticed the scent, but I had no reason to believe it had diminished.

We made it to the ship and slipped through the electrostatic field into the hangar. As soon as the shuttle had come to a rest, we filed into the common room to retrieve our bags. Toran dropped the ramp.

Breathing in the filtered air of the hangar, I realized how foul an atmosphere we'd been in for the last day.

Tami rounded the shuttle, then quickly brought up a hand to cover her nose and mouth when she saw us. "Stars! What happened?"

I sighed. "Marsh monsters."

She lowered her hand, but her nose remained wrinkled. "If I didn't know better, I'd think you'd spent the last month in a bio reclamation tank."

"Oh, I'm sure the swap was on par with a decades-old waste bin," Kaiden replied. He rubbed his shoes together and some of the drying mud flaked off in a clump on the deck.

Tami frowned. "Maybe you should strip down before you go through the ship."

I looked down at my own filthy self. "Solid plan."

We removed everything but our white base layers, which were now closer to a light taupe, and left the other soiled items piled on the deck.

"I'll reach out to the maintenance crew and get all this cleaned up for you," Tami told us.

I flushed. "Sorry about the mess."

Tami shrugged. "I think I have it easy compared to you, considering what you must have gone through to end up looking like that."

We thanked her again and then headed up to our respective quarters—pausing to acquaint Maris with her own room in line with ours.

I'd never experienced such a glorious shower in my entire life. While I'd spent plenty of time playing in the dirt as a kid, most of Erusan was dry, so dust was our biggest problem. This mud was sticky, and the scent of decay lingered even after two thorough scrub-downs. If I never had to traverse another bog in my life, I'd be happy.

As I exited the shower, I realized that I'd neglected to check for clean clothes; there was no way I was putting on my old shipsuit until it had been thoroughly laundered.

I wrapped a towel around myself and went to investigate the

wardrobe. Inside, to my relief, were three white suits and undergarments. It was generic sizing, unlike my other custom-fitted suit, but I'd take anything clean and dry at that point.

After dressing, I exited my cabin and wandered down the hall to the room we'd designated as our combination hang out, planning, and rendezvous place. Toran was the only one present, and he appeared to be absorbed in an inspection of his magical signature locator device. With only a generic shipsuit at his own disposal, he had the top portion of the suit folded over with the arms tied around his waist.

"Hey," I greeted when he didn't appear to notice me enter. "Looks like a trip to the equipment room is in order."

"Oh, hello, Elle." He looked down at his bare chest. "Yes. Feeling better?"

"Much." I moseyed over to him. "What are you working on?"

Toran set down the device and frowned at it. "I was wondering if there might be a way to have the device tap into a nearby signature rather than needing direct physical contact, so Kaiden or Maris wouldn't need to remove their pendant each time."

"That would be handy."

"Unfortunately, I don't see a way to make any quick modifications." He sighed.

"Well, bright side is that we only have one more world to visit to get the remaining artifact."

"Yes, very true. We can always work on it more depending on what our future missions entail."

I leaned my hip against the table and crossed my arms. "I still can't believe they want *us* to go up against the Darkness."

"It would be like any other task—break it up into steps and take actions that progress toward that end."

"This isn't just a random project. We're talking about maybe dealing with advanced alien tech here. *You* at least have training. I don't know how much I can offer."

Toran smiled. "Don't sell yourself short, Elle. You've held your own quite well. I seem to recall many of our successful ideas coming from you."

I dropped my gaze, blushing. "Maybe."

"Feeling better?" Kaiden asked from the doorway, stepping inside.

"Much, aside from a draft," Toran replied, running one hand down his other exposed arm. "I was just telling Elle that she has no reason to doubt her worth on our team."

"Oh, stars no!" Kaiden exclaimed. "Using peat in place of firewood was a stroke of genius."

My lips parted in a bashful smile. "Thanks."

"Not to mention, you're getting pretty good with that sword," he added.

"That part is weird," I admitted. "I haven't really practiced with it, but these new forms just come to me in my mind, and it's like I have muscle memory of doing things I've never done before."

"I think it might have something to do with how our bodies were re-formed," Kaiden said. "It's like that with the magic, too."

"Same." Toran leaned against the table next to me. "I'm thankful for the help, wherever it came from."

"Yeah, no kidding." I sighed.

"Speaking of help, what are you working on there?" Kaiden asked Toran, gesturing to the device the other man had been fiddling with.

"Nothing that matters at the moment—"

Toran cut off when an announcement sounded on the central comm. "Jump in T-minus ten minutes."

I pushed off the table. "Back at it again."

"So much for getting a night's rest in our own beds." Kaiden headed for the door.

"The only consistency is that nothing is predictable," I commented while following him out of the room.

"I don't expect that to change any time soon," he replied.

"There you are!" Maris exclaimed from down the hall as soon as we left the room. She ran over.

"Hi," I greeted.

Her dark hair was still damp from a shower, and she fluffed it with her fingertips. "Jumping again already?"

"Final artifact world," Kaiden replied.

She looked to me. "This one's for you?"

I nodded. "That's the plan."

"Then back to the Archive." Kaiden continued toward the pod room to get prepped for the impending jump.

As much as I hated jumps, the thought of this one didn't bother me nearly as much knowing that the end was in sight—at least, I told myself it was. I recognized that the situation with the Darkness wouldn't be resolved when we sealed the Archive, but at least I would have a sense of security once a backup of my world was safely sealed.

We strapped into our usual pods and endured the stomach-churning jump. When it was complete, I sat up in my pod eager to face our next challenge. This one would be on me, but I was ready to prove myself.

"Ugh, I hate jumps," Maris moaned across the room. She popped up above the lip of the pod then lie back down.

"You all right?" Kaiden asked.

"Yeah," she said, though her tone indicated otherwise. "Just gimme a minute."

"Any bets on what the Valor trial might be?" I asked the group while her stomach settled.

"Hmm." Toran got a ponderous expression. "Something requiring strength and courage."

"Um, yeah—" I stopped when I noticed him smirking. "You don't say?" I finished, smiling back.

"It's probably fair to assume something will try to crush, suffocate, or eat you," Kaiden chimed in.

I grinned. "It will be sorely disappointed when I disembowel it instead."

"Let's get a look at the world," Kaiden suggested.

Maris was just hauling herself out of her pod. "I'll be right there."

We left her to finish getting her bearings and headed down the corridor to our staging room. Kaiden removed his pendant and placed it on the device.

"I hope finding this location is as straightforward as the last," Toran murmured while he activated the device.

The characteristic soft blue light illuminated in the pendant. After a moment, readings appeared on the touch-surface tabletop.

Toran frowned. "That's strange."

"What?" I asked.

"This isn't showing anything."

"Like, no magical signatures?"

"No, as in *nothing*," Toran clarified. "It's like there isn't a proper planet here."

My brow furrowed as I looked out the viewport, but there was only a typical starscape. That didn't mean anything, since the room was often orientated away from any planet we may be orbiting. "Did we jump to the right place?"

Kaiden backed away from the table. He pressed behind his ear. "Commander, we—"

"Please come to Central Command," Colren replied over the general channel through the comms in our ears.

"We'll be right there." Kaiden ended the link. "I don't like the way this is going."

"Yes, agreed." Toran removed the pendant from the device and handed it to Kaiden.

The three of us returned to the hall. Maris was still in the pod room as we passed by on our way to the lift.

I poked my head through the door. "Maris, did you hear that? We need to go to the bridge."

"Yeah. Is something wrong?" she asked.

"The planet is giving some weird readings. We need to get a visual on it," Kaiden replied.

Maris frowned. "What about getting back the rest of our clothes? I feel naked in just this shipsuit."

"It'll have to wait," I said, though I could relate to how she was feeling. Before she could protest further, I strode toward Central Command.

We were buzzed inside, and Colren greeted us in the center of the bridge. "I trust you tried to use your device to examine the planet?"

"Yes. Are you having difficulty getting readings, as well?" Toran asked.

The commander gave a grave nod. "We hadn't prepared for this contingency."

"What contingency?" I questioned. My stomach twisted. Things were just started to go in our favor; it figured something would go wrong now.

The commander beckoned us closer to the viewscreen on the forward wall. I gazed out at the beautiful spacescape, drawn in by the stars, but then I noticed something at the bottom of the view. There was a planet there, except it was dark.

The tension in my gut spread to my entire chest. "Wait, is that…?"

"This world has already been consumed by the Darkness," Colren stated. "We're too late."

"TOO LATE FOR *what*?" I asked, though I already knew the answer. If the planet had been consumed by the Darkness, that meant the final artifact we needed to open the Master Archive was now beyond our reach. We had failed our mission.

Kaiden's brow furrowed. "Is that it? There's nothing we can do?"

"Perhaps there is an alternative way to seal the Archive," the commander suggested. "We need to explore every available option."

"But, why can't we just go down to the planet?" Maris asked.

"Look at it! It's been almost completely consumed," I said, pointing at the depressing image on the screen.

The reddish world was crisscrossed with dark smoke-like lines, and the tendrils were continuing to expand. I had no idea how long it took a world to be overrun, but based on what little I'd seen, we only missed our window by hours. If we had been able to land closer to the Spirit icon and hadn't lost a day, or if we hadn't slept, then maybe—

I stopped myself. Thinking in those terms wouldn't change what we were facing now. It's not like we could reset across multiple star systems and do it over again.

"But, that doesn't matter, right?" Maris continued.

"Of course it does," Kaiden said. "That's a dead planet now."

"No, we talked about this before," Maris insisted. "We're supposed to be immune to the Darkness, right? We can go there."

I stood in silence, my gaze flitting between my companions and the commander. "What *happens* to a world when it's consumed?" I asked tentatively.

"We don't know," Colren admitted. "When we first encountered the Darkness, we sent in teams to investigate and they didn't come back."

I eyed him. "You said we're different—that we should have an immunity. How do you know that?"

The commander shook his head. "That isn't important."

"I don't know, seems pretty relevant to me." Kaiden crossed his arms.

"Commander, if you would like our continued cooperation, being forthcoming with us will get you the best results," Toran stated. Despite the soft heart I knew he had on the inside, I had to admit that any firm statement from Toran carried additional weight due to the intimidation factor of his stature.

Colren evaluated us. "All right, come on." He led us to the private conference room, and we stood around the table. "Remember when I told you that the Darkness appeared three months ago? Well, you weren't the first people we extracted."

That wasn't the least bit reassuring. "Who were the others?" I asked.

"We first had the bioprinter ready for the extraction procedure a month ago," he explained. "The details about how it functioned were vague in the ancient records we were referencing, but the technical team was able to piece enough of it together to give it a shot. The first results were… not viable."

My stomach turned over again. "How do you mean?"

He shifted in his seat. "The consciousness never properly knitted with the physical form. That's why we ended up developing the initiation procedure you all experienced."

"Don't need the grisly details, but okay, they died," Kaiden said. "Were you able to make it work with others before us?"

"We did. And that's how we discovered the secondary feature of Darkness exposure resulting in a sort of tolerance for future encounters," the commander continued. "The team—there were three of them—were on a Hegemony world that served as a research post; in fact, it was where the bioprinter was first developed and tested. Due to the sensitive nature of the activities, the data was saved on local servers rather than backed up through the subspace relays to the Hegemony's central data repository. When the Darkness came to the world, the team volunteered to retrieve it. We sent them in with half a dozen armed guards.

"The team was composed of two Spirit casters and a Protector. When the Darkness arrived at the research site, the Protector stayed behind to finish the data upload to this ship. The two Spirit casters proceeded to the extraction site, but they were overrun by the Darkness mid-travel. The guards accompanying them were all frozen, but the two casters were able to make it to a shuttle to escape."

He swallowed. "I suppose it would have been more accurate to say that we believe someone with abilities such as yourselves can withstand *temporary* exposure. We don't know how long they could have lasted; we never wanted to risk sending them back in."

I folded my hands on the desktop. "Okay, if they made it out of that encounter, then where are they?"

"They crashed while trying to land on Crystallis," Colren revealed.

"Hold on, you'd tried to send people down there before us?" Kaiden glared at him.

The commander backed up a little. "We attributed the crash to a legend that only a team representing all of the disciplines could land on the world. So, we set about waiting for you."

"This is insane," I muttered.

Kaiden shook his head slowly. "You lied to us."

"I conveyed what was useful in the moment," Colren corrected. "Based on this reaction, I should have kept those details to myself."

"You use people and move on when they're no longer helpful. That's the kind of behavior I've always actively fought *against*." Kaiden scoffed.

The commander threw up his hands. "What else should we do? Our conventional weapons are useless, our trained soldiers freeze into columns of black soot when they come in contact with the Darkness, and we lost our last two best hopes by what we now realize was just a freak weather-related shuttle crash. We don't have a lot of options here. We need to stop this, and as far as I know, you're the only people who can get close enough to give us any clue what we're dealing with.

"I apologize for keeping the details from you, but it didn't seem like divulging that information would sway you in the direction of helping. I'm only saying anything now because I have nowhere else to turn. We know how important this world was for the mission at hand. I don't know what to suggest."

I was struck by the commander's raw emotion. I'd always thought of military types as being stoic no matter what, but I was reminded in that moment that even the most serious of officers were still people. And *we* weren't trained soldiers. This was an emotional appeal to fellow citizens. Our worlds and our very existence was being threatened, so we needed to join forces to be more than our singular selves. We had to rise to the occasion and become the heroes our people needed.

"If there's a chance we can still retrieve the artifact, then I'll take the risk and go down there," I said.

"Elle," Kaiden started.

"No, I mean it," I shot back. "We didn't ask to be placed in this position, but we're the only ones standing between the Darkness and the total annihilation of everything we love. If there's even a *chance* of saving my family, I'll risk getting turned into a column of soot, or whatever it is that happens when touched by the Darkness."

My new friends sat in stunned silence.

Surprisingly, Maris was the first to speak. "Elle is right. We're already invested this much. We need to do everything we can to see this through."

"I will gladly give my life to this mission, if it comes to it," Toran agreed. "However, I trust whatever technology—or magic—enabled us to escape the Darkness in the first place. I believe we will be able to travel to that world and not be harmed. Well, at least not by the Darkness directly."

"I'm in, too, of course," Kaiden said. "I won't turn my back on that commitment." He cast another glare in Colren's direction. "But in the future, I hope for continued transparency. We need to work together. Secrets won't help get the job done."

The commander nodded. "And you'll have it. I assure you, you now have all of the information we do."

I swallowed. "Okay, so, the original team was able to escape a planet overrun by the Darkness on a shuttle. Does that mean that it doesn't alter manufactured materials?"

Colren shook his head. "Yes and no. Organic matter is the most susceptible, as far as we know, but everything eventually succumbs. In terms of going down to the planet, my suggestion would be for the shuttle to drop you off, and we'll send it to retrieve you once you have the artifact."

"What about our comms?" I asked. "Those are inside us, but not exactly a *part* of us."

"An excellent question to which I don't have an answer. I would hope that it being completely encased in your skin that they would be protected from the Darkness' effects. In the event the electronics become corrupted, we can arrange a rendezvous place and time," the commander stated.

"Right, about that." Toran folded his huge hands on the table. "The device we've been using to locate the artifacts didn't pick up a signal because of the Darkness. We have no idea where to go."

"If the artifact is intact, it will likely still emit a signal," Colren replied. "Perhaps you can adapt the device to interface with the shuttle's sensor suite and do a high-altitude sweep of the planet."

"That could take hours. At the rate the Darkness advances, we may not have that long," Kaiden objected.

The commander shook his head. "I have no other solution to offer you."

"Then let's stop talking and start doing." I stood up. "Even our clothes and equipment might not stand up in that environment. We'll need to move quickly."

"Is it, like, contagious?" Maris asked. "Can we track it back to the ship?"

"As far as we know, no," Colren replied. "However, we'll follow a full decontamination protocol for your return, and the shuttle will drop you off without touching down on the surface. The atmosphere is clearly tainted, as well, but it seems to spread much more quickly on the ground."

"Contact between solid matter, versus the more spread out structure in air," Kaiden hypothesized.

"As reasonable an explanation as any. I'm sure scientists will be seeking answers for years to come." The commander sighed. "But, for now, the Master Archive remains the priority."

I nodded. "We're on it."

"Safe travels, and good luck."

After Toran grabbed his search device and extra tools, we hurried down to the hangar to get our laundered equipment from Tami. While the preflight check was underway, Toran began his modifications to the device so it could interface with the shuttle. Since he was busy, I ran to the equipment room on his behalf to get him a new custom shipsuit from his saved profile, which he graciously accepted. Once we were dressed, the other preparations completed within minutes of each other, and Tami saw us off with well wishes.

Speeding toward the dark world was a decidedly unnerving experience. Every part of me screamed that it was wrong to head toward something which was so obviously tainted.

Next to me, Kaiden's face was drawn with concern. He still sat in the pilot's chair, though the auto-pilot was solely responsible for this voyage.

I tried to set aside my own worries and focused on the positives. After all, there was still a *chance* that we could get the final artifact. A slim chance, but some hope remained. Too much was riding on it for me to give in to doubts. The certainty that there would be a secure backup of my world was the only thing keeping me moving forward. If I didn't have that... Well, I didn't know *what* I'd do. But the fight wouldn't be there. It just wouldn't be the same if I was only trying to save myself.

The initial descent into the atmosphere was bumpier than usual. It would seem that whatever was causing the Darkness was somehow impacting the air currents and the shuttle's inertial compensators. That made the dark tendrils snaking through the sky even more ominous.

I shuddered. Everything about it was creepy. I couldn't wait to be back on a planet far away from the Darkness' influence.

The shuttle followed a preset flight path designed to optimize our aerial search for a signal using the modified device. Maris handed over her pendant this time, and Toran kept a watch on the readings to double-check the automated search software's findings. At an elevation of thirty kilometers, the shuttle leveled out and began its search pattern above the umber landscape.

"I know what you're thinking, and I hope we don't have to go around the entire planet," Toran stated to break the uncomfortable silence.

"Not that you have much control over the situation," Kaiden replied.

"Actually," Toran countered, "the previous sites were all within a several degree spread to the north of the equator. If that pattern holds, we will have a much smaller search area to cover."

"Here's hoping." I settled deeper into my seat.

Half an hour passed in relative silence.

I propped my feet up on the front console and would have dozed off if it wasn't for the occasional jolt from a shifting air current.

At last, Toran came to attention. "I think I might have something." He used his console to indicate a point on the holographic map overlaid on the front viewport. A red point was highlighted approximately eighty kilometers from our present location. According to the topographical map, it was on top of a steep hill, which offered no easy drop-off point, even without landing—especially due to the wind gusts.

"Let's check it out from the air," Kaiden said. "We don't want to commit to the wrong site." He programmed the destination into the autopilot.

The moment the destination came into view, any doubts about it being the correct location vanished. Whereas the other sites on past planets had been a crystal situated in a predominantly natural landscape, this crystal sat atop an eight-story tower at the summit of a steep hill covered in dark orange grass.

"How in the…" Words escaped me.

"I have no idea," Kaiden murmured. "But look at these wind readings—there's no way we can set down at the summit."

I reviewed the scan data he was pointing to. Gusts of wind as great as eighty kilometers per hour weren't insurmountable, but between the risks of smashing into the tower, touching the ground, and sending us accidentally rolling down the entire length of the hill, it was in our best interest to find an alternative.

"How about we have the shuttle drop us off at the base and we can hike up?" I suggested.

"Except *that* might be a problem." Maris pointed down to the left.

While the hill face was still untouched by the Darkness, one of the sinister tendrils was snaking its way toward the slope from the west. I hadn't been watching it for long enough to get a sense of the time to interception, but my gut told me we didn't have long.

"We'll figure it out. Let's go." I unstrapped from my seat and steadied myself against the wall using my hands as the shuttle rocked in the wind.

In the common room, I removed the mess kit and bedroll from my pack to lighten it but was sure to leave in the rope and flashlight knowing that we had a tower to negotiate. The side ramp didn't make for a reliable midair egress, so I headed to the airlock at the rear of the craft. I opened the interior door and waited for my companions.

They followed my model of removing the items likely to be unnecessary for this mission and then put on their packs.

I kept watch out the side viewport and saw that the shuttle was hovering at a holding elevation, awaiting our final instruction to descend for a quick drop-off.

"Ready?" Kaiden asked with a smile as he joined me in the airlock.

"As I'll ever be." I patted my sword hilt. "I have this."

"Assuming it doesn't disintegrate in your hands."

I frowned. "Wait, what about the artifacts?"

Kaiden hesitated. "I'd really hope that whatever gives us special immunity would apply to them, too."

"But we're organic and were altered by a brush with the Darkness. That has nothing to do with them."

"Yeah, but they were encased in crystal and then floated to the ground. Magic is different. I don't have any logical reason I can point to, but my gut tells me that it's not an issue."

I nodded. "Considering that I became a blade master overnight, I can't argue with the power of unexplainable knowledge and hunches."

"So, my circlet stays?" Kaiden asked.

I smirked. "Oh, I get it. You just don't want to give up your crown."

"I have no comment."

"Uh huh…" I eyed him suspiciously while Toran and Maris joined us.

When we were all in the tiny chamber, I closed the interior door and cycled the exterior hatch. Kaiden tapped on a control console within the chamber to initiate the next phase of the automated flight sequence for our drop-off.

Wind ripped through the chamber the moment the exterior hatch cracked open. I gripped a handhold to steady myself as we descended. The shuttle stopped just under three meters up from the ground, swaying as it struggled to compensate for the winds ripping down the slope.

Keeping a firm grip on the handhold, I leaned out to spot my landing. Scrubby grass covered the vicinity, so at least we wouldn't be landing on rock.

I took a deep breath. "Here goes!" I leaped.

The ground raced toward me. I bent my knees as I touched down to absorb the impact, then transferred my weight and rolled to a stop. I rose to my feet.

Kaiden and Maris dropped down nearby, following a similar technique. Toran, the last to leap, just took one big jump and landed with both feet like it was nothing.

"How are we going to get back up?" Maris asked.

"I can reach it and haul myself up then help you," Toran said.

She didn't look entirely convinced but nodded anyway.

The shuttle quickly gained elevation and then accelerated back into space.

No longer under the influence of the artificial gravity on the shuttle, I felt lighter. "Is the gravity lower here?"

"I felt the shift, too," Toran said.

"Maybe it's a product of the Darkness," Kaiden suggested. "Or could just be the planet."

"That first notion is deeply unnerving." I took a step and found that my movement was easier, but there wasn't any significant extra bounce.

"Okay, we have six hours until the rendezvous, if we can't get in touch before then," Kaiden stated. He peered in the direction of the approaching Darkness. "But we don't have a lot of time for other reasons."

"No need to tell me twice!" I started jogging up the slope.

The combination of my lighter pack and the reduced gravity made for an easier ascent than I'd anticipated. However, the winds were against us, and I found myself leaning up the hill to maintain a good equilibrium.

From a distance, the slope had seemed relatively featureless aside from some orange foliage, but as we trekked up the open exposure, I spotted the openings to caves mixed in among rock outcroppings.

"Think anything lives here?" I asked.

"Maybe, but potentially not for long."

My heart sank. "I hadn't thought about that part. I've been thinking about the people on the infected worlds, but all of the wildlife…"

"Don't go there, Elle," Kaiden cautioned. "We're already actively pursuing the best—and maybe only—way we can help them."

"Yeah, I know." I took a deep breath.

Another cave was up ahead. As we approached it, movement drew my attention. I tensed. "Uh oh. I think there's something in that one."

KAIDEN READIED HIS staff and Maris grabbed a dagger from a sheath at her hip, apparently not yet ready to rely on offensive magic alone.

I drew my own blade. Whatever was in the cave might be dangerous, and I wasn't about to take any chances after our most recent encounters. I altered my path to dip to the left so we'd have better coverage of the cave mouth.

Scuffles and tapping sounded within the shadowed recess. My muscles tensed as I prepared for a beast to leap out.

When I was four meters from the cave opening, I caught a flash of gold as a tiny, scaled head poked out from the shadows.

Brilliant green eyes that reminded me of my own looked at me with curiosity, and the creature tilted its head. It crept forward, revealing a long neck that flared into a scaled body with four legs, folded webbed wings, and taloned feet. Dorsal spikes ran the length of the creature from the crest of its head to the tip of its slim, scaled tail. Its belly was a lighter shade than the top, and it had a glowing orange patch at the base of its throat.

"Uh, guys… is that a dragon?" I felt ridiculous asking, but there it was staring at me.

"Those are just a legend, aren't they?" Maris asked.

I raised an eyebrow. "Like magic?"

Kaiden examined the creature. "I mean, it *looks* like I'd expect a dragon to look, but isn't it a bit small?"

The cute little thing *was* tiny, no more than seventy centimeters from nose to tail. I got a sudden impulse to pick it up and bring it with us. "It's not bothering us. Let's let it be," I said instead.

No sooner had the words left my mouth than four more heads appeared—blue, green, red, and black. They all had the same vibrant green eyes.

The red dragon squawked and jumped on the blue one, and the two tumbled off of the rock ledge onto the grassy hillside.

"Aww, they're playing!" Maris squealed.

"I think these might be babies," Toran conjectured.

"They're adorable, I won't try to deny it, but we don't have the luxury of playtime right now." Kaiden glanced down the hill at the advancing Darkness.

"No, we don't." I smiled at the baby dragons and then took a brisk pace up the slope.

After fifteen minutes, we reached the brow of the hill. The relatively flat area around the base of the tower was only four meters wide, and it was as windy as the shuttle's sensors had indicated.

My hair kept smacking me in the face, so I quickly bundled it into a braid and tucked it inside the back of my coat to keep it out of the way.

Kaiden's cloak beat around him in the wind. "I don't see an entrance to the tower on this side."

I inspected the smooth stone face. We could probably find a way up using the rope in our packs, but I really hoped it wouldn't come to that.

"Let's walk the perimeter." I set off to the left.

The winds remained strong as we rounded the northern side of the structure. There were no windows in the stone face, as far as I could see, and the ground level had no ingress points along the first half of the building's circumference.

Finally, rounding the east side of the tower, a three-meter-tall reinforced metal door sealed an arched entryway. I grabbed the door handle and gave it a good tug. Nothing happened.

"Locked?" Kaiden asked.

"Or magically sealed. Who knows?" I frowned at the door.

"May I?" Toran asked.

I held out my hand. "Please."

The large man gripped the door handle and pulled. Unlike with my attempt, the metal groaned, but it still didn't budge.

"I can try to force it," he said.

It was a tempting offer, but I wasn't sure that was the best move. All of the tasks to retrieve artifacts on the other worlds hadn't involved forcing open a doorway. Yes, we'd needed to engage in fights, but the built structures had all responded to the touch of someone aligned with the corresponding discipline. If that pattern followed, then I needed to be the one to open the door.

I motioned Toran aside. "Let me try again."

The question was, why hadn't it opened the first time I tried?

I thought back to our previous challenges. Toran had activated the columns with his bare hands, which is also how he fought. Likewise, Kaiden had had to cast magic at the stone pillars to activate the pathway to the island. Since I fought with a sword, maybe...

I drew my blade. In one swift motion, I slashed the steel across the metal door, leaving a golden streak where it scratched. The golden line glowed brightly for a second, and then the door dissolved before my eyes.

Kaiden smirked. "Well, that's one way to open a door."

"I do love to make a showy entrance." I smiled back.

Inside, the tower was dark beyond the shallow pool of light cast from the doorway. I cautiously peered inside.

"Help me," a woman murmured from the shadows in a voice so faint and cracked the words were barely intelligible.

"Stars!" I ran into the chamber.

Kaiden was a step behind me. He ignited a ball of light in his palm, illuminating the room.

The woman was chained to the far wall. Seated on the floor with her legs outstretched, her hands were cuffed at head level and she looked as though she'd been dragged across the ground and beaten.

Anger swelled in my chest thinking about what kind of horrible person would do that to her. "It's okay, we're friends." I approached her slowly, checking for signs of a trap.

"We'll get you out of there," Maris said, rushing up behind me.

"Maris, wait." I held her back.

"Why?" she glared at me.

I don't know why I hesitated. It sickened me to see the woman suffering, yet something didn't feel right about the situation. She could be dangerous, for all we knew.

"You have to assume this is part of the test," Toran interjected. "Who is this woman and why is she here?"

"Exactly." I stopped three meters from her. It was too suspicious that anyone would be chained inside a tower on the top of a hill in the middle of nowhere—especially considering that there were no nearby signs of civilization aside from this singular structure.

"Why are you here?" I asked the woman, as much as I wanted to free her from her shackles and heal her. Just looking at her battered face made my own skin throb.

"Please. Release me. Before they come back," she whispered.

I couched down. "Who put you here? Why?"

She shook her head, the motion jangling the chains binding her wrists.

"Look, I hate seeing you like this. I *want* to help you, but trust should be earned."

The woman scoffed. "You wouldn't trust a poor woman chained to a wall?"

"No one deserves to be treated that way, but that's also something people don't often do to others without reason—however misguided the action may be." I looked her in the eyes. "Now, how did you come to be here?"

She cracked a smile, some vitality seeming to return to her. "Do you always question innocents?"

"How do I know if you're innocent? If you've been wrongfully imprisoned, then you should at least have a story to tell. But you keep dodging my questions."

"It takes wisdom to know when to act and when to observe," the woman continued. Her voice was definitely getting stronger; there was no mistaking it now. Even her skin appeared more vibrant.

"Who are you?" I asked again.

She looked me square in the eyes—her intense, luminescent emerald irises now far different from the vacant appearance she'd had only moments before when we entered. "The more important question is, who are *you*?"

In the blink of an eye, she vanished, leaving behind no trace of the chains or her presence.

I took an unsteady breath. "That was weird."

"Man, I thought were we just going to attack stuff. I wasn't planning on mind games again," Kaiden said.

"Shouldn't expect anything to be so straightforward," I replied.

"I thought maybe the encroaching Darkness was complication enough."

"Whoever set up these trials didn't know that would be the case."

He shrugged. "Maybe they did, maybe they didn't."

I massaged my eyes with one hand. "I'm too on edge to think about records of events that haven't happened yet."

"Or maybe they *have* happened and we don't know," Toran cut in.

"Nope, not gonna think about it." I shook my head.

"Help!" another voice called from the story above.

"Stars, not again." I jogged toward the stairs.

"Elle, it's not real," Toran said.

"That doesn't mean ignoring it is the right thing to do. It's a test, and we need to participate if we're going to get that artifact." I bounded up the stone stairs two at a time.

The staircase curved around the outer wall of the tower, passing through a hole in the floor at the second level. With no windows, it was too dark for me to make out any details until Kaiden came up behind me with the light floating above his palm.

"Flashlight time," I muttered, stopping to retrieve it from my backpack. I clicked it on as my companions all made it to the second story.

The space was relatively plain, with only a stone bench along the outer wall and a single, low stone column in the center of the room. What made it strange, however, was there was no sign of the woman who'd cried out for help, nor did there appear to be a way upward in the tower.

"Help, please!" the woman cried again.

"Where are we supposed to go?" I mused aloud. With nothing else appearing out of place, I approached the stone column at the center of the thirty-meter-wide room.

Upon closer inspection, the meter-tall column was a pedestal table sporting a broad, flat top engraved with foreign characters. The language was familiar, however.

"Hey, Kaiden, is this Laeric?" I asked.

He walked up beside me to examine the marks. "Yes, it is, but I don't know what to make of it." He swung his backpack around so it was hanging on one shoulder to his front and rummaged around in bag. After several seconds, he located an electronic handheld device. He smiled. "Translator. We're getting better at this 'planning ahead' thing."

I smiled back. "Please, enlighten me."

Kaiden held the device over the top of the pedestal, and a screen on the back displayed a translation of the ancient words. There were six wedges, each labeled in order: *Vengeance, Conceit, Valor, Humility, Cowardice,* and *Duty.*

"No idea what to make of that." I frowned at the translation. "Except, Valor is the name of this discipline, so maybe that means something?"

"Of those options, that seems like the one to pick," Kaiden agreed.

Toran raised his fists defensively. "Why do I feel like a fight is coming?"

Maris drew a dagger. "I don't like this."

"Has to be done," I replied. I pressed the stone labeled *Valor* with my right hand.

Nothing happened.

"Maybe you have to use a sword like with the door?" Kaiden suggested. He took a step back from the pedestal.

"Could be." I started to draw my blade.

No more than two centimeters were exposed when the tower began to tremble. The walls opened up on all sides, revealing six identical stairwells leading into darkness. The stairs extended far beyond the outer walls of the tower, yet they were completely enclosed.

"Oookay, this is officially weirding me out," I admitted.

"This one is all you, Elle. Where does your gut tell us we should go?" Kaiden asked.

Valor was again the obvious choice, being the namesake of this discipline. However, just like something had told me to hold back from helping the woman, I had a feel that wasn't the correct answer.

Assuming the staircases were representative of paths—not a stretch, since it was pretty literal—*Vengeance, Conceit,* and *Cowardice* were all obvious rejects. *Humility* and *Duty,* though, had appeal. After all, strength could easily be misdirected if it wasn't balanced out by humility, and even otherwise vicious acts could be honorable when performed in the line of duty. Still, I wasn't sure if the straightforward answer of *Valor* was the way to go or if I should pick one of those supporting components.

I stared at the pedestal, frozen by indecision. "I don't know what to do."

"Pick something," Kaiden urged.

"Help!" the unseen woman cried again from all directions.

"Elle, not to rush you, but the Darkness—"

I held up my hand to cut Toran off. "I know. I'm thinking."

None of the singular paths felt right to me. There was more to heroic acts than a one-dimensional characterization.

Without thinking, I slammed my hands down on the pedestal, pressing *Valor* and *Humility* with one and *Duty* with the other while holding the flashlight.

The stairways blurred as they merged into a singular path leading in the direction across from *Valor*.

Toran nodded. "A bold choice."

"Looks like it paid off," Kaiden added.

"Come on. There's no telling what we'll find up there." I jogged toward the stairs.

The stairwell wove around the outside of the tower, despite having appeared to go straight outward from my vantage inside the second-story chamber. It spiraled for another six stories at a steep angle until it reached the tower's roof.

I shut off my flashlight as we stepped out into daylight. I expected to get a spectacular view of the surrounding landscape, but instead I was surprised to see that the tower was surrounded by a strange mist. The light filtered through like it was a clear day, but everything beyond fifty meters away was blurred like looking through an out of focus camera.

"What's with this place?" I murmured.

"I don't know, but let's get out of here fast," Kaiden replied.

The focal point of the rooftop was the crystal monument we'd seen from the shuttle. It radiated a soft blue light like all of the others we'd come across, and I was relieved to see that it wasn't yet clouded by the Darkness spreading throughout the rest of the land.

Floating in its center was a slim sword with a slight curve to the blade. The sabre beckoned to me, drawing me toward the monument at the center of the rooftop. I reached out toward it.

"Are you sure you want to do that?" a woman asked from behind me.

I pivoted toward the voice.

Standing before me was the same woman who'd been chained in the basement, but she was now dressed in a regal crimson gown and her golden hair was styled in ringlets. Her red lips were curled into a knowing smile and she evaluated me with her piercing green eyes.

"I'm here for the artifact," I stated.

She nodded. "You have passed the first test. You desire to help, but you have learned since your youth that actions have consequences."

"Don't pretend to know what's in my mind," I replied.

"I needn't pretend. I *do* know." She clasped her hands in front of her, and I noticed she wore golden finger caps, which ended in sharp points.

My eyes narrowed. "Who are you?" I asked once more, though I didn't expect an answer.

"A better question may be about *what* I am." She began to walk slowly toward us. "And the answer to that is that I am a guardian created out of necessity. For all of the powers the ancients mastered, they were not immortal. I, and the two others like me, were created to pass on the knowledge that all others would forget, so that the worlds could be saved in the time of their greatest need."

The woman gazed to her left, and for a moment, the mist parted around tower and the encroaching Darkness was visible below. "You have been chosen, but that doesn't necessarily make you worthy."

"Then let me prove myself, as my companions have," I replied.

"If you fail, then this place will be locked to you. Are you sure you're ready?" The woman tilted her head.

"This place will be inaccessible, anyway, once the Darkness reaches it," I replied.

"There are forces stronger than the Darkness."

I came to attention. "There are? There's a way to stop it?"

The woman smiled. "You haven't answered my question. Are you ready to face the challenge?"

"Yes. I'll do anything I need to in order to stop the Darkness."

The woman inclined her head. "Very well. Prepare to face your challenge."

She dissolved into scarlet mist, which flowed over the stone railing behind where she had been standing.

I placed my hand on my sword hilt.

Behind me, Kaiden, Toran, and Maris tensed.

A roar echoed from somewhere below the tower, followed by a concussive whoosh of massive wings beating. My heart skipped a beat as a red, scaled head with jaws two meters wide came into view.

The massive beast roared again and thrust its wings, creating a strong enough gust to almost knock me off my feet. It flew past the tower on the side and a patch on its throat glowed bright orange. It opened its jaws, releasing a plume of fire.

I squinted against the heat of the flames. "I think we found those baby dragons' mom."

I BACKED AWAY from the stone railing. Setting aside the surprising revelation that dragons were real, the part about them being able to turn into mist and take the form of a human was definitely a new one. "How did it...?"

"Doesn't matter." Kaiden hoisted his staff. "Just need to fight it."

My heart sank. "It doesn't feel right to kill it." A dragon... a creature that was by all accounts mythical. And it had babies...

Kaiden nodded. "Then you better find some other way to make it say that we won so we can get that artifact."

Toran rushed up next to me. "We will follow your lead, Elle."

The crimson dragon roared again and then disappeared into the mist. I gulped as I stared in the direction that the creature had gone; it would undoubtedly return in any second. "Okay, aim to disable."

Despite giving the order, I had no idea what I meant by it. The dragon was fifteen meters long and breathed fire. I had no clue how to disable a creature of that size without killing it—or even how to kill it, for that matter. But, I couldn't admit to my friends that I thought we were doomed.

I dropped my backpack on the ground and drew my sword. "Maris, can you figure out some sort of protection spell for us?"

She looked unsure, but nodded. "I'll see what I can do."

The others set down their packs, as well, and held their weapons at the ready.

While I stood poised for the dragon's return, Maris clutched her crystal pendant in one hand. A shell of purple light appeared around me.

"If that did what I wanted it to, we should now have some fire resistance," Maris said.

"Hey, I'll take anything." I looked to Kaiden next. "Going along with the plan to not kill the dragon, maybe some ice attacks would be helpful against the flames?"

He nodded. "I'll give it a shot."

"How would you like me to proceed, Elle?" Toran asked.

"I don't think punches will be deadly against a creature that size. Hit it as hard as you can, and hopefully we can stun it," I replied.

He inclined his head. "I'll try."

"Say we do stun it. Then what?" questioned Kaiden.

I checked to make sure the dragon wasn't back in sight, then set down my sword to access my backpack. I retrieved my restocked length of rope.

"Tie it up? Seriously?" Kaiden raised an eyebrow skeptically.

"I know, I know. But if we can demonstrate dominance and mercy, maybe it will declare it a win."

Kaiden's gaze alternated between the rope and me. "If you say so."

A roar drew our attention to the sky overhead. The dragon was diving from above.

"Kaiden, hit it!" I shouted.

A ray of frost streamed from his staff, striking the dragon square in the face. It blinked as the ice made contact, then shook its head slightly like it hadn't even been bothered. To my horror, the patch on its throat glowed brightly again and it opened its jaws.

The flash of heat was too intense to look at. I was convinced I must be burning alive, but as I diverted my gaze to the stone rooftop, I saw the flames curving around the purple protective bubble.

The onslaught subsided, and the dragon flapped away into the mist to make a loop back toward us.

"Way to go with that shell!" I cheered to Maris.

She grinned. "I think I'm getting the hang of this."

The brief exposure to the intense heat had wiped me out, but a sparking green wave washed over me and I felt a surge of energy.

Maris smiled. "Figured you could use a pick-me-up."

"You read my mind."

Toran and Kaiden also appeared to be recharged.

"We need to lure it in close," Toran said. "I will try to stun it."

My mind raced as I thought about how we might be able to get it to land. Suddenly, I wished I'd brought a goat to sacrifice. Dragons liked goats, right?

I returned my thoughts to the present and what I had at my disposal.

"I'm going to offer myself to it," I stated before I could second-guess the idea. Granted, rethinking the action was probably *exactly* what I should have been doing.

"Elle, no," Kaiden said, firm.

The protective barrier is up, I'll be fine. I really don't think we're supposed to slay it. I need to show that I want to work with it."

"I don't like that plan, either," Toran said.

"This is what we're doing," I replied. "This is my discipline and you said you'd follow my lead."

The large man released a slow breath. "Very well."

"I'm going to have an ice ball ready in the event it tries to eat you," Kaiden said.

"Thanks."

Another roar sounded to my right as the dragon returned from the mist. I lowered my sword and ran to the stone railing on the far side of the roof away from my friends, wanting to distance myself to keep them out of danger as much as possible. "What do you want me to do?" I shouted.

The crimson dragon tilted its head. If I didn't know better, I'd think it was smiling at me.

It dove lower, but this time made no sign of breathing fire. Only four meters above me, it broke from its collision course dive, flapping its enormous wings to pull up.

I lost my footing in the gust, falling backward. My back struck the railing, and the momentum carried me over the lip.

My sword hand flailed as my torso dipped over the railing. Time seemed to slow down for me, even without a spell from Maris. I knew I had only a moment to act. I could drop my sword and catch myself, or hold onto the sword and likely fall to my death.

As poor form it seemed for a Valor challenge, I opted to ditch the sword.

In one motion, I released the weapon and managed to snag the inside lip of the stone railing with my index finger—a sole digit keeping me from toppling over the edge. As the sword plummeted down the side of the tower, I tried to secure my grip with my other hand, but the awkward semi-sideways angle had pinned my other arm underneath me.

I was terrified to move. My finger was slipping, and any attempt to swing my legs to shift my weight back toward the roof caused me to slip further.

This wasn't how I pictured the end.

A strong hand gripped my wrist. "I've got you."

I breathed a sigh of relief as Kaiden pulled me up. I shimmied my hips back to the proper side of the railing and slid to my feet. "Thanks."

There was genuine concern in his eyes—the kind I'd seen from my father while my mom talked about a particularly bad day at work. Even with a dragon looping back toward us, he set me at ease.

"That didn't look like it went to plan," he said.

"Yeah, no, not really."

"Maybe more working together and less using yourself as bait?"

"Yeah, we've got this." I gave him a confident smile and he nodded back.

Together, we turned to face the dragon as it came for another pass.

With my hands empty, I'd be next to useless in a fight. But, I was still determined to end the engagement peacefully.

"There is no honor in senseless killing," I shouted, stepping forward with my hands held wide. "I wish to protect others, not take the lives of innocents."

The dragon halted its descent, flapping its wings to hover above me.

"There are times to fight, but this isn't it," I continued. "We have bigger concerns." I pointed in the direction of the plains below which I knew were being consumed by the Darkness. "I'd rather help save you and the rest of your kind."

The dragon planted its taloned feet on the rooftop, crumbling the stones beneath it. It gazed at me with its brilliant green eyes, somehow seeming to see inside and through me.

Twenty intense seconds passed in silence as it stared at me unblinkingly. It took all of my willpower to stand with my hands at my sides, completely at its mercy.

Just when I felt like I could take it no more, the dragon bowed its head.

As quickly as it had taken shape, the dragon dissolved into red mist. It swirled in the air for a moment and then reformed as the regal woman.

"You have shown both duty and humility in your actions today. A virtuous leader knows what the true fight is." She bowed her head.

"How can we help you and your babies?" I asked.

"Do not worry about us," the woman replied. "Our magic is more ancient than even the crystals. We have withstood greater calamities. All will be restored in due time."

I hesitated. "What of us and our worlds?"

"You will soon have what you need to face the menace. But that is something you must discover for yourself. Good fortune until we meet again." The woman faded into mist.

A tingling wave passed through me, and I was left with a renewed sense of strength and focus. The call of the crystal at the center of the roof was even stronger.

I turned toward it. "Is that it? Is that all I had to do?"

Toran nodded. "Not every victory requires a fight. You proved that today."

"Final artifact, Elle. It's yours," Kaiden said.

I stepped forward. A pace from the crystal, I stretched out my hand.

An electric tingle spread from my fingertips up my arm and throughout my entire body. The crystal shattered into glassy sand and fell to the ground. Before me, the sword hovered in the air for a second before slowly drifting onto the mound of crystal fragments.

I bent down and gripped the hilt in my hand. Another tingle ran up my arm, almost like the sword was an extension of myself. When it was fully in my grasp, a blue flame ignited along the length of the blade.

"Whoa!" I almost dropped it in surprise.

Maris crossed her arms. "Gotta say, guys, Elle gets the award for the coolest artifact."

I grinned. "No argument here."

Kaiden adjusted his circlet. "Yeah, whatever."

"We should get back," Toran advised.

"Yes, we got what we came for." I tested the blade in the scabbard from my old sword and found that it was a close enough fit to work temporarily, though it would be better to get one custom made once we got back to the *Evangiel.*

"I'll call the shuttle to come pick us up," Kaiden said.

With my sword stowed, I retrieved my backpack from where I'd dropped it and headed for the stairwell while the others gathered their gear.

When Kaiden had completed the call, we jogged down the steps to the bottom of the tower. As we rounded the final curve to the ground floor, it seemed far darker than it should. I slowed my pace.

"Does anyone else feel that?" I asked.

"Yeah, and I don't like it," Maris replied.

Toran nodded. "We shouldn't be on the world any longer."

We reached the ground and headed for the door.

I froze the moment I caught my first glimpse of the world beyond the tower. Gone was the orange-tinted landscape of rolling foothills. Now, there was only black—and something was moving within the Darkness.

"STARS! WHAT'S DOWN there?" My heart pounded in my ears as I stepped outside on the windy hilltop outside the tower.

"I don't know, but it's standing between us and our pickup point." Kaiden's eyes were hard and his face was lined with worry.

The Darkness had almost reached the hill's summit and was continuing to advance. The strange movements in the shadow were still at a distance beyond the base of the hill, but it was headed in our direction.

Toran took a slow breath. "I had hoped we wouldn't need to test our supposed immunity to the Darkness."

"Yeah, no kidding." I sighed, then tapped behind my ear. The comm chirped, and I opened the link with my team and Central Command. "Commander, we have the artifact, but this area has been overtaken by the Darkness."

He didn't reply at first. "The shuttle is already on its way."

"What do we—"

"Get to the pickup point."

"But—"

"Fight your way out if you have to. Just get there." He ended the commlink.

"That wasn't the least bit helpful," I said.

"No, it wasn't." Toran evaluated the Darkness swirling below.

"We only need to make it twenty minutes," Kaiden encouraged. "We can do this."

I nodded. "Okay." I took off down the slope and the others followed my lead.

A hundred meters down the hill from the tower, we reached the first patch of ground tainted by the Darkness.

I hesitated. "I really don't want to touch this stuff."

"We don't have a choice. There's nowhere for the shuttle to retrieve us up here," Kaiden said. He continued forward, though his movements were cautious.

Watching his steps, he passed over the threshold to the tainted ground. The blacked grass crunched underfoot, the blades disintegrating into black dust when disturbed.

"I don't understand how it could have advanced so quickly," Maris said. "We weren't in there for long at all."

"There was some strange magic in that place. Maybe time perception was different," I hypothesized.

"Yes, whatever was going on with the pathways and rooftop, I do not believe we were perceiving the reality that we experience out here," Toran agreed.

"I'm looking forward to getting back to a place that isn't infected like this world." Kaiden continued forward. "Are you coming?"

"Yeah, sorry." I jogged forward, trying not to think about what I was walking on.

Seeing it in person, I realized that the moniker of 'Darkness' was more a term of convenience than an accurate description of what it had done to the world. Everything *had* turned black in color, but it wasn't pitch black in the sense of there being a lack of light. Rather, it was like smoke blanketed the land and mini cyclones had ravaged trees and other once-living things that now looked like they had been turned to charcoal in a fire.

The upper expanse of the hill was only short grass, but I cringed when I saw up close what the Darkness had done to larger foliage. Bushes that had been covered in orange leaves on our way up were now black, and the slightest brush up against them caused the entire structure to fall apart into what looked like a pile of soot.

My stomach turned over. "Is this what happened to our worlds?"

Despite his tough exterior, Toran appeared to be on the verge of tears. "That's why protecting the Master Archive is so important."

I hadn't really understood until that moment. In my head, my family was frozen in time—Colren had been careful in his phrasing to give that impression. I had pictured them standing in the town square right where I'd left them, concerned expressions on their faces and the members of our town around them. If I'd visited, I'd imagined I could walk around them and give my parents a hug, even if they didn't know I was there.

But now, seeing what happened to a world that had been consumed, I realized the truth was very different. The planet was lost—as destroyed as it would be if it had been hit by an asteroid. The inhabitants and all other life were dead, but their backups lived on in storage. What that meant for their consciousness, I didn't know. Resets were only supposed to take a moment. Were all the people who had been on those worlds now floating in perpetual darkness, their consciousness searching for a physical form that no longer existed? Or was their hyperdimensional consciousness roaming freely outside of spacetime unaware of the body they once had?

No matter the case, I hoped they were at peace. If anyone had awareness of what was happening to their world, I couldn't imagine they'd ever be able to psychologically recover. I had a feeling my mom would agree if she'd been there to comment.

The pressure in my chest swelled, making it difficult to breathe. I just wanted to know they were going to be okay—that when we could restore our world, things could go back to how they were.

But I knew that was impossible. I'd already been through too much. Even if *they* were all the same, *I* wouldn't be.

I caught Kaiden's gaze as I ran up next to him on the journey down the hill. He was off somewhere distant in his own mind, even though he looked right at me.

"I know," I murmured. "I didn't get it until now, either."

There wasn't a family for me to go back to—as of right now, they were gone. The only hope was to perform a global reset to restore the world.

He nodded solemnly. "We'll figure out what's causing this and stop it. We'll get them back."

"I won't stop trying until we do," I affirmed.

We were almost to the cave where we'd encountered the baby dragons. I braced myself for the horrific sight of their tiny bodies turned to black soot, but instead, a perfect dome surrounded the cave and everything within it was like we'd seen it before—the grass still vibrant orange and it even seemed to be lighter inside the dome.

The baby dragons stood on the stone outcropping outside the cave mouth, concern in their mesmerizing green eyes. When they caught sight of us, the red one bound across the grass toward the perimeter, stopping half a meter short from the invisible barrier. It tilted its head questioningly.

"We'll get you your world back," I told it as we rushed by. "I don't know how, but we'll figure it out."

I couldn't tell if it understood me, or maybe it just picked up on my positive intentions, but it bounded back toward its siblings while making a chittering sound.

The other baby dragons joined in the chittering, and the blue one flapped its wings as it started hopping.

I wished we could stay to watch them, but we had to keep moving. I tore my gaze away so I could watch my footing.

"I think they like you," Kaiden said.

"I'm glad their mom decided to cooperate."

"Assuming they're even related."

That hadn't occurred to me. "You think there might be other dragons on this world?"

"If there are, I hope they've been able to make other sanctuaries like this—" Kaiden cut off. "What was that?"

"What was what?" I'd been looking down at where I was stepping, but I snapped my head up to look ahead.

"That movement we saw when we were up above," he said. "I think the creatures are almost here."

The shadows had only seemed like tiny specks from our previous vantage, but the top of the hill was a long way away. Up close, the creatures coming into view through the dark, approaching mist were two meters tall and three long. I couldn't get a clear view of the dark beasts against the black backdrop, but they seemed to slink like a cat despite being sized like a horse.

I drew my new sword, and the flame instantly ignited along the blade. "Keep moving forward. Get to the pickup site and watch each other's backs."

"Time for the Dark Sentinels to finally fight the dark," Toran said.

I had to think for a second. "Oh, yeah! Team name."

"What?" Maris asked.

"Our intrepid trio at the time nicknamed ourselves the Dark Sentinels," I explained. "Seemed fitting."

She nodded. "The trio is now a quartet, but I like the branding."

I smiled. "Glad you approve."

My pleased expression only lasted for a second. One of the black creatures bounded forward through the dark mist, heading directly for me.

I brought my new sword up in one swift motion, ready to cut down the loping beast.

However, as it cleared the mist, I hesitated—its skin was rippling like something underneath it was trying to break through. I stared at the bizarre sight of what appeared to be hands and limbs pressed against the skin from the inside. It didn't seem possible for the creature to be functioning.

Despite my disbelief, it was almost on top of me.

At the last second, I leaped to the side and flourished my sword. The flaming blade sliced the creature's sleek side. But rather than blood and innards, six small, black bodies burst through the wound. The original creature turned to black dust around them.

I recoiled with horror. "Stars! What—"

"Not going to wait to find out." Kaiden launched a fireball from my right side.

The blast struck the front two of the meter-long creatures. They let out high-pitched shrieks and bared a double row of needle-sharp teeth.

"How did that not take them out?!" I shouted.

Kaiden paled. "What *are* they?"

I had no answer for him. Their four limbs and a head were within my frame of reference, but their movement seamlessly alternated between using two and four feet as they undulated across the ground, their chalky, black skin hiding the details of their physique. Coupled with their tiny fangs and the lack of visible eyes, they were the most alien creatures I had ever seen—not that I'd been on other worlds before four days ago.

Kaiden's magic had been ineffective, but my sword worked better. I rushed the two beasts he'd hit with the fireball, swinging my new blade like a scythe at neck-level.

One of the creatures ducked. The blade struck true with the other, severing its head.

I braced for another wave of even tinier creatures to leap out of the body, but there was only thick, dark blood.

The five other creatures hissed in unison.

My skin tingled as a purple barrier appeared around me, presumably cast by Maris. As soon as the spell was in place, Toran rushed forward to punch the creature closest to us that was still standing.

It yelped as the blow collided, knocking it to the ground. The four others condensed their bodies then pounced, launching themselves a meter or more into the air to grip Toran with their paws.

"Gah! Why did you do that?" I ran forward so I could attempt to help him tear the creatures off.

They snarled at us and tried to snap at my fingers.

Toran was able to pry one off of his chest using his metal gauntlets, and I beheaded it the moment it was on the ground.

He managed to fling another to the side, out of my reach.

Kaiden concentrated a beam of electrical energy on it with his staff, and the creature fell motionless.

We tore the two remaining creatures free, and I sliced one while Toran stomped on the other.

The one remaining creature, which had managed to survive Kaiden's first fireball and Toran's attack, made one final attempt to sink its teeth into my thigh. I kicked it back and then buried my blade in its chest.

"What are these things?" I asked no one in particular.

"I don't know, but I think more are coming." Kaiden gulped. A herd of the larger creatures were advancing—too many to count.

I tightened my grip on my sword, heart racing. "When is that shuttle going to get here?"

"Two minutes," he replied.

Toran evaluated the approaching herd. "We might not make it that long."

"Not with a scattershot approach like what we just did," I agreed. "Backs together! Maris, can you bolster that protection spell?"

"I'll try," she said.

"Toran, hang back on this one," I continued. "We need to keep them at bay with ranged attacks. I'll slice 'em if they get too close; get any behind me."

"Got it." He spun around to face the opposite direction.

Kaiden came in close on my right and Maris to my left.

Maris held up her hands and a second purple dome shimmered around us only seconds before the first wave of large creatures broke through the dark mist.

They charged forward, seemingly unaware of the barrier. When the first of them struck it, the beast stopped cold with a yelp like it has run into a wall.

Kaiden took the opportunity to blast it with a concentrated beam of electricity, like what had been effective on the other. Energy crackled around the creature until the beast collapsed to the ground, then it arced to another coming up from behind. When a third beast neared, the beam split.

"That's it!" I cheered, thrilled with the increased strength of Kaiden's spells since he got the circlet.

I glanced at Kaiden and saw the strain on his face—he wouldn't be able to keep it up for long, artifact or not.

Another beast looped around our protective ring and pressed against it. The barrier stretched at the pressure points, threatening to tear.

I stepped forward from my place in the ring to impale it through the neck. As I pulled my blade back to drive it home, the snarls from the creatures outside stopped as a descending engine roared overhead.

"That's our ride!" Kaiden shouted over the rumble.

"How are we supposed to get up there with all these creatures around?" Maris asked.

"I don't know if my original plan to jump up and pull you inside is feasible anymore," Toran said.

"Don't have another choice," I replied. "You'll have to make it quick."

"Can you make the barrier bigger, Maris?" Kaiden asked.

She laughed. "I don't even know how I'm making this one!"

I glanced at her over my shoulder. "Not helpful."

"Just being honest." She shook her head. "I already feel pretty drained. I don't think I can do the big, grand thing you're after."

My mind raced. "Okay, Toran, get Maris inside. She can maintain the shield from in there, and then Kaiden and I will follow."

"But—" Toran cut off his protest as the shuttle made its final descent.

"Just go!" I shouted, barely able to hear my own voice over the engine.

Loose strands of fuchsia hair whacked against my face from the turbulence.

The creatures appeared to be over their initial shock from the shuttle's arrival, and they crowded in around the perimeter of the protective sphere.

Out of the corner of my squinted eyes, I saw Toran hoisting Maris into the shuttle. As she grabbed hold of the airlock handles, the protective shell started to flicker.

"Hold it!" I shouted, but my voice was lost.

The barrier collapsed.

Creatures rushed in from all sides, a black mass moving as one. Each of their bodies contorted with the same pressing of limbs and heads inside. It was only a matter of time before the smaller creatures broke free, even if I didn't cut them out to speed up the process.

One of the large beasts reared in front of me, flailing hooved feet. I slashed my sword across its legs; amazingly the flaming blade sliced clean through the bone.

The creature toppled to the side, its undulating torso still intact.

Two more came for me. I swept my blade without thinking, twisting and bobbing through the creatures as they advanced.

I lost track of how many there were or how much time had passed—it was just me and my sword. It found its mark every time. I was entranced by it. With my old sword, I had been using a weapon. Now, I felt like the sword was an extension of my own being.

The creatures kept coming. I leaped over the bodies of the disabled creatures to fight the new wave. My friends needed to get to safety; that was the most important thing. I had to give them time.

I ducked to avoid a hoof and then spun around to de-limb the creature. The wounded beasts writhed around me. The abdomens of the first to fall looked like they were about to burst.

"Elle!"

I didn't hear the voice at first, thinking it a phantom in the wind.

"Elle!" the shout came again.

I snapped to attention.

The bodies. There were so many of the felled creatures around me—dozens. Had I really done all of that myself?

"Take my hand!" Toran shouted at me. He was up above, leaning down with his right arm extended.

"Kaiden—" I started to ask, looking around for him.

"He's inside. Come on!" Toran shouted back.

The abdomen of one of the felled beasts ripped open and six vicious creatures jumped out.

Without hesitation, I sheathed my weapon and then leaped up to grab Toran's arm with both hands. His fingers wrapped around my right wrist.

"Go!" he yelled.

The shuttle quickly gained elevation.

Toran heaved me into the airlock. It was just the two of us, and the interior door was closed.

He hit the control panel and the outside door cycled shut.

I realized I was shaking. My heart pounded in my ears and I could barely fill my lungs.

Toran placed a hand on my shoulder. "You're okay, Elle. Breathe."

Closing my eyes, I took several slow, labored breaths. My pulse slowed and my breathing came more easily.

"What happened?" I asked when I felt able to speak. My voice trembled.

"I don't know, it was like you were in a trance," Toran replied. "I got Maris up and then climbed inside, myself. When I bent down to get Kaiden, you were slashing your way through anything that moved. We both shouted at you to come inside, but you didn't seem to hear us. Kaiden and Maris went in to take manual control of the shuttle, and I kept shouting your name until you responded."

"What?" I leaned against the wall, shaking my head. "How long was it?"

"A few minutes? I don't know."

"I…" It had only seemed like seconds, *maybe* a minute, tops. How could I have zoned out like that?

"We all made it out. That's the important thing," Toran said. "That was some good fighting down there."

"It's all a blur," I murmured.

"And it looked it from up here, too, even without Maris' special spell."

"What's happening to me?"

Toran shrugged. "These artifacts have special properties. Beyond that, I can't say." He opened the internal airlock door.

I slowly rose to my feet. "This is going to be a wild ride."

"Speaking of which…" Toran motioned me toward the bridge.

"Right." I jogged toward the nose of the vessel.

In the bridge, Kaiden and Maris were in their customary seats.

"Nice of you to join us," Kaiden said.

"Yeah, sorry." I strapped in.

He glanced at me questioningly, switching the shuttle over to autopilot for the journey back. "What happened back there?"

I shook my head. "Got in the zone, I guess."

He chuckled. "Was there even anything left down there? I think if Toran hadn't pulled me up, I may have met a swift end by your blade."

"No, of course I wouldn't hurt you."

"I dunno, you seemed like you were somewhere else."

I crossed my arms and slumped in my chair. "It was weird. I remember it, but it's like it was a dream."

"More like a nightmare," Maris interjected. "What were those things, anyway? Native to the world, or were they part of the Darkness?"

Kaiden shrugged. "There aren't any records of the lifeforms on this world—it's not in the database, which is probably why it was such a safe place to store the artifact."

"Until this Darkness," I murmured. Or maybe the artifact had been sealed away because it caused the user to go into a murderous trance. After what just happened, I wasn't about to rule out any possibility.

"Considering the state of the other organic matter, I'd hypothesize that the creatures were somehow born of the Darkness," Toran chimed in.

Maris drew into herself. "Where did they come from?"

"Who knows?" I shook my head. "And I hate to say it, but there might be a lot more of those things. We'll need to figure out the most effective attack against them."

"Unfortunately, that will require proximity," Toran said, "and I'm not looking forward to being anywhere near them."

"We can deal with that later," Kaiden said. "As long as Crystallis hasn't been overrun, we shouldn't need to face any more of them in the near term."

"And if the planet already *is* infected, we have bigger problems," I added.

"Exactly."

The shuttle traversed the remaining distance to the *Evangiel*. As it spun around to dock, I caught a glimpse of the planet we'd just left. It was now almost entirely dull black.

I shook my head slowly. "Why do this to a world? Is it deliberate or just some awful disease?"

"I can't imagine this happened on its own," Kaiden said.

"If it's caused by an enemy, then where are they?" Toran asked.

Maris shuddered. "I don't want to meet whoever could do this."

"With you there, but we likely won't have a choice," I said.

The shuttle passed through the electrostatic field into the hangar, but rather than its typical docking location, it instead taxied to an open area away from the other craft. Crew members in hazsuits ran to meet us.

"What a lovely welcome," I said.

"Can't say I blame them for the precaution," Toran replied.

We walked to the shuttle's common area and dropped the ramp. Workers were securing a tent around the shuttle.

Tami, dressed in a hazsuit, approached the base of the ramp through a temporary tunnel. "Strip to your base layer. Leave everything else here and head straight to the decontamination booths." She pointed to a marked tent ten meters away at the end of the tunnel.

"Even the artifacts?" I asked.

She nodded. "Trust me, Elle, we all want you to complete this mission. Everything is safe with us."

I nodded and did as I had been instructed.

The decontamination process was as unpleasant as its name suggested, but within fifteen minutes the chemical scrub was complete. Afterward, I had to admit I felt really, really clean—the ultimate full-body exfoliation. A fresh shipsuit and undergarments were waiting for me in my stall, and I dressed.

Kaiden stepped out from his booth moments after me. He grinned. "You look radiant."

I smiled back. "So do you. I guess having an outer layer of skin burned off will do that to a person."

"Good times." He crossed his arms. "Can we get out of here?"

I shrugged. "I assume so, since no one is telling us to stay."

Toran stepped out from his booth. Based on the way he exited the door sideways, I could only imagine how tight of a squeeze it had been for him to maneuver inside. "We should jump back to Crystallis as soon as possible."

"Yeah," I agreed. "Let's go check in with the commander."

COLREN RELEASED ME from an awkward bear hug. I was a little stunned by that reaction to our story, but I guess successes had been in short supply for the past three months.

"Well done," he said for the seventh time.

"Thank you. Just doing our part," I replied as a variation on my previous acknowledgements.

While we'd given him a recap of the events on the surface, he'd listened even more attentively than during our previous meetings. When we got to the part about the black creatures, he'd seemed particularly intrigued.

"This information about the lifeforms is invaluable. We've never known if there was anything on the surface before now," he continued. "This is the evidence we've needed."

"Evidence of *what?*" Kaiden asked.

The commander took a deep breath and leaned his hip against the conference table. "We've suspected this was an attack, but we never knew for sure. Now that there's a lifeform involved, it supports that this was by design."

"Those were a far cry from an intelligent invasion force," I replied. "Seemed like mindless beasts to me."

"Maybe, maybe not," Toran interjected. "Watching you at the end, they were coordinated. Granted, many wild animals also use coordinated attacks, but that gets into a whole other matter of instinct versus intellect."

I crossed my arms. "Even if they're 'smart', there's a big difference between being an effective killing machine and being able to design tech that can blanket a world in Darkness. Those things down there don't strike me as the scientist type."

"But, it sounds like they *were* very well designed for their task," Colren cut in. "And the Darkness is, as well."

"That sounds like a leap in logic. There's no evidence that those creatures were designed to do anything; it might just be a side-effect of the Darkness infection. We don't know if they originated on that planet or not."

The commander sighed. "Perhaps I am just trying to see connections where there are none. It's been so many months with no answers."

Kaiden pursed his lips. "Say that they *were* designed, though. Why have such a creature when the native population has already been turned into a pile of soot?"

"We don't yet have enough information to even hazard a guess," Colren replied with a dejected shake of his head. He gathered himself. "Let's just get you back to the Archive. That's one part in all of this we *can* control." He rose from the table and smoothed his black uniform jacket.

"We'll be ready to head out right away," I said.

"It'll be at least another three hours before we can jump," he replied. "They're still tending to the shuttle. We don't want to leave anything to chance, and we can't jump until the crew is finished and can go to their pods."

Kaiden cracked a smile. "A little R&R, then?"

I nodded. "I could certainly use it. And a stop by the equipment room to get a new scabbard."

"Tend to your business. We'll announce the jump time when the maintenance crew is nearing completion."

"Thank you, Commander. We'll see you on the other side," Kaiden acknowledged.

We departed the conference room in Central Command and nodded to the crew on our way out. There were smiles on their faces and their eyes were alight with hope that hadn't been there when I'd first met them.

Though I didn't feel like we'd accomplished much, we were delivering on the promise we'd made to *try*, and that counted for something. I wouldn't feel better until the Master Archive was sealed—the artifacts were next to meaningless without that step.

"I'm going to see if my sword has been cleaned yet so I can size a new scabbard for it," I said once we were out in the main corridor.

Kaiden nodded. "I'd like to browse through the equipment inventory again now that we've been through a few fights. Mind if I join you?"

"Of course not."

"Well, *I'm* going to relax," Maris stated, not shocking me in the least.

"I could use some down time, myself," Toran admitted. "I'll be in our common room."

"Okay, see you there later," I said.

Kaiden and I headed for the lift.

"Are you feeling better?" he asked me when we were alone. "You seemed pretty shaken up after that fight."

"Yeah, I'm fine."

He didn't say anything else for the lift ride down, only casting me the occasional sidelong glance. When we reached the lower deck, we strolled down to the hangar. Tami and the crew were out of their hazsuits, and we found them arranging our equipment near where our shuttle was typically berthed.

"What can I do for you?" Tami asked when she saw us approaching.

"I was hoping to get my new sword," I said. "I need a scabbard for it."

"Ah. Well, it's all cleaned up," she replied with a frown. "Looks like things got messy down there."

"It's been quite an eventful day or three." I forced a smile.

"We'll be back to the Archive soon, as I understand it," she said.

Kaiden nodded. "Not sure what will happen after that, but we're making progress."

"And we're grateful for it," the engineer responded. She paused. "Well, help yourself to your things. Holler if you need anything else."

"Thanks."

I grabbed my sword and Kaiden took his circlet.

"I *knew* it!" I teased. "You're addicted to your crown."

"It's not a—" He sighed, shaking his head.

I nudged him. "Come on, let's go see if any new items are available to us now that we have some combat experience.

We traced the corridor back to the equipment room with the 3D printer.

As soon as we were inside the privacy of the room, Kaiden stopped and looked me in the eyes. "Elle, are you sure everything is okay? You've seemed a little... off since Maris joined the team."

"We've had a lot going on," I replied.

He crossed his arms. "Don't be evasive. I can tell something is bothering you."

"I don't think you've known me for long enough to be able to read my mind."

"Who says I'm not telepathic?"

My mouth fell open a little, and my pulse spiked as I recounted some of the things I'd thought over the last several days. "I—"

He laughed and reached out his hand to place it reassuringly on my shoulder. "Relax, I'm just messing with you. But seriously, what's wrong—aside from everything?"

I took a deep breath and looked down. His touch on my shoulder was warm and comforting, and I fought the impulse to go in for a hug. So much had happened over the past few days, I could feel myself fraying around the edges. But the group dynamic was already strained as it was, and the last thing I needed was for him to react awkwardly about it. It was better to keep my concerns to myself and let my emotions fall back in line on their own.

"We had our trio thing going, and it worked. Now, the balance is weird," I replied, trying to sound diplomatic.

"Yeah, that addition caught me by surprise, too."

"And, if I'm being honest, it bothers me that she'll just kind of give up midway through. A moment of brilliance followed by 'I can't' rather than trying to push through."

He dropped his hand from my shoulder and shook his head. "Yeah, she's an odd one, isn't she?"

I eyed him. "What do you think of her?"

"A little too high maintenance for my taste. You and Toran have taken everything in stride, and she... hasn't. Then again, you seem more resilient than most."

"I thought maybe I was just being petty."

He nodded. "No, I hear you. I do think she's starting to get it, though."

"I'm..." I hesitated. "I'm concerned about you with her—"

Kaiden raised an eyebrow. "Oh, *really*?"

My cheeks flushed. "You cut me off! I'm concerned about her as a fellow caster—being your backup for an offensive spell. I worry that she could freeze while we're in the Archive when the pressure is really on."

"That could happen to any of us, Elle. Are you *sure* that's the only thing on your mind?"

I sighed.

"Come on, if we can't be honest with each other, then how are we supposed to work together?"

"Well," I mumbled, "I've seen the way she looks at you. You haven't exactly stopped her."

"Ah."

I crossed my arms. "What I mean is, this isn't remotely the right situation to be having those kind of thoughts. We can't afford distractions."

"Is it bad of me to point out that you're distracted by worrying about potential distractions?"

I glared at him.

"Sorry." Kaiden cracked a smile. "In all seriousness, though," he continued, "there's too much going on right now to have attention divided. Yeah, Maris puts on a show, but that's just how she is. It doesn't change what's important—what we're trying to do here."

"Yeah, you're right."

Kaiden dropped his voice to a whisper and looked me in the eyes. "Besides, Elle, if anyone had a chance of distracting me in that way, it wouldn't be her."

My heart warmed with the words—the kind of fulfilling flutter my friends had described but I'd never experienced for myself. I stayed focused on his intent gaze and I gave him a coy smile. "That's good to know."

He returned the smile. "You shouldn't have had any doubts."

"I have a bad tendency of overthinking things."

Kaiden brushed his hand down my arm. "Don't. We should probably focus on getting through this Archive sealing before... whatever might happen happens."

I nodded. "Getting all happening-y..." I bit my tongue. "Sorry, that went better in my head."

He chuckled. "It's fine. You're just overthinking it again."

"I'm bad at this stuff."

"Clearly I am, too, if you genuinely thought I had a thing for Maris."

"Okay, maybe not *that* much," I admitted.

"Still, I could have handled things better so you'd never have doubted my interest in you."

"It's only been a few days. I wasn't expecting anything."

Kaiden searched my face. "But it's been plenty of time to form an impression."

"That can happen in a moment."

"I know that feeling." He took half a step closer to me. "Any thoughts you'd like to share?"

There was a lot I wanted to say, though I knew I shouldn't... How at first I'd been drawn in by his looks, then questioned the attraction when his initial cavalier attitude came to light. But then I'd gotten to know his intelligence and heart, and it was clear he cared—not just about what we were doing, but those around him. And the more I learned, the more I liked what I saw.

We hadn't known each other for long enough to gauge how our viewpoints aligned on all matters, but there was no denying that a spark had been there from the beginning. I'd ignored it at times and misinterpreted it at others, but standing centimeters apart now, it was the most certain thing amid the present chaos.

I swallowed. "Didn't we *just* say what bad timing this is?"

"I'm also bad at listening to my own advice."

"Hey, we have that in common." I smiled.

He leaned closer to me the slightest measure. "I mean, if a distraction is there anyway, it might be better to get it out in the open."

I ran my fingers through the ends of my hair, suddenly feeling exposed with only my white shipsuit on. "Won't it be weird for the others if we..."

"You can only spend so much time worrying about other people before you go crazy."

"That's true." My heart pounded in my chest.

He brushed my hair away from my face with his index finger. "What would make the next trials easier for *you*? You don't have to ignore your own needs while looking after others."

"I don't know." A tingle spread throughout me, radiating from his touch. I wasn't sure exactly what I wanted to happen next, but I knew I wanted more.

His eyes locked on mine. "Well, *I'd* like—"

The door slid open, breaking the moment.

Maris barged in, and Kaiden and I instantly took a step back from each other.

"I decided I really need more practical sho—" She cut off when she saw us standing away from the scanner. "Sorry, am I interrupting?"

"Not at all. New shoes are always top priority," I replied, hoping the dim lighting in the room hid the flush in my face. Whatever had almost happened, she didn't need to know about it.

She gestured to the scanner. "Have you already…?"

"No, go ahead," I told her.

Maris looked us over again but wisely said nothing.

When she turned her back, Kaiden cast me a knowing glance and subtle smile, which I returned.

I didn't have much experience in relationships of the romantic nature, but I did know that a solid friendship was the foundation of any worthwhile partnership. If nothing else, the challenges ahead would be very informative about what kind of future we could possibly have together; if this madness didn't test a bond, nothing would.

Maris stepped into the scanner and made her new footwear selection while we waited. She picked a pair of boots with only a slight heel, not too dissimilar from mine. I wanted to make a snide 'I-told-you-so' comment about her original footwear, but I didn't since I knew it wouldn't be helpful—especially since I hadn't cautioned against it before when I had the chance.

She sent the production request to the 3D printer. "All yours. Thanks for letting me jump ahead."

"Yeah, no problem," Kaiden acknowledged. "Elle, you want to get set up?"

"Sure."

While Maris waited for her new boots to print, I held up my sword in the holographic scanner and used the interface to customize a scabbard for it using one of the base designs.

"May as well see if anything else catches your eye," Kaiden suggested when I'd sent the scabbard to the printer.

"You don't mind?"

"That's all I came down here to do. I'll watch for anything that looks interesting."

A chime at the back of the room beeped and the panel slid open to expose Maris' new black boots.

"These will do," she murmured, admiring them. She scooped them up in her arms. "Have fun with your shopping. See you upstairs."

"See ya," I bid her as she left the room.

I waited for the door to close. "Browsing the inventory is the *only* thing you came down here to do?" I asked Kaiden.

"Well, I did also want to make sure you were doing okay."

"Then the conversation kind of took a turn."

"It did." He paused. "Should I finish saying what I was about to when Maris showed up?"

Almost every part of me wanted to shout a resounding 'yes', but the logic part of my brain had had a chance to regain a foothold. "I want to see where this can go, but we'll be at the Archive in a few hours. We can resume this after it's sealed."

He nodded. "Okay."

I sensed his disappointment, but it was the kind that came from accepting a harsh truth. And, realistically, we were only hitting pause for a day. If we couldn't exhibit that measure of self-control, then we had no business getting involved in the first place.

With the tension temporarily diffused, I turned my attention to the holographic menu system. I was content with my present clothing, so I decided to focus on potential accessories.

Most of the items were useless for our mission, but a glove caught my eye. It was classified as an accessory, but the description struck me as a weapon.

"Is this right?" I questioned. "Can it really fire a blast capable of knocking an enemy back?"

Kaiden read the description from next to me. "Certainly makes it sound that way."

The rendering of the glove was dark gray in color with teal accents along the fingers and knuckles. Its palm contained a white patch ringed in the same teal accent color.

"I don't get how *that* could produce a physical blast," I insisted.

"Maybe it has something to do with your abilities? This magic-tech likes to bend the rules."

"That it does." I shrugged. "Well, only one way to find out if it works, right?"

"Very true," Kaiden agreed.

I sent the item to the printer.

"All right, let me take a quick look to see if there's anything else open to me that wasn't showing up for you." Kaiden took my place on the platform and started browsing through the inventory to see what was available for the skills in his discipline.

"Huh, that's weird," he said after a minute.

"What?"

"That glove you got is marked in my menu as being only for casters."

"Really?" I walked up behind him. "That can't be right."

"Take a look." He pointed to it.

There was no mistaking the notation. My brow knit. "Then why did it let me select it?"

"That's a very good question."

OUR RELAXATION TIME was short-lived before the jump, but I was eager for us to get back to the Archive. I tried to nap as much as possible during our time in hyperspace in my pod; though it was next to impossible to sleep unless one was passed out, I at least managed to clear my mind.

We were about to enter the final push. There could be anything waiting for us in the Archive—a single button to push, an endless string of monsters, a labyrinth. I wasn't about to rule out any possibility after what we'd been through over the past several days.

I was also happy to have the time to reflect on my conversation with Kaiden. After thinking it through, I decided it was ultimately a good thing Maris had shown up when she did. As curious as I was to explore our growing connection, this *really* wasn't the time to test that out; after all, if we decided we hated each other, it'd make for a pretty awkward trek through whatever caves or fields we might find ourselves traversing in the future. Still, I looked forward to a time when we were settled enough to give a relationship a chance.

When the *Evangiel* arrived at Crystallis, we exited our pods and began dressing in our clean gear, which we'd retrieved before the jump. In the case of my boots, however, apparently the treads had been so caked in guts from the alien creatures that the crew had deemed it easier to manufacture a new pair using my saved template rather than clean them.

I wiggled my toes in the replacement shoes. "Damn, I'd *just* gotten the other ones properly broken in."

Kaiden buckled his belt. "I'm sure these will be seasoned in no time."

"Please tell me there isn't another ten kilometer hike in our future," Maris moaned.

I slipped my coat over my white base layer. "Oh, come now! Don't you want to test out your new boots?"

"I can do that quite successfully by staying within a reasonable distance from the shuttle," she replied.

"We can land close to the cave," Toran said as he secured his pauldrons. "However, we have no idea how deep we'll need to go inside."

"Great." She sighed. "The only thing better than going on a long hike is going on a long hike into a creepy cave."

"I wouldn't call it creepy, per se," I interjected. "More… mysterious, perhaps?"

"Yeah, let's go with that," Kaiden agreed.

"Creepy, mysterious, whatever it is, I don't like confined places," Maris said.

"It'll be fine," I tried to assure her. "I'm sure we'll be in and out in no time."

We finished dressing and then headed for the hangar. Our bags were waiting for us at the base of the shuttle's ramp, and we gathered them.

"Good luck down there," Tami said to us. "We made some upgrades to the shuttle's sensor suite, which should help with your landing. We'll be cheering you on from here."

I placed my hand on my sword's hilt. "Thanks. We'll see you— Oh!"

"Forget something?" the engineer asked.

"Yeah, the monument. We were going to bring cleaning supplies to get it back to how it should be."

Kaiden shook his head. "Elle, I have to say that I'm impressed. After everything we've done over the past week, you still care about scrubbing some sealant off of an old stone."

"It's a *crystal*," I corrected, "and it's connected to an ancient artifact. We should be respectful."

He smiled. "I appreciate that you care."

"Sealant, you said?" Tami frowned. "That stuff is a pain to get off, but I have something that should do the trick." She motioned to one of her maintenance techs and gave instructions about what to bring back.

A minute later, the tech returned with a container of cleaning solution, some wipes, and gloves.

"This should get it off." She handed it to me.

"Thank you. We'll see you soon."

I dropped my bag and the cleaning supplies in the common room and then went to the bridge to assume my usual seat.

A somber mood settled in the bridge while we strapped in.

"Do we need a pep talk?" I asked while the shuttle taxied out of the hangar.

"This does seem like one of those times for a speech," Toran replied.

"I think you just volunteered yourself, Elle." Kaiden smiled at me.

I sighed. Giving speeches wasn't typically my thing, but I was feeling oddly inspired. "Okay, well… I know we haven't known each other for long, but the past week has shown we're here because of a common goal. It has nothing to do with where we're from or what we were before we were called, but what's in our hearts. We will do anything to help our loved ones and the other victims.

"We didn't ask to be chosen for this role, but we were. It hasn't been easy, and I'm sure it won't get easier, but we have each other." My gaze met Kaiden's for a moment. "Everyone is counting on us now, and we need to push forward for them. We're going to go in there and do whatever it takes to seal the Archive, because that's the only way we can be sure our loved ones are safe. I know that won't be the end of it—the Darkness isn't going to go away just because the Archive is sealed—but it's a big step forward. It's a step that shows we can work together and do this.

"We may have started off as strangers, and maybe not all of us wanted to be fighters, but we've all risen to the occasion. I know *I've* done things I never dreamed I could do. Whoever I thought I was going into this, I now know I'm so much more. All that we need to do is try."

The others stared silently at me as I concluded.

"Was it that terrible?" I asked.

Kaiden shook his head. "No, that was actually really good. You sure you didn't prepare that?"

"No, just got all psyched up in the moment." I glanced behind me at Toran and Maris, both of whom still looked stunned. "You know, when someone gives a rousing speech, typically you cheer, or, you know, *react*."

"I was moved by your words," Toran stated matter-of-factly.

I shook my head and slouched in my seat. "I'm definitely going to dial back my expectations for speech reception in the future."

"Might be the setting," Maris said. "Like, we're not facing each other, and arm-pumping is a little awkward in these harnesses."

"I am not a cheer-er," Toran said.

Kaiden chuckled. "Guys, the Dark Sentinels need to work on our team spirit."

"I'll say." I crossed my arms. "Well, I tried."

After clearing the *Evangiel*, the shuttle began its descent into Crystallis' turbulent atmosphere. Kaiden took manual controls as the clouds thickened outside the viewports.

The shuttle jerked as the first of the winds hit.

"What was that?" Maris asked.

"Oh, did we not mention that part?" I glanced back at her. "This whole planet it a mess. The inertial compensators don't work here for some reason, and we need to go in for a semi-blind landing."

She paled. "You *what?*"

"Nah, it'll be fine with the upgrades, I'm sure," Kaiden assured her. He frowned at the control panel. "Well, I mean, we'll figure it out."

"What's wrong?" I asked.

"The destination won't lock in the nav system," he replied.

"That's not the same issue we had last time, is it?"

"No, before we knew where we were going but couldn't see it. Now we have sensors to see where we are but the destination isn't standing out."

My chest constricted. "We saw something like this before… on the last planet that was touched by the Darkness."

"Shit, you're right." Kaiden paled.

"There's no visual sign of it," Toran stated in an assured tone, but his drawn face belied his inner concern.

"Maybe the magical signatures are the first to be affected," I hypothesized.

Kaiden nodded. "Let's hope there's an extra layer of protection around the Archive like the dragons had."

"Stars, I hope we're not too late." I sunk as deep into my seat as I could.

"First we have to *get there*," Kaiden said. "I'll head us toward the spot where we entered the valley last time." He entered in our previous stopover location and adjusted the shuttle's course.

I nodded. "We found it once before that way."

We descended through the thick cloud cover, bracing ourselves against the turbulence. Maris moaned most of the way down, but I tuned her out, distracted by thoughts of what we might find at the Archive.

It hadn't occurred to me before that the Darkness might reach Crystallis before we returned. It had felt like we were making good time in our quest to retrieve the artifacts from the other worlds, though, in truth, we had no idea how the interstellar infection was transmitted. The affected worlds followed no clear location pattern or commonalities that were readily apparent. The only reference guide was the information the Hegemony had been able to extract from the Archive, and that was far from complete.

After an uncomfortable ten minutes, the shuttle dropped through the lowest cloud layer, revealing the barren landscape of the world.

I saw no hint of the Darkness, giving me hope that perhaps that wasn't the reason for the navigation issues. In my heart, however, I knew that was wishful thinking; this world was at risk like any other, and its time may have come.

"I think those are the rocks where we fought the lizard things," Toran said while pointing out the front viewport from his seat.

"That's correct based on this nav log," Kaiden confirmed. "Which means the valley should be up this way." He altered the craft's trajectory to head toward the mountain range to the east.

Kaiden followed the readings from the new sensor suite to navigate the shuttle through the foggy mountain pass to the hidden valley.

The cloud cover cleared as if a veil had been lifted, revealing the sheltered valley filled with thousands of crystals. To my relief, there was no sign of the black speckled infection I'd seen on my own world right before the reset. Maybe the Darkness *wasn't* here yet.

"Stars, this is amazing!" Maris gasped.

"Pretty incredible, isn't it?" I agreed.

"I've never seen crystals this size."

Kaiden shook his head. "Didn't even know it was possible before we came here."

"It's no wonder this place is kept hidden. I can only imagine what would happen if the location of this world got out," Toran said.

I nodded. "Regardless of your political opinions, I'm glad the Hegemony has more sense than that."

"They have reverence for the crystalline network, that much is clear," Toran murmured. "Their motivations behind it might be another matter, given what little information they've been willing to share."

"Can you blame them?" Kaiden asked while navigating the shuttle toward the landing site. "We're a bunch of random people they bioprinted after extracting our consciousness from… wherever it is we go between resets. Would you really trust us with your secrets, either?"

I laughed. "When you put it like that, I wouldn't, no."

Toran inclined his head. "We're only here because they were desperate, that's true. Perhaps after we complete this task we will have earned their trust."

"*I* think we've already done a lot for them," Maris stated.

"Well, *we* have," I corrected. "You pretty much just got here."

"Two days after you!"

"That's an eternity in this business." I grinned.

Kaiden landed the shuttle, with only a slight bump to indicate we were on the ground. "We'll all be veterans after we face this. Ready to go to the place no one has been for hundreds of years?"

I unbuckled my harness. "That *does* make it sound even cooler and more exclusive."

"The coolest and most exclusivist." Kaiden smiled back while he powered down the engine.

"I don't believe that's how I'd characterize this mission," Toran said, unbuckling his own harness.

"Just keeping it light, my friend." I patted him on the shoulder while I passed by his seat on my way to the common room.

I was about to put on my backpack but then thought better of it; whatever we might face inside, I wasn't going to need camping gear. I opted to instead grab the flashlight, a length of rope, and a tablet from the pack. I was able to fit the small tablet and flashlight in my coat's pockets, and the rope I slung diagonally over my arm and torso.

By the time I was finished, the others had joined me in the common room and had retrieved select items from their own bags. Only Toran opted for his full backpack.

"I'll bring a med kit," he stated. "May as well be prepared for a fight."

"I can take care of that." Maris replied.

"What if you're the one hurt?"

"Oh, right." She frowned. "I don't want to get hurt."

"I think that's a pretty universal sentiment," I responded.

Kaiden slipped a flashlight into his pants pocket. "We might not even have to fight anything. The artifact guardians may have been the worst of it."

"Hopefully." I didn't believe it for a second.

"Everyone ready?" Kaiden asked.

I checked my pockets. "Yep." I paused. "No, wait." I jogged over to where I'd left the cleaning supplies.

Kaiden sighed. "Elle, I appreciate what you want to do, but can't we deal with that later?"

I smiled. "Just saving us a trip. We can take care of it on the way back out."

"All right," he agreed. "Everyone else good to go?"

Toran and Maris nodded.

"Okay, let's go."

Toran released the exit hatch, and we filed down the ramp into the sand-like ground covering of crushed crystal.

The diffused light through the fog gave the valley a strange purple tint I hadn't noticed on our previous venture, likely because I was distracted by visiting an alien world for the first time. Even having spent the last week in space and on other planets, walking among the giant crystals remained the most awe-inspiring location of all those we'd visited.

We wove our way through the groups of crystals and rock formations toward the slope up to the cave entrance. I was mesmerized by the subtle hum in the air, which seemed to come from the crystals themselves. I was barely paying attention to where I was walking when a snarl from the shadows next to some rocks snapped me back to focus.

The sound was familiar. "Freaking stone lizards," I mutter, drawing my sword from its new scabbard.

Kaiden sighed. "Ugh, I hated those things."

Three of the spiny creatures emerged from the shadows at the base of a giant crystal five meters to our left.

"We really don't have time for this." Kaiden raised his hand, and a fireball shot out from the end of his staff. It divided into three, each headed directly for one of the stone lizards.

The fireballs struck each center mass, and they all but vaporized into ash.

I sheathed my blade. "You've gained some skills since the last time we were here."

"Crazy how far we've come, isn't it?" Kaiden strolled toward the cave's entrance.

When we reached the foot of the incline leading to the cave, we took a running start to get up the scree. The task was more challenging with my hands full of cleaning supplies, but I managed to make it to the top on my first attempt.

At the cave mouth, Kaiden illuminated a light orb in his palm and led the way inside.

We walked in silence on the way down to the inscribed column that had sent us on our hunt for the artifacts. When we arrived, everything was just as we'd left it, with the black sealant still marring the opaque crystal.

I set down the supplies at its base. "We'll get you back to how you should be."

"I don't think it can hear you," Maris said.

"Considering the artifact guardians, some kind of sentient force here wouldn't surprise me, actually," Kaiden said.

"Even if there isn't, good cosmic karma is never a bad thing," I added.

Toran nodded. "Indeed."

Maris sighed. "Okay, whatever."

Kaiden approached the back wall of the cave. "How do you think we get this open?"

"Maybe touch our artifacts to the symbols?" Toran suggested.

"Sounds reasonable." I drew my blade.

Together, Kaiden, Toran, and I extended our respective artifacts toward the stone wall, touching each to its corresponding symbol. I held my breath with anticipation.

Nothing happened.

"Okay, there goes that idea." Kaiden returned his circlet to his head.

I lowered my blade. "Maybe we need to use the items?"

"Punch the wall?" Toran raised an eyebrow.

"I dunno." I shrugged. "All of the other worlds we visited required us to interact with the crystals."

"Hmm, I wonder if that's the problem." Kaiden walked back over to the central column. "Maybe we need to do something with this?" He brushed his hand against the crystal's surface.

The white monolith glowed pale blue in response to his touch.

"I think you're onto something!" I jogged over and placed my hand on the opposite side. The light intensified.

Toran joined us. As soon as his hand touched the crystal, the light flashed blindly bright and then returned to a subtle light blue glow.

"Did that do it?" I wondered.

A moment later, the symbols on the wall started to glow. To the left, the central crystal that the tunnel wrapped around began to glow, as well. The light took on more definition as the outline of an archway formed in the surface of the crystal wall, then pressed backward through the crystal to form an arched passageway.

I stepped toward it. "Well, shall we?"

"YEP, HIDDEN PASSAGEWAYS aren't the *least* bit ominous," Maris muttered when we entered the ethereal crystal corridor.

The walls were as smooth as a plane of glass. I wasn't sure if there had been some sort of camouflage over the entryway or if the pathway had actually formed right before our eyes. Given the transformative feats we'd witnessed over the past week, I was inclined to believe it was the latter.

The corridor sloped downward at a subtle angle, presumably passing underneath the spiraling tunnel we'd entered on the way in. It continued straight for twenty-five meters and then there was only blackness.

Kaiden held up his hand and increased the intensity of the light orb. The illumination cast on our faces got brighter, but the light faded three meters from us.

"Okay, yes, it's a little creepy," I acknowledged.

"Is the space so large that we can't see the walls, or is something actively suppressing the light?" Toran asked.

I looked behind us; the passageway through the crystal was visible, but it was only darkness all around us. "This is going to sound a little weird, but I don't know if here is *here*."

Kaiden spun around to look where I had. "What do you mean?"

"Remember on the last world in the tower where we fought the dragon? The geometry didn't work," I said. "I think there was some kind of magic at play, where reality was... distorted."

"Like, portals?" Toran asked,

"Maybe. Or perhaps distances aren't what they seem." I walked back in the direction of the passageway but stayed to the right. "There's one way to test the idea."

I stretched out my hands in front of me when I neared what should be a wall, but there was only emptiness. I continued forward until I was parallel with the mouth of the passageway; standing next to it, I saw only blackness.

The sight freaked me out, and I hastily stepped backward. "That isn't right."

"What?" Kaiden prompted.

"The corridor is there, but it… isn't." I steeled myself and returned to the parallel position. I extended my hand toward where it should be, feeling nothing. "Okay, if I'm not crazy, this is about to get even weirder."

I turned to my left, directly into where the crystal-lined corridor should be, and walked forward. I took five steps through the darkness, then turned left and continued walking. When I glanced over my shoulder, I saw that I was now on the left side of the passageway.

Kaiden was staring at me, dumbfounded.

"I just walked through—or behind—or whatever that supposedly solid thing we all came through, didn't I?" I questioned.

My companions nodded silently.

I shuddered while I returned to the group. "Okay, yeah, this place is officially messed up."

Toran frowned. "So, if we're here-but-not-here, then where do we go?"

"That's assuming *here* is a place and not a… *not*-place?" Kaiden's statement ended more like a question.

"In other words, we may no longer be on Crystallis," Toran said with more certainty.

"Or, at least, maybe not the Crystallis we know," I replied. "This could be another reality entirely."

"How are we supposed to seal the Archive if we can't see anything?" Kaiden asked.

"I'd really love a 'how to' guide right around now," I muttered,

Maris wrapped her arms around herself. "I don't like this place."

"You can say that again." I took a few tentative steps deeper into the blackness away from the passageway. To my surprise, the doorway didn't seem to get any further away, though my friends did. "Hey, I think it's okay."

"*Nothing* about this is okay," Kaiden grumbled.

"No, come on. We just have to trust it," I said.

Kaiden eyed me suspiciously. "Did the Darkness get to you on the last world?"

I sighed. "No! The passage is there, even when I move away from it. I think it's a test—'only those willing to take a risk will advance' kind of deal."

"If you say so." Kaiden walked forward to my position. He looked back over his shoulder. "Huh. I see what you mean."

"I'll trust you," Toran said, coming to join us.

"Wait up!" Maris hurried after him.

We continued forward through the blackness for what felt like half a kilometer but it was impossible to tell. The passageway entry remained at a constant distance behind us as we moved forward, and whenever we backtracked, we were able to get to the opening.

I had no explanation for the magic at play, but it was one of the most fascinating things I'd ever witnessed. Had the situation been less dire, I could think of a dozen ways to play around with my friends using the unique properties of the place.

At last, something in the environment changed—so subtle I didn't notice it at first. A breeze was picking up around us, ruffling my long hair.

"Where's that coming from?" I asked.

Kaiden licked his finger and held it up in the air. "That way, I think." He pointed to the left.

"Wind means an opening," I said. "Maybe we should head that way?"

"I'll buy that logic." Toran altered his course to head in the direction Kaiden had indicated.

The arched passage continued to follow us to our left, moving perpendicular to us. As unnerving as it was to have something behave in such an odd fashion, I was thankful for the presence of its subtle white light amid the otherwise oppressive blackness—a lone constant to offer grounding.

After several dozen meters, the wind intensified until it was clearly coming from a specific point.

Kaiden's light didn't illuminate any walls, but I could feel the currents. The wind was coming from what I perceived to be a narrow tunnel.

"Onward?" I asked.

Kaiden nodded. "We've come this far."

"All right." I clicked on my flashlight and led the way inside single-file.

Like the light orb, the beam from my flashlight dissipated after three meters. However, the further I went into the tunnel, the ground began to take on more definition—transitioning from pure blackness to textured, dark stone.

Gradually, the walls began to take shape, as well. They started as an arched corridor and deeper into the tunnel flared outward until a cavern took shape. Behind me, the crystal passageway remained.

"Under any other circumstances, I would totally be freaking out right now," I said.

"I still might," Kaiden murmured. "This is *weird*."

"But fascinating," Toran stated.

"On a positive note, I'm loving my new walking boots," Maris chimed in.

I rolled my eyes. "Thrilled for you."

"Hold up." Kaiden grabbed my shoulder, stopping me.

My heart skipped a beat. Half a dozen paces ahead, the ground dropped out in front of us; I'd become so accustomed to walking through the blackness that I hadn't even noticed. "Thanks."

He came up next to me and smiled. "Gotta have each other's backs. Friends don't let friends walk off of cliffs."

"You never met my friends."

"Right, you and your cliff-jumping for *fun*."

"I would advise that we not recreate those antics here and now," Toran cautioned.

"No argument here." I cautiously approached the lip of the precipice.

There was only blackness below. Looking outward, I could tell the cavern continued, but I couldn't gauge how far back it went.

"Nothing down he—" I cut off as the ground started to rumble.

I hastily stepped back from the ledge as rock fragments broke off and fell into the depths. "What's happening?"

"Either we did something wrong and the place is falling apart around us, or we're about to be tested again," Kaiden murmured. His orb of light morphed into a fireball.

"That figures." Maris sighed.

A purple protective shell appeared around me. "Thanks, Maris."

She smiled. "Here to help. You guys do… whatever it is you're supposed to do."

"Fight the thing?" Toran speculated.

I drew my sword. "Sure. Let's go with that."

The rumbling intensified, then a series of distinct concussive thumps shook the ground underfoot.

Poised with my sword at the ready, I braced for whatever monster might emerge.

Yellow light illuminated in the dark depths before us, casting a shadow of the creature climbing upward along the rock wall. It appeared to be shaped like a person, only bigger—or maybe that was a trick of the light.

When a hand sporting fingers longer than I was tall cleared the lip of the cliff, it was clear the lighting had not oversold the feature attraction.

Kaiden staggered backward. "Is that a rock titan?"

"It appears to be," Toran concurred.

"Wait, *that's* what you fought before I came?" Maris squeaked.

"Well, maybe one half this size," I replied.

"How… No. No way." She backed away.

"Relax, we probably don't have to actually fight it," Toran said.

Maris stared at him blankly. "What?"

"The other one just required us to demonstrate the principles of the discipline—protecting others," he explained.

The creature's head cleared the cliff and it fixed us in the vacant stare of its glowing yellow eyes.

"Should we skip the slashing and blasting bit?" I asked.

He nodded. "Mind being the bait again?"

"Not at all. I just hope this is right." I sheathed my sword and stepped forward.

"Elle—" Kaiden started to protest, but Toran placed a hand on his shoulder.

"I won't let it harm her," he said.

The titan glared at me as I walked forward until I was two paces from the edge of the cliff. Heart pounding in my ears, I waited.

The giant raised its hand to strike.

I stared into its yellow eyes, glowing with the same light I'd come to associate with ancient power. While I watched intently, waiting for the blow to come, I thought I saw the light flicker—a touch of Darkness clouding the brilliance.

"Did you—"

Before I could ask my question, the hand was rushing down to squash me, and time decelerated.

The hand's motion slowed as the world tinted orange. Toran ran up from behind me and held up his right fist above his head.

The rock titan's palm struck Toran's fist. From the point it made contact, the bonds holding the rest of the titan together disintegrated in a slow-motion wave, and it shattered into dust. The debris rained down around us.

"Well, that was easy," Kaiden said.

Maris looked dumbstruck. "I thought it was going to smoosh you."

Toran gently patted my back. "I told you that wouldn't happen."

"Good thing you were right." I sighed with relief. "Hey, I don't know if you saw it, but I think I noticed a dark spot in the giant's eyes."

"Like, the Darkness kind of dark?" Kaiden asked.

I shrugged. "It was just a flash. I'm not sure."

The light emanating from the depths beyond the cliff shifted, drawing my attention. The rays consolidated and began to sway. After several seconds, ribbons of spiraling light drifted upward, heading for Toran.

He stood transfixed by the swirling light. The golden ribbons wove around him, then merged into him.

Toran gasped and fell to his knees.

"Are you okay?" I bent down over him.

He stared ahead, terror on his face as he seemed to see something that wasn't there. "The Darkness," he murmured. "It transmits through the crystals. I see it."

"A vision?" Kaiden asked.

Toran staggered to his feet. "Yes, sort of. But it's more like I know things now. It's too much to process at once."

The orange hue in my vision faded as the haste spell wore off.

"Where does the Darkness come from?" Maris asked.

Toran shook his head. "I don't know."

A strong wind ripped through the cavern, almost knocking me off-balance. Light illuminated once more in the dark depths, this time blue.

"Oh, boy. Here we go again." I placed my hand on my sword's hilt but didn't draw it.

"Another repeat of last time?" Kaiden pondered.

"Let's hope so. That was the least kill-y of all of them," I replied.

"It tried to drown me!"

"Only because you did the pattern wrong." I smirked. "You learned the right way real quick after that, didn't you?"

He shook his head. "You're impossible."

"Just speaking the truth."

The sound of rushing water overpowered the wind, and a tidal wave rushed up to form a wall before us, seemingly suspended in midair above the lip of the canyon. It shimmered with soft blue-green light.

"All you." I flourished my hand toward Kaiden.

He stepped toward the water, his staff raised.

A blob of water a meter tall plopped out from the wall and landed on the rocky ground in front of Kaiden.

"Okay, let's hope the pattern holds." He froze the blob into a column of ice and it shattered.

Two more blobs emerged in sequence, which he quickly dispatched with a fireball and lightning bolt, respectively. Then, three blobs appeared together, and he dealt a different elemental blow to each. When they had been dispatched, a fourth blob plopped down. He set down his staff and approached the water column, holding a hand to either side of it.

He stood there for thirty seconds with no magic.

"Uh, Kaiden?" I prompted.

"I'm trying! This healing thing doesn't come naturally."

The blob shuffled forward.

I frowned. "I think it's getting impatient."

"Yes, thank you." Kaiden sighed with obvious frustration.

I walked over to stand next to him and placed my hand on his back. "Hey, you've got this."

He glanced over at me. "Easier said than done."

"Don't overthink it. You did it once. You can do it again."

Kaiden took a slow breath and faced the blob. "Yeah." He closed his eyes.

Green light appeared between his hands, permeating the column of water. It glowed brightly and then lifted from the ground, floating back toward the wall. When it reached the water wall, it merged into it, and the light spread.

The water vaporized, leaving only the light behind.

In the final moments before the water vaporized, I thought I saw a glimpse of Darkness within it. The light was dim, though, so I couldn't be sure.

The ribbons of blue-green light glided toward Kaiden and I stepped back from him. The light wove around him, then seeped inward.

He took a choking breath and doubled over. After a couple of rapid breaths, he straightened. "I saw something," he whispered.

"What?" I asked, wondering if it was the same dark flicker I'd seen.

"It was—" He didn't have time to answer before wind ripped through the cavern once more.

"Talk later. It's dragon time," I said.

"Yeah. I'm a little less clear on the trick with this one," Kaiden said. "As I recall, you almost fell off of the tower."

"I totally had that under control," I lied.

"But what should we do?" he pressed. "Are you going to try to talk it down like you did last time?"

"I mean, the others went down like they did before, right? May as well try," I replied.

Red light lit up the dark depths and a vicious roar echoed through the chamber.

"Yeah, talking to it is a *great* idea," Maris grumbled.

The purple protective shell returned around each of us.

"Watch, we'll be out of here in no time." I drew my sword but kept it angled down in what I hoped was a non-threatening stance.

Another roar cut through the quiet, followed by the flapping of immense wings.

The dragon cleared the cliff, beating its wings to hover five meters above us. This one was darker red, and its scales almost appeared to glow in the scarlet light shining from below.

"We've come to protect the Archive," I shouted. "Please, tell us what we need to do."

The dragon tilted its head questioningly. Then, its brilliant green eyes widened. It spasmed.

"Uh…" I stepped back from the cliff.

"That doesn't seem right," Kaiden murmured.

The giant beast thrashed its wings to stay aloft, writhing in midair. To my horror, its skin began to darken, changing from crimson to inky black. The dark transformation flowed over it like paint until it was completely transformed.

It gained control of its movements and turned its head to face me. The green eyes morphed to black.

"The Darkness!" I started to warn.

A blast of fire surrounded us, with only Maris' protective shields keeping it from scorching us alive. Even through the magical barrier, my skin seared.

"Okay, so maybe no talking!" I gulped.

"Was that supposed to happen?" Kaiden shouted back.

"I think the Darkness has infected it," I replied. "Who knows what this place was supposed to be like."

"Is it too late to seal the Archive?" Toran asked.

"I have to believe it's not. Not everything was corrupted, just this form. We can still do this." I raised my sword. "Come down and fight us!" I shouted at the dragon.

"Way to invite trouble, Elle." Kaiden readied a ball of ice on his staff, poised to deploy it.

"I'm just reacting to what I'm given," I said.

The dragon swooped down, its talons outstretched.

Toran punched at one of the feet as it passed by overhead, the only part of the creature low enough to reach.

Kaiden blasting a rapid volley of ice balls at it, aiming for the orange fire pouch in its throat. The blasts connected, but the dragon seemed unfazed.

"Another haste spell would be great!" I yelled while jumping and thrusting my blade upward toward the dragon. Being shorter than Toran, the blade only grazed the dragon's foot when I jumped.

"I'm on it," Maris replied.

My surroundings tinted orange again, though it was a subtle difference in the already red light.

The dragon circled around for another assault, now seeming to move in slow motion.

"Toran, boost me up when it comes by," I suggested.

He nodded his understanding and cupped his hands to give me a stirrup.

When the dragon approached again, it was much lower and its talons were extended like it was ready to grab us.

I assessed the timing, and when the moment felt right, I ran toward Toran, planting my foot in his hands. He heaved me upward, and I raised my sword. With the extra height, the blade plunged into the dragon's belly.

It roared and tilted sideways, one of its massive wings dropping toward the ground as the body rotated.

My boost from Toran carried me forward through the air as the beast fell. I landed on my feet and transitioned into a roll to diffuse my momentum.

When I leaped to my feet and turned around, the dragon was recovering its balance while taking a beating. Toran was administering rapid punches to its side while he had access, Kaiden was lobbing ice balls and electrical charges, and even Maris was slashing at its wing with her dagger.

I ran back to help them.

I'd gone two steps when the orange tint faded and my time perception returned to normal.

The dragon snapped its wing back in one swift motion and slammed it onto my companions. They flew backward and hit the rock wall hard, the protective shell spent. All three of them crumpled to the ground, motionless.

"No!" I ran toward them.

Their chests were moving with breath, to my relief, but they appeared to be out cold. It was just me against the beast.

I stared it down. "Let's end this."

THE DARK DRAGON roared at me, tendrils of smoke rising from its nostrils.

I couldn't hesitate. It was all down to me.

My sword was useless from this distance; I needed a different approach. I ran through a mental inventory of everything I had with me. The rope wouldn't be helpful for me alone, and everything else required being close. Then, I remembered the blaster in the palm of my new glove. I looked at the device and saw that it was now glowing with white light.

In one motion, I dove to the side to distract the dragon from my fallen friends and blasted an energy orb from the new hand device. I expected it to be a little light show, but to my surprise, a blast comparable to one of Kaiden's fireballs shot from it.

The blast struck the dragon beneath its eye, and it rounded on me with a snarl.

I shot another blast, which seemed to do nothing other than annoy the dragon. To take it down, I'd need to hit it in a vulnerable place, and I'd need more than a weapon that only went skin deep.

The orange glow beneath the dragon's jaw caught my eye. Having watched how the creature moved, I could tell it was guarding that part of itself—its one weakness.

But I'd have to get close, and the heat would be a major issue. I hoped my magical blade would be able to withstand it, but my hands would be burned to a crisp before I ever got close enough. I'd need protection, and normal armor wouldn't do.

Toran was only three meters away where he still lay unconscious. I dashed over and grabbed his gauntlets from his hands; the magical items just might be enough to withstand the heat without melting. They were far too big for me, but I could still grip my sword through them.

I was about to turn back to face the dragon when Kaiden caught my eye next to Toran. He was starting to stir.

"Take it," he murmured.

"Are you okay?" I asked, crouching down.

He winced. "Take it," he repeated with a motion toward his head. "The circlet."

"It's useless to me."

Kaiden shook his head. "You're a caster, Elle. I saw what you just did."

My heart skipped a beat. "I am?"

"The three disciplines. That's what this was always about. But not three distinct people—three in one." He managed to remove the circlet from his head. "Take it!"

The dragon roared.

"Stay here." I took the circlet from him and placed it on my head. A surge of energy flowed through me. My hands tingled, and my senses were sharp. I felt like I could tackle anything.

I charged toward the dragon, raising my sword for a strike. Two strides from it, I leaped into the air, jumping higher and faster than I ever had before. I drove the blade into the dragon's throat and used my momentum to rip downward.

The orange fire liquid flowed from the wound, burning the dragon's flesh everywhere it touched.

I fell free of the splatter zone only centimeters from the edge of the cliff.

The dragon sputtered and it fell into the depths.

I panted and it turned into a laugh. "Is that it? Did I do it?"

"I think so." Kaiden staggered to his feet behind me.

Toran and Maris began to rouse.

"What happened?" Maris moaned, gripping her head.

The red light beyond the cliff consolidated and began flowing toward me. I couldn't help tensing as it wrapped around me. It seeped into my skin.

Images flashed before my eyes and my head pounded.

I saw the Darkness snaking its way through a world, permeating everything in its path. The matter morphed to fit the image of the Darkness, becoming twisted to its form. But there was more behind it— not a mindless infection, but design. The beings born from the native wildlife were hybrids, a mutation combined with the genetic makeup of the alien beings behind the Darkness. The worlds weren't being consumed, they were being *transformed*.

My eyes shot open. I realized I was lying on my back on the cold stone. Kaiden was bent over me.

"Are you all right?" he asked.

"Yeah." I sat up, bringing my hand to my head. My gloved fingertips clinked against the circlet. "You can have this back now, thanks." I handed it to him.

"What are you doing with that and my gauntlets?" Toran asked, coming over.

I smiled. "Just saving the day."

Kaiden helped me to my feet. "I think Elle got something of a special treatment when she was formed—a little of everything rather than just one discipline."

Toran's eye widened. "Oh, really?"

I shrugged. "A matter for future investigation. The important thing now is that the dragon is dead."

"What about sealing the Archive?" Maris asked.

"Still trying to figure that part out." I looked around the dark cavern. "There has to be a path, or monument, or something."

"Unless we're too late," Toran said. "I know none of us want to consider that possibility, but we *are* surrounded by darkness right now. Whether it is *the* Darkness, I don't know."

"You're right: I *won't* consider it." I removed the gauntlets and thrust them toward Toran. "There's something here."

I retrieved my flashlight from my pocket and followed the edge of the cliff toward the left and it dead ended in a rock wall. I went the opposite direction and found that it continued. After fifty meters, the ledge narrowed to a two-meter-wide path.

"Elle, where are you going?" Maris asked, running up behind me.

"We're about to find out."

"They certainly make this complicated," Kaiden said.

"Nothing worthwhile is easy," Toran told him. "I only hope our efforts will pay off."

The path widened again after thirty meters to a seven-meter-diameter platform, which was surrounded on all sides by blackness. At the center of the platform was a solitary two-meter-tall crystal.

"Together," I said, motioning to Kaiden and Toran.

We each extended our right hand and touched the crystal.

A soft blue glow rose throughout the cavern. As it got brighter, the shapes of crystals began to take form. They blanketed every surface for as far as I could see, with no bottom or ceiling in sight.

I took it in, awed. "This is incredible!"

"Wow." Maris shook her head with disbelief next to me.

"Greetings, Chosen," a voice said from all directions in a warm, neutral timbre.

"Hello?" I replied.

"You have made it past the trials and proven you are pure of heart. Why do you journey now to the Master Archive?"

"There's a Darkness spreading. It may already be here, but the Archive needs to be sealed."

"A protocol is in place," the voice replied. "Before the act is complete, you must understand what it means for the worlds connected to the crystalline network. When the Archive is sealed, no new records can be added until it is unsealed. The crystals on the worlds will be useless until then."

I looked to my companions. "Not like they're doing us a lot of good now."

They nodded.

"We understand. Proceed with the sealing."

"Acknowledged."

The crystals flashed briefly, and then the light dimmed to dull gray.

"Sealing complete," the voice stated. "The Archive will remain in this state until the Chosen return."

"All right, so we should probably not die," Kaiden quipped.

I raised an eyebrow. "I would have hoped that was the plan, anyway."

"Is there anything we must know to unseal it?" Toran asked.

"Only purity of intentions," the voice replied.

"What of the Darkness?" I asked. "Can you tell us anything about it?

We heard that the Archive might contain information about events that haven't happened yet."

"It is true that this place exists outside of time as you know it. But truths must be discovered in their due course."

"Not even a hint?" Kaiden asked.

"You have already been given the knowledge you need."

"Those visions!" I said. "That was you? I thought the Darkness had infected it."

"The challenge is designed to prey on your fears to test what is in your heart. The Darkness is your greatest threat, and so that is how it manifested. This place is safe, and so it will remain now that you have completed your task."

"Thank you," I said. "Hopefully, next time we meet it will be under better circumstances."

"You will never be far."

The crystal column at the center of the platform flashed, and a shard the size of my thumb flaked off.

"A gift to aid you in the trials ahead," the voice said.

I picked up the shard; it was opaque white and glowed slightly with a soft blue light. I placed it in my pocket. "Thank you."

"Go now. The entry will re-seal behind you."

"All right, Dark Sentinels! Mission number one: accomplished." Kaiden grinned.

"Yeah, I guess so." I expected to feel more excited, but there was still so much ahead. A backup of my world was now safe, but the world itself was lost until we could restore it. We had scored a victory, but it was only the first step.

We walked back single-file along the narrow path.

"Why don't you look happy, Elle?" Maris asked when we reached the wider area near the entry. "It's over."

I shook my head. "It's *not* over. Yes, the Archive is safe now, but the Darkness is still out there and we need to figure out how to stop it."

"About that... I saw things. Right after the Spirit challenge," Kaiden murmured.

"What did you see?"

"Ships," Kaiden replied. "Alien ships. They were traveling to the worlds consumed by the Darkness."

"And I saw the Darkness spreading through the crystals," Toran added. He turned to me. "What about you, Elle?"

"The Darkness was transforming the worlds." I gave them an account of my vision.

"Hmm. So, maybe the Darkness is like some sort of advanced preparation for the aliens?" Kaiden posited. "Transform the world to their specifications."

"And, based on your vision, it would seem that the creatures we encountered may have been transformed by the Darkness," Toran stated.

"If those are hybrids, then what are the beings behind it?" Kaiden wondered aloud.

"Evil, whatever they are," I muttered. "This is a war. A full-on invasion."

"But we did it," Maris said. "We sealed the Archive. It's safe. Our worlds can be restored."

"Not until the threat is gone," Kaiden countered.

I crossed my arms. "Yes, but how do we do that?"

"Not sure, but I suspect it will be up to us to figure out."

"And we won't do that standing here." Toran gestured toward the exit.

We took the doorway to the crystal corridor, which had embedded in the back wall of the cavern, and trudged out of the Archive, exhausted. When we reached the column at the end of the stone tunnel leading from the cave mouth, the cleaning supplies were waiting at the base of the monument.

"I know we're tired, but I think we should put this back how it's supposed to be," I said.

"A few extra minutes won't kill us," Kaiden replied.

"I can help with the tiredness." Maris waved her hand and a rejuvenating wave washed over us.

Kaiden helped me clean off the crystal, returning it to its natural milky white. Though no magical being appeared to thank us for cleaning the ancient artifact, I felt in my heart it was the right thing to do.

When we were finished, the four of us returned to the shuttle.

The mood for the ride back was lighter than it had been in recent days. I suspected that would change as soon as we debriefed with the commander, but it was temporary relief.

We docked on the *Evangiel* in our usual berth.

Tami came to meet us as we exited the shuttle. "Did you do it?"

I grinned. "Archive sealed."

She placed her hand on her chest. "Thank the stars!"

"The Darkness is still out there, but the backups are safe. We'll find a way to restore the worlds," Kaiden said.

The engineer nodded. "I have no doubt you will." She took a shaky breath. "The commander is expecting you."

"We're on our way." Toran headed for the hangar door and we followed.

We took the lift up to the bridge level and walked down the corridor toward Central Command.

When we passed by the entry to an ancillary pod room, Kaiden motioned to me. "Elle, hang back a minute."

Toran looked back questioningly.

"We'll be right there," Kaiden told him.

When the others had gone ahead, and Kaiden motioned me inside the pod room.

"You were amazing today," he said when the door had closed. "I don't mean to say that in private because I wouldn't say it in front of them. It's not that." He stepped closer to me.

"Then why?" I searched his face.

"Because when I was lying there looking up at you, thinking it was all over, all I could think about was that we'd left things at a 'maybe someday'. But we have no idea what's coming tomorrow or a minute from now, so what's the point in waiting?"

"There might always be a 'next mission'."

"Exactly." He continued toward me until we were only centimeters apart. Slowly, he brought one hand up to my shoulder and then gently slid it upward to cup the side of my face.

His touch warmed me, sending an excited tingle to my core. I gazed into his radiant blue eyes. "Then let's not wait."

Our lips met and he wrapped his arms around me. I returned the hug as we shared the tender moment, forgetting our troubles in the universe beyond. We had each other, and in those seconds that was all I wanted.

When we parted, I gave him a bashful grin. "I have to say, that was worth the wait."

"I heartily agree." He gave me another soft kiss.

I wanted nothing more than to lose myself in the bliss, but I knew others were waiting on us. I pulled back slightly and entwined his fingers in mine. "What now?"

He laughed. "I have no idea."

"Should we say something?"

"Seems like a formal announcement would be weird."

"Yeah, so…"

He cupped his other hand around our interlaced fingers. "Maybe we just drop a few subtle hints and let them figure it out for themselves?"

"I like that approach." I placed my free hand over the crystal shard in my pocket. "We should probably go debrief with the Commander."

"Right."

Hand-in-hand, we walked up to the conference room in Central Command.

Our comrades gave us a questioning look when we entered, but we casually dropped our hands to our sides like there was nothing to see.

"So, you did it? The Archive is sealed?" the commander questioned, romance clearly the last thing on his mind.

"Yes, and we learned some things in the process," Kaiden began. He gave a recap of our visions and what we'd been able to piece together, while we interjected anecdotes as seemed appropriate.

Colren shook his head with amazement when we finished. "That explains so much."

"Unfortunately, that doesn't really help us know how to stop the Darkness and whatever beings are behind it," Toran replied.

The commander nodded. "Well, it's a start. And now we know this was a first wave and ships may be coming next. That's more information than we had before."

Maris crossed her arms. "But still, *all* of that and it didn't give us any other hints about what to do next? For a place that supposedly holds all the answers, we didn't get much."

"There was nothing else?" Colren asked.

"Well, there was one other thing," I said, pulling the crystal shard from my pocket.

The commander gingerly took the crystal from me. "Where did you get this?"

"It broke off from a crystal within the Archive," I replied. "The voice said it would aid us in the trials ahead."

"Stars!" Colren exclaimed. "Could it be…?" He stared with wonder at the tiny crystal fragment.

"Does that mean something to you?" I asked.

"If I'm not mistaken," he began, "this might be a shard from a Master Crystal. I didn't think we'd ever get access to one."

I tilted my head. "What is it, exactly?"

"If legend holds, it's connected to the Master Archive," Colren explained. "Such a shard provides a direct tether to the only storage medium that allow backups beyond our inhabited worlds."

Kaiden crossed his arms. "That sounds fancy, but how does that do us any good?"

The commander's eyes lit up. "Oh, it changes *everything*! This gives us a control point."

My heart skipped a beat. "You mean…"

Colren nodded. "This will allow us to access the Master Archive from anywhere." He held up the crystal. "With this, we can perform a universal reset."

"That's great!" Maris exclaimed. "Now you can do a reset and save our worlds."

Toran drooped. "No, having this tool doesn't eliminate the underlying threat."

Colren nodded solemnly. "This gives us hope, but it's not a magical fix." He activated the desktop and brought up a holographic recording of four worlds marred by incremental stages of Darkness infection. The dark clouds swirled around the planets, devoid of any signs of life. "This is what's become of your worlds."

My stomach turned over, realizing that I hadn't even recognized my home of Erusan.

"This is only the beginning," the commander continued. "The aliens will just come back if we do a universal reset now. We need to *stop* them."

Kaiden's gaze hardened. "We have some special abilities, yeah, but how are *we* supposed to go up against *that*?"

"I don't have an answer, but we've exhausted all of our other options," Colren stated. "You may have viewed your last task as a fun adventure, but the real invasion is coming. We currently have no way to stop the aliens' advance. What's happened to your worlds," he motioned to the holograph, "will happen to *every* world in the Hegemony if we don't find a way to fight back. You four are our best hope."

"How long do we have?" Toran asked.

Colren shrugged. "Weeks? A month, maybe? The rate of infection is accelerating. I didn't want to distract you from your task of sealing the Master Archive, but the truth is that we're past desperate. Though I wish I could send you home and say everything is going to be okay, that's not the reality."

I fought back a wave of guilt. I'd spent the last week living a super-charged version of my dream to be a Space Ranger, ignoring the unpleasant facts of my circumstances. The Hegemony was at a critical juncture, and I had the chance to make a difference. I couldn't shirk that responsibility when it mattered the most.

"Whatever's need, I'm in," I declared.

"Me too," Kaiden affirmed, then he whispered just loud enough for me to hear, "I guess you're stuck with me for a little longer."

I smiled back. "I'm okay with that."

"I never turn away from a challenge," Toran said.

Maris drew a deep breath. "Guess I can't lose my nerve now."

The commander gazed at each of us in turn. "We can't afford to lose any more worlds. We don't have any time to waste."

I steeled my resolve. "Tell us what we need to do."

A LIGHT IN THE DARK

DARK STARS: BOOK 2

1

LIMBO WAS MY least favorite state of being.

I drummed my fingers on the touchscreen surface of the conference table, not sure if I could sit idle in our lounge aboard the *Evangiel* for a moment longer.

The other members of my team seated around the table looked as anxious as I felt, their brows furrowed and lips drawn into scowls. In the week since we'd sealed the Master Archive, we'd hit dead end after dead end with our investigation into the Darkness' origin. If we didn't have a breakthrough soon, there wouldn't be any worlds left to save.

"We can't just sit around here doing nothing," I insisted.

"We've been training and preparing," Toran replied.

I shook my head. "But practicing isn't *action*."

Kaiden sighed in his seat next to me. "Elle, we've already been over this."

I raised an eyebrow. "We agreed to give it a week, and it's been a week."

"As I recall, *you* set that timeframe, not the rest of us," Toran countered. He crossed his muscular arms and fixed me in a level gaze.

"Yeah, it's a terrible plan," Maris agreed, flipping her dark hair behind her shoulder. "I say we keep waiting."

"Look, if our visions in the Archive were even remotely accurate, then an alien invasion force could be coming any moment," I continued. "Do we really want to sit around and wait for them to come to us, or are we going to *do something*?"

I turned to Kaiden for backup. I wasn't sure if our budding romance was enough to buy me favor for my crazy idea, but if I could convince one of my three companions to go along with it, it'd be him.

He shifted in his seat. "I don't like the 'wait and see' approach, either, but intentionally exposing ourselves to the Darkness is reckless."

It wasn't an outright 'no'. I could work with that.

I smiled disarmingly. "We've already faced it once. This is what we were called to do."

"No, we were brought together to seal the Master Archive—which we've done," Maris said.

"You don't need to come," I told her. "But this is something *I* want to do, because I think it's the right move. If there are any clues to be found about the Darkness and how to stop it, we'll find them on the first world that was consumed."

Kaiden sunk deeper into his seat. "It's been more than three months since the Darkness appeared. There's no telling what that world might be like by now, considering the transformations that have happened on other worlds in *hours*."

"All the more reason for us to investigate," I replied.

He examined me. "You won't let this go, will you?"

I shook my head. "I'll go alone, if that's what it takes."

Toran sighed. "I can't endorse this plan, but I also dislike the idea of any one of us going off on our own."

"So, you'll come with me?" I asked.

The huge man nodded. "Very well."

Kaiden threw up his arms. "All right."

I looked to Maris. "What about you?"

She frowned. "This is a terrible idea."

"So you've said." I started to stand up. "All right, we'll see you when we get back."

"I didn't say I wouldn't go." She folded her hands on the tabletop. "You'd all probably die without me."

I smiled. "Let's talk to the commander."

The lines of reporting and leadership had been somewhat blurred since our arrival on the Hegemony's ship, the *Evangiel*, two weeks prior. We were civilians, yet we'd been tasked to serve the government and military in an attempt to stop the Darkness slowly consuming our worlds.

With the leadership having nowhere else to turn, we'd been given a degree of autonomy far outside standard operating procedures, and I knew it would ruin me for life.

We made our way to the top deck and proceeded to the nose of the vessel, where we were buzzed into Central Command through the main door.

Commander Alastair Colren rose from the lone seat at the center of the bridge when we entered. "Do you have news?" he asked.

The dynamic threw me off every time I talked with him. A hardened military commander in his fifties, and yet he was looking to me—a teenager from a backwater world—for a plan of action. My universe had been turned upside down in more ways than one when my consciousness was extracted and downloaded into my new, enhanced body bioprinted to my personal specifications.

"Not news, exactly, but a proposed plan," I replied.

He motioned us toward the conference room adjacent to the bridge on the port side of the ship.

When we were seated around the table, I took a deep breath and spread my hands on the tabletop. "I know this is going to sound crazy, but I think we should go to the world that was first consumed by the Darkness."

Colren's eyes widened. "Why?"

"Well, we've only been to one world that was tainted, and that was when the Darkness was still in the process of spreading across the planet. With what we learned on Crystallis in the Archive, we now know the Darkness is some sort of alien invasion—transforming each planet to suit them. But we've never seen the finished product. If we go to one of the first worlds, we can see the result of the transformation, and maybe we can learn more about the enemy we're facing."

"While I don't disagree with the reasoning, it's a huge risk to go into that unknown environment," the commander replied after a slight pause.

"You brought us here to help. Shouldn't we be doing everything we can?" I pressed.

The commander shook his head. "Yes, but there are other factors."

It didn't take much to read between the lines. The Hegemony needed representatives from all three disciplines—Valor, Spirit, and Protection—to un-seal the Master Archive once the Darkness was defeated. Losing all of us would mean starting over. I hated to think of myself as replaceable, but the fact was that we were resources, not just people.

"What if two of us went to scout it?" Kaiden suggested, clearly thinking along the same lines as me.

"But the team—" Maris started to protest in a surprising turn from her earlier objections.

"I can't in good conscience send all four of you into a dangerous, unknown environment on a whim," Colren cut her off, firm.

I understood the commander's reasoning, but I didn't like it. We were stronger together, but I was desperate to have *any* forward progress, even if it meant only half of us got to go. "That might be a good compromise."

"Magic casting would be a good complement to Elle's skills," Kaiden continued. "Plus, we already have two Spirit casters, so that minimizes the risks."

Maris eyed the two of us. "Yeah, I'm sure that's the *only* reason the two of you want to go alone together."

My cheeks flushed in spite of myself. "This is about what's best for the mission."

"Sure," she muttered.

I couldn't tell if her reaction was coming from a place of envy about our relationship or just her incessant need to be contrary. Either way, I figured it was better to ignore her.

Colren steepled his fingers while he sat in thought. "Very well. That's a reasonable course of action," he agreed.

"Where is the first world, anyway?" Kaiden asked.

"The first planet touched by the Darkness was Windau," the commander replied, seemingly unfazed by the other comments. "It's one of the outer colony worlds—fewer than ten thousand residents."

I straightened in my seat. "How long did it take before the Hegemony realized what had happened to the world?"

"That was before my involvement in the matter," Colren stated. "As I understand it, several days passed. There was a report of a cloud in one of the crystals, and then it wasn't until a supply freighter arrived three days later that anyone outside realized the seriousness of the issue. The world was already fully shrouded in the Darkness."

"I guess it's time we find out what's happened on the surface in the three months since then," I said.

He inclined his head. "I was hesitant to suggest it myself, given the dangers, but an investigation does seem like the best course of action at present."

"And what about the alien ships?" Toran asked. "Can we help prepare?"

The commander folded his hands on the tabletop. "The accounts of your visions are everything we need at this time. The admiralty has already begun planning."

"The aliens are close. I know it," Toran murmured.

I shared his concerns about a potential invasion. However, as much as I wanted to prepare, we had no idea what timeline may have been attached to our visions. Beyond that, we didn't have a way to fight the aliens unless we got more information related to the Darkness. Our new recon mission was the best bet for both countering the Darkness and fighting whoever was behind it.

"We'll be ready," I tried to assure Toran, despite my own doubts.

His eyes revealed that he didn't believe the assertion, either, but he nodded.

"I'll make the jump arrangements to Windau," the commander said, rising from the table. "As always, thank you for the proactive attitude. I hate that all of our moves are now acts of last-resort, but I'm willing to try anything."

"We're committed to the cause," I replied.

He nodded absently then departed the conference room.

Kaiden sighed. "I already regret this."

Toran sat in silence for several moments. "It still unnerves me every time to see someone in Colren's position unsure about what to do."

"Can you imagine what it was like for him before we got here?" I asked. "He was in a command of a group who were sent down to planets and killed without warning. I don't blame him for wanting people to volunteer rather than order anyone to go into a dangerous situation."

"That's the job of a commander—to make those tough calls," Kaiden said.

"But we're not soldiers; we're private citizens. The most he can do is request we do something, unless it's an order related to him captaining this ship. I think we'll need to keep driving the investigation forward ourselves."

"It'd be great if some of that involved worlds *not* already overtaken by the Darkness," Maris interjected.

"Don't count on it. If Kaiden's and my upcoming field trip doesn't kill us, that means we'll have a lot more worlds we can explore," I replied.

Toran paled. "That means we could visit our homeworlds."

I nodded. "Not sure if I'm looking forward to that prospect or not."

"Let's not get ahead of ourselves," Kaiden cut in.

"Yeah, we have to survive our visit to the first planet." I rose from my seat.

Kaiden crossed his arms. "That's not what I meant."

"I know, I know. One planet at a time—systematic investigation and all that."

"The scientific method has been drilled into me, what can I say?" He cracked a smile, but it didn't touch his eyes.

"We'll get to the bottom of this. Soon." I took a deep breath. "Should we get out of here?"

Maris jumped to her feet. "Yes, please. The sooner you go do your thing, the better."

We headed for the exit.

"I wish we'd done this a week ago," I said.

"A week ago, I would have called you a crazy person," Kaiden replied.

I frowned. "Actually, I think you did when I first mentioned it—in those exact words, no less."

"That sounds about right."

We walked through the bridge and out to the main corridor.

"There's something I don't get," Maris said when we were in the empty hallway.

I looked over my shoulder at her. "What's that?"

"We got that shard of the Master Crystal... so, why haven't we done a universal reset?" she asked.

Kaiden and I exchanged glances.

"It would be pointless right now," Kaiden stated.

Maris placed her hands on her curvy hips. "But why?"

"Yes, the crystal gives us a control point," I replied. "That does no good, though, when we don't know where the Darkness is coming from. It would just spread again as soon as the reset is complete."

"But we know where it's going and what it will do," she insisted. "We can reset, evacuate the affected worlds, and then deal with the problem without everyone's bodies getting turned to black soot while their consciousness is who-knows-where."

I shook my head. "I don't think a universal-scale reset would be *nearly* that straightforward."

"Agreed," Toran broke his long silence. "Having worked on the interface stations for local crystals, I have a decent understanding of what it takes to get to an exact reset point. We have a crystal, but we *don't* have an interface console for it. If we attempt a reset, we won't have much control over where it resets *to*. Unless Colren knows something he hasn't shared with us."

"Can you make an interface?" I asked.

He released a long breath. "I could try. Unfortunately, the only way to test out if it works would be to use it."

I frowned. "And if it's wrong…"

"People could find themselves a decade too young, or it might be after the Darkness has already arrived," he continued. "That kind of reset would place enormous demand on the crystalline network—I'm not sure how it would respond. I also have no clear idea of what will happen to *us* at the epicenter. We could be unchanged, or we might end up back in our old bodies, too. This wouldn't be the kind of reset we're used to."

"Maris does have a point, though," Kaiden countered. "Wouldn't it be better to save people now if we can?"

"I'd think Colren would have jumped all over that idea if it was reasonable," I said.

"Agreed, and it's not just about the risks," Toran added. "There's also a large logistical component. If we were to reset with the intent of evacuating the affected worlds, where would all of those people go to?"

"And which worlds will the Darkness spread to next?" Kaiden added.

"Wasn't there information about that in the Archive?" Maris asked.

I nodded, thinking back on what we had been told regarding the information the Hegemony had been able to extract using their mysterious 'viewing' device. As far as I knew, they had been able to use the remote hyperdimensional link with the Archive to anticipate which worlds would be infected by the Darkness, but the information was too vague to draw conclusions about specific timing. "Not enough details," I replied. "We don't know how long it will take to stop this invasion, so if we were to start evacuating people, how long would we be able to keep moving them around to avoid the spreading Darkness?"

"Not to mention, is the crystal shard a one-time use thing, or do we get multiple shots to get it right?" asked Kaiden.

"Good question." I pursed my lips.

Toran took a deep breath. "Given that, I'd say we should wait to use the crystal shard as a last resort. If we *do* only get one shot, we would need to make it count."

"Yeah." I looked to him. "Maybe you should start working on a potential reset interface for the shard, just in case."

He inclined his head. "I suppose that would give me something to do while you and Kaiden go exploring."

"What about me?" Maris asked.

"I guess you get to go back to lounging around and doing whatever you do when we're not planetside," I replied flippantly.

Maris bristled. "I could use the time to test out my healing magic in the infirmary."

I wanted to ask her why she hadn't been doing that for the last week rather than repeatedly going over the same skills with us in an empty cargo hold, but I kept the comment and eye-roll to myself. "Sounds good," I replied instead.

"Jump in T-minus ten minutes," a female voice stated over the central intercom.

"The commander moved fast," Kaiden said.

"We should get to the jump pods." I picked up my pace down the corridor.

Toran took a deep breath and shook his head. "No turning back now."

I smiled. "Hey, you'll have it easy."

"Being the one left behind isn't always easier—too much time to think and worry," the large man replied.

Despite his tough exterior, it warmed my heart that Toran was such a caring guy on the inside. I really couldn't imagine having a better companion to watch my back. "We'll be in comm contact," I assured him.

"So we can learn in real-time if something goes horribly wrong. Great." Maris quipped.

I smirked. "Guess we'll just have to avoid it getting to that point, won't we?"

We descended the lift two decks to the level with our living quarters, lounge room, and jump pods. Several crew members were jogging down the hall toward their own pod rooms in preparation for the upcoming jump.

When we reached the pod room, we stripped off our outer clothes and weapons, storing the items in cubbies behind each pod. Hyperspace jumps were by far the most disorienting experience I'd had since leaving home. The first several jumps, I'd loathed getting into the pod. This time, however, I was excited—though nervous—to finally be taking proactive steps to stop the Darkness. Everything up to this point had been efforts to safeguard worlds so they could be restored after the menace was defeated, but I felt like we hadn't done anything to fight back. As risky as it was to visit an infected world, I hoped it would take us one step closer to defeating our faceless foe.

"See you on the other side." I reclined on the ergonomic couch in my pod.

"Can't wait." Kaiden smiled at me from the next pod over while he got settled in.

I secured my harness, then placed my arms at my sides and breathed steadily in preparation for the jump. Hyperspace was uncomfortable and disconcerting no matter how much I mentally prepared myself, but I'd found that being calm and centered did help minimize the bizarre synesthesia side effects.

The announcer gave a final countdown through the speaker in my pod as the translucent hatch extended to seal me inside. Moments later, I was pressed against the floor of the pod as we transitioned into hyperspace. My heart felt like it dropped into my feet and my vision blurred. I kept my breathing as slow and steady as I could throughout the jump, entering an almost dream-like state as we traveled without a clear sense of time passing.

When we finally arrived, the pod hatch retracted and I unbuckled my harness. Shaking slightly, I propped myself up on my elbows until my head stopped spinning, and then I sat up the rest of the way.

Kaiden had also roused. "Hey," he greeted.

"Hey yourself," I replied, climbing out of my pod.

"Ugh, I hate jumps," Maris groaned while sitting up in her pod across from me.

I steadied myself on my feet. "They really need a better jump system."

"The fact that FTL travel is possible at all is amazing," Toran interjected. He shimmed his broad shoulders through his pod's open top.

"Yeah, yeah." I stepped behind my pod to retrieve my clothing and weapons. I slipped the black pants over my white base layer and then donned the black, belted overcoat. Knee-high boots with purple accents and my Valor artifact—a sword—completed my ensemble.

I pulled my long, fuchsia hair outside the coat's collar when I'd finished dressing. "I hope Tami doesn't freak out when she learns we're taking another shuttle down to an infected world."

"Oh, I'm sure she'll be having a fit on the inside while never letting it show." Kaiden grinned.

"I don't envy her maintenance crew having to deal with the mess," Toran murmured.

"Hey, *we're* the ones who've been down on the frontlines," I pointed out.

He shook his head. "Elle, everything we've done up to this point is just a prelude. The real engagement is about to begin."

"Yeah, I guess it is."

Kaiden finished fastening his cloak. "You ready to do this?" he asked.

I placed my hand on my sword hilt. "I was literally made for this mission."

Kaiden raised an eyebrow. "Really, you went there?"

I shrugged. "Hey, who said you can't try to have some fun while saving the universe?"

THE FOUR OF us descended a lift to the hangar deck in the belly of the ship.

"You don't need to see us off," I said to Maris and Toran, whose mouths were contorted into scowls as we walked down the corridor.

"I still don't like the idea of breaking the team apart," Toran replied.

I shrugged. "This will just be a quick scouting mission."

Maris scoffed. "Yeah, on a planet where everything wants to kill you."

"If something goes wrong, we'll need people who are able to un-seal the Archive after this thing is defeated," Kaiden said.

"The likelihood of something *going* wrong increases exponentially if we don't stick together," the other man insisted.

I stopped and looked him over. "You know... we don't *have* to listen to the commander."

Toran raised an eyebrow. "Disobey orders and have the four of us go anyway?"

"They weren't 'orders' exactly," Kaiden mused.

"You two are going to get a hero complex if we don't keep you in line," Maris said while eyeing me and Kaiden.

"I have no objections," I said. While I'd been trying my best to act like a responsible adult, given the challenging circumstances we were facing, I was still the youngest on our team. If my older, wiser counterparts were okay bending the rules...

Kaiden nodded. "I'm all for keeping the team together."

We continued down the corridor until we reached the double doors leading into the hangar.

Technicians were in the process of completing a pre-flight check on our typical shuttle while the chief engineer, Tami, consulted a tablet nearby.

"Long time no see," I greeted when we were within earshot.

Tami looked up, her eyes bright. "Hey there. Do I want to know why we're prepping for a full decontamination protocol when you return?"

I smiled. "Probably not."

The engineer sighed. "You're going down to another infected world, aren't you?"

"The first one, in fact," I replied.

Her eyes widened. "We're at Windau?"

I raised an eyebrow. "That infamous, huh?"

"Probably not to others. I had family here," she revealed.

"Oh, I'm sorry."

She forced a smile. "Hey, each of us have family and friends at risk. All the more reason for us to work together to beat this thing."

"Do you ever get ruffled, Tami?" I asked. "When we've trashed a ship you've stayed calm, and even now you seem so collected."

The engineer laughed. "Oh, Elle, when you've seen as much crazy shit as I have over the years, you learn to keep things in perspective."

I cocked my head. "And what perspective is that?"

"If you're not going to die in the next five seconds, things could always be worse."

"Can't argue with that," Kaiden agreed.

She nodded. "So, the commander said just two of you are heading down, right?"

"Change of plans," I lied. "All four of us are going after all."

"Stronger together," Toran added.

Tami looked us over. "This is probably something else I shouldn't ask about, huh?"

"We're just striving to give ourselves the best possible chance to succeed," I replied.

"Complementary skillsets, and all that," Maris chimed in.

"Well, your four packs are already in the common area of the shuttle, in addition to pressurized hazsuits for each of you," Tami said.

"Maybe just wait to report our departure to the commander until we've left," I advised.

She rolled her eyes. "Yeah, I figured that was coming."

"You're the best, Tami." I grinned.

"Better make this trip worthwhile." She backed away from the shuttle. "Safe travels. I'll give you a five-minute head start."

Kaiden ascended the ramp. "Plenty of time."

"Not like anyone else would be able to follow us, anyway." I followed him on board.

We passed through the compact common area where our supply backpacks had been arranged near the built-in dining table, and then continued down a short corridor on the starboard side to the bridge. I took my typical seat in the front right while Kaiden took the pilot's seat on the left, with Maris behind him and Toran behind me. The shuttle's automated systems would normally do most of the work, but the unique properties of the Darkness had a bad tendency to interfere with the navigation and stabilizer systems. If this planet was anything like the others, Kaiden would likely have to take manual control.

"What's the plan?" I asked. "Risk landing the shuttle or set it to drop us off and come back later?"

"I maintain that landing it would be bad," Toran stated.

"But if we need to make a quick escape, we'd be trapped," Kaiden countered.

I nodded. "That's what I was thinking, too. Except, what if we *do* land the shuttle and need to make a quick escape, but the vessel has been compromised and we can't use it anyway?"

"That's assuming we need to land at all," Maris pointed out. "We can learn a lot just by flying around."

"True," I admitted. "I guess we can play it by ear."

"Because things never go poorly when we do that." Kaiden buckled his flight harness.

"You have another idea?" I asked.

"Nope, just laying the foundation for a future 'I told you so'."

I rolled my eyes. "This relationship is off to a great start."

Maris raised an eyebrow. "Trouble in paradise already?"

"*Nothing* about this is paradise," I shot back.

"Wow, thanks." Kaiden started up the engines.

"I don't mean you, just the situation." I reached over to pat his knee. "*You're* great."

"None of this is relevant," Maris huffed.

I glanced at her over my shoulder. "Sorry, but I can't promise new relationship-y stuff won't creep in now and again."

"Oh, well aware of that." Maris crossed her arms.

I couldn't tell if her exasperation stemmed from this exchange directly or if it was a more general frustration with the position we had been placed in with the Hegemony, but I owed it to the team to minimize drama. We were risking our lives, and the last thing any of us needed was unrelated interpersonal dynamics getting in the way of the mission. Nonetheless, Kaiden and I had already crossed a threshold by admitting we had feelings for each other that went beyond professional comradery. Neither of us seemed interested in going back to how things were before, so we'd have to find a balance between team morale and our own desires. Since it'd only been a week, we hadn't worked out exactly what that would be.

All I knew for sure is that out of all the people I'd met, he was the only one worth the effort. If that relationship could give me one shred of normalcy amid all the other craziness, I felt I could be that much more effective doing what I'd need to do. The fact that the 'normal relationship' was with someone who'd manifested magical abilities was beside the point.

The shuttle followed autopilot commands across the hangar and through the electrostatic field out into space. Only blackness and distant stars were visible at first, but then the shuttle arced over the bow of the *Evangiel* and the planet of Windau came into view.

Previous worlds I'd encountered that had been consumed by the Darkness had ribbons of swirling black snaking through the atmosphere, muting the normal luminescence of the planets against the dark backdrop of the void. In frightening contrast, I could hardly recognize this world as a planet at all. The Darkness blanketed every centimeter of the world, almost as though ominous clouds from a horrific thunderstorm now covered the entire planet. Unlike a storm, there were no flashes of lightning or calm patches of sky to break it up, only marbled shades of black and dark gray.

"I suddenly feel much less-good about heading down there." I gulped.

Kaiden shook his head. "Pictures couldn't do this justice."

"Why did I ever agree to come?" Maris moaned.

"Because that's the last place anyone should go alone," Toran stated. "We need to look out for each other—that's why we are a team."

"All the same, sorry for talking you into my crazy idea," I said.

"We had no leads about how to stop this thing. You're not wrong that a more hands-on approach might give us a clue," Kaiden replied.

Toran grunted behind me. "And here we thought our role might end when we sealed the Archive."

"Did we *really*, though?" Kaiden countered.

"As soon as Commander Colren said we had a special immunity to the Darkness, I figured we were in this for the long haul," I said.

Maris sighed. "Just my luck to be placed on a team of people who run toward the danger rather than from it."

I smiled. "We have a chance to make a difference. Not many people get the opportunity to save an entire civilization."

"Elle, your hero complex is showing," Kaiden joked.

"Right, like I'm the only one in this shuttle who gets any satisfaction out of saving the day."

"It's true," Toran admitted. "If I can't be with my family, then I want to take an active role in making our worlds safe for them again."

"Yeah, but there's trying to solve a problem, and then there's going *into that*." Kaiden made a sweeping gesture toward the planet below us.

"Yet, you were the first to agree to come with me." I eyed him with a playful smirk. "Don't deny that part of you likes the thrill of danger."

"There is something empowering about venturing into the unknown," he admitted.

Maris nodded. "Well, yeah! Why else do you think I came along?"

I chuckled. "All right, so all of us are a little crazy."

"More than a little, by my estimation," Toran replied. "Some might say we have a death wish, visiting a planet like this."

"Nah, we've got this." I grinned.

"Pretty sure that casual dismissal is exactly what would make people call us crazy in the first place," Kaiden pointed out.

"Without that attitude, we'd still be back on the *Evangiel* and the Archive wouldn't be sealed."

"I suppose you're right," he agreed.

"Too late to turn back now," Toran muttered when a glow formed around the shuttle as the nose pushed through the outer layers of the corrupted atmosphere.

The comm on the front console flashed, accompanied by a beep.

"Shuttle 1, the four of you going was *not* the plan," Commander Colren stated tersely.

Kaiden and I exchanged glances. He shook his head and sighed.

I pressed the comm controls. "We decided we were stronger as a team," I said.

"Then you should have maintained that point in our meeting earlier," the commander replied. "Changing plans without expressing that intent is a great way to get yourselves killed."

"It seemed like a better idea five minutes ago," I mumbled.

"It's reckless. Turn back now," he instructed.

"With all due respect, Commander, no," Kaiden stated. "To beat this thing, we need more information. Our best chance of getting the insights we need is by investigating the planet, and sticking together as a team is how we'll do that safely. Yes, we agreed, and then we went behind your back, which was wrong. However, wasting time arguing isn't going to accomplish what we need to do any faster. We're taking action, because that's what the situation requires. We could have gone about doing that in a more 'official' way, but the outcome would be the same."

Colren sighed. "I suppose I shouldn't be surprised that you take advantage of the fact that I have no direct command authority over you."

"Nothing personal," I said. "We just want to see this through as quickly as possible."

"I can't fault you for that. Just... please don't run off again in the future."

"Yes, sorry. It won't happen again," I assured him with the full intent of keeping my word, though I was well aware that circumstances could change at any moment.

"Be careful down there," the commander added. "We'll be awaiting your safe return." He ended the commlink.

"So it begins..." Kaiden said melodramatically.

The shuttle shuddered as the high-altitude air currents swirled around our tiny vessel.

Toran gripped his armrest. "I must trust in the belief that this is what we're supposed to do."

"Yes, definitely going to keep telling myself that." I cinched my restraints tighter and then gripped my own armrest as another jolt wracked our shuttle.

As much as I did want to be a hero, I couldn't shake the nagging doubt at the back of my mind that I was hopelessly out of my depth. We'd won a handful of fights and had successfully sealed the Master Archive, but those few activities didn't make us seasoned pros. I hoped my grand aspirations would make up for some of what I lacked in practical skills and experience, though I knew my ambition would catch up to me eventually. With any luck, others would be there to help me make it through whatever ordeals I might face.

As we descended through the atmosphere, the oppressive Darkness seemed to close in around us. My heart leaped every time the shuttle jostled in the turbulence. Worse, my inability to see more than a few hundred meters ahead through the black clouds gave me a strange sense of claustrophobia I'd never experienced before.

"How close are we to the ground?" I asked Kaiden.

He shook his head, concern knitting his brow. "I can't tell."

"That seems bad," Maris commented from the seat behind him.

"The ground appears to be quite unstable," Toran reported. I glanced over my shoulder and saw him consulting the workstation along the starboard bulkhead behind me; a planetary model was displayed on the screen. "The mass and density of this world is not what it should be."

"We encountered that before, right?" I said, thinking back to the planet where I'd fought the dragon for my sword Valor artifact. At the time, I'd hoped that the planet had naturally lower gravity than the small handful of other worlds I'd encountered during my brief travels. However, the more we experienced the ravages of the Darkness, the more I was convinced that the infection changed the very composition of the worlds.

"Yeah, but this is far more pronounced," Kaiden said.

"It's been months," Toran replied. "Whatever we witness here is likely a preview for what to expect on the other infected worlds."

"Is the Darkness hollowing them out?" Maris questioned.

I shook my head. "No idea. But I'd really like to know what the end game is." No matter the methods of the planetary transformation, mass just didn't disappear; it had to have gone somewhere. Given everything we'd observed, whatever was controlling the transformation of the infected planets seemed to follow a set of rules. If we could learn enough, we might be able to gain control of that system so we could put everything back to how it was supposed to be. Just as importantly, we could make sure it could never happen again.

Toran didn't say anything more on the matter, which I took as a bad sign under the circumstances. As the most scientifically minded member of our team, I relied on him to be the voice of reason when it came to throwing out random hypotheses related to what alien force we were up against. It was worrisome that he had no commentary on the bizarre conditions, even though geophysics was somewhat far afield from his engineering background. If even he and Kaiden were out of their depth, then anything I might say on the scientific front may as well be pure fantasy.

We continued the descent in silence for another minute until the occasional jolts wracking the vessel turned into constant rattling.

"Nav system is glitching," Kaiden reported. "It's just like what happened on the other worlds—can't maintain a lock." He took the manual controls.

"We need to set down," Maris said.

"I advise against setting down at random," Toran cautioned. "The ground is too unstable in some places to support the shuttle's weight."

"Plus, the entire point in coming here is to look for clues," I added. "We should try to find one of the crystal monuments."

Toran nodded. "Agreed. Since the Darkness appears to spread through the crystalline network, studying one of the monuments makes the most sense."

Kaiden focused on the controls. "I'm flying blind here, so start searching!"

"Already working on it," Toran replied. "I'm vetting reaction pings from prospective crystals."

I swiveled around in my seat to give him a questioning gaze. "Don't you need Kaiden's or Maris' pendant for that?"

"I've been busy for the past week figuring out how to make it work remotely," he responded without taking his attention from the monitor.

The search method he'd devised using one of the caster pendants and the ship's sensor suite had allowed us to locate sites by pinpointing the concentrated energy signatures associated with crystals. Previously, one of the pendants needed to be placed in a cradle on the device for it to work. Toran's new innovation would certainly make our new searches more convenient.

"There are several strong signatures around the planet, but the closest is ten kilometers to the northeast," Toran continued. "I believe it may be the crystal that serviced the capital city."

"Sounds like a great place to start," I said.

"Let's do it," Kaiden agreed. "Send me the coordinates."

Toran relayed the location to the nav console, and Kaiden identified the point on the holographic map that was overlaid on the front viewport.

"This should be easy to get to," he said while redirecting the shuttle's course toward the new destination.

"It's getting back *out* that worries me," Maris muttered. As much as I wanted to project an aura of self-assurance, I had the same fears.

We sped through the blackness outside the viewport. As we neared the destination, Kaiden decelerated and directed the shuttle toward the ground. However, even as we descended, there was no ground in sight. My heart lodged in my throat as the readings on the proximity sensors continued to jump around.

"Shouldn't we have touched down already?" I asked.

"Yes," Kaiden acknowledged, confirming my worries. "Prior comments aside, we can still bail."

"No, we owe it to our loved ones to vanquish this menace," Toran replied.

"Yeah, no risk, no reward," I said.

Kaiden took a slow breath. "All right." He inched the shuttle downward.

Out the front viewport, the blackness around us began to take on more definition. I squinted into the dim surroundings, trying to make sense of the forms. "What is that out there?"

I reached forward to adjust the overlay settings, hoping to increase the contrast so we could navigate by sight. After fiddling with the slider for several seconds, the view out the viewport took on an amber hint, which brought out previously hidden details in our surroundings. My chest constricted as I realized we had descended into a chasm with steep cliffs rising at least a hundred meters above us.

Kaiden sucked in a sharp breath. "That's not good."

"How did we miss ground level?" Toran mused.

"No idea. Up. Now." I pointed toward the sky.

"Don't need to say it twice." He hit the yoke to gain elevation. The shuttle continued to descend.

My stomach turned over. "Why aren't we...?"

Kaiden paled. "I think we're trapped."

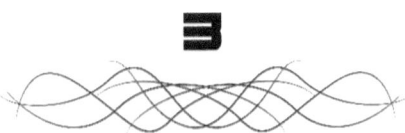

I SWALLOWED HARD. "We can't be trapped."

"Well, the shuttle isn't responding." Concern pitched Kaiden's voice while he continued trying to direct the craft upward. Despite throttling the engine, the vessel continued to descend deeper into the black chasm.

"What's pulling us down?" I asked, panic setting in.

"I don't know!" Kaiden's hands raced over the controls.

Maris' face drained. "Is it, like, a gravity well or something?"

"I don't think it works like that," I muttered in reply.

"The sensors aren't picking up anything in our surroundings to indicate we're trapped in such an anomaly. This shuttle's engines are strong enough to break orbit, so there's no reason we'd be unable to pull away now," Toran explained.

"Unless we've been tethered," Kaiden said.

My heart skipped a beat. "By *what*?"

"I don't know, but see if you can identify anything." Kaiden continued fighting with the controls. The shuttle swayed side to side, but it was unable to gain any elevation.

I used the console in front of me to bring up detailed sensor data around the shuttle, including pressure points on the hull that may indicate a grapple. The aft frame of the vessel did appear to be stressed, though I couldn't make out a singular point where an anchor might be tethered. "Does this thing have a rear-view camera?"

"Not for close-range observation," Kaiden replied.

"Then we'll need to get a look the old-fashioned way." I unbuckled my harness.

His eyes widened. "Where are you going?"

"To look out the rear airlock," I replied, bracing myself on my seatback as the shuttle rocked. "Hold it steady."

"Elle, don't—"

"I convinced all of you to come down here, so I better figure out what's preventing us from going home." I jogged toward the common area with my arms outstretched to either side to catch myself as the shuttle bucked. My heart pounded in my ears. It was my fault we were in the mess. I couldn't let anything bad happen to my friends, especially not before we had a chance to accomplish our mission.

I passed by our packs and the four hazsuits on my way to the aft airlock beyond the sleeping cabins. If things took a turn for the worse, those suits might be the only thing standing between us and the unstable environment... Not that I had a lot of faith that the thin material would last long against the corrosive properties of the Darkness.

At the end of the corridor running the length of the shuttle, the airlock entry door was sealed. I checked the panel to confirm it was pressurized and then opened it. The outside hatch had a one-meter-wide square viewport at its center, and I pressed my face against the thick plastic to see if I could spot whatever seemed to be tethering us inside the chasm.

To my horror, a thick, vine-like structure appeared to be wrapping itself around the shuttle. The vines thickened toward the base, though I couldn't make out the anchor point through the blackness. "Hey, guys! There's a bad thing going on back here," I shouted toward the bridge.

"What do you see?" Kaiden shouted back.

"Black vines, or something," I replied.

A moment later, I heard the heavy thud of footsteps, and Toran came into view down the corridor. He squeezed into the airlock next to me, motioning me aside so he could look outside.

"Stars!" he exclaimed. "What is that?"

"Certain death... if I'm not being overly dramatic."

He frowned. "That's a little too on-point to be a joke."

I looked down, all too aware of my predisposition for ill-timed humor. "We need to detach it," I said to get us back in the right headspace.

"I have no idea what to suggest, given we don't know what that *is*."

"Cut it?" I suggested.

"With what? We need to use a laser cutter from a completely different angle."

"To cut the tendrils from the base, yeah. But what about sheering them off from where they're attached to the shuttle?"

He examined me. "What do you have in mind?"

"What if we make it impossible for the vine-things to grip the hull?"

"Like an electrified fence?"

"Yeah, along those lines."

"That general idea could work if we had time to play around with it, but it's too risky to try as a one-shot."

"What else, then?" I asked.

Before Toran could reply, Kaiden shouted again from the bridge. "What's going on back there?"

"Trying to figure out how to sever the evil, alien vine-things," I shouted back. I returned my attention to Toran. "If we can't science this thing on short notice, then it'll come down to magic."

He nodded. "But how?"

I shrugged. "Giant fireball?"

"Sounds like a job for Kaiden."

"It does, but he's flying." I braced myself as the shuttle rocked. "Do you know enough from your engineering classes to take over for a few minutes?"

Toran scowled. "Not really, but I suspect we may not have another option."

There were two more possibilities—either Maris could try offensive magic, or I could—but neither one of us had Kaiden's degree of control. Given the surgical nature of the task at hand, I decided against voicing the alternatives. "Take over in the bridge and get him back here. I'll get a suit ready."

The large man nodded, then took off toward the bridge.

I followed him as far as the common room, where I started putting on one of the hazsuits and unfurled another so it would be easy for Kaiden to don. He appeared in the common room just as I'd secured my suit up to my hips.

"What are you doing?" he asked.

"Getting ready."

He warily examined the suit. "For what?"

"You use a fireball or lightning, and I slash and make sure the vine-things don't snatch you. Easy."

Kaiden picked up the prepped suit and frowned. "And where are we going to do this from?"

"The back airlock," I replied.

"Elle, that's crazy!"

The shuttle rocked again, knocking me into the dining table. I caught myself and used my hands to steady myself until the ship's internal stabilizers compensated. "Sounds like a better plan than waiting until the tendrils either pull us all the way to the bottom of the chasm or we run out of fuel."

He started dressing. "Point taken."

I slipped my arms into my hazsuit's sleeves. "Gotta say, this isn't what I had in mind when I suggested we come down here."

"Really? Because I figured we'd be screwed."

"Oh, I did, too, but I was thinking more like tar pits or shadow beasts, not giant tentacle monsters."

"Wait, you said vines…"

"Yes, but I have no idea what they're attached to. I thought maybe it would sound better to say we were being attacked by a giant monster rather than being eaten by a demon plant."

Kaiden stared at me with disbelief. "How would that be *any* better?"

"Now that I say it out loud—"

"Never mind." He slipped the hazsuit helmet over his head and then grabbed his magic staff. "Let's try to get free."

I finished securing my own helmet, grabbed my sword, and then quickly followed Kaiden into the aft airlock. We sealed the interior door and then pressurized the compartment to the outside. When the indicator light turned green, Kaiden released the rear hatch.

The roar of the shuttle's engine filled the chamber, and a gust of wind knocked me backward. I gripped one of the handholds near the hatch opening with my right hand and readied my sword in my left. The black vines made no motion in our direction.

Kaiden's mouth fell open as he took in the sight of the alien tendrils writhing around our vessel.

"Blast 'em," I urged.

"Those things could take us out in a second!"

"That's why we need to get to them first!"

He shook his head. "No way I can blast them in one go."

"Do your best. I'm here in case they try to counter-attack. We need to try."

Kaiden looked far from convinced, but he nodded. With one hand gripping the wall inside the airlock, he directed his staff toward the most concentrated bundle of black vines. A flaming, blue orb formed on the end of his staff. When it had swelled to twice the side of Kaiden's head, he released the fireball into the blackness.

The orb struck its mark and exploded in a flash, scattering smaller blue flames throughout the vines. In each place touched by the flames, the vines spasmed, but no tendrils appeared to have been severed and none released from the ship.

"Try again," I said.

Kaiden cast another fireball, even larger this time, but it was just as ineffective. "We need to try something else."

"Yeah, you're right." Without hesitation, I locked in my grip on the handhold and then swung my body outward behind the shuttle. Following with the momentum, I slashed with my sword arm toward the nearest vines affixed to the hull.

My blade sliced through the vines, and the severed segments fell away into the blackness below. The ruined ends of the vines, however, lashed out toward me. I swung back into the comparative safety of the airlock just in time to avoid one of the vines whipping toward my sword arm.

Kaiden quickly hurled a fireball toward the vines, and they recoiled.

"Thanks." I smiled at him before taking a cautious look out the open hatch. The ends of the vines were re-forming into points where I had sliced them off. "Stars! These things don't quit."

"Shit, we never should have come down here. No more indulging your crazy ideas!"

"Hey, I wouldn't have suggested it if I expected *this*." I slashed at the vines as they stabbed toward us, slicing them off again.

"Any other ideas for how to get us out?" Fear filled Kaiden's eyes.

We'd faced some terrifying things in our brief time together, but we'd always at least had solid ground underfoot. To have our one means of escaping the planet now grappled by the alien force placed us in a totally new kind of danger. I didn't want this to be the end. We needed to find a way back to safety.

"My blade works against them," I said, trying to suppress my own fear and doubt. "I just need better reach."

Kaiden's eyes widened. "You can't be serious!"

"I need a way to get out there and cut that big one. The shuttle might be able to break free of the others."

"No." He shook his head. "No way. You couldn't hold on through that."

"I won't have to if I'm tied down."

"But the engines—"

"Shut them down, I swing out and do my thing, then use the EVA winch to pull me back in, and Toran punches it."

"Elle..."

"There's no time to argue."

Kaiden swallowed, then activated the suit's comm since he couldn't touch the integrated comm behind his ear. "Maris, get to the interior airlock door. We need you to cast a protective shell."

"See?" I said. "I'll be in a safe, happy bubble." Despite my attempt to make light of the situation, the notion of swinging out behind the shuttle terrified me. But what scared me more was being drawn down into the blackness where the tendrils were coming from.

"What the...?" Maris' voice filled my helmet as she stared out the interior airlock viewport at the scene.

"Elle has gone mad," Kaiden stated. "But her plan might be the only thing that can save us right now."

I grabbed the end of the winch tether outside the airlock and secured the control belt around my waist. "A shield would be great."

Maris gaped at me for a second, then nodded. She waved her hand and a translucent purple shell appeared around me. "Be careful."

"Yeah, that runs contrary to this entire maneuver." I altered the suit's comm to include the whole team. "Toran, I'm going to need you to cut the engines on my mark."

"But that will—" he started to object.

"I need to sever these vines and I'd rather not be incinerated in the process," I cut in. A new wave of snaking vines were rising from the depths; they'd reach the shuttle within twenty seconds, and then my swordsmanship might not be enough. I prepared to leap from the door. "Kaiden, follow with fireballs behind me so the severed ends can't grab hold while I swing."

"You don't have to."

I looked him in the eyes. "This is our only move." I shifted my gaze down to the approaching vines. "Ready, Toran?"

"Standing by."

"Cut the engines!" The roar ceased. In the sudden silence, I dove from the hatch into a freefall toward the black depths. Ten meters out, I hit the winch's brake using the control belt. The cable went taut, causing me to swing in an arc toward the bundle of tendrils. I slashed through as many as I could reach with my sword as I swung by. The slicing-resistance of the blade slowed my trajectory, and by the time I reached the thickest of the strands, I was only able to cut halfway through. I could only hope it would be enough.

Kaiden's fireballs blasted behind me and the shuttle was losing elevation without its engines firing. There was no way I could try for another pass.

I hit the winch controls to reel me in at maximum speed. Despite the short distance I had to go, the shuttle was falling too fast, and I wouldn't be able to make it back inside before the craft would be snared by the tendrils once more.

"Go now!" I shouted to Toran. Maris' shield had withheld fire breathed from a dragon at close range, so hopefully it would protect me from the engine's wash.

"Wait!" Kaiden shouted, but Toran had already activated the thrusters.

The waist belt dug into me as the shuttle pulled away from the remaining black vines, breaking free when I was still three meters out as the winch reeled me in. Heat from the engines hit me like I'd stepped into an oven, despite the shield and the protective layer from the hazsuit. Fortunately, the winch was positioned far enough from the engines that the cable wasn't in the direct path of the exhaust, and the mechanism was able to reel me in the rest of the way.

Gripping a handhold inside the doorframe, Kaiden extended his free hand to help me inside. "That was some move!" he said as his hand wrapped securely around my wrist.

I grinned up at him while I scrambled inside. "I swear I wasn't trying to show off."

"Nice work and all, but we have other problems," Maris said over the comm.

I looked up at her still staring through the viewport, pointing behind us. Looking over my shoulder, my stomach dropped as I saw the walls of the chasm closing in.

"HURRY!" KAIDEN PULLED me the rest of the way into the airlock. He hit the hatch controls the moment my feet were inside.

"Get us out of here, Toran!" I shouted over the comm.

"I'm trying!" he replied with a frantic tone that made it clear he'd seen the walls inexplicably closing in.

I slammed against the side wall of the airlock as the shuttle apparently changed direction. Out in the corridor, Maris cried out as she toppled away from the door. Kaiden struck the wall next to me. I pawed the side wall, searching for a secure handhold.

The shuttle tilted upward as we started to climb. The shuttle jolted twice, then I sensed smooth acceleration as the black pit receded behind us.

"We're clear!" Toran cheered.

I rose to my feet and released my helmet. "Okay, yeah, that was *not* part of my plan."

Kaiden removed his own helmet and hugged me. "Are you okay?"

"Yeah, I think so." I checked myself over, seeing no apparent injury. "It all happened so fast. I didn't think."

Kaiden's sky blue eyes shone with concern. "Elle, you can't throw yourself out an airlock like that."

"I had no interest in finding out what the tentacle monster had in store for us."

"Well…" He faded out. "I was worried I was going to lose you."

"You won't get rid of me that easily." I leaned close, staring into his eyes until he relaxed. His lips met mine in a reassuring kiss.

The ship shuddered, bringing us back to our surroundings.

I pulled away from Kaiden. "We should get back to the bridge."

"Yes, please!" Toran replied over our ear comms.

My pulse spiked. I checked the comms and realized that we'd left the channel open. Maris and Toran had been free to listen in on our private exchange. "Be right there," I muttered, then muted the channel.

Through the inner airlock door's viewport, Maris smirked at us before turning to walk back toward the bridge.

Kaiden sighed. "They heard that?"

"And saw, apparently." I shook my head. "Well, us being a couple isn't a revelation."

"No, but making out in the airlock in the middle of a mission isn't 'keeping things professional' like we agreed."

"That was hardly 'making out'."

"You know what I mean."

"In all fairness, we just almost died," I stated. "A celebratory moment is allowed."

Kaiden stripped off his hazsuit. "We'll need to do more of that once we're not almost-dying."

I smiled coyly. "I like that plan."

"Again, really don't know how to fly this thing…" Toran said over the shuttle's central comm.

"Sorry, on my way!" Kaiden replied, then hit the inner airlock door. It hissed open and he jogged into the corridor.

"What's the plan now?" I asked, following him.

"We have a decision to make: either proceed with an investigation, or head back to the *Evangiel* and apologize for being foolhardy."

"That second option doesn't sound like our style."

"I figured you'd say that." Kaiden entered the bridge, and Toran rose from the pilot's chair. "Thanks for getting us out of there," Kaiden said, taking over the controls.

"What happened back there?" Toran asked while he returned to his own seat behind mine.

"Angry foliage," Maris replied.

Toran screwed up his face. "What?"

"The vine-things that may or may not have been monster tentacles,"

I clarified.

"This place is a nightmare," Toran muttered.

"We're going back to the *Evangiel*, right?" Maris asked.

I buckled into my seat next to Kaiden. "We came here to do research, and we haven't learned anything useful yet."

"There was a pretty resounding message of 'this place is terrible',"
Maris shot back.

"And what good does that do us for stopping the Darkness? We still need to get access to one of the crystals," I insisted.

Maris crossed her arms. "What's to stop more of the vines from roping us in as soon as we get close to the surface?"

"I think those were just in the chasm," Kaiden chimed in, though his tone was distant. "I can't believe I didn't see it before."

I turned my attention to him. "See what?"

"The pattern of the Darkness' impact isn't random," he explained. "Look at it." He motioned toward the front viewport, which was still tinted amber. "We must have already been down in the chasm when you activated the filter, but seeing it now, it's so obvious."

I examined the surrounding landscape, mystified. There *was* a strange order to it all, and not in the way I would have expected. The chasm we'd escaped was part of a larger canyon that encircled the remains of what appeared to be Windau's capital city. An even larger canyon surrounded the inner canyon, and another beyond that. Each were perfectly formed circles, too precise to appear natural and certainly not random. However, the presence of the mysterious, concentric circles alone didn't catch my eye as much as the way tendrils of Darkness flowed outward from a central point in the city like spokes on a wheel; we had crossed through one spoke and been snared.

"What is it?" I scrunched up my nose.

"I have no idea," Kaiden murmured.

Maris wrapped her arms around herself. "I retract my endorsement for coming here. This is all wrong."

"It's so ordered…" Toran mused, seemingly lost in his own thoughts. "I always thought of the Darkness as chaotic, but the precision of this pattern suggests a high level of refinement and intelligence."

"Great, so whatever aliens are behind it are smart and organized." I sighed. "Question is, can we go to the epicenter of the activity without getting attacked?"

"I guess the only way to tell is the test it out," Kaiden replied. "Maybe we can start by bringing the shuttle into one of the more open areas to see if the vine-tendril things react to our presence?"

"Sounds much better than going into the middle and getting trapped again," I said.

"So, the hypothesis is that the tendrils will find a way to maintain connections through their path no matter what and we just got in the way?" Toran clarified.

I shrugged. "Unless you have any other ideas."

"I do not," he replied. "I can't say I have any solid ideas about anything at the moment. The behavior of our foe has caught me by surprise."

"I'm not sure what I was expecting, either, but I'm with you—I somehow thought it would be more chaotic."

"Exactly. For a bunch of swirling, black smoke, this almost looks like it's programmed."

I hesitated. "But that's crazy, right?"

"No crazier than us manifesting magical abilities. DNA is just a set of biological instructions. Granted, transforming a planet is more complicated than directing the growth of a plant, but the processes are hypothetically the same."

"So, the Darkness is some kind of biotech?" Maris asked.

Kaiden shrugged. "Maybe. It's all speculation until we take a closer look."

"Speaking of which," I frowned at the scene outside the viewport, "how *are* we supposed to do that, given the tentacle-vine-monsters?"

"Well, if our problems before were, in fact, caused by interrupting the energy flow, then we should fare much better if we set down in an open area," Kaiden replied.

"Except, when we visited an infected planet before, creatures came to attack us," I pointed out.

"They were moving before they saw us," he countered. "Maybe we were standing in their travel path and that caused the attack."

"It's a big assumption to think that they'll stay out of our way if we leave them alone," Toran chimed in.

"Not saying they will *entirely*, just that they may be less… aggressive,"

Kaiden clarified.

"Anything we say is a guess," I stated the obvious. "We already committed to seeing this through, so arguing about whether or not we might die is kinda pointless."

"We, collectively, seem to make terrible decisions," Maris observed.

"As a result, we keep being reckless and doing things no sane person would do." Kaiden sighed.

"Is it crazy, or heroic?" I asked.

Toran shook his head. "I've absolutely no clue."

"Debates for another time. We need to land," Kaiden interjected.

"Right. The part about not dying." I surveyed the landscape. "You said we need an open spot away from the bands of Darkness, right? What about the triangular patch beyond that wall-like structure?" I pointed toward what appeared to be a former field, or perhaps a plaza; it was impossible to tell which, given how much the Darkness had transformed the surroundings. What I could make out, however, was that the city's crystal was at the hub of the twisting, black tendrils which now pervaded the landscape.

"We'll be surrounded, but that also means we won't have to get around those dark tendrils on foot," Kaiden said.

"No need to convince me," Toran replied.

Maris nodded. "Let's get this over with."

"Going in." Kaiden directed the shuttle toward the fairly open area I had identified.

The craft pitched and rolled on the turbulent winds as we came in for the landing. I gripped my armrest while I tried to keep my breathing slow and even. As frightening as the wild shuttle ride was, I suspected that it was nothing compared to the horrors we'd face on the surface; the tentacle monster in the trench had made that clear.

As we neared the landing site, the details in the twisted landscape became clearer. I realized that the dark tendrils fanning out from the central crystal weren't solid objects, as I had thought from a distance, but were rather a steady flow of tiny black particulates—the same fine cloud I'd witnessed in the canyon crystal on my homeworld shortly before I'd been recruited by the Hegemony. In fact, very little in the environment looked to be completely solid, with even former buildings and vegetation appearing to be riddled with holes that resulted in a sponge-like texture.

The oddity supported the other evidence about lighter gravity—and reduced planetary mass, by extension—but it still offered no explanation for *where* that extra material had gone. For as thoroughly as the Darkness had consumed the planet, there was no outward evidence of it extending into space or elsewhere.

Kaiden deftly maneuvered the shuttle into position above the plaza and directed it straight down. "Stars willing, nothing will swallow us..." he murmured while descending the final meters.

I held my breath and braced.

The shuttle bumped slightly and then all was still. Out the front viewport, the dark tendrils were unchanged. For now, the Darkness appeared to be ignoring us.

I unstrapped my flight harness and jumped to my feet. "Clock's ticking. This nasty stuff might eat a hole through our ship or clothes."

"I'll get my supplies." Toran raced ahead of me toward the common room.

Kaiden and Maris exchanged glances. "We'll need as much protection as we can get," Kaiden told her.

She nodded. "I'll do what I can."

My stomach flopped. We were out of our minds to enter this kind of environment, but we didn't have any other choice. With no way to learn anything remotely, we needed direct access to that central crystal. Though I wished circumstances were different, it was better to make the most of it rather than dwell on thoughts of alternatives that could never be.

I rushed into the common room to gather my own hazsuit and pack of supplies. "These suits are already tainted," I grumbled while slipping on the garment I'd used several minutes earlier. "There's no way we can retain any sort of contamination containment."

"Yeah, I figured that would be a losing battle the moment we agreed to come here," Kaiden replied with a weak smile.

Maris paled. "Let's hope legend holds and we *do* have an immunity."

I strapped my sword over the hazsuit. "Hey, if nothing else, we'll find out quickly." I wasn't sure if my own words were comforting or not. While a swift death would be preferable in theory, there was no telling what it might feel like to be turned into a column of ash, especially when one's final thoughts would be about how the mission had failed. I shook my head, chastising myself. That kind of thinking wasn't productive.

The others were uncomfortably quiet after my statement, likely running through similar scenarios to my own bleak vision of what our final moments might be like.

"We're going to make it through this," I said. "It won't stop us this easily."

"That's right." Toran looked around the room. "Is everyone ready?"

I checked the seals on my suit. "Ready."

Kaiden and Maris nodded, their suits secured and supply packs slung over their shoulders.

"Let's go." Toran led the way into the airlock and cycled it once we were all inside.

My breath was loud in my ears inside the suit while I waited the ten seconds for the outside hatch to open. Finally, it released with a hiss.

Without the roar of the shuttle's engine to drown out the surroundings, I was struck by how quiet the planet was. Wind whipped through the open hatch, but there were no other audible sounds emanating from the mysterious black tendrils or anything else nearby.

"Be careful out there," Maris said. She waved her hand, and translucent purple shells appeared around each of us.

"Thanks." Steeling myself, I hopped out of the shuttle onto the black ground. My feet sank in five centimeters as the aerated ground compressed beneath my boots. I took several firm steps to make sure I wasn't going to sink in further, and it appeared to be solid enough. "This is weird."

Toran paced next to me. "I have no idea what to make of it."

"I'm pretty far beyond trying to make scientific sense of this," Kaiden said. "Let's get to the crystal." He set off in the direction of the monument two hundred meters to the north.

Maris wrinkled her nose as she followed. "If I could smell anything right now, I bet this would reek."

Toran nodded. "I'm inclined to agree."

"That other world didn't," Kaiden pointed out while he forged ahead.

"But that one had *just* been infected. This one has had months to marinate in its own destruction," Maris countered.

I kept careful watch on our surroundings, looking for any signs of movement by creatures that could attack us. "What a delightful thought."

"Doesn't matter. Let's get out of here before we become one of the permanent fixtures." Kaiden picked up his pace.

I jogged ahead to walk abreast to him. Catching his gaze as I approached, I gave him a reassuring nod. It was clear his nerves were starting to fray; we'd need to support one another and not give in to our imaginations' worst case scenarios.

Kaiden's outward demeanor didn't change, but he took a slow breath and nodded back. Nerves or not, he was still there in the moment with me. I had nothing to worry about.

The first hundred meters from the shuttle, our path toward the crystal was fairly clear. We plodded across the black ground, leaving a path of footprints behind us. As we neared the destination monument, however, small tendrils of the Darkness started to sprout from the black ground.

"I didn't notice these from the air," I admitted.

"Neither did I." Kaiden frowned at the pulsing energy pathways of the dark particulates.

"Let's try to step around them." I eyed our path ahead, but I couldn't tell if the ground closest to the crystal monument was the black spongy material we had been walking on, or if it was a mat of the tendrils.

It was possible that it didn't matter either way. However, given our working hypothesis that we were attacked because we'd interrupted the energy flow of one of the larger tendrils, it was reasonable to assume that the attributes would scale down, as well. My companions had all instinctively stepped around the small tendrils when they'd first appeared in our path, so I definitely wasn't the only person thinking in those terms.

By the time we'd gone another twenty meters, it was clear that avoiding the small tendrils might be unavoidable. I slowed my pace. "Decision time."

Kaiden looked at the path ahead and then back to me. "We can't give up now."

"Agreed, but we should be prepared for a fight if the ground turns on us," I replied.

Maris groaned. "How in the stars are you supposed to prepare for *that*?"

I shrugged. "I don't know, but I have a sneaking suspicion it's about to happen."

"Elle," Kaiden took a step backward and a fireball appeared in his palm, "move!"

I TENSED AS my gaze shot down to my feet. Four of the slim, black tendrils had started to wrap around my boots. I tried to raise my right foot, and the tendrils elongated but didn't let go.

"Stars!" I took two rapid steps back the way we'd come. The tendrils maintained their hold.

"I'll get it!" Kaiden said, bringing back his arm to throw a fireball.

"No." I held up my hand. "If we start attacking, everything around us might go on the offensive."

I took several slow, cautious steps, and the tendrils continued to let me move, though the Darkness remained wrapped around my boots up to my ankles. "Look, it's not stopping me."

"We should just let it latch onto us?" Maris didn't look convinced.

Kaiden took a hesitant step into the patch of tendrils that had snagged me, and they flowed over the toes of his boots. "We might not have another choice."

Maris refreshed the protective shells around us, but the new magical barrier appeared to have no effect on the tendrils or ground. "You're all out of your minds."

"Takes one to know one, Maris." I smirked.

She rolled her eyes and stepped forward into the now-writhing tangle of dark tendrils. "Just go already."

Without further delay, I continued toward the crystal monument, taking slow, gentle steps to avoid disturbing the ground too much. The tendrils seemed content to wrap around my feet and then move aside as new tendrils rose to take their place. I kept watch on the behavior as I pressed onward to make sure it wasn't getting any more aggressive.

Toran brought up the rear of our party, looking extremely concerned about the risky strategy. As the strongest of us, I'd expect him to be less worried about being snared by something as narrow as my pinky finger. Nonetheless, the strange properties of the Darkness were enough to put even the largest warriors on edge. And, despite his appearance, I needed to remind myself that Toran was an engineer and family man at heart, not a veteran fighter.

We shuffled our feet across the ground like we were wading through ankle-deep water. By the time we were thirty meters from our destination, the strange ground covering had wrapped us up to our knees. It took all my concentration to keep from panicking. So long as we could move, there was nothing to worry about... though that could change at a moment's notice.

"Almost there," I said. "Toran, you ready to hook into the control system?"

"Assuming it still works, yes," he confirmed.

The crystal monument loomed before us, standing nearly three stories. Though it should have been glowing blue, the crystal was now off-white and was filled with a swirling cloud of the dark particulates. Dark tendrils seemingly flowed out from the crystal, thickening and merging into the apparent energy conduits crisscrossing the landscape. What had once been a chrome enclosure surrounding the crystal with a touch-surface access panel was now dull black and beginning to crumble.

I scowled at it. "That doesn't look like it's in very good shape."

"It's not." Toran swung his pack forward on one shoulder so he could root around inside. He retrieved a screwdriver and proceeded to prod at the interface panel; the corroded metal flaked away. "These wires are shot."

"Dead end?" Kaiden asked, his brow tight with concern.

"Didn't say that." Toran dug deeper into the ruins. "The components next to the crystal still look functional—I need to cobble together a bypass around the typical interface protocol."

My concerns receded the slightest measure. "But it will work?"

"It should." He got out more tools and started chipping away at the corroded metal until the salvageable interior components were exposed.

There was nothing for us to do but wait. I moved my feet on occasion so the tendrils wouldn't work too far up my legs.

"This is so eerie," Kaiden said under his breath while he paced next to me.

"I'm kind of getting used to us being the only ones roaming around an alien world," I replied, trying to bring some levity to the situation.

"This was a thriving colony," Maris shot back. "We're not alone."

"There's no one here anymore, Maris," I said.

Her face reddened. "Those dark columns over there? I think those used to be people."

My heart skipped a beat. I'd been so focused on the ground and the crystal up ahead that I hadn't been paying attention to the other features in the surroundings. The columns Maris had pointed out had seemed like any of the other mass of dark tendrils stretching in every direction, but I could now make out the heads and shoulders atop the vertical shapes. They were posed in combat, some with arms up for an attack while others were bent over, shielding their heads with their arms. At first, I thought that they were defending the crystal. As we got closer and I was able to assess the arrangement, it instead appeared that they were in the process of fighting something coming *from* the crystal.

"I'm sorry, I didn't mean to diminish anyone's sacrifice," I murmured.

"Don't think about that now." Toran said.

Kaiden swallowed. "Everything is backed up in the Master Archive. That's the important thing."

"Let's focus on what we're doing now." Toran cast me a cautionary glance before pulling his interface equipment from his pack. I rarely saw strong emotion from him, and I definitely wasn't eager to be on the receiving end of a reprimand in the future.

I kept my distance while Toran continued to work. Not knowing what may be lurking in the Darkness around us, I rested my hand on my sword hilt, ready for action.

Kaiden shuffled over to stand next to me, then turned sideways so he was facing me while also being orientated away from Toran's and Maris' sightlines. "Everyone's on edge," he said over a private comm channel. "You didn't say anything wrong."

"I could have phrased it better," I replied over the same private link.

"Even so, Toran is having an especially rough go of it because today is his daughter's birthday."

My chest constricted. "Oh, I didn't know."

"He mentioned it to me while we were walking to breakfast. Don't say anything to him about it, but I thought that context might explain some things for you."

"Thanks."

Kaiden brushed his gloved hand down my arm. "Hang in there. We'll be back to the ship soon."

"Yeah." I glanced over my shoulder at Toran, who appeared to be finished hooking up his equipment. I switched to the general comm channel. "Were you able to access the crystal interface?" I asked.

The large man grunted. "Sort of. The connection is working, but I haven't been able to decipher the data logs."

"Will you be able to?" Kaiden asked.

"If this is just a security safeguard, then yes," Toran replied. "If it's because the data is corrupted, then there's nothing I can do."

I looked out at the Darkness swirling around us. I wasn't sure if my eyes were playing tricks on me, but I thought I saw movement in the shadows. "And how long before you know either way?"

"I have absolutely no idea, which I know isn't helpful," Toran replied. "It'll take as long as it takes."

"Can't fault honesty." I kept my attention on the place where I'd seen movement moments before. "Work as quickly as you can." I realized just how stupid the obvious statement sounded as soon as I heard it out loud, but no one called me on it.

Two minutes passed in the unnatural silence of the world. At last, Toran made a satisfied huff. "I think I'm finally getting somewhere."

I perked up. "Really? What have you found?"

"No specific *what* yet, but maybe part of a *how*," he replied. "It traces back to my vision."

"About how the Darkness spreads through the crystalline network?" Kaiden asked.

Toran nodded. "I believe I may have identified the signal that controls the Darkness' spread."

"That's huge!" I exclaimed. "Now we can counteract it, right?"

"Maybe eventually, but that would take so much more research that it's not worth thinking about yet."

My excitement faded. "Okay, what *do* we know, then?"

"I'm copying the records to a portable drive, but at first glance, this signal looks to have segments similar to the records used for crystal backups," Toran revealed.

"Wait, you know how to read the backups?" Kaiden interjected.

"I can't decode it myself, no," the other man clarified. "There are maybe three people alive who know enough about the storage medium to decipher a fraction of a backup record without the crystal interface. I've just seen enough interfaces to recognize the organizational structure of the code when I see it."

"That's weird that it's coded," I commented. "I always thoughts the records were a physical thing... You know, crystal-y."

"Yeah, me too," Maris agreed, looking over Toran's shoulder. "Really, can you even call that a 'code'?" She tilted her head.

Toran held up his tablet so I could see the contents of the screen. From a distance, it reminded me somewhat of a complex molecular model from chemistry class. "It's a code in the sense that it's an alphanumeric representation, though there's also a relationship component. Really, it's too complex for a person to understand—even super computers only know how to interact with the crystal storage medium, not recreate it."

"What does that mean for the Darkness—or alien tech, however we want to refer to it?" I questioned.

"I know too little to say," Toran replied.

"And if you had to guess?"

He hesitated. "My hunch is that this alien code taps into the crystalline network's reset ability and overwrites it with its own instructions to restructure the physical reality inside each crystal's zone."

I let the words sink in. "That's pretty out there, but it weirdly does explain everything."

"I don't like that hypothesis," Kaiden said. "That means that these aliens understand the tech on a level that is far beyond ours."

"Not liking the implications doesn't make it incorrect," Toran replied. "But, like I said, it's a wild guess."

I took a slow breath, sorting my thoughts. "This confirms some of the ideas we've been tossing around about what the Darkness is and its purpose, but that doesn't get us much closer to stopping it. We somehow need to trace where the signal is coming from."

"Well, I can tell you for sure that it's being sent via the crystalline network, so it's a planet somewhere in this galaxy," Toran replied.

"Narrowing it down to a whole galaxy, that *really* helps." I sighed.

Kaiden thought for a moment. "Come to think of it, does anyone actually know how big the crystalline network is?"

I shrugged. "No idea. Does the Hegemony have a map?"

Maris activated a comm link to the *Evangiel*. "Commander Colren," she greeted when the communication connected.

"Is everything okay?" the commander replied, sounding anxious through the static on the link.

"Ran into a bit of trouble, but we're unharmed," she continued. "We've reached the central crystal and are extracting the data logs now. Say, do you know about any sort of map of the crystalline network?"

He was silent for several seconds. "Why do you ask?"

"We need to trace a signal being transmitted via the network. Knowing how far-reaching it is might help us narrow down where it's coming from," Toran chimed in.

"We have a partial map, yes," Colren replied. "It was extracted from the Master Archive using the interface system on the *Evangiel*. Now that the Archive is sealed, though, there's no way to get updated records."

"A partial map is better than nothing," I said.

"Maybe, but I don't know how useful this one will be. There aren't any outer boundaries to the network—it's as expansive as known space," the commander clarified.

My sense of hope that had been building over the past several minutes crashed. "It really could be anywhere…"

"There might be answers buried in the signal," Toran said, his enthusiasm returning even as mine dwindled. "We won't know for sure until I get this data back to the *Evangiel*."

"Then get back here," the commander instructed. "I don't want the four of you down there for a second longer than necessary."

"Just another minute or two and this download will be complete," Toran acknowledged.

"We'll be waiting for you. Central Command out." Colren ended the commlink.

"One step forward, two back," I muttered.

"I don't know, we may have actually had a net gain of half a step forward with this one." Kaiden smiled.

Maris snorted. "This is really testing the definition of small victories."

"Yeah, I guess it's something to investigate, at least," I realized. "Leads are better than dead ends."

Kaiden nodded. "For sure."

Toran checked on the transfer. "We can be on our way soon. Just another minute or so until—" He cut off. "What's that over there?" He set down the tablet on the monument's edge and brought up his fists in a defensive pose.

I noticed the approaching figure a moment after him. The creature slinked through the black tendrils with the grace of a cat, one moment on four legs and the next on two. Its sleek pelt and powerful jaws reminded me of the creatures we'd encountered a week earlier after I'd retrieved my Valor artifact. Given that I'd watched those other creatures birthed, I could only draw one conclusion. "Is that what those things from the Valor world grow up to be?"

Kaiden readied a fireball. "An alien hybrid."

"This day just keeps getting better." Maris refreshed the protective shells around us.

"We need to hold it off for another minute," Toran said. "As soon as the transfer is complete, we can make a run for the shuttle."

"Yeah, except the ground might eat us," I pointed out.

The shadowcat snarled and bounded toward us, ending any hope of avoiding an engagement that might aggravate the vines.

Kaiden released a fireball as soon as the alien made its move. The blast struck the shadowcat in the center of its broad chest, but the creature barely missed a stride.

I ripped my legs free from the nest of vines as quickly as I could, not worried that I may aggravate them. I needed to move; my sword had proven to be one of the few effective weapons against similar shadowcreatures in the past.

Wading through the dark tendrils, I raised my blade, its magical blue flames rippling around the steel. After six strides, I was within striking distance. The shadowcat reared to maul me, and I ducked, thrusting my blade into the base of its ribcage and slashing downward.

The alien beast roared with pain and fury as it struggled to distance itself from my attack.

"Hit it now!" I shouted.

Fireballs launched from the end of Kaiden's staff as I ripped my blade free and dove to the side. I rolled over my left shoulder and jumped back to my feet to face the creature, which was still standing but looked weakened.

Kaiden struck it with an electrical attack, which branched into three separate beams to simultaneously hit its head, torso, and hindquarters. Smoke rose from the charred hide at the points of impact, and the creature swayed on its feet.

I needed to finish it off while it was stunned. I ran forward until I was a pace away, then swung my sword downward at the base of its skull. The flaming blade sliced clean through the flesh and what must have been the equivalent of bone in the alien hybrid. Its jaws flexed wide as it sucked in a dying breath. Knees buckling, it crumpled to the ground. The moment it fell, the black tendrils blanketing the ground began to encase it; within minutes, it would be nothing more than an unrecognizable mound.

I lowered my sword and released a relieved sigh. "I really hate these things."

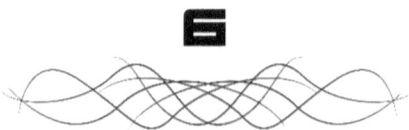

"YOU OKAY?" KAIDEN asked me, lowering his staff.

"Didn't even touch me," I replied, checking myself over. It was then, however, that I realized my moves during the fight had foolishly exposed most of my suit to the infected ground. I quickly checked myself to make sure that none of the tendrils had latched onto my torso, and at least I seemed to be unscathed in that respect. What might happen to my suit remained to be seen.

I flicked my blade and then wiped it off using a cleaning cloth from a pouch next to my scabbard. "Are we ready to get out of here?"

"Yes, transfer just completed," Toran confirmed as he detached his equipment from the interface.

"Good, let's go." I shifted anxiously on my feet while Toran finished packing. Dark forms kept darting through the shadows around us. As much as I wanted to hope I was just on edge from the last engagement, I knew better; we were being hunted.

Once Toran had secured his equipment and the data backup in his pack, we began making our way back through the tendril-covered plaza at a steady pace. Though the way toward the monument had been easy going, I now found that the tendrils were beginning to tug more at my feet whenever I tried to take a step.

"Is anyone else feeling a little restricted here?" I asked.

"Then it's not just me." Kaiden frowned at his feet as he continued to plod forward. "I don't think it wants us to go."

"That might be the most disturbing thing I've heard all day—and there've already been some doozies." Maris shook her foot as one of the tendrils threatened to climb up her leg. In response, the vines already around her feet and ankles cinched tighter. "Agh!"

"Don't fight it!" I cautioned, trying to keep my own movements measured despite my pulse spiking. "Relax. See if they let go."

Maris paled, her breath quavering over the comm. "It's getting tighter."

"Shit." Kaiden glanced from Maris to the shuttle a hundred fifty meters away. The last two-thirds of that distance were relatively open ground, but we still had another fifty meters of the tendril field that now seemed intent on keeping us as part of its personal collection.

"I don't think we can make a run for it without turning this entire field against us," I said. "Let me see if I can cut it off. Keep moving."

I shuffled over to Maris with far more difficulty than I would have had even a minute prior.

Kaiden and Toran continued along the path to the shuttle, watching me over their shoulders.

"Stay calm," I told Maris when I reached her.

"Easy for you to say when a demon-plant isn't cutting off the circulation in your foot," she replied through gritted teeth. Terror filled her eyes in the light cast from the hazsuit's facemask.

I pointed my sword blade toward the ground and slowly pressed it through the knots of black tendrils at the side of Maris' right foot. The steel sliced straight through the vines, but they recoiled from each severed point and snapped back in an attempt to re-snare her legs. A new tendril snaked up her thigh.

Maris conjured a fireball in her palm. "Stand back, Elle."

"Maris, don't! This whole field might turn on us."

She looked me in the eyes through the facemask of her hazsuit. "It already has."

A beam of fire streamed from her palm toward the dark tendrils closing around her. I brought up my arm to shield my eyes against the blaze, regaining my vision just in time to see a wave of the black vines rising up before me.

I took a hasty step back and sliced at them with my blade. "Run!" I shouted to Kaiden and Toran, hating that we might fail in the mission after being so close to succeeding. It might be too late for Maris and me, but maybe the two men could make it back to the shuttle before they were snared.

Only, rather than the sound of receding footsteps, my attention was drawn by a fireball thrown by someone other than Maris. The orb hurtled past Maris, who was still desperately trying to beat back the vines attempting to weave their way around her.

"You missed!" she yelled at Kaiden.

"I wasn't aiming for you."

Then, behind Maris, I saw his intended target—a pride of six shadowcats slinking from the shadows of the city ruins. Their expressionless black eyes were impossible to read, but their inky lips were curled back to reveal three rows of needlelike teeth.

"Great, that's all we need." I sliced the black vines at my feet and bolted back toward Maris.

She was still rooted to the ground, casting weak fireballs in an attempt to get free. "We're not going to make it." Her tone had gone from frightened to defeated, not a good sign.

"Don't even start." I glared at her. "Buck up and fight back. We're the heroes, remember?"

Maris worked her mouth while she no doubt searched for the right objection, but instead she nodded. "You're right. Screw this planet."

Our eyes met and I suddenly knew what we had to do; I couldn't explain where the feeling had come from, but Maris' eyes lit up. She cracked a smile. "Ready?" I asked on instinct.

"Do it."

I slashed my sword around her and she spun, simultaneously casting a continuous beam of fire from her hands. As the movements unfolded, I couldn't shake the feeling that we'd done it before, even though it hadn't occurred to me until a moment earlier. Wherever the idea came from, the move worked. My sword severed the bonds holding Maris in place, and the vines recoiled from the heat radiating from the flames. As Maris spun, she picked up her feet and jumped to a new patch where the vines appeared to be dormant; they certainly wouldn't stay that way for long, but a half-second delay was everything with the tools at our disposal.

My world tinted orange as Maris cast haste magic on our party. My own movements appeared in real-time to me, but everything except for my companions in the outside world now looked like it was moving in slow motion. The vines unfurled from the groundcover like a time-lapse video, and I carefully stepped around the tendrils slowly extending toward my feet.

"Stars, this would have been really handy earlier!" Kaiden exclaimed.

"Sorry, I was distracted," Maris replied, flushed. "Stop complaining and fight!"

Our banter ceased and two of the shadowcats parted from the others to circle around behind us. Their movements were swift, even with our altered perception from the haste magic. We wouldn't have any advantage, but this at least gave us a fighting chance.

I got into battle position. Just one of the shadowcats had proven to be a reasonable foe for our group, but I had my doubts about half a dozen. While physically I knew we could take them on, the real challenge came from six individual targets. We needed a way to keep them working together as a unit so we didn't have too many separate fronts to track.

"Maris and Kaiden, keep those four distracted," I ordered. "Toran, those two will be coming up behind us. We can't let them catch us by surprise."

"Okay, we'll try," Kaiden acknowledged.

I wanted to correct him that 'try' wasn't an option, but I decided that went without saying. We were about to fight for our lives, and we all knew it.

With our backs to Kaiden and Maris, Toran and I arranged ourselves so we'd have full visibility of the area around us; there was no way the two shadowcats could sneak up behind us without us knowing. One of them was bound to make a move at any moment, we just had to wait.

Except, nothing happened.

"Where are they?" I asked in a low voice when thirty seconds had passed with no sighting.

"I don't know," Toran replied.

"How long are we supposed to distract these things?" Kaiden called out.

I kept my feet moving to avoid being snared. "Until these two aren't behind us."

He grunted "Well, these four are getting impatient."

It didn't make any sense. The other shadowcat had pounced on us the moment we saw it. Why had these two disappeared?

The orange tint faded from my vision, the haste spell having expired. "Maris, time to—"

My vision spun and a sharp pain radiated from my right shoulder. I struck the ground, my vision black as tendrils washed over me in one horrifying wave. My arms were bound by the vines in an instant. I was trapped.

Heat radiated above me. I couldn't see it, but I could feel two taloned paws pinning my shoulders to the ground. The shadowcat's jaws must have been centimeters from my face. "It's got me!" I shouted into my comm, not sure that anyone would hear me or know where I'd fallen. I needed to free myself.

My arms felt impossibly heavy with the vines wrapped around them, but I yanked my sword hand with all my might. The vines had just enough give to free it a little, and then I used the slack to see the movement through the rest of the way. I pivoted my wrist as much as I could to stab the end of my blade upward into where the shadowcat's abdomen should be based on it pinning me with its front legs. Unable to raise my shoulder, I knew the attack would be weak, but the flaming blade of the sword would do the work for me.

Just as the blade met resistance, the world tinted orange around me again. The weight released from my shoulders and I sat upright. As I rose, some of the tendrils that had covered my facemask fell away, and I saw the shadowcat stumbling backward, viscous black blood spurting from a wound in its side. Amazingly, I'd hit it right where I'd intended.

A smile played on my lips. "You messed with the wrong group." I leaped to my feet, slicing back the vines around me to keep them at bay.

The shadowcat I'd wounded snarled, but when it tried to lunge toward me once more, it stumbled. I took the opportunity to deal it a lethal blow, severing its head at the base of the skull like I'd done with the first. Its lifeless body collapsed, the pool of blood invisible amid the bed of vines.

"Well, that wasn't so bad." No one replied to my quip. I pivoted to face my friends and was horrified to see that four shadowcats were racing toward Maris and Kaiden while Toran was gripped in the talons of the fifth.

My heart dropped. I couldn't aid in both defenses at the same time.

Toran was closer to me, but I also had more faith that he'd be able to beat the solitary shadowcat into submission. A fight of four against two—especially given Maris' weak offensive capabilities—was where I was needed the most.

I bounded across the intervening terrain, still under the influence of the haste magic. Kaiden's and Maris' fireballs appeared to have almost no effect on the attacking shadowcats. The creatures' movements were almost as quick as ours, but I could still close the distance in time.

"Jump clear!" I shouted when I was right behind Kaiden and Maris.

They looked over their shoulders, then quickly took a step to the side as I charged past them.

"What are you—" Kaiden started to ask.

In response, I jumped over the head of the middle shadowcat and flipped midair. When I was directly above it, I plunged my sword into its back and used it as a pivot point to kick the shadowcat on its left, and then swung back around to the right. As I completed the rotation, I removed the sword, bringing it around at an angle to decapitate the other middle shadowcat as I flew horizontally through the air. I didn't have enough momentum to repeat the move on the fourth, but I was able to embed the tip of my blade as I passed over its back, opening up a gash that stretched from its shoulder to the center of its ribcage on the other side.

I landed on my side and then rolled up to my feet in one motion. By the time I was upright, the first shadowcat I'd stabbed had fallen to the ground and was disintegrating, and the decapitated creature was already halfway turned to soot. The remaining two shadowcats looked worse for wear but were still standing.

"Holy shit…" Kaiden whispered in stunned disbelief.

"Don't just stand there!" I lunged back for the shadowcat nearest me, which I'd slashed across its back. Just as I made my move, the orange tint faded from the world around me, along with the protective purple shell.

The shadowcat seemed to sense the change, and it rose on its two rear legs, bearing its teeth and flashing the dark talons on its front paws. I thought it was just a display at first, but then it compressed its hindquarters and sprung toward me. I tried to dodge it, but the talons had latched onto me before I fully registered the movement. The hazsuit's fabric ripped. I sensed pressure on my back, but there wasn't the searing pain of the nails in my flesh that I expected to follow; my coat beneath the hazsuit had done its job once again. The shadowcat, however, wasn't deterred by the thin fabric.

It snapped at my facemask, wrapping its jaws around the transparent plastic. The faceplate fogged from its warm breath and smeared with slobber. Rancid air leaked in through the tear in my hazsuit's shoulder. There was no telling it if would hasten the corruptive properties of the world on my equipment, but at least there was still oxygen I could breathe.

I struggled to get my arm into position to stab at the beast, but my sword was too tangled in the tendrils covering the ground for me to get it free from my current position. Instead, I kicked up with my right knee, aiming for the wound in its side. I couldn't connect. I was pinned, and it was only a matter of time before the creature broke through my remaining defenses.

A sudden glow of energy surged through me, and I balled my right hand into a fist to punch at the creature. As I brought my hand up, my eyes snapped shut on reflex as a fireball smashed into the shadowcat's side. I opened my eyes to see Kaiden holding his staff. Several seconds earlier would have been nice, but I appreciated his help all the same.

The shadowcat recoiled from the fireball, loosening its hold on me just enough to roll free. The tendrils on the ground slithered over me, and I bolted to my feet as quickly as possible to keep them from getting any purchase. As I stood, I noticed that my three companions had disposed of the other shadowcat already, leaving us the one final foe.

Kaiden launched a series of fireballs at the shadowcat as soon as I was out of range, and it cried out. When he paused his attacks, I made my move to end the fight.

I took a running leap toward the beast and flipped over it, swinging my sword at its neck as I passed overhead. The shadowcat shuddered, its legs buckling. I landed on my feet on its other side as it started to dissolve into soot.

"Just like that!" I cheered. But my celebration only lasted for a moment.

The ground covering, which had remained fairly subdued during the fight, now looked intent on finishing what the shadowcats had been unable to do. The tendrils had all straightened up to almost waist-level, and they were reaching for us.

"Run!" Kaiden shouted, casting a solid stream of fire from his palm in an arc around us. The tendrils shrank back just enough to leave a path. He took the lead, clearing the way, the intentions of making a quiet retreat now a distant memory.

I took the third position after Maris, with Toran at the rear. I kept enough distance between myself and Maris to hack at the tendrils with my sword after Kaiden thrust them back. We ran at full speed toward the relative safety of the open area around the shuttle. Just another twenty meters to go.

The tendrils tugged at my ankles, but I wasn't about to let anything stop me. I checked over my shoulder to make sure Toran was safe, and he nodded to me.

We were almost to the end of the black field. The ground covering was shorter and sparser now, allowing Kaiden to ease up his flame attack. After another ten meters, we were free from the last of the tendrils.

Maris let out a relieved chuckle. "And *that's* why I didn't want to come with you."

Toran patted his backpack over his shoulder. "We got what we came for."

"Yeah, but I expect the rest of this world will turn on us at any moment." I looked back at where we'd come from. The tendrils were still writhing on the ground, and some were beginning to snake toward us.

Kaiden continued running in the direction of the shuttle. "What are you waiting for?"

We picked up our pace and closed the final hundred meters to the craft. Kaiden was the first to arrive, and he halted two meters from the back airlock.

I stopped short when I saw the look of horror on Kaiden's face. "What's wrong?" I asked.

He pointed at black pits in the shuttle's thermal plating. "We have another problem."

7

"NO! IT CAN'T have corroded this quickly." My stomach turned over.

"I don't know what to tell you." Kaiden took an unsteady breath.

Maris gulped. "Is it flyable?"

Kaiden shrugged. "No clue. It might be superficial damage, or there might be no structural integrity whatsoever."

Toran cautiously approached the craft. "As long as the support structure is intact, it will be space-worthy. We'll just need pressurized suits."

"Are the hazsuits enough?" Kaiden asked.

"Perhaps, for a short time, but the emergency EVA suits would be better."

I pointed at the tear in my shoulder. "I'll definitely need one of those."

Kaiden's eyes widened. "Elle! Why didn't you say you were hurt?"

"I just did. I've been a little preoccupied with not dying. And, I'm not hurt—just my suit."

"That means you're contaminated directly, not just the outer layer," Toran said.

I shrugged. "I already took off my suit once inside. We lost containment a long time ago."

Toran took a slow breath a nodded. "We'll deal with it once we're back on the *Evangiel*. Come on."

He opened the exterior airlock hatch and beckoned us inside. We squeezed in, and Kaiden cycled the interior airlock. The door opened with a hiss.

"I'll get it started up and see what kind of damage we're facing," Kaiden said, rushing toward the bridge. He began stripped off the hazsuit.

"Maris, help me with the EVA suits. They should be in storage back here," Toran instructed.

"I'll help Kaiden with the inspection," I said and followed him toward the bridge. I paused in the common area to remove the hazsuit, then jogged the rest of the way to the front of the vessel.

Kaiden was seated in the pilot's chair and was busy looking over the preliminary system scans. "...Yes, Commander. Understood." He ended the comm link.

"What's the word?" I asked.

He didn't glance up from his work. "It's not looking good."

"Was that Colren? Is he sending help?"

"I told him to hold off. We have a shot at being able to achieve orbit even with the damage; the reduced gravity works in our favor."

"I'm sorry I got us into this," I mumbled.

"We needed that information. It was worth the risk."

"But we haven't gotten it back to them."

He shook his head. "We have a datalink. Central Command is waiting for an upload."

"That's great the data will be safe, but *I* don't want to get stuck here," I replied. "Things were just starting to get good."

"Me either."

"But if this shuttle is too damaged, they can send another, right?"

He didn't respond.

"Right, Kaiden?" I pressed.

"That's what I was talking about with Colren. I had to manually pilot us down here. I don't know that the automated systems could do it. Any pilot without our resistance to the Darkness would likely only last a few minutes here, even with protective gear, based on what Colren said."

"So, even *if* they could make it here, it'd be a one-way trip."

"Yeah. Let's hope it doesn't come to that."

I'd never placed one life at a higher value than any other, but when it came down to it, we have unique skills that would be difficult to replicate. I had no doubt that Colren would send someone to their death if it meant saving us, and I didn't want that on my conscience. "Is there anything I can do to help you?" I asked.

"I'm getting a warning error on the amidships starboard bulkhead next to the side hatch. See if there's any corrosion visible on the inside yet," he replied.

"I'm on it." I headed back toward the corridor, then paused and turn around. "We're going to get out of here, Kaiden."

He glanced back at me. "I know we will."

I returned to the common room to find Toran and Maris donning EVA suits. "Good, you found them!"

Toran moved stiffly in his, the outfit far too tight on his broad frame. "They'll keep us alive, provided the ship can fly."

"Kaiden thinks we have a shot," I replied. "He said we still have a datalink, so you can upload the info you pulled from the crystal."

"Oh, good. I'll do that right away." Toran rushed toward the bridge.

"Did Kaiden talk to Central Command? Are they sending a replacement shuttle?" Maris asked.

"That's complicated," I replied. "Short answer is that we're on our own until we have no other options."

Maris frowned. "But won't we not know this one isn't space-worthy until we're, you know, up in space?"

"That's my worry, too."

"I mean, these suits are just a precaution, right? We won't actually need them inside the shuttle…"

I didn't want to lie to her, so I instead turned my attention to the bulkhead Kaiden had sent me to inspect. "Just make sure your suit is sealed, Maris. We'll be fine."

The other woman worked her mouth. "I really shouldn't have gotten out of bed this morning."

"You're tellin' me." I turned my attention to the problem bulkhead. Leaning in until I was only a few centimeters away, I looked for any signs of the dark corrosion we'd witnessed outside.

My initial assessment didn't reveal any concerning patches, and I was almost ready to breathe a sigh of relief. Then, I noticed a dark area with small pits in the metal at the base of the hatch. "Uh oh."

"No. No 'uh ohs'!" Maris exclaimed while she hurriedly donned her suit.

"Would you prefer 'that doesn't look good'?"

Her face flushed. "How screwed are we?"

"I don't know." I turned toward the bridge. "Toran, how important is the starboard-side bulkhead?"

There was only silence for several seconds, then the rapid thud of footsteps. Toran came into view down the corridor. "What did you find?"

I pointed to the problem patch.

He approached and crouched down, frowning at it. "This might be superficial or the interior of these walls might be as brittle as charcoal."

"Yeah, that's what I was afraid you'd say." I took a steadying breath. "I didn't see anything else over here, but I haven't looked over the rest of the shuttle."

"Well, conditions are guaranteed to deteriorate. We should probably try to take off while we still have functional engines," he replied.

"We're all going to die," Maris moaned.

I cast her a silencing glance. "No, we're not."

"Finish suiting up," Toran instructed. "The upload will be complete in two minutes."

"That's way faster than it downloaded from the crystal," I said with surprise.

"This connection actually works properly."

Maris took a deep breath. "I'll try to cast a shield around the shuttle in the meantime." She clasped her crystal pendant in her left hand and closed her eyes.

I bit my tongue to keep from questioning her about why she didn't do that the moment we got back; it hadn't even occurred to me, but it wasn't my responsibility to do her job for her. Instead, I turned my attention to putting on the EVA suit.

The garment was, thankfully, straightforward to secure, even for a novice spacefarer like me. However, as I brought it over my right shoulder, which had taken the brunt of the shadowcat attack, I had to hold back a grimace of discomfort. While I was used to having limited shoulder mobility, it was always my left arm; to be injured on the other side was disorienting and annoying. I was fairly confident that I was only banged up, though, and the discomfort would be temporary.

By the time I was finished dressing, the upload was complete and we were ready to go. I sealed everything below my neck, then picked up the helmet and returned to my seat on the bridge to strap in.

"All sensors indicate we have structural integrity," Kaiden announced over the front speaker on his EVA suit.

I clicked my helmet into the neck collar and switched to the interior comms. "This is the part where we ignore the maybe-hole back there, isn't it?"

He kept his gaze straight ahead. "Yep."

"Nothing could possibly go wrong." I tightened my restraints.

"Let's get out of here." Kaiden made the final necessary entries on the front control panel, and the shuttle lifted off the ground.

"So far, so good." Maris sounded more cheerful than she had all day.

Toran and Kaiden remained silent, watching the readouts on their respective stations. I kept my gloved fingers wrapped around the end of my armrests while I focused on staying calm.

When we were at an elevation of five hundred meters, the comm chirped, indicating an incoming call.

"Glad to see you're off the ground. Wishing you a safe return flight," Colren said.

"Thank you," Kaiden acknowledged.

"We're already recoding the data you gathered," Colren continued. "It's invaluable."

"Glad to hear it. I look forward to reviewing it myself," responded Toran.

"We'll see you soon." The commander ended the link.

"That totally felt like he was calling to say goodbye," Maris said.

I rolled my eyes. "Everything's fine. We're off the ground—that was the hard part."

Kaiden glanced over at me, his expression telling me that wasn't the case.

"What else is there?" I prompted.

"I haven't kicked in the main boosters yet to get us up to the *Evangiel*'s orbit altitude."

My stomach dropped. "That's what will stress the structure."

"Yeah." He took a slow breath. "We're about to find out if it will hold." He activated the controls.

Sudden pressure pinned me against the back of my seat. I ran through the scenarios in my head for what I'd do if the shuttle started to fall apart around me, contriving an epic plan to leap from the doomed craft and somehow make it safely to the ground, where I'd defeat any enemies that dared to mess with me. In reality, I figured that if anything went wrong, we'd be goners before we realized what'd happened.

Even as my mind raced with disastrous possibilities, there was no sign of trouble. Once we made it past the first critical minute of the boost and the pressure eased, I started to relax. "So far, so good."

Kaiden nodded, but he was still tense. "We're entering the upper atmosphere now. We should be past the worst of it."

"I don't like what I'm seeing on some of these structural readings," Toran chimed in. "This isn't my area of expertise, but some of the integrity measures are getting close to their warning levels."

I was even less of an expert, but Toran's tone told me everything I needed to know: we were in trouble.

My heart thudded in my chest as the EVA suit closed in around me. If the hull failed, the suit's thin fabric would be the only thing separating me from the void. "What do we do?" I asked, panic pitching my voice.

"It might be fine. Hang on," Kaiden replied. His own tone was still calm and level, but his frantic movements belied inner worry.

Through the front viewport, the planet's atmosphere dissipated, and pinpoints of light from distant stars greeted us.

"We're almost to the *Evangiel*, right?" I asked tentatively.

"Yeah, out of the atmosphere—they can pick us up?" Maris added.

Kaiden and Toran remained silent.

"*Right*?" I emphasized.

"We're out of the atmosphere, but we're still in the gravity well," Kaiden said at last. "I don't know how much maneuvering I'll be able to do before we lose structural integrity."

"The corroded components are right around the mid starboard thruster," Toran explained. "It's the main boost we need for landing. If it fails while we're coming in, part of the infected material could break off and hit the ship. Without being able to decontaminate it properly…"

My chest constricted further. "What are you saying?"

Toran took a shaky breath. "It's too dangerous to land, but if we don't land soon, the shuttle will fall back to the planet's surface and we'll be stuck for good, assuming we don't burn up in the process."

"No. Nope." Maris shook her head, squeezing her eyes shut.

I looked to Kaiden. "There has to be another way."

His gaze flitted between the shuttle controls and out the viewport. "Maybe."

"What do you have in mind?" Toran asked.

Kaiden swallowed. "We can't use the maneuvering thrusters too much, but I may be able to feather them enough to get us *close* to the hangar entry."

I tightened my grip on my armrests. "Close enough to land?"

"No. Close enough to make a jump for it."

"You *have* to be joking!" Maris exclaimed.

"There's still risk of contaminating the outer hull of the *Evangiel,*" Toran pointed out.

"Not if we're coordinating with them," Kaiden countered. "They just need to pull away to avoid the craft colliding—that's way easier to avoid than thousands of tiny fragments from the ship disintegrating."

"This is completely insane," I muttered under my breath.

"Well, we either make a break for it or let the ship fall apart around us. Want to vote?" Kaiden asked.

"I don't think there's any room for contention," Toran replied. "Are you thinking the side starboard hatch?"

The other man nodded. "Angles wouldn't work with the rear airlock."

"But the corroded area is around the side hatch!" I looked over my shoulder at Toran. "Won't it—"

"There's a way to work the angles and approach so the hatch and debris will eject away from the *Evangiel,*" Toran said. "The nav computer can handle the calculations and piloting."

I shook my head. "It couldn't possibly have been designed to do that."

"It was, actually." Kaiden's hands raced over the controls. "All sorts of emergency evacuation procedures are embedded in the system. We almost crashed one time as a kid and the disaster protocols saved us."

My mind raced, trying to think of any other way to get out of the predicament. But I couldn't kid myself. I knew nothing about what we were facing, only that I wanted to live. I had no choice but to trust the opinion of the two people on my team who knew what they were talking about when it came to ships.

"Tell us what to do," I said.

"Stars! This can't be happening," Maris moaned.

"Seals on your suits are good?" Kaiden asked. He began to gently turn the shuttle toward the *Evangiel.*

"Yeah," I confirmed, followed by acknowledgments from Maris and Toran.

"Okay, unstrap and brace yourselves in the common room," Kaiden instructed. He hit the comm controls while I released my harness. "Commander, we have a situation."

I worked my way down the short corridor while Kaiden briefed Central Command on what we were planning. I listened in on the conversation, though I glazed over when they got into the technical jargon. To my surprise, the commander supported the proposed approach, agreeing that it was too risky for the shuttle to make contact with the larger ship given its level of contamination. It would be left to burn up on reentry into the atmosphere where the Darkness would claim it.

They rapidly completed the planning, and Kaiden made the necessary entries to the nav system to enable Central Command to remotely control the shuttle. He joined us in the common room, his face drawn with worry. "I know this sounds nuts, but it's going to be fine."

"I've never been in a spacesuit. This—"

Kaiden gripped my shoulders. "You've got this, Elle."

I looked out the side viewport at the *Evangiel* rapidly approaching. "It's so far away."

"It won't be by the time we make our move. Just consider it hands-on training for that Tactical School you were so eager to attend," he shot back with a forced smile.

"Well, *I* didn't want to be a Ranger," Maris said, it almost turning into a wail.

"Put that worry to good use and conjure us up a protective shield," Toran suggested.

"Hey, I'll take anything." I hugged myself. But, another thought broke me from the worries about my mortality. "Stars! Our gear."

When we'd donned the EVA suits, I'd set down my Valor artifact sword and my other armor, thinking that it would be safe in the common room until we landed. However, if we were to abandon the shuttle, the items would be lost with it. A quick glance at Toran confirmed that he'd, likewise, set down his gauntlets. Only Kaiden had been able to wear his artifact—the delicate, silver circlet, inside his EVA suit's helmet.

"Forget about the clothes, just get the artifacts," Toran said, racing toward his gauntlets.

I ran for my sword. Just as I took my first steps, the shuttle lurched. I stumbled sideways, and Kaiden caught my arm. "What was that?"

"Shit! The thruster didn't fire how it was supposed to," he replied, looking at our approach out the viewport.

"Shuttle 1," a female voice said over our ear comms, "we'll compensate for your flight path. We'll get you. Don't worry."

"Right, 'don't worry'!" I finished my dive for the sword and wrapped the scabbard's waist strap around my hand. "Really helpful."

Toran grabbed his gauntlets and shoved them inside his backpack. He looped the pack's straps around his arm. "Better than 'you're probably going to die, but good luck anyway'."

Maris gaped at us. "You're all terrible!"

"Look at us, still bantering even in the face of death." I couldn't help cracking a smile.

"Yep, we've officially lost our minds." Kaiden shook his head.

The shuttle lurched again, and I stumbled back toward where I'd been bracing against the port bulkhead. "When is this thing happening?"

"Any second," Kaiden murmured, keeping his attention out the viewport. "The *Evangiel* is turning now."

"But, what's the plan?" Maris asked. "We're just leaping from here to the ship, or…?"

Kaiden shook his head. "Not exactly. We'll blow the side hatch, and the sudden pressure change will suck us out. If we've timed everything right, that will put us on a trajectory to pass through the electrostatic shield into the hangar, and then the *Evangiel* can pull away from the contaminated shuttle."

"Then we get scrubbed down along with all of our stuff?" I completed.

"That's the idea."

I eyed him. "You're making it sound too easy."

"Am I? Sounds pretty tricky to me," he replied.

"But totally doable, right?" Maris pressed.

Kaiden shifted on his feet. "Yes, absolutely."

I wanted to call him out for lying to our faces, but I figured that wouldn't do anyone any good. The commander had signed off on the plan, so that meant it was the best course of action under the circumstances. "Just tell me when to let go and I'll follow." I said.

Kaiden took my hand in his. "Get ready."

KAIDEN AND I gripped handholds along the bulkhead in our free hands and prepared to make our move. Toran and Maris also took each other's hands for extra stability, and Maris cast a purple shell around us to hopefully offer added protection against debris or radiation the EVA suits might not shield against.

After a tense forty seconds, we finally got the signal from Central Command over our comms. "Remotely releasing the hatch in three... two... one... breach!"

My perception tinted orange around me, and I realized a haste spell had been cast the moment the countdown ended. The hatch across the shuttle from me released in slow motion, sending a cloud of oxygen into the void as the common room rapidly depressurized. Kaiden let go of his handhold and allowed the pressure change to suck him toward the opening. Reluctantly, I released my own handhold and we careened toward the opening. Toran and Maris were only a meter behind, and the four of us flew into the open void.

With my altered perception, I was able to take in the unobstructed view of space for the brief moment I passed between the shuttle and the *Evangiel*. The stars were even brighter than they seemed from inside a craft, and for that instant I felt the true vastness of space. I was a speck in the universe. Yet, my purpose made me an important speck, and I needed to do everything I could to survive.

Our course was true as we hurtled across the void toward the large ship. The shimmering gold of the electrostatic field raced toward me. Kaiden's firm grasp offered my only sense of grounding as I cartwheeled on an uncontrolled vector through the barrier. The energy passed over me in a wave and bright light assaulted my eyes.

Artificial gravity kicked in the moment I passed all the way through, pulling me toward the hangar floor—which happened to be above me based on my awkward entry angle. I thudded to the deck face-first. Kaiden released my hand the moment before impact, allowing me to catch myself a little and absorb the worst of the fall.

Cries of surprise and relieved chuckles sounded over the comms as my teammates settled on the deck. We carefully rose and checked ourselves over.

"Everyone all right?" Toran asked.

Remarkably, the event had left me no worse for wear. "I'm alive. That's good enough for me," I said.

Maris brushed herself off. "I am *never* doing that again."

"I don't know, it wasn't that bad." Kaiden cracked a smile.

I raised an eyebrow. "You really do have a hero complex, don't you?"

He shrugged. "I mean, I suppose it was me who got us back here safely."

"Right, yeah, the Central Command crew had nothing to do with that."

"Elle," he leveled his gaze on me, "I'm just messing with you. This was a team effort."

I popped off my helmet and brushed my hair back from my face. "Right, sorry. Guess I'm still on edge."

Toran smiled. "We accomplished our mission. We got the data we set out to retrieve."

"We should go—" I cut myself off as I looked down at my EVA suit. We still needed to go through decontamination. The tents where we'd need to scrub down were waiting for us on the other side of the hangar.

"Are you okay?" Tami shouted from my left.

I turned to face her. "Think so."

The engineer stopped seven meters from us. "Were you... exposed?"

"Unavoidable," Toran replied.

She nodded. "All right, you know the drill."

I began stripping down to my white base layer shipsuit. "Yep."

Kaiden pressed behind his ear while he started to undress. "Commander," said to the comm, "we're back on board. We'll come see you as soon as we've finished the decontamination procedure."

"Glad all of you made it back," Colren replied in our ears. "I want a full med eval, as well. We're working through the data you gathered and should have a summary of the preliminary findings to share once you've finished."

"Okay, see you soon," I acknowledged.

We filed into the decontamination booths and completed the scrubdown. It was just as unpleasant as I remembered, but I gladly took it over the chance of having some of the corrosive Darkness remaining on me. Unlike the previous time in the booth, however, duplicates of our custom-sized shipsuits were waiting for us. After dressing, we were directed from the decontamination booths into a temporary medical examination area next to it. A nurse looked me over inside the tent, pausing on some bruises forming on my limbs and torso from the fights, but everything checked out to her satisfaction.

When I emerged from my medical screening, Kaiden was waiting for me. "You have a radiant glow about you again," he teased.

"You too. I think this time the chemical scrub took off an extra layer."

"We were right up in it on the planet. I won't complain about anything that keeps the Darkness far away from us."

I nodded. "Think we'll finally be able to get answers about what it is and where it's from?"

"Stars, I hope so! The longer this drags on, the more antsy I get." He crossed his arms.

Toran emerged from the tent next. "I would like to second Maris' vote to avoid corrupted worlds in the future."

"If that information is as good as you made it sound, we won't have to," Kaiden replied.

"Here's hoping," Maris said as she stepped out from the tent, her hair still perfectly styled through some mysterious magic she'd no doubt deny using.

"Let's get up to Central Command and find out," I suggested.

Kaiden held out his arm for me to lead the way.

The bridge crew snapped to attention as soon as we arrived. They'd always examined us with curiosity, but this was one of the rare moments that their professional regard bordered on awe. We'd just successfully come back from a planet that would have destroyed anyone else. While part of me appreciated the attention, it was awkward to be idolized for something I didn't have any control over. We had been called to fulfill our role—that didn't make us special, we were just performing our duty.

Colren beamed at us from next to his seat at the center of the bridge. "Welcome back. I'm almost willing to forgive you for disobeying our agreement considering what you managed to retrieve."

My cheeks flushed slightly. "Sorry about that."

"It's done now. Let's talk in the conference room." The commander led us into our standard meeting space, then took a seat on the far side of the table.

The four of us sat down facing him with Kaiden and me in the center.

I folded my forearms on the tabletop and leaned forward. "Did you get anything good from the data Toran extracted?"

Colren nodded. "We're still working through exactly what it means, but the preliminary findings are promising."

"What have you learned?" Toran asked.

"Well, the signal embedded in the data is quite curious." Colren tapped on the touch-surface tabletop and an ethereal melody began to play. Underneath the enticing tones was a dissonant hum that caused everyone at the table to scowl. The commander silenced the recording and continued. "At first we thought it was a specific set of instructions, like a looping set of orders. But when the techs looked deeper, they realized that there were actually multiple layers to the signal."

Kaiden tilted his head. "In what way?"

"Well, there does appear to be a high-level message on one layer, but there's also a complex code we were able to pick up from other parts of the world that were well outside the vicinity of the crystal you accessed. In some manner, it appears to be a control system for the Darkness."

Toran nodded. "I suspected that might be the case."

"How did you arrive at that?" the commander asked.

"Based on how everything behaves on infected worlds, I thought maybe the Darkness was tapping into the crystal's unique properties—to use them as a means to re-form a world." Toran spread his hands on the table. "Now, I can't be certain that's how the crystals work, but that's been the prevailing hypothesis."

I hadn't fully processed what Toran had said down on the planet's surface, but now that I didn't have the black tendrils snaking up my leg, I allowed the words to properly sink in. "What are you saying… that a reset is actually rearranging matter?"

"As far as anyone can tell, yes," Toran replied.

"How?" Kaiden asked.

Toran bowed his head. "Scientists have debated that for decades—arguing everything from nanotech to a controlled release of hyperdimensional energy. The important part has always been the outcome, not the mode. However, if the Darkness is interrupting the process and inserting its own variations for how to restructure the environment, then we might need to dive deeper."

Matter rearrangement. I'd always taken the crystalline network for granted, never thinking about what actually happened during a reset. Having it spelled out, though, it all made so much more sense—why materials needed to remain within the crystal's zone in order to come through after a reset. It wasn't so much that the raw material needed to be the same, as I was certain state changes happened, but there needed to be enough material and energy present for the crystals to recreate the physical state from when the reset point was set.

What still didn't make any sense to me, though, was why an alien race would want to tap into that process to alter a world, let alone how they could accomplish such a feat. It was clear they had access to ancient technology that was well beyond our comprehension, so that would suggest they would have the firepower to wipe our worlds if they saw fit. Why go to the trouble to taking worlds one by one through the Darkness?

Commander Colren seemed to have similar thoughts as he leaned back in his chair with steepled fingers. "What might the aliens want with these worlds?"

"Clearly, they want us gone," Maris said.

"Yeah, that much is obvious," I agreed. "Everything on those worlds is designed to kill us."

"But maybe not intentionally," Kaiden chimed in.

Colren tilted his head. "Go on."

"Well," Kaiden continued, "I tend to look at everything the way I would with an agricultural problem. There's the natural state of the world, and then there's what happens when some outside force starts directing the natural progression—like when there's an infection. For example, a virus that attacks blood cells isn't trying to kill the host, per se; rather, it is trying to redirect the hosts' resources to fulfill a different role. Though that can result in death, that wasn't the virus' specific aim. I think the Darkness may operate in a similar fashion."

"Like the animals," I realized. "Not all of them died. Some were transformed into those other creatures that attacked us."

He nodded. "Exactly. And the plant life and other things turned to soot, but then new forms took their place. It might not be intended as an attack, but rather some sort of bio-optimization."

"Perhaps transforming the worlds to match the aliens' preferred habitat?" Colren posited.

"That's my best guess," Kaiden replied. "Especially since the gravity of the planets has been altered somehow. I can't think of another explanation that covers all the things we've observed."

"The ships," Toran murmured.

The commander's brow furrowed. "Pardon?"

"In Kaiden's vision, there were ships," he explained. "If they've been preparing these worlds for habitation, then…"

"Eventually the beings themselves will come," I completed for him. A chill gripped me as I thought through the implications. We weren't just up against the faceless Darkness—an entire invasion force of unknown beings might be coming for us.

Colren snapped to attention. "We have little chance of standing up to an adversary we know nothing about—especially one with the kind of skills these aliens seem to possess."

"We must be able to learn more from the code," Toran said. "Trace it to an origin."

The commander made several entries on the touch-surface tabletop, and a holographic star map appeared above it. "The techs have been unable to trace its origin, but they did observe something interesting. The full code has never been recorded before, but when it was broken down into its components, they realized that part of the signal had appeared on the other worlds."

"All parts, or only some of them?" Toran asked.

"There wasn't an apparent pattern," the commander replied.

Toran held out his hand toward the holographic model. "May I?"

Colren inclined his head with assent.

"Where do you have the data stored?" Toran asked.

The commander navigated to a directory, and then Toran began sifting through the information displayed on the tabletop in front of him.

I leaned over Kaiden to watch him work, but it was all foreign codes and graphs that made no sense to me. To my left, Maris took one glance and then leaned back in her chair with a mystified sigh.

After two minutes, Toran's hands stilled. "That's curious."

"What is?" Colren prompted.

"The fragments of the signals you recorded—there isn't a pattern, exactly, but there are two instances of some of the same code segments." Toran's brow knit as he stared at the data. "It may well be that duplicates of other segments of this full pattern may appear at other locations in the future."

I massaged my temple. "You mean, the signal was broken into pieces, and each world has one part of that larger signal?"

"Sort of. Rather, there are six instances where the same signal segment appears on two different worlds."

"Adjacent locations?" Colren speculated.

Toran shook his head. "Quite far apart, by the look of it. Let's see how they map." He manipulated the star map to display each of the locations of infected worlds with lines drawn between the six worlds that had emitted a signal that duplicated part of the full pattern they had retrieved.

As soon as the red lines were in place, it was clear the seemingly random arrangement of impacted worlds wasn't so random at all—the lines all intersected through a single point two systems over from Yantu, Maris' homeworld. I had no doubt where the other lines would pass if the worlds with no duplicated signal-segment had their doppelgängers identified.

"What's over there?" I asked.

Maris shook her head slowly. "Nothing. It's empty space."

"This arrangement is too consistent and widespread to be a coincidence. I can't believe we missed it," Colren murmured.

"In all fairness, you've only had this data for, what, half an hour?" Kaiden said. "Toran has spent more time analyzing signals related to the crystals than anyone else on the ship."

"It was a lucky, educated guess." Toran took a deep breath. "The relationship between the worlds is certainly clearer now, but I have no hypothesis to offer about the significance of that intersecting location."

The commander crossed his arms. "It's important in some way—I can't imagine any other reason why these paths would all converge in the same place."

"Could there be a planet there we don't know about?" Kaiden asked. "The source of the signal?"

Toran zoomed in on the location using the holographic display. True to Maris' assertion, there was nothing nearby.

"Maybe it's so corrupted by the Darkness we can't see it?" I suggested.

"Perhaps." Colren nodded. "In any case, this is the lead we had hoped to find. We should investigate it and see if we can learn anything more up close."

Kaiden leaned back in his seat. "There is another possibility. What if this is where the aliens are going to appear?"

INTENTIONALLY JOURNEYING TO the location where advanced aliens might emerge was simultaneously thrilling and terrifying.

I'd always been one to fantasize about meeting other intelligent life. The Hegemony had never made direct contact, as far as I knew, but I'd heard about discoveries of ruins that suggested we weren't alone in the universe. Whenever I heard about such things, I'd always pictured a glorious, peaceful meeting where we'd share our greatest developments and be welcomed into the fold of another interstellar civilization. Knowing what little I did about the Darkness, however, I suspected that the aliens we could potentially be meeting in the near future were almost certainly aggressive and probably weren't out to make friends. Being on the frontline for that first contact sounded like a surefire way to have things end badly.

All the same, my friends and I had been touched by the Darkness propagated by the aliens, and that connected us to them more than anyone else. If anyone had a chance of successfully interacting with them, it was probably us.

Still, as I left the meeting with Commander Colren on the bridge, I couldn't help but feel like we were about to fly into a trap.

"Just when I thought this day couldn't get any crazier..." I muttered to my companions.

"I know, I'm not crazy about going there, either," Kaiden agreed. "When the best case scenario is that we find a planet no one has observed before, you know you're in trouble."

"What if a whole alien fleet appears around us?" Maris asked, looking a little pale. "This isn't a warship."

"Like the whole Hegemony fleet would do any good against these guys." I took a deep breath.

Toran cast me a stern glance. "That attitude won't get us through this."

"Hey, I know, I didn't mean it that way." I looked down at the deck as we walked down the corridor toward the lift.

Maris held her hands at waist level. "Let's just get some rest before the jump."

"Yeah, good plan." I kept quiet for the remaining journey to our residential area, lost in speculations about what we might find at our destination.

When we reached the lower deck, Toran and Maris headed straight for their quarters. Kaiden took a slower pace, and I hung back when he motioned to me.

"Are you planning to go to sleep right away, or do you have a few minutes?" he asked when we were alone in the corridor.

I smiled coyly. "I could be persuaded to stay up for a bit." I opened the door to my quarters and beckoned him inside.

We stood together in the narrow space between the bed and side wall. A flutter of nerves hit me as he took a step closer.

"It's been quite an eventful day," I said to break the tension.

He laughed. "Yeah, you could say that. Those were some pretty impressive moves."

"I held my own."

He eyed me. "Come on, Elle. I know you're dying to gloat. Let it out."

My anxiety from earlier dissipated as I thought through everything I'd done that day—feats I never would have dreamed were possible. I tried to contain my excitement for a few more seconds, but it burst out. "That thing with the rope? That was insane! I still can't believe it worked. And then, when I took out those four shadowcats in one pass—"

"Shadowcats?"

"Yeah, I figured we should name the alien things. I thought it sounded cool." I placed my hand on his toned chest. "You had some shining moments, yourself. That was some good thinking with the shuttle escape—jumping from there to the ship."

"I can't believe it worked."

My mouth dropped open. "You told us it would be fine."

"Well, yeah. That's what you're supposed to say to get people to go along with a crazy plan."

"Colren supported it."

Kaiden shrugged. "We didn't have another choice. It was the best out of a series of bad options."

"So, we really did almost die today?" My momentary excitement faded as the reality sunk in. Despite all the remarkable things I'd been through in the last couple of weeks, I hadn't been able to shake my conditioned thinking that there were always reset points and experts were in charge to make sure something terrible didn't happen. Even facing mortal danger, part of me felt invincible—that it was all part of the plan and things would work out even if I screwed up. I knew that was foolish and naïve, but such a radical shift in thinking took time. Maybe now, with so many dire events occurring in rapid succession, it was finally enough for me to see that the stakes were real this time, and the outcome permanent. We no longer had a safety net of local resets, now that the Master Archive was sealed.

"I think we had at least three proper near-death moments today," Kaiden replied. "I hope the universe continues to side in our favor."

I chuckled. "Yeah, right? Let's see, the tentacle monster, the insane shuttle ejection back to the *Evangiel*..."

"And the shadowcat things," he filled in. "I didn't really think they'd do us in, but they *could* have, so I figure it counts on the list."

"Yeah. Thanks again for fireballing that shadowcat. I wouldn't have gotten away if you hadn't."

Kaiden looked down. "About that... That wasn't me."

"Who, then? Maris?"

He shook his head. "No, Elle. It was you."

My heart skipped a beat. "Me? But—"

"You cast magic on Crystallis. This wasn't the first time."

"Yeah, but that..." I still couldn't wrap my head around the idea that I had fragments of abilities from all three disciplines. I'd chalked up what happened on Crystallis to the pressure of the situation, the imperative to defeat the dragon guardian so we could seal the Master Archive. The notion that I could still tap into those abilities... I wasn't sure I was ready to wield that level of power.

"Why are you so hesitant? It's amazing you can do those things," Kaiden said.

"And I bet Hegemony scientists will have a field day studying me for years to come as soon as we're not in crisis mode."

"They wouldn't do that."

"Since when does a one-of-a-kind person *not* become the center of attention? Stars, I didn't even realize I'd cast that magic! If Colren finds out what I can do, there's no telling how he might react."

Kaiden looked down. "This is a big thing to keep secret."

"Can I trust you to do that?" I asked. "Whatever anyone pieced together about what happened on Crystallis, I want to leave it at that. As far as anyone is concerned, that was a one-time thing."

He hesitated, then nodded. "I have your back, Elle. And that's not just because of what's going on between us. You're right that Colren might single you out, and I don't want there to be anything to mess with our team dynamic."

"We're already throwing that off enough as it is."

He smiled. "Well, *that* part is okay."

"You would think so."

"I've gotten the distinct impression you don't disagree."

I tilted my head and shrugged playfully in response. The movement sent radiating pain down my right arm, and I winced.

Concern spread across Kaiden's face. "Hey, are you hurt?"

I brushed it off. "Just a little bruised. Medical cleared me."

"Why didn't you say anything?"

"I can handle a few bumps and scrapes. It's nothing to worry about."

He caught my gaze. "I'm going to worry all the same."

Admittedly, I knew I'd react the same way if I found out he'd been hurt. And, furthermore, I knew that part of the reason I'd gone for the four shadowcats rather than helping Toran was because Kaiden was at risk. We'd vowed to not let romance get in the middle of duty, but I knew that was impossible; subconscious desires were too powerful.

"It's happening," I said.

"What is?"

"The thing we said we wouldn't let happen. I like you, and now I'm thinking about *you* rather than the *mission*."

He took my hand. "I like you, too, Elle. I'd be lying if I denied being more concerned about you than the others."

I shook my head. "But this is crazy! We just met two weeks ago."

"Sometimes that's all it takes, especially when you've been through the kind of stressful situations like we have. That kind of thing can bring people together."

"What are we going to do? Isn't this some kind of huge liability putting everyone else at risk?"

"Why? Because we like each other as more than casual friends? I don't think that's going to destroy civilization." He raised an eyebrow.

"But the Hegemony is counting on us to be focused. And if we're distracted by non-mission things, then—"

Kaiden placed his hands on my shoulders. "Elle, take an objective look at what you're saying. This isn't a disaster that's going to compromise the team; it's a chance for us to be closer so we can work even better together. And, you told me a few days ago that you wished you had something constant in your life, knowing that even once we defeat the Darkness, you're still moving away from your family and friends. Well, maybe this thing with us could be that for you."

I gazed up at him. "Isn't it a little soon to be thinking about that?"

"Maybe. Probably. But all I know for sure is that I've been lonely for a really long time. I thought it was because I'd moved around too much, so settling on a world would give me a sense of grounding. When it didn't, I figured I just hadn't been there for long enough. Except, in the brief time I've known you, I feel more fulfilled than I ever have before."

"I do, too, but—"

"Then why question it? Relationships don't have to be a distraction, they can be an asset."

A thousand thoughts filled my mind, about how I'd always been more of a loner but had been secretly envious of the couples around me. How I'd watched my parents while I was growing up, and how I'd always hoped I'd find my own partner who complemented me as well as my parents worked with each other. And how I was sick of being alone, but I was afraid to get close to someone because I wasn't used to being vulnerable, and I was worried that once someone saw the inner me, maybe there'd be something that they didn't like.

As much as those worries swirled inside, there was still a sense of calm deeper down. What I felt for Kaiden wasn't a superficial crush like I'd experienced before, but was instead the kernel of what could grow into a lasting bond. If there was anyone worth overcoming my fears for, it was him—not *in spite* of our larger team efforts, but *because* of it. To get through that, we needed to trust each other.

I swallowed. "You're right. I guess I'm just nervous."

"About what?" He smiled. "It's not like some switch flipped when we admitted we have feelings for each other and now you have to do anything different."

"But it *is* different. I don't know how to do this relationship thing."

"As you've said. But you know how to be a friend, right?"

"Well, yeah. I mean, I have friends, and we've hung out for years."

He nodded. "Right. Well, I'd say we're on our way to being friends, too."

"Agreed."

"Okay, that's pretty much it. Dating is essentially just being friends, but with some other physical stuff added on. All the serious stuff comes with time, and there's never a guidebook for that. It's something you have to discover as a couple."

"And you know this from experience?" I eyed him.

"No, but living in close quarters on freighters growing up, I watched a number of relationships go from stolen glances in a corridor to people starting families. In all those cases, the friendship bond is what saw them through the rough patches."

I chuckled. "You know, my mom would really like you."

"If I can get a therapist mom to approve of me, I must be doing something right."

"A lot." I inched closer, gazing up at him. "I like that you're honest and speak your mind. I have a bad tendency to bottle things up when I get uncomfortable, but you help me want to face those things head-on."

Kaiden brushed my hair away from my eyes. "That's what friends do."

The gentle touch of his fingertips on my face sent an excited shiver through me. "Thank you for being here with me. I mean, I know we were all randomly assigned to this team, but thank you for wanting to take a chance on 'us'. I'd probably lose my mind if I didn't have you as a friend through this."

"I think I'd be feeling pretty lost without you, too." He leaned closer, his breath warm on my cheek. "You really are incredible."

"You're not bad yourself."

Our lips met. He entwined his fingers in my hair at the base of my neck and wrapped the other around the small of my back. We'd kissed several times since our first a week prior, but those had mostly been passing pecks—touches to gain familiarity and comfort. This was different, passionate in a way I'd never experienced. I gave into the desire, happy to let him direct me to the bed so we could lie together and forget the troubles in the outside universe.

I reveled in the contact as he kissed down my neck and caressed me. The soft touch set me at ease, never pressuring for it to be more than the next progression in the gradual process of getting to know one another. Based on these initial impressions, I liked where things were headed.

Faces flushed and breath heavy, we eventually settled into a cuddle with one of my arms on his chest and my head nestled on his shoulder.

"Well, that was nice," I said, breaking the silence.

He chuckled and stroked my hair. "Yes. Yes, it was."

"I take it that was some of the 'other physical stuff' bonus one gets from dating as opposed to other friendships?" I winked.

"Just a preview, really."

"That is definitely something I am eager to explore further."

Kaiden pivoted to face me. "Eager, huh?" He gave me a light kiss. "I have nowhere I have to be until the jump, so I am all yours until you say otherwise."

"Is that so?" I kissed him, scooching my hips closer to his.

"I could do this all day." He kissed me back, slower and deeper.

The desire that had just started to subside came back full force, and I pressed against him as our arms wrapped around each other once more. His hand traced down the side of my shipsuit. Suddenly, the garment felt far too restrictive—

"Dark Sentinel Team, report to Central Command," a female voice said over the intercom.

Kaiden pulled back from me slightly. "Really? *Now*?" He sighed.

I frowned. "This better be for something meaningful with real action items."

"Action to offset the interruption of other action?" Kaiden smirked.

I rolled my eyes. "I guess I should probably get used to your terrible word play."

"I have it on good authority that you love it, and, in fact, probably would have said something very similar yourself."

"No comment." I slid off the bed.

"Uh huh. Thought so."

We smoothed our mussed hair and then entered the hallway after checking that Maris or Toran weren't already in the corridor. I'd gotten used to the idea of holding Kaiden's hand around them, but I didn't want to share much more than that about the state of our relationship just yet.

When we began walking toward the lift up to Central Command, Toran and Maris emerged from their cabins.

"Calling us back already?" Toran said as he jogged to catch up to us.

"I'd *just* fallen asleep." Maris sighed. "I guess we'll all need a pick-me-up."

A moment later, a green wave passed over me, leaving me refreshed. "Thanks, Maris."

She smiled. "Anytime."

The healing magic wouldn't sustain us long-term, but it would buy extra hours in between proper sleep. Not knowing what we were about to walk into, I'd take any advantage I could get.

We were buzzed through the entry door to the bridge when we arrived, and Colren was talking with the helm officer. One of the techs motioned for us to wait in the corral of workstations near the entry door.

After concluding his conversation, Colren turned around to acknowledge us. "I know I promised you some rest before the jump, but we've uncovered some new information buried in the signal."

"We're ready to help in any way we can," Toran replied.

"It may be nothing, but I wanted to get your impression of something since you're the only ones to have visited a world in Darkness." The commander swept his hand, and the front viewport changed from the view of a starscape to a split screen image depicting the darkened surface of three infected planets from a high elevation. "We left probes at the worlds we visited with you," he continued. "We just received footage from Yantu, Erusan, and the Valor artifact world. In and of itself, the footage isn't that remarkable. However, when we synced the time stamps and compared it to your combat log, it took on new perspective."

He waved his hand again and the three videos began to play. At the same time, an audio clip played. I instantly recognized my voice and the sounds of fighting during our engagement with the shadowcats earlier. The images of the planets were each of dark, swirling clouds. On the surface, tendrils of dark energy like we'd seen on Windau flowed across the landscape. The moment I slayed the final shadowcat in battle, however, there was a shudder in the energy flow on the other worlds— almost imperceptible.

My eyes widened. "That's not a coincidence, is it?"

"Was there anything significant about that battle?" Colren asked.

I flashed to my use of a fireball, but quickly shoved it aside. Kaiden has used plenty of magic before. Unless... "Were there any other instances like this in the recording?" I asked.

"Nothing from during your most recent mission. We haven't checked others," the commander replied.

That confirmed it wasn't the use of magic itself. But me wielding it couldn't be all that different. At least, that's what I insisted on telling myself. There were plenty of other explanations.

Kaiden glanced at me, but he said nothing.

I swallowed. "We were tapped into the crystal at the time. Maybe that augmented whatever natural link exists between the worlds through the crystalline network." Logically, that made more sense than the odd behavior being the result of me casting magic. The timing, though... I couldn't explain why the Darkness has reacted at the moment it did rather than showing constant signs throughout the sync when the other shadowcats had been slain.

"Given that the signal seems to be everywhere, that makes sense," Kaiden agreed.

Toran nodded thoughtfully. "If we can learn how to tap into the crystal's controls ourselves, we may be able to fight back against the Darkness."

"It's something for us to observe further, I suppose," the commander said after a pause. "Nothing more we can do at present. Now, I've kept you from your rest for long enough. I'll see you after the jump."

We bid our farewell and filed out from the bridge.

"Really, they had to wake us up for *that*?" Maris grumbled.

"It was a very strange observation indeed," Toran stated. "I can't think of anything that stood out in that moment compared to any other."

"Definitely strange," Kaiden said quietly. He caught my gaze again, and I gave a subtle nod.

Whatever was happening with my abilities, it may have given me more of a connection to the Darkness than anyone realized.

I STARED OUT at the alien starscape, hoping for a clear sign of why the signal had pointed to this specific location. The aftereffects of the spatial jump still clouded my mind, but the adrenaline rush from reaching our destination was quickly bringing me back to full awareness.

Next to me, Kaiden frowned at the void. "Something doesn't feel right about this place."

"I know what you mean," Maris agreed, arms crossed. "I feel like I'm being watched."

I wanted to tell her it was all in her head, except I wasn't sure she was wrong. The aliens *could* be watching us, waiting to strike. I hated feeling like I was waiting in a trap. "How long are we going to hang out here?"

Toran shook his head. "At this point, I believe the commander intends to wait until we make contact."

My heart skipped a beat. Was I really going to be on the welcoming committee for the first alien contact in generations? "How long might that take?"

"Stars if I know." Kaiden sighed. "Say, doesn't this ship have some sort of interface with the Master Archive?"

"That won't do any good now that the Archive is sealed—same reason we didn't use it to get any leads over the last week," Toran replied.

Kaiden waved his hand. "Not for new leads—looking backward. Before the Archive was sealed, did they extract any more information about which worlds would be affected?"

"Pretty sure Colren would have mentioned if they had anything like that," Maris said. "Sounds like the information source was cut off as soon as we were done."

"But they knew there were blank points in the Archive," Kaiden insisted. "So, they must have *some* information beyond what was real-time a week ago."

Maris screwed up her face for a couple seconds, thinking. "I dunno. Maybe, I guess."

"Well, if there *is* something the commander didn't share with us, it might be in the same directory as data we extracted since it's all connected to the Darkness," Toran suggested.

"Do you remember where that is?" I asked.

"I think so." He stepped over to the table in the center of our lounge room and began navigating through the computer network.

"Why haven't we gone looking for this info before?" Maris wondered aloud.

"Probably because we thought we were being told everything," Kaiden muttered.

She tilted her head. "And what makes us think they're keeping anything from us now? We were promised last week that we had been told everything the Hegemony knows."

"As much as I want to believe that's the case, Colren was way too casual about coming here into an unpredictable situation facing likely alien contact," Kaiden replied. "Do you really think we'd be here with no backup if the circumstances were as uncertain as they seem?"

"That's a good point," I realized. "What do you think they're keeping from us?"

Maris' eyes widened. "Do they know what the Darkness is?"

"Doubt it. Colren has seemed genuinely surprised by every bit of information we've brought him," I said.

"Then what else?" she prompted.

I looked to Kaiden. "Any thoughts?"

"I think it has something to do with the Master Archive or the records," he began slowly. "Every time he's been especially cagey, it's been connected to records of past events—or the things that are in the record that haven't happened yet."

Maris frowned. "I still don't get how that's possible. If it hasn't happened, it can't be history. Time travel isn't a thing."

"Not time travel. A reset," Kaiden said.

"Yes, the Archive appears to exist in a different plane that might not be subject to the physical resets," Toran stated while he browsed through files via the tabletop interface.

I eyed him. "Meaning, there *has* already been a universal reset."

"I'd believe that sooner than I would time travel," he replied.

"If there's been a reset, then why don't we remember it?" That was how it always worked—our cognition remained intact.

"It could have been well before our lifetime," Kaiden replied. "Resets don't have to be limited to going back only hours or days."

"But decades or centuries would mean..." Maris massaged her temples. "Nope, can't do it."

"Makes my head hurt, too." I rubbed my eyes. "But it's all speculation. We might be reading way too much between the lines."

"Except, we're not," Toran murmured. He fanned out a set of documents on the touch-surface tabletop. "Bandwidth issues in the crystalline network could explain the memory issues. And, they *do* have evidence of a prior reset."

"Wait, really?" I came to attention. "From when?"

Toran released a long breath. "That's not clear—but a long time ago. They also noted something strange, like the same record had been overwritten multiple times... and that anomaly matches up with the present, as near as anyone can tell."

My chest constricted. "Are you saying that we might have gone through a reset we don't remember?"

"It's possible," Toran replied. "There are scientific models to support it, but it's still in the realm of theory."

I groaned. "I'm getting really sick of speculation. We need *answers!*"

"Let's take a step back here," Maris cut in. "The reason we were looking into this is so you could see if there's talk about the alien fleet, or whatever. These other potential resets are another matter entirely."

Kaiden huffed. "There are too many threads to chase."

"You're right, Maris," Toran conceded. "We need to focus on clues related to what we're about to face—the distant past isn't important right now."

"And what *can* you glean about that?" asked Kaiden.

Toran laughed. "Absolutely nothing."

I did a double-take. "You're joking, right?"

He held out his hands to encompass the tabletop. "When I said they have evidence, I mean there's a single note on this file where someone circled some weird data points and scribbled, 'Universal reset???' with, yes, three question marks." He pointed to it.

Sure enough, the red text stood out from the jumble of nonsense displayed on the screen. Dots and bars formed lines, which had gaps and intersecting branches, but each of the points could mean anything. Codes were attached to some of the lines, though it was unclear if that was a product of the data extraction procedure or if Hegemony researchers had added the notations. My head swam as I tried to wrap my mind around the implications of resets on top of resets, but I didn't know where to begin.

"Can you make any sense of this?" Toran continued. "I hate to say it, but I think Colren is just following whatever clues we give him. There is no grand strategy here. They weren't truthful in the sense that they *do* know there was a universal reset at some point and didn't tell us, but they don't know anything else about it. The code from the Archives may as well be random splatters of paint on a wall."

I stared at the data he'd spread out in front of us, and I was inclined to agree. "So, that's it? We just have to sit around and wait again, hoping that everything works out okay?"

My friends' shoulders rounded.

"The only thing I can tell you is that, like Colren told us before, there are records indicating events past our present time," Toran said. "Assuming that's true, then at least some people must survive whatever's coming."

"But if everything works out okay, then why was there a reset?" I asked.

Kaiden's brow knit. "Yeah, that's a good point."

"There's too much about this that we don't understand," Toran said. "We may be looking at this all wrong."

"Then what are we supposed to look at? I have no idea what to suggest we should do." Kaiden sighed.

"The commander thinks we should wait and see," Maris pointed out.

I nodded. "But he'll listen to us if we bring another suggestion."

"I still think we must be missing something in the signal," Kaiden insisted. "The commander may have come here on faith alone that things will work because of what's recorded in the Archive, but that's not good enough for me."

"Yes, there is still the question of *why here*," Toran stated. "With so many systems to choose from, there must be significance to why the aliens selected this location."

"That's assuming the intersecting lines *do* have any significance," I said.

"It was all too perfect," Kaiden countered. "You saw it—there was nothing random about it."

Maris paled. "What if it was a test?"

I looked at her. "What do you mean?"

"What if they embedded all of that in the signal as a test to see if we were smart enough to figure it out. Create a map, see if we follow it."

"And if we show up here, we pass?" Kaiden asked.

"Or lose, depending on what they might be trying to measure," Toran replied.

I swallowed. "If that's the case, this wasn't us hacking into their secret plans at all… we might be playing directly into their hands."

Kaiden bit his lower lip. "If so, what do they want?"

"Well, it gives them information about our reasoning ability as well as technological capabilities," Toran said.

A chill passed through me. "None of that matters when we're delivering a whole ship. An investigation of the unknown—any civilization would put their best foot forward. They may have been trying to bait us into handing them the Hegemony's best tech, signed, sealed, and delivered."

"Stars, if that's the case—" Kaiden cut off as a warning claxon sounded.

My heart leaped into my throat. "No…"

"Spatial anomaly seven thousand kilometers to port. Crew to battle stations," a woman announced over the central comm.

Maris' face twisted with terror. "What do we do?"

I looked down at my white shipsuit—hardly battle-ready attire. "We need to get our gear."

"Tami's going to be a little preoccupied," Toran said.

"Do you want to only be wearing this is we're boarded?" I gestured to my onesie. "Yeah, no."

"Can't argue with that. Let's go." Kaiden headed for the door.

"We should stay here and wait for instructions, not go wandering around the ship," Toran insisted.

"Sure, I'm all for waiting this out—*after* I have my sword in hand." I followed Kaiden to the exit. Foolish or not, I wasn't about to leave my fate entirely in others' hands. It seemed especially prudent for me to retrieve my weapon considering our 'no magic' rule on the spaceship, but I also suspected those rules might be bendable under the new circumstances.

As Kaiden and I entered the corridor, Toran and Maris jogged to catch up. Though I never had any doubt that they'd accompany us to the hangar, it was still a relief to have the team sticking together. Now, more than ever, was the time to make sure we didn't get split apart.

The corridors, which were typically devoid of too many passersby, were now abuzz with activity as crew members ran toward their various posts. Most individuals barely seemed to notice our presence, but now and then, I caught a sidelong glance from the occasional higher-ranked crewman. On the fourth such instance on our way to the lift, a dark-haired man with a petty officer insignia held up his hand as we passed by.

"Where are you going?" he asked.

"To retrieve our gear," I replied.

His dark eyebrows drew together. "That can wait."

I stood my ground. "Can it? What's the reason for the alarm?"

"A spatial anomaly—"

"Yes, we heard the commander's announcement. But if that anomaly turns out to be an alien ship, we need to be ready."

"We're under orders to keep you secure," the petty officer replied.

"Great, then that supports our objective of being able to defend ourselves. We'll come back here as soon as we have our gear."

The crewman looked like he was about to protest further, but Toran cut him off, "We can look after ourselves."

"Fine, just stay out of everyone's way." The man continued to jog down the corridor.

I pressed forward. "I kind of feel like we could get away with anything on this ship."

"We do seem to have more freedom than I'd expect," Toran agreed.

"No complaints from me." Kaiden pressed the call button for the lift when we reached it.

"I guess the 'last, best chance designation' does afford some autonomy to do things 'our way'," I said.

Maris chuckled. "Which appears to be getting in the middle of the mess and then miraculously finding a way out."

The lift doors opened and Kaiden stepped inside. "The part about overcoming the challenges is key."

"Sounds like we're about to face a whole new mess," I replied. "We've sort of gotten a handle on fighting the Darkness creatures planetside, but how in the stars are we supposed to fight something in *space*?"

"Assuming the aliens behind the Darkness are anything like those creatures," Toran countered.

"Why else would they make those changes to the planets if it wasn't to make it hospitable to them? Yeah, they might not be exactly like those black monster things, but I bet some of the attributes carry over." The lift arrived at the hangar level and I led the way out.

"That's true, the form of the creator often does transfer into design," Toran agreed while we hurried toward the hanger. "Like, our bipedal robots."

Kaiden frowned. "Let's hope that they didn't make those shadowcats to be cute little pets in the way we'd breed hamsters."

"Yeah, nope." I shook my head. "Not going to think about it." I knew from experience that I could have an active imagination and assume the worst, so there was no way I could let myself start thinking about what a guard dog might look like if the shadowcats were the equivalent of little fuzzballs that liked to munch on carrots.

We entered the hangar to find it more crowded than it ever had been since our arrival on the *Evangiel*. Crew members were busy inspecting all the fighters lined up on the far side of the hangar deck, and two of the remaining three shuttles were being prepped. I tried to pick Tami out of the forty or more people darting around the cavernous room. After thirty seconds of observation, I spotted her at a control station near the port bulkhead.

"Let's find out where to get our stuff," I said, jogging toward her.

We slowed to a walk as we neared the control station.

Tami was absorbed in her monitor, but as we walked up, she pivoted to one of her techs. "Have you completed the initialization sequence?"

"Yes, the P-85s are idling. Awaiting the launch order."

"How about—" Tami cut off when she saw us, her face flushing. "What are you doing here?"

"We came to get our gear," I replied.

"Your—" She sighed and it turned into a swear under her breath. "All right, fine. The decontamination cycle should be finished. It's over there in the tent."

"Thank you." Toran paused. "Is there anything we can do to help you?"

She laughed. "Tell me what kind of loadout I should give to our fighters? Stars, we may as well be staring into a blank black box."

"What's going on out there?" I asked her.

"All I know is that the engagement protocol Colren issued is for the highest risk scenarios with likely loss of life."

Maris sucked in a sharp breath next to me.

"We need to find out what the commander knows," I said.

"Whatever it is, I don't want to know. I just keep the ships flying," Tami muttered.

"It will all work out," I told her. I hated generic platitudes, but it was all I could think to say in the moment.

She nodded. "Thanks. We'll do what we can."

"Incendiary rounds," Kaiden said as he headed toward the decontamination tent.

"Hmm?"

"The loadout for the fighters. Incendiary rounds," he repeated to Tami. "The creatures in the Darkness don't like fire."

GETTING MY SWORD and other gear hadn't set me at ease the way I'd hoped it would. We were still on a ship, reliant on the craft and crew.

"I want to see what's going on," I stated.

"Didn't we agree to go back to the lounge and wait this out?" Toran protested.

I smiled. "Since when do we stick to the plan?"

"And things have gone *so* well for us whenever we improvise." Maris rolled her eyes.

"I think we'd all like to understand what's happening. It's not like we're reinterpreting orders this time," I replied.

"I'm not confident they will let us on the bridge, but I'd like to try," Kaiden agreed.

"Only one way to find out." Hand on my sword's hilt, I strode toward the hangar exit.

"Colren is totally going to yell at us," Kaiden murmured, walking abreast.

"Yeah, but maybe we can learn something in the process."

"You know," Toran said behind me, "we might be able to tap into the feed from the front viewport and the general sensor suite. Given the directory I accessed earlier, I'm pretty sure I have the right permissions."

I smiled back at him. "But what's the fun in that?"

"For the record, I have no problem observing from a distance," Maris interjected.

"Noted. Now, let's go find the middle of the action." I continued forward with renewed purpose.

As much as I pretended to be the reluctant hero, I loved being in the thick of it. I'd dreamed of being a Ranger on the Space Force, and this was my chance to skip Tactical School and live out my fantasies. Granted, the mortal danger wasn't ideal, but I couldn't imagine sitting back and watching from afar while more worlds were consumed by Darkness. As we stood on the precipice of direct contact with the aliens behind the attack, I wanted to see it firsthand.

Kaiden and I led the way up the lift to the command deck. The corridors had cleared out while we retrieved our gear, giving us a straight shot to our destination. At the entry door to the bridge, Kaiden pressed the buzzer. We were normally buzzed in almost instantaneously, but this time, no response came.

"I don't think they want to talk to us," Maris said.

Toran nodded. "Let's go back to the lounge room."

"Not yet." I tapped the comm activation point behind my left ear. "Commander, we're here to help."

"Elle, I'd expected your team to remain in your quarters."

"Well, you *didn't* say that, and we're here now, so..."

The comm cut out for a few seconds. "Honestly, we could use another set of eyes on this." The door buzzed open.

I disconnected the comm link and smiled at my team. "See?"

Toran shook his head. "I can't believe that worked."

Kaiden eyed me. "Have you always been this assertive?"

"Stars, no! But having a badass magic sword is a major confidence booster." I was still somewhat surprised by the ongoing changes in myself. I'd done reckless things and always had a bit of a rebellious streak, but outright standing up to authority and making myself heard was a new attribute. At one time not long ago, I hadn't even wanted to tell my parents that I wanted to attend Tactical School; now, I was expecting a Hegemony commander to include me in decision-making. The changes seemed to become more pronounced every time I tapped into my new abilities. Eventually, I wondered if I'd even recognize myself.

We entered the bridge, and the crew members didn't even glance at us. Commander Colren's attention was glued on the front viewport.

At the center of the starfield, an almost imperceptible distortion warped the appearance of the stars behind it. I squinted, trying to make it out. "What is that?" I whispered to Kaiden.

"Must be the 'anomaly'."

We slowly approached the back of the command chair, waiting for Colren to acknowledge us. He finally turned around, looking more openly distraught than I'd ever seen him in our two weeks on the *Evangiel*.

"We've never seen anything like it," he murmured.

I gestured at the distortion. "Was it here when we arrived?"

The commander nodded. "We didn't notice it at first, but when we scanned the area, it showed up on all of the non-visual displays. What you see on the screen is augmented with a holographic overlay; there's nothing to see with the naked eye."

"I *knew* this place felt wrong," Kaiden said to me.

"Is it related to the Darkness?" Toran asked.

Colren stood up from his seat. "Considering we can't see it against the void, in some ways it seems like *pure* Darkness. The anomaly is disturbing because it's radiating gravity like a black hole, but there is no event horizon or debris field."

My stomach flopped. "If it's not a black hole, could this be the location of a system that was completely consumed by Darkness?"

"If it was, we'd have no way to verify it," the commander replied.

"But we *do* know our tech came from another civilization. This may have all happened before," I said.

Kaiden nodded. "We saw what looked like weapons fire on Crystallis, remember."

"Yes, remnants of past wars could be all around us," Colren said. "But whatever this is, it's not dormant. It's emitting a signal that's made up of components from the others we've observed."

I tilted my head. "But not the same?"

"Not exactly, no. There's another code segment we haven't observed before."

"May I see it?" Toran asked.

Colren accessed a panel next to his command chair, bringing up a hologram in the open area between the seat and the forward bulkhead. "Can you make any sense of this?"

Toran stepped forward toward the projection, his eyes flitting around the displayed data.

As usual, it was all nonsense to me, though I did pick out waveforms that I recognized as components of the signal emitted from the crystals, which we'd also observed coming through the infected crystal on Windau. "How is a signal coming from a thing that's essentially nothing?" I asked.

"Probably a wormhole," Kaiden replied.

"There's a hyperdimensional connection between the crystals, which exists outside of our normal spatial perception; that much has been clear for a long time," Colren stated. "Whatever that link is, we might be witnessing it here in its true form without a crystal to enclose its terminus."

That concept stopped me cold. There was much we didn't know about the technology we took for granted in our everyday lives, but I'd always associated the crystals with connections between the worlds. It hadn't occurred to me that any connections might extend beyond the known crystalline network.

"I'm not sure what to suggest," Toran said. He took a deep breath. "The signal we picked up on Windau was only detectable through a hard connection, and other signals can be picked up in the vicinity. I don't know where this one would be coming from."

"From whatever the anomaly is connected to." I looked at him. "I mean, it has to be connected to someplace else, right?"

"That is the only explanation," he agreed.

"How do we find out *where* that is?" Kaiden asked.

Colren placed his hands on the back of his command chair. "I was hoping you might have some suggestions."

"I don't—" Toran began.

"What I meant is that you developed the detection system using the crystal pendants. Could that be adapted for longer distances?" the commander clarified.

Toran shook his head. "It's only a proximity indicator. I don't see how we'd use it to trace the signal anywhere."

"Maybe you don't need that approach at all," I said in the ensuing pause. "Why go after the aliens at all when we can have them come to us? Force the engagement to be on our home turf."

"Preemptive strikes have an advantage," Colren replied.

"But only if you know what you're facing, right?" I countered. "Even if we *did* trace this signal back to somewhere, that probably wouldn't give us any more details about the aliens who sent it out. We're here to study and assess the potential enemies themselves, not just where they might be from. Right? So, let's observe, find a weakness."

"Wait for them to come to us?" Colren asked.

"For now. All signs point to this being a hub of some sort for them. My guess is they'll show up here eventually—and probably soon. The *Evangiel* and whatever other ships you want can be waiting here."

He considered my statement. "The only reason I'd shied away from that approach is we have no way to predict what kind of ships they'll possess or how many they'll send."

"What I saw in my vision was an entire fleet," Kaiden said. "Not that those visions necessarily reflect reality, but there's at least potential for more than a hundred ships."

"Topping those numbers would be a huge commitment for the Hegemony's resources. Our fleet is stretched thin with evacuation efforts on the infected worlds," the commander responded.

My heart skipped a beat. "Evacuations? You never said anything about that before."

"That information was outside the scope of your responsibilities and activities," Colren stated.

"Yeah, wait, you never mentioned any ships being around to get people offworld when we went to get Elle or Maris," Kaiden said.

"There weren't any there," the commander said.

"Then who? Where?" I pressed.

"Certain high-asset individuals and their families have been taken to secure locations," he said slowly.

"Meaning government and military personnel," Toran filled in.

The commander nodded. "Those decisions are made well above my paygrade. Most evacuations have been from the Capital as a preemptive measure."

"I hope they at least threw in a few scientists," Toran said. "I'm out of my depth with all of this—I've just gotten lucky."

"More than luck," Colren replied. "But yes, there are scientists who've been briefed on our latest developments. We'd hoped to rendezvous with them after the investigation here, but it looks like we may be sticking around here longer than I'd anticipated."

Toran tilted his head. "We don't need to meet in person. A vid chat via hyperspace relay would allow us to share ideas."

"Good thinking," the commander agreed. "I'll talk with the admiralty about making a stand at this location against a potential invasion force. In the meantime, I'll put you in contact with the research team so you can compare notes."

"Sounds like a reasonable approach to me," I said.

"What are the rest of us supposed to do?" Maris asked.

"Stay vigilant, but you're free to pass the time however you see fit," Colren said. "We'll be at Threat Imminent status until further notice."

"And, when things go down, should we... wander up here?" I asked.

He sighed. "I have a feeling that even if I said you should remain in your quarters you'd show up here anyway."

"Most likely."

Colren shook his head. "Then we may as well just make it your standing instruction to report here if and when any alien craft appear."

I cracked a smile. It looked like we'd get a front row seat to the next show after all.

THE RED WARNING lights had changed to yellow by the time we were back in the corridor outside the bridge. "Anyone else have an overwhelming feeling of impending doom?" I asked my team.

Kaiden chuckled. "That's been a pretty constant state for the last few weeks."

"It just doubled down," Maris replied. "I don't know how we're supposed to relax."

"I, for one, will be trying to learn everything I can about this anomaly and how it works," Toran stated. "I suggest you find your own ways to contribute."

I wanted to help, too. It was the reason I'd wanted to venture down to Windau and was the same reason I'd embraced my transformation rather than trying to run away. But I felt like I was backed against a wall with my hands tied in this moment. Everything I'd learned about my new abilities related to skills that I'd be unable to exercise on a spaceship. So long as we were here, I had no idea what kind of 'contribution' I might be able to make.

"I guess I'll head back to the lounge," I said at last.

Kaiden nodded. "I'll join you, unless some space plants appear that you need analyzed."

We reached the lift and stepped inside.

Maris eyed us. "Would it cramp your style if I joined in?"

"Of course not," I replied on reflex, only afterward realizing that it would have been nice to get some more couple time with Kaiden.

However, maybe it was for the best we slowed things down a bit, especially given the new complication related to the potential alien fleet.

Momentary disappointment flitted across Kaiden's face, but when his gaze met mine there was understanding in his eyes. "I still feel awkward just sitting around waiting."

"Me, too. But, we don't have the right skills to bring to this one. We need to leave it to the scientists," I said.

Maris nodded. "I'm *definitely* out."

The lift doors opened, and we stepped out into the corridor on the level housing our cabins and lounge.

"Well, you three sort that out. Reach me on my comm if you need anything. I'll be in my cabin." Toran walked quickly towards his cabin.

I sighed, plodding behind him at a slower pace. "More waiting. I had enough of that last week."

"You know, we don't *have* to wait in the lounge," Kaiden said after we'd only gone a few steps. "We could get in some combat practice."

Maris crossed her arms. "I thought there was a 'no magic on the ship' rule?"

"In all fairness, that was self-imposed rather than any official ruling from Colren," Kaiden clarified. "If we can find an interior storage room or something, it might be a good opportunity to keep working on our combat skills."

"Toran would say that's a terrible idea," I replied.

Kaiden smiled. "Toran isn't with us right now, is he?"

Maris evaluated us. "I get the impression it's a bad idea to ever leave the two of you unsupervised."

"Nonsense! We're completely responsible one hundred percent of the time," I lied.

"Right, like when you dove out the back of the shuttle earlier," she countered, missing the irony in my statement.

"Hey, I *saved* us." That was the truth. The move was dangerous, yes, but we hadn't had a lot of options. If I was going to be berated, it should be for doing something genuinely reckless—like when I climbed up the rock titan's arm without a plan.

"I promise to not use any of the strong magical attacks," Kaiden stated. "Besides, we made that rule when we were just starting to learn about our abilities; we all have a lot more control now."

Maris smirked, looking us up and down. "You two have lost control in other ways." She sauntered back to the lift and pressed the call button. "Are we going to practice, or what?"

Face flushed, I followed her back to the lift. "I'll check with the commander."

I'd prepared myself for some gentle ribbing about the new relationship, especially from Maris. She had always struck me as the kind of young woman who'd get wrapped up in other people's relationship drama. Just like I had a tendency to joke around when I was stressed, she was seeking her own distractions to ease anxiety about the terrifying unknowns. Nonetheless, the teasing was annoyingly out of place amid our present bid for survival.

After a quick call to Colren about our desire to practice, he directed us to use an unoccupied storage room on the hangar level. After exiting the lift, we headed to the right, past the fighter pilots' quarters, until we reached a series of larger doors labeled numerically as cargo holds. All the nearby doors had a biometric lock, currently in red 'locked' mode.

I frowned at the lock on the first door. "I wonder if our credentials will open it?" I extended my hand to the scanner and placed my palm flat against the surface. The device let out a harsh beep.

"That would be a 'no'," Kaiden observed. He peered down the hall. "Hey, I think I see a green light further down."

The three of us continued another twenty meters to a door that did not appear to be locked like the others. Kaiden brushed his hand over the control panel, and the door opened with a hiss. Beyond, a five-meter-by-ten-meter storage room was completely empty.

I smiled. "Now we're in business."

Kaiden stepped inside. "Point any attacks toward the inside. We don't want to blow a hole in the outer hull."

"What if there's something combustible on the other side of these walls?" Maris asked.

Kaiden and I exchanged glances. "Well, let's not bust through any walls, then," he replied.

Maris was silent for a moment. "Maybe this is an opportunity for me to try something out. We've needed a lot of shields around us, right?"

I nodded.

"This might be a good time for me to practice some of that defensive magic," she continued. "Like, put a shield around this entire room."

Kaiden placed a hand pensively on his chin. "You know, that's not a bad idea. It would contain my magical attacks so we wouldn't have to worry about damaging the ship."

"Except, we'd be trapped in the shell *with* the fireballs or lightning or whatever," I pointed out.

Maris' eye lit up. "Unless I can maintain different sets of shields—one around the room and individual ones around us."

I raised an eyebrow. "That's kind of a jump from what you've been able to do in the past, isn't it?"

"We're down here to learn new skills, aren't we?" She strode confidently into the center of the chamber.

"We are, indeed." Kaiden followed her inside. "Elle?"

I sighed. "Guess the only way to find out is to try." I stepped inside and spotted an interior control panel next to the door. After flipping the lights on and closing the door, I joined my friends in the center of the chamber. "Have at it, Maris."

She took a slow, deep breath and closed her eyes. "Okay, a shield. A big shield."

Purple sparks danced around her hands, casting a cool glow on her form-fitting clothing. The sparks shot upward toward the ceiling and arced in all directions to form a circular dome. With the rectangular shape of the room, the dome's edges brushed up against the side walls while open floor space remained in front and behind.

"I don't think it would be a good idea for the bubble to extend into the other storage rooms," I stated.

"Can you do anything about the shape of the shell, Maris?" Kaiden asked.

"I'm not sure." Her brow furrowed with concentration. Slowly, the shape of the shell began to elongate to better fit the proportions of the chamber, reaching almost to the ceiling and stretched into a curved oval footprint that covered most of the deck space.

I smiled. "Hey, not bad!"

She grinned. "It's actually not that hard now that I'm doing it."

"See how else you can augment the spell," Kaiden suggested.

A second wave of sparks passed over Maris' hands, but as soon as they reached her fingertips, the larger shield began to shudder. "Gah!" she groaned. "So much for this being easy."

"It's just like when you have the individual shells around us," Kaiden said, though I suspected he was making it up to keep Maris from giving up. "Since Toran isn't here, pretend the room is him."

Maris raised an eyebrow. "He's big, but he's not room-sized."

"Then make this one smaller and work up from there," he replied. "Practice the nesting and then bring it to scale."

She took a steadying breath. "Okay."

The shell brushing the confines of the chamber shrunk until the dome was only five meters wide. Then, Maris' hands glowed once more with purple sparks. They extended from her fingers and fed into three smaller domes, one around each of us.

"It's working!" she exclaimed with a giggle.

"Shed the self-doubt, Maris." Fire danced across Kaiden's palms. "Now make this area bigger so we can start to play."

Maris fed the larger shell until it filled the room. "I'll just have to keep it simple for now."

"All right," Kaiden agreed. "Now, we need to let attacks pass through our personal shells and get blocked by the room shell and the other personal shells."

"And how am I supposed to do *that*?" Maris sighed.

"I don't know. The same way we can do anything else." Kaiden sent a tiny fireball toward the side wall—no bigger than the end of his thumb, but enough to help Maris focus on controlling the properties of each shield. The lower-temperature orange flame passed through both barriers and struck the wall, leaving a black smudge. "That's what we *don't* want to happen."

Maris rolled her eyes. "I got that, yeah."

"Again." Kaiden repeated the move with another tiny fireball. The orb shot through the inner defensive shield but then sputtered when it reached the outer layer.

Maris grinned. "Just need to picture what I want it to do!"

"While you two keep up with that, I'm going to work on my flips." I drew my sword in preparation for my own practice activities.

We spent the next half-hour playing around with our various skills. Maris was only able to maintain each shield for two minutes initially, but she eventually improved her concentration enough to keep the large one active for nearly five minutes at a stretch. I hoped we wouldn't need those skills in the future, but it was comforting to know it was an option for any prospective engagements.

Kaiden eventually grew tired of practicing with scaled-back fireballs and stood back to watch me practice my forms. "You're looking like a seasoned pro with that sword."

I smiled over my shoulder while I continued to practice lunges. "Feels like it, too." I flourished the sword over my head and pivoted on the ball of my right foot to face him. "This ancient muscle memory or whatever it is we got from the artifacts is awesome."

"Some of these skills we woke up with in the bioprinter, which is even weirder," he replied, tossing a loose flame between the palms of his hands.

"It doesn't make any sense, but this magic is a part of me," Maris said. "I can't believe I went most of my life without it."

I stopped my exercises. "Looking back, it's like something was always missing."

"I know what you mean." Maris swelled the latest iteration of the outer shield until it touched the side walls. "After this practicing, I feel even stronger." The sphere continued to expand, its edges passing through the bulkheads into the adjacent chambers.

"Whoa, Maris, dial it back," I cautioned.

Her faced paled. "I'm trying" she exclaimed. "It's like something else is fueling it." Purple sparks danced on her fingertips.

The flame Kaiden had been playing with suddenly flared to the size of his torso. "Stars! What...?" He threw his hands wide and the flame dropped toward the deck, fizzling out.

Maris' shield, on the other hand, continued to grow. Hoping to break her concentration, I ran over and grabbed her right wrist, twisting her arm behind her back as gently as I could.

She sucked in a sharp breath, and the purple shields dissolved. "What just happened?"

I shook my head. "It was like an energy surge or something."

Kaiden frowned. "I've never had that happen before."

A chirp sounded in my ear, startling me. "Dark Sentinel team to the bridge! We have contact."

I RACED DOWN the corridor toward the lift with my comrades. "Contact with *what*?"

"The aliens?" Kaiden speculated.

My heart skipped a beat. "Is that what caused the magical energy surge?"

His frown deepened. "If it was, then we know even less about them and their capabilities than we imagined."

"I can't believe this is happening," Maris moaned.

I couldn't, either. Not only was my civilization about to meet genuine aliens for the first time in recorded history, but I was going to be a part of that experience. No matter how many times I thought about it, I couldn't help feeling giddy despite the danger. No longer was I some anonymous girl from a backwater world—I would be in the history records as someone who was present during what would no doubt be a landmark moment in our civilization, no matter how the events unfolded.

Taking a deep, steadying breath, I tried to mentally prepare myself for whatever was about to happen. "We need to say something about the magical surge."

Kaiden nodded. "Yeah, I was thinking the same thing."

We took the lift to the bridge level. As we exited, I spotted Toran marching down the corridor ahead.

"Hey!" I called out.

He glanced over his shoulder then halted when he spotted us. "Good, you got the summons."

"Do you know anything about this 'contact'?" Kaiden asked.

The large man shook his head as we reached his position, and we continued down the hall toward the bridge. "I've just been going over the data about the anomaly. I was about to have a conference with the team working on it in the Capital, but then the alert sounded."

"I kind of thought we'd have to wait a long time for something to happen," I admitted. "There are still several unpaired worlds, so I was thinking that pattern would be complete before the aliens appeared."

"Maybe our presence here has altered the plans," Kaiden suggested.

"Let's hope the aliens are happy to see us," Maris said.

"Yeah, here's hoping." I didn't have any faith that would be the case.

We reached the entry to the bridge and were buzzed through the door. The usually calm techs were visibly rattled, eyes darting and a slight tremble to their hands. Colren stood in front of his seat, dividing his attention between the holographic data display and the enhanced image overlaid on the front viewport.

The previously faint anomaly was now a bright point of light. When my eyes adjusted to it, my breath caught in my throat as I realized that the light wasn't the only change. An object was coming through. "Stars!" I gasped. "What is that?"

Kaiden tensed next to me. "I think it's a ship."

The craft was recognizable as such only because of its present location and behavior. From its appearance, I would have thought it a clump of organic matter, like moss viewed under a magnifying glass. Thin tendrils looped around each other to form a roughly cylindrical shape, and the craft's dark coloration was only visible because of the bright light from the anomaly behind it. The more I looked at the form, it reminded me of the tentacle monster and ground covering we had encountered that morning.

"Is it alive?" I murmured.

"I don't know, but that's what I saw in my vision," Kaiden said. "It's coming true."

I swallowed hard. I couldn't get a clear sense of scale from my vantage, but I got the impression the ship was nearly a kilometer in length—far larger than our own vessel, and with unknown firepower. All the same, seeing it put me in an aggressive mood. "We can't let them invade. We need to stop it!"

"They've already begun the invasion, Elle," Toran said with uncharacteristic grimness in his tone.

"It's not too late to turn them back." I stepped forward to the dais with the captain's seat. "Commander, we're here."

Colren didn't take his gaze off the ship as the final section of it cleared the anomaly. "This is the moment that will define our future."

"Whoever they are, they mean us harm," I said.

He nodded. "I know."

The alien ship had no visible engine wash, but its movements made it clear that it wasn't traveling on inertia alone. It moved away from the anomaly, looking like it was coming for us, but then halted twenty kilometers from where it had emerged.

"Helm, pull back to fifty thousand kilometers and hold," the commander ordered.

"Aye," the helmsman acknowledged, and the front view began to shrink as the ship pulled away.

"We're just going to let them hang out here?" I questioned.

"Of course not," Colren replied. "We'll do our best to drive them back through whatever that anomaly is, but the Hegemony fleet hasn't arrived yet. We thought we had more time to prepare."

My heart pounded in my chest. "What if the rest of the alien fleet comes before our backup?"

"We'll evaluate our options at that time," he replied.

I took a deep breath. "Commander, there's something else going on. We were practicing magic on the lower deck, and there was some sort of magical energy surge. It happened right before we got the alert from you."

Colren's scowl deepened at the end of my statement. "We noticed some strange activity, too, in the device we use to interface with the Master Archive."

"What *is* that, anyway?" Kaiden questioned.

I'd been curious, myself. The commander had mentioned it on several different occasions, but never more than a reference in passing. Considering that he had disclosed there were only four such devices known to our people and this ship had one of them, I would have thought he'd make a bigger deal out of it.

Colren glanced out the front viewport, the site of the anomaly now only a bright point in the distance. "I suppose it's time I showed you." He led the way off the bridge. "I must admit that I wasn't entirely forthcoming about this device and its supposed capabilities."

"We can't help you if you don't share information with us," Toran said.

"And that's why I'm showing you now. It wasn't necessary before," the commander replied.

Kaiden brushed his hand across the small of my back as we turned to follow the commander out. "We'll get through this," he whispered just loud enough for me to hear.

I flashed a slight smile. "I know we will."

Colren led us back in the direction of the lift and then continued past it. I'd originally thought the corridor dead-ended just after the lift, but the commander touched the wall panel and a compartment opened to reveal a biometric scanner. He placed his palm on the device, and a portion of the wall slid to the side.

I exchanged surprised looks with my team members. "A secret passageway on a spaceship?"

The commander cast me a cautionary glance. "And it will remain need-to-know." He stepped through the opening into the chamber beyond and we followed him inside.

The room had a similar aesthetic as the bridge, with control stations situated around the perimeter of the seven-meter-wide round room. At its center was the device that was clearly the main attraction—a transparent orb suspended on a chrome pedestal. The meter-wide orb glowed with soft blue light.

"Is this crystal?" I asked.

Colren sealed the entry door behind us. "All analyses point to yes, but we have never been able to carve crystals. This device and the three others like it are the only instances we've ever seen the crystals in a form other than their natural shape."

Kaiden twirled his pendant in his fingers; the crystal at the end of the chain glowed brightly with proximity resonance. "What does it do?"

"More than you could ever imagine." The commander approached the orb and placed his hands on either side of it. As he made contact, the intensity of the glow increased momentarily, then darkness filled the center of the sphere.

"Stars! It's infected," Maris exclaimed.

"No," Colren replied. "This is a 'no signal' notification, of sorts. Before the Master Archive was sealed, this is how we extracted information."

"How?" I asked. It looked more like a giant crystal ball than anything capable of downloading information about past-or, potentially, future—events.

"There's a visual interface for the hyperdimensional link," Colren explained. "The user would navigate through a series of visual cues. For example, a digital maze with multiple branches, and at each turn, a world. The selected planet could be spun backward through thought commands to view its past states at the saved reset points."

"Thought commands? Like, telepathy?" Kaiden asked.

Colren nodded. "The crystal forms a sort of cybernetic connection with the user so long as they are in physical contact with the sphere."

"Just like how we make a reset point by touching the crystal," I realized.

"*Any* world can be viewed?" questioned Toran. "Even uninhabited worlds without a crystal interface?"

The commander inclined his head. "There appears to be a passive record stored at regular intervals, though we'd have no way to access it for a reset without the interface. Anyway, this system sounds more interesting than it was useful in reality. Over the years, researchers figured out how to translate the visual feed into raw data for analysis. That's how we observed the record gaps we eventually connected to the Darkness."

As crazy as it sounded, all of the questions that had been floating in my head for the past two weeks were slowly getting answered. Colren *had* been telling the truth earlier when he said he'd told us everything, just not enough details for us to understand the full extent of his statements.

"Okay, so, this device doesn't work now that the Archive is sealed," I said. "You said there was some strange activity with it earlier. What happened?"

"We received a momentary data feed, but it was jumbled—like data had been overwritten multiple times on the same file, so only fragments were readable."

"What did they say?" Toran asked.

Colren turned around to access the workstation behind him. "It was only a few minutes ago, so we haven't run a full analysis. What little information the techs could make out looked like code snippets."

Toran joined him by the monitor integrated in the wall. "These look similar to the waveforms I was analyzing, actually."

The commander perked up. "Can you plot them?"

"Maybe." Toran took over the controls. After a minute of entering commands, he shook his head and frowned. "No, these are too incomplete for the results to be accurate. I could easily extrapolate and plot *something*, but there'd be too much guesswork involved to trust the result."

I drummed my fingers pensively. "It's strange... this seems to be the origin point for the signal, but there isn't a crystal here. I don't know how it would interface at all."

"We *assume* there's not a crystal here," Toran interjected. "What if there's one inside that anomaly?"

"I guess there could be, since it's all... anomalous," I stated awkwardly.

"But what about everything else going on here?" Colren prompted. "Why would the aliens have interest in this place if there's no world to consume?"

I thought through everything I had learned about the crystalline network over the past two weeks and how everything operated. It *didn't* make sense that the aliens would select this as a staging ground for their fleet when there were more than a dozen worlds they had already shaped to their specifications using the Darkness. But, when I failed to rationalize the actions using my conventional understanding, I flipped it around. Suddenly, the pieces started to fall into place. "You said the gravity was high here—meaning there could be dense mass we can't see?" I asked, breaking the silence in the room.

Colren nodded.

"So, what if the signals we keep picking up are instructions for that matter? On the other planets, the crystals were used to rearrange matter to create whatever environment the aliens want for their bio..."

"Bio-optimization," Kaiden supplied for me.

"Right. And that process could be done anywhere there's sufficient raw material, correct?" I asked, and Toran nodded. "So, what if the ships aren't coming through that anomaly, but that they're being *manufactured* in it?"

Toran paled. "That's all the crystals do—follow a set of instructions and use whatever is at their disposal to complete the structures."

"Stars! If that really is what's going on…" Colren raced to the door. "We need to shut it down!"

14

"COMMANDER! ADDITIONAL ALIEN craft inbound," the helm officer announced as soon as Colren returned to the bridge with my team following close behind.

"It might not be inbound at all," Colren muttered.

"Sir?"

He shook his head. "Set ship to combat-ready. Move into high-precision firing range of the anomaly."

"Aye!" the helm officer acknowledged.

"This could totally backfire," I whispered to Kaiden.

"If your idea is correct, then there aren't a lot of other options. The longer that thing is active, the bigger the enemy fleet we'll be up against."

"What's the ETA on our backup?" Colren barked.

"Jump logs indicate they should arrive in six minutes, sir," the comm tech replied from one of the rear stations near where I was standing. She was the most composed of the support staff, but I could still plainly see the worry in her eyes.

"Ten kilometers to engagement range," the helm officer announced.

"When you have a lock, fire a Class I barrage at the anomaly," Colren ordered.

My hand found Kaiden's, and we entwined our fingers. The warmth of his presence took the edge off my worry as we braced for combat.

"Target in range. Commencing Class I barrage," the helmsman announced.

"May the stars be with us," Colren murmured.

Twenty torpedoes launched from the bow of the *Evangiel* and streaked toward the anomaly. It still seemed too far away to fire on, but I had to remind myself that the physics of space battles are different than on a planet. In terms of this environment, we were practically breathing down the enemy's neck.

Four excruciating seconds passed while we waited for impact. As the torpedoes neared their mark, the single alien craft that had fully emerged from the anomaly fired what looked like an inky cloud, visible only thanks to the visual overlays on the front viewport. The black cloud intercepted the torpedoes two kilometers short of the anomaly's event horizon, and the twenty bombs vanished.

"Report!" Colren demanded.

"The torpedoes are gone, sir. No detonation," the helmsman replied, a quaver in his voice.

Kaiden's grip on my hand tightened. "They can command the Darkness," he whispered.

"No. This can't be happening!" My throat constricted as tears stung the corners of my eyes. We had been making progress, we had a plan. Now, all of those efforts seemed to be meaningless. How could we stop an enemy who makes weapons vanish?

Colren seemed equally at a loss.

"Sir?" the helmsman prompted when no further orders were given.

"Plasma cannons," the commander instructed.

"That gets us too close," Toran murmured.

"What do you mean?" Maris asked, drawing the four of us into a huddle.

"Plasma cannons are a short-range engagement weapon," Toran clarified. "If we're close enough to fire at the anomaly, we would be well within range of their Black Cloud of Death."

"Yeah, I don't want to go anywhere near a thing you'd give that nickname." I glanced at Colren. "Should we say something?"

"He is no doubt aware of the risks already," Toran said. "My guess is that this move is to determine which strategy will be best for the rest of the fleet to follow. Torpedoes appear ineffective, so we need an alternative means of attack."

"Then saying something won't help." I sighed. "For being here on the bridge, we're not doing much."

"We're civilians on a military vessel. It's a wonder we're here at all," Kaiden replied.

With a sudden and horrific death now too near a reality for comfort, I was beginning to agree with Maris' assessment that I should have never gotten out of bed that morning. Agreeing with Maris… the end really was nigh.

No, thinking like that wasn't going to accomplish anything. "Come on," I said, beckoning my friends toward the exit.

"Where are you going?" Toran asked.

"Back to that special room," I said. "If that thing can pick up signals from the aliens, maybe we can learn something about them during the attack."

"Wait, we'll need a way to see what's going on out here," Kaiden countered. He jogged up to Commander Colren and whispered something to him, which I assumed was my plan.

The commander nodded. "I'll give you access and patch through the feed."

Kaiden bounded off the dais and headed for the door.

"It's not as fun now that we have permission," I jested, jogging up next to him.

He cracked a smile. "Only you would say something like that at a time like this, Elle."

We dashed down the corridor to the secret entry.

Toran placed his palm on the hidden biometric scanner, and the door opened. "This is why we ask for permission."

"Oh, right." My cheeks flushed. "I wasn't thinking about that part."

Once inside, we sealed the door and then turned our attention to the various stations around the room. Toran began fiddling with one to get the live feed from the bridge's viewport while Kaiden examined the sphere.

"I can't believe Colren trusts us with this," he said.

"In all fairness, we have more experience with this ancient tech than anyone, after we went through the artifact-gathering," I pointed out.

"I guess there is that. We haven't broken anything yet."

I smiled. "That we know of, anyway."

"The cute banter can wait. Figure out how this thing works!" Maris cut in.

"Sorry." I inspected the device. There were no obvious controls. "Colren said the viewing was controlled by thought, didn't he?"

"That's right, he did." Kaiden eyed the device. "Should I...?"

"Be my guest." I held out my hand.

Kaiden placed his palms on either side of the sphere. The glow intensified for a moment before the blackness returned. However, one of the idle workstations along the wall sprang to life.

"I think we have a link!" I ran over to it. "Try to focus on the anomaly, Kaiden."

"Great, that's the *last* thing I want to think about."

"Hey, you volunteered to do this part." I checked the workstation's monitor, which had code scrolling across it. "How are you doing getting the feed set up, Toran? I'll need you over here."

"Almost ready," he replied.

I looked over my shoulder to see what he was working on just in time to see the video stream from the bridge appear on the monitor at his station. The *Evangiel* was rapidly approaching the alien ship and the anomaly. By my estimation, we had to be getting close to firing range for the plasma cannons. Any nearer and it would be a suicide run; maybe it already was.

"Come, on they'll fire soon!" I urged.

Toran ran over to my position, immediately locking his eyes on the monitor. "Okay, good, this is steady and matches what I was observing earlier. If there's any change when we strike, we'll know why."

"They'd better make a move soon." I took an unsteady breath. I had no interest in finding out firsthand what it felt like to be disintegrated by that black cloud.

With Toran focusing on the code, I went back to the station with the feed from the bridge. Four additional alien ships were starting to appear in the anomaly, and two earlier ones were almost complete. The tapered noses of the vessels protruded from the bright glow like they were predators rising from a pond, elegant and sinister.

A new glow appeared on the screen, originating from the *Evangiel*. With a sudden flash, two blinding plasma beams crackled across the blackness toward the anomaly. The beams struck one of the half-formed ships, sending a ripple of lightning over its hull. At first, it appeared the energy blast was dissipating without causing any damage, but then the tendrils that comprised the hull slowly began to unfurl from their proper places. The black bands dropped and began to shrivel, eventually disintegrating. With gaps in the structure, the rest soon fell apart.

"Hey, it worked!" Maris cheered.

I kept my own glee at bay, knowing this was only the beginning of the engagement. We were still within range of the completed alien craft. "What does the readout say, Toran?"

"There was a marked spike at the time of impact," he reported. "One of the waveforms dropped in amplitude."

"Does that mean the more ships there are, the stronger it is?" I speculated.

"As good a guess as any at this stage." Toran pressed behind his ear. "Commander, the signal changed when the ship was in distress. We'll keep an eye on it."

"That's a relief to hear. We'll take care of the rest of these in short order," Colren replied. The comm link ended.

"How can we use this information to our advantage, though?" Kaiden chimed in. "It's obvious the ship was hurt when it fell apart. Does this thing with the waves and signal actually help us?"

"What if the impact *hadn't* been so obvious? The waves would have told us something," Toran replied. "And now, even if a ship shows no exterior damage, we know we can assess the health of their fleet using this method."

"Well, we better take out the rest of those ships before it becomes a proper fleet," Kaiden said.

New ships popped onto the screen with a blue flash. Information tags popped up above each on the screen. "The Hegemony fleet is here!" This time, I did cheer.

Colren no doubt had relayed the information about the plasma cannons because the new Hegemony ships were accelerating toward the anomaly. I counted at least three dozen craft—a sizable fleet to take on the four remaining alien vessels and the anomaly itself.

When the Hegemony ships were close enough, plasma beams lanced out from the bows of the ships toward the targets. The beams rippled over the hulls like they had when the *Evangiel* fired, and the dark tendrils began to fall away from the ships' forms. However, the attack had placed the Hegemony ships close to the completed alien vessel, which obviously wasn't going down without a fight.

"It's getting ready to fire!" My heart pounded in my ears. If its weapon could do to a ship what it had to the torpedoes, the Hegemony fleet could be leveled in a matter of minutes.

"Why aren't they pulling away? Didn't Colren warn them?" Kaiden's voice was pitched with concern.

"They're getting ready to fire again—waiting for the plasma cannon to recharge," Toran replied. "I don't know if they have enough time…"

Everything seemed to fall silent around me as the scene unfolded on the screen. The mouths of the cannon glowed in preparation to fire, but before they could, a black cloud engulfed the forward line of ships. I could barely make out the alien attack itself, only brief explosions as the destroyers lost integrity. Within seconds, there was no evidence the ships had ever been there.

The cloud of Darkness was all but invisible against the starscape, and it wasn't until the next wave of Hegemony vessels began disintegrating before my eyes that I could make out its path of destruction.

"Stars! They have to get out of there," I choked.

"They can't outrun it," Kaiden murmured.

Three of the Hegemony vessels that had been farthest from the alien ship attempted a hasty retreat, but before they'd gone four ship lengths, another cloud of the Darkness enveloped their hulls, each glowing for a moment before falling dark.

Tears glistened in Maris' eyes. "The crews…"

I wanted to honor them for their sacrifice, but we had more pressing issues. New alien vessels were beginning to form within the anomaly, and the *Evangiel* was now the only ship standing in between the enemy front and the Hegemony worlds. There was no reason to believe our ship would fare better than the warships the Darkness had already dissolved as if the reinforced hulls were tissue paper in a sandstorm.

"There's no way out of this," I realized. The rest of fleet was annihilated and we were next. We were all going to die.

Kaiden swallowed. "At least we tried."

I opened a comm channel with the bridge. "Commander—"

The view on the screen changed as the *Evangiel* rapidly pulled away from the anomaly.

"We have to retreat," Colren confirmed over the comm. "Stars help us. Those ships were the most advanced in our fleet."

My stomach turned over. We could run now, but to what end? Any future engagements couldn't possibly have more promise with our lone ship against such a formidable enemy. The war was over before it had truly begun.

I slowly shook my head, not wanting to believe. "This can't be it."

"We'll regroup with the reserve fleet at the Capital. We need to consolidate resources," Colren stated. "Prepare to jump."

Maris turned to leave the chamber to head toward our jump pods. "If only we could start over," she murmured

Except, there *was* a way to start over...

"We can!" I exclaimed. "The shard."

"Elle, we have no idea what that will do," Toran cautioned.

"Can it be any worse than this? We're dead, our worlds are lost. Us dying here would very likely doom the rest of our civilization, too. If we have any chance for a do-over, I think we need to take it."

The commander didn't say anything over the comm at first. "Yes, we do need to take that chance. Come to the bridge."

Kaiden shook his head. "This is nuts."

"It is, but it might be the best shot we have," Toran replied.

"If we go back far enough, we can save our worlds," Maris said while we jogged down the corridor to the bridge.

"We'll find a way to do that no matter what," I told her.

The bridge door was standing open in anticipation of our arrival, and Colren was in his customary position at the center of the domed command area. He bore a grim expression, but a sliver of hope shined in his eyes as he turned to face us.

"Our fate falls to you." He pulled out a locket hanging from a black chain underneath his uniform jacket. The spherical locket reminded me of a multi-pointed star, crafted from an exotic blue-tinted metal. He pressed one of the spikes and the sphere split in two, revealing the crystal shard inside. He handed it to me. "If I don't remember any of this, thank you in advance."

"How do we use it?" I asked, taking the crystal from his outstretched hand.

"If the lore is correct, bring it to the viewing device and merge it with the crystal," the commander said. "You hold our future in your hands."

"We won't let you down."

I ran back to the viewing room with my team, not bothering to close the door since this physical reality was about to vanish. We huddled around the crystal orb.

"We just stick it in there?" Maris asked.

"I guess so." I looked between the shard in the palm of my hand and the orb.

Worry filled Kaiden's eyes. "How will it know when to reset to? If it only goes back five minutes, we're still dead."

"The cybernetic link!" I hovered my hands side-by-side two centimeters above the crystal. The shard felt tingly and warm in my palm so close to the sphere. "Maybe if we all think about where we want to reset to, it'll do that."

"I don't know what else to suggest," Toran said.

"It needs to be sometime when we were all together and we weren't about to die," Kaiden said, his brow knit.

"What about right after we sealed the Archive?" I suggested.

"Yeah, that could work." He nodded.

"Why not go back before that?" Maris said. "If we could see into the Archive for clues."

"Going back to an older reset point might not un-seal it," I said. "In fact, the point was made that the Archive exists outside of our reality."

"Wouldn't it be worth trying?" she insisted.

"For that matter, go back to before the Darkness appeared," Toran said.

"But we weren't in our new bodies yet," I protested. "It needs to be after we met."

A shudder wracked the ship.

"There's no time to argue!" I continued. "We'll go with right after we sealed the Archive."

"Okay," the others agreed.

With thoughts of the significant moments from the past two weeks still drifting through my head, I prepared to merge the shard. My friends each held their hands above the crystal's surface like mine.

I looked each of them in the eyes. "See you on the other side." I pressed my hands against the sphere, and the shard held against my palm was absorbed into the orb.

The crystal was warm against my hands, radiating not only heat but also an aura of power I couldn't fully comprehend. All I knew was that the sphere was my connection to both past and future. I needed it to save me and my friends while there was still any hope.

I pictured the moment we finished sealing the Archive—the elation and relief I felt having accomplished a task that had seemed impossible. I tried to envision the cavern with the seemingly endless rows of crystals. In that moment, I was thankful for my family, my new body, the artifacts, and the skills that had enabled me to accomplish those things. I had been born anew, and that moment was affirmation that I had become my full self.

Blackness closed in around me. I held the images in my head as best I could, trying to trust in the crystalline network—that it would detect our good intentions and aid us in accomplishing our goal. I floated in nothingness in the way I had after the reset on Erusan before I awoke on the *Evangiel*. As much as I wanted to remain confident, part of me wondered if this time I wouldn't wake up, that I might be trapped in the darkness forever.

THE MOMENT STRETCHED on. I sensed myself drifting away, pieces fading into the surroundings.

Just when I was worried there might not be anything of myself left, light crept in at the edges of my vision. I pulled myself toward the bright point in the distance.

At last, I sensed air in my lungs and my vision cleared. I was standing in front of a meter-tall crystal column, and a small crystal shard was in my hand. The crystal was at the center of a ten-meter-wide platform inside a giant cavern covered in millions of crystals. I was overcome with a sense of joy as I took it in.

"We did it!" I said. "We sealed the Archive." There was something else nagging at the back of my mind, like I'd forgotten something.

"We should get back to the *Evangiel* and give Colren our report," Kaiden said.

Colren... there was something I was supposed to tell him. I looked at the crystal shard in my hand. It had something to do with that.

Toran led the way back to our shuttle while I tried to remember whatever it was I had forgotten.

"You okay, Elle?" Maris asked me.

I looked around at the eerily familiar surroundings. "Have we been here before?"

"Well, yeah, on the way in," she replied.

Kaiden placed his hand on my back. "You sure you're feeling all right?" His touch was familiar, setting me at ease in a way I didn't expect.

"Yeah, just worn out, I guess," I replied.

We exited the Archive, pausing only to clean the monument we'd defaced earlier in our quest. As we stepped outside into the diffused purple light of Crystallis, I was overcome again with the feeling that I'd been in that place before. The towering crystals scattered throughout the two-kilometer-wide valley were alien to my eye, yet I couldn't shake the impression that I'd stood in that exact place admiring the view. I shook my head slowly, hoping the déjà vu would pass.

"It's a magnificent sight, isn't it?" Toran commented.

"Yeah. Don't think I could ever get tired of it," I replied.

He nodded. "All the same, I hope we never have to come back here."

"With you there." I followed him down the scree slope toward the shuttle.

We entered the craft and got situated on the bridge. My friends were visibly relaxed compared to the tension we'd been under for the past week, and it warmed me to see genuine smiles on their faces.

Kaiden, in particular, had a lightness about him I had only witnessed in the briefest moments during our time together. As he secured his flight harness, his gaze caught mine. "I can't believe we actually pulled that off."

I smiled back. "Never thought I would slay a dragon."

"First time for everything." His gaze lingered on me for a moment longer, then he turned his attention to the flight controls.

Jovial small talk continued during the flight back to the *Evangiel*. By the time we entered the hangar, I had convinced myself that the odd feeling of familiarity was just the adrenaline from the days' events coloring memories of the other missions with my team. So much had happened in such a short time, it was no wonder that the experiences had started to blur together.

After being greeted by a joyous maintenance crew, we took the central lift to the command deck. As we passed by the ancillary pod room across from the weapons vault in the corridor, Kaiden caught my eye and nodded toward the door to the pod room. "Elle, hang back a minute."

Toran glanced over his shoulder with a raised eyebrow.

"We'll be right there," Kaiden replied to the silent query.

My heart skipped a beat as we waited for the others to go ahead, and I followed Kaiden inside the pod room.

When the door had closed behind us, Kaiden took a step closer to me.

"You were amazing today, with the dragon and everything. I'd say that in front of them, too, but there's something else that's more… private."

"What's that?" I stared into his sky-blue eyes.

"When I was lying there on the floor of that cavern, thinking it was all over, all I could think about was that we'd left things at a 'maybe someday'. But we have no idea what's coming tomorrow or a minute from now, so what's the point in waiting?"

Those same thoughts ignited in my own mind. Or, they felt like my thoughts. Somehow, it was almost more like a memory. "There will always be another reason to wait."

"Exactly. And I don't want to miss the chance to see what we could have." Kaiden stepped toward me until we were almost touching. Gently, he brushed the fingertips of his right hand along my shoulder and then cupped the side of my face in the palm of his hand.

"I don't, either." A tingle of desire surged through me as I stared into his eyes. I slid my left hand behind his head and locked him in a passionate kiss.

We melted into each other, the stress and uncertainty of the previous week fading into the background. I was eager to lose myself in him and forget what we had been through. In that moment, it was only us, and I'd want it no other way.

Even though we'd never done more than hug or hold hands before, I somehow felt like I knew him—how to touch, how to move. As I followed my instincts, I could feel him respond how I sensed he would, and he somehow knew exactly how to caress me even though I didn't consciously know myself what I wanted.

Eventually, we separated, breathless.

Kaiden's lips parted in a stunned smile. "Wow."

I grinned. "Good wow?"

"Definitely." He paused. "That didn't feel like a first kiss."

"It really didn't." While I didn't have much experience on the matter, my friends back on Erusan had talked about enough awkward encounters for me to know that instant physical sync was rare, to say the least. There should have been some level of awkwardness or uncertainty. Either we were soul mates, or… I gnawed on my lower lip. "*Was* it our first?"

He chuckled. "Considering we were interrupted by Maris the last time we almost did—"

"No, not then." I shook my head. "Never mind."

Kaiden cocked his head. "You can't start a statement like that and not finish."

I sighed. "I dunno, ever since we left the Archive I just can't shake the feeling that we've done all of this before."

"Yeah, I remember what you said earlier."

"I know it sounds crazy."

He swallowed. "It would, except being with you just now, I couldn't help thinking the same thing."

I took an unsteady breath. "How would that be possible?"

"The only thing that comes to mind is a reset."

"But we remember those."

"We're *supposed* to remember them."

I tugged on the end of my braid. "I wonder if Toran or Maris have had any of these same feelings?"

"Only way to find out is to ask," Kaiden replied. "And they're probably wondering where we are."

"Oh, right! Colren." I glanced toward the door. "Should we say something?"

"About a potential reset or what we were doing in here?"

"Both."

He linked his fingers with mine. "Regarding this, I think we can drop a few subtle hints and they'll figure it out. As for the other thing, let's give it a little bit and see if anything else unusual sticks out."

"Works for me."

Still holding hands, we exited the pod room and continued down the corridor to Central Command. When we entered, we found that Toran and Maris were already with Commander Colren in the conference room. Kaiden and I rushed to join them, dropping our hands to our sides as we entered.

"Nice of you to join us," Colren stated, his gaze fixed on us as we found our seats.

"Sorry, Commander." My cheeks flushed.

Maris smirked. "We were just getting to the part about the rock titan outside the Archive."

"Yes, that." I nodded.

Kaiden and I interjected bits about our battles with the rock titan, spirit elemental, and dark dragon while Toran took the lead on the explanation. When Toran finished the description of the Master Archive and our talk with the mysterious voice, Colren leaned back in his chair.

"That explains so much," the commander said, shaking his head with amazement.

"Unfortunately, the information doesn't help us know how to stop the Darkness and whatever beings are behind it," Toran said. "All we can say is the records are safe."

Colren nodded. "That's what we hoped to achieve. Also, now we know this assault on our worlds was a first wave and ships may be coming next. That's more information than we had before."

Maris crossed her arms. "Even after *all* of that, we still don't have any other hints about what to do next? For a place that was supposed to hold all the answers, we didn't get many."

"There was nothing else?" Colren asked.

I snapped to attention. "Well, there was one other thing." I pulled the crystal shard from my pocket. It tingled in my palm, almost like it was resonating with the magical energy inside of me.

The commander carefully took the crystal from my outstretched hand. "Where did you get this?"

"It's a piece of a crystal in the Archive," I replied. "The voice said it would aid us in the trials ahead."

"Stars!" Colren exclaimed. "Could it be...?" He examined the tiny crystal fragment with awe in his eyes.

"Do you know what it is?" I asked.

Colren cracked a smile. "It appears to be a shard from a Master Crystal. I didn't think we'd ever get access to one."

I tilted my head. "What it is, exactly?"

"If there's any truth to the legends, it's connected to the Master Archive," Colren explained. "Such a shard provides a direct hyperdimensional link to allow backups beyond our inhabited worlds."

Kaiden frowned. "And what does that mean for us?"

The commander's eyes shined with renewed hope. "This is the tool we needed. It gives us a control point."

"It would enable a universal reset," I murmured, meeting Kaiden's gaze.

"That's right." Colren nodded. "With this, you could access the

Master Archive from anywhere and use it as the locus of the reset event."

"Even with the Master Archive sealed?" Kaiden asked.

"With the Master Archive sealed, a shard like this would be the *only* way to conduct a reset, as I understand it," Colren replied. "But, as powerful as this tool is, there are so many unknowns that I'm not sure if it's viable."

Toran nodded. "A last resort, then."

Kaiden and I exchanged glanced again. "So, if we did use it, there could be side effects?" he asked.

The commander shrugged. "I couldn't even begin to predict what might happen. Controlling the timeframe of the reset would be a challenge even with the tools at our disposal. Furthermore, there's no telling how a reset on an interstellar scale would work." He stared at the crystal in his palm. "I look at this and see a way to restore the worlds that have already been lost, but it could also mean going back in time before any of us exist. As much as I want to use it, we need to try to find another way."

I shifted in my seat. "I guess we would have to be pretty desperate if we decided to use it, then."

Maris smiled. "That's for our future selves to worry about. For now, I say we should call today a victory."

"Indeed, it was," Toran agreed.

I forced a smile. "Yeah, totally."

"Take the rest of the day to celebrate and rest," Colren told us. "We'll regroup in the morning and figure out our next steps."

"Thank you, Commander. See you then." Kaiden rose from the table.

The bridge crew offered us thanks and congratulations as we passed through, but I barely heard the words. All I could think about was the potential side effects of a universal reset and wonder if what I was experiencing might be related to that. Based on Kaiden's intense expression, I suspected he was thinking about the same thing.

"So, how are we going to celebrate?" Maris asked as soon as we were in the corridor outside Central Command.

"Not sure if I'm up for much of a party," I replied, far too preoccupied with other thoughts.

Maris eyed me, an amused smile playing on her lips. "Just hoping for some alone time with Kaiden?"

"No, that's not—" He started in response then cut off. "Yeah, we've grown close, but there's something else going on."

I nodded. "You know earlier what I asked if we'd been in that cavern before? Well, those same feelings of familiarity keep happening."

"I started noticing things, too," Kaiden added. "We were talking about it before the meeting. That's why we were late."

"Have you experienced anything out of the ordinary?" I asked Toran and Maris.

Toran frowned. "Nothing specific."

"But there's a feeling, right?" I pressed. "Like we've had these conversations before. Not *precisely* the same, but similar."

Maris sighed. "Next you're going to say that this has something to do with that crystal shard thing."

"It might," Kaiden replied.

"Colren said there could be side effects after a universal reset," I continued. "What if there was one and we don't remember?"

"That would mean something went wrong and our consciousness didn't reknit correctly," Toran said.

"We have nothing to go on other than a hunch," Kaiden continued. "It might be nothing—just a bizarre byproduct of being in the Master Archive. But what if we *did* do a universal reset? What had happened to make us try something so extreme?"

"Maybe we learned how to control it?" Maris speculated.

Toran inclined his head. "Perhaps. Or, we were so desperate we'd try anything to get another chance."

I swallowed. "Whatever the circumstances, what we do next will dictate whether we go down that same path or have a different, better outcome."

Maris' brows drew together. "How can we have things turn out differently if we don't remember what we did the first time around?"

"We need to *try* to remember," I implored. "Keep track of all of those little things that seem familiar. Assemble the pieces."

"We should bring this to Colren," Toran suggested.

"And we will, as soon as there's anything actionable," I assured him. "Right now, all we could say is that we think we get into trouble at some point and resort to a universal reset. That sounds more stress-inducing than helpful."

Maris glared at me. "You don't say?"

"Elle is right. The commander has enough on his mind right now without piling on an issue this vague," Kaiden agreed. "The four of us need to figure out what we can so we have something solid to bring him."

"Very well," Toran conceded.

Maris sighed. "All right, fine. Where does that leave us with the celebratory party?"

Kaiden shrugged. "Well, if we hadn't had this something-isn't-right realization, I expect a party would have been in order."

I still wasn't thrilled by the idea of having to be social while I was working through what kind of problem we were up against, but I did have to agree with Kaiden's logic that we should try to recreate the circumstances as much as possible. The more similar we could make it, the more we might be able to jog our memories about the alternate reality from which we had potentially reset.

"Something in the Mess, maybe?" I suggested.

"Oh, *now* you're in the mood for a party?" Maris cast me a sidelong glance.

"I think other-me would have been, that's all."

"Trying to guess what we would do under other circumstances is a recipe for madness," Toran cautioned. "We shouldn't try to overthink this."

Maris got a devious glint in her eyes. "I know one surefire way to help you relax."

NOT SURPRISINGLY, BARTENDER Maris' solution to our worries revolved around shots. However, we soon learned through various inquiries that, being a military starship, the *Evangiel*'s booze selection was limited to a single bottle of whiskey in Colren's quarters, which was a rare vintage and declared to be strictly off-limits.

With that plan thwarted, we instead found ourselves gathered around one of the tables near a viewport in the Mess. We'd each taken extra helpings of the least offensive variety of gruel on the menu, the orangey-brown one. When I didn't think about it too much, I could almost convince myself it was proper chili.

"Really festive, guys. Definitely pulled out all the stops with this one," Maris muttered as she gathered a portion of the paste onto her spoon and dribbled it back into the bowl.

"Okay, so we didn't take into account that everyone else is still on duty," Kaiden said.

"Think the original celebration was like this?" I asked.

"I can't imagine significantly different circumstances," Toran replied. "After all, the rest of the crew remains unaware of our situation."

I set down my spoon. "You know, that's a good point. Do you think anyone other than us is having the déjà vu thing happen?"

Toran nodded thoughtfully. "True. If we keep this to ourselves, we won't know if the phenomenon is limited to us."

"Some subtle question-asking might be in order," Kaiden said. "Wasn't that the plan anyway?"

"It was." I pushed my mostly empty plate away. "Sitting around here isn't exactly festive, as Maris said. Why don't we go mobile?"

Maris raised an eyebrow. "Bring the party to those who can't leave their stations?"

"That's good thinking." Kaiden smiled. "See people in their element where they're comfortable, find out if anything feels off to them."

I nodded. "Precisely."

"This would be way better with a party tray." Maris sighed.

"Booze isn't necessary to get people to talk, Maris," Kaiden said.

"No, but it certainly makes things easier."

I stood up and grabbed my meal tray to bus it. "We're not trying to get people to spill their deepest secrets here."

"Okay, so maybe I want the drinks for *me*," Maris admitted. "Come on, it's been a rough day! We were almost eaten by a dragon."

I placed my leftovers in the receptacle. "Well, we *weren't* eaten, so there's that."

Kaiden laughed, joining me at the bussing station. "My list of 'things to be thankful for' has gotten incredibly strange."

"Best not to think about it too much." Toran rose to take care of his own plate.

While the others finished clearing the table, I scoped out the rest of the Mess. Only three other tables were presently occupied. The diners at two of the tables were completely absorbed in their own conversations, but those at the third kept glancing over at us. I decided they might make a good warmup for our planned investigative discussions.

"Let's start over here," I said, leading the way to the target table with the two men and a woman.

"And these are…?" Kaiden whispered.

"People who seem to have an interest in us." I whispered back. "Hopefully that means they'll talk."

I plastered on what I hoped was an approachable smile as I neared the table. "Hey, I couldn't help but notice you watching us. What's up?"

"Real subtle, Elle," Kaiden said under his breath behind me.

The first of the two men, a crewman in his late-thirties with dark hair and amber eyes, folded his hands on the tabletop and tilted his head. "Why might have we taken an interest in you?"

"We *are* the heroes around here, after all," I replied in a smug tone.

"I'm actually surprised no one else wanted to join us in our celebration."

"Oh, that's what that was?" the red-headed woman asked. "Looked like any other meal."

"We had hoped for some company, but everyone is busy," Kaiden chimed in.

Maris squinted. "Not to mention, how do you get by without a stocked bar?"

The fair-haired second man raised his water glass. "Cheers to that!" His two companions cast a stern glance in his direction and he lowered the glass.

"Some of these days really start to blend together, you know?" I continued. "I don't know how you do it."

"You have no idea," the dark-hair man replied. "Sometimes, I could swear I'd already processed the same readings."

"Oh, is that so?" That sounded remarkably like the situation we were presently facing, but his phrasing made it sound like it was an ongoing situation, not a recent development.

"I've been doing practically the same thing for seven years. You've got to expect the days to run together now and again." He cracked a smile, though it didn't seem heartfelt.

"Already happening to me and I've only been here for two weeks," Kaiden chimed in.

The blond man snorted. "I don't know how anything could feel routine for you while you're off galivanting on those planets."

"It's usually more 'trying not to die', if we're being honest," Maris corrected.

"Sure, whatever you want to call it," the first man replied. He swirled the purple contents of his glass. "In any case, we were wondering what's going to happen to the rest of us when you do get yourselves killed."

The breath left my lungs like I'd been kicked in the chest. "Pardon?"

"You heard me. It's only a matter of time your lack of experience catches up with you and you don't come back from one of your little missions," he continued, sweeping a lock of dark hair from his eyes.

The woman at the table crossed her arms. "Sorry, does it come as a surprise to you that everyone on the ship doesn't worship the deck plates you walk on? The commander has put his faith in you for whatever reason, but some of us would prefer to place our trust in seasoned soldiers who don't play dress-up and play with swords."

I had half a mind to draw my blade and see what she thought of it up close, but Kaiden placed a calming hand on my elbow.

"Why were you watching us, then? Taking bets on which one of us would die first?" he asked the three crew members.

"More or less. We were wagering a weeks' worth of dessert about which one of you would crack under the pressure first," the blond man said. "My bet is on her." He nodded toward Maris.

While I didn't disagree with his assessment that she was the potential weak link on our team, I wasn't about to let anyone get away with talking about my new friends that way. I glared at him. "None of us asked to be placed in this position. No, we don't have a lot of experience, but so far we've already accomplished things no one else has been able to do. If we end up dying on a planet, at least it won't be for lack of trying—for stepping outside of what's safe and familiar. This isn't a conventional enemy, so maybe an unconventional team is *exactly* what's needed."

He inched back in his chair as I spoke, fear evident in his wide eyes. It surprised me that I could come off as so intimidating, but I realized that the attack glove I normally wore on my right hand had started to glow even though it was only hanging at my side rather than on my hand. I suppressed my concern about the remote activation; right now, I was busy defending the honor of the Dark Sentinels.

"I told you not to bet against this one," the woman said to the dark-haired man, seemingly unfazed by the magical item clipped to my belt.

Kaiden rounded on the man. "What happened to make you so hostile?"

"What happened?" The dark-haired man laughed bitterly. "Our worlds have been destroyed, and yet we're chasing down so-called 'legendary artifacts' and letting a handful of kids call the shots."

"I'm not as young as I appear," Toran spoke up for the first time, his booming voice grabbing the crew members' attention.

"Doesn't matter. Why aren't we fighting back against the Darkness?" the blond man said, leaning forward in his chair. "Why haven't we done anything to reclaim our worlds?"

I narrowed my eyes. "We *are*. We've done nothing but try to find a solution for the last week. Just because you don't know everything we're up to, don't assume nothing is happening."

The woman shook her head. "I work in Communications. I know

exactly what you've done, and it amounts to sealing the Archive—the thing we need to restore the worlds. You haven't made any progress, it's just been a giant step backward."

"That's not an accurate assessment," Toran said, his voice still level and calm.

The dark-haired man downed the remaining contents of his glass. "The Hegemony is doomed if they truly believe in placing their faith in the likes of you. The sooner you aren't around, the sooner they'll get back to solving this problem with soldiers like they should have all along."

Acrid annoyance welled in my chest as I thought about how much was wrong with his statements. The Hegemony *had* tried a direct physical approach and all those people had died. Even though it might look like we hadn't accomplished much, we'd made sure the records of our worlds were safe. Without that, there never would have been a hope for a reset to fix everything. We'd made a tangible contribution for the better, even if these people didn't want to see it.

I wanted to yell at the three crew members and set them straight, to show them that I wasn't a helpless teenager who didn't have the guts to fight in a war. I was putting my life on the line, and they needed to see that I took it seriously. My friends and I were a formidable team, and we would stand together to the end.

But I held my tongue. These people didn't want to have their opinion changed; escalating the conflict wouldn't solve anything.

"I guess we'll just have to show you why we're the best team for the job," I said as calmly as possible. "Oh, and for the record, swords and capes are awesome." I spun on my heel and stormed out of the Mess.

I didn't turn back to see the reaction on the crew members' faces, but a snort from Maris suggested that they were at a loss for words.

Once in the corridor, I took a slow, deep breath. "Okay, so maybe talking to people outside the inner circle was a bad idea."

"Yeah, no way around it, that could have gone a lot better," Kaiden said.

"I had no idea anyone had resentment toward us," I continued. "Tami and Colren have been so welcoming, I thought that carried through to the rest of the ship."

"High-tension times aggravate people's fears," Toran replied.

Maris frowned. "They weren't just afraid, they were angry."

"I'm angry, too," I admitted. "This is a terrible situation. Our worlds might be lost, we don't know what to do, and now we might be stuck in a reset loop without knowing it."

"Our very presence here asking questions has changed things," Toran said. "Perhaps it is better we return to our quarters as we would have otherwise."

Maris stifled a yawn. "Fine by me."

"Yeah, we can do more investigating in the morning," I agreed.

We took the lift to our area and moseyed down the corridor. As we neared the common room, I slowed my pace. "I'm not quite ready for bed. I think I'll hang out for a bit and enjoy the view."

"Mind if I join you?" Kaiden asked.

"Of course not."

Toran gave us a knowing smile. "Stay out of trouble, you two. See you in the morning."

"Good night," I bid him and Maris, then wandered into the lounge.

The planet of Crystallis was just visible out the viewport, approaching the leading edge of dawn. White light flared from behind the planet's shoulder, creating a dramatic aura above the purple-hued atmosphere.

"I don't think I'll ever get tired of viewing a planet from space," I murmured while taking it in.

Kaiden came to stand at my left hip. "Even having grown up on starships, I still haven't."

I turned to look up at him. "Are we really just foolish kids in over our heads?"

"Oh, Elle, we're definitely in over our heads, but to be *foolish* I think we'd need to not recognize what we're up against. I have no doubts that we each understand what's at stake."

"That's true."

He wrapped his arms around me, and I laid my head against his chest. The embrace had the same familiarity and comfort I'd experienced during our kiss before. If there had been a reset, whatever bond was developing between us seemed to transcend our other memories. I couldn't help wondering where we might have left off with things in the alternative version of our future.

"It feels right, doesn't it?" Kaiden murmured into my hair. "I don't know how, but I feel I know you more than I should."

"For all we know, we could have been together for years before the reset."

"No, there's still something new here." He pulled back slightly to look into my eyes. "I can't explain it, but I somehow sense that we're still figuring things out. It's like we went through something that brought us closer, but the amount of time together hasn't caught up with the closeness of experience."

"You're right, there's comfort to a point and then… the unknown." If that instinct held, we weren't an old married couple. I found myself strangely relieved as I processed the half-memories, realizing that there were still unexplored elements to our relationship. The happiness worried me for a moment as I thought it might stem from second-guessing the romance, but then I realized it was rooted in a desire to have a natural progression uncolored by echoes of another path. There was still a chance for us to have firsts together—proper new experience, not re-creations. I would hate to think that important moments in my life could have been erased without memory. When those moments did happen, I wanted to have it forever as a part of myself.

"You still with me?" Kaiden asked softly.

"Sorry, just thinking." I traced my hand down his chest.

"About what?"

"You. Us. That maybe despite everything going on, there's a sliver of a chance that we can still get to know each other like a normal couple."

He gave me a light kiss. "I'd like that very much."

I kissed him back, longer and deeper. "But I don't want to forget any of it. How can we move forward when all of this could go away again?"

"We've been resetting for our whole lives."

"Always with our memories. This isn't the same."

He studied me. "I think I know what you're hinting at."

"Are you okay taking things slow?"

"Considering we just had our first kiss, I had no expectations."

I looked down. "It's probably way too soon to bring that up, sorry."

"No, never apologize for being honest. We need to be able to be open and trust each other."

"I do feel I can trust you."

"Good. You can." He placed his hands on my shoulders. "And after seeing you take on a dragon single-handed today, I have no doubts about being able to trust you with my life."

"Heh, yeah. Let's hope battles like that aren't an everyday occurrence."

"This, on the other hand," he gave me a kiss, "I'd be happy to have as a regular thing."

"I was just thinking that." I closed my eyes and shut out the world around me, happy to be there with him.

When we eventually parted, I linked my arm through his and we watched the sun rise over Crystallis. There was so much light... I was filled with a sense of hope that we still had a chance of defeating the Darkness.

"We saved this world, and there will be others," Kaiden said, holding me close.

"I believe that, even if everyone isn't on our side."

"Those people in the mess hall didn't know what they were talking about. They don't know us or what we can do."

"As petty as it is, that makes me want to try even harder to prove them wrong."

Kaiden laughed. "I appreciate that about you."

"I suspect you're much the same way." I leaned against him,

He kissed the top of my head. "Having a little fighting spirit comes in handy."

As we stared down at the light-bathed planet, my mind drifted to the Darkness I'd seen consume other worlds. It took this kind of vantage—being in orbit—to appreciate the scale of what we were up against. Entire planets, systems, a civilization... Images of the Darkness tore through planets in my mind's eye, twisting tranquil landscapes into corrupted, savage environments and morphing native creatures into vicious killers. But as I thought about Erusan, Wantu, and the horrors of the Valor artifact world, new visions began to surface of a place I'd never seen before. I saw myself in the environment. Felt it. It was like I had experienced it myself and the memory was only now surfacing.

"No." I pulled away from Kaiden, heart pounding in my ears.

"What's wrong?"

I massaged my temples. "It can't be."

Kaiden stood silently and waited for me to collect myself.

I took several deep breaths, trying to relax my racing heart. "I think I just remembered something that hasn't happened yet."

17

KAIDEN PROCESSED MY words. "That's good, though, right? Weren't we hoping to remember what might have happened before the reset… assuming there was one?"

I wiped my hands down my face. "Yes. Except, now I wish I didn't know."

"What did you see, Elle?" He took a step toward me, his eyes fill with worry.

"We were on a world—completely consumed by the Darkness. But it wasn't the Valor world. This one has been infected long ago, and all of the terrible creatures we've seen were mature." I described the tentacle monster and the fields of tendrils. The visceral element of the memories had me on edge. Only Kaiden's presence kept me centered.

"Do you have a sense of where this planet was?" he asked me when I finished going over the scattered recollections.

"No idea. I got the impression that it was our first time there, wherever it was."

"If the corrupted environment was mature, then it has to be one of the first Hegemony worlds to be infected by the Darkness."

I frowned. "Assuming my memories were recent. What if we make that visit two months from now?"

He smiled coyly. "I don't think so."

"Why?"

"Well, we already established that we have a good thing going between us, but it hasn't advanced too far, near as we can tell. Based on what we're feeling now, I doubt it wouldn't have advanced by two months from now."

I couldn't argue that logic. I was already craving to be closer to him; I couldn't fathom delaying those explorations. I'd been waiting for years to find someone I could trust, and I was eager to make up for lost time. Plus, having the looming cloud of potential death being around every turn, I could really use another outlet to help me decompress.

"Okay, so we're maybe dealing with a timeline of a few weeks?" I said.

He nodded, a smirk playing on his lips. "Assuming you can resist me for that long."

I rolled my eyes, hating that he had a valid point. "All right, so, a week or two," I amended.

Kaiden looked pleased with the adjustment but said nothing.

"Anyway," I continued, "if I've correctly interpreted the nonsense going on in my head, at some time in the next two weeks we're going to find ourselves on an apocalyptically terrible world to attempt to access a crystal. Then, it would seem something soon afterward makes us resort to a universal reset, which results in... this."

"Lots of hypotheticals in that explanation."

"Do you have anything better to offer?"

He shook his head. "Having not had a new vision—or memory burst, whatever you want to call it—of my own, I can't comment. But I do believe something along those lines is happening. I still can't explain it, but I feel it."

"Why haven't Maris or Toran been as affected by it?" I wondered.

"Maybe they haven't had the right stimulus to jog their memories. You didn't start to remember until we... you know."

I took several paces, thinking. "Okay, so we might be able to spark other memories with the right experience. In that case, should we do as many things as possible to see what's familiar, or just forget that other timeline and do our own thing now?"

He smiled. "Well, I suppose that depends on what 'experiences' you have in mind."

I rolled my eyes and groaned. "Not with *us*. I mean, going around the ship, or—"

"I know, I'm just teasing." Kaiden turned more serious. "I keep going back and forth about whether I really *want* to know what happened before."

"And what are you thinking now?"

"That we should go to bed and worry about it in the morning. Maybe a path will present itself."

"That's a classic non-answer if I've ever heard one."

"I've heard it's a necessary survival skill in any relationship."

I smiled. "Like when I ask you what you want for dinner but I've already made up my mind?"

"Exactly."

I laughed. "With that kind of wisdom, I can't believe you were single."

"Mostly by choice, but I'm ready to not be."

"Good. In that case, I'm inviting myself over for the night."

His eyed widened with surprise. "Not that I mind, but why?"

"Do I really have to explain?"

"Of course not." He placed an arm around my shoulders, and we headed for the door. "Honestly, I didn't want to be alone staring at the ceiling of my cabin tonight, either."

I stopped by my cabin to brush my teeth and then slinked over to Kaiden's cabin next door. Despite the vastly different circumstances, I was reminded of going to sleepovers at Adrianne's house as a kid. I wasn't sure if my former self from before the reset would have opted for a sleepover in this moment, but it's what *I* wanted.

Kaiden's eyes lit up when he opened his cabin door. "Welcome. It's exactly like yours, so I don't think you'll have any trouble finding your way around." Even if the space was unfamiliar, the compact design with a bed, wardrobe, and wash room at the back didn't leave much opportunity for getting lost.

I stepped inside. "Thank you for humoring me."

"I didn't want to be alone, either, to be honest. It feels like everything could fall apart at any moment."

"I can't shake that feeling, either."

He glanced between the bed and me, then began taking off his outer clothing like we did before every jump. The white base layers made for comfy pajamas, I'd found, so I'd brought nothing else over to wear.

When we'd finished stripping down, we sat down on the bed next to each other.

"Forget everything that's going on out there," Kaiden said. "Right now, we're here together." He reclined on the bed, gently pulling me with him. With our heads sharing the pillow, he wrapped one arm around me.

For the first time in days, I felt truly secure. I'd expected dark thoughts to keep me awake all night, but Kaiden's warmth at my back and his arm around me really did help me forget the outside world.

Pounding on the door snapped me to attention. "Wha…?"

The clock indicated two hours had passed. I hadn't even realized I'd fallen asleep.

Kaiden bolted upright next to me. "Who *knocks* rather than paging on the comm?"

"Not thinking clearly?" I speculated, shaking off the grogginess of sleep.

He slipped off the bed then stepped over to the door and cracked it open. His posture relaxed. "Maris, what—"

"You have to come!" she exclaimed. "It's Toran. He keeps muttering about 'ships'—" She cut off when she saw me sitting on the bed through the cracked door. "You…?"

Kaiden started to close the door. "Where is he?"

"Mess Hall," she replied.

"We'll be right there." He latched the door, letting out a long sigh.

I started hastily dressing in my outerwear. "What are they even doing up at this hour?"

"No idea." He started dressing, as well.

"That was nice, by the way," I said as I slipped on my overcoat. "Even though I didn't mean for anyone to see me over here. Not that I mind, just…"

"Yes, it was, and I know what you mean. I didn't want them to make this into a big deal, either."

"Maybe this thing with Toran will be enough of a distraction."

"For Maris? No way. Relationship gossip is her lifeblood." Kaiden finished slipping on his shoes.

"I had to dream."

Once dressed enough to look presentable, we hurried to the Mess. Maris was nowhere to be seen, but two women and a man stood outside the Mess entrance, looking concerned.

"Do you know what's going on?" I asked them.

"We were unwinding after late shift when he came in—sleepwalking, maybe. She came in right after him," the first woman said.

"He started talking about 'dark ships' and how they were coming," the second added. "Freaked us out."

"Then the brunette came in and told us to leave," the man said.

"Thanks. We'll get Toran calmed down," Kaiden replied.

I approached the entry door with him. "Talk about a setback on our reputation campaign with the non-believers," I whispered.

"We have bigger issues to worry about than our social standing."

The door slid to the side, revealing the mostly empty Mess. Toran was standing in front of the wide viewports, trembling, and Maris was patting one of his broad, bare shoulders in what appeared to be an attempt to comfort him. With his back to us, I couldn't see his face or get a sense of his disposition.

"Hi, Toran, what's wrong?" I said in my friendliest tone.

Maris glanced toward us for a moment before returning her attention to Toran. "You were right earlier," she said. "We're starting to remember now."

My heart skipped a beat. "What have you seen?"

"A world. Death. I don't know where it was, but it's dangerous," Maris replied.

"Sounds an awful lot like what I saw." I approached the viewport. "We should compare notes and see if we can put together a narrative for what happened—or might happen, however you want to put it."

"Nothing we can do to stop it," Toran murmured.

I was finally close enough to see his face, and to my shock there were tears welling in his reddened eyes and his flushed cheeks were damp. I wasn't sure how to react; comforting had never been my specialty, let alone tending to the person who'd always been the rock on our team.

"Toran, hey, what's wrong?" Kaiden asked, visibly shaken by Toran's state.

The huge man sniffled. "I don't know. It hit me all at once—almost like I stepped outside of myself."

"The crew thought maybe you were dreaming," I said.

"No, this wasn't a dream." He dried his eyes with the backs of his hands.

"Tell us what you saw. We've been having flashes, too. Maybe we can make something of it," Kaiden urged.

Toran took a steadying breath. "I'm not so sure there's anything we can do this time."

"The last week has taught me that there's always a way," I told him. "Now, what is it about these ships?"

"We don't stand a chance against them," he said, his voice cracking again.

I swallowed hard. Alien ships… something about that was so familiar. I could envision them in my mind even though I only had a vague description from the Archive visions to go on.

Kaiden and I exchanged glances. "Could these have been the ships I saw in my vision inside the Archive?" he asked.

"Probably, but there's one particular ship I keep seeing. I'm terrified of it and I don't know why." The flush in Toran's face was fading and his eyes were more focused.

"Right now, gut feelings are all we have," Kaiden told him. "Trust that impression."

"I do, but…" Toran shook his head. "What if this *is* a memory from before the reset? What if that ship made us desperate enough to try anything?"

"This time, we have a heads up. We can be more on guard and not let it happen again," I said. But what had transpired? I could feel the answer somewhere in the back of my mind, but it was just beyond my grasp.

"How?" Maris threw up her arms. "We don't know anything new! We already knew there are dangerous things out there."

"If some memories have surfaced, the rest are buried in there, too," I insisted. "We just need to figure out a way to access them so we can stay a step ahead of the enemy."

"Unless they also know what's coming," Maris countered.

"Things have already started to change," Toran said. "This is a fresh start for both sides."

"Except, now we've seen some of what they can do. We can have countermeasures in place." I didn't know *what* countermeasures were feasible against giant shuttle-snaring Darkness tentacles, but the Hegemony's military needed to have something that stood a chance against them.

"It'd be helpful if we could shake off this amnesia," Maris said.

"No, I don't think it's like that at all," Toran replied, sounding much more like his usual level-headed self.

"If not amnesia, then what?" I asked.

"An incomplete download resulting from the limitations of the distributed hyperdimensional crystal-link."

I stared at Toran and blinked.

He took a deep breath. "Sorry, I was reading up on it before I got distracted by alien ship visions, and all the techno-babble is still in my head."

Kaiden smiled. "A plain-speak explanation would be great."

Toran was silent while he collected his thoughts. "Okay, so, there are two basic parts to it," he began. "Foremost, the crystals are a link to a higher dimension—we've known that for decades. Based on what's commonly accepted, the hyperdimensional link between the crystals is governed by restrictions similar to the limited bandwidth of a computer network. While hyperdimensional storage is theoretically limitless, only so much information can practically be funneled through the crystalline network at one time. Consequently, it gets hashed and compressed when each reset point is established, with the individual crystals functioning as a sort of 'cache' to aid in the recall."

"Okay," Kaiden began, "so when the cache is full, that's why old information is eventually removed from the hyper-memory, and entire prior resets may disappear from a crystal interface?"

Toran nodded. "Exactly."

"What does that have to do with our memories?" Maris asked.

I cast her a silencing glare. "Let him finish."

"This is where things get more contested," Toran continued. "Some scientists believe that a part of our consciousness suspends outside of spacetime during the resets. Usually, that part of ourselves can come right back to our reconstructed bodies and it feels like we reverted to a prior time, reconciling the previous-future *and* the memories of everything leading up to that moment. I think in the case of the universal reset, though, those previous-future memories didn't download."

Kaiden scowled. "Why?"

"To put it simply, bandwidth issues," Toran went on. "For a local reset, the data requirements are fairly small, allowing a long past span of time to be perfectly recovered. A planet-reset is still possible, but the risks of losing some memory of the previous-future increase; this might be one reason why large-scale resets are so rare. Now, beyond that, a universal-scale reset is a huge undertaking—way more information than the crystalline network can reconcile with its limited 'bandwidth', if you will. The hyperdimensional transfer through the crystal-interfaces is simply insufficient to allow full restoration of anything other than the matter, energy, and memories up to the time of the reset. The fragment of consciousness that exists outside of spacetime didn't have a chance to resync, so the previous-future memories are inaccessible."

I tilted my head. "Then how do the four of us remember?"

He shrugged. "Proximity to the locus of the event. The crystalline network might prioritize re-syncing of memories for people closest to the reset crystal."

"So, the further away from the locus, the less a person would remember of the previous-future?" I asked.

"That does fit with what we observed," Kaiden said. "Those crew members talked about the days running together—which could have been from routine, or maybe there was the slightest hint that we'd looped back."

Maris nodded. "That's true."

"The effects in others are weak, even on the same ship. Lightyears away—in the Capital, for instance—would they sense any déjà vu at all?" Kaiden wondered aloud.

"If it scales like anything else we've observed here, then no," Toran stated. "But the scientific models would suggest that the other memories weren't lost, exactly, just that they couldn't be recalled during the reset. They should still exist in the part of our consciousness that dwells in hyperdimensional space—a theory which is supported by us being imbued with abilities we hadn't learned yet."

Suddenly, I wish I'd paid more attention in physics class. "Okay, where does that leave us?" I asked.

"Aware but still disconnected," Toran murmured.

"We need to access those memories that didn't resync," Kaiden said.

"That not something that can be forced," Toran replied. "Regardless, we still need to figure out what to tell the Hegemony's decision-makers. Nothing in our visions points to a specific time or place."

"You're right." I turned away from the others, wracking my mind for the answers I knew must be somewhere within me. The ships... Toran was onto something there. Why couldn't I remember what?

The feelings of familiarity and fear were coming from somewhere. If I knew to be concerned, there was a reason why. For my own sanity, I needed to believe that I was in control. Maybe Toran was right and the details had been lost during the consciousness reintegration, but I wasn't ready to believe that the memories were beyond my grasp.

I focused on the elements I had remembered so far, trying to put them in order so I could develop a sequence of events for what had happened leading up to the presumed reset. The dark planet must have come before the ships, since those seemed to be the end of that timeline. But what had happened in between?

Hazy recollections of something bright against the dark backdrop of space began to come to me. I was mesmerized at first, and then fear crept into the corners of my mind. "A light," I murmured. "Did the ships come from a light?"

Kaiden gripped his head. "Gah! It's right there, but I can't remember!"

An overwhelming sense of destruction filled me as I thought about the light. It was a point of creation, and yet I somehow knew it would take everything from us.

"That place." My brow knit. "That's where we lose the fleet, I think."

"That place keeps appearing to me, too," Kaiden said. "There's a bright point. Beautiful, but danger surrounds it."

The jumble of images in my mind became sharper: an alien fleet birthed for the sole purpose of our destruction, and a weapon that could level the Hegemony defensive line in an instant. We needed to stop them.

I snapped to attention. "Call Colren. We're about to be invaded."

18

THE COMMANDER LISTENED intently across the conference table as I told him what I had remembered. I kept waiting for him to dismiss the statements and say that my imagination had gotten the better of me, but he kept nodding with understanding as I piled on the outlandish claims.

"I wish we had more to give you," I concluded.

"Any information is good information," Colren replied. "I only wish we knew where this place was."

"We might be able to figure it out with a little help," Kaiden said. "Which worlds were the first taken by the Darkness?"

Colren frowned. "Windau, Azura, Tarden. Why?"

"Maybe seeing some records of those worlds will help jog our memories," I said. "If the creatures on the planet were mature—"

"Then the corruption has to have been from some time ago, I follow." He stood up from the conference table and glanced out the glass door toward the bridge. "Access any records you need. Figuring out the site of these engagements is the first step toward finding a different outcome."

Kaiden stood up and nodded. "We'll do our best, Commander."

Colren took a step toward the door then stopped. "Say, would there be any way to tell if we've had this conversation before?"

"Not that I've been able to figure out," Toran replied. "I believe the hyperdimensional component of our consciousness wasn't able to re-link with our physical selves during the reset. But, our memories and abilities still exist in that part of ourselves outside of spacetime. I think, perhaps, this might explain how we have muscle memory for things we've never done before. Part of our hyperdimensional consciousness—that 'self' imbued with our future abilities—imprinted when we were re-formed in the bioprinter. However, I can't tell you if this may have happened before or if this is the first reset."

"That's the most fitting explanation I've heard." Colren smiled wearily. "Are you sure you were only a crystal interface maintenance tech?"

Toran laughed. "I've always had an interest in the metaphysical. I guess this experience turned out to be a good fit for both skills and experience."

The commander appraised us. "We got very lucky with the four of you."

"You've allowed us to come into our own," Kaiden said. "We have everything to lose in this fight, too."

"Keep at it. Let me know if you identify any locations." Colren left the conference room.

"Do you really think looking at pictures is going to help us remember?" Maris asked when the door had closed behind the commander.

"It's about more than that," I replied. "We need to try to immerse ourselves in those worlds. If we can picture ourselves there, then maybe the memories of actually *being* there might come to the forefront."

Kaiden sat back down at the table and tapped the integrated touchscreen to active it. "I'm willing to try anything."

"All right. Let's look at the files on those worlds Colren mentioned." I turned my attention to the holographic display.

Toran navigated to the onboard database of Hegemony worlds and brought up the details of his investigation into the Darkness. I'd suspected that a compiled file existed, but I'd never wanted to try to find it before. Acknowledging its very existence—and especially reading it—meant admitting the scale of the threat we were up against. I'd done my best to avoid any concrete information about how many worlds had been consumed by the alien infection. Seeing the records now, my worst fears were confirmed: more than two dozen worlds had been affected. Hundreds of millions of people's lives hinged on us finding a way to fight back.

"Stars! I didn't know it was so many," Kaiden murmured.

"I honestly thought it might be more." Toran brought up the timeline of when the known worlds had been infected. "These records might not be complete, since we wouldn't have known about the Valor world unless we'd gone there for the artifact."

"If we have memories, that means we went there, which means we know about the place," Kaiden said, looking over the timeline. "That means Windau is the first we know about."

"Logically, that does seem like a place we might investigate," I said.

"It does." Toran selected the planet's file.

In its natural state, Windau was a garden world of forested mountains and deep valleys paired with sophisticated urban developments. Its capital near the equator was a thriving city situated around a central square, with a large crystal at its center.

I recoiled in my chair as the images loaded on the holographic projector. The sight in front of me was a pristine city of sculpted stone and glass, but in my mind the scene was covered in writhing, dark tendrils and a perpetual black haze. "Stars, this is it." I wanted to be excited, but the contrast of the images had my stomach in knots.

"It's familiar to me, too. We went here and something bad happened," Kaiden said.

"We were attacked." Maris' voice was assured, and her gaze was fixed on the projection. "The Darkness didn't want us to leave."

"We should avoid this place," Toran suggested.

"Yeah, I'm all about avoiding places where we almost die," I agreed.

Kaiden pursed his lips. "I wonder why we went down there, though?"

I sifted through the images floating through my mind. "I think it had something to do with that crystal."

"Yes, you're right." Toran let out a long breath. "I believe we were trying to learn about the Darkness and how it transmits through the crystalline network."

"Is there any way to get that information without a direct interface?" Kaiden asked.

"No way that's currently workable. I've been toying with the idea of creating a remote connection using the waveform resonance of your magic pendants, but I haven't been able to make it work yet," the other man replied.

"This might be the time to try again," Maris advised.

"Is there really time to mess around with that?" I asked.

"All of our guts are telling us to avoid this place," Kaiden said. "Weren't you just saying we should listen to those instincts?"

"Yeah, I guess so," I admitted. Still, I couldn't shake the feeling that we'd learned something important there. If we didn't get that information, I had no idea what to expect for our future. But, by that same token, maybe it was that information that led us into the bad situation before, and now we could find another way around it.

"See what you can do, Toran," Kaiden said. "You're welcome to my pendant any time you need it."

"Thank you. If you don't mind, I'll begin work in the morning."

I couldn't believe they were ready to call the matter resolved so easily. "Shouldn't we look at the other worlds, too, to see if anything jumps out at us?"

"Yes, but it can wait a few hours," Toran said. "We'll work better after a night to process, regardless of what Maris' restoration spells can do for our bodies."

Taking a moment to assess my physical state, a wave of tiredness washed over me. Letting myself drop out of work mode, I realized that I was still going on the two hours of sleep we'd snagged before Maris got us up. "You're right. Work always goes better when rested and clear-headed."

"I don't expect my head to be clear any time soon, but sleep, at least, I should be able to manage." Toran ventured a smile.

"Yes, I'm sure you two are eager to get back to whatever it is you were up to," Maris added, eyeing Kaiden and me.

"Did I miss something?" Toran asked.

I rolled my eyes. "I told you she wouldn't let it slide," I muttered under my breath to Kaiden next to me.

"I found Elle in his cabin when I went to get them," Maris revealed.

Toran nodded. "I'm glad something good has come from this situation."

I blushed. "Yeah, it's not all bad."

"We're still a team first and foremost," Kaiden assured them. "What's going on between us will stay between us."

"I trust you," Toran replied.

I detected a twinge of envy from Maris, but she nodded her

understanding.

"We'll figure this out." Kaiden rose from his seat. "Meet in our common room in the morning?"

"Sounds good," Toran agreed, and Maris murmured her assent.

We adjourned from the conference room and bid good night to the overnight watch on the bridge, finding that Colren had already returned to his quarters. After taking the lift down to our residential level, Kaiden and I let Toran and Maris go ahead.

"Should I go back to my cabin, or…?" I asked when we were alone.

"I liked having you over, if you're still amenable."

I smiled back at him. "I'd like that very much."

I AWOKE FEELING more refreshed than I had in quite some time. To my relief, Kaiden had proved to be a quiet sleeper, and I looked forward to spending more nights together.

Though the relationship was already out in the open, I sneaked back to my cabin next door to get ready for the day. Once showered and changed into a clean shipsuit, I wandered down the corridor to the lounge.

Toran was already at work on the holographic display above the tabletop, reviewing what appeared to be waveforms like those we'd analyzed during our previous investigates into the crystals. "Good morning," he greeted when he noticed me enter.

"Hey. How was the rest of your night?"

"Took me a while to get to sleep, but I feel better now," he replied. "And you?"

"Things are good." I couldn't help a bashful smile from slipping out.

"I'm happy for you two. You seem good together."

"Yeah, we are. I think he's the kind of complement I've always needed but didn't know what to look for."

He smiled. "It's funny how those people find us. My wife is an extroverted master of social situations. Before her, I would have been content to remain at the edges, looking in on any event."

"How long have you been together?" I asked.

"Almost thirteen years, though sometimes it feels like we just met. We took our time before having our daughter."

"My parents had me young. My mom hadn't even finished graduate school yet. I got the impression sometimes that they wish they had waited."

"I trust you'll find your own timeline. Don't ever let others tell you what you should do," he advised.

"I won't. When we make it through this, I think I'm going to take some time to focus on myself and what I really want."

He raised an eyebrow. "Having second thoughts about Tactical School?"

"No. Maybe. I don't know." I shrugged. "I kind of like having freedom and being in charge. After being able to call the shots like this, I can't imagine going into boot camp and being a grunt."

"That's very true. Colren has given us amazingly free rein. I wouldn't expect most posts as a Ranger to offer that level of autonomy."

"Yeah. So, I dunno. Maybe there's some way to get that adventure without going down that path. Or, maybe I'll be all adventured out."

"I know you'll accomplish great things no matter what you decide to do, Elle," he told me.

The statement warmed me in the way praise from my parents always did. "Thanks, Toran. I expect to see you on the cover of a major scientific journal after all of this. I don't think you'll remain an anonymous maintenance tech after the ingenuity you've shown to gain understanding of the crystals."

He chuckled. "Perhaps. I guess it's good my wife will be able to help me mingle at all of the fancy awards dinners."

I laughed. "All of the recognition will be well deserved."

"Who's getting recognized for what?" Maris asked, stepping onto the room.

"Just thinking about the good times ahead," I told her.

"Aren't we having good times now?" Kaiden asked from a meter behind. "Or is having things try to kill us not fun?"

"Not ideal, no." I smirked.

"Being showered in fame and fortune for saving known civilization is cool," Maris said. "But, really, I just want my home to be safe."

My heart ached. "Me too."

Kaiden slipped his pendant off his neck. "Here, Toran, you probably need this for the cradle, right?"

"Yes, thank you." The other man took the pendant and placed it on the specialized device he'd connected to the ship's sensor suite. "I don't know why I couldn't get it to work last time, but let's try hitting it with the full spectrum and see if I missed any resonance points before."

While Toran worked, I plopped down in one of the lounge chairs and brought up records about the other worlds consumed by the Darkness. As powerful as the images were, none aside from Windau stood out to me with any clarity.

After half an hour, Toran finally pushed back from the table and groaned. "I don't know what I'm missing."

"You were working on this for days before the reset. I wouldn't expect you to solve it in less than an hour," Kaiden said, who'd settled into a seat next to me with a tablet of his own.

"I know, but I was hoping for an easy solution all the same." Toran sighed. "I wish I understood more about how the network transmits data. I'm not surprised we decided to go down to a planet—a direct link would bypass the need for a remote workaround like this."

"Would it have to be an infected world?" I asked.

"To read the alien signal on the network, yes." He paused. "But, you know, maybe a direct line to a crystal would still yield more insights than analyzing the pendants. We could tap into the network that way and identify the different components of the signals. I could then parse out what's different with the pendant to isolate the elements associated with the remote connection."

I blinked at him. "I'm going to assume you know what you're talking about and I don't have to."

"Yes."

"Okay, so, what do we do?" Maris asked.

"Back to Crystallis?" Kaiden ventured.

"We're already here, and there are more crystals than any other world I know about," Toran replied. "Seems like the best place to be."

Kaiden set down his tablet. "All right. Let's tell Colren and head down."

After relaying our intended plan, we gathered our gear and headed down to the hangar. For once, Tami was nowhere to be seen—finally taking some leave after the grind of the past several days—but her crew got us situated on our shuttle and sent us on our way.

Being our third trip down to Crystallis' surface, Kaiden had figured out the best way to minimize turbulence from the planet's tumultuous atmosphere and adjust for the inertial compensators malfunctioning due to the planet's unique properties. We followed our prior path to the valley containing the Archive, since it held the largest number of crystals we were likely to find anywhere in existence.

Despite seeing the valley before, it still took my breath away as we entered. The towering crystals gleamed in the purple light of the planet, majestic and timeless.

"I'll set us down on the other side of the valley away from the Archive entrance," Kaiden said as he looped the shuttle around. "That should hopefully minimize interactions from the Master Crystals, if that's even an issue."

"Good thinking," Toran agreed.

Kaiden located an open area with minimal slope near the canyon's northeastern edge and landed the shuttle.

I unstrapped from my usual co-pilot's seat. "What's the plan?"

"I brought a standard crystal interface kit from the *Evangiel*, but it'll take some time to hook up before I can start gathering readings," Toran replied.

"Need any help?" Maris asked.

"Not right now." Toran gathered his equipment. "This shouldn't take too long."

"You know where to find me." Maris wandered back toward the sleeping cabins at the aft of the shuttle.

Kaiden and I followed Toran outside into the alien landscape.

"Want to get in some combat practice while we wait?" Kaiden asked me.

"Sure. Is that okay, Toran?"

"Sounds good. I'll call you when I'm ready," he acknowledged.

I followed Kaiden toward the canyon wall. "Are you *really* planning to lob fireballs in a delicate crystal valley?" I asked when we were beyond Toran's earshot.

"Maybe a couple for good measure, but I figured a romantic nature walk might be a nicer way to spend the morning than listening to Maris whine on the shuttle."

We strolled through the crystals until we found a collection of rock boulders that shielded us from the surrounding crystals. It seemed as safe as place as any to unleash a few attack spells without fear of harming the surroundings.

"Actually, I had an ulterior motive for bringing you out here," he revealed.

"We *just* spent the night together."

He smiled. "Not related to that. I indicated I was going to be practicing magic so that you could give it a shot."

"Kaiden…"

"I know you've been reluctant to admit you have casting abilities, but you do, Elle. Maybe you should try tapping into that."

"Maybe," I realized. We'd glimpsed the enemy we were up against, and it would take every advantage we could get to defeat them. If I had new skills locked inside me, I owed it to my team to prepare myself for the upcoming fight.

"There's good energy in this place. The magic comes freely. Just try it out and see if anything comes to you."

I took a deep breath. "Okay, I'll give it a shot."

Having magical abilities had always sounded fun to me, but as I prepared for my first intentional use of magic, I found myself more terrified than excited. It probably stemmed from having no idea where the magic came from or what it was. The idea of manipulating the world around me with unseen force went against the laws of nature that had been a cornerstone of my life.

Yet, I'd seen the bliss on Kaiden's and Maris' faces when they were casting. I wanted to taste that sweet power for myself.

I turned away from Kaiden to face the collection of boulders that were to serve as the object of my target practice. While Kaiden had initially been drawn to fire, I found myself called in a different direction. Competing forces of light and dark filled my mind—not the Darkness, but something else… Something even more powerful.

I extended my gloved hand toward the boulder, palm open. A white orb formed between my fingers, shining brightly even in the daylight. It swelled in my palm for two seconds and then released. The orb shot toward the boulder and struck it at my chest-level. At the impact site, a fist-sized chunk of stone broke away and hovered in the air, seemingly defying gravity.

My mouth fell open. "How…?"

Kaiden's eyes widened. "Well, that's a new kind of magic."

I lowered my outstretched hand, and the rock dropped to the ground. "What…?"

"Hmm." Kaiden crossed his arms. "I'm not sure what to make of that."

"Is it the glove?"

"No, that's just a channeling tool, like my staff. I *maybe* snuck down to the equipment room this morning after you left to go check out the details about the item," he admitted.

"Hence the invite on this nature walk."

"Yep."

I let out a slow breath. "So, what, I can levitate things?"

"After smashing parts of them to bits, apparently."

"I'm not so sure about this magic thing," I replied with a frown. The kind of magic I'd fanaticized about was filled with colorful light and elemental-themed attacks, not… whatever I'd just done.

Kaiden tilted his head. "Elle, you tried *one* thing. I think it's a little premature to draw conclusions."

I shook my head.

"What's wrong?" he asked.

"I'm scared to see what I can do. And if I'm scared of myself, what will others think?"

He softened. "Hey, you don't have to worry about me going anywhere, at least. And besides, anyone who'd ditch you over you manifesting magical abilities wasn't a very good friend to begin with."

"I don't want to hurt anyone."

"You have to trust yourself, Elle. These abilities can catch you by surprise sometimes, I can attest to that, but it doesn't come out of nowhere. *You're* in control. Be clear in your intentions and the abilities will follow."

"You make it sound easy."

"It's natural… it's a part of you."

I scoffed. "Right. This thing that only three known people in existence have is completely 'natural'."

Kaiden paused. "Okay, I could have phrased that better."

"Uh huh."

"How about…" He thought for a moment. "You now have access to something ancient, and unique, and special, shouldn't you embrace that gift?"

I evaluated him. "All right, that's a sentiment I can get behind."

He smiled. "Besides, I know you secretly want to be a mage."

Excitement welled within me as I heard the word. "Okay, yes!" I burst out. "I really do want to learn about this, even if it does scare me."

"Good, harness that desire," Kaiden said. He nodded his head toward the boulder. "Now, see what else you can do."

I held my palm open toward the rock once more, concentrating on the place I'd struck on my previous attempt. This time, I tried to picture what I wanted to happen—for the entire boulder to lift from the ground. I figured it was way too big of a spell to take on, if it *ever* would be possible, but I may as well aim high.

Another white sphere formed in my palm. It swelled until it was the size of my head, then launched toward the boulder. The light dispersed on impact, enveloping the top half of the rock monolith in light. Cracks scored the stone, and fist-sized fragments levitated along with dust from the destruction. The boulder broke apart before me, the fragments at my command. If an enemy were in sight, there would be no escape from my assault.

"Stars!" A deep voice drew my attention to the edge of the path we'd taken from the shuttle.

My head snapped around. Rock fragments fell to the ground in a thunderous cascade, echoing through the alcove.

Toran stood between the crystals at the path's edge, his heavy brow raised with surprise. "Elle, you can cast magic?"

MY HANDS DROPPED to my sides. "Toran, we thought you were going to call us."

"I did. Apparently, you didn't hear me, and the comms don't work down here." The large man turned his attention to Kaiden. "Did you know about Elle?"

"What's the big deal?" I interjected. "Kaiden and Maris are both casters."

He held up his hands defensively. "I'm just surprised you didn't say anything."

"I wasn't sure I actually *could* do anything," I said, looking over the destroyed boulder. Its top third was missing. Given more time, I may have ripped apart the entire thing.

"This was an experiment," Kaiden said.

I nodded. "Yeah, like I said, it's not as though I'm the only one with magic casting."

"Yes, but Maris and Kaiden don't also have your physical skills," Toran replied.

"That doesn't mean they couldn't. Is there actually a rule against having skills in multiple disciplines? Just because we picked one when we were extracted doesn't mean we should be limited, does it?" I honestly had no idea. If our skills were based in some sort of ancient lore, I'd never read it as a kid. All I knew was that I felt multiple abilities within myself and I was done ignoring certain parts. Kaiden was right: I *did* always want to be a mage. I had been so close to selecting the Spirit discipline during my extraction, maybe part of that desire had manifested, along with some of Protection due to my defensive attitude.

Toran nodded. "You're right, there's no reason to think we can't have multiple skills. That part doesn't bother me. What I do find concerning is that you felt you needed to come out here and test those skills in secret."

I didn't know why I had been so intent on keeping it to myself. I appreciated that Kaiden had honored my wishes, but in this matter, perhaps he had been too accommodating. My mantra to my team had been that we needed to be open and trust each other, yet I had been trying to hide a huge revelation about myself.

"I'm sorry," I murmured, hanging my head. "It wasn't fair or right for me to not say anything."

"In all fairness, it was only yesterday during the battle in the Archive when those abilities came to light," Kaiden said in my defense.

"Yet, somehow the equipment room scanner on the *Evangiel* knew to make this caster-specific device available to me," I said, flexing the glove on my right hand.

"Maybe there's some common marker it picked up in me and Maris, and then also saw in you," Kaiden suggested.

"Whatever the reason, this is still all new to me." I sighed.

"Please don't hide things in the future, Elle," Toran said. "You can trust us."

I nodded. "I know."

"Anyway, we're keeping you from the important work, Toran," Kaiden interjected. "What did you come find us to say?"

"Right." He looked me over again. "I found something interesting through the crystal interface."

"Show us," Kaiden gestured for Toran to lead the way.

"I still want to hear more about this apparent telekinesis," Toran said while we walked.

"I'm not sure what to say," I said. "Caught me completely by surprise! I was kind of going for a lightning attack—I always like the way those looked."

"This definitely wasn't elemental-themed like my magic, but it seems incredibly powerful," Kaiden said.

"Indeed. Especially for an initial attempt." Toran paused. "I can't help but wonder… if you can lift, can you also crush?"

"I have no idea." It hadn't occurred to me to try; I wasn't sure I *wanted* to try.

"Once we get back to the *Evangiel* and have a better sense of the alien fleet, you should test out your new magic the way you encouraged us to do," Kaiden told me.

I eyed him. "Yeah, well, if you thought fireballs were a bad idea on a spaceship, then a boulder-disintegrating gravity-defying light orb thing seems like an even worse idea."

"Might need to come back to a planet like this," he amended.

"You may get practice time before we leave," Toran stated as we reached the open area near the shuttle. "I have more investigating to do. The unique properties of this crystal canyon have resulted in some interesting interactions with the crystal interface."

"What do you mean?" I questioned.

Toran strode to a crystal with equipment hooked up to its base. He pointed toward the portable readout screen. "The signal seems to be augmented. I'm picking up something strange in the background that I can't explain."

I examined the data. I didn't understand what the components indicated, but it was clear that there were strong waveforms at the forefront and something different at a low level in the background. "Have you ever seen anything like this before?"

Toran shook his head. "Looking at the signals emanating from reset crystals wasn't exactly my job before this madness started. But with that said, I never came across anything anomalous before now, including the scans over the last week."

"Does it have something to do with this place? The connection to the Master Archive?" I suggested.

"Or, could this be interference from the Darkness?" Kaiden asked.

"That's the most likely explanation. It appears to propagate through the crystalline network," Toran replied.

I frowned. "And let me guess… to properly analyze it, you'd need to go right to the source on an infected world?"

Toran nodded. "That would offer the greatest insights, yes."

"No wonder we took the risk." Kaiden sighed.

"There might be another way…" Toran began slowly. "I may be able to enhance the signal using the amplification from this place. I don't think

I would have even picked up the signal on another world even if I'd been looking for it."

I frowned. "This is very bad."

"It's a *lead*. That's good!" Kaiden said.

"That part, yes, but not what it means," I said. "We suspected the Darkness infects worlds through the crystals, but if we can pick up a signal here, that means it might be throughout the *entire* crystalline network, not just the worlds where it's already shown up."

Kaiden paled. "Or, at a minimum, this world is next."

"But the Archive isn't actually *here*," I reminded him.

"All the same, this is the only way we know to access it."

Toran took a deep breath. "There are no signs of corruption on this world, so I do suspect the signal I'm picking up is from the broader network rather than something specific to this world. It's faint."

Kaiden's shoulders rounded. "So, it's everywhere? I'd always thought of it as hopping from one world to another."

"Yeah, but…" I bit my lower lip. "What if it's not an infection of the *crystals* like we thought, but rather of the hyperdimensional network itself?"

"In that case, it could appear on any world without notice," Kaiden murmured.

"But we can find it," Toran said. "I believe that further analysis of this signal might tell us where it's coming from."

"And once we find the source, we can go on the offensive," I realized.

"Exactly."

I threw up my hands. "Then why are we still talking? Analyze!"

"There's a problem," Toran said. "I don't know how to decode the signal. I can isolate certain components, sure, but I can't interpret what each segment of code does without having more information."

"I thought you said you could trace the signal to its source?" I asked.

"Yes, if I can cross-reference it with some other readings on the *Evangiel*. But as for the big 'how exactly does the Darkness work?' question, I'm afraid this might be another dead end."

My heart dropped. "I'll settle for learning where it's coming from so we can stop it." Yet, I found myself more concerned than excited about Toran's plan. The déjà vu that had been haunting me for the last day struck once again in its vague an unhelpful way that danger was up ahead.

I almost said something about it, but we already knew full-well that there would be risks. These actions were likely what had led us down the path that culminated in our confrontation with the alien invaders. As scary as it was, we needed to move forward.

"Any new insights are more than we have now," Kaiden agreed. "Can we do anything to help?"

"No, if you're good with this plan, I'll get back to it. You may as well resume your practice," Toran replied.

I hesitated. "This work always seems to fall to you. I wish we could do more."

"Never doubt your own contributions, Elle. We all pull our weight in different ways," he assured me.

"You're quite literally the heavyweight around here," Kaiden said with a smile. "We'd be lost without you."

"I'm happy to play my part. I want us all to get back to our families."

An ache gripped my heart with the reminder that my homeworld of Erusan now only existed in the Master Archive, beyond my present grasp. "We'll leave you to it." I turned back toward the path I'd taken earlier with Kaiden.

He followed me. When we had gone several meters in, he jogged forward so we were walking abreast. "Why do I have a bad feeling about this new investigation of Toran's?"

"You too?" I shook my head. "I was really hoping it was just me."

"No, this situation is way too messed up." He sighed.

"I want to be ready for whatever confrontation is coming."

"You did great in the last one."

"But that wasn't against the core of the Darkness—it was tests the crystalline network's creators *wanted* us to pass," I countered. "The next fight is for real."

Kaiden stopped as we reached the open area serving as the practice grounds. "We'll get through this Elle. I trust that those trials were designed to prepare us for facing whatever danger may come our way, and now we have the skills, fortitude, and bonds to take on whatever those alien bastards may throw at us."

I tilted my head. "I kind of like seeing you all fired up."

"I believe in what we're doing."

"Me too, though it's not like we can say 'no'… We're it—we're the plan."

"I can't think of a better quartet to save the day."

I laughed. "Except maybe a quartet of trained, experienced people who actually know what they're doing."

"For faking it, we're doing a pretty spectacular job."

"I suppose we are. Speaking of which," I sized up the boulder I decapitated earlier, "I should probably get back to pretending I know magic."

"An excellent plan." Kaiden leaned against a nearby rock.

I held out my hand toward the boulder and tried to clear my mind. However hard I tried, thoughts of the oppressive force of the Darkness kept creeping in. I closed my eyes and shook my head in an attempt to clear it. When I re-opened my eyes, I discovered that an energy orb was starting to form in my palm. Unlike the others I'd cast, though, this one was black.

"Um... Kaiden?" I wasn't sure if I should try to dispel the new magic or find out what it could do.

I heard him take a step away behind me. "We came out here to learn new skills." His tone was less than assured, but I was just as wary of the black cloud swirling in my palm that looked suspiciously like the Darkness.

"All right, here goes." I released the orb.

It shot from my palm and enveloped the boulder just like the levitating spell, but this time there was no immediate result. I kept waiting for the rock to be mutated into something else, given what we'd witnessed the Darkness do, but three seconds passed with no apparent effect aside from the black cloud.

Then, my sense of reality warped. The boulder began to compress, like it was dough in a baker's hands being flatted into a biscuit. When the boulder was half of its original height, the sides also began to draw inward. As it condensed, the blackness surrounding it became more intense until there was only a black mass the size of my fist where the three-meter-tall boulder once stood. The perfect, black orb dropped onto the gravel with a thud.

"Whoa," Kaiden murmured behind me.

"Was not expecting that," I whispered. I took a steadying breath. "I think I'm a freak. It's official."

"Jury is still out on all of us, but you're fascinating and talented if nothing else." Gravel crunched underfoot as Kaiden walked past me toward the black orb resting on the ground. When he reached it, he nudged it with his toe. It didn't budge. "What the…?"

I jogged up next to him and crouched down to inspect it. There were no distinguishing features on the smooth, matte black finish. "Is there a whole boulder somehow packed in there?"

Cautiously, Kaiden reached out to touch it. Though his fingers easily wrapped around the form, he couldn't get any purchase on it. He tried with both hands. "Gah! This thing must weigh a ton. Or several, maybe."

We tried to lift it together, but it still didn't budge.

Kaiden shook his head and stood up. "I don't think that's going anywhere."

"This magic doesn't make any sense." Kaiden's and Maris' abilities had clear roots in the ancient magic of lore, but I couldn't imagine where mine stemmed from. If our abilities truly were a manifestation of our hyperdimensional consciousness, then it scared me to think what had transpired to make we want this as a part of myself.

"Strange or not, this is a powerful ability, Elle. Based on how you took out that rock, imagine what you could do to a bunch of those monster things that attacked us on the Valor world."

"That's true." Except, it was one thing to rip apart or crush a rock. I didn't love the idea of doing that to a living creature, but that was my reality.

Kaiden seemed to sense my discomfort. "But hey," he continued, "just because you have these abilities doesn't mean you need to use them. We already have a good team dynamic going with the slashy, punchy, magicy-ness. This can be a… last resort."

"Yeah, having a special bonus offense can't be a bad thing," I realized.

"Rocks made for good target practice. You can stick to that as long as you want."

"I guess I'll need to find another victim." I evaluated the black sphere that used to be a boulder. "Too bad, since this one was perfect."

"Maybe the sphere itself can be a target?" Kaiden suggested.

"Not sure what I'll be able to do with that. I doubt I can condense it further. What else is there?"

"Break it apart like you did with the boulder?"

Breaking apart and crushing the same unfortunate piece of rock sounded like a tedious way to spend the afternoon, but I suppose I didn't know what was possible until I tried. "All right, stand back."

We returned to where we had been standing when I'd compressed the sphere. I held out my hand while I concentrated on the light from my first attempt, committed to push back the dark that wanted to close in around my mind. Slowly, a white orb formed in the palm of my hand. I launched it toward the black sphere.

The sphere was encased in white light. I focused on it, willing the form to expand into the boulder that once stood in its place. But, that creation was lost—crushed out of existence. I could feel it.

However, the black sphere began to tremble on the ground. Kaiden and I together hadn't been able to nudge it. The trembling intensified. My brow furrowed with exertion as I attempted to rend the sphere apart. Instead, it began to levitate.

"Elle, that's amazing!" Kaiden whispered behind me.

"I don't know how…" Excitement rippled through me as I thought about the power literally at my fingertips. This new ability combined with my enhanced physical strength and agility would enable me to do almost anything. If I ever came face-to-face with the aliens, they would be in trouble.

I spent the next half-hour trying variations of the techniques—levitating, splitting, and compressing using various rocks around us. None of it felt natural to me, but by the end, my initial reservations had subsided; I had new powers, and I was ready to use them.

The practicing was eventually interrupted by a call from Toran in the distance. "Elle! Kaiden! Come here."

"Coming!" Kaiden yelled back.

I presently had the black sphere suspended in the air, trying to see how long I could hold it. So far, it'd been three minutes and twenty seconds. "Can he wait a few minutes? I'm on a roll," I said. The sphere dipped a little as my concentration faltered.

"You can try again later, Elle."

I glanced toward him. "But this time—" My attention lapsed as I turned away, and the sphere launched in the direction I was looking: right at Kaiden.

He ducked just in time to miss the super-dense orb hurtling toward him. "Whoa!"

The sphere struck the base of a crystal spire, letting out a piercing ringing as the crystal vibrated. I brought my hands up over my ears to deaden the sound, but it pulsed inside me. That trill… I'd heard it before. It was within the Darkness.

Finally, the intense ringing faded, and I removed my hands from my ears. "Sorry! Are you okay?"

Kaiden took a deep breath. "Yeah, I'm fine."

I was horrified to see that the black sphere had been embedded ten centimeters into the hard ground. If it had hit Kaiden, he would have been killed instantly. "I didn't mean to."

"Accidents happen." Kaiden looked shaken.

"Still, I shouldn't have been playing with—"

"It's fine, Elle," he insisted. "Let's just get back to Toran." He turned to leave.

"Hey, did you… sense anything when that crystal vibrated?" I asked as I started to follow.

He nodded after a few seconds. "Yeah, it's weird. Some images popped into my mind, but I don't know what to make of them."

Now that he mentioned it, there had been a faint visual component to my reaction to the sound. I'd thought it was a vision blackout, but as I reflected, I detected the signs of a starscape.

We hurried back to the shuttle's landing site. Toran and Maris were standing next to the crystal Toran had been observing.

"What was that sound?" he asked as soon as he saw us.

"I accidentally hit a crystal. It's okay—"

"I saw something," Maris murmured. "Why would that make me see anything?"

I had no idea, but the image kept solidifying in my mind. A memory. And the place… it was so familiar to me.

Dread closed in at the edges my mind. My chest constricted, and my heart pounded in my chest. I could barely breathe through the panic. The memories flooded back to me—Darkness ripping through the fleet and disintegrating the Hegemony ships before my eyes against the bright backdrop of the spatial anomaly.

That place… that was where we did the last reset, moments before we were about to die.

My breath caught in my throat. "Stars! I remember." I looked around at the horrified expressions of my friends.

Tears filled Maris' eyes. "I do, too. It all happened so fast."

Kaiden took an unsteady breath.

"How is that possible? *One* vessel took out a fleet of Hegemony ships?" It didn't seem real to me even though the memory was as strong as if I'd lived it moments before.

"This explains why we reset," Kaiden said. "What chance do we stand against an enemy where one of their ships can level dozens of ours in a matter of minutes?"

I didn't know what to say. I wanted to dismiss the concerns, but the truth was I believed the worries were legitimate. We *didn't* stand a chance against an enemy that powerful. At least, not facing them head on.

"Let's talk to the commander," I said. "If we're going to beat these bad guys, we need to set a trap."

21

"THEY'RE GOING TO... manufacture the ships?" Colren gave me a quizzical look from across the conference table in Central Command.

"In all fairness, we don't know for sure if they were being generated in real-time or if it was some kind of gate technology," I admitted. "But the point is, if we wait for one of those ships to finish coming through the anomaly, we're done for."

"But we *do* know where they're going to be," Kaiden emphasized. "And if things play out like they did last time, we have a limited window to get the upper hand."

"How do you know the location?" the commander questioned.

"Well, we don't *exactly*," Toran replied. "But I remember the method we used to determine the point. As soon as I've cleaned up and isolated the signal we recorded on Crystallis, we'll be able to segment it and cross-reference it with the other worlds' signals."

"If we need military aid, then I'll need something more to bring to my superiors than a hunch," Colren said.

"It's not a hunch, Commander. I remembered that I'd analyzed the signals emanating from each of the worlds consumed by the Darkness," Toran explained. "They're paired in a way to denote a set of coordinates. But it's incredibly complex. We need a master key." He tapped on the tabletop where the signal from Crystallis was displayed. "*This* is that key. The amplification from the crystals allowed us to pick up the full pattern without going directly to one where the signal is strongest—an infected world. The network is all... well, connected. Crystallis gave us a strong enough antenna to listen."

The commander considered the explanation. "Without getting bogged down in the technical details, I think I understand the concept well enough to support the case to the admiralty. Finish documenting where we need to go and I'll make sure we have our fleet meet us there."

"I will," Toran acknowledged.

Colren rapped his fingers on the tabletop. "And the timing?"

"Vague," I admitted. "We had a discussion about that on the flight back from the planet, and we suspect the encounter happened maybe a week from now in the other timeline." Using terminology about timelines bothered me since we hadn't actually time-traveled, but it was the easiest way to characterize what we were experiencing. Resets were supposed to be straightforward—to change the outcome of a specific incident. But when that incident affected the fate of interstellar civilization, I suppose matters were bound to get complicated.

"If a week is the target, then we'll shoot for three days to give some breathing room." Colren rose from the table.

"Is there any way we can help with the preparations?" I asked, standing to face him.

"Nothing at the moment, but stand by. You've given us a fighting chance, thank you." He departed.

"I need to get to it." Toran pushed back from the table.

Kaiden nodded. "I guess we should get in some practice while we wait."

It took Toran nearly seven hours to complete his isolation of the Darkness transmission signal. Kaiden, Maris, and I divided our time between combat practice in an empty storage room and offering feedback to Toran whenever it was requested of us. When Toran had finished segmenting the signal and used the pairings to determine the coordinates, we passed off the information to Colren. Then, the real waiting began.

I expected us to make a jump soon thereafter, but a check-in with Colren revealed that we wouldn't make our move until the rest of the fleet was ready to mobilize. Given the enemy threat we were expecting, the Hegemony's leadership thought a unified front would be best.

Three days passed while the interstellar preparations were made. Two worlds that had been identified before we sealed the Archive as future targets for the Darkness completed evacuations early so the assigned ships would be available for the alien engagement. As the time for action neared, we were told that a scouting party had been sent ahead, and they'd given the all-clear for the fleet to move in. All we could do was hope that nothing changed in the time between the report and when we dropped out of our jump.

Shortly before the scheduled jump, we were summoned to Central Command to meet with Colren. We joined him around the conference table in our usual fashion. Unlike most meetings, however, he adjusted the glass walls facing the bridge to make them opaque.

The action immediately put me on alert, and I exchanged worried glances with Kaiden as we took our seats.

"Thank you for coming," Colren began. "In half an hour's time, we'll jump to the coordinates where we expect the spatial anomaly to appear. We'll be joined by eighty of the Hegemony's warships. The rest of the fleet has been assigned to the most strategic worlds to provide whatever protection they can should this engagement not end well."

"As long as we prevent the anomaly from completely forming, there won't *be* an engagement," Kaiden replied.

"Right. About that..." Colren folded his hands on the tabletop. "That's why I called you here."

My heart dropped. The commander's sober tone was one of reluctant resignation. I braced for the news.

"After stating the case as clearly and in as many ways as I could, the admiralty drew their own conclusions. Whereas I insisted we needed to strike fast and hard, they'd like to attempt a peaceable resolution."

Kaiden laughed. "No! You can't be serious."

Colren's grim nod said it all. "I believe what you've told me. You've earned my trust. That's why I'm telling you this now. I genuinely believe their ordered course of action is not in the Hegemony's best interest, but I'm obligated to obey. After all, if a peaceable solution *is* viable, we could save countless lives. That's too great a chance for me to ignore."

I shook my head with disbelief. Maybe the reset had somehow messed with their heads.

"But when talking to the aliens doesn't work?" Toran prompted.

"I need you ready to perform a reset so we can get another chance and hopefully get things right," the commander stated.

"How?" Kaiden asked. "I only have a vague recollection of some sort of device."

Colren nodded. "The observation crystal—it's near the bridge. If you performed a reset before, it would have been with that."

"Right, but even if we do…" I faded out. He knew full well that we'd face the same situation with the aliens that we were in now. There was no need to spell it out.

"Which is why you need to figure out a way to remember whatever happens here," he said. "It's imperative we find a way to prevail and end this reset cycle. This is your task."

"No offense, but you're just telling us now?" Kaiden shot back. "We've been sitting around twiddling our thumbs for three days."

"The order just came through—probably so I wouldn't have time to submit a formal protest," Colren revealed. "I hate to ask more of you, but as the sole civilians on this ship, you four are the only people not bound strictly to the admiralty's orders."

I imagined even telling us his misgivings was a violation enough as it was, so I didn't press the issue. "We'll do our best to brainstorm a solution before the jump," I said.

He inclined his head. "Thank you. I hope that solution doesn't become necessary, but we need to be prepared for all contingencies."

"We'll get started right away," Toran told him.

Colren looked us each in the eyes in turn. "I'll show you where to find the observation room and set up your access credentials so you'll be ready. We'll meet again after the jump."

After a short tour of the room near Central Command, my team adjourned to our lounge, processing the news that the prevailing plan was now to attempt contact with the aliens.

"There's, like, zero chance they're going to respond in a friendly way, right?" Maris asked, breaking the silence as we gathered around the table.

"Yeah, I can't imagine any other outcome," I agreed.

"That's so stupid. Why would they try to *talk* to them?" Kaiden shook his head and groaned.

"They know we're overpowered," Toran replied. "The Darkness expanding through the crystals is faceless and vicious. Ships mean there might be intelligent life on board. If we can't beat them with force, the next best hope is to appeal to reason."

"Do you think it's the right call to talk to them, then?" I asked.

"Oh, stars no!" He scoffed. "They're going to get everyone killed."

"So, a reset is almost guaranteed to be necessary. How do we make sure we don't make these same mistakes again?" I looked at my friends' faces around the table. They were scared and concerned. We should be.

"Well, maybe going through this more than once will help us remember faster than we did last time," Maris suggested.

Kaiden shook his head. "This to too important to leave to chance."

It was. Somehow, the vital information had to be part of us—a powerful imprint that would still be at the forefront of our consciousness even after a reset.

"We need intentional touchstones," I said, a plan starting to form in my mind. "Focus on things we know we'll see right away after the reset and tie them in our consciousness to the important information we need to remember."

Kaiden lit up. "You may be onto something with that. Like how we started to remember when we kissed."

"That's touching, but how in the stars are we supposed to build memory associations for complex coordinates and information about fleet movements?" Maris asked.

"We don't need coordinates, only a prompt to seek out the lead to that information," I replied. "And we need to know what hasn't worked, but witnessing the destruction seems to help that come through just fine."

"What kind of alternative plan should we suggest?" Kaiden questioned.

"That's for our alternate selves to figure out," Maris said.

Toran didn't look convinced. "That's a difficult situation to put ourselves in, isn't it?"

I was about to take Toran's side, but then I thought it through. "Maris does have a point. Our new selves will potentially have two sets of memories to pull from as they start to remember. I believe in myself and us. They'll figure it out," I said.

"They won't even have a chance if we can't make the memories stick," Kaiden stated. "How do you propose we go about making these 'touchstones'?"

"Hold clear, distinct memories in our minds that are tied to specific places," I began. "We need to think through what actions we'll likely take right after the reset—preferably with a strong emotional component, so we can tie the memories to those actions. We also need to decide what the vital information to convey is. It can't be anything too complex, but it needs to get the point across."

"Let's start with the information," Kaiden said, bringing up a notetaking interface on the tabletop. "First, we need to know the process for determining the coordinates to the anomaly site."

"Yes," Toran concurred. "Really, just directing us to the surface of Crystallis with interface equipment will set me on the right path."

"Let's try for more—like the signal and planet pairings—but you're right about simplifying it to the bare minimum," I said. "We also need to convey that we have to beat the aliens to the anomaly site. No delays, no talking. If we end up resetting, that didn't work."

"Gather a fleet, get there as fast as possible," Kaiden agreed.

Toran nodded. "Keep the anomaly from forming."

"What else?" Maris asked. "There has to be more than that."

"Is there?" I thought about what we'd encountered on the last go-around and what we had experienced so far this time, but most of it was incidental. All the important moments could be traced back to finding the signal and the initial moments of our encounter with the alien ship.

However, there was one other piece of information I wanted to bring forward: my new telekinetic abilities. That would be on me to remember.

"Yes, that's what's most critical," Kaiden agreed with me. "Anything else is bonus, but that's what we *need*."

"Okay, so the touchpoint part," I went on. "What places did we go after the reset that we could tie memories to?"

"It's the pod room near Central Command for us," Kaiden said.

"My memories triggered in my cabin when I lay down on my bed," Toran said. "That's the place I always think about my family before I go to sleep."

"What about you, Maris?" I prompted.

She shook her head. "I didn't remember much of anything until I heard that tone down on Crystallis. I'd just come out of the shuttle to talk to Toran when I heard it."

"Won't be able to recreate that. But maybe there's another auditory trigger you could use." I thought for a moment. "What about the lift's chime?"

"Too common," Kaiden said. "That's a background sound at this point. It should be distinct."

"What about the entry tone on the bridge?" Maris suggested. "We go to see Colren as soon as we get back from sealing the Archive."

"Yes, good!" I took a deep breath. "We have a little over twenty minutes before we need to get ready for the jump. Go to your places. Think about the signal and the alien fleet as much as you can. Sound, touch, visuals—tie those memories, build the association."

"See you for the jump," Toran acknowledged.

Kaiden, Maris, and I ran back to the lift so we could return to the Central Command level. Upon reaching the deck, Maris continued to the bridge's entrance while Kaiden and I entered the pod room along the corridor.

"Okay, that first kiss is what's important, not so much this place itself," I said.

Kaiden smiled at me. "So, you're saying that kissing you will help save the universe?"

I rolled my eyes. "Get over here."

I pulled him close to me and our lips met. I was tempted to revel in the moment, but I focused on the memories I would need after the reset. I hated building a connection between something so terrible with an act that would normally be happy, but it was the strongest feeling at my disposal. There'd be plenty of time once we got through this to overwrite the bad association.

Crystallis, the alien signal, coordinates, the anomaly, the alien ships— I tried to pair each memory with a specific touch. The images seared into my mind.

We spent fifteen minutes soaking in as many details as we could. At last, a ten-minute warning sounded for the impending jump, signaling that crew members would be flooding into the pod room at any moment.

"I'm sorry to ruin this for us," I murmured as we pulled apart.

Kaiden gave me a final light kiss. "Nothing could. We'll make new memories."

With the alien threat at the forefront of my mind, we made our way to our own pod room. Toran and Maris were already stripping down to their shipsuits when we arrived.

"How'd it go?" I asked.

Toran shrugged. "I did what we discussed. Hopefully it will be enough."

"I think I drove the comm techs crazy by opening and closing that bridge door dozens of times," Maris said. "The sound is still reverberating in my ears."

I wrinkled my nose. "That sounds awful, but in this case, I think that's a good thing."

Maris eyed me. "You two definitely had it best."

I began taking off my outer clothes. "Not as good as you think." I didn't expect her to understand how much it tore me up to taint the memory of a significant, happy moment in my life. Even if she did understand, there wasn't time to get into it. I trusted in the bond I was developing with Kaiden, and we'd free ourselves from the association eventually.

We climbed into our pods and strapped in.

"See you on the other side," I wished my friends.

"Keep the memories fresh," Kaiden advised. "Everything will happen quickly once we arrive."

I did my best to hold thoughts of the aliens and the signal in my mind throughout the disorienting jump. As the synesthesia kicked in, I began feeling the visual elements of the memories, even hearing and tasting what had never been a part of my experience before. It made it all the more salient.

Finally, the pressure pinning me against my couch began to diminish. We had reached the jump coordinates.

I stretched my arms as the translucent pod cover slid down. "All right, time to see how terribly this 'conversation' with the aliens goes!"

"May as well go straight to the observation room to reset," Kaiden replied, sitting upright.

"I choose to hope that there's at least a chance this will—" Maris was cut off by a warning claxon.

"Enemy ships inbound. Battle stations," Colren announced over the comm.

"Shit, what?" Kaiden hurdled out of his pod.

Toran squeezed out of his own pod. "How are they here already?"

I scrambled to my feet. "There's not time to get dressed, come on!" I ran toward the door.

We dashed to the lift and piled inside.

"This can't be happening," I murmured under my breath.

Kaiden shook his head. "We should have had days."

"But we didn't do things the same," Toran pointed out. "We went to Crystallis, not Windau."

My head felt like it was about to explode. There were too many variables. It could have been any number of things that led to this different sequence of events.

The lift door opened on the Central Command level and we raced down the corridor to the bridge's entrance. Maris winced as the door unlocked and slid open.

Inside, Colren leaned forward in his seat at the center of the bridge, his attention fixed on a fleet of two hundred alien ships arranged in a defensive spherical formation around the anomaly.

Hegemony ships dropped out of hyperspace around us. Any that were too close to one of the alien vessels were immediately enveloped in a black cloud that began disintegrating the target vessel within seconds.

"They knew we were coming," I realized. "They were *expecting* us."

Kaiden looked sick as he stepped through the open doorway. "What could have clued them in?"

Toran shook his head. "Maybe they could tell we were reading the signal on the crystalline network and they decided to accelerate their plans."

Maris frowned. "That would imply that they knew how we would react."

"They must remember what happened during the last timeline, too— maybe even better than us," Kaiden said.

That was the last realization I wanted to have, but I couldn't disagree with the conclusion. My heart dropped. "If we reset again, they'll also remember whatever we do here."

We exchanged glances. Our plans hadn't taken into account the possibility that the aliens would have any recall of events after we reset. No matter what we did now, they would still have the upper hand.

"Does that mean the reset plan is off?" Maris asked.

The Hegemony fleet was getting slaughtered outside the viewport. I couldn't face that outcome. "No, we need to try again while we still can."

"What will a reset change if the enemy remembers?" questioned Toran.

"We need to do something completely different and unexpected," I said. Once again, it would come down to us. But, maybe we didn't have to be alone. "Except, we need to hedge our bets."

Without hesitation, I ran up to Colren. "Commander, we need to reset."

Defeat was written on his face as he turned to face me. "Good, you're here." He pulled out the locket containing the crystal shard from under his uniform. "Go. The observation room is—"

"You have to come with us," I stated.

He shook his head. "My place is here."

"Us relaying information to you isn't enough. You need to remember for yourself."

"I haven't prepared like you did before the jump. Watching Maris—"

"No, but you've seen this!" I made a sweeping gesture toward the space battle depicted on the screen. "I can't think of a stronger reminder than sitting down in this chair with this view as your most recent memory."

"My duty demands I don't abandon this post," he protested.

"You're not. This will let you come back and prevent all of those people from dying!"

On screen, four of the alien ships disintegrated a defensive line of Hegemony destroyers standing between the enemy and us. We had maybe a minute to act.

I grabbed Colren's arm. "Commander, we need to go *now!*"

He took one last look at the horror unfolding on screen and gave in. "Next time," he whispered to the bridge crew as I urged him toward the exit. The officers gave resolute nods and salutes as he passed by.

He led the way out of Central Command and down the corridor toward what I presumed was the observation room he'd mentioned.

"They began attacking as soon as we arrived," Colren said while we ran. "We were lucky to be far enough away from them."

"They must remember," I replied. "That's why we need you. We'll need a different approach."

He nodded. "Stars be with us."

At what appeared to be a dead-end to the corridor, Colren used a disguised control panel to open a hidden doorway. He held the crystal shard in his hand. "Do you remember what to do?"

I took the crystal fragment from him. "Enough. Think about where you were while we were down in the Master Archive."

"When, exactly, was that?" Colren asked.

"No, that point won't work with him," Toran stated. "We need a time when all of us were together. Maybe the first meeting after we got back—when we gave him the shard?"

"That's after Kaiden's and my touchpoint," I countered.

"No time to argue. It will be the easiest point for the five of us to picture," Toran insisted.

"All right," I yielded, pressing the crystal shard into my palm and holding it in place with my thumb. I extended my hand over the observation sphere. "Everyone ready?"

My friends put their hands in place, and Colren followed suit.

I started the count down. "One.... two... three!"

On my mark, we all placed our hands on the orb. As I released the crystal shard, I held the memory in my head of when Colren first took it from me during our debrief—the sense of hope that we had a tool to let us fight back. As the feeling flooded through me, the world dissolved to blackness.

REALITY RESOLVED AROUND me.

Relief. Joy. Hope. I couldn't put my happiness into words as I processed what Colren had just told me. We now held the key for a universal reset.

I looked over at the faces of my companions seated around the conference table adjacent to the bridge. They seemed as happy as I was feeling. Yet, something nagged at the back of my mind.

Across from us, Colren continued to admire the crystal shard. "You could use this to control a reset event from anywhere," he said.

"But the Master Archive is sealed," Kaiden said. "I thought it couldn't be accessed for resets?"

"If the lore is correct, then a shard like this would be the *only* way to conduct a reset," Colren replied. "Except, those are only legends. There are too many unknowns to be sure how a universal reset could play out."

"A measure for desperate times," Toran murmured.

Desperate times... Sudden tension gripped my chest. I should be happy; why did I feel stressed?

"Could there be side effects from a reset like that?" Kaiden asked.

Colren shrugged. "It would be impossible to predict. I can only imagine that with something that complex, there could be complications." He smiled. "But no need to worry about that. Today was a victory."

"Yeah, it was," I agreed, my vanquishing of the black dragon still fresh in my mind.

"Take the rest of the day to celebrate," the commander said. "You've earned it." He rose from his seat.

We stood up.

"Thank you, Commander," Kaiden said.

Colren headed out the door. He stopped a pace outside the conference room and turned back. "Have we…?" he faded out, then shook his head. "Never mind. Enjoy your celebrations." He continued toward his command seat at the center of the bridge.

"All right! A party is in order," Maris cheered.

"Not that we have a lot of exciting options," I mumbled.

"Mess hall?" Kaiden proposed.

"That's pretty much it," Maris replied.

Toran nodded. "I'll need to take some time to unwind before I'm up for any festivities."

"That'll give me time to find out if there's anything worthwhile to drink on this ship," Maris placed a hand on her hip. "The selection thus far has been sorely lacking."

"It's a military ship, not a pleasure yacht," I said. The Darkness was still out there; it hardly seemed like a time for a party.

"People have to unwind all the same!" She waved her hand. "We'll meet at… 17:00?"

"Sounds good. Maybe we'll even be able to round up some people to join in the fun," Kaiden said.

A big celebratory bash still felt like the wrong thing to do, but I wanted my friends to be happy—especially Kaiden. If a party was what they wanted, I'd suck it up.

We exited the conference room. As we walked through the bridge, crew members smiled and bowed their heads in acknowledgement for what we'd done. As invisible as our actions were to most, we'd given our civilization its best chance to rebuild once the threat had passed. Seeing their reactions and putting it in those terms, maybe a celebration *was* in order.

When we passed by Colren in his command seat, however, I was surprised to see a very different expression on his face. He seemed almost horrified.

I was about to ask him what was wrong, but Kaiden brushed my arm. "Do you have a few minutes to talk?" he whispered.

"Yeah, of course," I replied, gesturing toward the Central Command exit. "Back in the pod room."

Kaiden nodded.

The four of us continued through the bridge getting a proper hero's treatment from the crew, receiving acknowledgements ranging from nods and smiles to salutes. At any other time, I would have felt the swell of pride from a job well done, but Colren's expression had shaken me. Something had tainted this apparent victory.

When we reached the doorway leading to the outer corridor, the door automatically slid open with a hiss and soft chime.

"Stars!" Maris exclaimed, placing a hand on her stomach.

"What's wrong?" I asked.

"This…" She shook her head. "This isn't right. We've been through this before."

Kaiden's brow knit. "What do you mean?"

She stared at the open door. "I know this sound."

"We've been through here several times," I replied. "It's not—"

"No, not just a casual visit," she insisted, her voice raising. "That chime is embedded in me."

Colren looked around from his command seat. "Do you feel it, too?"

Maris' gaze met his. "I don't know what I'm feeling. It's like I'm in a dream."

"Elle." Kaiden's fingers brushed against my left hand. The feeling was so familiar—far more than I expected for someone with whom I'd only minutes before shared a first kiss. And there was something else in the touch I couldn't explain that made me want to pull away, though not from him, exactly.

Our eyes met. "What's happening?"

"I don't know, but we need to go—"

"—to the pod room," I completed for him.

He looped his fingers through mine and led me down the corridor, leaving a confused Maris and Toran in Central Command with Colren.

The moment the pod doors opened, I sensed a shift within me. I knew this place—really *knew* it. A scuff on the side of one of the pods, a scratch in the white paneling next to the door, the placement of rivets along the baseboard. I couldn't bring up the images in my mind on command, but there was the strangest sense of déjà vu as I looked around the space.

"Now I get what Maris was saying. Something weird is happening," I said.

"I couldn't shake the feeling that I needed to come back here with you," Kaiden replied. "I don't know why."

I took his hands. "We'll figure it out."

His touch reassured me, drawing me close. I leaned in for a kiss, but as our faces neared, a deep-seated sense of discomfort washed over me. I pulled back, releasing his hands.

"What was it you wanted to talk about?" I asked, taking a step back.

He cleared his throat. "Just, about what happened earlier. I—"

"Kaiden, Elle!" Maris shouted from the corridor. She burst into the pod room. "Do you remember?"

"Remember what?" I asked.

"The invasion."

Kaiden frowned. "Does this have something to do with our visions in the Archive?"

"Yes, and so much more." She sighed. "This wasn't supposed to be our reset point. You missed your trigger."

My brow knit. "What in the stars are you talking about?"

"We've been through this before—at least two times, maybe more," she said. "We tried to make ourselves remember. I don't think I would have had Colren not been experiencing a similar feeling of familiarity."

"And what does that have to do with our 'trigger'?" Kaiden asked.

"Your touchstone," she replied, though that didn't clarify anything for me. She looked between us. "You really don't remember yet?"

"I have no idea what you're talking about," I confessed.

She groaned. "Recreate that moment when we first came back from sealing the Archive—that's when we were supposed to reset to. Come find us in the conference room when you remember."

"What happened to having the night off?" questioned Kaiden.

"Now we know about the invasion. We don't have a lot of time." Maris waved her hands. "Do your thing. Hurry!" She left the room, the door sliding shut behind her.

"What just…" I sucked in a slow breath.

"Either she's totally lost it, or there's our explanation for the weird feelings," Kaiden said.

I nodded cautiously. "What was that about recreating the moment we came back?"

"Last time in here, we kissed."

"How'd she even know about that?"

"We didn't exactly hide it," he pointed out.

"True. But what does it have to do with anything?"

"We can find out."

I eyed him. "You don't really think…?"

"After the week we've had, I'm willing to believe just about anything."

"All right. No harm, I guess." The aversion I'd felt was still at the forefront of my mind, but it competed with the attraction I'd felt for him since we first met. Only a few minutes earlier, we'd shared a first kiss that had been the culmination of those feelings. I didn't understand why I was apprehensive now.

Kaiden approached me. "I think we were standing just about like this." He gently placed his hands on me and leaned in.

Our lips met, sparking a flurry of images in my mind. A fleet of black alien ships, the spreading Darkness, twisted creatures, a bright anomaly standing out against the void surrounded by an unfamiliar starscape. The fleet was coming. They would destroy us.

Kaiden and I parted.

"Did you…?" I asked.

He looked shaken. "Yeah. I think those were memories. But how could we have memories for something that hasn't happened yet?"

"Not in *this* timeline maybe," I realized. "But if we reset…"

Kaiden opened his mouth like he was about to protest, but instead he nodded. "That's the sensation I couldn't place. We *have* done this before."

The images began to sort in my mind, a narrative forming. "We made ourselves remember. That space battle is the 'make or break' moment for us. We need to find a different strategy."

"We don't have a lot of time. They can get their fleet there faster than we can."

"Where is 'there'?" I rubbed my temples. There was still more I couldn't remember. The memories were so tantalizingly close to my grasp.

"Let's go talk to the others," Kaiden suggested.

I wished I had been able to remember on my own, but I could tell something was off. I needed the rest of my team.

We returned to Central Command. Maris, Toran, and Colren were already back in the conference room. The bridge's crew members no longer had the happy expressions they had displayed minutes earlier, having witnessed the shift in Colren's demeanor.

Kaiden closed the conference room door behind us after we entered. Our three associates were already seated in their customary places around the table.

Colren folded his hands on the tabletop. "Do you remember?"

I glanced at Kaiden then nodded. "Enough."

Toran shook his head. "How can the four of you have these memories when I don't?"

"That's hardly the primary concern at present," the commander cut in. "If my visions are to be believed, we have just been through a universal reset. An alien offensive is preparing to slaughter the Hegemony fleet. If we don't take immediate action, we will be doomed to repeat that fate."

As he spoke, the hazy memories continued to sort in my mind. The aliens had been waiting for us. We hadn't stood a chance. "How can we fight back if they know we're coming?"

"They'll be expecting a fleet," Colren replied. "It's our turn to catch *them* by surprise."

"We should disrupt the anomaly to keep any ships from emerging," Toran stated.

The commander nodded. "Yes, but that alone is a short-term solution; they could always emerge elsewhere. What we really need is a way to fight back."

"What do you have in mind?" Kaiden asked.

"A stealth mission," the commander began. "As soon as the alien ships are fully formed, their weapons can take us out before we even have a chance to fire. But, if we want to learn how to counteract those weapons, we need to gather more information about them. That gives us a very narrow window between when the ship starts to form in the anomaly and before it's operational."

I wasn't sure I liked where this plan was going. From what I could recall, the alien ships appeared to have similar properties to the planets that had been consumed by the Darkness. There were only four people known to have a measure of immunity against the Darkness, and I was one of them. "Let me guess: you want *us* to go investigate?"

Colren nodded. "We need to know the face of our enemy—what's going on beneath the surface."

"It's too risky to allow the anomaly to remain," Kaiden insisted. "There won't be time to destroy it if something goes wrong—we don't even know that we *can* destroy it."

"I have no intention of allowing the ship to emerge completely," the commander continued. "Board, extract information, then destroy the ship and hopefully the anomaly along with it."

Maris raised an eyebrow. "Like, plant a bomb?"

"Not just any bomb, a spatial disrupter," Colren clarified.

Toran breathed out between his teeth. "That could destabilize the whole area."

Colren nodded solemnly. "It's the only thing guaranteed to interact with the anomaly. And we can't deploy it remotely."

"Not even a remote-piloted shuttle?" Toran asked.

"Too many variables for getting it close enough," Colren said. "Placing it by hand on the alien craft is the only way to be sure."

My brow drew together. "Sorry, but what's a spatial disrupter?"

"A weapon I thought was only conceptual," Toran explained. "Theoretically, it can rip the fabric of space through multiple planes, not just affect the matter in this plane we know as 'reality'."

"It's extreme, but since we only have one shot at this and don't know the details about this anomaly, we need to throw everything we have while there's a chance to strike," Colren said.

I frowned. "I'm a little unclear on the part of this plan where all of us *don't die*."

"Yeah, I have to second that sentiment," Kaiden agreed.

"It's simple," Colren said. "You'll board, use your knowledge of the Darkness' signal to tap into the ship's systems, extract any data you can, plant the spatial disrupter, and return to the *Evangiel* for a jump before the disrupter activates."

"Yeah, see, that's still sounds like the kind of insane plan where everyone dies," I said. "There's a slim chance we'd be able to interface with the alien ship's systems, let alone on a time crunch."

"Not to mention, how do we get on the ship? There's no way the environmental controls are the same," Kaiden added.

Maris nodded. "Assuming we can even get close enough to board."

"Insta-death all around," I concluded.

"I'm aware of those factors," Colren insisted. "First, the ship won't be able to attack you if you're already on top of it when it begins to emerge from the anomaly. Furthermore, the ship's environmental controls are irrelevant if you're in an EVA suit. As for timing, yes, interfacing with the ship's systems might be overly aspirational, but you don't know until you try. If nothing else, this mission would enable you to see firsthand what's inside the hull while also planting the spatial disruptor."

"That last part alone makes the risk worthwhile," Kaiden said.

I hated that he was right. We needed to destroy the anomaly, and I had to defer to others who knew far more about these matters than I did about the best way to do it. If they said this was the only way, then we needed to make it happen. "All right. How exactly are we going to do this?"

Maris' eyes widened, and she leaned forward on the table to look over at me. "You aren't actually considering this plan, are you?"

I stared back, resolute. "I'm sick of getting pushed around by these guys. Let's show them what we've got."

EVEN THOUGH I was psyched up to storm the alien ship, there were a lot of preparations to make. For starters, we didn't know *where* the anomaly was, only some vague recollection that we needed to go to Crystallis to get a clue. Even without the reset, it still felt like we were running in circles.

We adjourned from the meeting and prepared to return to the planet's surface. Since we hadn't had any decompression time since our battle in the Master Archive, we agreed to take fifteen minutes to freshen up in our cabins.

I felt much better after a quick shower, and when I stepped into our lounge to reunite with my companions, I was ready to take on any challenge. No sooner had I entered the room than Toran burst in after me.

"I remember!" he declared. "I sat down on my bunk and…" He shook his head. "We're kind of screwed, aren't we?"

"Can't think about it that way," I said. "There's at least a little chance we can pull this off, right?"

Toran pressed the heel of his hand to his temple. "I remember how to find the spatial coordinates we need, but there's no telling if those signals have any bearing on the system interface for the ship."

I shook my head. "Don't worry about that part. Planting that bomb is the important thing."

The large man fixed me in a level gaze. "Since when are we a covert ops team, Elle? Breaching an enemy ship to plant a space-ripping weapon—it's crazy!"

His sudden, raw emotion caught me by surprise. "I know, Toran. We're doing the best we can."

"This plan does not put us on the path of success."

"Then what do you propose we do?" I crossed my arms. "We're the only ones who can get near the Darkness without getting turned to soot, and we have maybe five minutes to act between when the alien ship first appears and when its weapons will be operational. What's a better way to use our time?"

"I don't know," he replied after a pause.

"I don't like this either, but we entered Crazy Town a week ago. Maybe getting up close and personal with the bad guys is exactly the kind of action we need at this stage."

"Don't tell me you're actually excited about this plan?" Kaiden asked from the doorway.

I smiled at him as he stepped into the room. "Only excited that this might be over soon."

"This one engagement won't change the larger circumstances," Toran said solemnly.

"But it's a start," I said. "Right now, we need a win."

Colren had tried to make sealing the Archive sound like a big victory, but I continued to think of it as 'maintaining'—it was a fallback, not a step forward. Taking out an alien ship, though… That was the first step toward reclaiming what had been taken from us. The fact that we might finally be able to put a face to the murderous monsters who'd destroyed our homes was a welcome bonus.

Maris joined us moments later, and we headed to the hangar to board a shuttle back to Crystallis. Tami seemed a little confused about why we were heading back so soon, but the reset loops were far too large of a subject to broach in passing.

We boarded the shuttle and took our typical landing approach through the mountain pass. As we neared the crystal canyon, I was overcome by another intense wave of déjà vu.

"How many loops have we been through?" I asked.

"I seem to have snippets from two floating around," Kaiden said while he looped the shuttle around toward a landing site. "Not to say there weren't more."

"And the enemy remembers," Toran emphasized. "That means they might be preparing to deploy their fleet through the anomaly. We need to beat them there."

"How long will it take to decode the coordinates?" Maris asked.

Toran's flight restraints jangled as he shrugged in the seat behind me. "Hours? Hopefully I remember some shortcuts once I get into it."

Kaiden set down the shuttle on the opposite side of the canyon from the Archive entrance, and Toran immediately got to work.

While Toran connected to the crystals, I wandered through a collection of crystal formations nearby. After a few minutes, I came across a boulder. The rock stood out in my mind, stopping me in my tracks. It'd seen it before, but I also sensed that I'd done something to it.

"What's wrong?" Kaiden asked from a few meters behind me.

I jumped, not realizing he'd followed me away from the landing site. "Nothing."

"You've been acting strange since we've started to remember."

"Isn't it *stranger* that you haven't? This entire thing is nuts," I replied.

He came to stand next to me. "It's affected me plenty. I'm just trying to stay focused."

I shook my head and scoffed. "I don't rightly know what happened when anymore."

"With reality resetting, does it even matter?" he asked. "It's like it didn't happen."

"Except, it *did*. And we can't pretend like it didn't, because our enemy remembers and they're going to use that information against us."

"Then we have to use those memories, too, so we can end this." Kaiden took my left hand. Now, away from the pod room, the touch was reassuring, grounding me.

"What have we been through?" I murmured. "It's all there, right beneath the surface, but none of it's clear."

"Soon we'll know where we have to go, and we'll figure out what we have to do. The rest... maybe it's best we don't know all the details about what happened. After all, it didn't end well."

"What about learning from mistakes?"

He shrugged. "The critical information will come to us as we need it. For now, there are only two things on my mind. First, we need to find that anomaly and stop the bad guys. Beyond that, I know I care about you."

"We barely—"

"Maybe this time around, but there's something between us, Elle. For me, that makes putting up with all the other crap in between worthwhile."

I softened. "Yeah, it does."

He smiled. "As much as I wish we could get to that 'afterward' part, we should probably take a step back for the time being."

I nodded, though I wished circumstances were different.

"Now," he continued, "why were you staring at that rock like you had a vendetta?"

"I think I destroyed it," I replied.

"With your... sword?" Kaiden raised an eyebrow.

His skepticism was well-founded. I couldn't imagine how I'd be able to level a boulder that size with my skills. Even Toran would be hard pressed to smash something on that scale. To further complicate matters, I had a vague recollection of doing something to the rock other than smashing it with physical force.

Kaiden eyed me. "Is this about that other thing you don't want to talk about?" He glanced over his shoulder. "You know, the *magic*," he whispered.

I checked around us and took a step closer to him. "Whatever you think you saw in the Archive, this isn't something I can control. It may have just been some magical version of 'hysterical strength'."

"You don't know if you can control it until you *try*," he urged.

The boulder may as well have had a target painted on it, I had to admit. "Fine," I yielded. "Stand back."

As if on instinct, I raised my hand and a white orb formed in my palm. It launched and enveloped the boulder, breaking it into bits. To my amazement, those rock fragments began to levitate, slowly drifting away from the impact site as if in slow motion. Before I could fully grasp the wonder of it, another orb formed, this one dark. Curious, I released it and a black cloud washed over the remaining boulder and the tiny rock fragments floating above it. The material began to condense, shrinking to a single, black sphere the size of my first.

A sensation of power washed through me. I knew that feeling—it transcended the resets and any time that had passed since those abilities had first become a part of me, even if I didn't know it. "Stars... I know magic!"

Kaiden grinned. "Told ya."

I experimented with the telekinesis for a few more minutes, but Toran soon called us back to the landing site to share the results of the analysis. Reluctantly, I lowered my hands.

"Keep this between us?" I requested.

Kaiden frowned. "Why don't you want to tell anyone about this magic, Elle?"

"I don't want anyone relying on it—it's too new," I insisted.

He held up his hands. "Fine, suit yourself." I could tell he wasn't happy about that arrangement, but I appreciated that he respected my wishes on the matter.

Frankly, I didn't know why I was so reticent, either. The best explanation I had in the moment was that I didn't want anyone to look at me like I was different or special. Right now, we needed to be a unified team. If I was called out as having alignment to multiple disciplines, I'd be set apart. The bonds with my teammates were what would get us through the coming trial, not showing off. I'd use my new abilities to help if the circumstances demanded it, but otherwise, unity was paramount.

And, more than that, the nature of my magic scared me. The ability to crush and rend—that wasn't strength I took lightly, and I vowed that I would only use it when there was no other choice.

Kaiden and I returned to the landing site to find Toran and Maris staring at the portable display screen for the crystal interface equipment.

"Find what you need?" Kaiden asked the other man.

Toran nodded. "I believe so. Once I got over the initial shock, I located the signal a half-memory hinted I should be able to identify." He went on to explain something about segmenting the signal and pairs of fragments across different worlds. I only partially listened, knowing it wasn't relevant to anything I had to do.

He finished what he needed to gather the necessary data, and then we returned to the shuttle.

"This might take hours to analyze," Toran said as we strapped into our seats.

"Don't have that long," I replied. "We need to beat that first alien ship. And, we have no idea how long it takes them to mobilize."

"Wanting things to go faster doesn't change reality," he replied.

I slouched in my seat. "Do what you can."

The ensuing hours were torture while I tried to be patient for Toran to finish the analysis. His initial projection was eight hours, but after two and a half, the pairs were well enough established for us to load the data into a spatial model.

"Should be right… here," Toran said as he made the requisite entries.

The holographic interstellar model above our work table refreshed to show color-coded highlighted worlds with lines linking each pair. The lines intersected to converge on single location outside any known system.

"I guess that's where we need to go," Maris said.

Kaiden nodded. "I'll alert the commander."

Within minutes, we were in our pod room stripping down to prepare for the jump. I still hadn't quite wrapped my head around what we were about to do—taking a shuttle to board an alien vessel that contained tech capable of disintegrating a ship. Even if our bodies were resistant to the Darkness, our suits would be slowly eaten away. Granted, the enemy ship would have formed and the aliens would have taken us out well before the suits failed, but still. I liked living, and the odds weren't in our favor for making it out of this next encounter unscathed.

"Have a good jump," Kaiden said as he climbed into his pod.

"Jumping to our *doom!*" Maris exclaimed with even more melodrama than usual.

Toran sighed. "I choose to believe we'll prevail."

"Of course we will." I dropped onto the ergonomic couch within my pod. "See you soon."

However, as I strapped into the harness, my private worries and doubts continued to multiply in my mind. I did my best to propose counterpoints about the capabilities of my team and my own skills—both those familiar and still being discovered—but the isolation and disorientation of the jump through hyperspace left me running through contrary arguments. One part of me wanted to take what we knew and go back to the Capital to regroup with whatever experts the Hegemony could locate, while the other part of me was convinced we needed to forge ahead with our insane plan. However, the closer we got to our destination, the more I wondered if a more conservative strategy was a better move. Though only a few hours had passed, the alien ships could have already traveled through the anomaly. We very well may be walking into another trap, only this time, alone.

When the *Evangiel* began its transition back into normal space, I tried to refocus on the task at hand. The decision had already been made. We were doing this, last-minute reservations or not.

As soon as our pods opened, we sat up to stretch while our senses normalized.

I smoothed my hair away from my face. "When do—"

The central alarm sounded, and Colren came over the intercom. "Battle stations! Dark Sentinel team to the hangar immediately."

We vaulted out of the pods and started to dress as quickly as possible. "Shit!" Kaiden exclaimed. "Did they beat us here?"

I shook my head. "Must be."

Toran groaned. "I thought we would be fast enough."

"They didn't need to find the coordinates like us," Maris pointed out unhelpfully.

With my pants and boots donned, I grabbed my coat and sword to carry with me; I'd just have to take them off again when I put on the EVA suit. "Come on, let's get to the hangar."

The others gathered their remaining gear and followed me at a jog out of the pod room. We hurried to the lift and took it down to the hangar level.

Tami was waiting for us next to one of the shuttles—a different craft than the one we'd used on previous missions. "There might still be time," she said by way of greeting. "We loaded the bomb and your other equipment before the jump. I'll explain the activation on your way over."

"Are the alien ships here?" Kaiden asked while we were ushered up the shuttle's entry ramp.

"The anomaly is forming," Tami replied. "Hopefully you can make it to the site before the first ship."

At least we still had a chance. "See you when we get back," I said.

The engineer nodded. "Good luck."

In a flurry of activity, the shuttle's outer door was sealed and we set down our handheld gear in the common area. A black crate and four EVA suits were spread out on the deck.

"Should we get dressed now?" Maris asked.

"Need to get underway first." Kaiden directed us toward the bridge to get situated.

"How long is it going to take to get into position?" I asked while strapping into the co-pilot's seat.

"Should only be a few minutes. Looks like Tami got it warmed up for us," Kaiden said as he looked over the controls. "I guess we're doing this."

I nodded. "Yeah, let's get it over with."

Kaiden activated the auto-pilot to guide our shuttle to pre-programmed coordinates near the anomaly. "I'll take over once we're near the alien ship and know what we're working with."

Maris sighed. "So much for a briefing... or a plan."

"The plan is that we wing it," I replied. The truth, though, was that I hadn't pictured the moments before our mission being anything like this. I thought we'd complete the jump, have an opportunity to scout out the anomaly before it opened, and be able to get into an ideal position to board the enemy ship. Now, we'd be lucky if we made it close enough before the enemy ship's weapons were functional.

The shuttle taxied from the hangar and glided through the electrostatic field. The moment we were clear, a chime sounded in my left ear.

"Sorry for the abrupt departure," Colren said. "We observed an energy spike as soon as we came out of the pods."

"You're right—can't risk it," Kaiden responded.

"I'll be standing by here to reset using the shard if anything goes wrong," Colren said.

The promise of nearby backup should have been reassuring, but I knew better. "We need to treat it like this is a one-shot deal, because it is," I replied. "After this, they'll know this strategy. We can only catch them by surprise this way once."

"That's true," the commander acknowledged.

Toran unstrapped from his seat. "We need instructions about how to deploy the disruptor."

"Yes, Tami will be on in a moment with her technician," Colren stated.

"Let's get dressed in the meantime," I suggested, unbuckling my own harness.

Kaiden glanced between me and the controls. "All right."

The four of us hurried single-file into the common area to claim our EVA suits. The form-fitting suit felt constrictive once I tugged it on, but I suspected that was more in my head than reality. A vague memory tickled the back of my mind about wearing the suit another time and things not ending well. I could only hope this scenario would play out better.

"Placing the disruptor will be the most challenging part," Tami said, joining the comm link. "Brian, one of the weapons techs, is here to explain."

"The disruptor will work best if attached to a large physical mass, ideally the hull of the alien ship," an unfamiliar male voice said over the comm. "The goal is to destroy the anomaly-portal, so you'll want to place it on the ship as close to the spatial event as possible."

"Great, but how are we supposed to accomplish that in... what, two minutes?" I asked.

"That's why I said, 'as possible'," Brian replied. "You can only do so much. Just flip the red switch once you have it in place—that will activate the remote trigger."

"And then you wait for us to get clear?" Kaiden said.

Brian paused for much longer than I would have liked. "Yes," he responded eventually.

"While setting the disruptor, observe anything you can," Colren instructed. "This may be our only chance to get close and learn about these beings... whatever they are. Feeds from your EVA suits will report in real-time. And, Toran, you'll find a device sitting on top of the disruptor that might assist in interfacing with the alien ship's system."

"I see it," Toran acknowledged.

I exchanged glances with my team, now even more concerned than before that this was a suicide run. "We'll do our best, Commander."

A rapid beep sounded from the bridge. "That's our cue!" Kaiden said, running back to the front of the vessel.

I followed close behind him. Out the viewport above the nose, the spatial anomaly had taken on a white glow, and an ethereal sparkle was rippling across the space that had appeared matte black moments before. "Stars, what...?"

"It's beautiful," Maris murmured.

Before I could wonder too much, a dark form began to emerge. My breath caught in my throat. "The ship is coming through."

24

THE ALIEN VESSEL was more menacing up close. Even with only a few dozen meters exposed at the horizon of the anomaly, it already looked sinister. Inky tendrils intertwined to form the support structure, and a fine mesh with a fibrous appearance spanned the beams. There were no viewports or other openings, just blackness inside and out.

I stared at the ship with distaste. "We're going in… there?"

"Assuming we can find a way in." Kaiden took over manual control of our shuttle and directed it toward the spatial anomaly.

"Don't get too close," Toran cautioned.

Kaiden cracked a wry smile. "Sorry to break this to you, but the entire *point* is to get close."

"Why did I agree to this?" Maris moaned. She waved her hand in the back seat and a shimmering purple wave of light extended outward, encasing all but the shuttle's engines.

I nodded back at her. "Thanks. Good thinking."

Kaiden accelerated toward the outer edge of the spatial disturbance until we were twenty meters from it.

From so close, the sparkling light had the nuance of a cloud, swirling with highlights and shadows. The alien ship really did seem to appear from nothing—dark particles appeared against the white background moments before they joined together in their proper places to form the ship. Of all the amazing things I'd witnessed over the past week, this was one of the most incredible based purely on the scale. The ship rose at least two hundred meters tall, and here it was, apparently being 3D-printed from a glowing cloud.

"Stars, we need to find a place to get inside," Kaiden muttered under his breath, eyes darting across the uneven surface of the ship.

"There's no time to search," Toran said. "We need to *make* an opening."

"Helmets on," I announced.

Maris frowned. "What—"

"Kaiden, bring us around so the side door is facing the ship. Get as close as you can," I instructed.

He nodded and then did as I'd instructed.

We clicked our helmets into place and switched to the suit comms.

"Toran, with me," I said. "Secure the disruptor. We need to open the side hatch."

Fortunately, he didn't protest; seconds might make all the difference.

"Maris, keep that shield active," I continued while I strapped my sword to my waist around the outside of my EVA suit. "I'm going to see what I can do about making us an opening. Everyone hold on to something!"

As soon as Toran had secured the disruptor, I released the emergency seal on the side hatch. The door flew open, and I held on for dear life as the compartment vented. The purple shield around me swelled as I moved away, flickering for a moment during the decompression and then stabilizing again.

"The shield keeps wanting to expand," Maris said with a frown. "Something feels different."

"Might be the anomaly," Kaiden said over the comm. "I remember something about that from another timeline."

"Hold it as steady as you can." I grabbed a length of emergency cord from the supply locker next to the door and hurriedly tied it around my waist. The action was so familiar to me, but I couldn't think of why. I just knew I needed to get outside of the shuttle and make us an opening.

Ninety seconds. We'd barely have any time inside.

Without hesitation, I gripped my sword in my left hand and pushed off from the doorframe, launching myself toward the side of the ship five meters away. As I approached the alien hull, I angled my sword to pierce it.

The blade embedded. I could sense resistance for the first two-thirds of the length of the blade, then an open cavity beyond. With all my strength, I wedged my feet into the uneven covering on the ship to get enough leverage to pull down. I ripped a meter-long gash. It wasn't nearly enough. I'd maybe be able to create a person-sized opening in time, but there was no way we'd be able to get the shuttle inside, and the alien vessel was far too large for us to have a chance to make it anywhere into its depths on foot. But, I'd take getting inside at all over complete failure. Even so, I'd need help.

"Kaiden, fireball now!" I yelled into my comm.

"Maris, get the disrupter," Toran instructed. I could just make out the telltale signs of him running back to the bridge to take the flight controls.

A moment later, Kaiden came onto the comm, "Elle, get clear!"

I shoved off the hull of the alien vessel and swung back toward our shuttle using the tautness of the cord. When I was mid-arc, a bright flash of blue overpowered the white light cast by the anomaly, and in the corner of my vision the largest plume of flames I'd ever seen Kaiden cast erupted from the end of his staff. As I reached the side of our shuttle, the flames were dying back, leaving a charred tunnel into the alien ship. If the anomaly was enhancing our magic, at least we could use that to our advantage.

Kaiden's staff illuminated with a light orb on its tip. "I've got the interface device. Come on!" Gripping his staff in one hand and the equipment pack in the other, he launched himself from the hatch toward the new opening into the alien ship.

"You're all crazy!" With the half-meter-long disruptor box in her hands, Maris followed him in the mad flight across the void.

I needed to get to their position, but my own entry angle was way off. I untied the cord from around my waist and hoped for the best. Steadying myself with a handhold, I squatted against the hull. I leaped toward the opening.

Mid-flight, I realized I was going to overshoot my mark by at least two meters. "I need something to grab!" I shouted. The section of hull was full of the spongy substance that seemed to writhe in interlocking layers, reminding me of tentacles that echoed deep in my memory. I feared if I embedded in it, I might not be able to claw my way out.

Just in time, Kaiden's staff shot out into my flight path. I managed to grab it in my right hand and hang on. He pulled me inside.

"Hurry!" He began scrambling inward as soon as I was safe.

The interior was much like the outside—black structural fibers that looked more grown than manufactured. The open cavity that I thought I'd detected inside when I jabbed my sword through the hull was actually just a pocket of the moss-type material forming a connective mesh between the structural beams. As far as I could tell, the vessel wouldn't be able to hold an atmosphere, unless there were other containment systems not readily visible. There also didn't appear to be conventional corridors or interior components. Frankly, I wasn't sure how the ship could even operate.

"Let's get in there," Maris said. An orange wave overlaid on the purple, and the subtle pulsing of the ship's walls around me slowed as my own movements and perception accelerated.

The haste spell would get us extra seconds, but not enough to make up for the other delays. We needed to move. Fast.

Kaiden took the lead, shooting occasional bursts of blue flame to clear the path ahead, the apparent influence of the anomaly enhancing the flames.

The gravity inside the ship left us midway between weightlessness and normal. Gentle pushes sent us rocketing forward, and we soon found we could run along the walls and floor through the cylindrical opening left by Kaiden's flames. He angled us backward in the direction of the anomaly while tunneling deeper into the ship.

We'd gone nearly one hundred meters when we entered a chamber that appeared to be a natural structure within the ship rather than simply the tunnel Kaiden had bored. It wasn't large—approximately four meters on each side—but it felt spacious after the tight confines of the flame-forged path. At the center of the space, a bulbous mound protruded approximately two meters from the floor, layered with a tighter weave of fibers than the surroundings. I was inexplicably drawn to it, sensing a power within.

"Do you think this place has any significance?" I asked.

Before anyone could answer, something suddenly grabbed my ankle, stopping me short. I looked down to see black tendrils snaking out from the singed walls to reach for us. Even under the effect of the haste spell, the tendrils were still moving quickly.

"What the...?" I slashed at them with my sword.

"Gah! The ship wants to eat us!" Maris exclaimed, re-upping the protective shell. However, the tendrils pierced right through the barrier, undeterred.

I swiped at the ones reaching out for her legs, and I was able to slice them off at their base along the wall.

"We need to keep moving," Kaiden urged.

Another one gripped me. "Yeah, and these aren't making it easy!"

I cut my sword across the new batch, but before I had completed the swing, another set was already forming. "Try scorching them, Kaiden," I said.

"These walls were already burned. I won't hold them."

"We need to try something!" I insisted.

Kaiden set down his staff and pressed his hands together. When he pulled them apart, the surface of his gloved palms was glowing like molten lava.

My jaw dropped. "That's… new."

He smoothed his hands down the walls around us, leaving a smooth, glass-like finish from which no new tendrils emerged. "You're not the only one learning new skills."

And for that, I was very thankful.

Kaiden quickly dealt with the origin points for the tendrils we had been unable to tame inside the chamber. Finally, the path ahead was clear.

I checked the control display on the wrist readout of my EVA suit: the ship had appeared almost three minutes prior. We were already over our budgeted entry time. "This location will have to be good enough," I said.

"You're right." Kaiden unslung the interface device from around his shoulder. "Confession: I have no idea how this thing works."

"The interface? Turn it on and start the sync," Toran said over the comm.

I looked over Kaiden's shoulder at it. The controls appeared to be straightforward enough, so I left him to it. "Come on, Maris, let's set this disruptor." I gestured to a place at the base of the tunnel where there was a soft, fibrous bed surrounded by a cluster of the more solid support beams. We wedged the crate into the nook and flipped open the lid.

"Are you in place?" Brian asked over the comm.

I startled, having forgotten that anyone else was listening in on the channel. "Yes, got it."

"You see the red switch in the upper right? Flip that," he instructed.

I hesitated, glancing over my shoulder at Kaiden. "How's it coming with the interface?"

"The system seems to have linked with something, but I don't know what," he reported. "I'm recording, or downloading... I dunno, but it's doing something."

I kept an eye on the strange mound in the center of the chamber. The shadows were jumpy under the lights cast from my EVA suit, but it also seemed like the fibers were unfurling.

"Elle, is the disruptor activated?' Colren asked. "We don't have a link."

I didn't reply at first. Not activating that device was the only thing keeping them from turning it on before we escaped. We'd have to flip the switch before we left, but I had no intention of doing it a nanosecond before we were ready to race back to the shuttle.

My eyes kept darting to the mound. There was no mistaking the movements now. The fibers were pulling back to reveal a pod with interlocking segments forming a seal down its length. The pieces were starting to separate.

"Almost ready," I said over the comm while giving Kaiden a look that told him to wrap it up fast. I nodded toward the thing in the center of the chamber, and he nodded.

After an awkward five-second pause, Kaiden nodded that whatever the interface device had been doing seemed to be complete. He secured it in its case.

"Okay." My hand over the red switch. I flipped it. "It's on."

We propelled ourselves down the corridor as fast as our arms and legs could carry us. Without the cumbersome disruptor or needing to open the path with flames, we made exceptional time on the way back. However, two dozen meters from the exit, the corridor started to close in, brushing against the edges of the protective shields Maris had placed around us. Worse, I sensed a presence stalking us from behind.

"Need those flames!" I told Kaiden while looking behind me. Something red flashed through the darkness of the corridor, and as it passed, the walls vibrated.

He cast a column of flame forward without hesitation. The opening cleared for a moment, but then began rebuilding itself in double-time.

Maris' eyes widened with horror as our escape path closed. "What's it doing?"

"There's something here," I murmured, tightening my grip on my sword.

"Maybe an emergency damage control system finally activated," Kaiden said, casting more flames to keep our path open, but our pace had slowed to a crawl.

"The ship is waking up." Whatever that thing in the chamber was, it might not be the only one. We needed to get out.

"And it must almost be clear from the anomaly," Kaiden added. "We're almost out of time."

The thick silence on the comm didn't set me at ease. I knew Colren was aware of what was at stake with this mission.

Kaiden cast more flames, but each spell did less damage than the last; either the influence of the anomaly was waning, or the ship was adapting. "I can't give it any more," he admitted. His eyes met mine, pleading. None of us wanted to die here.

"Let me try." I repositioned in front of him. I'd never tried to cast magic without my palm device, but I'd had to leave that behind when I put on the gloves of the EVA suit. But, if the magic was truly a part of me, that tool was only a way to focus, not the source of my power.

I held out my hand in front of me, concentrating on the almost-filled path ahead. White light shot from my hand, piercing through the dark tunnel. The black tendrils recoiled, and those that didn't move from its path quickly enough disintegrated.

"Whoa," Maris gasped behind me. "You...?"

"I'll explain later." I dashed ahead, desperate to get back to the shuttle.

"The ship is almost complete," Colren warned.

"We're almost out!" I shouted. The end of the tunnel was in sight.

We bolted through the remaining section of the tunnel. I stopped myself short just before reaching the open gap of space between the ship and the waiting shuttle. It was too far to jump.

"Toran, can you get it any closer?" I asked over the comm.

"I'll try."

The shuttle neared the alien ship, the side door aligning with the crude entryway we'd made. All the same, it would be a four-meter-long leap. I took a few steps back and got a running start. At the last second, I kicked off the alien ship and flew toward the shuttle's hatch. The kick at the end set me on a slight spin, but I was able to track my flight lines and grab one of the handholds around the hatch to keep myself from bouncing off my mark.

I swung inside but stayed next to the hatch to help the others inside.

Maris was next to make the leap. She followed my lead to take a running start, but she miss-timed her final steps and didn't get a good kick off, instead drifting off the alien ship.

"I've got you!" I leaned out the hatch to grab her, but my reach came up short.

Maris flailed. "Get something!"

I popped back inside to look for an object to extend my reach. My scabbard might work.

As I looked down to detach it from the waist belt, two forms spiraled through the opening—Kaiden apparently having made the leap and grabbed Maris along his path. They hit the deck hard with their limbs a jumbled mess.

Maris shook her head down near Kaiden's right knee, climbing off him. "Thanks."

"Close the hatch," Toran ordered from the bridge over our helmet comms.

I quickly pressed the emergency seal, and the door snapped shut. The moment it was closed, a vibration surged in the floor as the shuttle accelerated. I checked the timer on my wrist band again. Our five minutes was almost up. A quick check out the side viewport confirmed that the alien ship was almost fully formed. If the weapons activated, the shuttle and the *Evangiel* would have no means of defense.

With my EVA suit still on, I ran to the bridge. "On our way, Commander."

I took my seat, and Toran moved aside for Kaiden to take over for the landing. With time short, it would almost certainly be a hard, combat-style landing rather than the methodical autopilot control.

"We did it!" Maris cheered from her seat.

"Yeah, we did." However, I couldn't bring myself to celebrate. Though we'd accomplished our objective to plant the disruptor and gather data from the ship, we were far from safe.

The shuttle was accelerating toward the *Evangiel*, but we didn't seem to be closing any distance. They were pulling back from the anomaly, even as we tried to reach them.

We weren't going to make it back in time.

"I'm sorry," Colren murmured.

With a flash and ripple across the surrounding starscape, the *Evangiel* disappeared.

"THEY LEFT US?!" Maris exclaimed.

My heart dropped. We were alone in the void within kilometers of where a spatial disruptor was about to detonate. Was this the end?

I shook myself. No, I wasn't going to give up.

"We have to brace!" I shouted. "Hold back the disruptor wave."

"Elle, this weapon—" Toran began.

"It breaks apart matter, I know. But we have magic. If the dragons can make sanctuaries outside of normal reality, maybe we can too."

Maris looked like she was about to object, but she nodded. "It's that or die."

"Fight to the end," Toran agreed.

"Come on." I rose from my seat and motioned everyone toward the center of the bridge.

Kaiden hurriedly set the shuttle's autopilot to full throttle along the escape vector and joined us.

"How do we do this?" Maris asked.

I had absolutely no idea. However, I was certain that if anyone could generate a shield to counteract the disruptor wave, it would be us; we were imbued with ancient powers from a past age, representing the disciplines destined to make us heroes. The answer lay somewhere within ourselves… we just had to find it.

"Maris, you need to create a shield around the shuttle," I instructed. "The rest of us need to feed energy into it. Don't think about it, *feel* it."

"We need a focal point," Toran suggested. "Something we can all concentrate on to help channel the energy."

I glanced around the bridge, not seeing anything that seemed fitting. Instead, I unsheathed my sword and held the glowing blade in front of us. "Grab the hilt and focus on the blade," I said.

Kaiden glanced over with a knowing smile as he wrapped his hands around mine on the hilt, followed by Toran and Maris. We were in a tough spot, but if we didn't make it, at least it would be over quickly and we'd be with each other.

I remained fixated on the sword's blade with my friends, as much as I wanted to watch the alien ship coming through the anomaly. Based on my memories, the ship must almost be clear. I wondered if the creature I glimpsed had somehow removed the disruptor, but maybe the *Evangiel* hadn't set the detonation before they—

A blinding flash forced me to squeeze my eyes shut. When I sensed the brightness diminish through my eyelid, I squinted back toward the viewport.

A black, rippling wave was folding the space around the anomaly. The alien ship disintegrated and twisted against the starscape behind it, its ruined fragments disappearing into the wave. As each fragment struck the wave, it illuminated in a pinpoint flash before being snuffed out. The ship was gone, and so was any sign of the anomaly, but the wave was still rushing outward, and it would reach us in moments.

I squeezed my sword hilt, reaching out with my extrasensory abilities to detect Maris' shield around our shuttle. The barrier didn't stand a chance against the destructive wave. I needed to make it stronger.

As I reached within myself, I sensed Kaiden and Toran directing their own magical energy toward the shield. Toran's pure, protective spirit hardened the shell, and Kaiden augmented it with an electrical charge to help deflect the approaching wave. However, even with those enhancements, I knew in my gut it wouldn't be enough. We needed a different kind of magic, something to manipulate the very underlying forces in our universe.

The disruptor wave ripped apart, but I had the ability to bind.

I tied my sense of self to the shell around the shuttle. I could feel the change in my surroundings as the disruptor wave approached—rending the bonds across spatial planes. My skin tingled with anticipation.

The leading edge of the wave struck the shell, rocking our shuttle to the side. The distance from the epicenter and our forward momentum diminished the blow, but my tether to the shell still made me feel like I was being ripped apart. I struggled to remain on my feet and not lose my concentration.

I focused on the outer shell and holding it together. The bonds threatened to rip apart, but every time they started to fray I pulled them back together. Everything important to me that I had left in the universe was inside that shuttle. I'd do anything to hold onto my friends and keep them safe, even if it meant burning myself up in the process.

The disruptor wave continued to rip into my extended self as the leading edge of the wave passed by our location and we were left in the center of the affected zone. But, the shell held—a tiny sanctuary surrounding by nothingness.

I was slipping. I couldn't hold it for any longer.

The disruptor wave began to dissipate, a gravity well formed at the detonation site. The shuttle's engines were ineffective within the shell, and our bubble was yanked toward the black maw that had opened at the epicenter. The shell had proven successful in keeping us safe, but we'd need the ship's engines if we wanted to avoid getting sucked into the black pit.

"Drop the shield!" I ordered while keeping my own magic active.

"We'll—"

"Just do it!" I cut Maris off.

The shell collapsed in its previous form, but I redoubled my efforts to maintain the structural integrity of the shuttle.

The backward pull of the shuttle ceased as the engines were freed from the shell. Slowly, we began accelerating away from the detonation site.

Even as we pulled away, the ruins of the alien ship and everything else in the vicinity were condensing onto a singular point. In a sudden burst, a secondary wave fanned out from the epicenter, this one re-condensing rather than breaking apart. I quickly shifted my spell to counteract its effects and keep us from smooshing.

I wasn't fast enough. The shuttle shook as its frame twisted and cracked. The engines cut out, leaving us traveling forward on inertia at a slow spin.

The remaining disruptor wave collapsed. It was over.

I released the telekinetic shield and dropped to my knees, panting.

"Elle!" Kaiden couched down next to me and placed a hand on my back.

"I'm okay," I gasped, wishing I could rip off my helmet and get some fresh air. "Just gimme a sec."

"What was that you did?" Toran asked.

"Elle, maybe it's time you said something," Kaiden whispered to me.

"Okay, confession: I have some sort of telekinesis-style magic," I revealed, slipping my sword into its scabbard.

"That's…" Maris faded out.

I nodded. "I don't understand how it works. I just… knew what I had to do."

Toran and Maris stared at me with raised eyebrows.

"Well, thank you," Toran said at last.

I staggered to my feet with Kaiden's help. By the time I was upright, I realized that the artificial gravity was starting to fail, and I was lifting slightly off the deck. "Unfortunately, now we're trapped here with no escape."

"There must be an emergency signal," Toran stated.

"Right, yes." Kaiden glided back to the front control panel. Only a handful of items were illuminated on the backup battery power. He activated the emergency transponder.

"The commander wouldn't have jumped too far away," I said, hoping that wasn't just wishful thinking.

Maris wrapped her arms around herself. "How long do we have?"

"We have backup oxygen and power for the suits," Toran replied. "We'll be able to make it at least sixteen hours, maybe more."

I prayed to the stars we wouldn't have to wait that long.

Despite my best wishes, the hours dragged on. I spent the first two hours telling myself that the *Evangiel* would be there any second. By the end of the fourth hour, I was beginning to doubt we'd ever be rescued.

"They should have picked up our distress signal by now, right?" Maris asked.

"Yeah, I'd think so," I agreed.

"Maybe they're out of range, or…" Kaiden faded out.

"Or *what*?" I pressed.

"Or they have no intention of returning to this place," Toran completed for him.

I swallowed. "Why wouldn't they, though? I mean, we activated the beacon—that means our ship wasn't destroyed and we made it through."

"That's a straightforward explanation, yes," Toran agreed.

I frowned. "What else would it be?"

"That the enemy found a way to mimic our signals and is trying to lure them back into another trap."

My heart sank. "Oh." I paused. "Can't we have a custom message saying it's us?"

"I don't know enough about these emergency systems to do that," Kaiden said. "They'll need to authenticate once they send a scout vessel back to check the scene."

"So, we have to keep waiting," I concluded.

And so we did. We remained silent for the next half hour, both to conserve oxygen and because we had nothing to say. In the next several hours, we'd either be rescued or suffocate. All things considered, it was one of the bleaker moments in my life.

I stayed closed to Kaiden, hating that our EVA suits prevented us from being able to seek comfort from closer contact. As I stared out the front viewport, I rested my helmet on Kaiden's shoulder. My eyes had glazed over after looking out into the nothingness for so long, but then a point of light caught my attention.

I sat upright. "Hey, what's that?"

The others roused, following my sightline.

Kaiden squinted. "Can't tell from here." He propelled himself across the bridge in the zero-*g* to the front control panel. "Stars, it's a Hegemony ship!" he cheered.

My ear comm crackled. "Shuttle 2, do you copy?" a male voice asked.

"Yes, we're here!" I replied. "All four members of the Dark Sentinel team accounted for."

"Thank the stars!" the man said with an audible smile. "The commander and rest of the crew will be thrilled to hear it. We're on our way to grab you, hang tight."

The rescue shuttle maneuvered to us and extended an umbilical from their airlock to allow us safe passage out our side hatch. I'd never been quite so happy to be back in artificial gravity and to be able to remove my helmet.

As it turned out, the *Evangiel* had jumped back to wait several hundred kilometers away while the rescue craft went searching for us and to look for any evidence of the alien ship or anomaly. The shuttle would have been deployed sooner, but Colren had called for backup in the event the disruptor hadn't destroyed the anomaly. Waiting near the *Evangiel* were two dozen of the Hegemony's warships poised for action.

"Okay, so they came prepared," I said as I looked over the fleet.

"Glad they weren't needed this time," Kaiden replied.

"But this isn't over yet."

Our rescue craft entered the *Evangiel*'s hangar and came to rest in a decontamination tent. True to form, Tami, dressed in her hazsuit, was the first to meet us as we exited.

"I'm so happy to see you're okay!" she greeted.

I smiled. "It'll take more than an interdimensional bomb to get rid of us."

She laughed. "I have no idea how you did it, and I'm sure you have quite a story to tell. The commander is waiting for you; I'll have to get the inside scoop later."

"And you'll have it," I assured her.

"But first," she pointed to booths at the end of a tunnel leading from the tent, "decontamination, sorry."

I looked down at my EVA suit that had been immersed in the innards of the alien ship. "No complaints here."

We endured the uncomfortable chemical scrub and emerged from our respective stalls to find clean, custom-sized shipsuits waiting for us. I always hated walking around the ship in just the base layer, but I'd grown rather attached to my outfit and would rather the garments get cleaned rather than have new ones made; even if the style was identical, it just wasn't the same.

Once we were dressed in the white suits, Kaiden pulled me aside and wrapped me in a tight hug. I gladly hugged him back.

"We did it," he murmured into my hair.

"Yeah, but what in the stars are we up against?" I asked, pulling away. "Did you see that thing in the chamber?"

He paled. "Yeah, I did. Just a flash of red eyes and more limbs than I could count. It didn't look friendly."

I took his hands. "Whatever it was, we'll face it together."

Kaiden leaned in and gave me a kiss. The unpleasant associations that had tainted our intimacy since the reset had now faded into the background. Once again, it was just the two of us sharing a special moment. For that instant, my worries and fears melted away.

Toran cleared his throat. "Anytime…"

We parted. "Right," I said, flashing a happy smile at Kaiden.

Our party left the hangar and took the lift to Central Command. Applause greeted us as soon as the bridge door opened, led by Commander Colren.

He beamed at us from the center of the room. "I don't know how you survived the disruptor, but thank you for seeing the mission through. Welcome back."

Anger rose in me, hearing his casual words. He'd left us to die. An apology didn't cut it.

"What happened to resetting if something went wrong?" Maris snapped. I was happy for her to say it so I didn't have to.

Colren shifted on his feet. "We first had to see if the anomaly was sealed."

He needn't say more. That was the mission: to stop the alien invasion. Losing us would be a setback, but it would have been a worthwhile sacrifice to ensure that the alien fleet didn't make it through the anomaly. If he had reset in an attempt to save us, our efforts may not have been successful on another go around. We needed to take any victory we could, in part or full. Casualties along the way were to be expected.

Kaiden and Toran nodded with understanding, but Maris only scoffed and tossed her head in response.

"Elle has been holding out on us," Toran said. "She has telekinetic magic, apparently."

Colren's eyes widened and he tilted his head questioningly.

I blushed. "I'm still trying to figure out what I can do with it."

"Whatever the methods, you've demonstrated once again that you were exactly the team we've needed," the commander replied. "I can't express enough how difficult it was to give the departure order without you. But, the data you were able to transmit was too valuable. We had to make sure it got to the capital."

Kaiden came to attention. "What did the interface equipment pick up?"

"A series of codes and signals," Colren explained. "When we compared it to the other data we've gathered, we were able to confirm that alien tech uses the crystalline network's reset ability to restructure physical reality within a crystal's zone. There must have been a crystal inside that anomaly. But, we captured the origin point of the signal, and we believe it will lead us to the location of the alien's homeworld."

"That's… wow," I murmured.

"The anomaly—or hidden crystal… was it destroyed?" Kaiden asked.

"The rescue crew picked up none of the usual readings we had detected before. It's gone, or at least dormant," the commander said.

The others grinned.

"That's excellent news," Toran said.

"Elle, come on, this was a big win today," Kaiden said when he saw I wasn't smiling.

"Was it?" I shook my head. "Yeah, we prevented *this* invasion, but they'll try again. I'm certain of it."

"It bought us time," Toran said.

"But how much? We don't know how that spatial anomaly was formed in the first place," I continued. "For all we know, they could have already opened another one somewhere else, only now we have no idea where."

Colren nodded. "That's why we need to end this while we can still get the upper hand. We've confirmed that we have an effective weapon against them."

"That's true." I finally allowed myself to revel in our temporary victory. "And now we know where to hit them so they'll never come back."

MASTERS OF FATE

DARK STARS: BOOK 3

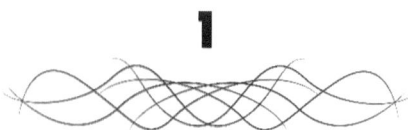

PRACTICE COMBAT WASN'T the same as a real fight, and I had a thirst for battle.

As I twisted and flipped around the mock battlefield with my three friends, I couldn't help but wish that we were on a world fighting creatures born from the Darkness rather than attacking rocks on an uninhabited planet.

Envisioning a shadowcat in my mind, I lunged to the side while swinging my sword in what would be a decapitating blow. I landed lightly on my feet then spun around to spot my next target.

"Nice move," Kaiden complimented.

I grinned back, still poised for action. "I can't wait to take them out for real."

The planet Commander Colren had selected for our exercises was one of the least interesting places from our travels to date. Rather, it was beautiful—impressive mountain peaks and expansive forests—but it wasn't... magical. I craved for the intensity of the crystals on Crystallis or the hum of the Darkness signal in the background. To be on a purely ordinary world felt like a part of me was missing.

Toran sighed, heaving his broad shoulders. He lowered his fists. "If our attacks are focused on individual creatures, we're going about the war all wrong."

"That's true. Any word on the larger strategy?" asked Kaiden, bringing his staff to a resting position on the ground.

Toran shook his bald head. "My conversations have been about the technical nature of the Darkness and the potential form of the aliens. We haven't gotten far enough to know how to take them out for good."

"Are you *ever* going to figure it out?" I asked, realizing only after I'd spoken that it sounded whiny. But, in the days following our engagement with the alien ship at the anomaly, Toran and the other scientists had concluded that the signal's origin wasn't nearly as clear as they'd once believed. It was coming from a specific location, and they knew where that place was, but there didn't appear to be anything there.

"It's a complex situation. There are forces here beyond our current understanding," Toran replied.

Maris tightened the ponytail holding back her dark hair. "Because it's *magic.*"

"Just because we don't yet understand it, that doesn't make it magic," he retorted. "Frankly, some theories the Hegemony's science team has presented are pretty exciting."

"Because they're magic," Maris insisted.

"No, just higher dimensional sp…" I faded out, not remembering the term Toran had used yesterday.

"Hyperdimensional entities manifesting in our plane," Toran corrected. "But that's only one hypothesis. They just as easily could be beings that have learned to control matter using whatever mechanism the crystals use for resets."

"Regardless of what they are, we need to figure out how to stop them," Kaiden stated.

Torn inclined his head. "Which is what we're trying to do. But, it's difficult when we don't rightly know what they're after."

"I still say it's matter—or dark matter," I posited. "All of the worlds infected by the Darkness were hollowed out."

"I still don't believe that's the case," Toran countered.

"Then what—" I was cut off by a chirp in my ear from the embedded comm.

"Dark Sentinel team, return to the *Evangiel*," Colren instructed.

"Is everything okay, Commander?" Kaiden asked.

"New information. Meet in the conference room," he replied, then cut the commlink.

I looked to my friends. "Good information or bad information?"

"That tone didn't *sound* good," Maris observed.

Kaiden let out a deep breath. "Looks like you may soon get your wish for a proper fight after all, Elle."

"We'll see what the commander has to say." Really, it wasn't that I desired to be at the center of the conflict, it was that I hoped for an end to the madness that had been our lives for the past several weeks. I wanted to put a face to the enemy who'd forced me away from my family and made so many people suffer at the hands of their planet-killing weapon. I didn't want to confront them because of bloodlust—rather, I wanted to end the war so we could return to our loved ones and once again have control over our own lives. Though my future path was now unclear, not having the threat of an alien invasion hanging over my head would certainly make matters easier.

The four of us hiked back to our shuttle in a grassy field two hundred meters from our practice area. My chest was tight with eager anticipation to hear Colren's news. The commander had been strangely silent in the four days since our near-death encounter with the alien ship, so I looked forward to a face-to-face meeting to assess his current frame of mind. I could only imagine he was as anxious for the conflict to be over as I was— maybe even more so, having been in the thick of it for a longer time. However, he was our connection to the rest of the Hegemony, so I wanted to make sure he was still on our side. After all, he'd already left us to die once, when he jumped the *Evangiel* without us.

After a brief shuttle ride, we docked in the hangar and made our way to Central Command on the upper deck of the *Evangiel.* Colren rose from his seat at the center of the bridge and motioned us toward the glass-walled conference room.

"How was practice?" the commander asked as we took our typical seats.

"Good," Kaiden replied.

I nodded. "We feel prepared, if that's what you mean."

"It was," Colren said. "So, there shouldn't be any issue with carrying out our new orders."

Toran's brow knit. "The Hegemony has made a decision?"

Colren nodded. "We've been ordered to mount an investigation of the world where the alien signal is originating. Since nothing is showing up on long-range scans, we have no option other than to get closer."

My stomach flipped as I thought back to the last time we'd gone to an

alien-controlled world to investigate the Darkness. I hadn't experienced
it in this timeline, but my memories from the previous-future had become
clearer with time. The multiple independent timelines with their own
sequences of events wove through my mind; I couldn't tell quite how
many resets we'd been through, but there were at least three clear versions
of events where we hadn't stopped the alien fleet. In those timelines,
worlds infected by the Darkness had proved almost deadly. I could only
imagine a journey to their central hub would be the most dangerous of
all.

Kaiden caught my eye from the seat next to me. He cracked a subtle
smile, knowing how much I had been asking for a direct alien encounter
over the past several days. However, in usual fashion, those aspirations
sounded a lot crazier to me now that we were up against that reality. Our
brush with death following the spatial disruptor had shaken me, and I
suspected my friends had also been changed by the confrontation with
their own mortality.

Still, sending the Hegemony's flagship into enemy territory… my
own nerves aside, that sounded reckless.

"The *Evangiel* is going?" I asked in response to Colren's orders. "I
mean, I know we're on board and our team is the most logical choice to
check everything out, but isn't a ship this size a little… obvious?" Since
Colren had always been surprisingly accommodating with answering our
questions and us challenging his orders—at least when we were in good
favor—I figured the best way to test his current regard for us was to needle
him a bit.

The commander seemed ruffled for a moment by my question, but
the cloud passed from his face almost immediately. "Yes," he admitted,
"only larger vessels are capable of executing a jump of this distance. This
crew has come closer to the enemy than any other. We're the best choice
in a number of ways."

A thorough, on-topic answer. That was certainly a good indication
that we hadn't permanently been relegated to cannon fodder status. "I'm
up for the challenge," I replied, though my new nerves hadn't subsided.

"Good, because I mean it quite literally when I say that everything is
riding on this mission," Colren continued. "The aliens could be back at
any time with greater numbers. We got lucky you were able to get onto
that ship and plant the disruptor, but those strategies only tend to work

one time. To end this war, we need to go after the core of their civilization and do everything in our power to make sure they don't ever come looking for us again."

"No argument here," Kaiden said.

Colren folded his hands on the tabletop. "This will need to have a final resolution unlike any other conflict we've faced. If we're successful, it will mean that the war effectively never happened."

"We'll reset," Toran stated.

"Exactly," Colren acknowledged with a nod. "We need to figure out how to defeat them and then reset to before the Darkness ever arrived on a Hegemony world."

"Attack them before they can attack us," I mused.

"Yes, but they've demonstrated that they maintain awareness of other timelines through the resets," Kaiden pointed out. "Won't they be expecting us to do that?"

"Almost certainly, which is why so much is riding on this next mission," Colren replied. "The way I figure it, we have one shot to find their weakness and go in for the kill."

"That's not the right approach." Toran shook his head. "If we reset to before the Darkness arrived, there's no telling what will happen to *us*. We can't rely on deploying an end game strategy after a universal reset—though we got lucky last time, that was only going back a week. But months? To before we were transformed? I worry this whole mess would start all over again."

Colren frowned. "What other options do we have? We need to restore the corrupted worlds."

"Yes, but we should have full reset controls once we un-seal the Master Archive," Toran countered. "We can initiate the reset *after* we've defeated the enemy."

"But then they'll just come back..." Maris said, casting him an exasperated glance.

Toran straightened in his seat. "Not necessarily. That's why we need to learn more about them. If the hypothesis pans out, then we won't need to go through yet another timeline to beat these guys."

Colren came to attention. "Are you talking about the hyperdimensional origins theory?"

"Yes, exactly. I've been talking it over with the research team at the

Capital, and it's the only explanation that accounts for all of our observations."

I normally zoned out when the technical speak came up, but 'dimensional origins' sounded a lot more interesting than signals and frequencies. "Was this what you were about to get into planetside?"

He nodded. "The key bit of information we have about the aliens is that they seem to have remembered information from before prior resets. While it's *possible* they have a direct link to hyperdimensional storage that we don't, another possibility is that they're simply unaffected by time."

Maris raised an eyebrow. "Wait, what?"

"We might be dealing with higher dimensional beings—perhaps 5D, existing 'above' time, if you will."

I ran my fingers through my hair, brushing it back from my face. "Hold on a sec. If these are fifth-dimensional beings—assuming I remember anything from my physics class—then why in the stars would they have any interest in our measly spacetime reality? That'd be like us becoming obsessed with a stick drawing."

"Correct, which is where the transformed worlds come in," Toran continued. "You'd posited, Elle, that they were after matter or dark matter. I don't think that's precisely it, but they do seem to be after *something*. Perhaps they can only access it through this plane for whatever reason."

"Regardless of their objective, we're not going to learn anything more waiting around here," Colren stated. "It's time to see how they like someone pounding on *their* front door for a change."

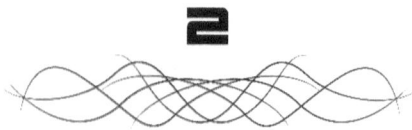

THE *EVANGIEL* DROPPED out of hyperspace beyond visual range of the alien planet. I was still nauseated from the jump when we reported to the bridge, the hyperspace transit having been a longer ordeal than normal. I had no idea where we were or exactly how far we'd traveled, but it was clear we were very much on our own.

Taking a series of slow deep breaths to try to settle my stomach, I turned my attention to the front viewport. Even with holographic augmentation, I still couldn't make out our target. "Is it like the anomaly site from before—a dark gravity well?" I whispered to Kaiden.

"No, we're just a long way from the planet," he replied. "I have a horrible feeling they're going to send us across the system in a shuttle."

"Great. Now that you've said it, it's sure to happen." Even the five-hundred-meter-long *Evangiel* was tiny compared to the vast emptiness around us. The notion of venturing out in a shuttle was downright terrifying.

So much for being ambitious and brave. I'd picked a great time to let nerves get the better of me. Or, maybe I was just wising up to the bleak realities of the situation.

"Hey, it's going to be fine," Kaiden tried to assure me, seeing my worried expression.

"I liked our odds better before I knew we might be going up against higher dimensional beings."

"Nah, it's exciting!"

I cast him a skeptical glance. "Not quite the word I'd pick."

Colren rose from his seat at the center of the bridge, interrupting our private exchange. "Preliminary scans indicate no sign of activity on the planet's surface," he began. "If there's a civilization here, it's well hidden."

"Or beyond our means of detection," Toran said.

"Yes. So, I'd like you to take a closer look," the commander instructed.

"Alone on a shuttle," Kaiden muttered under his breath.

"I don't want to take the *Evangiel* any closer," Colren continued. "You'll travel on the *Sanctum*. Meet up in the hangar in fifteen minutes."

Kaiden pursed his lips. "I stand corrected."

"All right, let's go," I said to my teammates.

We stopped by our quarters to clean up. I waited for Toran and Maris to enter their cabins, hanging back in the corridor with Kaiden.

"I didn't think we'd head out so quickly," I told him as soon as we were alone, wishing there was time for more than a fleeting conversation.

He took my hands. "We can get all the time together we can stomach once this is over."

"That better be soon. I don't know how much more of this I can take."

"You're not alone." Kaiden pulled me into a hug. "We'll get through this together."

We parted with a kiss and then went to our cabins to get ready. After a quick shower, I departed for the hangar with my team.

I'd recognized the name of the *Sanctum* as being the scout ship that rescued us following the spatial disruptor detonation at the anomaly site. The vessel was tiny by most measures, but our standard shuttle could fit inside its cargo hold. The first time I'd seen the *Sanctum*, it had been a welcome sight—a connection to what had become my home away from home during our fight against the Darkness. As we prepared to board the ship this time, however, I instead felt like we were taking a step into the dangerous unknown.

"Welcome aboard," a dark-haired man in his thirties greeted us at the top of the ramp.

"Try to bring it back it one piece, Richards," Tami called from the deck outside, her lips pursing into a worried pout.

"You know we always do, Chief," Richards replied with a slight smile. He returned his attention to us, his gaze pausing on our weapons and modified physical features—a common reaction among crew members meeting us for the first time. "So, you're the infamous Dark Sentinel team, hmm?"

"And you're Richards, it would seem," Kaiden replied with an equally evaluative look.

The man nodded. "*Sanctum* is normally Samwell's baby, but I volunteered to escort you instead—couldn't turn down the opportunity to see you in action."

"And Samwell was okay with that?" I asked, remembering the name of one of the officers who'd picked us up in our disabled shuttle.

"Let's just say that no one is particularly excited about heading into enemy territory like this. Didn't take a lot of arm-twisting," Richards responded.

"We've always liked living on the edge." A short-haired blonde woman poked her head out from the bridge and grinned. "I smell a promotion if we get you four back alive."

"This is hardly a time for career ambition," Toran stated.

The woman shrugged. "To each their own."

"To say Kess has a competitive streak would be a gross understatement," Richards said with a nod toward the woman. "Don't get her started."

"Hey, anyone willing to accompany us is good by me," I said. "I'm Elle."

My teammates introduced themselves in turn.

"Do you really have... magic?" Kess asked after the introductions, examining us.

"That's what we're calling it, anyway," Kaiden replied. "I know you want to see it, but if you do, that means things have already gone wrong."

Kess smiled. "Bring it on."

"Save it for the baddies, Kess." Richards paused. "Hey, what are we calling these alien bastards, anyway?"

I looked to my teammates. "You know, we haven't really been calling them anything."

Kess raised an eyebrow. "Seriously, you gave yourselves a team name and didn't name the bad guys?"

Kaiden shrugged. "I dunno. I guess we figured the Hegemony had a name for them, or we'd find out what they call themselves."

"It's always been 'the Darkness'," I added. "The beings themselves didn't come into it until recently."

Kess rolled her eyes. "Whatever. Strap in back there." She nodded toward a bank of seats along the outer bulkhead above the cargo hold.

"I'll get her fired up," Richards said, shimmying through the bridge entrance past Kess.

I took a seat next to Kaiden in the indicated seats and started to strap in. "You know, they do have a point about a name for these bad guys."

"Well, 'Creepy Alien Bastards Who Want to Destroy Us' has been working for me," Maris said.

"Yeah... 'cab-woo-du' doesn't exactly roll off the tongue or sound particularly menacing," I said.

Kaiden laughed. "Nor does 'cabbies' or anything else that comes to mind from that abbreviation."

"I suggest we table this issue for another time," Toran advised. "Personally, I don't care what we call them. Let's just focus on the not-dying part of the mission."

"I can get behind that," I agreed.

As soon as we finished securing our flight harnesses, a low vibration spread through the floor of the vessel, and the scene out the side viewport shifted as the ship glided through the hangar. We passed through the electrostatic field into open space, and the *Sanctum* boosted toward the destination world.

"All right, clear. We're looking at about four hours of transit time," Richards said over a central comm. "Get comfy."

Kaiden sighed. "I kinda miss being up front and in charge."

I swiveled my head, keeping a neutral expression. "This is my shocked face."

Toran chuckled. "It seems we've found our places."

"I feel all fancy getting transported around," Maris said with an excited shiver. "My mom always told me that you know you've 'made it' as soon as you have a chauffeur."

"Not your chauffer," Richards said over the comm. "You know we can hear you, right?"

I cracked a smile. "Just friendly banter. We can keep this up for hours!"

"Have fun with that. We'll let you know when we're nearing the planet," Richards said. A chirp over the comm indicated that the channel had been muted.

I scowled. "Okay, on a scale of 'one' to 'annoying', I'd say we were only at a three."

"Yeah, I'm surprised they cut us off like that," Kaiden agreed. "Seemed friendlier when we met."

"They're soldiers on a mission," Toran reminded us.

I slumped in my seat. "So long as they don't ditch us on the planet, fine with me if they don't want to chat."

Kaiden nodded. "I have no doubt they'll come around once they witness our awesomeness firsthand."

"Not that they *will* see it. I mean, they aren't coming down to the surface with us, are they?" I asked.

"I'd hope not," Toran replied. "I believe they meant that they'd be monitoring the feed from the recorders on our packs."

"*Thrilling*," Maris said sarcastically.

"Hey, that footage is probably restricted access normally," Kaiden told her. "I guess I'd be pretty curious to see what allegedly magical abilities looked like in practice, too."

Maris got an excited glint in her eyes. "Well, guess we'll need to put on a show."

We made small-talk for most of the journey, comfortable in each other's company. I couldn't resist taking Kaiden's hand on occasion or giving him a pat on his arm or leg when he made a particularly eyeroll-worthy comment, but I tried to keep the contact to a minimum since I knew it made Maris and Toran feel awkward. I'd promised to make sure our team came before the relationship; I hadn't been able to keep that promise one hundred percent of the time, but I still tried my best.

For the final half hour of the voyage, Richards and Kess invited us to the bridge so we could watch the final approach to the planet on the holographic display overlaid on the front viewport. I appreciated the gesture, though I suspected it was a matter of practicality rather than them wanting us there.

"It really doesn't look like anything special," Kaiden observed as he studied the augmented image of a barren, brown-gray planet.

"Well, you have a breathable atmosphere, moderate temperature, and $0.9g$, so it's pretty spectacular in the grand scheme of things," Richards replied.

"Hey, at least we won't die just from stepping outside the shuttle, so there's that!" Maris said with forced enthusiasm.

"What's more curious is the signal." Toran deftly moved his hands over the communications control panel at an auxiliary station.

"Still can't figure out where it's coming from?" I asked.

He frowned pensively. "You could say that... It's really like it's coming from everywhere. But it's not a signal, exactly, more like a... signature."

"As in, a radiological signature?" Kess asked.

"In a sense, yes, but not in that same core classification," Toran confirmed. "I believe this may be a sort of quantum echo—something I'd discussed with the Hegemony's research team. If that is the case..." he trailed off.

"Then what, Toran?" I prompted.

He took a slow breath. "Then that might indicate the presence of significant alien activity, only on a plane we can't see."

Kaiden frowned. "I don't like the sound of that."

Kess swore under her breath. "I should have known something was up with this whole op."

Richards snorted. "Yeah, like this info would have made you second-guess the assignment."

"Irrelevant distinctions," she replied.

"It's all speculation," Toran continued. "If we want to confirm that hypothesis, we'll need to get a closer look."

"Last I checked, we don't have hyperdimensional vision," Maris stated.

"Not exactly, but I believe we've been in contact with hyperdimensional access points in the past," he went on. "The Master Archive, for example, we agreed wasn't on Crystallis in a conventional sense."

I thought about what we'd observed. "That's true. There was also the weird tower on the Valor world."

"Exactly. There's a hyperdimensional connection between the crystalline network and the higher planes, so maybe that manifests in other ways," Toran said.

"What do the aliens have to do with that, though?" Kaiden asked.

Toran shrugged. "That's what we're here to find out."

Maris propped her elbows on her thighs and leaned forward. "Those other places had connections into the higher planes. Do you think there might be an access point on this world?"

"If there is, it's likely connected to a crystal," Kaiden said, twirling his pendant in his fingertips. "We already know how to find those."

Toran inclined his head. "Indeed, we do. Let's take a look."

"What's this, now?" Richards asked.

"Think of it as a sort of magical crystal-detector," Kaiden said.

Kess' expression brightened. "All right, now we're getting to the interesting stuff."

I raised an eyebrow. "The idea that a civilization might extend into another dimensional plane wasn't interesting enough?"

"But… magic-detector," Kess replied.

I couldn't argue with her logic. "Yeah, fair enough. Do you have everything you need for the interface, Toran?"

"Mobile setup should be in my pack, hold on." Toran disappeared into the cargo area of the ship.

"How did you come up with this tech?" Richards asked.

Kaiden gave a dismissive flip of his wrist. "Lucky guesses, mostly. Toran seems to have an instinct for this stuff."

"You've certainly won the commander's respect," Kess said.

"Didn't feel that way when he jumped without us," I mumbled.

Richards swiveled to face me. "You survived the disruptor wave, but the *Evangiel* wouldn't have stood a chance. Only reason we're here is because the commander made that call."

I knew in my heart that the soldier was right, but it had still distressed me to witness firsthand that we were disposable. "I know he didn't mean it personally," I muttered in an attempt to smooth things over with our escorts.

"This is war, not summer camp." Richards eyed me. "But," he took a deep breath, "you *have* made it this far, which is more than can be said for many soldiers. That's why I volunteered to come—to see you in action, and to help you see this thing through. I've heard some crew members say you're not up to it, but I think actions matter more than age or experience."

"After all, you survived a *spatial disruptor* detonation," Kess cut in. "Considering that's pretty much impossible, you have more than luck on your side."

"And, seriously, I've known the commander a long time. You can trust him," Richards added, softer.

I nodded, dropping my gaze to my hands. "I know. I get why we were left behind. Just… made everything more real, I guess."

Kaiden rubbed my back. "And showed us we can do what we thought was impossible."

Kess smiled. "We're on your side. Anyone who doesn't have faith in you is an idiot."

Perhaps I'd misread the soldiers' intentions before when they'd relegated us to the cargo area for most of the journey; they were just focused on the mission, it wasn't about excluding us.

I wasn't sure what had been going on with me over the past few days—moodiness, paranoia. Ever since the incident at the anomaly I'd been on edge. Based on how Kaiden kept glancing over at me with his brow creased, it appeared he was concerned about me, too. I suppose it had just been a matter of time before the stress and pressure got to me. Maybe I was finally cracking. Considering what we were about to do, the timing could be a lot better. I took a deep breath and tried to center myself.

"All right, here we go," Toran said, returning to the compact bridge carrying a device the size of his substantial fist.

"What does it need to operate?" Richards asked.

"I can tap it into the communications console. It'll piggyback on the ship's sensor suite to identify the specific signature of crystals on the planet," Toran explained. "We'll see if any of those look like a key location and investigate accordingly."

"Proceed." Richards gestured toward the console. "We're under orders to remain on the *Sanctum* while you take the shuttle to the surface, so you'll be on your own once you know where you're going."

"Used to it, no problem," Kaiden said.

"It doesn't look like this world is infected by the Darkness, so at least we won't have to worry about contamination when we come back," I added while Toran began syncing the equipment with the shuttle.

"Thank the stars for that," Kess murmured.

We fell silent as Toran studied the data feeding into his specialized receiver, using the unique properties of Kaiden and Maris' pendants to identify resonant signatures on the planet's surface.

After two minutes of calibrating the equipment to the *Sanctum*,

Toran sat back and frowned at the screen. "That's odd."

"What now?" Kaiden asked.

Toran sighed. "Well, every other time we've tried this sort of scan, specific crystal locations have been called out. On this world, though, it's like the entire planet is pinging. But that's strange, since we had difficulty getting readings on the Darkness-infected worlds unless we were close to one of the crystals."

"There's no evidence of the Darkness here," I pointed out.

"True, but I'd expect this planet and the others infected with the Darkness to demonstrate the same properties," he replied.

"Maybe there's something about this planet that isn't on the others?" Maris suggested. "An 'x factor'."

"I suppose." Toran examined the visual representation on the screen, illustrating a glow around the planet. "This does support the hypothesis that there's a civilization here we can't see."

"How are those connected? I thought this detected the presence of crystals," Maris asked.

"It's doesn't detect crystals precisely," Toran corrected, "more like it picks up a sign of their presence via unique signatures. But, it's possible that those signatures aren't unique to crystals and are actually signs of something else we can't see."

"Higher-dimensional energy?" I supplied.

Toran took a slow breath. "Perhaps, though I can't with certainty say it's connected to the aliens."

Worry spread across Richards' face. "Assuming there *are* higher dimensional beings, won't they know we're here?"

"Almost certainly," Toran replied.

"But, they haven't attacked us," Kaiden pointed out. "So, either they don't care, or they don't see us as a threat."

"Or, they're waiting for us to walk into a trap," I said.

"Regardless, we're not going to learn anything significant about this planet from here. We need to pick a site and investigate," Toran stated.

I nodded. "I'm not disagreeing, but I don't have a good feeling about this."

"Me either, but we don't have a choice," Kaiden said.

"Where do we target, then?" Maris asked.

"How about an old-fashioned visual survey?" Richards suggested. He modified the front viewport to display a holographic representation of the planet with augmented topographical features. Blue outlines appeared around specific sites, which contained signs of a built environment.

My brow knit. "City ruins?"

"Looks like it," Kess said. "Nature doesn't make straight lines like that." She traced her finger over a grid pattern on the largest southern continent.

"Any sign of a crystal?" Kaiden questioned.

"No, but the energy readings indicate there could be one at that location, perhaps underground," Toran replied. "Since the city ruins are more intact there than anywhere else, that's my suggestion for where to begin our search."

"Works for me," I agreed. Ancient alien city ruins somehow upped the spookiness factor of the mission, but there was no turning back now.

"All right, let's get our stuff and head out," Kaiden said.

My friends and I climbed down to our shuttle berthed in the belly of the *Sanctum*, which completely filled the small cargo hold. Richards and Kess remained on the bridge in comm contact.

"We'll keep a low orbit, ready to rendezvous whenever you're ready," Richards said over the shared comm channel while we entered our shuttle.

"Shout if you need anything. We'll be watching," Kess added.

"And if the comms don't work?" Kaiden asked. "We've had issues before."

Richards didn't reply immediately. "Then we'll give you ten hours before we head back to the *Evangiel*."

It sounded like enough time to give us a comfortable buffer. With any luck, we'd complete our task well before that. "Okay, see you soon," I acknowledged.

We got situated on the bridge in our usual seats and strapped in. Kaiden took the controls in anticipation of our release from the docking grapples.

"I have a lock on the destination," Toran stated from the seat behind me.

"Confirmed," Kaiden said. "Nav system is online."

"Safe travels," Richards wished us over the comm. "Releasing the clamps."

A shudder passed through the craft as the docking grapple released, and a moment later the view changed to a starscape with the brown-gray planet below.

"All right, here we go," Kaiden murmured under his breath, aligning the shuttle for atmospheric entry.

I gripped my armrests as the shuttle reached the outer boundaries of the atmosphere. At the same moment, I became aware of a strange feeling in the air, almost like an electrical charge.

"Anyone else feel that?" I asked.

"Yeah, it's weird," Kaiden replied.

Maris grasped her pendant. "It feels like it did next to the anomaly."

"What's going on?" Richards demanded over the comm.

"There's a strange—" I cut off when my comm gave a 'disconnection' warning chirp in my ear. "Great." I leaned forward to try the shuttle's communication system; only static met my attempts to raise the *Sanctum*.

Kaiden let out a long breath. "Here we go again."

EVEN WITHOUT FUNCTIONAL comms, at least we weren't flying blind, unlike some past journeys.

Kaiden was able to maintain a nav lock on our target, and we slowly descended toward the city ruins, taking in the surrounding landscape.

The former city was spread out on the floor of a valley surrounded by mountains and rolling foothills. However, with no vegetation or snow, the landscape was lacking the kind of drama I'd expect from rocky peaks. What appeared to be a dry riverbed bisected the city ruins, the western side seeming to have weathered time better than the east.

"Land inside or outside the city?" Kaiden asked, circling around at a low elevation so we could scope it out.

"I like the idea of landing in the open," Toran replied.

I raised my hand. "Second that."

"Yeah, definitely," Maris agreed. "This place gives me the creeps even from up here."

There was something profoundly disquieting about the ruins. Only gray stone—possibly the remnants of cast concrete—and bits of metal support structures rose from the windswept landscape. I couldn't see any specific evidence of weapons fire or other attack from afar, but the irregular distribution of destruction around the city suggested that the damage wasn't simply from natural decay.

"What do you think happened here?" Maris voiced my own curiosity.

"Not sure, but whoever used to live here left a long time ago," Toran replied.

"Or *whatever*," Kaiden emphasized.

"If it's sentient, wouldn't it still be a 'who'?" Maris questioned.

I crossed my arms. "I'd rather not think about it."

Kaiden selected a landing area half a kilometer beyond the obvious outskirts of the city ruins.

I suspected that the area had once been a suburb, though only amorphous mounds remained where structures may have once stood. The sense of disquiet welling inside me intensified as the shuttle touched down. I unstrapped my harness and stared out the viewport at the desolate landscape. "I guess we should get to it."

"Yeah, the sooner we can get out of here, the better," Kaiden agreed.

The four of us shuffled into the common area to grab our packs. I hoped we wouldn't need any of the extra supplies stashed inside, but I'd rather have them than not.

Toran checked the readout next to the side hatch. "Atmospheric readings all look to be within tolerance, just like we observed from orbit."

"Minus microbes that will gestate inside us and hatch new baby aliens to take over the galaxy," Maris said.

I frowned. "Maybe we *should* wear EVA suits."

"If we get into a fight, that will put us at a serious disadvantage," Kaiden pointed out. "If our enhancements can withstand the Darkness, I don't think microbes are a huge concern for us."

"Yeah, good point," I conceded.

"Shall we go, then?" Toran asked.

I nodded. "Ready."

He released the seal, and the hatch folded down and extended a ramp to the ground.

I stayed in position for several seconds, waiting for the first wafts of the alien air to reach us. True to our equipment readings, we didn't instantly die. "Let's see how it is outside."

We descended the ramp and then re-sealed the hatch from the outside, not wanting to risk unseen rogue wildlife wandering into the shuttle. Standing on the grainy soil, I could tell the gravity was lighter than I was used to, though not enough to try anything too exciting.

"I say we head into the center of the ruins," Kaiden suggested. "That central square we saw might be a good place to start—probably the city center for a reason."

I nodded. "Likely a place to find an old crystal."

"Sounds good to me," Maris said, bounding toward the city.

We ran easily in the lower gravity, making quick time over the flat terrain. As we reached the first toppled structures in the ruins, I realized that I'd missed a crucial observation in our flyby.

"The scale seems strange with these buildings."

My friends studied the structures, slowing their paces along the former boulevard.

"You're right," Toran said. "Everything seems at least fifty percent larger than what we're used to."

"Not just that," Kaiden added, "but I'm not sure this was designed for a bipedal society."

I looked closer at the building he was studying. There did seem to be something off about the design of the stairs—like there were two sets of steps next to each other at alternating intervals. At first I'd thought that the steps had broken in half and shifted vertically, but they were intact upon closer examination. Though I'd seen designs like that on occasion in my own culture, for it to be everywhere was surprising—especially when coupled with the benches staggered along the strip between two flat roadways. The benches each had a distinctive slope at the bottom, joining to a ledge at the height of my shoulders.

"Maybe those are… sculptures?" Maris offered.

"I'm not so sure." My stomach knotted as I thought about the creature I'd seen on the alien ship four days before—an undulating torso, seamlessly transitioning from two to four legs as it skittered through the ship. I could picture the creature perched on the strange bench, as staggering as it was to think about those monstrosities being part of a society that would go for a walk in the park.

"Maybe we can find some art that shows what they look like," Kaiden said, picking up his pace.

"Yeah." I met his stride.

We encountered few other clues as we continued toward the city center, most buildings being too decayed to offer insights. I found it strange that there was anything left of the city ruins, but apparently the ravages of time weren't as harsh without vegetation or significant rainfall.

At last, the structures became larger and more elaborate, indicating we were entering a part of the city that may have once been the center of the economy. Most of the buildings were now piles of rubble standing three stories tall, but some rusted metal superstructures rose ten stories or more—the last remnants of what used to be. Unfortunately, it was impossible to get a proper sense of the culture's design aesthetic with so few intact elements.

"The town square should be just up ahead," Toran announced, breaking the eerie silence of the place.

"It's so similar to one of our cities," Maris murmured. "I thought it would be more... alien."

That did seem odd to me, too. While certain features did strike me as being designed for a different sort of creature, the overall layout of the place was bizarrely similar to what I'd expect from one of the Hegemony's worlds. It was almost like the city had been taken over and retrofit.

"Wait... what if this wasn't *originally* an alien city?" I said.

"Like, they invaded it?" Maris asked.

"Yeah, like they made some changes to suit them, but didn't change everything," I clarified.

Toran stroked his chin. "An interesting thought. I suppose this could have been a world they invaded before they mastered how to transmit the Darkness through the crystals."

"But if this is their homeworld now, of sorts, wouldn't they have gone back to transform it now that they *do* have that tech?" Kaiden asked.

"Not if they didn't need to," I replied. "Maybe the Darkness isn't for bio-optimization at all. Maybe we've been looking at everything the wrong way."

Kaiden frowned. "What happened to the native population here?"

I shrugged. "No clue. Maybe they enslaved them, or ate them, or transformed them in some way."

"Or they didn't need physical forms anymore." Toran shuddered. "They're probably watching us right now, laughing at us feebly trying to put together the pieces."

Maris paled. "Yeah... maybe let's not talk about it anymore?"

"Wait, look." Kaiden pointed ahead of us. A distinctive tower was visible over the top of a nearby rubble pile.

"That's the monument in the town square," Toran said. "Come on."

We picked up our pace, eager to complete our mission as quickly as possible. I hated the notion that unseen beings may be watching us—

creatures beyond my comprehension, existing outside the flow of time as I knew it.

As we rounded a bend in the street we'd been following, the central square came into view. Six roadways intersected like spokes on a massive wheel with a tower at its center. The top had appeared smooth from a distance, but I now saw that it was broken. It appeared that a statue had once been perched atop it, though the figure was now only broken shards around the base.

"I bet that would have given us some clues," I said with a sigh.

"There's still a lot to see." Toran peered at the tower's base. "I believe that may be a doorway."

I took another look behind the rubble, spotting the archway he was referencing. It did, indeed, look to be an opening. The tower itself was only five meters in diameter, so there couldn't be a chamber of any substantial size inside. However, if it went *down*…

"Do you think the crystal is underneath there?" I asked.

"As good a guess as any," Kaiden replied

Maris rummaged in her pack and produced a flashlight, grinning. "And, we're finally prepared."

Kaiden conjured a light orb in his palm. "Really, Maris? I thought more of you."

"Hey, if you want to serve as a living beacon of magical energy, go for it. Personally, I'd rather try to blend in."

He extinguished the light and swung his backpack forward over his shoulder to get inside. "On second thought…"

"I'm not sure how incognito we can be with these artifacts, but I suppose some precautions wouldn't be a bad thing," I realized. My instinct had been to draw my sword to have it in hand, but that might enhance its signature. I decided to wait until there were clear signs of a threat before I activated the weapon.

Toran and I also retrieved our flashlights as we approached the archway, climbing over small piles of debris. I kept an eye on the rubble for clues about what type of figure had topped the column, though I saw no remaining evidence of its form. The only hints were recesses in textured pieces of stone with an intricate organic pattern that reminded me of moss—or the fibrous webbing I'd previously observed inside the alien ship. The fragments were too small and eroded to tell for sure, so I decided to keep the observation to myself.

The archway was framed by an ornate rendering of twisting vines reaching toward stars and planets above. Maybe I wasn't reading too much into the other fragments after all. "Does that remind anyone else of anything?"

"Our visit to Windau," Maris stated without hesitation. "I'll never forget those horrifying vines that attacked us."

A rotted wooden door still hung in the recesses of the archway, but when Toran pushed against it, the remaining fragments turned to dust. "Looks like we have our way in," he said, shining his light into the blackness within. "There appears to be a path down."

I couldn't help thinking back to the Valor world and the strange staircase in the tower that didn't obey spatial reality as I knew it. It was possible that this passageway itself was a dimensional transition point. "I'll lead the way," I volunteered, figuring that my combined skills made me the best prepared to react to any threat.

"No argument here." Maris took a step back, allowing Kaiden to follow behind me and have Toran take the rear.

I steeled myself for whatever we might find and stepped inside.

The interior was adorned with similar motifs to the exterior carvings, with vines snaking along the walls and a celestial representation overhead. Rather than a staircase, as I'd expected, a ramp spiraled downward along a central axis, leaving clearance for even Toran's tall frame. Beginning the descent, I held my flashlight in one hand while keeping the other on my sword's hilt.

"You know, Elle," Kaiden began, "I think you may be onto something with that idea about the aliens conquering another civilization. This looks suspiciously like a temple."

"Do you think the people were… worshiping them?" I asked.

"I don't know, but if I saw evidence of a higher-dimensional being, I could see how it might seem to be a deity."

After we'd spiraled fully around the central column, the ornate carvings on the walls and ceiling transitioned to a single vine and star pattern along the outer wall. It continued in that manner as we progressed down three more stories, where the corridor opened into what appeared to be a natural cavern.

"Wow." I sucked in a breath, taking it in. The ceiling was at least three stories overhead, covered in shimmering crystal.

"All right, so I'm beginning to understand how your pendants might be resonating with this entire planet," Toran said.

Kaiden couldn't take his gaze off the ceiling. "What is this place?"

"Clearly somewhere important to these people, considering the effort it must have taken to carve out that entry," I said.

"It's strange that so many of the images includes stars, yet their sacred place is underground," Maris observed.

"These crystals might be more to them than pretty decoration," Kaiden countered. "Maybe they understood that the crystalline network connects the planets."

"Do you think the vines represent those connections?" I pondered.

"Could be." He shrugged. "We may never know."

"Let's see what else is in here," I suggested, continuing into the cavern. However, I was only able to go a short ways before I encountered a four-meter-tall wall spanning the width of the cavern. A single archway to my right allowed passage through it.

"That's strange." Kaiden stopped behind me. "Why would they build a wall here?"

Toran approached the archway and looked inside. "Not a wall. I think this might be a labyrinth."

I frowned. "That makes even *less* sense."

Kaiden's face contorted. "Why in the stars would they build something like this?"

"Ancient culture, different philosophies," Toran said.

"Not that ancient, based on the state of the ruins," Kaiden pointed out.

"This labyrinth may have been down here for a long time before that construction," Maris point out.

"True. Labyrinths have been used throughout history for many things. Perhaps it's symbolic," Toran suggested. "Some ancient religions viewed mazes like this as a meditative exercise, or to represent a journey toward the inner self."

"Find peace and serenity with your evil alien overlords!" Maris jested.

"I'll pass." I kept my voice low, not liking how it reverberated in the chamber.

"How complicated do you think this maze is?" Kaiden wondered aloud.

"Depending on the value of what lies at its terminus, it could be anything from a simple exercise or a trap we may never escape," Toran replied.

"Not a great argument for going inside," Maris muttered.

"Agreed." Toran nodded. "This isn't what I expected to find in here. I suggest we look elsewhere."

"Come on! This is even more intriguing than what I thought might be down here," I countered. "This is way too promising a lead for us to turn back now."

"I really can't imagine us coming across a structure that might give better clues about what happened to this world," Kaiden seconded.

Maris shook her head. "I don't know…"

"Look, it's not like we can actually get trapped," I reminded them. "The top of the maze is open, right? We can just climb up and walk along the top—we'll see the path all the way to the end."

Toran considered the proposition. "I hadn't thought about approaching it that way. It could work."

"Might anger the evil overlords to outsmart them," Kaiden quipped.

Maris tsked. "Don't joke about that!"

"Relax, everyone. Let's just get to the end of this thing and figure out what it is." I searched in my pack for a coil of rope.

"I hope you're right." Toran took a steadying breath and then retrieved his own rope. He tied one end to my pack to use it as a weight, then hurled it over the top of the stone wall near the entrance.

I cautiously ventured through the arch to secure the rope. As I rounded the corner through the archway, I caught a glimpse of movement in the shadows deeper inside the labyrinth. "Is someone there?" I called out.

"Everything okay, Elle?" Kaiden peeked through the archway after me.

"Not sure. I thought I saw something."

"All the more reason for us to walk *on top* of the walls. Good thinking," he replied, coming to join me.

"Yeah." I went to where my bag had dropped and anchored it to the wall using the climbing gear in my pack.

Kaiden stayed with me while I finished, to my relief. Once the rope was secured, I grabbed my pack, and we ran back to the other side of the wall where Maris and Toran were waiting.

"All set?" Toran asked me.

"Yep."

"I'll go first," he said. "If it can hold me, the rest of you will be no problem."

I stood back to give him room.

Despite his proportions, Toran nimbly scaled the rope, bracing his feet on the wall. He hoisted himself over the top lip and looked around.

"The walls are nearly a meter wide, and the maze isn't too large," he reported. "I think we'll be able to find a way across, though it's difficult to see. I believe the maze terminates at the end of this chamber."

"And on to another cavern?" questioned Kaiden.

"Perhaps. I suppose we'll find out when we get there."

Since it was my idea, I climbed up next. True to Toran's assessment, there was no obvious break in the maze before us. I could barely make out the tops of the stones at the furthest edges of the chamber with my flashlight. "I'm not sure how well we'll be able to chart a path through here," I said. "We need something brighter.

Kaiden climbed up next to me. "I can fix that."

"Magic may draw unwanted attention," I reminded him.

"It's that or we waste time backtracking because we couldn't see well."

"All right, up to you," I conceded.

He conjured a light orb and released it into the center of the chamber. It hovered near the ceiling, illuminating the tops of the stone walls.

"Thanks." I flashed a smile at him and then turned my attention to scouting a path. "Okay, we should be able to follow along there and then take a left."

"Looks good," Toran agreed.

Leading the way, I took the proposed course at a quick but cautious pace. The wall was less than a meter wide, and while sufficient to provide adequate footing, it felt like a long way up to be walking on a narrow path. Despite my past jumps into the canyon on Erusan, I'd never liked heights. I especially didn't relish the prospect of falling here, not knowing what may be lurking in the shadows.

Occasionally, I shined my light downward to see if I could catch another glimpse of whatever I may have seen near the entrance. I sensed something nearby, though that may have been nerves getting to me again.

Even though I tried to stay focused on my footing and following the path along the wall, my gaze kept wandering toward the shadows below. We were cheating by walking along the top like this. It's not how it was supposed to be.

"Elle, watch out!" Kaiden's strong arms pulled me back from the edge.

A section of wall had begun to crumble beneath my feet, throwing me off balance. Kaiden kept a tight hold of me, and Toran pulled us both backward away from the damaged section.

"That was close." Maris let out a shaky breath.

Kaiden released me, turning his attention to the path ahead. "It's not much further. Stick to the middle of the wall."

"I was, I—"

"You almost walked off the edge, Elle," he stated.

"I did?" I stared into the shadows. "There's something down there. I can feel it."

"Now that you mention it…" Maris wrapped her arms around herself.

"We need to stay focused," Kaiden said, though the words sounded forced.

Only Toran remained his usual, calm demeanor. "One foot in front of the other. We'll be back on the ground soon."

I still didn't *want* to be on the ground. All the same, I continued forward, watching my footing. We only had one more switchback of the wall to traverse before we'd reach the end of the cavern.

"Almost—" The wall gave way underfoot. I was falling, and the shadows were jumping up to greet me.

4

MY BACK SLAMMED into something hard, and I rolled over into a soft, sticky mass. Stunned, I lay motionless. It wasn't until I sensed tendrils coiling around my legs that I tried to react.

To my horror, my attempt to get up revealed that my arms were already wrapped in tendrils, as well. "Help!" I gasped, not sure where I was or if anyone could hear me.

"Close your eyes!" Kaiden shouted in the distance.

I squeezed my eyes shut moments before bright orange flames erupted around me. The tendrils loosened, and I jumped to my feet. "What the...?"

I was standing in a mass of writhing vines, similar to those I'd seen on planets infected by the Darkness. The vines were temporarily stunned, but I saw them slowly unfurling, preparing to lash out at me again.

A rope dropped down next to me. "Grab hold!" Toran shouted.

The end of the rope was tied into a loop, and I slipped my foot into it while holding on above with my hands. Toran pulled me up just in time to avoid another assault from the vines.

Their presence here made no sense, especially since we hadn't seen any other vegetation on the planet, and we were several stories underground. I'd always thought that the vines were a warped version of existing plant life, not... whatever was going on here.

"Stars! I don't know what happened." My heart pounded in my ears and my breath was labored.

Kaiden helped me up at the top of the wall. "I told you to be careful."

His face was drawn with worry, seeming exhausted.

"I thought I was." I shook my head. "There's something about this planet—this entire system. It doesn't feel right."

"I know, I sense it, too." Kaiden took an unsteady breath.

"We need to get to the next cavern," Maris urged. "Learn what we can and then get out of here."

"It was a mistake to venture inside," Toran murmured.

"Too late now—" Kaiden cut off as the wall beneath us began to tremble. Dust rose into the air as chunks of stone tumbled down to the ground. "Shit, it's collapsing!" he shouted.

We dashed along the top of the wall, planting our feet anywhere that seemed remotely stable. Gaps opened in our path, and we leaped over the collapsing sections in our desperate race to safety.

Only six meters to go. The wall began to cave toward the opposite direction of the interior cavern. I grabbed Kaiden's hand, and we leaped together in the direction of the exit.

When I hit the stone floor, I bent my knees and rolled to the side, releasing Kaiden's hand. He popped up next to me, wincing, but otherwise appeared unharmed.

Maris and Toran were still running along the upper ledge four meters above us. A purple bubble appeared around them, and then Toran scooped Maris into his arms. He leaped down to where I'd landed, taking the full impact of the jump with only a slight knee bend. The moment he was on the ground, he set Maris down and resumed running toward the arch.

"Hurry! It's all collapsing," he shouted.

I couldn't see beyond the immediate cloud of debris, but I had no interest in waiting around to assess the destruction. Racing after Toran and Maris, I glanced behind me to see the vines lashing out after us.

Kaiden sent a blue fireball flying, enough to buy us the seconds needed to escape. The stone walls continued to fall, burying the dark vines in debris.

I dashed the final steps through the archway into the next chamber. The moment we passed through the archway, the vines stilled. The last remnants of the maze walls collapsed behind us, and then the chaos was over—a cloud of dust was the only indication that something had just happened.

Maris coughed. "I really hate this place."

I wiped dust off my face using my coat sleeve. "Was that a trap, or were the walls just old and ready to come down?"

Toran shook his head. "I could see it going either way."

Maris looked back at the destruction in the cavern. "Are we trapped in here?"

I evaluated the piles of rubble. "No, we can get over it." I waggled my fingers. "Besides, I have that fancy telekinesis magic."

"Too bad you couldn't have levitated us all the way here," Maris said.

"I don't trust my abilities enough yet to risk hurting you," I replied. "Besides, I don't think I can levitate myself."

"Have you tried?" she asked.

"No, but—"

"Elle, you might want to take a look at this," Kaiden interrupted.

I turned in the direction Kaiden was facing. He'd released a light orb into the center of the chamber, illuminating details I'd missed when I ran in. The chamber was easily the size of the previous cavern, but it was wide open space. Strikingly, the entire floor was glittering.

"What is that?" I stepped closer and crouched down. The sparkling sand appeared to be crystal fragments like we'd seen on Crystallis. "Are these?"

Kaiden squatted next to me, the glow in his pendant intensifying. "I think so, but these still have a charge to them."

I looked up at the ceiling; it was similar to the one in the first cavern and appeared to be intact. Wherever these crushed crystals had come from, it wasn't because they fell from the ceiling. "Could this civilization have been connected to Crystallis?"

"Or they pissed off the same group of hyperdimensional aliens and got wiped out." Kaiden stood up.

"Why shatter these and not scrape everything off of the ceiling, too?" Maris questioned.

"Not all crystals are the same," Toran reminded her.

"Well, this doesn't bode well for us finding a crystal to use as a dimensional transition point," I said. "Seems like whoever came through here had a grudge against the very thing we're looking for."

"That, or…" Kaiden trailed off.

"Hmm?"

He shook his head. "I was just thinking back to when we first came across the crushed crystals on Crystallis. At the time, we'd wondered if maybe there had been a war."

"Right." I nodded.

"Well, in war, a lot of strategy comes down to the territory you control, and access points. If there *were* battles being fought that spanned multiple dimensional planes, and if certain trans-dimensional interface points made it easier to move within the overall framework, it would make sense to restrict the number of those access points."

"Hmm, that's an interesting way to look at it," I said.

"I agree with that logic," Toran said. "And, if that's the case, perhaps there is a still a trans-dimensional interface access point somewhere down here."

"Hey, we've gotta have a shorthand term for that," Maris chimed in. "How about TDI?"

"Yes, much better," I agreed.

"That might explain where those vines came from," Kaiden said. "It's in here, too." He motioned toward the dark corners of the room. The black vines were barely distinguishable in the shadows, but they clearly recoiled from the light orb.

"Ugh, I hadn't thought of that." My heart sank. "That means that if we use a crystal as a TDI to the higher dimension, we'll be going through a gateway infected by the Darkness."

"Considering we're on the planet we think is the aliens' homeworld, it wouldn't be at all surprising if the TDI was connected to the Darkness," Toran pointed out.

"Doesn't make it any less disturbing," I replied.

"No, it does not." Maris looked around the chamber with distaste. Something caught her eye, however, and she perked up. "What's that?"

She jogged over to a low mound a few meters away, which was even shinier than the surrounding crystal powder. "Ooooo!"

We ran over to where she was standing over the object. Partially buried under the crystalline gravel was a jewel-encrusted shield half a meter in diameter. The rainbow of stones was breathtaking, creating the image of a cosmic scene with a yellow star, blue and green planets, and purple-black starscape backdrop.

"This is totally mine," Maris declared, bending to pick it up.

I stopped her. "It might be a trap."

Kaiden looked around. "Yeah, this is literally the *only* object in this room that isn't a part of a structure."

"But it's so shiny!" She glared at us. "It's not fair—you all get special artifacts, and I have nothing."

"Three artifacts for three disciplines," I said.

"Doesn't mean there were *only* three," she pointed out.

I rolled my eyes. "Wanting the thing doesn't change the fact this is a super-fancy item in a destroyed, infected cavern under a ruined city. There is no way that *isn't* super-suspicious any way you look at it."

"It doesn't *feel* evil," she said.

"Maris, this is almost certainly a trap, come on," Toran urged, trying to motion her away.

"Or, it's a special thing that's been waiting for someone with special abilities to come along and find it," she countered.

"If you want to kill yourself, fine," I said flippantly, backing away with the hope she'd drop the matter.

Instead, she gave me a challenging look. "Fine."

Before anyone could stop her, she bent down to touch the shield.

I braced for an explosion or Darkness tendril to lash out at us. Instead, Maris simply picked it up.

"It's light," she commented, holding it in both hands.

I didn't let my guard down. "You're insane."

"No, just really sick of the three of you getting to do everything cool." She started to loop her arm through the strap at the back of the shield. "It fits—"

She cut off with a yelp of surprise as a shimmering silver forcefield appeared around her.

I jumped back from it. "Whoa…" The silver-hued bubble extended from the edges of the shield to make a protective barrier around her, moving as she moved.

"This is amazing!" she exclaimed. "See, told you!"

"You are so frickin' lucky," Kaiden muttered.

"I think you're envious." Maris grinned.

He only shook his head with exasperation in response.

"There's no telling what this thing does, Maris," Toran cautioned.

"I can sense it," she replied. Her fingers traced along the jewels with a contemplative expression. "It wants me to have it."

I sighed. "If you say so."

I couldn't explain how the shield came to be in that place, but I knew what she meant about the artifact feeling 'right' in her possession. I'd felt the same way when I first received my Valor artifact sword, and I felt like a part of me was missing whenever it wasn't at my side. As bizarre as it was, maybe Maris *was* supposed to find this shield here.

Or, it would slowly drive us all mad until we killed each other through some horrible curse. Despite us not instantly dying, I wasn't ready to take 'trap' off the table until I learned more about the artifact.

Either way, I didn't want to linger. The shadows continued to shift in the dark edges of the room, almost like they knew we were talking about them. I couldn't tell if my eyes were playing tricks on me, but some of them seemed to be moving independently from the vines.

"You have your thing now. Let's keep going," I suggested, returning my hand to the hilt of my sword.

Kaiden, likewise, tightened the grip on his staff. "This chamber is even more unnerving than the last."

"Speak for yourselves!" Maris practically skipped forward, the glimmering silver forcefield still around her.

I had to admit, a portable magic shield was a spectacular find.

I feigned confidence as I followed her deeper into the cavern, sweeping my gaze around the walls and ceiling every few seconds. I was certain there was something following us, even though I hadn't been able to get a clear look. Any kind of creature that had been locked in a dark cavern for stars-knew-how-long wasn't something I wanted to meet—especially not while I felt like I was losing my mind.

We continued forward at a steady pace. Halfway into the two-hundred-meter-long chamber, a breeze rustled my hair; I hadn't sensed any air currents since we descended the ramp. I spun around to check for signs of movement behind me. Before I'd pivoted a quarter of the way, a solid form bashed into my left side, knocking me to the ground.

Grunts of surprise sounded from my friends, and they collapsed next to me.

My combat instinct took over, and drew my sword in one swift movement while leaping to my feet. Kaiden's light orb still illuminated my surroundings, but there was nothing there.

"What hit us?" Maris asked, raising protective shields around each of us.

I felt a touch safer with the purple shell around me, though I was still on edge. "I don't see anything."

Kaiden jumped to his feet, hefting his staff. "It's like it came out of nowhere."

"I thought I saw something in the shadows, but I wasn't sure," Toran said.

"Same." I shifted my position so my friends were facing away from my back.

"Okay, so it wasn't just me." Maris gulped.

A dark mass passed across the corner of my vision. Without thinking, I sent a telekinetic disintegrating pulse from my focusing glove toward the movement. As if in slow motion, even without one of Maris' time-bending haste spells active, the creature dodged the attack and then disappeared, seemingly into thin air.

"What?" I tensed, looking around for it. "Where did it go?"

"You saw it?" Kaiden asked.

"Yeah, it was right—"

I cut off when Maris yelped. Her shield clattered to the ground and she lurched sideways with a cry of agony, falling—three bleeding claw marks raked the left side of her abdomen. She gasped in pain.

"Over here!" Toran ran to stand over her, his fists armored by their magical gauntlets, raised in defense.

Kaiden and I pivoted so the three of us formed a protective triangle around Maris.

"Are you okay?" I asked her.

"I'll live," she replied, pressing her right palm over the wound. Green healing light spread from her fingertips to the gashes, and the wounds began to close. "New rule: don't drop your shield when something unexpectedly slams into it."

"Also, I thought these clothes were supposed to be slash-proof!" Kaiden exclaimed.

"Yeah. They have been for everything else," I said.

"Shit, it was moving faster than I could see," Kaiden murmured, a quaver in his voice. He picked up Maris' shield where she'd dropped it and handed it to her.

"Thanks." She looped her arm through the shield's back strap again, so it re-formed a forcefield around her.

"The creature is still out there, and there might be more." I scanned the shadows, looking for any sign of where it may have gone. I'd never seen anything move like it—lightning-quick attacks and then vanishing completely.

"We need a haste augmentation," Kaiden urged Maris.

Her wounds had healed, leaving bright pink scrapes down her side, but she still looked pale. "I'll try," she replied weakly. When she raised her hand, I didn't see the characteristic orange cast to my surroundings to indicate that the haste spell had activated. "I'm not…"

"Finish healing, and hold onto that shield," I told her. "We'll handle this." How, exactly, I had no idea. At the moment, I didn't even know *what* we were fighting.

My wonder didn't last for long—a sleek, black creature materialized in front of me, swiping a three-clawed limb toward my head.

I leaned backward just in time for the razor-sharp tips to miss my neck, simultaneously attempting to drive my sword into its belly. The creature arched its midsection to avoid my counterattack, then partially dissolved as it spiraled sideways toward Kaiden. He was ready with an electrical attack, sending a lightning bolt at the alien creature.

It froze in place, allowing me to get a proper look at it for the first time. The creature had elements of the other beings we'd encountered that were products of the Darkness. Its body was similar to the shadowcats from Windau, though it had a more elongated head and fanged jaw like the first creatures we'd fought on the Valor world. Its four, powerful limbs ended in what looked like a dexterous cross between a paw and a talon, with three retractable claws on the front and a shorter one facing backward; pads on the palm would allow for silent movement when it walked on either two or four limbs. A tail extended from its hindquarters—not entirely organic in appearance, but rather transitioning from apparently solid flesh to shifting, black smoke. Perhaps the most distinctive feature, though, was its red eyes positioned at the front center of its face, which sparkled with the depth of staring into the cosmos, mesmerizing me.

I'd seen those eyes before on the alien ship. And those limbs, the movements… it was exactly the kind of form I'd expect to occupy the modified city on the surface above us.

"Elle, get—" Kaiden had barely spoken before the creature disappeared again.

"Where—" The wind was knocked out of me as I flew forward, my back on fire where a paw had thwacked me. Next to me, Kaiden was toppling toward the ground.

As I fell, I glimpsed the creature lunging at Toran while he tried to protect Maris.

I realized the attack on me and Kaiden had been a distraction all along. The creature was going after Maris, our healer—who was also the weakest member of our team—and Toran—the physically strongest combatant—aiming to take both of them out of the equation first and minimize our chances to fight back. This wasn't a mindless assault like the shadowcreatures from the other world, it was demonstrating a smart, careful strategy to disable, not kill. It wanted us.

We'd finally come face-to-face with our real enemy.

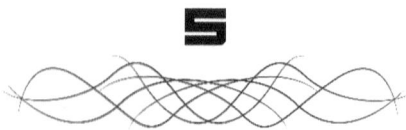

TORAN'S EYES LOCKED with the creature's as it pinned his shoulders to the ground. It leaned in closer, eyes flashing.

"N-no," Toran stammered, trying to pull away.

The creature tilted its head while digging its front claws into his shoulders.

I wanted to yell at him to fight back, but I couldn't bring myself to move or react. It was as though I was frozen, somehow at peace with what I was seeing. The impulse to break free surged in my mind, yet I could do nothing.

Maris and Kaiden appeared to be equally frozen. Their gazes were fixed on the creature.

A series of percussive clicks sounded next to me and from behind. My pulse spiked, fearing another of the creatures had appeared to finish us off. However, I detected no physical presence, despite the sound seeming to come from multiple directions at once. It was then I realized that I'd only heard the sound in my mind.

The clicks repeated, morphing into a low trill, almost like a cat's purr. The sound sent a shiver through my body, pulsing in my head. I was transfixed.

Without stepping from where it had Toran pinned, the alien creature came to examine the rest of us while we were immobilized. Ghostly copies of the creature separated from its physical form, one gliding over to inspect each of us. I could see through the beast as it approached me, yet I sensed heat radiating from it. Dazzling red eyes bore into mine as the ghostly figure leaned in until it was only centimeters from my face.

Dark, nimble tendrils unfurled from where they had been folded against the creature's sleek torso. The dozens of tentacle-like tendrils attached to its lean chest and shoulders traced their way over my face and down my body, seeming to search for something. When they reached my sword, the tendrils recoiled, and a new series of clicks filled my mind.

My heart pounded in my chest. I could sense the creature was angry, but I didn't know why. I willed my mouth to work so I could yell at it to get away, yet I was still unable to move any more than was necessary to draw breath. It could kill me right now and there would be nothing I could do to stop it.

"Leave me alone!" I shouted in my mind. It took all the energy I could muster to articulate the words. Even then, I wasn't sure they would come through or if the creature would understand.

Another flurry of clicks sounded and the purr intensified. The tentacles quivered and swirled in what may have been nonverbal communication outside my frame of reference.

"Why are you doing this to us?" I tried to ask it telepathically, hoping that it could glean some meaning from my thoughts. The Hegemony had hoped to communicate with this race and find a peaceable solution without war; while I still didn't believe that was possible, maybe we could at least learn their motivations and use that information to minimize loss of life on both sides.

The creature tilted its head, and a new chittering sound filled my mind. The clicks and tonal purr began to morph, turning into whispering voices. I couldn't make out what they were saying, but it sounded like it could be a language produced by my tongue, if only I knew what to say.

"I don't understand," I told it.

The whispers rose again. *"Steal."* The single word stood out from the din.

"Steal? Steal what?" I asked.

"Never enough."

I couldn't tell what the creature was saying. Did it want to steal something, or was it accusing us of being thieves? Everything we possessed we'd come by honestly, and I certainly wasn't about to let the alien take something from me, regardless of the reason.

"You can't control us." I tried to put force behind the words, but my

present situation of being pinned in its presence hadn't given me a lot of confidence in myself.

The creature's expression changed into what I interpreted to be a sneer. *"So weak, so limited. Doesn't even know what it is."*

The last part of the statement caught me by surprise. Was that a comment about me, specifically? Did it know why I had a combination of abilities? *"What do you know?"* I asked it.

Its red eyes flared, and the whispers in my mind fell quiet. The creature pressed its face toward mine. *"Kill."*

Messages didn't get much clearer than that. I needed to break free—immediately.

The telepathic hold still had me pinned in place. I told my legs and arms to move, but the commands could never fully form in my head. I tried to scream, to cry out. Try as I might, no more than the faintest whimper escaped my lips.

I'd been a warrior only minutes before, able to leap and fight. Now, I was helpless, even though there was nothing physically holding me.

My friends still seemed unable to move. But, if we didn't do something, this creature seemed intent on killing us.

"You can't control us," I told the creature again, believing it more this time. If the being was so strong, it could have ended us already. Either it was waiting to play with us more, or it knew we couldn't be taken out as easily as it wanted us to think. I chose to believe the latter.

"Kill."

"No!" I shouted back in my mind. *"You can't stop us."* More than anything, I wanted to break free. I willed myself, trying to believe it was possible. The only thing holding me in place was my own mind.

I still couldn't do it. I was trapped.

The creature extended its strange tentacles to surround me. *"Death."*

Toran's fists shot upward from where he had been splayed on the ground, driving his metal gauntlets into either side of the creature's head. It reared, and the echoed versions of itself were sucked back into its body.

The paralyzing hold was broken.

Kaiden hurled a fireball at the creature from where he was lying on the ground, engulfing it in blue flames.

The creature leaped off Toran, unfazed by the flames, and rounded on Kaiden. Most of its tentacles smoothed back to form a protective armor over its body, but four remained at its side, which morphed into spearheads angled forward on the flexible tendrils.

While it was focused on Kaiden, I took the opportunity to jump to my feet and run toward it, sword in hand. It seemed to sense me coming, disappearing in a blink only to reappear behind me a moment later.

"Some haste magic would be great!" I shouted to Maris.

This time, my vision tinted orange in response to her magic. I rounded on the alien creature and found that my faster movements were now a match for the creature's abilities. It was trying to disappear again, but I could see the transparency beginning to form a moment before it transitioned. I could maybe reach it in time.

I lunged at it with my sword, going for speed over precision. The blade barely missed the top of its shoulders.

The creature disappeared and I paused, waiting to see where it would reemerge.

An electrical bolt cast by Kaiden clued me in that the creature was manifesting to my right. It was only halfway solid, the electrical assault apparently interfering with its ability to fully materialize in our spacetime. But, we needed to kill it, or at least wound it enough so it wouldn't want to come back. I assumed it would have to fully materialize for any physical damage to be effective.

"Hold it there," I told Kaiden, running into position.

I approached on its right and Toran ran over to the left while Kaiden continued to cast a continuous electrical bolt.

"I can't keep this up!" Kaiden warned.

"Let go!" I told him.

The moment he released the bolt, Toran pummeled it from one side while I sent a telekinetic blast from my glove. The creature bucked and undulated, its skin shimmering as the tentacles folded around its torso absorbed the blows. I sent another telekinetic blast, but the creature compressed and rose onto two legs, then bent over itself to turn the other direction.

"No you don't." Maris lobbed an electrical orb at it—weak compared to Kaiden's, but enough to get the creature's attention.

Clicks and trills filled my mind again, and the creature took a step toward Maris. Her face went blank, falling back into a telepathic trance.

"Maris, stay focused!" I ran after the creature in an attempt to distract it. I'd gone no more than two steps when the coloration of my vision returned to normal; the haste spell had been broken.

At the edge of my perception, the creature's body started to become semi-transparent, allowing me to see the world behind it. It was about to slip away.

I lunged forward and drove my sword through the broadest part of its torso. As the flaming blade passed through, the creature's body re-solidified. Its flesh disintegrated as the corpse dropped. Before it reached the ground, the entire body had turned to dust, leaving no trace behind.

I stood in shocked silence, working my mouth until I could form coherent words. "What in the stars just happened?"

"That was… an alien, I guess?" Kaiden replied. "I have no idea what's going on."

"Why did it disintegrate like that?" I checked my sword for blood, but there was nothing to clean. "Some of the other creatures we've fought did when they died, but this was instant—and it didn't bleed."

"It may have to do with it being a higher-dimension creature," Toran replied. "We've fought hybrids before, but a true higher-dimensional being… that's a different matter."

"It was in my mind. I couldn't move," Maris murmured.

"I've never felt so helpless." I caught myself. "Well, not since we were modified."

"Yeah, no kidding. I couldn't even form a complete thought," Kaiden said.

Maris shuddered. "Me either."

"I tried to talk to it in my head, but I'm not sure it understood," I said. "I asked it what it wanted, and it just said 'kill'."

"How friendly!" Kaiden's attempted sarcasm felt hollow in the moment.

"I tried to communicate with it, too," Toran said. "I sensed it was frustrated with me."

"Really? How?" I asked.

He frowned. "I'm not sure. I believe it had hoped that I'd be completely submissive, and my ability to resist it caught it by surprise."

Kaiden scowled. "What was it after? If it was to 'kill', like Elle's encounter would indicate, why didn't it take us out when it had the chance. It was toying with us."

"We're different," I said. "We have abilities the rest of our kind don't. I think it was curious about us."

"But it also found us weak," Toran added.

"Yeah, said something similar to me, too." I nodded. "I think it figured it could take all the time it wanted with us and we wouldn't get the upper hand."

Toran's brow knit, but he didn't say anything.

"I could see why it was so confident. The way it moved... it was there, and then it wasn't." Maris shook her head. "How is that possible?"

Toran stared at the space the creature had occupied. "It never left."

"What do you mean?" I asked.

"I believe we were watching a dimensional shift. We couldn't 'see' it when it moved through a higher dimension, but it was still governed by our spacetime rules when it existed in our 3D framework," he explained.

"It used those shifts to corner us," I said. "That was smart."

"Not *that* smart," Kaiden countered. "If it was, indeed, at least a fourth-dimensional creature— able to move across the fourth-dimension of time, or in an even higher dimension—then it should have been able to know our movements and avoided being struck."

I thought over the battle. "It did seem to always be ahead of us."

"But it's dead, we saw it dissolve. Wouldn't a creature residing in a dimension above spacetime be able to see the outcome and know how to avoid dying?" Maris insisted.

Toran smiled with wonder. "Not necessarily. To such a being, the past and present would be solid, but possible futures would still be foggy. All the same, it may not be dead—only the physical form existing in our spacetime destroyed. There's no way to know."

Kaiden sighed. "Anything we say here we're just making up. We have next to no information to go on."

"Our observations will help to reveal the full picture," Toran mused.

"You've gotten way too philosophical in the last few minutes," I interjected. "What went on back there? Were you communing with that thing?"

Toran's brows drew together. "I did feel strangely linked to it. It wanted to enter the deeper parts of my mind."

"I couldn't feel anything," Maris admitted. "I was trapped within myself. I didn't know how to have a thought of my own in that moment."

Kaiden nodded. "Yeah, it was like there was another presence there, subsuming me."

The accounts were eerily similar to what I had experienced. I found it curious that Toran and I had been able to maintain a sense of identity during the encounters while Kaiden and Maris had been completely lost, but I didn't know what it meant. Toran had certainly fared the best of all of us, able to break free while the rest of us were helpless. I had to say that I really appreciated the span of skills on our team; it seemed like one of us was always able to come through for the others, regardless of the situation.

"I hope we never come across another one of those things again," Maris murmured.

"Don't count on it," I replied, trying to be realistic. "I still don't know if those are the alien masterminds or just a brand of their minions, but I can only imagine there are a lot more where that one came from. And, if we *did* kill it, the others will be pissed."

"Stars, pretty sure they're going to be pissed, regardless. If that thing was supposed to kill us but didn't, we're unfinished business," Kaiden said.

I frowned. "Speaking of which, why haven't we been swarmed?"

Toran was about to reply then hesitated. "That's a good point. If they can transition between the planes at will, then dozens of them could have come the moment the creature was in trouble."

Maris looked around the chamber suspiciously. "So why aren't they here?"

"The transition might not be straightforward for them," Kaiden suggested. "Maybe this one was already here and others can't just do it on the fly?"

I shrugged. "Regardless of the reason, I'm quite happy not being attacked."

"I always get talked into going places, and then evil aliens from a higher dimension get involved..." Maris sighed.

"Didn't we say that the only predictable thing is unpredictability?" I said. "Or maybe I made that up just now, I can't remember."

Maris pressed the heel of her right hand to her temple. "My brain feels mushy."

"Well, we can either turn around and have the evil aliens come after us while we get nothing in return, or we can forge ahead and get what we

came for, and hopefully figure out how to take them out in the process,"
I stated.

"Ahead," Kaiden replied.

Toran nodded.

Maris rolled her eyes and sighed. "You know my complaints never go
anywhere."

I ventured a smile. "Forward it is."

6

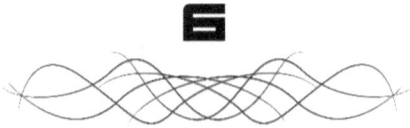

MARIS CAST ANOTHER haste spell now that she was healed, and we jogged toward the far end of the chamber. The dark tendrils still writhed in the shadows by the wall, but I saw no larger shapes lurking among them. I still wasn't confident if there had been more than one of the creatures in the chamber, but it either *had* been alone or the others had since fled. Either way, I was happy we didn't need to face another battle immediately.

As we approached the final quarter of the chamber, the volume of dark tendrils multiplied and extended further from the walls. By the time we were traversing the final meters, only a narrow path remained through the crystal dust on the stone floor, framed on either side by the weaving tendrils infected by the Darkness.

The ceiling and walls of the chamber also tapered, ultimately funneling us into a tunnel that was fully lined with the black foliage.

"Can't say I'm excited about going through there," I said, eyeing the two-meter-wide space. The ceiling of the tunnel would allow Toran to pass through without stooping, but only barely.

"I think we're almost to the end," Kaiden said.

"Might be wishful thinking," I replied.

"I don't know… there's a strong energy coming from the other side of this tunnel." He indicated his pendant, which was now glowing as brightly as it did when in the crystal canyon on Crystallis.

"I hope you're right." I stepped through the opening.

The tunnel continued for six meters before opening into another cavern. This chamber was on a more intimate scale than the two others we'd been through, with a four-meter-tall ceiling and approximately six-meter diameter. At the center of the space, a spherical crystal sat atop a carved stone pedestal. The dark tendrils wove around the base of the pedestal, seeming to merge with the crystal sphere at its base.

Despite the unnerving sight of the Darkness flowing out of the crystal, I was heartened by the sight of the sphere. I immediately recognized it as being a viewing device like the one in the secret room on the *Evangiel*. "That's promising."

"It is," Toran agreed, "though not what I was expecting."

I checked around the room to make sure there were no creatures lurking in the shadows. The spherical crystal at the center of the space was certainly the prize, and it wouldn't surprise me at all if it was guarded.

"Looks clear," Kaiden said, completing his own assessment with the aid of a light orb.

"What are we supposed to do with it?" Maris asked. "I kinda figured there's be, you know, a *doorway* somewhere. Don't we already have one of these?"

"This is one of the most powerful pieces of technology known to our civilization," Toran said. "If it's also here, I suspect we haven't been using ours to its full potential."

"Well, *we* haven't actually used it. Or, this version of us..." Kaiden faded out.

Maris raised an eyebrow. "Haven't we?"

Kaiden wilted. "You know, I've kind of lost track of what it means to be 'me' at this point, honestly."

"Doesn't matter." Toran stepped forward, focused on the device.

"Do you think we could use this to get information out of the Master Archive that we weren't able to get before?" I asked.

"I don't see why it would be any different," Kaiden replied.

"There are many reasons why it could be," Toran said, crouching down to look underneath the sphere. To my eye, it was suspended inside the stone cradle with no other attachments.

I crossed my arms. "You clearly have something in mind. Care to enlighten us?"

He frowned at the sphere. "There's no guarantee that this world is on the same crystalline network."

"Wait, *what*?" I gaped at him. "There are multiple networks?"

"We don't know for certain," he admitted. "I was talking through potential theories with the Hegemony scientists, and Lisa tossed that out a as a possibility."

"Lisa?" Kaiden questioned.

"A quantum physicist—at least, that's the closest field of study with a readily pronounceable name. She specializes in the subatomic mechanics we believe are related to the crystalline network's hyperdimensional links."

I stared at Toran. "You seriously either had no free time in your life before, or there's a lot more to being a maintenance tech than you're letting on."

He finally softened. "Why is everyone still so surprised I'm not illiterate in science? I majored in physics for a couple of years before I switched to engineering, okay?"

Kaiden eyed him. "If you say so. Now, what was that about multiple crystalline networks?"

"Well, the idea was that bandwidth would eventually tap out, as we've discussed before. While the hyperdimensional storage itself is theoretically limitless, there are still bottlenecks when it comes to retrieving data through the crystal interfaces. So, in an infinite universe, it may become impossible for a crystalline network to process all requests—it might need to be segmented," Toran explained.

"Different networks, but linked?" I asked.

"Yes, they would need to communicate with one another, such as to implement a universal reset. But, different sets of worlds may operate on different sub-networks from one another to streamline localized resets."

"And, what does that have to do with this device?" Kaiden prompted.

"Maybe if there *are* different subnetworks, that also means there are different Archives," Toran replied.

"But, the Master Archive is—"

"The only one that the Hegemony knows about," Toran cut me off. "That doesn't mean it's the only one in existence."

Maris pursed her lips. "If these aliens function on a different network, that might explain how no one has come across them before—at least not in recent history."

"That was my thought," Toran said. "But, keep in mind that this is all hypothetical. There *may* only be one network and the bandwidth issue is handled through other means. Decades more research will be needed to understand these systems."

"Could that explain how the aliens knew about the space battle and were able to head us off after our first reset?" I asked.

"Yes, being on a different network could explain the difference in recollection. More likely, however, that was a product of residing in a higher dimensional plane. Given what we saw with the creature today, I'm still leaning toward that being the most likely scenario."

"Which, again, means that they're watching us right now," I said. "We shouldn't stand around here doing nothing."

"While I agree wholeheartedly, I don't think it would be wise to attempt to use this device without some careful consideration," Toran countered.

"If you want to study it, then study it," I said, unable to keep a touch of exasperation out of my tone. He'd already said it was impossible for us to know what the device did without direct contact, so staring at it wasn't going to get answers—we needed to just *use it* and figure out the rest later.

Toran sighed. "I know this is frustrating, but I don't want us to walk into a worse trap than we're already in."

"Noted, but leaping first and looking later is kinda how we roll," Kaiden said.

"In this matter, I highly advise against it," Toran continued. "The way I see it, there are three possible outcomes for interacting with this device. First, we might be able to use it as a viewer, either for the sealed Master Archive—in which case, we'd only get a 'no signal' type response—or we'd confirm the presence of at least one other Archive, thereby indicating that we're now under the influence of a separate crystalline network.

"Secondly, we might inadvertently trigger another universal reset. We know from experience that these devices are used as a control mechanism for those. Though I know we don't have a Master Crystal shard with us, there's no telling if there are other factors that could initiate a reset."

"That's a disturbing prospect," I said.

Kaiden frowned. "And this sphere has the Darkness vine-things coming out of it, and it might be connected to those beings. If we initiated a reset from this point, that might... I don't know what, but it seems like it would be bad."

"Yes, very bad," Toran said. "For all we know, it could be a master plan to trigger a complete restructuring of all the Hegemony's worlds at once, completing the transformation by the Darkness."

"That…" I didn't know what to say. It sounded like a brilliant master plan, in theory, except it was missing a crucial 'why' justification. I also had no explanation for how the aliens would know we would come here—aside from a fuzzy-future vision that we did—or why we would need to be the ones to activate the viewer rather than doing it themselves. Unless… I stopped trying to rationalize it. There were too many offshoots to chase; I needed to take it one thing at a time.

"And what's the third option?" I asked instead, hoping to complete the picture of likely possibilities before delving into the details of each scenario.

Toran took a deep breath. "This might open a dimensional doorway to allow us access to a higher plane—or multiple planes."

That was certainly the most mind-twisting of all the explanations. "Okay, let's table that one for a moment," I suggested. "Back to the idea about it triggering another universal reset. How would that be possible?"

"Well, different crystals have different properties," Toran said. "Colren spoke about Master Crystal shards being used in concert with the viewing devices to spark a reset, but there would be no way to tell if a shard was already inside one of the spheres, right? We used the shard at the same time as we touched it to activate the reset, but maybe we could have melded the two before and programmed it with special properties, so the next person to touch it—however far off in the future—would activate it."

I stared at Toran. "Not saying that you're wrong, but that sounds *really* paranoid and far-fetched for what this sphere thing might do."

"Normally I'd second that assessment, Elle, but we *are* talking about potential fifth-dimensional beings," Kaiden said.

"Regardless, it doesn't make sense," I insisted. "Why set a trap for us to initiate a reset?"

"They could just do it themselves," Maris said, echoing my own thoughts from earlier.

"Unless they can't, for whatever reason," Kaiden pointed out. "Maybe the interface doesn't work for higher dimensional beings."

I considered the thought. "Maybe, but still. What possible purpose would a reset serve? I don't buy the idea of them using a reset to transform all the worlds at once; they're already well on their way to accomplishing that end, and speeding up the process would be irrelevant for beings that aren't locked into a unidirectional flow of time as we know it. For that matter, what in the stars do they even care about spacetime?"

"I don't know," Toran admitted after a pause.

"Which probably means that's *not* what's going on here," I concluded.

"Yes, thinking it through, that does seem the most unlikely of the three scenarios," Toran stated.

"All right, so that leaves the option of it being a viewing device that may or may not work, or it being a dimensional doorway," I summarized.

"Or Option D," Maris said. "I'll just note that as 'unknown doom'. The letter even syncs up!"

"Or 'death'," Kaiden added.

I gave them each a horrified look and shook my head. "Moving on… The remaining options are either benign, such as the viewer, or going to turn our universe upside down as we know it."

"Sounds like it," Kaiden agreed.

"So, I say we just go for it," I said.

Toran shook his head. "Elle—"

I shrugged. "Yeah, it's probably dangerous and foolish, but what else is new with us?"

"I know I'll regret saying this, but I think we should do it," Maris said.

Kaiden let out a long breath. "I've got nothing else. Sure, why not? I always used to say how much I wanted to go sightseeing on another dimensional plane one day."

Maris eyed him. "You were a weird kid."

"I'm joking!" Kaiden rolled his eyes. "You in, Toran?"

The other man looked between us and the sphere. "I suppose that is the only way to find out."

"That's the spirit!" I drew my sword. "We should probably be ready in case this teleports us into some crazy alien fighting ring."

"I *wasn't* hoping for a dimensional access point, but I'll take that over an alien death pit," Maris said.

Kaiden chuckled, readying his staff. "Elle, you have entirely too active an imagination."

Something told me reality was about to get a whole lot weirder than whatever I could dream up. "Everyone ready?"

My friends nodded.

Weapons in hand, we reached out to touch the crystal.

7

MY SWORD RADIATED heat in my left palm as I made contact with the crystal orb. Reality distorted around me, appearing to unfold—or maybe *I* was unfolding.

For a moment, everything around me became blindingly bright, overwhelming my vision with white light. Then, there was only blackness.

I tensed. Had we initiated a reset after all? I searched around me, desperate to find a clue about what had happened. Nothing seemed to be there. My friends were nowhere in sight. Panic welled in my mind, but I had no physical form to respond to the emotion.

Reality unfolded around me yet again, almost like I was turning to the opposite side of a window and the blackness I'd floated in was the side edge. Forms slowly resolved, and I found myself standing next to my friends.

"What just—" I cut off when I noticed our surroundings.

If I didn't know better, I'd thought I had walked into a house of mirrors. Every surface was a semi-reflective window, as though I was inside a crystal prism looking at a cross section of moments in time. Catching the angle of the reflective windows just right, infinite variations of the events from that moment branched like fractals inside it. Past moments were clear, but branches toward the future were foggy.

The sight was beautiful, but the sheer magnitude of possibilities was enough to make me lightheaded. "How did we get here?"

"Through the crystal," Toran stated. "Well, not *through* it. We transitioned to a higher dimension. This is fascinating."

No wonder my head ached.

"If the devices are the same, why didn't this happen when we did the resets before?" Maris questioned.

"It might be a matter of intention," Toran replied. "We *wanted* there to be a reset before, took efforts to think of a specific moment in time when we wanted to reset to. In this instance, we wanted to gain awareness of the higher planes."

I stared around me in wonder. "The crystals really can read our thoughts."

"It's all energy," Toran said. "The network—and the viewing devices, specifically—are attuned to picking up on the subtleties in those energy patterns. The biomechanics of it are really quite remarkable."

Kaiden spun around, taking in our surroundings. "It doesn't seem possible."

I studied the images. "What are these?"

"Windows across time and space." Excitement filled Toran's eyes. "I can't believe I resisted touching the sphere—to miss out on coming here. This confirms everything."

Kaiden looked as frazzled as I felt. "What are you talking about?"

"Follow any one thread, and it could lead to any past time or place," Toran murmured. "Each dimension telling its own story, with paths intersecting across time."

I stared at the images around me. They seemed to only be of the chamber where we had been standing moments before. "That doesn't seem right, Toran."

"Just because we can't see it yet, it doesn't mean it's not there," he said cryptically.

"Did that creature mess with his head?" I whispered to Kaiden.

"Maybe. None of this is making sense."

I cleared my throat. "Are we... inside the crystal?"

"Not inside, no," Toran replied. "That was only a means to help us see what was already around us. The crystal is still here, see?" He pointed to a semi-transparent sphere. "We're just now aware of the levels that exist above that spacetime reality. Right now, we're outside—or, rather, above—the flow of time as we know it. Six-, seventh-, eight-dimension, maybe? It's difficult to say."

"All right, so the crystal *was* a hyperdimensional portal," Kaiden said. "Yay us?"

"Not a portal," Toran corrected. "A trans-dimensional interface—"

"A TDI, we know," I said. "But 'portal' is *so* much easier to grasp conceptually, Toran."

"But it's not accurate."

I sighed. "*Anyway,* I was right. You didn't think it was," I ribbed Kaiden.

"Can you blame me?" he replied. "It sounded nuts."

"More than us having magic?"

Kaiden groaned. "That can't be your retort for everything unexpected."

"Hey, we don't have our packs," Maris realized.

I reached for the straps on my shoulders and found them suspiciously absent. "That's weird Why did our clothes and weapons come but not the packs?"

Kaiden shook his head. "I don't—"

"Quiet." Toran held up his hand, listening. "I'm not sure we're alone."

"Don't tell me this is where those creatures live," Kaiden said in a lower voice.

Toran listened for several more seconds and then shook his head. "Not to be pessimistic, but I suspect we're in a higher dimensional plane than those beings reside. What we may encounter here could be worse."

"Thanks, Toran. I feel *way* better." I tightened the grip on my sword.

"Wait, a *higher* dimension than them? How?" Kaiden questioned.

Toran ignored the question. "We shouldn't stay in one place."

"No, we're not going *anywhere* until we know what's going on here," I insisted.

"I told you," Toran began, "we're now, at a minimum, in the sixth- or seventh-dimension—"

"No, Toran, not just labels for things. That is completely meaningless to me right now as I stare through hyperdimensional windows into infinity! How does anything function in this place? How do we get *back*?"

Kaiden placed a gentle hand around my upper arm. "I'm freaking out, too, but *literally* freaking out isn't a good idea right now."

"I don't know, this does seem pretty freak-out-worthy," Maris said, though her tone was surprisingly level.

It seemed impossible that I was the one losing my composure. Maris was supposed to be the high-strung person on our team, not me. Was I overreacting?

I took a deep breath. It *was* a breath, right? There was still air in the higher dimensions? My head swam as I started to think about the bizarre mechanics of the world around me. Was I actually under the influence of gravity, or was this entire place a construct formed by my team's combined preconceptions about what reality was supposed to be? Would it all vanish if we were to suddenly stop believing in it?

My heart was racing. The clothes on my back were suddenly too heavy for me to bear. I panted for breath.

"Elle." Kaiden tightened his grip on my arm—firm, but still loving. "Elle, look at me." He stepped into my sightline, bending his knees to look me square in the eyes, leaning close to block out the dizzying views all around me.

His familiar face and touch took the edge off my anxiety, allowing it to recede enough for me to catch my breath.

"Hey, that's more like it," he said when my breathing normalized, offering a reassuring smile. "You're okay."

I swallowed, my cheeks flushing from embarrassment. "Sorry, I can't believe I lost it."

Maris waved her hand like it was nothing, flashing me a sweet, concerned smile.

"I don't think this was a random panic attack," Toran said pensively. "This is out of character for you."

"Heh," I grunted. "I thought it was." So much for being the calm warrior wise beyond my years.

Toran shook his head. "No, that creature we encountered—I believe that your... reaction may have been a result of its telepathic influence."

I did a double-take. "What?!"

"I sensed it in my mind, trying to introduce doubts," he explained. "But this wasn't the first time you encountered one of them, right?"

I thought back over the past week, recalling when my attitude had started to change. "True, I saw that one on the alien ship before we detonated the disruptor. Could that one have done something to me?"

"Perhaps. And, you said you've been feeling 'off'?" Toran asked.

I nodded.

"Maybe the creature we just encountered picked up on that kernel left behind by the other and exploited it, to mess with your emotional regulation. How are you now?"

"I dunno." My panic was receding and my thoughts were becoming more lucid. "Definitely getting better."

Toran evaluated me. "Well, it's possible that the dimensional transition may have broken its mental influence—we don't know what kind of changes our bodies may have undertaken during the transition, but it's clearly significant."

"Then why did I freak out *after* we got here?" I asked.

"Perhaps it was the sudden purging of the mental influence, bringing all of the subconscious thoughts they'd implanted to the surface at once."

"They had subconsciously re-programmed me?" I shivered. "That's a terrifying thought."

Toran shook his head. "That might be an overly dramatic characterization. It seems like they did little more than introduce some self-doubts—likely with the intention of making you easier to control. It seemed to want to subdue and study us."

"It also said 'kill'," I reminded him.

"Yes, but it could have easily killed us. I believe it wanted something from us first."

I swallowed. "I think that's actually *worse*."

He smiled warmly. "You've always been calm under pressure, Elle. This wasn't like you. I'd wager a small fortune those creatures had something to do with it."

The notion that I had been under psychological assault shook me even more than if I'd had a blade to my throat. What would have happened if I'd broken down in the middle of battle when my friends needed me the most?

"I might still be dangerous—" I started.

"Elle, all of us are probably just as mind-warped as you," Kaiden cut in.

"Very true," Toran agreed. "But, like I said, this dimensional transition likely disrupted any telepathic influence we may have been under."

"Regardless, you can't call yourself out as being the weak link here, Elle," Kaiden continued. "None of us are. The Dark Sentinels are a quartet, and we take care of our own."

It was funny to think of such fierce loyalty after only a few weeks together, but the experiences we had shared were more intense than what some people would endure in an entire lifetime. Even if I didn't fully trust myself at the moment, I did trust in the integrity of my companions. As long as we stuck together, we'd find a way to make it through each challenge as it came.

I took a few more slow, deep breaths. The nausea and dizziness were passing. "Thanks, guys. I hope it doesn't come up again, but I know I'm in good hands if it does."

"We'll watch each other. We're not in this alone," Maris said.

I managed a weak smile. "Thanks."

Toran froze again, listening. "I maintain that there's something else here," he said softly.

Temporary insanity or not, I remembered my original objection. "If we leave this place, how will we be able to find our way back?"

Our team's resident scientist remained unnervingly silent.

"Toran...?" Kaiden prompted.

"I don't rightly know how to get back from here, I'm afraid," he admitted.

"Should we maybe test that before we wander out into the unknown expanse of a higher dimensional plane?" I asked, unable to keep a sarcastic bite out of my tone or wording.

"Back to your old self, I see," Kaiden murmured just loud enough for me to hear, giving me a playful nudge with his shoulder.

I did feel a million times better, and I'd be on guard to make sure I didn't crack like that again. Crazy emotional breakdowns didn't work well with my image.

Image... Another wave of disorientation swept over me when I took the wrong moment to look into one of the windows. I squeeze my eyes shut and took a breath, allowing the feeling to pass. I could do this. I was in control.

When I opened my eyes again, Toran was standing at the sphere.

"Do we touch it like we did last time?" Maris asked.

"I'm not sure if the sphere functions the same way here," Toran mused. "The sphere is here, but also everywhere."

"What do you mean?" I shook my head. "Why wouldn't it behave the same way?"

"What I should have said is that the sphere in our spacetime reality led here to the hyperdimensional plane—or 'frame', to be more accurate,"

Toran replied. "The different planes aren't sandwiched, but rather nested. So, accessing that same crossover point from here, though, doesn't mean we'd return to spacetime where and when we left—it's not a one-to-one portal. We could find ourselves in an even higher dimension, or a lower one somewhere between home and here. Or... well, anything is possible."

"So, we *are* trapped," I concluded.

Toran didn't counter the statement.

"And you didn't think about that possibility *before* we came here?!" Maris squeaked.

"I was quite against the idea of activating the sphere without further study. You all overruled me." Toran sighed.

"Those possibilities aside, this access point is still our closest connection to getting back home," Kaiden jumped in.

I shrugged. "I guess if we got here once, we should be able to get back."

"That's what I was thinking," he replied. "Well, *hoping*."

"Perhaps only one of us should try, in the event it doesn't work in the intended way," Toran suggested.

"What happened to sticking together?" I asked.

"Given the potential for all of us to get *more* trapped, or just one of us, it seems like having people on the outside to help might be a good thing," he said.

"Does that mean you're volunteering as gateway-tester?" Kaiden questioned.

Toran nodded. "I, frankly, have a better theoretical understanding of where we are, so I'm the most likely to fare well on my own if we get separated."

It was the truth, and I had no productive counterargument to offer; knowing Toran, his mind was already made up. "If you're going to do this, then you should probably get it over with," I told him. "If something new is stalking us, like you said..."

"Right." Toran glanced at the sphere then gave us each a heartfelt smile. "Hopefully I'll see you again soon." He reached out to touch the crystal.

Nothing happened.

"Toran?" I asked when he didn't react.

"I don't understand," he murmured at last.

"Yeah, have to say, I expected it to do *something*," Kaiden commented.

"It should have." Toran frowned. "Direct contact took us here, so reversing the procedure should have solicited a reaction of some sort."

"No finger tinglies, even?" I asked.

He cast me a look of admonishment. "Never a term I'd use, Elle."

"Hey, you just confirmed we're stuck on a hyperdimensional plane. Trying to bring a little levity to the critical situation here," I shot back.

"There has to be something else we can try," Maris said.

"I don't know what," Toran admitted.

"Well, at least we're together?" Kaiden's tone was still light, but I could see the worry in his eyes—on the verge of panicking just like me.

"I don't want to be trapped in a higher dimension forever," Maris whimpered.

We couldn't afford to feed into each other's worry and lose our heads. I'd given into that once already, and it hadn't helped anything.

While the three of us dealt with the news in our own ways, Toran seemed strangely calm about the entire situation. "I trust that we'll find a path," he said, breaking the silence. "We made it here because this is where we needed to come, and we'll find our way back when our task is complete."

The words caught me by surprise; this new philosophical Toran was a little too much about going with the flow rather than action. "Yeah, sorry if that doesn't exactly set me at ease."

"Fate might be intervening." The end of Kaiden's staff glowed brightly as he spun away from me.

A moment later, I caught sight of his target. The creature—if I could rightly call it that—floated among the windows twenty meters away, though distance didn't seem to work the same way in that place. More like a blob than a living being, the semi-transparent form sparkled with a rainbow of light, bands of color rippling over its surface in complex patterns. Surrounding the central, transparent mass was a fine mist, giving the impression of a droplet of water evaporating in the sun— except, the drop of water was at least two meters in diameter and it could move on its own accord.

"Is that a jellyfish?" Maris whispered.

"We're not underwater," Kaiden replied. "I think it's more of a blob."

"Fine, a cosmic jellyfish," she amended.

"I was going more the 'cloud' route, myself," I said, not sure if the creature was friend or foe.

"Cosmic jellycloud," Kaiden offered.

Toran held up his hand. "What are you talking about?"

"There's a floating cloud-creature thing," I explained. "You don't see it?"

Toran shook his head.

"Weird. Why—" I cut off. "It's spotted us."

The nimbus, as I elected to dub it instead, glided toward us, its light pattern twirling and reversing every half-second. I wondered if the lights might indicate a sort of language or attempt at communication.

"It looks agitated," I said to my friends, then added louder to address the nimbus, "We're friends. We don't mean any harm."

The nimbus' lights stuttered and then initiated a new pattern of colored dots and zigzags.

"I suddenly wish I spoke Cloud," Kaiden quipped.

So did I—at least enough to know if the creature meant us harm. "Maybe we should get out of here," I suggested, backing away.

Four additional nimbuses glided from behind windows near the first, fanning out to frame us in a semi-circle.

"I don't like this at all," Kaiden murmured, his staff still glowing. "Three more just appeared, Toran."

"Stars! Why can't I see them?" Toran flushed.

I hadn't sheathed my sword since entering the higher plane, and I now wondered if I should. Perhaps if the nimbuses didn't see us as a threat, they'd leave us alone. On the other hand, I'd be at a disadvantage if they chose that moment to attack. I decided to try for the middle ground, lowering my weapon into what I hoped was a non-threatening position.

"What are you doing, Elle?" Kaiden hissed.

"We're the invaders here," I reminded him. "These things look like the opposite of Darkness. Assuming they're not connected to the other aliens, there's no reason for us to make new enemies."

Hesitantly, Kaiden lowered his staff.

Toran adopted a neutral stance with his gloved hands at his sides. "I hope they can sense our good intentions."

"They might not be dangerous at all," Maris said. "They're just big, puffy cloud things."

At first glance, maybe, but I disagreed with her assessment. These were intelligent, higher-dimensional beings, as far as I was concerned, and I didn't want to get in a fight with them. Now that we were on their turf, we couldn't rely on our experiences; we'd essentially entered a new reality with its own rules.

"Let's just back away slowly," I said, trying to stay calm. I made the first move and my team followed.

After we'd gone only two steps, violent pulse of light radiated from the four nimbuses, and they began to swell, electrical bolts of energy crackling inside.

The calm and steady approach was off the table. I spun on my heels. "Nevermind. Run!"

"SHIT, THIS IS *not* how I thought this was going to go!" Kaiden exclaimed as we barreled through the maze of mirror-like windows.

All of my thoughts about keeping track of our exit point were forced aside as the storming nimbuses chased us through the endless prism faceted corridors. I tried to keep track of the turns, but the strange angles made it impossible to maintain any frame of reference.

In that moment, I didn't care. We were being chased by angry cloud monsters, and I had no intention of finding out what their electrical bolts could do to me.

The view through the windows lining the walls changed from the ruined cityscape above the caverns to open plains. We couldn't have run far enough to have left the city in our spacetime reality, supporting my instinct that distance and scale followed different rules in that place. If we kept running for long enough, we could find ourselves near gateways to an entirely different planet.

Even though we managed to stay ahead of the nimbuses, they tailed us step for step. "How can we shake these things?" I asked, once it became clear they weren't going to stop following us.

"And why haven't they just jumped in front of us?" Kaiden questioned.

I'd been curious about that part, too. The other higher-dimensional beings we'd encountered had been able to glide through the planes and seemed to know everything we were about to do.

"I wish I could see what you're talking about," Toran said while running alongside me. "But I can maybe explain their movement—they're likely native to this plane."

"Native to here?" Maris said.

Toran nodded after we made another sharp turn through the maze. "Yes, seventh- or eighth-dimensional beings, wherever we are. They can't jump in front of us because they don't have access to a higher plane to use as a shortcut. I don't quite understand the rules of this place, but they are bound by them in the way we'd be back on our plane."

"Except with our magic," I pointed out.

"Yes, we do seem to be able to bend the rules," he admitted.

I had no clue where my abilities came from, ultimately, but I could sense that the hyperdimensional component of my consciousness that regulated my abilities was still above my present place in the dimensional hierarchy. That meant that we had an advantage with our abilities over the nimbuses—even if we were 'lower beings' in every other sense. If they wouldn't leave us alone, then we'd need to fight.

"Do you think they're a security guards of some sort?" Kaiden questioned. "Or, maybe they can recognize we're lower life forms and are trying to exterminate us like we'd kill ants in our house."

I wasn't crazy about those possibilities. Either way, it wasn't looking good for us.

"Let's take a stand," I said, preparing to stop so we could face our would-be attackers. "Try not to hurt them, but we can't keep running forever."

"I'm not even tired," Kaiden said. "But you're right, this is pointless." Maris nodded.

"All right," Toran agreed. "You'll have to tell me what to do."

"Just hang back. We'll handle this." I looked to Kaiden and Maris. "Okay, now!"

I leaned back on my heels to stop my forward momentum and pivoted to face the nimbuses, raising my sword. They had expanded to more than twice their original size, now oblong four-meter-wide clouds with an internal lightning storm. Bolts of electricity struck the reflective walls, leaving no signs of damage. As my friends and I closed the distance between us and the nimbuses, the bolts lanced toward us.

Toran ducked and ran to the side. "Now *that* I can see!"

I gauged the reach of the bolts and halted just out of range. "Maris, haste!" I instructed.

"You've got it." She waved her hand in the usual fashion to initiate the spell.

My surroundings were unchanged. "What happened?" I took rapid steps backwards to keep myself out of striking range of the enemy electrical storm.

"Stars, of course!" Toran said. "We're higher than the fourth dimension—of course time manipulation wouldn't work here."

"Oh, that's bad." I ducked and dodged to the side as one of the lightning bolts came dangerously close to striking me.

Kaiden retaliated with a wave of his staff, and the outer layer of the nimbus started to freeze.

"Good thinking with the ice!" I said.

The nimbus had slowed, but it was far from disabled. The others continued advancing toward us, the colorful light patterns taking on a decidedly menacing quality.

"There's has to be something I can do." Maris waved her arms again, and a purple shield appeared around each member of our team in addition to the silver forcefield around herself courtesy to her new shield.

Before I could wonder about if Maris' magical shields around us would stop the hyperdimensional creatures, I got my answer. One of the lightning bolts branched outward and struck the edge of my protective dome. The electrical current was reflected off the dome's surface, to my relief, and then struck one of the innumerable windows. I was surprised to see the reflected electrical bolts left singe marks—that hadn't happened when the nimbuses' bolts hit the mirrors directly.

"Their bolts are interacting with our magic!" I exclaimed.

"So they are," Toran concurred. "I wouldn't have expected that."

"Wonder later. We need to take these things out!" Kaiden urged.

"Killing them is a bad idea," I insisted. "We have no idea what they are. We're the outsiders here."

"I know, but *they're* trying to kill *us*." Kaiden dodged another bolt, then expanded his freezing spell to all four.

The lightning continued to bounce off the protective domes, striking the walls and ceiling. None of the bolts had yet hit the creatures. Given that the electrical attack had come from inside them, I figured it might not be a deadly blow, but maybe it would offer the kind of stun attack we needed to allow us to escape without killing the nimbuses.

"Maris, can you use your new shield to reflect their attacks back at them?" I asked.

"Yes, I'll give it a shot," she confirmed.

"Kaiden, keep that freeze ray going," I went on, moving forward now that I knew I was protected by the shield.

"Elle, what are you doing?" Toran asked.

"I'm going to provoke them," I said. "Stir up an electrical storm so they shock themselves."

"What should I do?" he replied.

"Be ready to grab me if I get electrocuted, I guess?"

"Careful, Elle," Kaiden said softly as I pass by him.

I flashed a daring smile. "I've got this."

"Ready with the shield when you are," Maris said.

"All right... now!" I raced forward with my sword while Maris simultaneously raised her jeweled shield so she could tilt the surrounding forcefield to the appropriate angle.

The nimbuses reacted just like I'd hoped, sparking a new electrical storm. The bolts shot out all around them, many striking Maris' shield and bouncing back. With Kaiden's freezing spell, the nimbuses' advance had slowed to a crawl, trapping them in the middle of their own storm.

Their external patterns shifted again to a chaotic display of colors and lights, which was undoubtedly a sign of distress.

"That's enough!" I called out to my friends, wanting to gauge the damage to the nimbuses before taking more aggressive action.

However, just as I started to back away, the nimbus in the right-center of the group broke free from its freeze and rushed toward me, releasing a flurry of electrical bolts as it ballooned to fill the corridor.

I dove for safety, my sword arm flailing as I fell.

As the nimbus expanded, a portion of it brushed against the tip of my blade. Light flared at the point of contact, then spread through the entire creature. With a bright burst, the nimbus vanished.

"Stars! Did I just do that?" I exclaimed.

"Your sword... why did it...?" Maris trailed off.

"The others, Elle! I can't hold them!" Kaiden shouted.

My stomach twisted with the thought of potentially destroying these creatures, but my friends were right—it was us or them. I ran forward and glided my blade over the other three nimbuses while they were frozen. The magical shield Maris had cast around me offering protection from their electrical attacks. They each vanished like the first, leaving us alone in the eerie corridor.

I lowered my weapon. "I didn't want to hurt them."

"What happened?" Toran asked.

"They came apart as soon as Elle's sword touched them," Kaiden summarized. "They picked the fight, Elle. We didn't have a choice."

"Still…" I stared at my sword. Only a graze from the blade had disintegrated the nimbuses—no other creature had been instantly destroyed with so little contact.

Toran followed my gaze. "That sword does seem to have some unique properties."

"Yeah, you can say that again." I watched the flames ripple along the edge of the blade before sliding it into the scabbard at my waist, not wanting to think about what else it could do accidently. "I wish we hadn't had to fight them."

"It might not be my place to speak since I didn't see both sides of the fight," Toran said in a fatherly tone, "but I can say for certain that our presence on this plane is about more than just the four of us right here, right now."

"*Why* couldn't you see them? That makes no sense," I replied.

"I'm sure there's an explanation, I just haven't worked it out yet," he went on. "What I do know is we have a mission to complete. To do that, we need to survive. More than that, we need to become masters in this place so we can use it to defeat the beings behind the Darkness. Other creatures may have been here first, but that doesn't mean we don't also have the right to be. We tried to leave them alone, they fought us, and you did what you needed to do for us to live. Maybe others of their kind will now regard us on their level so we can coexist. Either way, we need to establish ourselves as smart and capable—worthy of our place here. Sitting back and taking what we're handed won't get us where we need to go."

"I guess fighting and killing are the reality of our situation," I admitted, though I still didn't feel good about it.

Maris nodded slowly. "Those could have been highly intelligent, evolved creatures."

"Maybe so, but this team beat them," Toran stated. "Does that make us better? Not necessarily. Stars, I couldn't even see them! But, sometimes the little guy comes out on top, like a wild cat taking out a hiker. On the whole, survival of the fittest causes species to fall into an unavoidable hierarchy. The rest of our people may never glimpse this place, but the four of us…"

Kaiden nodded pensively. "What about the fight with the aliens behind the Darkness?"

Toran chuckled. "We're at an important juncture, aren't we? You could argue that being fifth-dimensional beings makes them superior to us, so maybe it would be fair to say that they should win. Personally, I think we have the right to fight for our survival. If we can overcome the odds, we will have proven our right to live another day."

"Considering the alternative is us dying, I have to agree," I conceded.

"There's this bizarre thing about being the more evolved entity in a scenario," Toran mused. "You can see everything the lesser forms are doing wrong, but from their own vantage, they're lost and helpless. It's like a bug getting trapped in the glass of an open window. You can see the path for it to escape—all it has to do is fly around the side and it will be free. But it doesn't—just keeps beating itself against the glass. We need to see that alternate path, to earn our right to survive. We're here in this place, we have the tools. It's up to us the seize the opportunity."

"I'd like to think we're more than bugs," Kaiden said.

Toran nodded. "Yes, but it's still up to us to fly around the side of the open window."

"Debating morality isn't important right now," Maris stated. "We need to get back to our home spacetime."

"I think this fight may have given us a clue," Toran said.

"Please share, because I have no idea," I replied.

He nodded toward me. "Your sword. I didn't make the connection until I saw how it affected those cloud beings."

"Let's call them 'nimbuses'," I interjected. "Couldn't get behind 'cosmic jellycloud', sorry."

"Stars, yes, much better!" Toran said

Maris looked a little miffed but said nothing. Kaiden shrugged.

"So, the nimbuses," Toran continued, "I maintain are native to this plane since they didn't just jump in front of us. However, since a brush with the sword disintegrated them, I believe the weapon must exist in a higher dimensional plane even than this—and that's also why it disintegrated the creature we fought in the chamber before making the transition, because it was a higher-dimensional being rather than something native to our spacetime."

I suddenly had to urge to rip the sword off me. "Are you saying this is, what, an eighth-dimensional object?"

"Possibly higher. I'm still not positive where we are now. I suspect our other artifacts may, likewise, be higher-dimensional items, though I'm not sure in what order."

Kaiden gaped at Toran. "What...?"

"It explains how we have been able to accomplish seemingly impossible tasks in the past," Toran continued. "For instance, opening the Archive, creating the shield around our shuttle during the disruptor detonation, entering this plane—Elle's sword is the common denominator. If she had been the one to touch the sphere, perhaps it would have worked, rather than when I did it alone."

My heart dropped. "But now we have no idea where that sphere is, relative to where we are now."

"I know, so that doesn't do us any good now. But, I think your sword might be the answer to us getting back to our usual reality. May I have a look at it?" Toran asked.

Despite our weeks of travel together, we'd never spent much time studying each other's artifacts. Once we each had 'ours', that had been it—we guarded our personal items loyally and only gave them up for decontamination cleaning when necessary. In particular, Kaiden and Toran had always seemed a little wary of my sword, and the one time Maris had asked to hold it during one of our practice sessions, she said it made her feel nauseated.

Even now, I didn't like the idea of handing it over to Toran. All the same, if it might help get us home, I couldn't decline. "Sure, here you go." I drew the sword and handed it to him by the hilt, careful to avoid the blue flames.

The moment it was in Toran's hand, the flames extinguished, looking just like any other weapon. "That's odd," he said.

Maris nodded. "Same thing happened to me. Give it a second."

Toran tilted his head questioningly, then his face contorted with discomfort. "Urgh," he moaned. "That's so disorienting—like I'm not connected to myself. Does this make you feel sick all the time, Elle?"

"Really, you too?" I shook my head. "Not at all. Makes me feel great, actually—like, supercharged."

Still wincing, Toran hefted the blade and gave it a thorough visual inspection. "It really doesn't seem that different, to be honest." He held it out toward me.

I took it back from him; the flames instantly reignited when it was in my hand. "Guess I just have a special bond with it."

"What are you thinking, Toran?" Kaiden asked. "Does this have something to do with our artifacts being on different planes?"

"Perhaps."

"Well, where does this leave us?" I looked between the faces of my friends. Since it seemed like Toran's inspection of my sword had hit a dead end, we were still trapped and directionless.

"I guess we should—" Kaiden cut off as a strange cry sounded, almost like a neigh. "Wait, did anyone else just hear a horse?"

"That can't be right," I replied, despite having heard it myself. Strange cloud monsters were the kind of oddity I'd expect to find in a higher dimension, but a horse?

"I think it came from over here," Maris said, her tone determined and excited. She ran to the left. "Come on, we have to find it!"

WE FOLLOWED MARIS through the twisting corridors of endless windows.

"I think I now understand why they built that labyrinth," I said. "Maybe someone glimpsed this place and it was a symbolic tribute."

"Could be." Kaiden nodded.

"Are you sure that sound was a call to us?" Toran asked.

"Yes," Maris replied emphatically. "It was so clear. I keep catching glimpses of it through the windows, too."

I wasn't as certain, but I had heard *something*, even though I'd yet to see any visual confirmation. Frankly, I wasn't keen on the idea of following the sound, since the last creatures we had encountered was far from friendly, but Maris was insistent. If this plan didn't work out, at least it wouldn't be on me.

While I recognized that I shouldn't look at things in those terms, I was still feeling drained and overwhelmed. The realization that my weapon was likely a higher dimensional object and our key to unlocking higher planes for our minds to access was throwing me in ways I hadn't expected. I'd barely gotten used to the idea of aliens, but this dimensional element was proving to be even more difficult to wrap my head around.

"I think I saw it again," Maris said, pulling my attention back to the present. She took a sharp right and paused, looking around. "I *know* I did."

Another soft neigh and a snuffle sounded in my mind. "Where is that coming from?"

"I don't hear it," Toran maintained.

"I think it's... in this one?" Maris examined one of the nearby windows, searching.

Toran seemed to be having a difficult time keeping his exasperation in check. "Why would there be a horse here?"

"Didn't say there *was* a horse, just that it sounded like one," Kaiden pointed out.

I sighed. "Fine, then—"

"Shh!" Maris cut in. "You're scaring it."

I froze and fell silent, trying to spot what she'd seen.

Maris approached a window to my right. "Hey, it's okay. We heard you. Do you need help?"

From my vantage, she was talking to herself. The sound was distinctive, though, so I gave her the benefit of the doubt.

"Why are you hiding?" Maris asked. "You can trust us."

Another soft snuffle filled my mind.

"What are you talking to?" I asked, coming toward Maris.

"Stop! You'll—" She drooped. "You'll scare it away."

Nothing was behind the window except a dim, indistinct landscape.

"What kind of thing is it?" I asked.

Maris shook her head. "Maybe he'll show you. Be nice." She held out her hands in front of her, palms up and cupped. "It's okay, they're my friends."

We remained motionless for nearly a minute. Then, a white nose and snout came into view through the infinite planes fanning out inside the window. The tapered head led to an arched, muscular neck and long body atop four slender legs ending in crystal hooves. Its entire body was covered in tiny, scalloped scales that appeared as thin and light as feathers. A golden mane flowed from the crest of its neck and matching tail flowed almost to the ground. Though mostly solid in appearance, I could make out the faint outline of the backdrop behind it, and it shimmered with a soft, golden glow. Its most striking features, however, were its luminescent golden eyes and a spiraling, crystal horn at the center of its forehead.

"No frickin' way!" I exclaimed louder than I'd intended.

The creature bucked and quickly retreated into the shadows within in the window.

"Hey, it's okay! Come back," Maris soothed.

"What was it?" Kaiden asked, having been at the wrong angle to see.

"You wouldn't believe me if I told you. Come here." I motioned Kaiden to me and pointed toward where I'd seen it.

Several seconds later, after more gentle coaxing, the creature came close enough to Maris for it to enter our sightline.

Kaiden sucked in a shocked breath. "Is that a… unicorn?"

I'd been hesitant to call it that, myself, but the description was too close to lore to not call it like I saw it. "Yes, I believe it is."

To my eye, the unique coat gave it a touch of griffon or maybe dragon, but the overall impression was decidedly equine. I would have been more shocked by the discovery if I hadn't previously encountered decidedly dragon-y dragons on the Valor world, but the realization that there was truth behind the existence of legendary animals thrilled me.

"He's so beautiful," Maris murmured.

"How do you know it's a 'he'?" I asked, not seeing any distinguishing physical traits either way.

"He told me," she replied.

I'd heard some whinnying, but that was about the extent of my interaction with the unicorn. "Like, telepathically?" I clarified.

"I think so," she responded, a fond smile brightening her face. "I think he likes me."

Toran slowly came up behind Kaiden and me. "What are you looking at?"

I swiveled my neck. "You don't see it?"

His brow drew together. "There's a… unicorn?"

I nodded. "Yes, all white and golden and ethereal—inside the plane within that window."

"Maybe you need to 'believe'," Kaiden jested in a clear play on childhood fairytales. I knew he was joking, but I couldn't help wondering if there might be a measure of truth to the statement.

Toran shook his head. "It's just like before. I can't seem to perceive things on the same planes you can."

"You'll just have to take our words for it, I guess," I told him, trying not to sound patronizing.

"Has the unicorn told you anything else?" Kaiden asked Maris.

She was silent for several seconds. "He's… trapped."

"What? How?" I questioned.

Maris' brow furrowed. "I'm trying to piece it together. It's not words, more like a jumble of images. I think he… got lost somehow, separated from his kind. They used to take shortcuts through this plane using special routes connected to the plane below this one, where he's from. Except, when the Overlords came, their normal routes closed."

"Overlords?" Kaiden raised an eyebrow.

"The aliens behind the Darkness, maybe?" Maris shrugged. "Anyway, he got left behind and the rest of his herd were forced to go on without him or else also become trapped."

"Can he get back?" I asked, empathizing with the unicorn as I thought about how I was separated from my own family.

Maris hung her head. "Oh."

"What is it?" Kaiden pressed.

"He wasn't talking about the recent invasion of our spacetime. I think he's been trapped since whatever went down that killed this planet."

"Stars!" I couldn't fathom being trapped alone, with nowhere to turn, no one to hear my cries. It must have been terrifying.

"What can we do to help?" Kaiden asked.

"We need to try to get him out. He can enter this plane if we can open the doorway." She shook her head. "That's the best I can explain it. I don't know exactly what he means."

"I wish I could see what you're talking about." Toran grunted.

"You still might be able to help," Maris said. "Your gauntlets—you've been able to shatter other things. Maybe you can break one of the windows?"

"This isn't normal spacetime," he replied.

"Still, it might do something. Can you try?" she asked.

Toran sighed. "Very well. You said it was this one?"

"Yes, hold on." Maris leaned in close to the window. "We're going to try to get you out. Back up, but don't go far."

The unicorn pawed one of his crystal hooves and then backed up until he was only visible at the edge of the window.

"Okay, go ahead." Maris stood aside.

Toran stepped up to the window and raised his fists. He pounded them into the surface in three rapid blows. The surface shuddered but didn't appear close to breaking.

Kaiden frowned at it. "Well, that doesn't seem to work. I'd suggest throwing some magic at it, but I'm afraid it would bounce back."

"No offense, but I don't think your magic is particularly effective here," I said. "It barely did anything to those nimbuses."

"Yeah, that's true." He stepped back. "Do your thing with your sword."

I smiled. "I swear I'm not trying to show off."

"You got the coolest artifact, we get it." Maris smiled back, clearly happier now that she had a special item of her own. Honestly, there were times when I'd rather have her new shield.

I unsheathed my sword, debating whether I should try bashing the window or take a more surgical approach. In the end, I decided to start with finesse, as I could always work my way up from there. I gripped the hilt in both hands and placed the tip on the center of the window.

The surface began to shimmer and flicker, fracturing the view through the window. As I pressed my blade deeper, each facet vibrated with increasing intensity until it was shuddering so fast that the view through the window once again became a single image. At the moment it coalesced, the pane dissolved.

I gasped, drawing back my blade from what was now an opening. The area beyond defied my expectations for a reality, with islands of solid-looking matter seemingly floating in a void. The unicorn was standing on one of these islands connected to the others by narrow bridges made from translucent filaments. "What is this place?"

"Another layer of reality above our own," Maris said. "He doesn't know how long he's been here—time is fluid above the fourth dimension. But he said this isn't how it used to be—it should be filled with light. This pocket got cut off when the Overlords came, and it's been dark ever since."

"I'm so sorry he was trapped here. That must have been awful," I said.

"He thanks you," Maris interpreted. She stepped to the edge of the opening through the former window. "You're free now. Come with us."

The unicorn didn't move.

"He's scared. He's not sure he can trust us." Maris frowned.

"We want to fight the Overlords," I told him directly. "Can you help us learn about them?"

The unicorn snuffled, sounding in my mind. Slowly, he picked his way down the narrow path from the island toward the door.

Maris motioned us backward as the unicorn reached the opening. He sniffed cautiously toward where the window used to be and extended his nose toward it. When it freely passed through, he made an excited hop and leaped through the opening into the corridor.

As soon as he was through, I noticed tiny crystals forming around the edges of where the window used to be, joining together to form a single, smooth plane as they spread inward.

The unicorn backed away from us as he got his bearings, glancing between Maris and the rest of us as he danced on his four crystal hooves.

"You're free now," Maris said.

He met each of our gazes with his spectacular golden eyes. *"Thank you,"* I heard in my mind, though the words were a construct of my own imagination. I was wrapped in a warm mental embrace of sunshine, filled with joy and the thrill of freedom. The intensity of the emotion almost brought tears to my eyes.

"You're welcome," I told him. "Is there anything else we can do to help you get back to your family?"

The unicorn shook his head with another huff, which I took to be a 'no' as a dark cloud filled my mind. They were long since separated, and there was no going back now. However, new images and sensations of warmth embrace me.

Maris brightened. "He wants to help us!"

"We'll take all the help we can get," I told him. "What should we call you?"

A powerful, ancient presence filled my mind once more. Though it still didn't convey spoken words, I automatically translated into my native tongue. *"I am known as Huefneril among my kind."*

I winced. "Okay, fair warning, I sense a nickname coming on."

Maris crossed her arms. "Yeah, that won't do." She looked the unicorn up and down. "I'm gonna call you 'Hoofy'."

I ROLLED MY eyes. "Really, Maris, you're going to call this majestic being 'Hoofy'?"

"Only as a delightful term of endearment. You don't mind, do you?" Maris asked the unicorn.

He snuffled. *"You have freed me. You may call me whatever you wish in your tongue."*

Maris spread her arms. "Matter settled."

Kaiden pursed his lips. "Feels a little on-point to me."

Toran pinched the bridge of his nose and shook his head.

Exasperating nickname or not, I'd take it over 'Huefneril'; at least it captured the right spirit. "So, Hoofy, tell us about yourself."

"First, I am curious about you," he said in his telepathic language of images and emotion. *"How did you come here? Your kind are not ascended."*

"It's… kind of a long story," I replied. "When the Darkness came, our worlds were lost. We were able to escape to these new bodies." I held memories in my mind to augment my words, and I could tell that Hoofy was absorbing their meaning, feeling them as I did.

"They never stop trying." I sensed the fear in Hoofy's statement.

"You know who's behind the Darkness?" Kaiden asked.

"They call themselves the Overlords. They seek to control, to dominate."

"Are they the ones who trapped you?" I asked.

"Yes, but not intentionally. It was a side effect of their alterations to the crystalline network. I was young and inexperienced. I hesitated, and I was

left behind." Hoofy shared his sadness and frustration.

"These beings… where are they? *What* are they?" I questioned.

"I have hidden from them so they cannot find me."

Maris softened. "I would, too. But we're friends. You don't need to hide from us."

Toran took in a sharp breath of surprise. "I can see him."

"Thank you," Maris said with an affectionate smile toward the unicorn. "How did you make him see?"

"I have hidden above them," Hoofy explained. *"They reside on a plane above time and thought, below this one. For years they have tried to ascend, but that is a place that cannot be reached by force."*

"Okay, so they're on a dimensional plane below yours and above our spacetime?" I clarified, trying to get back to my previous question.

"Yes, the plane beneath us. Once we used to commune with them on their level, but now we hide. Their ill intentions have corrupted the crystalline network."

I frowned. "Yeah, we've been seeing a lot of that."

"That's why I shied away at first—I could smell them on you. You were… changed."

I'd tried to forget how we'd come by our present forms—that we had been touched by the Darkness, and then our consciousnesses extracted and downloaded into modified bodies. I hated to think that any of the aliens or the Darkness was a part of me.

"We're not like them," Maris assured Hoofy.

"No, you have pure spirits. And you are more than them. Your kind is not ascended, but parts of you are. You can see what others cannot."

Toran brightened. "This is actually quite helpful—we can start narrowing down which dimension we're now perceiving. Can you help us understand?" he asked Hoofy.

The unicorn pawed a crystal hoof. *"There is time, and there is thought, then above that they dwell. We roam around them unseen, except when we pass through this place, over the bridges. They used to use them, too, but they started trying to change them and the bridges collapsed."*

These interpreted words on their own raised more questions than answers, but I probed the images and emotions that filled my mind, searching for the nuance of his messages. My perception expanded, and I saw what I knew as my reality flowing through time. Beyond that was an amorphous layer flooded by an infinite number of flashing thoughts; I realize this was the dimension through which Hoofy was communicating. Then, there was the dark plane where the Overlords, as Hoofy called them, resided. They manipulated matters of mind and time.

I recoiled. "That's how they were telepathically influencing me."

Kaiden pressed a hand to his temple. "Ugh, this is a lot to take in at once."

Toran grimaced. "It'd be really handy if we could transition between planes at will."

"Yeah." I paused. "I get it now—like, on a deeper level—what you were saying before about us having not actually *gone* anywhere. We're not stuck in a different place… our perception is just locked at a higher plane than what we're used to experiencing."

"Yes, but there is a spacetime component," Toran said. "Once we ran away from the entry point, our position in spacetime likely changed. Now I really *don't* know where we are."

"But, we *can* figure out which plane," Kaiden said. "Since time is 4D, that weird thought dimension must be 5D, making the Overlords on 6D, Hoofy and the other unicorns at 7D, and us presently at 8D, I guess?"

The eighth dimension—not a place I ever thought I'd experience.

"That count sounds right to me," Toran confirmed. "It makes sense, then, why telepathic influence broke down when we transitioned to 8D, since it's multiple planes away from 5D. Or, maybe that's a coincidence."

"I wonder where those dragons we met fit in?" Maris pondered.

"They live among us," Hoofy said in our minds.

"Okay, so sounds like the seventh dimension is the land of mythical creatures." I smiled.

Maris hopped giddily. "I can't wait to go there!"

"We have other things to deal with first," Kaiden told her. "Namely, figuring out how to take out those Overlord guys."

I frowned. "Okay, since it's come up a few times now, I guess I'll have to be the one to say it: 'Overlords', really? I mean, the ego on these guys!"

Maris laughed. "They clearly have some sort of 'lower dimension' complex. Like, 'We're only 6D so we should call ourselves something grandiose to compensate'."

Kaiden smirked. "No wonder their spaceships were so big."

Even Toran chuckled. "You three are ruthless."

"Hey, they brought this on themselves." I grinned.

"I believe the four of you have been chosen to set things right," Hoofy told us.

My smile faded, remembering the graveness of our circumstances. "We want to continue in our quest, but we don't know how to travel through this place."

"I would like to help you."

Maris clasped her hands. "Really?"

The unicorn bowed his head. *"It is only right that I do."*

"No complaints here," Kaiden said. "Welcome to the Dark Sentinels."

Hoofy pranced to the side. *"Come this way."*

We followed the unicorn—I still had to check myself each time I thought the name—through the mirrored maze of corridors. Now that I was gaining a better understanding of our environment and what I was seeing, I paid more attention to the scenes on the other side. Each of the facets appeared to correspond with a specific location, and the fractal branches within each followed the threads of time for each of those places. Additional facets revealed the different planes of reality, not all of them visual, but each unique. They shifted as the interconnected threads intersected with one another, a woven tapestry spanning time and space of everything that had been, everything that was, and even the somewhat fuzzy things that might yet come.

I wished I could find one of my own threads and follow it to see how everything worked out, but I knew that was impossible—or, at least, ill-advised.

"What more can you tell us about these Overlords?" Kaiden asked Hoofy while we walked.

"They thirst for power. They live in the dark and seek to shape others to be like them."

"Do you know where they came from?" I asked.

Hoofy shook his head, fanning out his golden mane. A series of images filled my mind, not translating into words in the usual fashion. It was clear that the Overlords were outside of time in the same way as the other hyperdimensional beings, but they were obsessed with the goings-on in planes outside their own. They tied themselves to time by virtue of their meddling, and that would be their undoing.

"We'll try to make things right," I told Hoofy.

"There is a chance," he replied. *"They descended once before to go after the crystals, but they were ultimately driven back."*

"What do they want with the crystals?" Toran asked.

"To ascend," Hoofy replied.

My brow knit. "How? What does that even mean?"

"They wish to be able to exist on a higher plane. I cannot say by which means or method they hope to achieve this goal."

"Sounds like something a bunch of power-hungry over-compensators would do," Maris said.

Kaiden chuckled. "That it does."

"You know the destroyed crystals we saw on Crystallis and in the caverns here?" Toran began. "I wonder if that happened the last time the Overlords descended."

"Very well could be," I replied. "There was clearly some kind of conflict."

"I still don't get why they would descend if they're ultimately trying to get to a higher plane," Kaiden mused.

"We have the crystal interface terminals, so maybe that has something to do with it," I suggested. "Considering that we jumped straight up to the eighth dimension from there, perhaps not all dimensions have clear methods to access them."

"Here." Hoofy stopped in the center of a particularly jumbled section of corridor with reflective windows arranged in odd angles. Even the gravity in the place seemed strange to me, though that may have been in my imagination.

The windows shimmered and seemed to tilt, revealing a landscape like the one where we'd seen Hoofy. The view through windows transitioned again, and I unconsciously moved backward.

Through the windows, there was a massive city spanning as far as I could see. Cylindrical towers rose from a nest of massive black vines at the base. The structures themselves were formed from the same latticework material I'd seen on the ships. Creatures similar to the one we fought in the cavern scurried through the alien city. The world was dark, only illuminated by a subtle, blue glow.

"Stars!" Kaiden breathed.

"I figured they'd have something like this, but actually *seeing* it…" I faded out, not able to find the right words.

At first glance, the activity reminded me more of an ant colony than anything I'd experienced with my own brand of civilization. However, as I followed specific creatures along their paths, I realized that they were actually interacting much like my own people would. They greeted some individuals as they passed by—acquaintances, but not everyone they happened to come across—and there appeared to be a brand of commerce. Certain areas were clearly designated social gathering places, which were adorned by organic pedestals that looked strikingly similar to the stone benches we'd observed on the planet's surface. Having made the connection, I even noticed that the black stairways bore a similar structural design to the modified steps retrofit in the ruined city.

I took it in with growing concern. "Did the aliens conquer the planet, or did the residents change into this new form?"

"Never satisfied, they always seek what they do not have," Hoofy said cryptically.

"There are a lot of similarities here," Toran agreed. "I could see it going either way."

"The point is, they're organized and have a lot of infrastructure," Kaiden said.

"And there must be even more than this, since they also have constructed and launched space ships," I said.

Kaiden frowned. "That's a good point. Why do they need ships at all if they can travel through dimensional planes outside of normal spacetime?"

"Assuming they're after something in our home plane, maybe that's a more efficient means to go long distances?" Maris suggested.

"Could be." I considered the information we had so far. "Maybe they could only create animals on the Darkness-infected planets but there was no way to get their own consciousness there?"

Kaiden nodded pensively. "They sent the Darkness through the crystalline network to prepare worlds, and then the fleet was to carry individuals to… do what?"

"That is the big question mark," I replied.

"I wish we knew the extent of their civilization." Toran stroked his chin. "Is there just a city, or are there multiple planets?"

"Do you know, Hoofy?" Maris asked.

The unicorn stamped one of its front hooves. *"This world is theirs, with the core at its heart."*

"Only this world, this city? Or is there more?" I pressed.

"It is more than it appears to be."

Toran nodded. "Right, yes. It's not limited to three-dimensional space as we know it."

"Hey, what about the anomaly site?" Kaiden asked. "Remember, the gravity around the site was weird, like an entire system was there, even though we couldn't see anything."

"I bet you're onto something with that. It would make sense for them to build up infrastructure around a place where they could transition their fleet into our spacetime," Toran replied.

Maris brushed her hair back from her face. "I can't think about it too hard or I'll want to curl up on the ground."

"I understand the impulse," I admitted.

"I'm curious what location in our native spacetime corresponds to this city's location. Do you know?" he asked Hoofy.

The unicorn shifted uncomfortably on his hooves. *"This is their place."*

"Yes, but it would help to know *where* this is," Kaiden said. "Is there any way to tell if this is a planet, or—"

"Can you go down to a lower plane and find a location there that relates to this city?" Maris asked in a soft voice. "We can't do it ourselves yet, and it may help us get back to our friends."

Hoofy continued his agitated side-stepping. *"They might see me."*

"Oh, I hadn't thought of that." I realized the conundrum. To get a clear view of our three-dimensional reality in this place at our appropriate time, Hoofy would need to descend to that plane. However, descending would require him to pass through the Overlords' domain and then remain at a lower level as he assessed the surroundings, making him visible to them and vulnerable to their attacks. It was a huge risk—not one we could ask him to take.

"Is there a way we can see for ourselves?" I asked.

"Too dangerous," Hoofy told us.

"I know, but we need to," Maris said. "You don't need to come with us."

Hoofy snuffled. *"There is a place that holds the answers you seek. Follow me."*

11

I FOUND MYSELF in even greater awe of the incredible eighth-dimensional landscape the longer I spent in the place. As we followed Hoofy through the corridors, I tried to peek through the windows to other planes, soaking in the wondrous sights.

"Now that I'm not on the verge of a nervous breakdown, this is amazing," I commented to Kaiden while we hung back slightly from the others.

"It doesn't feel as overwhelming now, does it?"

"No, it's just… wow."

He smiled slightly. "I'm glad to see you're doing better. I was worried about you."

"Yeah, unnerved me, too. I'm not used to being out of control like that."

"At least those Overlord guys can't get in our heads here."

I frowned. "You know, going along with the 'Overlords' thing is giving them too much credit. We need another name for them."

"That's pretty petty."

I laughed. "Oh, yes, I'm well aware."

He smirked. "And I like you even more for it. What do you have in mind?"

"Maybe the… 'Saps'. Create a self-fulfilling prophesy of them falling for whatever trap we set."

"You have a delightfully twisted mind."

"At least I use my talents for good."

"What are you two plotting back there?" Toran asked, looking over his shoulder.

"I propose a name change from 'Overlords' to 'Saps'. All in favor?" I asked.

Maris chuckled. "I like it."

Toran sighed. "Very well. 'Overlords' was too many syllables."

"Why do you find this new name amusing?" Hoofy asked.

I smiled. "Just a little word play. We mere lower-dimensional mortals have to entertain ourselves somehow."

We eventually reached an open area in the maze, which reminded me of a theater. Mirrors formed a dome overhead and down the walls in irregular hexagonal segments, transitioning to windows at floor level where they could be accessed. At the center of the space was a single crystal pedestal a meter tall, similar to the structure our Master Crystal shard had come from in the Archive.

"This is the infinity chamber. Here you may learn the ancient knowledge known to all ascended," Hoofy said. *"I cannot witness it myself, but if you can see, then you will know what must be done. You will be able to stop the menace."*

I swallowed. "No pressure, right?"

"Journeying to higher planes to glimpse the secrets of the universe—it's a regular Tuesday." Kaiden smiled.

"Yeah, hardy-har." Maris eyed the crystal pedestal like it was about to eat her. "How do we use this thing?"

Hoofy pranced with agitation. *"I will find you afterward, I cannot be here."* He galloped into the depths of the corridors.

I let out a long breath. "Totally reassuring."

"He'll be back," Maris said confidently.

"It's not that—what information is here that a being wouldn't want to know?" questioned Kaiden.

"I don't believe that's the issue. It's possible he *can't* access this information," Toran replied.

I raised an eyebrow. "How could *we* see something he can't? He's native to a much higher plane than us."

"And yet we're here now and were able to free him from a place he was trapped," Toran said. "I believe the four of us were changed more than we initially realized."

"Do you think our magic and abilities...?" I wasn't sure how to complete the statement, but I knew. Part of me had always known. Our powers came from somewhere, or *something*, and we were now close to understanding their origin.

Toran simply nodded in response.

"I guess we should activate this thing, or whatever we're supposed to do," Kaiden said.

"Do you think we just touch it?" I asked.

"Makes sense. All the other tech has worked that way," Maris said.

"Seems like a reasonable strategy," Toran agreed.

"Okay..." I approached the crystal pedestal. It hummed with the intense, sweet energy I'd come to associate with the crystalline network. I extended my hand toward it, and my fingertips brushed the surface.

The world fanned out around me, my senses richer and deeper than I imagined possible. I was surrounded by warmth and light amid an energy network connecting everything around me. At the edge of my awareness, I sensed my friends nearby. They glowed brighter than anything else in the vicinity—even more than the crystal pedestal at the center of the chamber—but there was still something even greater out there, just beyond my grasp.

As my awareness of my place within the energy network solidified, my consciousness expanded. The chamber, the eight-dimensional plane, were only one facet of my reality. At once, I was everywhere and nowhere. Darkness, light—it blended into a single sensory symphony. I knew that I was outside of time, yet I still had the urge to ground myself in a single place and moment from which to observe.

I searched around myself for some kind of foundation. However, there was only the color and light—beautiful, but I needed a connection to the familiar elements of my reality. Something, anything, to latch onto.

Beneath my present perception, I glimpsed a place teaming with life. I reached out for it, willing myself to pass through the dimensional veil so I could witness it for myself. As I descended through the layers of reality, I sensed my friends following me. Though we didn't bear the physical forms of our usual selves, I had no doubt it was them, visible or not. We gravitated closer to each other on the way to our destination until I felt like I could reach out and take their hands, if we had had bodies to touch.

The alien civilization we'd glimpsed through the window was now spread out before us, a fully populated planet and space dock beyond.

The scene spun backward. Now, a new world was forming before me. Signs of civilization formed and grew before my eyes, flashing at irregular intervals as physical reality was reset. Cities rose and fell, and then rose anew—bigger, more magnificent. They had achieved the pinnacle of development, and so the next phase began: to seek other life.

As I watched history play out in the spectacular cosmic time-lapse, the civilization learned to harness the crystal's power. They pierced the dimensional veil, to expand their consciousness to see everything that had been unseen. They found the other life they were looking for and welcomed the hyperdimensional aliens as gods.

However, the alien beings had aspirations of their own—to control the crystalline network and harness its power to regulate the unseen building blocks of our universe. All they needed was a direct link to the crystalline network: the interface crystals in our spacetime.

Blinded by ambition, the aliens tried to seize this power by force. In the end, their attempts to hijack the crystalline network backfired, shattering the crystals on many worlds. Interstellar society collapsed, with only a few scattered planets surviving to rebuild again. The aliens lost their gateway to the higher planes, but they knew that the keys to their ascension would emerge eventually. They would get another chance.

So, they retreated. They waited.

At last, civilized life in the lower planes—the reality my friends and I knew as our home—rebuilt enough to rediscover the keys that the ancient civilization had hidden for those worthy of gaining ascension to find.

The sword in my hand pulsed, and I knew it was one such key. The artifacts we now wielded opened access to the higher planes, and possessing them had forever changed us. Our time with the artifacts had enabled us to enter this dimension and to witness this ancient knowledge held within the fabric of the cosmos itself.

The aliens must not have realized our importance yet or we'd already have been killed. They were on the cusp of completing their plan to ascend, and we were all that stood in their way.

In that moment, I understood my place. I knew what I had to do. And I was terrified.

My consciousness returned to my physical form, and the multi-faceted dome came into focus around me. My friends were standing exactly where they had been when I touched the crystal pedestal.

We stood in stunned silence.

"All right, that's going to take some time to process," I said eventually.

Kaiden nodded. "Wow. Not sure I have more than that to say at the moment."

Maris looked like she was on the verge of tears. "I don't think I can look at anything the same way again."

"We certainly won't," Toran said, still staring into space. "So, these invading aliens have always resided at a higher plane?"

"As far back as that little history lesson went, anyway," Kaiden said. "Were the people on this planet our ancestors?"

"Maybe, in a slightly different form," I replied. "They looked like giants compared to us."

Maris shook her head. "They mastered the crystalline network only to have it be their undoing. Makes you wonder if we should be messing with any of this."

"Too late for that," Kaiden said. "The Hegemony made that decision for us when they discovered the ancient civilization's tech and started hooking up viewing devices and interface consoles for the reset crystals."

"Crazy how cyclical it is, isn't it?" I murmured. "Civilizations born and raised only to fall into the same traps generations later."

"These hyperdimensional alien bastards really know how to play a long game," Kaiden said.

"To timeless six-dimensional beings, one civilization is just like another," Toran responded. "But we're different, because now we know what they're after."

I raised an eyebrow. "Do we? Because 'controlling the crystalline network' still feels like a pretty broad goal. What do they want to *do with it*?"

Toran hesitated. "That part I still don't know."

"Well, we have the keys to accessing the highest levels of the crystalline network," Maris said, patting her shield.

I nodded. "Yeah, I guess we do." The vision hadn't revealed how the artifacts were made or where they had come from, but I could sense the power of my sword in its scabbard. It was almost like it was pure higher-dimensional energy compared to everything around us, but I figured that was an after-effect of the whirlwind tour through space and time.

"Well," Toran said, "I suppose we have learned what we came to find out. The aliens are concentrated on this planet in the sixth-dimensional plane. We won't be able to do any more until we regroup with the Hegemony."

"I'm all for getting out of here," Maris said. "Once they learn about our artifacts…"

"Yeah, we don't want them to catch us on a lower dimension, that's for sure." My hand instinctively went to the hilt of my sword. While the aliens might not usually take much interest in lower-dimensional beings, eventually they'd figure out that we were the same team that had been thorns in their sides in recent weeks.

"About the getting back to our usual plane of perception…" Kaiden said slowly.

"Hoofy might be able to help us," Maris said. "Let's go find him."

We retraced our path into the chamber and found the unicorn waiting nearby.

"Have you found the answers you seek?" he asked, trotting toward us.

"We got some answers, but we also have a lot of new questions," Maris explained.

Toran nodded. "Do you know anything more about the crystalline network, and specifically the Master Archive?"

"The network is above all else. It is what bridges space, time, and the higher planes. To understand more than that is impossible for a being of my level."

"Surely you must have heard—" I pressed.

"It is not my place," Hoofy interrupted within my mind.

"That's okay, you've already done so much for us," Maris hastily cut in. "Can you help us find our way back to an access point where we can transition to our home spacetime?"

"That I can do," Hoofy replied. *"This way."*

The unicorn led us through the confusing labyrinth of windowed corridors. Eventually, I spotted something recognizable. "That's the viewing-sphere!"

Maris breathed a sigh of relief. "Now we can go back home."

I drew my sword. "And this is the key, I guess?"

"Yes, I sense special strength in each of the artifacts you carry," Hoofy replied. *"That sword, in particular, holds great power."*

"We were discussing that right before we met you," Toran revealed. "Do you know anything more about it?"

"No, but I can tell you that it will facilitate your return home."

"Thank you for everything," Maris said. "You really saved us."

"It was you who saved me, truthfully," Hoofy replied. *"And in our short time together, I have become fascinated by your quest."*

Kaiden smiled. "Glad it's been entertaining to someone, because it's been pretty awful to live through."

"I was hoping I could journey with you," the unicorn went on. *"I will offer what support I can, but there are some things you must learn on your own."*

"That'd be great!" Maris exclaimed.

"No complaints here," I agreed.

Kaiden nodded. "Glad to get all the help we can get."

"Gladly. Will you be able to reside on our plane?" Toran asked.

"Not precisely, but now that you have witnessed the higher planes, I can make myself visible to you. Others of your kind, though, likely won't be able to see or hear me."

I chuckled. "Oh, this is going to go over *great* when we explain to Colren that we have a magical unicorn spirit guide."

"I *have* to be in the room for that," Kaiden said with a smile.

"Let's think that over before we say anything," Toran advised.

"All right." I looked between my friends and the viewing-sphere. "All together this time?"

We got into position and reached out to touch the sphere.

THE MIRRORED WALLS folded and warped, fading to black. When my vision focused once more, the underground cavern resolved around me. Our four backpacks were on the ground exactly where we'd been standing when we'd made the transition.

"Okay, that was officially the weirdest thing I've ever done," I declared, reaching down to retrieve my pack.

Maris scowled at our environment. "None of this feels right anymore."

"Yeah, I know what you mean." Everything around me seemed dull and lifeless after that amazing experience in the higher dimensions. It was simultaneously incredible and disturbing to know other beings could be observing me from a higher dimension without my knowledge. I tried not to dwell on it, knowing that it would be a path to madness, but I knew for certain that I'd never be able to look at anything the same way again.

"Hoofy?" Maris asked tentatively.

"*I am here,*" he said telepathically to the four of us. "*I do not want to reveal myself in this place so close to the Overlords.*"

"Don't blame you," Maris replied. "And, remember, we're going to call them the 'Saps' from now on."

"*They would not be pleased with this name.*"

I smiled. "Even better."

Kaiden headed toward the exit. "We shouldn't linger here."

I followed him. "Yeah, more of the Saps might be ready to transition to this plane now, however they do it."

Toran took up a position at the rear of our party. "This is not a place we want to find ourselves in another engagement."

I shared his concern. Now that we knew our artifacts were more than the weapons and defensive tools they appeared to be, we had to take extra precautions, lest they fall into enemy hands.

"Stars, I hope the *Sanctum* is still waiting for us," Kaiden realized. "How long were we in there? Or, sorta there. You know what I mean."

"I didn't check the time before," Toran said. "And, I don't know if we could trust the time readouts on any devices with us, anyway."

"I guess we'll see when we get back to the shuttle," I replied.

"Yes, no reason to delay," he concurred.

We jogged toward the exit, passing through the large cavern with its crushed crystal ground as quickly as possible. I kept a close eye on the black vines writhing near the walls, but no creatures came forward. I wasn't sure if they were wary of us after we took out the one earlier or if they had another reason to hang back, but it almost made me more nervous that we were able to pass through without incident.

Despite the amount of rubble in the chamber which formerly held the labyrinth, we were able to hop along the tops of the fallen wall slabs to quickly traverse the space, careful to avoid the shadowed recesses where the tainted Darkness vines may still remain. Beyond that, it was a quick journey up the spiral ramp to the surface. Passing through the corridor with its mosaics, this time I clearly saw the story depicted in the images, telling of the civilization welcoming the hyperdimensional aliens, only to be betrayed. The temple, the city, everything in their society had been changed to revolve around the Overlord's demands. I still didn't know exactly what had happened to bring about the society's ultimate demise after the crystals were damaged, but I was certain the Saps were to blame.

We hurried through the city ruins to our shuttle and took off as quickly as possible. As we reached the upper atmosphere, our comms chirped.

"Headed back already?" Richards said over the shuttle central's intercom.

"Good, you're still here!" Kaiden exclaimed from the pilot's seat.

"Yeah, of course we are. We agreed to wait ten hours," the ship captain replied.

Kaiden exchanged glanced with the rest of us. "How long has it been?"

"You only dropped out of comm contact about an hour ago," Richards revealed.

"Wait, that can't be right." Kaiden went into the flight record to see when we'd landed. The flight logs he overlaid on the front viewport clearly indicated that only a short time had elapsed—barely enough for our walk from the shuttle, to the sphere, and back again.

"No time passed while we were in 8D?" I asked.

"Fascinating," Toran murmured.

"I'm getting the impression that you have quite the story to tell," Kess chimed in over the comm.

"Oh, you have no idea." I let out a long breath.

"You can tell us on the way back," Richards said. "We'll open the cargo doors for you."

"Anything we say will have to be over the comms," Toran replied. "We came into contact with some of the Darkness. Best to follow contamination protocols just in case."

I slumped in my seat. "Stars, that's right."

"Does that mean we're heading back to the *Evangiel*?" Richards asked.

"Yes, we have what we need," Kaiden confirmed. "Trust me, we don't want to be around here."

"Roger that," the captain said.

Kess sighed. "I'm just bummed I didn't get to see your magic."

I chuckled to myself. "It's been a crazy day."

We flew the remaining distance to the *Sanctum* and docked in the belly of the ship. As soon as the docking clamps were in place, I felt the telltale rumble of engines as the *Sanctum* accelerated toward the rendezvous point with the *Evangiel*.

"Thanks, guys. Talk to you in a few," Kaiden said into the comm then muted the channel. He turned to us. "What are we going to tell everyone?"

"That's a very good question," Toran replied.

We moved from the shuttle's small bridge to the compact common room amidships and took seats in the dining table booth.

"We need to be honest about what we experienced," I said as soon as we were situated, "though I expect a good deal of skepticism."

"Agreed." Kaiden nodded next to me. "Between the hyperdimensional planes and time passage, a lot will come as a shock."

"They have no reason to doubt our word," Toran said.

"Yeah, but believing what we say and knowing what to do with that information are two different things," Maris pointed out. "Like, no matter what we say, telling them about Hoofy is going to raise eyebrows."

"You need not tell them about me unless you want to," the unicorn said in our minds.

"I suggest we keep to the most critical information about the Saps and their capabilities and play the rest by ear," Toran stated.

"Yeah, that works," I agreed. "The other major thing is regarding our artifacts."

Toran nodded. "They have become much more important than I initially realized."

"I'm not sure what we *can* say about them, other than they seem to be able to enable the sphere to act as an interface to higher planes," Kaiden said.

"But it's not just our original three," Maris pointed out. "My new shield seems to have an extra bit of fancy, too." She admired it. "And I don't just mean the bling."

"It does indeed hold great power," Hoofy confirmed.

Maris beamed with pride about her new possession. "I've always had exceptional taste."

"It is very 'you', no doubt. But, why didn't the Saps take the shield?" Kaiden asked. "If it's so powerful, why leave it down there in the cavern when the crystals shattered?"

"I think we've been very lucky," I said.

"That doesn't seem like a matter of luck, Elle," Toran countered.

"No, I mean, the Saps have huge egos, right?" I went on. "Well, a shield like that is defensive, which suggests the user has a vulnerability. I wouldn't put it past them to have looked at it and decided anyone carrying a shield must be weak, and therefore dismissed it. After all, what could possibly harm an 'Overlord'?"

Kaiden chuckled. "That's just ridiculous enough to be true."

"More likely, they can't wield the items," Toran pointed out. "After all, they are harmed when we touch them."

"True," I agreed. "In that case, we don't have to worry about them being stolen."

Toran shook his head. "Not necessarily. The items still hold great power, and the aliens—er, Saps—seem driven to tap into the crystalline network using any means necessary. I don't think we can assume our safety."

"And, are some items more valuable than others?" Maris mused.

Kaiden was silent for several seconds. "Okay, random thought: could the disparities we first experienced in our perception have something to do with our artifacts being at different dimensional levels?"

"Could be." Maris nodded. "Each of us, aside from Toran, did seem to see the cosmic jellyclouds—"

"Nimbuses," I corrected.

"—in slightly different ways," Maris continued without missing a beat.

"What if all of those visions were valid, just perceiving the creature on different planes?" Kaiden posited.

"But we were all in the same plane," I countered. "How could we not see a being native to it?"

Toran took on a pensive expression. "Just because we were in the same environment, that doesn't mean we'd be able to perceive everything in the same way—the more layers are added, the more complex the environment for our minds to grasp. Perhaps the artifacts assist with that mental evaluation in some way." He paused in thought. "You know, there really might be something to that, Kaiden. Just because we all have 'artifacts', that doesn't mean they're all attuned to the same dimension. Maybe spending time with each of them has made us particularly sensitive to perceiving the plane where they're based."

I considered it. "Could we figure out the dimensional order of the artifacts based on what attributes we saw of the nimbuses?"

"Yes, this hypothesis would suggest that perception would be layered—if part of the creature was in one plane, those with a higher plane of perception would see the parts on their plane and everything lower," Toran confirmed.

"Sorry, Toran, but you seem to have drawn the short stick for the artifact lottery," Kaiden said with a sympathetic smile.

"I already figured as much," he replied. "Now, what did each of you see?"

The three of us relayed the traits of the nimbuses we'd observed. Kaiden clearly had a less-formed vision than Maris and mine—little more than amorphous blobs that shot lightning. After some back and forth, I determined that Maris and I had actually seen the same cloud-like creatures, though the terminology we'd used initially was different.

"Does that mean our artifacts would be on the same level?" I questioned.

Toran shook his head. "No, Maris was only able to fight back against them, but your sword instantly destroyed them, Elle. That would suggest your sword exists on a higher plane than we were in at the time, and Maris' shield is native to their plane."

"I guess that's how it was able to cut through the window, too," I realized.

"Yes. That really does explain a lot."

Kaiden's brow knit with concentration. "Okay, so to summarize: we're normally living in 3D, traveling through time, 4D. The Overlords are 6D with the ability to manipulate 5D, thought. Toran's gauntlets are 6D, my circlet is 7D, Maris' shield is 8D, and Elle's sword is… 9D?"

I laughed. "I don't think all of that should be stated in a single sentence unless you want someone's head to explode."

Maris spread her hands. "All I got out of that is that we have a lot of stuff that's on the same or higher level as the baddies, and that means we can take them out."

Kaiden smiled. "I like that summary much better."

We spent the remaining hours of the voyage relaxing as best we could, thankful to be temporarily out of harm's way. Hoofy remained quiet and invisible, though I could sense his presence at the back of my mind, listening with fascination to our banter. I remained on edge as the time passed, still concerned that the Saps were somehow watching us.

It wasn't until we were within visual range of the *Evangiel* that I finally started to relax. "I'm looking forward to a hot shower and some sleep."

Maris glanced between Kaiden and me. "Yeah, I'm sure that's the *only* thing."

I flushed in spite of myself, hoping the low lighting in the shuttle hid it. I really *hadn't* been thinking in those terms, but snuggles did sound amazing after the day we'd had.

Kaiden brushed his foot against mine under the table. "I'm sure we could all use some downtime," he deflected on my behalf.

"Don't get too comfortable," Toran warned. "We still have quite the debrief to go through."

I sighed. "Oh, can't wait…"

After docking and completing the standard decontamination procedure, we headed for Central Command.

"Now I *really* hate leaving my sword behind," I whispered to Kaiden as we exited the hangar.

"I know, I was just thinking the same thing. But, if we can't trust Tami, we have bigger issues to worry about—she could kill us in a hundred different ways every time we step onto one of her shuttles."

"Good point."

Maris seemed miffed. "I wanted to show off my new shield."

"You'll get the chance soon enough," Toran assured her.

When we reached Central Command, we were immediately buzzed inside to find Commander Colren waiting for us. He looked us over expectantly. "Well, what did you learn?"

I took a deep breath. "Boy, do we have a story for you."

COLREN STARED AT us from the other side of the conference table, dumbstruck. "That isn't how I expected this recon mission to go."

"We didn't either, but there you have it," Kaiden replied. "The question now is... well, everything."

The commander steepled his fingers. "I wish there had been a clearer indication about what the 'Saps'—as you now call them—are after."

"Yeah, that's been a sticking point for us, too," Toran admitted. "It seems to have something to do with the properties of the crystalline network, which appears to function on a higher dimensional plane than we 'visited', if you will."

"Do the scientific models point to anything?" Colren questioned. "I know you've been in contact with the Hegemony's research team."

Toran shook his head. "We hadn't discussed anything beyond the idea that the aliens might actually be hyperdimensional beings. Guess that's been confirmed."

Colren gave a disbelieving chuckle. "I still can't wrap my head around what that means—the notion of a sixth-dimensional being existing above time."

"I assure you, it's even *more* disorienting to spend the better part of a day walking around somewhere only to discover that no apparent time has passed in your home dimension," I said.

He leaned back in his chair. "Yes, I could see that."

"So, Commander, we're at a bit of an impasse here," Kaiden said in the intervening silence. "We know *where* the aliens are—sort of—but the new knowledge about their hyperdimensional position means the previous attack plan won't work."

Toran folded his hands on the tabletop. "Yes. Unfortunately, the spatial disruptor is only a 5D weapon, and the Saps are 6D."

"What does that mean for the anomaly site we attacked?" Colren asked.

"It's still too damaged to traverse—this new information doesn't change that," Toran explained. "Think of it like paralyses due to scar tissue—the limb is still there, but it doesn't have feeling any longer, so it can't be used."

That analogy hit a little too close to home for me, and my right hand instinctively went to my left shoulder, remembering the injury that had shaped much of my outlook on life, before we were transformed.

"Meaning, we're still protected from an attack at that location," the commander determined.

"Yes, but that may now be one of the *only* places," Toran continued. "Our glimpse of the hyperdimensional plane on which the Saps reside showed that they have a densely populated world and a substantial fleet. I think the only reason they haven't sent more ships to our planets already is because there are only a few 'access points' for transitioning from 6D to our spacetime reality.

"Based on what we've observed, and learned—" he omitted Hoofy's presence, "—there are specific places that allow interaction across the different planes. The viewing crystals are one such trans-dimensional access point, in addition to their other functions. The local-reset crystals offer more limited points of access, and it seems like there's at least one main control crystal on each planet, which provides an intermediate degree of functionality; I think that's how the Darkness first spread, entering the main crystal and then spreading through the rest of the planet's network. But, there aren't many of these points in open space, which makes it difficult to move a fleet. Either the Saps will find another location to use as a jump point to bring their fleet into our spacetime, or they'll take a land-based approach through the crystals on each planet they want to conquer."

I thought back to the infection of my own world and how I'd seen the Darkness in the canyon's crystal but not in my town square. The planet's control crystal must have been in another city—maybe the planet's capital—and that's what prompted the order for a planetary reset.

"To determine which option they'll pursue—continue trying to find a solution for their fleet, or revert to a land-based assault—we need to know what their goal is," Colren mused. "As insightful as this information is, it doesn't actually help us."

I hated to admit it, but he was right. We'd learned more about the nature of our enemy, yet we still had no large-scale way to effectively fight back or even know where to head them off, since we had no idea where they were going. I couldn't keep a frustrating groan from slipping out. "You'd think learning the secret nature of the universe would answer a lot more questions."

"Yeah, if only we knew more about the dimensional planes above the Saps, maybe there's something that could help us there," Kaiden mused.

"There is someone who might," Toran said.

For a moment, I thought he was about to reveal Hoofy. However, Colren nodded. "Bounce some ideas off her. Something may stick."

"Excuse me." Toran rushed out of the conference room through the bridge.

"Sorry, did I miss something?" I asked.

"One of the Hegemony scientists Toran has been working with," Colren explained. "She has the kind of brilliance you can't train—incredible at making connections and bringing grounding to the extraordinary."

"In other words, exactly what's needed right now," Kaiden said.

The commander smiled. "I think we could all use some answers."

"Definitely." I recalled Toran mentioning a scientist acquaintance the other day, and I was happy to get a trusted outside perspective on our recent experience.

"Well, while Toran gets more into the science and engineering, can you offer any more insights into the tech you observed during your vision of the Saps' society?" Colren asked.

"*Something isn't right,*" Hoofy said suddenly in my mind. Based on how Kaiden and Maris tensed, I suspected he'd spoken to them, too.

"It was a lot to take in," I said, hoping the commander might reveal more of his intentions before I said anything too specific.

"Do you get any sense of their manufacturing capabilities, or their power source?" Colren pressed.

"He is asking on behalf of his superiors," Hoofy said. *"They want the core."*

I swallowed, not sure if I should listen to the commander or our new hyperdimensional companion. Though Colren had once left me to die, it was under unavoidable understandable circumstances; Hoofy, on the other hand, I didn't know at all. Yes, he'd led us through the 8D maze to the exit point, but could we trust him implicitly?

While I was still trying to figure out what to tell Colren, Kaiden brushed his foot against mine under the table, a signal I'd noticed him use over the past week when he saw me struggling to answer a relationship question and he was about to jump in to field it.

"Their structures all look organically grown," Kaiden said. "Couldn't say any more at this point with certainty."

The commander nodded. "Very well. I know that wasn't the focus of your investigation."

"Maybe we can take some time to sort through what we saw and talk more tomorrow," Kaiden suggested.

"Yes, of course, you must be exhausted." Colren rose, and we followed his example. "Thank you, as always, for your efforts."

I forced a smile. "Here to help."

Colren adjourned the meeting, and I led Maris and Kaiden to a private section of corridor outside Central Command.

"What was that about? Do you think the Hegemony is after the alien tech?" I asked after checking that no one was around.

Kaiden shook his head. "Why *wouldn't* they be? I can't believe I didn't think about that before."

"What do you mean?" questioned Maris.

"We've come across a race that's potentially figured out how to tap into the crystal control interface and use the crystalline network's innate properties to rearrange matter. Think about how valuable that kind of control would be to the Hegemony—you could remake an entire planet in a very short time, or maybe even scale the tech down to manufacture anything you could imagine."

I gaped at him. "Stars, you're right."

"The Hegemony is fairly stable and united at the moment," Kaiden continued. "But what if knowledge about this tech got out? Use it for the military, and private industry would get upset. Give everyone access and risk it falling into the hands of someone who'd use it to hurt others… It's a total gamechanger. Introducing this kind of tech is what sparks civil wars."

"Makes you wonder what really happened on Crystallis," I murmured.

Kaiden scoffed. "It wouldn't surprise me in the least if the civilization took out itself and the Saps had little to do with it."

Maris crossed her arms. "That's a disturbing concept."

I lowered my voice to a whisper. "Look, I think I trust Colren, but the people he reports to have shown some *really* bad judgment. We should be careful what we say."

"Agreed," Kaiden whispered back, and Maris nodded.

"Should we go see what Toran is up to?" I asked, returning to a normal volume.

"May as well. I'm curious what an outsider has to say about all this," Kaiden said.

We took the lift to the level that house our lounge and living quarters.

As we neared the door, Kaiden gently tugged my arm, holding me back. "Go ahead, we'll be right there," he said to Maris.

She raised an eyebrow and pursed her lips then sauntered into the lounge. The door closed behind her.

I gave Kaiden a questioning look. "Why did—" I'd barely gotten the words out before he leaned me against the wall, kissing me deeply. I happily relaxed into his arms, releasing my tension from our crazy day.

"I've been wanting to do that for hours," he murmured as we eventually parted.

"Same." I smiled up at him, still wanting more.

The doors to the lounge hissed open down the hall, and Kaiden hastily took a step back from me.

"Cool it, lovebirds," Maris said with a smirk as she poked her head out of the room. "The biology lesson can wait—Toran is all amped up to give us some schooling in quantum physics." She disappeared back inside.

Kaiden shook his head, holding in a snicker. "Wow, how long do you think she's been waiting to use that line?"

"Probably days," I replied.

Still chuckling, he gave me another kiss. "To be continued."

We followed Maris inside to find Toran leaning over the touch-surface table. A holoconference was in progress with a woman who appeared to be in her late-forties, graying hair pulled into a messy bun.

"Elle, Kaiden, this is Lisa Manswell," Toran introduced. "She'll be modest about it, but she's the Hegemony's top scientific mind when it comes to theoretical physics."

Lisa brushed off the compliment with a wave of her hand. "I muddle through. I must admit, Toran's account of your recent experience has introduced some interesting notions."

"Yes, I believe you were just about to offer an explanation for what we've been experiencing," Toran said. "I figured you'd all want to be here for that."

"Absolutely. So, what are we dealing with?" I asked.

"Dimensionally ubiquitous, zepto-elemental singularities," Lisa replied.

Kaiden raised an eyebrow. "Come again?"

"There was never any direct evidence of these singularities, but your observations are in line with what had been considered hypothetical models on the scientific fringe," the scientist explained. "They appear to be some kind of sub-fermion singularity with a quantum entanglement link spanning the dimensional planes."

I blinked at her. "Zepto-what?"

"Dimensionally ubiquitous, zepto-elemental singularities," the scientist repeated.

"Nope, that name is never going to work," I stated. "D-U-Z-E-S… How about we call them 'Duzies'?"

Toran sighed. "Elle—"

Lisa's brow knit. "That's so…"

I smiled. "A little ridiculous, I know, but it's short and memorable."

After a moment, Lisa smiled back. "You know, I actually kind of like it."

Toran flushed, casting the scientist a pleading look she seemed keen to ignore.

Kaiden smirked. "So, Toran, what were you saying about the Duzies?"

"I'm not going to call them…" Toran took a deep breath. "Anyway, these elemental singularities can explain everything we've experienced with our abilities. Theoretically, they are the building blocks of everything in our physical reality, extending into the hyperdimensional planes we recently visited. If we've been granted some sort of control-level access to those singularities, that might explain how we can now redirect the matter and energy around us into what appear to be magical effects."

"Did that happen when we were re-formed with the bioprinter?" I asked.

"Duzies almost certainly have something to do with the process, but I expect there's more at play than that alone," Lisa replied.

"Maybe something to do with our artifacts?" Kaiden suggested.

"Perhaps. The artifacts seem to be linked with the Duzies, maybe are even saturated by them," Lisa continued. "I couldn't tell you for sure without getting them into my lab, but I get the impression you won't be heading back to the Capital anytime soon."

"No, we won't, but we *can* say for certain that the artifacts exhibit strange properties," Toran said.

The scientist nodded. "I have no doubt about that. In lieu of the artifacts being in my lab for detailed analysis, I'll review the scans of them taken during the decontamination procedure and also look over your medical records with the biologists on our team. We may yet be able to get you more detailed answers about the mechanism behind your abilities."

"I really don't care so long as they work," I said.

For practical purposes, yes," Kaiden said, "but understanding *how* our abilities function might yield more information about the crystalline network itself—or what the aliens seek to control."

"We don't yet know what is above the eighth-dimensional plane we experienced," Toran said.

"Well, there are three options that we know about," Lisa replied.

I came to attention. "You know what's there?"

"In theoretical models, anyway. Before today, we never had any firsthand accounts of anything beyond 6D," she said. "The science suggests that 9D, which the sword seems to be linked to, is the crystalline network itself, 10D is consciousness—the part of ourselves that resyncs after a reset— and the eleventh dimension is the domain of the barely-understood dimensionally ubiquitous, zepto-elemental singularities. Duzies really are a *doozy*." She grinned.

I laughed. "I was waiting for someone to do it. Well done."

She bowed her head. "Delivering bad science puns is my second job."

While we were joking, Maris stood with her eyes wide. "Consciousness is *above* the crystalline network storage?"

Lisa composed herself. "It's important to distinguish between 'thought' and 'memory'," she explained. "Our memories are the organic constructs, which are recreated through neural pathways during the reset process. It's our consciousness—our internal self-awareness and volition—which utilizes our memories and creates our thoughts, bringing in the near-term feelings and recollections from the time after a reset point is established. Memories, consciousness, thoughts—all of those components make us ourselves."

"What about the universal resets?" Kaiden asked.

Toran nodded. "I'd pieced together some of it before, but I didn't have the dimensional map to complete the picture until now. See, all of our physical traits and memories are stored in 9D via the crystalline network backups. Restoring that much information during a universal-scale reset must eat up almost all of the available 'bandwidth' in the crystals—so there's only enough data for our 10D consciousness to recall memories for various past moments in time. Therefore, memories of previous-futures, which could be innumerable and incredibly complex, are lost or lose focus. Localized resets, by contrast, don't put nearly the same amount of strain on the crystalline network, so we are able to get an accurate 'download' of our memories from previous-futures, as well. That's why, after the universal reset, we could sense something was missing but couldn't grasp it. I think it was only due to our proximity to the locus of the reset event that our team was able to remember; the network dedicated a little extra bandwidth to enable a partial download of our previous-future memories since we initiated the reset."

"This reset thing is a whole lot more complicated than I realized," I said.

"Makes you appreciate what a thin line we walk to keep society from falling apart, huh?" Kaiden replied.

I shook my head. "Yeah, no wonder they minimize resets on the Capital."

"Oh, stars, yes!" Lisa said. "It's a wonder there aren't more mishaps. I mean, I have no recollection whatsoever about the universal reset. I wouldn't even believe it, except the rest of data Toran has presented lines up."

"Not to mention the potential for tampering," Toran said.

Lisa nodded gravely. "That's true. We've already seen what happens when the reset interface is highjacked. The aliens essentially hacked the crystalline network to modify planets however they saw fit. At least, that's our working hypothesis."

"Speaking of them," I began, leaning forward, "if the matter-rearranging is done through these 11D Duzies—which I'm guessing are completely invisible, then how can we see the dark cloud coming from the alien ships that dissolves anything in its path?"

Lisa nodded. "That's not the same. My guess is that the dark cloud might be some sort of 6D nanotech."

"And how are we supposed to disable it so we don't instantly die?" Kaiden asked.

"Easiest thing would be to work from a higher dimensional plane. Couldn't touch you that way," she stated.

"Ah, yes, of course." I caught myself and I sighed. "And there it is. My judgment for what constitutes a reasonable answer is officially broken."

"I HAVE NO idea what to do," I admitted to my friends as soon as we ended the holoconference with Lisa.

"The problem is we don't have enough information." Toran propped his elbows on the tabletop and leaned forward.

"How are we supposed to *get* information?" Kaiden asked. "We can't even see the Saps from our normal reality."

"Like Lisa said, we just need to be on a higher plane," Maris replied. "Don't you see? We can travel through 7D and pop in at the correct corresponding places in 6D. Aaand, we happen to have a guide who's native to 7D and can show us the ropes."

As much as I appreciated Hoofy's willingness to help, I wasn't confident we should place so much faith in our new friend. Aside from the fact that he was, well, a unicorn—a creature I'd been taught growing up wasn't real—Hoofy had gotten himself lost and trapped. I figured it warranted a bit of skepticism when it came to following a guide with that kind of track record.

Unfortunately, Hoofy's telepathy was a step faster than my brain's connection to my mouth. *"I would gladly guide you."*

"That's a generous offer, but is it smart for us to go back to that place, knowing what we know now?" Kaiden asked, to my relief.

"Yeah, we were lucky to get out of there the first time," I said. "The moment the Saps start looking for us, we'll be at a huge disadvantage."

Kaiden nodded. "Lots of exposure, both while we're landing and wandering around."

Maris rolled her eyes. "No, don't you see? We don't have to take a shuttle back to that planet at all. We have the viewing-sphere here on the *Evangiel*. We can use that as our access point."

Toran's eyebrows drew together in thought. "That *would* be an interesting approach. Since distance and time don't follow the same rules we're used to in this plane, I suppose it might actually be feasible for us to get there from here."

I eyed him skeptically. "Are you talking about *walking* back to that planet?"

"In 7D," Maris interjected.

"Yeah, but we're more than a four-hour ship ride from there in normal space," I objected. "Even with the differences in transit, is that reasonable?"

"Not to mention, I thought when we perceived the higher planes, we were also *here*—we don't actually 'go' anywhere," Kaiden said.

"That's not exactly true," Toran replied. "When we access the higher dimensions, we also theoretically gain the ability to act upon and take shortcuts across the lower planes. As such, I believe we can alter the degree to which we are seen in the lower planes, in the same manner we can't see Hoofy in our spacetime unless he wants to be seen."

Maris grinned. "I knew you'd come around to the nickname."

"I am simply using it as a matter of convenience," Toran replied. "That's hardly the issue at present."

I raised an eyebrow. "Yeah, more importantly, you're still glossing over the part where we walk across the star system in 7D."

Maris sighed. "That's *not* what I said."

Kaiden pursed his lips. "Now that I think about it, if we did a fly-by…"

I didn't like the sound of that. "Please tell me you don't mean what I think you mean."

"If you think I meant have the *Evangiel* swing by the planet at near orbit distance to drop us off, then yes."

"That's a terrible idea," I said. "We'll be stranded until they can loop around to grab us."

"No, remember, the time passage isn't the same in higher dimensions," Maris said. "When we transitioned before, it was like no time had passed at all in this plane."

"So, you're saying the *Evangiel* will fly in close, we use the viewing-sphere to transition to 7D, do our thing, get back to the viewing-sphere, all before the *Evangiel* leaves range?" I asked.

Maris nodded. "Easy."

"No, *not* easy. It's nuts." That was without even taking into consideration the part of Hoofy needing to successfully navigate for us.

"It actually might work," Toran said.

I stared at him. "You *can't* be serious." I was used to being the one to come up with crazy ideas. What did it mean that I was now the most rational person sitting in the room? Either I was missing something, or fear and desperation had caused my teammates to lose their minds.

"We do have unique skills, Elle," Kaiden said. "Shouldn't we use those to our advantage?"

"Yes, but…" I trailed off, not knowing what I could say that would make a compelling argument against the insane plan they were hatching. Truth be told, the more I thought about it, the more brilliant it was starting to sound.

We knew our fleet was no match for the Saps, and the four of us couldn't take on an entire civilization using our weapons. To win the fight, we needed to think outside the box—and operating from a different dimensional plane was *definitely* unconventional. If we could learn about the right weakness and make a targeted strike from a higher plane, no Hegemony ships or soldiers would come to harm and we'd be relatively safe ourselves.

"All right," I continued after a pause. "Maybe you *are* on to something."

Maris smirked. "Told you."

I took a deep breath. "One big concern does come to mind—"

"Only one?" Kaiden interjected with a smile.

I smiled back. "Just trying to keep things reasonable. But, Toran, didn't you say we can *theoretically* alter our presence? I mean, the Saps are native to 6D. Even if we can access 8D or above, does that really give us the ability to make it so they don't know we're there?"

"You have done this before, when you were in the dimension where we met," Hoofy said in our minds. *"I believe this strategy is your best chance."*

"That's all the confirmation I need," Maris said.

I took a slow breath. "I think we should take some time to process all of this and get some rest. I don't trust myself to make smart decisions right now."

"Yeah, I know what you mean," Kaiden agreed. "Why don't we meet up in... six hours?"

"Very well." Toran inclined his head.

Maris tossed her hands in the air. "Fine. But I think we should do something before the Saps decide to send another ship in our direction."

"I'm certain they would have done that already if they had a means of engaging us at this location on our plane," Kaiden said.

"Still, I'll advise Colren to keep the ship in motion," Toran murmured. "Anything we can do to make ourselves a more difficult target."

"No argument here." I headed for the door.

"See you in a few," Kaiden said to the others, following me.

I took a brisk pace down the corridor to my quarters with Kaiden close behind. I palmed open the door, and he slipped inside behind me before the others had emerged from the lounge.

"Inviting yourself over, I see." I smiled up at him.

"I believe it was an unspoken invitation."

"Perhaps." I placed a hand on his chest. "All sense of logic and reason has gone out the window, hasn't it?"

He laughed. "Yeah, I can't believe that plan is actually sounding like a good idea."

"I know, right? I thought all of you had lost it, but then..."

Kaiden placed his hands gently on my upper arms. "This is way too much for any one of us to comprehend on our own. I don't think we have a choice other than to trust our instincts."

"And your gut says we should follow a unicorn through a higher dimensional plane to somehow trap some hyperdimensional baddies bent on galactic domination?"

"I was actually thinking about how we skipped dinner, but maybe I was misinterpreting the sensation."

I rolled my eyes and shuffled toward the bed, drawing him with me. "You're impossible."

"You love my humor. I can tell."

That wasn't the only thing I liked about him. The more time we spent together and more we experienced, I found myself increasingly drawn to him. More than lust and attraction, there was a level of familiar comfort, similar to what I'd shared with my longtime friends. I felt safe with him, like the dangers in rest of the universe didn't matter so long as he was nearby.

As he traced his fingers down the side of my arm, I wanted to tell him those things. Except, I couldn't form the words. I wanted to show him.

"Now, where were we before?" I cupped the side of his face in my hand and kissed him.

He eagerly kissed me back.

We lay back on my bed, and I allowed myself to forget about our mission. Our higher dimensional selves may have no use for our corporeal bodies, but I certainly liked how he made mine feel.

There was no denying the ache of desire, yet I held back. Knowing a universal reset was coming, I hated to think that I might forget our time together. We'd already shared so many firsts, but such a big one for my lifetime... I wasn't ready. Not yet.

I inched back from him, not wanting to be too much of a tease.

Kaiden sighed when he sensed me pulled away. "Yeah, I know."

"I'm sorry, I—"

"Elle," he brushed my hair from my eyes, "there's nothing to apologize for."

Stars, he was so understanding it made me want him even more. "It's not that I don't want to."

"We agreed to wait, so we'll wait."

"And you're okay with that?"

He chuckled. "I think you're trying to entrap me."

"No."

"Come on, you know there's no good answer to that question."

I propped an arm under my head as I pivoted to face him. "I warned you I'm terrible at this relationship stuff."

He placed a hand on my thigh, biting his lower lip as he avoided my direct gaze. "This is always the tricky part, when the emotional and physical aren't quite in sync." He finally looked me in the eyes. "I like you a lot, Elle—from your personality and wit..." his gaze drifted downward, "...to you being absolutely stunning. And, frankly, I'd say we shouldn't be contemplating a relationship if there wasn't mutual desire—which is obviously not an issue. But the difference between straight-up lust and the makings of a proper partnership is that I know being fully with you will be worth the wait, however long that is."

My shipsuit seemed impossibly tight and warm. "I think I need a cold shower."

Kaiden laughed. "I really didn't mean that as a turn-on."

"Respecting boundaries is sexy. Don't you ever forget it."

He smiled. "I'll always strive to respect you."

I shook my head, grinned. "Now I think you're using my words against me to get yourself laid right now."

"Hey, you opened the door." He smirked, but then promptly sat up. "Seriously, though, we don't need to rush into anything. We'll know when the time is right."

I nodded and sat up next to him. "Like when the fate of the universe isn't hanging over our heads."

"I dunno… that seems like exactly the *right* time."

"Fair point."

"But not tonight." He patted my knee. "I can't make a speech about self-control and then cave."

"You're so principled."

"Well, stubborn, at least."

I smiled. "I appreciate your dedication to proving a point."

"The pleasure of your company does make it worthwhile."

"Such a charmer when you want to be." I shook my head.

"Only for you." His hand found mine.

I swirled my fingertips around his open palm. "I can't help but wonder what things are going to be like when this is over."

"What part?"

"What our lives will look like afterward, once we've won."

Kaiden didn't reply at first.

"What are you thinking about?" I prompted.

"I…" He sighed. "All right, I'll just come out and say it. I know we've been focusing on the Saps and this seemingly impossible task that was placed before us, but I never thought this experience would also mean meeting you. And even when the battles are over, I don't want that to mean I never see you again."

I scooted closer to him. "I don't, either."

"But with a universal reset as part of the endgame…"

"We remembered the other previous-futures eventually. I have to believe we will again."

He didn't seem entirely assured, but he nodded. "Once we do, I have no idea how it'll work—literally living on different planets."

"Yeah." I hadn't wanted to confront that reality, but it had crept into the back of my mind in the quiet moments over the past several days. I knew that us being together meant that one of us would need to give up our home. Since Kaiden was only on an internship, my initial reaction had been that he should come to me. However, thinking through it, I realized that I no longer felt the ties to Erusan I did before this experience. The time away had changed me, and I wasn't sure I *wanted* to go back.

"I guess that's jumping ahead a bit much, isn't it?"

I laced my fingers through his. "To the contrary, it's nice to know we're on the same page."

He brightened. "Okay, good."

I leaned over and kissed him, slow and deep. "We should probably get some sleep."

Kaiden stood up. "As much as I'd like to stay, I don't think sharing a bed would be particularly restful for either of us at the moment."

"On this occasion, I have to agree." I rose to see him out.

"I'll see you soon." He gave me a light parting kiss.

My heart fluttered as I showed him out the door. Despite the war, something good had come out of the recent drama, and I intended to hold onto my new future.

15

FIVE HOURS IN bed never felt like a proper night's rest. As I entered the lounge, I tried to shake off the remaining grogginess that my shower hadn't cured.

I hadn't been able to get to sleep straight away after my conversation with Kaiden. My mind had kept drifting back to Erusan and my uncertain life path—knowing that I wanted Kaiden to be a part of it but being overwhelmed by thoughts of the logistics. I'd reprimanded myself for losing focus on the mission, in the way I'd promised myself I wouldn't, which had then only stressed me out more. Ultimately, I'd thought through the key events that had happened since I'd been extracted from my world, and I reminded myself that there didn't need to be a clear distinction between my life before and my present. Everything we were doing was to fight for our *future*, and I shouldn't feel guilty about looking forward to what was to come after the final battles. If anything, that made me more committed.

"Good morning!" Maris greeted in far too cheery a voice for the hour.

I massaged my temples. "I don't suppose I could get one of those pick-me-ups of yours?"

"Of course." She smiled.

A shimmering, green wave washed over me, as I felt instantly energized as it passed. Unfortunately, the effects of the spells didn't last for as long as real rest, but it was marvelous at first. By the time it started to fade, I hoped I wouldn't remember I'd been so tired in the first place.

"You're getting good at these spells," I told her.

She beamed. "Not all that different from bartending in some ways—just tonics of a more magical variety."

"I can tell you must have been great at your job. How did you get into that line of work, anyway?"

Her smile faded. "Fairly easy money for someone with not a lot of other prospects."

I tilted my head. "What do you mean?"

She hesitated. "I was on my own since I was pretty young. My mom remarried this asshole when I was fourteen, and after three years I was sick of wondering if that would be the day he'd do more than just look at me." She took an unsteady breath. "So, I left at seventeen. I had to get used to taking care of myself fast. Realized I was good at putting on a smile, and looks helped. I'm not proud of using those assets, but I did what I needed to, you know? At least waitressing and bartending were on my terms, not *him* undressing me with his eyes every time I walked in the room."

My chest constricted. "Sorry, Maris. That sounds awful."

She shrugged it off, but I could see the distress was still deep inside. Living in that kind of environment changed a person in an enduring way. "A lot of people deal with much worse. I was able to get out before it got bad, and many aren't that fortunate."

I looked down. "Guess I had it pretty easy."

"You were hurt when you were young, right? Something with your shoulder?"

"Yeah, but that's not remotely the same thing," I replied, feeling a little ashamed that she'd draw any parallel between our experiences. "That was me making my own dumb decisions and paying the price. In retrospect, I'm glad it happened because it forced me to confront the reality that everything can change in an instant and we don't always get our own personal 'do-overs' when we mess up. I treated resets like a game. That round, I lost."

Maris nodded. "In many ways, it's the mistakes and hardships that shape us more than the victories."

"For sure. I can't imagine how insufferable I would have been if I hadn't learned some humility through that experience."

"That's what's important right? The person we grow into in the end. The path along the way is always rocky and unexpected."

"Some rockier and more treacherous than others."

She smiled. "The test of character is how we deal with those challenges."

"I'm impressed with your positive outlook, Maris. I honestly had no idea you had it so rough."

"Nah, could have been a lot worse."

I raised an eyebrow and leaned forward. "You were supporting yourself at seventeen. That's not insignificant. By comparison, I'm embarrassed by how spoiled I was."

"Having a good home life isn't something to be embarrassed by," she replied. "You clearly appreciate what you had and didn't turn out all stuck-up and self-centered."

"I'm sure it helped having a therapist as a mom. Hearing stories about what some of her patients were going through—anonymously, of course—did help keep things in perspective."

Maris looked me over. "It's more than that. You have the sort of innate confidence I admire, Elle."

I shook my head.

"No, really," she insisted. "You're the kind of person who's a natural leader—you have vision and focus, but you still think of the team and greater good. There was a time I would have said I was envious of those qualities, but considering that we were transformed into our 'ideal selves' or whatever, I know I must not need that in myself to be happy. But, it's... inspiring to have you on the team."

I smiled. "Thanks. For what it's worth, I can't imagine the Dark Sentinels without you." I paused. "I know we didn't get off to the best start."

She waved her hand dismissively. "I'm well aware I didn't make a great first impression."

"Those initial shoes you picked..."

Maris laughed. "I'll never admit there isn't always room for being fashionable, but okay... those were not a good choice. More than that, though, I didn't act like a member of the team. You tried to include me, and I resisted at every turn."

"It was a tough situation to be thrown into."

"That's no excuse. All of you faced the same thing." She took a deep breath. "I think I was just used to having to take care of myself and needing to have my guard up."

"I don't blame you."

She was silent for several seconds. "That's why I was so excited to get that shield. It's beautiful, but also powerful—a tool I could use to keep away anything that might hurt me."

I nodded with understanding. "It's not *just* a shield or an artifact. Something symbolic."

"Yeah."

I took a moment to reflect on everything she'd told me. I'd gotten the wrong impression about her. "I'm glad you opened up, Maris. I know some of that must be difficult to talk about."

She smiled weakly. "Thanks for listening."

"Always! I'm sorry for not making a better effort to be friendly earlier."

"Don't worry—that was on both sides." Maris got a wistful look in her eyes. "It's interesting which abilities we each manifested, even beyond our alignment with the disciplines. I always wished I could have a protective wall around me and to grow up faster so I could get away, and I ended up being able to cast magical shells and change time perception."

"Stars, I hadn't thought about it that way." I reflected on my own abilities in that context and realized that many of my abilities were centered around things I couldn't do because of my injury; I even wielded my sword lefthanded.

Maris held up her hands and studied them. "Maybe my desire to protect myself is what's driven me to help others. I hope I can find a way to use this healing magic."

I didn't have the heart to remind her that we would likely lose our abilities after the universal reset. "I know you will."

The lounge door hissed open and Kaiden entered, flashing a warm smile.

"Morning jolt?" Maris offered him.

He shrugged. "Sure, may as well." A green wave washed over him, and he noticeably perked up. "I don't know why we don't do this all the time."

"Because it's only special when it's a treat," Maris replied matter-of-factly.

"Yeah, I guess." Kaiden looked around. "Hey, where's Toran?"

"I was wondering the same thing," I said.

"He dropped by a few minutes ago and muttered something about 'contingency plans', then headed to Central Command," Maris replied.

I exchanged glances with Kaiden. "Should we follow him?"

Maris shook her head. "He said he'd be right back."

"All right." I plopped down at the table. "Any more thoughts on what we discussed last night?"

"I really think we should go," Maris responded, sitting down across from me. "I had a long talk with Hoofy."

"About what?" I asked.

"It started out as a discussion about our mission, but he ended up telling me more about his experience with the other planes, and about the Saps."

I raised an eyebrow. "If he knows so much, then why didn't he say anything sooner?"

Maris pursed her lips. "He wanted to make sure we wouldn't use the information for our own gain."

"How?"

She dropped her voice to a whisper, beckoning us closer. "Apparently, the Saps have some pretty interesting tech that's powerful enough the beings on higher dimensions have taken notice."

I cocked my head. "What does higher-dimensional tech look like?"

"I'm guessing it's more complicated than a toaster," Kaiden replied.

Maris groaned. "This isn't a joke. It's not just the tech itself but how they use it. It sounds like there's some kind of energy grid."

"Like, the crystalline network?" I asked.

"No, Hoofy said that's in a higher plane. This is something in 6D where they reside, but it does offer a link to the higher dimensions. The Saps themselves can't access the higher planes, but the energy grid is tied to them, and it will be a threat if it's left unchecked."

My brow knit. "How would that even—"

"Our sense of place and time is different," Hoofy interjected in my mind. *"Paths and doorways aren't the same to us."*

"Neither are thoughts, apparently," I muttered.

"I am not reading your mind, Elle. That would be a violation."

I wasn't sure I believed him, but I didn't want to belabor the matter. "Okay, so there's this 6D tech. What does that have to do with us and our mission?"

"Because I know where you can access the core of their energy grid," Hoofy replied.

Kaiden's eye widened. "All right, I'm intrigued."

"Okay, yes, that sounds like a genuine lead," I admitted.

Maris nodded emphatically. "Last night, he walked me through how we get there. We can do it."

"Did you tell Toran about it already?" Kaiden asked.

"Yeah, we both got here early this morning," she said.

I looked to Kaiden. "I'm guessing he jumped the gun and messaged something to Colren, and now the Hegemony is making plans without us."

Kaiden nodded. "Remember when Colren was asking about tech before? Any hint of a real lead and I bet they'll get all starry-eyed."

"Is Toran trying to get them to back off or collaborate?" I wondered aloud.

"He cares about his family more than anything. He wouldn't make a deal that undermined our ability to get back to our loved ones—I'm sure of that," Maris said.

I crossed my arms. "Well, he better not promise *anything* without running it by us first. When we're inevitably running for our lives after doing whatever it is we end up doing, I don't want him to say, 'Wait, we need to do this thing I said we'd do'."

"Like they can actually hold us to anything," Kaiden pointed out. "Our best-case scenario is performing a universal reset. No one is going to remember what we did or didn't do, anyway."

"I will remember," Hoofy said.

"Unless you plan to file a full report with the Hegemony about whatever we do, the unicorns remembering the fine deeds of the Dark Sentinels doesn't change much for us," I shot back with more bite than I'd intended.

"Elle…" Kaiden began soothingly.

I took a deep breath. "Sorry, I just really don't like the idea of us trying to get weapons or tech from the bad guys. We all saw what they're capable of."

"The Black Cloud of Death is awful any way you look," Kaiden agreed.

The door hissed open, and I snapped my head around to see Toran taking up the doorway.

"Sorry I'm late." He entered.

"Please tell me you didn't sell our souls to the Hegemony," I said.

Toran's brow knit. "I think I missed something."

"Your impromptu meeting in Central Command," Maris supplied. "Elle and Kaiden got it in their heads that you were striking a deal with the leadership about stealing alien tech."

He leaned on the table next to me. "I've been gone for, what, fifteen minutes? That didn't take long for you to jump to some strange conclusions."

"Not *conclusions*," I backpedaled. "Just, uh… notions."

Toran looked me over. "Right. Well, I wasn't making clandestine deals, sorry to disappoint. I actually went to talk with Colren about the comm issues we've been having on many of these worlds with alien activity."

"That makes a lot more sense," I murmured.

"Any remedies?" Kaiden asked.

"I couldn't sleep last night, so I was thinking about the interface for your pendant," Toran explained. "Before, we were only looking at the connection between the crystals in terms of frequencies and signals, but now that we know the network is hyperdimensional, I started wondering if we could augment the standard hyperdimensional comms using a crystalline connection."

Kaiden came to attention. "As in, use my pendant as a booster for the comm signal?"

"Yes, that's the gist of it," Toran replied. "And the viewing-sphere is already on board, so it could be tied into the ship's long-range communication suite."

"I have to say, I'd feel a lot better about our seventh-dimensional plan if we had a way to talk to the *Evangiel*," I said.

"Yeah, absolutely," Kaiden agreed.

"Okay. Then, I guess we're proceeding with the plan to do the flyby and trek through 7D," Toran said.

I suppressed the urge to second-guess our decision. "How long will it take to get everything set up?"

"Should have it ready by the time the *Evangiel* reaches the planet," he replied.

I nodded. "Okay, let's get ready to go."

Kaiden, Maris, and I spent the next hour chatting with Hoofy about his knowledge of the Saps and what we could expect to encounter in the seventh dimension along our route. Whenever he started discussing his home plane, I couldn't help imagining a fairytale land filled with unicorns and dragons and rainbows. I got the impression the last one was a reach, but the other two... Well, it started to get pretty clear where the ancient lore came from—maybe some travelers had somehow ascended to a higher plane or of the supposedly mythical beings had once dwelled in normal spacetime. I was looking forward to witnessing the ancient majesty firsthand.

As the time for our transition through the viewing-sphere neared, we met up with Toran in the secret chamber near Central Command. He was in the process of testing the new connection when we arrived.

"I think this will actually work," he said, admiring the product of his labors.

"Won't know for sure until we're wandering around 7D." I placed my hands on my hips.

"We'll be at the drop point in two minutes," a familiar voice said behind me from the doorway. I turned to see Colren watching us.

"If this goes as planned, it won't seem like we've gone anywhere," I said to him.

"Then it feels a little silly for me to say I'll see you soon." He cracked a smile.

"I'll never turn down well-wishes." I flashed a smile back, then approached the sphere.

"Good luck to all of you," Colren said, passing his gaze to each of us in turn. "May you find your way safely back to us."

We'd made a calculated decision to keep Hoofy's existence to ourselves, and this wasn't the moment to reveal that we'd have a hyperdimensional guide. "We'll do our best," I told him.

Maris got in position near the viewing-sphere. "It feels weird to be leaving without our gear packs."

"I dunno, this will force us to up our magic game," I said.

"That it will." Kaiden stepped up next to me. "So, how do we do this?"

"Same as last time, I suppose." I drew my sword, knowing now that it was a key aspect of making the transition to the higher planes. "Imagine what we want to happen, and hopefully it will."

"Here's hoping," Kaiden murmured.

"I'm all set with the comms," Toran announced. "We can transition whenever we come into optimal range."

Colren studied the info panel on the side wall. "Just over a minute to go."

"Okay, you know our target," I said to the rest of my team.

"I will guide you," Hoofy said in our minds, unbeknownst to Colren.

"Ready whenever you are," Maris replied aloud to both of us.

We stood poised around the viewing-sphere, waiting for Colren's acknowledgement that we were in position.

At last, he nodded to us. "It's time."

Gripping my sword, I reached out to the sphere with my free hand in unison with my teammates. "Here we go."

AS MY HAND made contact with the smooth crystal, a tingle ran up my arm then spread through my body. My vision fractured and unfolded into different facets. On one of the distorted planes, the majestic form of a unicorn came into focus.

"This is the path to the plane you seek," Hoofy instructed.

I willed myself toward the facet where he stood waiting for us.

Though I imagined myself passing through the facet like a doorway, I instead sensed my awareness expanding until I unfolded out into the seventh-dimensional plane. The sensation disoriented me, unhinging my sense of self. I fought to imagine a physical form—something familiar for me to latch onto. Slowly, a new perception of reality unfolded.

A bridge stretched out in front of me, seemingly suspended in midair. Soft, diffused light came from every direction, casting no shadows. The bridge itself was barely perceptible, a mesh of translucent filaments that reminded me of spider silk. Based on appearance alone, it looked like the bridge would bend underfoot, but it felt as strong as if I was standing on stone.

Toran, Kaiden, and Maris appeared around me in the same configuration in which we had been standing on the *Evangiel*, with the viewing-sphere suspended at the center of the bridge between us. Hoofy was standing in full view several meters away.

Kaiden immediately rested the end of his staff on the bridge and placed his free hand on his stomach. "That was way worse than last time."

Maris looked a little green. "You'd think going to a lower plane would be easier."

I took a steadying breath and sheathed my sword, seeing no immediate threat. "We still have a lot to learn about how these transitions work, but that can wait."

"Yes, clock's ticking." Kaiden caught himself. "Or, maybe not. I suppose we're outside the normal flow of time in our plane, aren't we?"

Maris shook her head. "I don't want to think about it. Hoofy?"

The unicorn tossed his head and snuffled. *"The energies of this plane are difficult for your kind to focus on. Now that you are here, the discomfort will dissipate."*

"Well, that's a relief," I said.

"And while, yes, we are above the flow of time here, it is not prudent to delay. Follow me." Hoofy loped across the bridge away from us.

I broke into a run, finding my movements easy and natural, just like they had in the eighth-dimensional window maze. If we found ourselves in an engagement, at least I'd know how to handle myself.

Just as I'd experienced on the hyperdimensional planes before, distance was distorted and difficult to judge. For that matter, my sensation of time passing was also impaired—like my internal clock was off. Were it not for my rhythmic strides as we ran across the ethereal bridge, I'd have had no confirmation that I'd traveled anywhere or that any time had passed.

"What is this place?" I asked to break the silence.

"This is a thoroughfare connecting the worlds," Hoofy replied. *"The closer to an inhabited place, the more possible branches and drop-out points."*

"So, we really *could* walk between planets," Kaiden murmured.

"Yes, though even here, I do not know if your kind would have the patience for the journey. To walk a path of that length leaves one alone with their thoughts, and not everyone would welcome that kind of prolonged introspection."

"Do you feel time passage?" I asked him.

"I sense time in the way you might dip your hand into the current of a stream. I can direct it and pause its progression for a time, but it will ultimately continue its advance the moment my intervention fails. Therefore, my kind focused on specific moments and experiences. If we wish

to capture a moment, we make a dam in the stream. When we are ready to move on, we allow the current to take over once more."

Maris smiled. "That's really beautiful."

"A wonder to you and a simple matter of existence for my kind."

"I don't know that I'll ever get used to this perspective," Kaiden said.

"Me either." I shook my head.

"Some matters are beyond our understanding," Toran murmured in the tone he used when discussing philosophical matters. "And it's okay for us to accept them as they are."

"Works for me." I picked up my pace, realizing that we'd started to lag behind Hoofy.

Eventually, the bridge widened and then split into a multitude of pathways, each branching into new bridges. The forms had an organic quality to them, curving gently around an unseen sphere.

"Are these bending around the planet?" I asked.

"In a sense, but it is not a direct parallel to your physical reality. Think of it as being structured around the natural energies of this world."

"Where do the rest of your kind live?" I was willing to suspend my disbelief, but I was getting unnerved by everything we'd seen so far. Though the lack of distinct 'place' was disconcerting, my more pressing concern was that we hadn't seen any other creatures since we arrived. Considering that this plane was supposedly Hoofy's home, I'd expected to see other unicorns by now.

"Yeah, it does feel a little… empty around here," Kaiden agreed.

"Oh, we are far from alone," Hoofy replied. He slowed his pace and veered to the right side of the bridge. He extended his horn beyond the boundary of the pathway, and a bright point originating at its tip burned through the diffused light, parting clouds I hadn't realized were there.

The fog dispersed, revealing a breathtaking pastoral landscape framed by towering, distant peaks and a forest with trees unlike anything I'd ever seen. Their overall forms were similar to trunks and branches as I'd expect, but their makeup and material, rather than being wood and leaves, appeared to be pure energy—white-blue trunks sprouted directly from the ground and morphed into branches, which eventually discharged into the air to create an electrical canopy. The 'ground' itself was a welcoming shade of green, though like the filament bridge, it was an apparently solid material floating in near-nothingness. Short, reed-like grasses covered the field, and their bases simply merged into the ambient light.

Three figures in the distant reaches of the field raised their heads while we observed—the unmistakable silhouette of unicorns.

Hoofy stepped back. The opening remained, though the edges began slowly closing in.

"Do you know them?" Maris asked.

"All of our kind are known to each other."

"Then why aren't you going to see them? Why can't you go home after being trapped?" I pressed. Hoofy's behavior didn't make any sense, and it was unnerving me even more now that we were relying on him to guide us.

The unicorn bowed his head, taking several moments to reply. *"I was not entirely truthful before. When you freed me, I could have gone home, but my choices have made me an outsider."*

Maris' brow knit. "What do you mean?"

The opening to the serene pasture closed.

"By aligning myself with you, I am no longer welcome among my kind."

My heart dropped. "Huefneril, I'm so sorry. I had no idea." Using his full name seemed more appropriate in the moment. My gut twisted at the thought of having doubted his intentions when he'd given up his home to help us.

Maris paled. "But why? What does helping us have to do with anything?"

"The truths I led you to are revered and guarded. You are young and untested; others of my kind would deem you unworthy. But I knew from my experience of being trapped, unable to do anything but observe, that you hold rare power and must continue in your quest at any cost. I have no shame in doing what I know to be right, even if the others do not see it that way."

"Sounds like good riddance to me," Kaiden muttered.

I shot him a warning glare.

"But being excommunicated sucks any way you look at it," he hastily added. "And we really owe you for helping us out."

"Yes, we do," I agreed. That was assuming Hoofy was telling the truth. The explanation still seemed too simple and didn't quite add up.

"Come, we are almost to the destination." Hoofy resumed loping down the bridge.

I took a deep breath. "Lead the way."

We followed the filament bridge to the left, taking an offshoot which twisted the path so we wound up walking upside down from our original orientation.

"That was a first," I quipped as soon as we'd completed the transition.

"A scientist could have a field day in here studying the physical laws of this place," Kaiden said.

"More like multiple lifetimes," Toran replied.

Maris grinned. "See? Aren't you glad we came? We're getting to see something no one else in our lifetime ever may."

"That is pretty special," I had to admit.

"Wish the circumstances were a little different," Kaiden said. "You know, not a desperate attempt to avert certain doom."

"I think we've been able to upgrade from 'certain' doom to 'possible', given that we now sorta have a plan." I flashed a playful smile.

"Oh, yeah, we've totally got this."

I brushed my fingertips along his as we walked, happy to steal a moment of clandestine contact while we had the chance. Though we were in extensions of our familiar bodies, I somehow felt even more connected to him through the gentle touch.

Hoofy stopped. *"This is the place."*

"Where is it, exactly?" Kaiden asked.

"This corresponds to a central location in the Overlord's domain," Hoofy explained, reverting to his term for them, I noted. *"Transitioning here will place you at the entry—the properties of the place make it too risky to go directly inside."*

I sighed. "Sounds like we'll be walking right into the middle of a nightmare."

"The Overlords will not expect you, and that will make you difficult to see. More importantly, you have something they do not—the ability to transition out of their plane at will."

"We were wondering about that!" I said. "One of them attacked us before we met you, and we couldn't figure out why more of them didn't come to help."

"They must use these trans-dimensional gateways to make the transition, such as the viewing-spheres," Hoofy explained. *"Even then, they must be charged to make the transition and maintain their abilities. They*

have been seeking a more efficient way to remain on your plane."

"Okay, that explains why we weren't overrun," Kaiden said.

"What is this 'charging'?" Toran asked.

"You will see," Hoofy assured us. *"If you run into difficulty, I will direct you back to here as I did before."*

Maris bit her lip. "If you're staying here, how do we get… down there?" She gestured vaguely at the ground.

"More of an 'over there', I think?" I made an equally vague swirling motion with my hard around me.

"Whatever, you know what I mean." She cast an imploring gaze toward Hoofy.

"I will guide you, but I can only stay a moment. They must not know any of my kind are aiding you."

"Why not?" I asked.

"It would upset the balance."

I wanted to question the cryptic response, but Hoofy had started to fade from my vision. *"Do not use your artifacts. They will sense them."*

"Don't we need them to change planes?" I asked.

"Your higher-dimensional constructs are restricted to one plane at a time. You are now saturated with enough Duzies to transition to adjacent planes without your artifacts, but larger transitions will still require the use of your artifacts," Hoofy replied. His presence filled my mind even as he continued to fade from my vision. *"Trust, Elle. This is not a time for doubt."* I could tell the words were meant for me alone.

"I'll try," I replied telepathically, doing my best to embrace the words as truth. Reservations or not, I needed to do whatever was necessary to make it to the next phase of our mission.

Holding Hoofy's presence in my mind, I followed him as he reached toward the lower plane. The bridge and light faded around me, replaced by blackness.

Subtle shapes came into focus—a black wall rising eight meters, several three-meter-tall columns, distant towers. I could barely distinguish the shapes from the surrounding darkness. After a moment, I realized the only source of light was Hoofy's soft glow.

"You are here. I will be watching and waiting to guide you back when your task is complete." The unicorn disappeared.

"Why is it so dark?" I whispered.

Percussive clicks sounded in the darkness from a dozen meters away, and one of the forms I'd taken to be a column moved. Eyes wide, I realized that it was actually a sentry.

"Shit," Kaiden swore under his breath, backing away next to me.

I kept my voice at a low whisper, "So much for a stealth approach." I reached for my sword.

"Wait." Toran held us his hand, stilling us.

The clicks ceased and the sentry shifted its position. Then, they returned to stoic stillness.

Toran pressed behind his ear, and I hear a chirp in my own ear as the comms activated. "I don't think they can see us," he said at the barely audible level the devices were designed to facilitate. "We need to find a secure vantage point." He pointed backward away from the sentries.

I turned my attention to the matter at hand. "They can't 'see us'—meaning they can't visually see, or they haven't spotted us?"

"We'll need to test that," Toran replied. "I don't want to do that here."

"He's right. Come on." Kaiden formed a dim orb in his palm to provide just enough light for us to find a path leading away from the guards.

The ground was covered in the same fibrous, mossy substance we'd encountered on the alien ship, and I noticed several vines snaking across the dark landscape. I could just make out the path of some of the vines leading into nearby structures, which I'd first mistaken for natural hills.

"Over here." Maris motioned us toward an alcove between two of the structures. Protected on three sides, we could get our bearings without having to watch our backs too closely.

"Okay, this is *exactly* what I should have expected, but it still seems strange," I said once we were in the relative safety of the alcove.

"It really does bear a striking resemblance to the infected worlds," Toran agreed.

Kaiden nodded. "Definitely supports our original hypothesis about the Darkness being for bio-optimization."

"Guess they wanted to spread the love and share all this… greatness." I looked around with distaste at the bleak surroundings.

"Regarding the light," Kaiden went on, "I seem to recall that the creatures on the Valor world didn't have eyes—or that the eyes were black."

"Yeah, that's right," I confirmed. "The thing I saw on the ship had red eyes, though, and it *definitely* saw us."

He pursed his lips pensively. "That may have been modified. For that matter, the thing we encountered on this planet in the chamber after the labyrinth had eyes, too."

"It would make sense that they'd be blind, being in an environment like this," I said.

Toran sighed. "But not having sight, their other senses are no doubt enhanced—possibly even senses we can't fathom."

"Well, they haven't been able to track us well in the past," I pointed out. "So, at least there's that."

"But we've also never been on their home turf," Kaiden countered.

"We came here to learn about them, so we should do that rather than speculate," Maris urged.

I peeked out the alcove, finding no visible creatures nearby. "You're right. Staying in a hidey-hole won't get us anywhere. I say we try to test out our detection theories first, but not on those sentries. Let's see if we can find somewhere a little less prominent."

"Hoofy, can you hear us?" Maris asked at a slightly higher volume. "Do you know where we can find one of the Overlords on their own?" Several anxious seconds passed with no reply. "Hoofy'?" she repeated.

"*I am searching,*" the unicorn said at last. "*There are not as many inside this facility as in the rest of the city.*"

"What is this place?" I asked. "Saying 'facility' makes it sound like some sort of industrial complex."

"*Yes, think of it as the outer yard of a power station. I will return.*"

While we waited for Hoofy's report, I took another peek outside the alcove to further orient myself. My vision had acclimated somewhat to the dark, so objects were easier to make out. It wasn't pitch black, as originally had seemed the case, but rather there were tiny pinpoints of light throughout each of the vines; they had probably been there all along on the other planets, but the brighter surroundings had hidden the detail. The pinpoints of light pulsed gently in a rippling wave.

"They're alive," I whispered to Kaiden, directing his attention toward one of the vines near us, a larger one nearly a meter in diameter.

His brow drew together. "You know, if this place is a power station, then these are likely power conduits."

"*I have found what you requested,*" Hoofy cut in. "*Leave this hiding place, and I will lead you to an Overlord that you can study.*"

Maris frowned. "I suddenly don't like this plan."

"We either proceed or go back to the *Evangiel* with nothing," I replied. "Gotta push forward."

She took a steadying breath. "I know."

17

WE CREPT FROM our hiding place and picked our way through the vines to the right, following Hoofy's telepathic directions. After what felt like several minutes, Hoofy's instructions abruptly stopped.

"I cannot follow along with you further. Any closer and they may detect our communications."

I started. "They can sense telepathy?"

"They can do much more than that."

Toran's eye widened. "Why didn't you tell us this sooner?"

"I have already interfered more than I intended. Some things you must discover on your own as part of your path. I am only here to point you in the right direction." Leave it to a unicorn to make a declarative stance on what extent it's okay to meddle with the future.

"Where do we go from here?" I asked.

"Continue in this direction. You're almost there." He paused. *"I have already spent too much time here—they can sense me. I will be waiting for you when you complete your mission."*

"Wait!" Maris cried, but I could detect that Hoofy was no longer linked with our minds.

"Come on, nothing we can do about it now." I forged ahead.

We soon encountered what Hoofy had undoubtedly intended for us to find.

"Stars…" Kaiden gulped.

This creature almost fit the embodiment of the 'Overlord' moniker. Standing three meters tall, it sat atop a bench made of dark vines. The ends of the vines were embedded in its flesh, with pulsing light emanating from each of the connection points. The resulting effect was both regal and terrifying. It had the same flexible body and smooth skin that we'd seen on others of its kind, with tendrils parted and draped along its torso where the vine-like cables connected.

"What's it doing?" Maris whispered through our comms, terror evident in her tone.

"It's almost like it's… charging," Kaiden said, his face twisted with disgusted awe. "Is that what Hoofy meant before when he was talking about them needing to 'charge' in order to transition between dimensional planes?"

Maris scrunched her nose. "But what's the power source?"

"Very curious," Toran murmured.

I evaluated the scene. "So, I'm guessing these vines are for more than decoration."

"Their purpose as some sort of energy transmission medium is different than I imagined," Toran replied. "I wouldn't have expected the creatures themselves to draw directly from it."

"Might not be *just* energy," Kaiden pointed out. "Could have an information component, or something else."

I considered the suggestion. "Maybe not all of them interface like this. I mean, that doesn't seem very practical. What if this one is… special?"

"You think that's why Hoofy took so long to locate it?" Maris questioned.

"I'd be nice if he'd stuck around for us to *ask him*," I muttered.

"Hey, he's putting himself at risk to help us," she shot back.

"Hardly as much as the risk we're taking, ourselves." I took a deep breath. "It doesn't matter. We need to make the most of the situation."

"Right, checking their perception of us," Kaiden said.

Toran pensively examined the alien being. "Despite Hoofy's intentions, this might not be a good subject. Though it's alone, since it seems to be connected to a network, disturbing it may immediately trigger an alarm if it spots us."

"Should we wait for it to disconnect?" I asked.

"If they're telepathic, do hardwire connections even matter?" Kaiden countered.

Toran frowned. "I don't like the idea of waiting here for an indeterminate amount of time, but I also don't like the idea of sneaking into their fortress without having a sense of what we can get away with."

"Agreed," Kaiden said. "Let's give it a little bit. If it doesn't make any sign of moving, we can reevaluate."

"I can live with that," I replied. Really, I hated the idea of staying in the creepy dark place a moment longer, but I liked the notion of getting into an unwinnable engagement with the hyperdimensional aliens even less.

We settled into a fairly protected nook between some of the larger vines where we had a decent vantage on our alien subject while still retaining multiple escape paths if we got unexpected company. The strange time passage in the plane made the waiting especially bizarre, and I soon had no sense for how long we may have been there. However, I felt none of the anxiousness I normally would have under such circumstances. I was so in the moment that I was surprised when the alien being roused on its bench.

"Here we go," Kaiden whispered.

I re-centered myself. "That didn't take long."

"Honestly not sure about that," Toran replied as he shifted his position to get a better view.

"What's the plan?" Maris asked.

I looked around to be sure there were no other creatures nearby. "I think we should start out with a basic visual test," I said.

Kaiden frowned. "Meaning?"

"Walk out in the open and see if it responds. Well, creep out quietly," I replied.

"There's no doubt these beings can detect our presence," Toran stated. "Even if it can't 'see' you in a traditional sense, heat, electrical impulses, magical energy signature, or any other factors will almost certainly bring you to their attention."

"But that's kind of beside the point, isn't it?" Kaiden asked. "What we *really* need to test isn't that they notice we're here, but if they view us as a threat—or if there's a way to behave that makes them ignore us."

I nodded. "Yeah, exactly. I don't mean to literally test if it can see me, but rather if we can walk by one of these things without getting into a fight."

"And if it instantly attacks you?" Toran questioned.

"Well, then there's a whole team here to jump in." I shrugged. "I know, not ideal. But we don't have a lot to go on here."

"True. And like Hoofy said, we can return to the higher plane if things get too intense," Maris said.

"Exactly." I took a deep breath. "My crazy idea, so I'll play bait."

"Of course you will." Kaiden sighed.

While I appreciated his desire to protect me, I wasn't about to let it distract me from learning what we needed to beat the Saps. "I'll see how close I can get without raising suspicion."

"Have fun being bait!" Kaiden's tone was playful, but I could see the worry in his eyes.

"I'll just obliterate it with my 9D sword of it gets too ornery." I smiled at him.

"Speaking of which, you might want to heed Hoofy's advice to keep it sheathed until you need it," Toran advised. "Activating our artifacts may bring… unwanted attention."

"Yes, thanks for the reminder." An item powerful enough to help us transition between planes *had* to stand out. But, we hadn't been swarmed—or even acknowledged—yet, so it would seem that the items must be in some sort of dormant state while not in active use.

Keeping the blade sheathed, I slowly stepped from our hiding place, approaching the alien creature as it slid from its perch atop the bench. Its sleek form fluidly shifted from two limbs to four as it touched down on the mossy ground. Blue sparks appeared underfoot with each step for the first dozen paces, then it was almost invisible again in the dim ambient light.

It went against my instincts to approach the enemy with no weapon drawn. I walked as slowly and silently as possible, hoping to minimize the variables in our test. There was no indication that it had noticed me during the initial approach, but when I was ten meters away, the creature suddenly halted and looked directly at me with its eyeless head.

I froze. "I think it sees me," I whispered just loud enough for my comm to pick up.

"There's no doubt it can sense your presence in one way or another," Toran replied in a calm tone. "Just try to be… nonthreatening."

"Gee, thanks." I tried to steady my racing heart. Maybe I'd watched too many monster movies as a kid, but I couldn't help thinking that the creature could sense my fear.

It glided forward, the tentacles along its torso lifting up to point toward me.

Doing my best to project an aura of calmness, I stepped to the side to avoid the creature's approach path. Its tentacles rustled, but it made no further motion toward me. I continued my slow semicircle around it, glancing occasionally to see if it was still watching me.

"You're doing great," Toran said over the comm. "Try to get near that bench where it was connected."

If anything was likely to upset the Sap, messing with the bench probably would. I tiptoed forward to get a closer look.

The structure was covered in the same strange, dark vines that were ubiquitous in the plane, but the ones on the bench had a higher concentration of the glowing dots. When I was within three meters of the bench, some of the tendrils unfurled and reached out toward me.

The Sap snapped its head around and fixed me in an eyeless glare, its tentacles shuddering. It stepped toward me, vocalizing a series of rapid clicks.

I reached for my sword. "Time for Plan B."

"Wait!" Toran commanded over the comm. "See what it does."

I remained still, my hand hovering centimeters from the hilt of my sword. The Sap slinked toward me with its tentacles fanning out to view me from multiple angles. Even on all fours, the creature was taller than me, blocking my escape path. Its jaws parted.

"Wait, Elle," Toran said again.

I took a slow breath, fighting every instinct to grip my sword.

The creature leaned forward, less than a meter from my face. Its tentacles swept around me, some nearly brushing my clothes and hair.

Then, the tentacles suddenly folded back against the creature's body and it turned to depart, loping into the darkness in the opposite direction from which we'd come.

"Stars! What the…" I placed a hand above my heart pounding in my chest.

"I have to say, I wasn't sure that would work," Toran admitted.

Kaiden nodded. "Yeah, I thought you were going to be lunch in a matter of seconds."

I glared at them. "All right, that's the last time I volunteer as bait."

"But why *didn't* it see you as a threat?" Maris asked. "I'd think they'd be all over anything unusual around here."

Toran took on a pensive expression. "Unless there's some aspect of us that *does* belong in this place."

I raised an eyebrow. "So we… blend in?"

"Perhaps." He shrugged. "Really, there's only one way to find out."

THOUGH A SINGLE encounter wasn't enough experience from which to draw definitive conclusions, even hours of testing might still lead to the wrong conclusion about what we could get away with near the Saps. So, we decided to go directly for the big prize: whatever was beyond the guarded wall.

"All right, slow and steady," I instructed while creeping from the hiding place near where we had first arrived. "Watch your footing."

The spongy ground made it easy to move quietly, but the tendrils snaking through the landscape introduced numerous tripping hazards. We'd elected to avoid showing unnecessary light that would draw attention to us, so our approach to the guarded facility was mostly on feel.

Having successfully made it past our test subject earlier, I took the lead. We didn't have much of a plan beyond watching each other's backs and trying to minimize noise, but there were too many unknowns for a more specific plan.

"Don't look directly at the guards," I whispered as we approached the wall.

The two sentries sat on their rear haunches, looking more like stone statues than living beings in the dim light. Half of their torso tentacles were raised in the position I'd come to associate with 'sensing mode', and their barbed tails were wrapped around on top of their front feet. Like the other Sap I'd just approached, they had no visible eyes in their skulls.

I kept my gaze on the path in front of me as I walked toward the facility wall. Our staging location was approximately thirty meters from the wall, and the ground in between was mostly open with nowhere to hide. Thin tendrils shifted underfoot as I walked, though none tried to climb my legs and tether me. Thanks to the soft ground, our movements were all but silent.

When we were ten meters from the nearest sentry, the creature's tentacles stirred and its head pivoted to face us while it make a series of low, percussive clicking sounds.

"Stay calm," I whispered, not breaking stride.

"I can feel it," Maris whispered back. "It's trying to get into my mind."

"We're just part of the landscape. Nothing special to see," I replied, hoping she could convert that sentiment into a convincing mental image. When the creature made no further movement and its vocalization subsided, I assumed she had been successful.

We came abreast of the sentries, passing between them while their tentacles swiveled to track us.

"Where's the door?" Kaiden questioned.

"Dunno. We'll have to inspect the wall," I whispered back. Part of me hadn't expected we'd get this far, so I hadn't planned what to do next.

Up close, I discovered the wall was a tight mesh of vines, and the blue pinpoints of light along their lengths pulsed in unison. The wall extended at least three hundred meters—the strange distance perspective of the plane notwithstanding—and there didn't appear to be any breaks that we could use to get through.

"We'll have to go over it," I realized.

Kaiden evaluated the wall from next to me. "It has to be eight meters tall. How do we get up there?"

"Climb." I pointed to the grooves made by the interwoven vines; they'd provide perfect hand and footholds.

"We'll be completely exposed," Maris objected.

"Not to mention, touching it may set off an alarm," Toran pointed out.

"Maybe. I mean, the security seems pretty lax, doesn't it? There're only a handful of guards," Kaiden commented.

I shrugged. "No natural enemies?"

"Yes, this is what I would expect to see from a society that is maintaining internal order rather than protecting against an outside threat," Toran said.

"Well, our options are to give up or press forward, and I know we're not turning around," I said.

Kaiden faced the sentries. "All right, start climbing. I'll keep watch."

I carefully reached out to grip the vines, bracing for an alarm or attack. Nothing happened.

"So far, so good," I told my friends. The vines wriggled under my fingertips, but I was able to get a firm grip. I hoisted myself up with my arms and found a toehold for my boot.

"Scout ahead for what's over the top," Toran advised.

"I'm on it." I easily scaled the wall, finding the woven texture quite suitable for the task.

I slowed as I neared the upper ledge, listening for any sign of more creatures. My fingers found the top of the wall, and I pulled myself up just enough to peek over the top. Unfortunately, there was nothing to see aside from a flat vine-mesh rooftop and a single, thick column rising into the blackness one hundred fifty meters away.

"I'm not sure we can get in this way," I told my friends over the comm, then described the view.

"There *has* to be a way inside," Toran insisted.

I pulled myself the rest of the way onto the roof, testing my weight on it; the mesh flexed but held. "I'll scope it out."

I jogged across the rooftop toward the vertical column in the distance. I'd gone no more than thirty meters when I noticed a dark area in the surface to my right. I changed course to get a better look and saw that it was a hole open to inside, only covered by a thin mesh of fibers. "Hey, I think I've found a skylight!"

"Can you see anything inside?" Kaiden asked.

"No, pitch black in there." I tugged at the fibers across the skylight, and they ripped away in my hand. "Not sure how we're going to get down there without rope, but it's a way in."

"Should we go for it?" Kaiden questioned.

"It's that or walk around the perimeter of the structure," Toran replied.

"I vote for skylight," Maris said.

"All right, we'll be right there," Kaiden told me.

I set about clearing the remaining mesh from the opening while waiting for them to arrive. By the time I saw Toran cresting the lip of the building, I'd opened a two-meter-by-two-meter hole. My three friends jogged over.

"We're about to go against everything I was taught as a kid about not crawling into creepy, dark places," Kaiden said.

"Pretty sure we've been ignoring that kind of advice for weeks now." I smiled.

"We need to know what's down there. Might be time for some light," Toran advised.

I sighed. "I *really* wish we could have brought our gear packs."

Kaiden shook his head. "I can do a light orb, but that'll mean using magical energy."

"Have to risk it," I told him.

Kaiden conjured a small orb in his palm—faint compared to his usual spells, but blinding after my eyes had become so used to the dark. He dropped the orb through the hole, directing it to drop slowly so we could see what was beneath us. No objects or architectural features were visible at first, but four meters down I spotted the outline of charging benches similar to what the lone Sap had been seated on earlier.

"Make it brighter," I urged.

He fed a little more energy into the sphere, giving us a better view of the room below. Based on what was visible from our limited vantage, multiple benches were arranged around a central, unseen structure. None of the seats were presently occupied.

"I hate the idea of dropping down there, but we'll never get a proper look around from up here," Kaiden said. He left the orb resting on the floor eight meters down.

"But *how* do we get inside?" Maris asked. "That's way too far to jump."

Toran sized it up. "I may be able to make it."

I shook my head. "Too risky if you get hurt. And that doesn't help the rest of us."

Kaiden rested his staff on the rooftop and leaned on it. "Options?"

I looked over at the pile of fibers I'd pulled from the opening. "I wonder if we could make a rope out of that stuff."

The others assessed the pile. "Where'd that come from?" Kaiden asked me.

"It's what was covering this skylight."

Toran picked up several strands, pulling on either end of the strands; they stretched but didn't break. "This could work."

I grabbed a bundle for myself and began braiding them together to reduce the flex and increase the strength. With my friends following my example, we soon had a healthy pile of two-meter-long segments, which we knotted together to form a single length long enough to reach the floor.

"I'll go first this time," Kaiden volunteered. "Second heaviest, so it should hold Elle and Maris if it'll support me."

"I'll anchor it," Toran agreed.

The two men got into position, and Kaiden tucked his staff into his back waistband so both hands would be free for climbing. He dropped through the hole and began lowering himself down.

"This is just one chamber—maybe twenty meters square," he said into his comm.

"Any doors?" I asked.

"Yeah, a couple of archways."

"Okay, I'll come down next." I looked at Toran. "We'll need to figure out where to tie off the rope when you come down last."

"I'll figure something out, don't worry," he assured me.

I climbed down, followed by Maris. The chamber contained six benches arranged around a bundle of vines in the center of the room. It seemed odd that the room was empty, but there was no way to know how frequently the creatures 'charged', if that's what was really going on. In line with the center of the room, archways opened to the right and left.

Toran began tying the rope to the mesh rooftop material.

"Stand back in case this doesn't hold," he advised. He swung through the hole and put his full weight on the rope.

For the first three meters, everything was fine. Then, he suddenly dropped down a half meter before the rope went taut again. "It's slipping!" He picked up his pace. A moment later, the rope came free.

He plummeted the final four meters, rolling as he hit the ground.

Maris ran over to him. "Are you okay?"

"Yeah." He rose, rubbing his side. "Ooph. Now I wish I'd just jumped."

I looked up at the skylight in the ceiling, now completely inaccessible without the rope. "I guess we aren't getting back out that way."

"Might not need an exit, anyway," Kaiden pointed out. "Just because we couldn't plane-transition *into* this place doesn't necessarily mean we can't get out by that method."

"True. I guess we'll need to wait for Hoofy to show himself to find out for sure," I said.

"He'll come through for us," Maris reiterated.

I still didn't share her certainty, but now knowing what he'd given up to help us, I had more faith in him than when we'd set out on the mission. "Let's find their weak point and get out of here."

"Isn't it a little overly optimistic to think there's *one* weak point for their entire civilization?" Kaiden questioned.

"Hoofy said that was the case," Maris replied.

I had to agree with Kaiden's skepticism on that point. "But isn't that a really, really terrible design?"

"From our perspective, yes," Toran replied. "However, if they have no natural enemies—as we hypothesized earlier—then there's no reason to not have centralized systems. After all, that's most efficient."

"Okay, so if we can destroy something critical at the core, that might cripple them?" I asked.

"Or at least be a major setback," he said. "The trickier thing will be to make sure they can't easily rebuild."

I nodded. "Trapping them on this plane would be ideal, if we can."

"Definitely easier said than done. But, I'd like to learn more about this energy grid of theirs," Toran went on. "Perhaps that will help us formulate a plan."

"For starters, what's the deal with these benches and the 'charging'?" Kaiden said. "Sounds kind of robot-like."

"I'd liken it more to photosynthesis, how plants get energy from the sun," Toran posited.

I thought about it. "If this place is indeed the central generator, I can see how taking it out would be pretty damaging."

"Temporarily," Kaiden cut in. "This civilization didn't come from nothing. They could rebuild."

"Hence the need to isolate them," I said, heading toward the archway to the left. "But, I'll settle for neutralizing the threat right now."

Kaiden sent a light orb hovering in front of us, illuminating a vine-lined corridor that led deeper inside the facility. The interior reminded me of the ship we'd boarded at the anomaly site, only the proportions of this space were at least twice the size. I sensed a hum of energy in the air originating from the depths of the place.

"Did you notice those columns rising from the rooftop?" I asked.

"Kinda difficult to miss," Kaiden replied.

"I bet those are above the energy core," I continued. "This corridor is heading in that direction."

"A reasonable assumption," Toran agreed.

"How can we destroy a place like this?" Maris asked. "We don't have anything aside from our artifacts and magic."

"Maybe that would be enough," I replied. "We've never tried to go all-out on an inanimate object before."

"We shouldn't attempt anything until we have a better sense for how this civilization operates," Toran cautioned.

I nodded. "That's why we're heading to the core."

Kaiden flitted his gaze around the hallway. "I still say something is wrong about all of this. There aren't enough Saps here… and there's so little security. Either the place isn't as important as we've been led to believe, or this is a trap."

The same feeling had been nagging at the back of my mind, too. It had all been far too easy. It didn't make sense that they'd just ignore us. "I don't know what we're missing."

"We'll find out soon. We're getting close," Kaiden said.

The hum of energy intensified. Eventually, the corridor terminated in what appeared to be a solid wall of vines.

I frowned at the wall. "This can't be right."

Maris tilted her head. "Hidden door?"

"Must be something like that." I approached the wall. "Remember how the tunnel started closing in on us when we were leaving the ship?"

"Yeah. Meaning, these walls might be 'alive', for lack of another term," Kaiden replied.

"How do we get them to move?" Maris brushed her right hand along the vines.

"There must be some sort of trigger… like a certain type of energy associated with the Saps," I mused. "It seems like right now we're registering as 'background', but if we could figure out a way to make ourselves seem like *them*…"

"I have no idea how to run that kind of analysis without equipment I don't have," Toran said.

Kaiden brightened. "We might not need it. Elle, you have telekinesis."

"You want me to rip the wall apart?"

"It's a lot more precise than a fireball. Just break apart enough vines to make an opening."

"I dunno…" Using any form of magic would certainly draw attention to us as being something other than ambient background blips, and that kind of attention seemed like a bad idea.

"Think about it," Kaiden insisted. "The Saps 'charge' using those bench things—concentrated energy. If you direct concentrated energy at the wall, it might spoof it into thinking that one of the aliens is trying to get through."

"Or, some as yet unseen security force will descend upon us in an instant," I countered.

"Either way, we're presently trapped at a dead end. Might as well attempt to move forward."

I couldn't object to that argument. "Fine, I'll try."

My friends turned around to watch the corridor behind me while I prepared my telekinetic attack. I extended my right hand with the special focusing glove, a white orb forming in the palm. I released the ball of energy, and it struck the center of the back wall. Radiating from the point of impact, the interwoven vines began to unfurl and move apart to form an arched doorway.

"That was too easy," I said, my concern growing that we were being directed exactly where they wanted us to go. It was impossible that somewhere so important had next to no security, whether the civilization had known enemies or not.

"This place doesn't make any sense," Kaiden said.

"Doesn't matter. What's *that*?" Maris pointed through the archway toward a massive chamber filled with thick, pulsing vines that shined with the brightest light of any we'd seen so far in the plane.

The chamber's roof was six meters above, covered in vines that met to form a thick column in the center. The arched entryway where we stood was two-thirds of the way up the side wall, with the rest of the chamber dropping away below into a massive nest of vines. The vines spread from a single, small device at the bottom of the pit, pulsing with a bright blue light.

"Stars! What the…?" I gasped.

"That must be the core," Toran said.

Kaiden shook his head. "There's no one here. This is so weird."

"Agreed." I checked along the walls for a pathway to the bottom of the pit. There was no obvious staircase or ladder, so we'd have to climb along the vines. "Let's get a closer look."

Maris gulped. "I was afraid you'd say that."

I took the lead climbing down the curved wall. It was easy-going with so many vines to grab, though the way they squirmed under my grasp was disconcerting.

We reached the bottom of the pit and climbed over the large vines toward the center. I'd thought perhaps that warped perspective had made the core of the device appear to be only a meter across, but I found that was accurate as I approached. A blue orb hovered at the center of the thick vines, simultaneously the origin point of them and also nestled inside them. Normally I'd consider it a trick of the light for the orb to appear both in front of and behind the same vines, but I suspected that there was actually a hyperdimensional component to what I was seeing.

Maris squinted. "Huh. I expected it to be bigger."

Kaiden frowned at the device. "That doesn't look like a normal power generator. What's the fuel source?"

"Nothing in this plane," Toran replied cryptically, squatting down to get a better look at the vines. "After everything we've seen, I believe the only answer is that this device draws power from a higher dimension, and the Saps feed on that energy."

"I came in here thinking we might get answers, but now I just have more questions," I admitted.

Kaiden shook his head. "An alien race with a hyperdimensional energy source… Why are they bothering to mess with us and the crystals?"

"Stars…" Toran murmured, his eyes widening.

I crouched down next to him. "What?"

"I think I just figured out what the Saps are doing," Toran said, then fell silent.

"Okay, you can't say something like that and not follow it up with an explanation!" Kaiden hissed, dropping down next to me.

Maris knelt beside us.

Toran pointed at the device. "If I'm right, back in our plane, we'd consider this to be a zero-point energy device. Based on what we've observed here, this energy source is integral to the Saps' existence—it's what makes their ships work, feeds them, and powers the mechanisms of their civilization. It's connected to *everything*. But they can't access the higher planes, where they want to go. The best connection to the higher dimensions is—"

"The crystalline network," I completed for him.

"And our spacetime has an interface system." Kaiden sat back on his heels. "Stars! Why didn't we see it before?"

"If that's what they're after, there are terrible implications," Toran continued. "The crystalline network controls and utilizes the infinite power of the eleventh-dimensional Duzies, the very building blocks of the entire cosmos! So, if the Saps found a way to tie their energy grid—the thing everything in their society is connected to— into the interface system for the crystalline network, that could theoretically give them full control of the Duzies *without* needing a separate interface console."

"Shit!" Kaiden gasped. "They'd be like… gods."

"Full control… rearranging matter and directing energy at will." I shook my head. "Nope, these guys are way too unstable for that kind of power."

"If that's what they're after, then why start with the Darkness and invasion fleet?" Maris asked.

"I don't know. That part still doesn't—" Toran cut off, snapping his attention upward.

The doorway we had entered through was now filled with half a dozen figures, and they were staring directly at us.

19

"STARS! WE'RE CORNERED down here." My heart leaped in my chest.

"Time to get away!" Maris said. "Hoofy?"

There was no reply.

"How are we supposed to transition to the higher plane without him?" Kaiden questioned, a panicked pitch to his voice.

"Stars if I know." I drew my sword. "Time to fight." The blue flames ignited as soon as the weapon was out of its scabbard.

The moment my weapon was exposed, the six Saps dropped down into the pit, gliding toward us on all fours.

I raised my sword into a defensive pose. "I told you this was a trap!" A purple protective shell courtesy of Maris appeared around me.

"Like we wouldn't have come anyway," Kaiden replied.

"Irrelevant." I charged for the two Saps barreling toward me.

My instincts took over as I swung my sword, faking out the first Sap so I could redirect a jab at the second. A moment before my blade was set to pierce the torso of my target, its barbed tail whipped around to strike me in the back of the knees. It was stopped by the protective shell around me but then unexpectedly broke through, knocking me to the ground.

The first Sap took the opportunity to pounce. I rolled to the side just in time to avoid it pinning me, one of its clawed feet landing a mere two centimeters from my right shoulder. I angled my blade upward to strike its belly. It let out a cry as the blade entered, and then it disintegrated into black ash.

Having seen its comrade fall, the second Sap edged away from me toward the four others, which were presently engaged with my friends.

"One down!" I said, chasing my second attacker.

The other Saps were alternating attacks on my friends, sometimes breaking through the protective shells and other times stopped. Only the forcefield cast from Maris' shield seemed to reliably deflect the assaults. Kaiden's lightning attacks appeared to be wounding the creatures, but Toran's punches only seemed to annoy them. My sword was by far the most effective weapon.

I extended my right hand and lobbed an energy ball toward the Sap running from me. It lurched to the side to avoid the blast, then it rounded on me.

Its eyeless gaze bore into me. "Stop." The command filled my mind.

Against every intention, I halted. I tried to will myself forward, but I was completely frozen, my arms dropping to my sides and legs unwilling to move. I'd never felt so utterly trapped, let alone without anything physically holding me in place.

Nearby, my friends had likewise ceased their fighting. Each was transfixed by one of the Saps, and the fifth creature sauntered between us, its attention lingering on each of our artifacts as it passed by. The protective shells, aside from the forcefield extending beyond Maris' shield, had collapsed.

"It is ours," a voice hissed in my mind. I sensed that it was coming from the Sap that was walking around rather than the one focused on me.

"What is?" I tried to mentally form the words.

The Sap didn't reply, but it tightened the telepathic vise locking me in place. It extended its tentacles toward my sword arm, poised to pry the weapon from my grasp.

Next to me, Toran kicked his captor, followed by a rapid series of punches to the creature's neck and chest.

The others started with surprise, their concentration broken.

I thrust my sword forward, piercing the chest of the Sap in front of me. Dark blood spilled down its front, and then it dissolved into black ash.

Kaiden cast a shower of lightning over the two Saps nearest him, while Toran continued to pummel the creature in front of him. I dashed to the creature clawing at Maris' shield, swinging my sword around to slash its side as soon as I was within range. My blade connected, and the Sap turned to ash.

"Elle, over here!" Kaiden called.

I ran toward him and vaulted over one of the vines, using the extra height to sail over the first of the attacking Saps. I plunged my blade into its back and ripped downward, and it disintegrated before I landed. As soon as I touched down, I jabbed my sword behind me into the rear haunches of the second creature engaged with Kaiden. Only Toran's opponent remained.

The final Sap let out an aggravated series of clicks as it charged for Kaiden. I sprinted forward to broadside it—not enough to knock it off its feet, but it halted when I raised my blade to its throat.

"What do you want from us?" I asked aloud.

The creature stared back at me with its invisible eyes.

"Tell us what you—"

I choked on the words as the creature snapped its neck forward to be sliced on my blade. It spasmed briefly before turning to ash in my hands.

"Stars…" Kaiden murmured.

Maris swallowed. "Guess they really didn't want to tell us."

I took several panting breaths, willing my heart rate to slow. "I really hate these guys."

"They're the worst," Kaiden agreed.

I glanced at the power core. "Others will probably come soon. Let's destroy this thing while we have the chance."

"*Wait,*" Hoofy said in our minds. "*Not like this.*"

"Oh, *now* you show up!" Kaiden exclaimed.

"*It was important for this scenario to play out to its end. I see that my faith in you was not misplaced.*"

"That's—" Before I could finish, the chamber unfolded, replaced with white light. A segment of filament bridge appeared beneath my feet, at the core of a complex intersection with innumerable branches extending into the mist in either direction.

"Why did you do that?!" I glared at Hoofy. "We were about to take these guys out."

"*Destroying the core in the way you intended would not stop them. There is still much for you to learn.*"

"It would really help if you told us what you know… or anything at all," Kaiden replied.

The unicorn bowed his head. "*I know my actions do not make sense now, but soon you will understand."*

"I understand plenty. You let us walk right into a trap!" I shouted at the unicorn.

"Elle—" Maris tried to soothe.

"Don't defend him," I cut her off. "He's been playing games with us."

"No, I did what was necessary for you to come into your true power."

I worked my mouth; that wasn't the response I'd anticipated. "What do you mean?"

"Your transformations were not complete the moment you were reborn," Hoofy replied. *"You have been growing and evolving. After your transformation had completed, your strength needed to be tested."*

"Normally that's done in training, or whatever. You sent us into the heart of their operations!" I spat back.

Hoofy tilted his head. *"You learned what you needed to, did you not?"*

"Yeah, we did," Maris replied. "And we all made it out okay."

"Barely," I muttered.

"We were at the core. We could have ended the fight right then and there," Kaiden said.

"It is more complicated than that," Hoofy replied. *"Now that I know you are ready, I can explain."*

I crossed my arms. "Okay, so talk."

"Not yet. I will tell you after you are back on your ship and can gather the tools you need."

I couldn't help rolling my eyes. The unicorn had done nothing but talk in circles. I wasn't sure we were ever going to get anywhere.

He fixed me in a level gaze. *"I sense your exasperation, but everything will fall into place soon."*

"It better." The reply came out as more of a threat than I'd intended, but my patience had worn thin. If Hoofy didn't offer a detailed explanation within the next several hours, I wouldn't listen to anything else he had to say.

Seemingly unfazed by my hostility, Hoofy trotted toward the left along the bridge. *"Come, the exit is this way."*

We followed him through a complex intersection of multiple bridge segments and continued along a path toward the left. Eventually, we reached a single long expanse—presumably the path by which we'd entered—and jogged for what seemed like an eternity in my antsy state.

"*We're here,*" Hoofy said.

Maris stopped in front of me. "I don't see the sphere."

"What, it's not there?" I passed by her to search for any sign of the viewing-sphere that had been visible when we arrived, but I couldn't see it either. "This is the right place, isn't it, Hoofy?" I asked.

"*Yes,*" the unicorn acknowledged. "*The ship must have moved.*"

I tried to hold back the panic threatening to take hold. "Well, where is it?"

That wasn't part of the plan at all. We should have only been gone a few moments in relative time in the lower planes. It was next to impossible that the *Evangiel* could move on so quickly.

"Uh oh," Toran murmured.

"No, Toran, 'uh oh' is *not* an okay thing to say in this situation." I peered further along the bridge, hoping that maybe we hadn't gone far enough.

"Well, last time we were in 8D and no apparent times passed in our normal reality," Toran said. "This time, though, we were in 6D and 7D. They're still above spacetime, but maybe it's… different."

Kaiden wiped a hand down his face. "Why didn't that occur to us earlier?"

"Because this idea seemed straightforward and easy at the time." Maris winced. "Sorry."

"That should have been our clue." I took a deep breath, committed to not lose my cool. "How can we tell when or where we are?"

"From here? I have no idea," Toran admitted.

"But we *do* know that the *Evangiel* should be here, and they know it," Kaiden said. "I'm certain they'd loop around for another pass as soon as they realized we weren't on board."

"Regardless, how do we get back?" I questioned.

"Can you help us find the ship?" Maris asked Hoofy.

"*I'm already trying. However, we will not be able to remain on this bridge. The ship is no longer in proximity to any of these hyperdimensional paths.*"

I didn't like the sound of that. "Okay, so where do we go?"

"*We will have to cut through another part of the plane,*" Hoofy replied.

"Can we do that? Is there anything there?" I asked. After all, we were technically in a place that corresponded to open space relative to our home plane of reality.

Hoofy trotted to the edge of the bridge and touched his horn to the mist. An opening formed in the clouds, revealing an open plane that seemed desert-like compared to the pastoral scene we'd witnessed earlier. *"Nothing is completely empty."*

Maris hesitated. "You said before that you were not welcome to enter that place anymore."

The unicorn shifted on his feet. *"Getting you back to your ship is more important. Come."* He leaped through the opening onto the scrubby grass.

"No argument here." Kaiden jumped through after him, and the rest of us followed suit.

As I passed through the opening, the light level flickered and I sensed a change in the ambient energy. Everything around me felt charged and vibrant, though there were no discernible landscape features or signs of life.

We raced forward in the general direction we'd been following on the bridge but angling away from it. Hoofy loped ahead with the rest of us running to keep up. It was easy to keep pace in the strange gravity of the place, but I found it disorienting to not have any landmarks by which to gauge our progress.

Hoofy stopped short. *"No, they are not supposed to be here."*

I leaned back on my heels. "Who? What?"

In answer to my question, ten heads with distinctive crystal horns appeared in front of us, and with a ripple through the air, the rest of their equine bodies came into view. I wasn't sure if they'd just entered through a transition point or had been cloaked in some manner, but these were clearly members of Hoofy's former herd based on how they were glaring at him.

"You were not supposed to interfere," the lead unicorn said, stomping forward.

Hoofy stood his ground. *"This was too important for us to stand back and do nothing."*

"It is not our place," the other insisted.

"So was declared last time, and look where it got us." Hoofy tossed his golden mane. *"I will not make the same mistakes you did."*

The other unicorn turned her attention from Hoofy to us. *"You do not understand the forces at work."*

I chuckled. "Yeah, you can say that again! No frickin' clue."

She squinted at us, to the extent her unicorn features allowed. *"You think this funny?"*

"No, not at all!" Maris hastily cut in. "We've had a really weird week. Well, several weeks. We're kind of at the point where we don't know what to believe or who to trust anymore."

"Yet, you have aligned yourselves with this traitor." The elder unicorn glared at Hoofy.

"Traitor?" So, Hoofy hadn't told us the whole story, after all.

"It is true, I was not forthcoming with you," Hoofy revealed.

"What do you mean?" Maris asked, her tone pained.

"Fanciful notions and rash actions," the elder replied. *"Stars know why you freed him."*

I held up my hand. "Whoa, wait. *You* trapped him on the other plane?"

The elder unicorn huffed. *"Nonsense. The fool got himself trapped by going where he did not belong."*

"Enough dancing around it. What happened?" Kaiden interjected.

Hoofy hung his head. *"For generations, the Overlords have been building their energy grid. We knew your kind were at risk, but the others insisted it was not our place to intervene. But during our migrations, I watched the echoes of ancient times, when we used to roam your forests and share our knowledge with your kind. I could not bear the thought of your falling victim to their evil—not after the friendship our people had shared.*

"I saw a chance to thwart the Overlords, by means of an anomaly that crosses the planes. I believe it has been expanding since they brought their power core online, and all it needs is the right nudge to wall them off. Unfortunately, I did not have the correct tools, and I found myself trapped."

The elder snuffled. *"That is what happens when you wander from the herd."*

Hoofy met her gaze. *"You would not take action."*

"Right or wrong, that's in the past now," I said. "Now, we're already a part of this. Sorry if a collaboration wasn't on your wish list, but we're invested now. And, we have a ship to get back to."

"They have overcome their influence. They are integrated now," Hoofy told the elder.

She evaluated us. *"Is that so?"*

"They have mastered the artifacts," Hoofy continued. *"They are the best chance to see this through."*

"We swore to not involve ourselves. You broke that code, and nothing can undo that. However, that also means we cannot stand in your way now." The elder took a step back.

Hoofy bowed his head. *"I hope eventually you will see that this was the best way forward."*

"If you are successful, then perhaps we will. What has already happened is not always destined to remain." The elder and rest of the herd faded from view as suddenly as they had appeared.

Kaiden scratched his head. "I have to say, that was one of the stranger encounters we've had."

"Agreed," Toran said. "I was worried that we might get stampeded."

"They would never behave in such a fashion," Hoofy said.

"Fine, then shoot us down with rainbows," I offered as an alternative.

Kaiden smiled. "Or choke us with magical dust."

"Do unicorns do magic dust? I always thought of that as more of a faerie thing," I said.

"Definitely pixies," Maris cut in.

Toran cleared his throat. "The ship is getting farther away with every moment."

"Stars! Unicorns are very distracting." I resumed running in the direction we'd been heading, with Hoofy once again taking the lead.

"I sense it is close," he said, followed by an image projected in our minds. An echo of the *Evangiel* was overlaid on the landscape in front of us, with a more distinct bright point where the sphere resided in the viewing room. The ship was pulling away from us ever so slightly.

"Faster!" I urged my friends. I could see the sphere now in my normal vision.

We picked up our pace and began gaining on the sphere. It was so close…

"Get your artifacts ready," Kaiden said. "We need to do this at the same time."

I drew my sword in preparation. Just half of the ship's length to go.

We sprinted the final distance, dropping our pace just enough to match the travel of the ship.

"On three," I said, extending my hand. I counted down, and we simultaneously touched the sphere.

Reality folded, going black for an instant before there was a bright flash. The viewing room resolved around me, with the solid sphere between me and my friends. My stomach flipped as I was struck by the sensations of being in my normal physical self.

"What happened? You disappeared," Colren asked from where he was still standing near the doorway. "It's been nearly two minutes."

"That's going to take some explaining," Toran replied.

"All right, so I guess we really do 'go somewhere' after all." I took a shaky breath, overcome with a wave of nausea. "I never want to go there again."

Kaiden gave me an apologetic smile. "Well, you're going to have to. Like, soon."

"At least we'll get the bad guys," Maris offered.

There was that. And I was definitely ready for it to be over.

IN HIS USUAL fashion, Colren listened patiently while we gave an account of our experience as the five of us stood in the viewing room. The explanation was fairly straightforward until we got to the part about the fight near the energy core.

"But then Hoofy wasn't there to help us transition," Maris said.

I winced. It was only a matter of time before one of us slipped.

Colren's brow drew together. "Hoofy?"

"Erm," Kaiden hesitated.

I took a deep breath. "So, we didn't tell you *everything* before."

The commander crossed his arms. "What did you leave out?"

"On our earlier venture into 8D, we came across a sentient being," Toran explained. "His name is Huefneril, but we've been calling him 'Hoofy'."

"You say that like you're still in contact," Colren stated.

"Because we are," I revealed. "He's been helping us negotiate the transition between the planes."

"And what kind of being is this Hoofy?"

I bit my lower lip. "A unicorn."

His eyes widened. "A...?"

"Turns out they're real and actually hyperdimensional beings," Kaiden said.

Colren worked his mouth. "Why didn't you say anything about this sooner?"

"Because we were worried it would sound like we'd lost our minds,"

I replied. "And we weren't sure it would be important, but it turns out that the information he's led us to is actually pretty critical to bringing down the Saps."

"And I'm supposed to trust you after you withheld details?" he eyed us.

"Well, we're telling you now," I pointed out. "We have every intention to do what's necessary to take out the Saps and restore our worlds. Do the details really matter so long as we're working toward that common goal?"

He paused in thought. "And you can trust... Hoofy?"

I nodded slowly. "His motivations were unclear at first, but now I believe we can trust him, yes. His heart is in the right place, though we need to keep his zeal in check."

Colren let out a long breath. "I suppose I'm in no position to pass judgement on this matter. You were given autonomy."

"It's been a crazy few days," Kaiden said.

"That it has," the commander agreed. "Now, tell me more about the energy core." There was a hunger in his eyes I hadn't seen before.

I exchanged worried glances with Kaiden. "It's at the center of everything for them," I replied. "Destroy that, and it will cripple them."

"Everything, even their ships?" Colren pressed.

"It appears to be hyperdimensional in nature," Toran explained. "We've witnessed the strange vine-like structures everywhere we've encountered the aliens. I believe the vines are networked conduits, which simultaneously draw on and transmit the energy. Since the network is hyperdimensional, that direct connection is not necessarily apparent as a physical tether in spacetime."

The commander nodded thoughtfully. "How do you know that core is the only one?"

"We have only the word of our guide," I said. "But, he took great risk to help us, so I believe he's telling the truth. As a hyperdimensional being from a higher plane than the Saps, he knows more about the Saps' civilization than we ever could."

"That kind of technology would be lifechanging for the Hegemony," Colren stated.

There it was. I knew the pronouncement had been coming, and now we were officially in a bind. While I agreed that an infinite power source would be revolutionary, I was also too acquainted with the Saps to want anything to do with their technology. For all we knew, it was constant contact with the power source that had twisted them into the evil creatures they were. Hegemony's wishes or not, I had no interest in helping them get hold of that device or get plans for how to make their own.

My friends seemed to have similar misgivings, based on their expressions.

"The energy technology and the Saps can't be separated from one another," Toran replied on our behalf. "If we make any attempt to preserve the core, we risk our worlds and future."

"That isn't a decision for us to make," Colren said.

Toran's face darkened. "You haven't seen what we have."

The commander shook his head. "And you have no idea what kind of threats the Hegemony has faced in our history. We go to great lengths to protect our citizens from the evils of this universe, but one of these days we won't be able to stop them. If we have a chance now to get something that will give us an upper hand in an inevitable future engagement, that's an opportunity we need to seize."

"I don't disagree with that sentiment, but this tech is not the answer," I insisted. "The Darkness, the beings, the vines, the energy core—it's all part of the same hyperdimensional organism. If we try to adapt that, we'll just infect our worlds all over again."

"You can't know that for sure," Colren responded.

"No, and you can't be sure that it won't. It's not a risk I'm willing to take." I wasn't sure what would come from standing up to the commander, but I figured we had little to lose. It's not like anyone else could actually go after the energy core if we refused.

Colren paced in a circle. "Leadership won't be happy about your lack of cooperation."

"The goal has always been to get our worlds back. Why the sudden interest in the alien tech?" Kaiden asked.

"We've always been a curious race, and greedy," Colren mused. "No one can remember where we came from or how we came to be—we're always focused on the future and the next phase of our development." He chuckled. "It's kind of funny, when you think about it, considering how much we rely on resets to fix our mistakes."

"And once we reset, no one is going to remember what we did or didn't do in this moment," Kaiden pointed out. "But our decisions now will affect what happens to our people in the future. Do we want to leave them—and ourselves—open to future danger, or do we want to end this once and for all while we have the chance?"

"There will always be danger," Colren murmured.

"And fighting one evil with another isn't the answer," I said. "If we really want to reach that 'next phase' for our society, we can't go stealing tech we don't understand. We need to make those discoveries for ourselves."

The commander glanced at the viewing-sphere. "I'm in an impossible position. I can't officially order you to do anything, and I also can't ignore my own orders."

"In that case," I said slowly, "we understand our instructions, and we'll do what we can to fulfill your request while completing the mission to the best of our abilities."

He cracked a slight smile. "Thank you. I trust you'll do what needs to be done."

My friends nodded.

"We will," Kaiden said.

"Now that that's settled," Colren continued, "I believe you were just about to explain this alien attack?"

I nodded. "Right, when they used their telepathy."

Toran gave an account of his experience with the rest of us interjecting anecdotes. Hearing the encounter from other perspectives, it was quite clear that Toran had had a very different experience than the rest of us.

"Why do you think you were able to resist them?" Colren asked.

Toran shook his head. "I have no idea. I could feel the creature trying to control me, but it just didn't... take."

The commander tilted his head. "Could this have anything to do with your abilities?"

"I honestly can't say," Toran admitted. "We didn't exactly get a User Manual to go along with our transformations."

"Fair enough." Colren chuckled. "Well, it might be worth another chat with the science team to see if they have an explanation. That seems like a crucial ability worth investigating."

"We'll do that," Toran agreed.

We finished recounting the end of the fight and our return to the

Evangiel. Since Hoofy was a sore topic, we glossed over the exchange with his herd, only noting a few highlights which supported our argument that the unicorn was on our side. My advocacy would have been halfhearted a day earlier, but after seeing how he stood up for his actions to help us, my perspective had changed. In many ways, I now saw him as an idealistic teenager like me—making rash decisions without thinking through every aspect of the plan, but those actions coming from a place of good intentions. Regardless of age, we were all entitled to mistakes. What mattered in the end was making it right, and that's exactly what he was trying to do with us.

When we had completed our account, Colren studied us. "While that was a rousing mission brief, you've made no indication of how you intend to destroy this energy core and then trap the aliens in their plane."

"Yeah, we're still working out the details on that," I hedged.

"I'll need more to go on than that," Colren replied. "I can't have the ship circle this system indefinitely, and the Hegemon himself is asking questions."

"We will discuss as soon as you are finished here," Hoofy said in our minds.

"Give us a few hours and you'll have your answer," Toran said.

Whatever solution we devised, I was certain it would require going back into the heart of the alien civilization. Except, this next time, they'd know not to underestimate us. It was a very real possibility that we wouldn't make it out of the next engagement alive.

"Very well." Colren agreed, then he dismissed us so he could give his superiors an interim update—no doubt including our intention to retrieve the energy core. There had been too much interest in his gaze for me to believe he had given up hope for us to follow through, but I think he at least understood the reasons for our resistance and wouldn't hold it against us personally.

We left the viewing room and returned to our lounge to strategize.

"We're in it deep now," I said as soon as the door was closed.

"I think that happened some time ago," Kaiden replied, taking his usual seat at the table. He propped up his legs on an adjacent chair.

Toran remained standing, arms crossed. "We're agreed that no alien tech makes it out, right?"

"Absolutely." I sat down next to Kaiden.

"Yeah, I want this *over*," Maris agreed.

"Okay, so we can blow shit up without worrying about finesse," Toran concluded.

I laughed. "Well, that's one way to look at it."

"Hoofy, do you want to fill us in on your plan now?" Maris asked, sitting down across the table from me.

A ghostly image of the unicorn appeared to my left next to the table. *"Thank you for trusting me. You are still missing one piece. Speak with your scientist friend again and explain what happened when the Overlord tried to control you. Once you understand, then we will talk."* He disappeared.

I groaned. "I've had it with cryptic non-answers."

Kaiden massaged the bridge of his nose with one hand. "Another chat with Lisa it is."

"Maris, you'd better make Hoofy come through for us after this," Toran said.

"He will," she assured us. "I know he's been a little cagey, but he's trying to walk the line between his vow to not interfere and his desire to help us."

"Sides always need to be taken in the end." Toran leaned over to activate the desktop so he could initiate a holoconference with Lisa in the Capital.

It took thirty seconds for the hyperspace relays to connect, and then a holographic image of the scientist appeared above the desktop. She smoothed back the stray strands of hair from around her face. "Hello, again. What can I do for you?" she asked.

Toran smiled. "We just completed another hyperdimensional expedition."

Her expression brightened. "Tell me everything."

We repeated the tale we'd told Colren, tailoring it to the most relevant details about the structures of the hyperdimensional planes we'd observed. The envy was clear in Lisa's eyes as she vicariously lived the experience.

"Amazing," she murmured when we finished.

"Can you think of an explanation for the telepathic resistance?" Toran questioned her.

"Well, it's all connected," she began. "Since our previous conversation, I've been doing a lot of thinking. It all comes back to the

Duzies. They're not just the building blocks of, well, *everything*, they're also pure energy—they're everything that *could be*."

I blinked. "You lost me."

"It's not like one of our cells that has a unique function," she explained. "Instead, they can be in a certain state, but also any number of other states at the same time. It's what allows you to redirect energy and 'cast magic', though really you're just ordering the Duzies to suddenly perform a different function."

Kaiden pursed his lips. "Okay…"

Lisa smiled. "But it gets more interesting. It's not just that you have been granted access to these Duzies, I believe you've also become super-saturated with them—like giant batteries. That's how you were able to cast magic in the vacuum of space without having much direct matter to draw on. And, I think that anything that's remained in your possession for some time also starts to get super-saturated."

"Like our clothes and stuff?" Maris asked.

The scientist nodded.

"Hmm. I guess that might explain why I felt so attached to my outfit," I realized. "A few times it would be easier to print a new one, but this one always felt… special."

"And our backpacks!" Maris exclaimed. "Those didn't come with us when we transitioned before, even though the other items did."

"We must not have spent enough time with them for those accessory items to have become saturated," Toran speculated.

"Exactly," Lisa confirmed. "Subconsciously, you've been aware of the Duzies for far longer than we've had a label to place on them."

"And what about the telepathic resistance?" asked Toran.

"Again, the Duzie super-saturation," Lisa replied. "The more your bodies get saturated with the Duzies, the stronger your abilities become. Your brains were the last part of you to become saturated. And, since Toran's abilities are about strength and resistance, I suspect that extends to his mind."

I stared at her image. "Wow." I supposed that also explained how I was still able to maintain some of my own thoughts, since I had the 'Protector Lite' treatment with my own abilities; Kaiden and Maris had indicated that they had almost no memory of the encounter, only a sense of being suffocated.

"Maybe the extra distance from the 5D thought-plane wasn't all of it!" Toran exclaimed. "The Duzie saturation may have been a part of why the Saps' telepathic influence broke so suddenly when we transitioned to 8D. It seems like that action of transitioning to a higher plane is what fully activated the Duzies that had been slowly saturating us. It must have flushed out the lingering telepathic link, so afterward we only remained susceptible to their control when in their presence—when their influence was stronger and faster than the natural 'repair' functions in our minds."

"Of course, I can't say with absolute certainty that this is what's going on with you," Lisa said, "but I can say that the evidence from your individual reports supports these conclusions. And, that means you should now be reaching your maximum potential."

"*Yes. Now do you understand?*" Hoofy interjected.

I took a deep breath. "I think that's the answer, Doctor."

The scientist smiled. "Call me 'Lisa', please. I'm happy I can help give you some clarity, if that's what this is."

Maris slumped in her seat. "Mind-melting stuff, but yes."

"Thank you, Lisa," Toran said. "We'll be in touch once we wrap our heads around this."

"Of course. I'll be here." The holoconference ended.

I massaged my eyes with my fingertips. "I have no words."

Kaiden shook his head. "I'm not sure what I find more disturbing—that this is the reality we're facing, or that it makes sense and I'm not all that surprised."

"You're not?" I snorted. "Stars, I don't know. Maybe I'm not actually as shocked as I should be."

"I appreciate that we now have an explanation of our abilities," Toran said. "This knowledge doesn't change our circumstances, but perhaps it will give us more control."

"Knowledge is power," Kaiden said.

"Yeah, something like that." I almost wished I didn't know what I did now. My abilities had seemed like simple augmentations at first, but realizing that I was saturated with these Duzies—that they were in my *brain*—was a lot to process.

Toran moved to sit down. "So, I was thinking—"

"I'm going to be honest," I cut in, "I can't talk about this anymore right now."

Maris nodded. "Me either. Just thinking about those Duzie things being in us…" She shivered.

"Let's take a break to digest this new info," Kaiden suggested. "After that, we'll work on our plan."

"I'll work on getting Hoofy to open up," Maris said.

Toran huffed. "Very well."

I rose from the table. "See you in a bit."

21

AFTER LEAVING THE lounge, I hung back in the hallway with Kaiden while Toran and Maris went ahead to their cabins.

"Mind if I invite myself over?" I asked.

He smiled. "I was hoping you would."

"That was a day," I said while we stepped into his cabin. "I don't think I've ever been so mentally exhausted."

"You haven't been through a college finals week."

I chuckled. "Yeah, that's true."

"This is different, though." He turned somber.

"I know… I want to say that I still know myself, that we haven't changed, but those things are in us. How different are we because of it?"

"That's bodies. What makes us who we are—our minds—that's above physical transformation."

"Is it, though? Can you really separate the two?" I sat on the bed.

Kaiden eased down next to me, placing a comforting arm around my back. "Whatever may have changed, we've gone through that transformation together."

"Yeah, there is that."

He took my hand. "We're in the final stretch, Elle. We'll get through this."

I shifted to lay my head on his shoulder. He tightened his arm around me—the kind of physical grounding I needed in that moment. Having seen the other planes, I realized just how small and insignificant our individual existences were. Yet, we'd been handed the power the change the direction of an entire civilization. I'd never wanted that kind of power, and now that the decisive moments had come, I was scared I wouldn't be able to follow through.

"I spent my whole life worrying about things that aren't actually important," I murmured.

"Importance is relative."

"Yeah, well, the color of my hair doesn't rank very high compared to the fate of the universe."

Kaiden laughed. "Okay, that would be silly to argue. But I do like this shade, for the record."

"Past me would have been thrilled about it. Now, I'd gladly give up my looks if it meant I could skip this fight."

"A few hours ago, you couldn't wait to get your hand on the Saps and put them in their place."

"That was before one of them bored into my mind. Don't get me wrong—I still want to whip their asses—but I don't take pleasure in this."

"Me either."

"This'll change us," I went on. "Even if we don't remember the details after the reset, this seems like the kind of experience that would imprint on our high-dimensional consciousness."

He reclined on the bed, and I lay back with him. "The universe will be better off without them."

"All the same, I hope we can trap them rather than have to do a full-on extermination."

"Yeah, I don't want that on my conscience." He paused. "I'm glad we're going through this together. If we remember anything after the universal reset, it'll mean a lot to have a friend who understands what happened."

I scooched closer to him. "I think we're more than friends at this point."

He turned so he could look me in the eyes. "I wish we hadn't met like this. I can't stomach the idea that I may never see you again after this is over."

"We'll find each other."

"I want to believe that, but…"

"I know." My throat tightened with the notion that our time together could be cut short at any moment. In just a few weeks, I'd grown closer to him than I'd ever anticipated. He'd given me a glimpse of a different side of myself and the kind of connection that was possible with another person. I realized how alone I'd felt for years, and I didn't want to give up the possibility of a future together.

I stroked the side of his face, and he drew me to him. Our lips met and I kissed him back, gently at first, then with the hunger of wanting to be as close to him as possible. My hands slid downward, working under his outer layer of clothes as he caressed me in turn. The more he touched me, the more I wanted.

This is when I'd always put on the brakes before, citing one excuse or another. But this time, I didn't want to stop. "I know I said before that I wanted to wait until there won't be any more universal resets, but what if we don't make it through this?"

"Elle—"

"We can't ignore that possibility. I…" I looked into his eyes. "I don't want to have any regrets."

Kaiden leaned in and kissed me deeply. "I don't, either." He pulled back just enough to make eye contact. "So I want to say now, while I can… I love you, Elle."

My heart jumped and my breath caught in my throat. A contented tingle spread through me.

"Maybe that's too soon to say, but—" he hastily added when I didn't reply.

"No, we threw conventional timelines out the window a long time ago," I said, smiling. "I love you, too."

Joy washed over me having finally been able to vocalize what I'd been feeling. I knew it was still early in the relationship and I was still *falling* in love rather than being all the way there, but that distinction didn't matter on the eve of our potential deaths. What I knew for sure was that I didn't want to spend my final moments—if this was the end—wondering what could have been.

I pulled him to me, and our lips met again. The threats and worries of the outside world didn't matter. We had each other, and nothing that happened in the future could take that away.

I savored every moment as we made love, knowing I'd only have one first time, and not sure if it would also be my last. I was thankful I waited for someone I truly cared about and who loved me in return. The connection came through in every kiss and caress. No matter what the future held, I'd be able to look back and know I had true happiness in that moment.

We lay together afterward, his arms around me and my head on his bare chest. I felt different—maybe not in a way anyone else would notice, but I sensed it in myself.

"You okay?" Kaiden asked.

I smiled up at him. "Yeah, I'm great. Just… reflecting."

"I have to say, I wasn't expecting this now."

"Me either, but that's probably how it should be."

He kissed the top of my head. "The eve of saving the universe *does* seem like a pretty appropriate time."

"That does have the makings of an epic love story." I snuggled closer to him. Being in his arms, I felt safe from the dangers awaiting us. "Hey, random question: why fire?"

He gave me a quizzical look. "What are you talking about?"

"Your magic. You were first drawn to fire. I jokingly said you must have been a pyromaniac as a kid, but is there any other story there?"

"Oh." He lay his head back. "Where is this coming from?"

"Just something I talked about with Maris earlier. We were reflecting on our abilities and why we were drawn to certain things with our disciplines."

"Hmm, well, I'm not sure there's a profound deeper meaning to my interest. Growing up on a ship, a runaway fire was always a worst-case scenario—we took every precaution to avoid accidentally burning ourselves up. Maybe I had some lingering desire to have control over it."

I slid my hand along his chest. "Maybe."

"What about you?"

"Oh, I just wanted to be a showoff." I laughed.

"Shocker, Miss All-Three-Disciplines."

"So high-maintenance, I know."

Kaiden chuckled. "I think I'm starting to figure you out." He traced a finger down my back and bent his head to kiss me. "You know… we don't have to go anywhere yet."

I kissed him back. "Is that so?"

He moved his hips toward me. "Uh huh."

The ache of desire rose in me again as his warm breath brushed against my neck. "In that case—"

"Come on!" Maris exclaimed in our comms.

"Gah!" I winced, wishing I could rip it out of my ear. "Of all the…"

Kaiden drew back from me, then tapped behind his ear to open the channel. "Maris, this isn't a good time."

"Stop napping. We have strategizing to do," she replied. "And if you're not napping, I don't want to know."

"Give us a few minutes. We'll meet you in the lounge," I grudgingly responded and then severed the commlink. "Seriously, they couldn't give us even an hour to ourselves?"

"Hey, at least she didn't interrupt in the middle of things."

"Yes, very true."

Making the mental shift from lover back to teammate, I suddenly felt exposed lying naked in his bed. I reached for my clothes. "We should get going."

Kaiden gently extended his hand to stop me from getting up. "Elle, I meant every word I said. I think you're incredible, and I can't wait to get to know you more."

I gave him a light kiss. "Me too." I paused. "I'm glad this happened."

"Same. Honestly, I'm surprised we were able to hold out for this long. Two super-hot young people with magical abilities? I mean, come on." He grinned.

"It was definitely worth the wait."

We dressed and tried to quickly re-style our hair so we weren't a giant, flashing beacon for 'Just Hooked Up'. It went without saying that it was a special experience between us, and we didn't need to broadcast it to anyone else.

Once presentable, we returned hand-in-hand to the lounge to find an impatient Maris and Toran waiting for us.

Maris looked us over. "Finally! About time you jumped each other. Okay, we have strategizing to do, so sit down."

"Happy for you two," Toran added.

My jaw dropped. I guess that happy glow I was feeling wasn't as subtle as I thought.

"Uh…" Kaiden hesitantly approached his usual seat.

I slowly sat down next to him, certain my face was bright red. "So, the plan…"

"Not to a plan yet," Maris continued like everything was normal. "We're still at the information consolidation stage."

"All right." I tried to melt into my chair, wishing we could have stayed in bed awhile longer.

"We've been discussing the relationship between the elements in play here," Toran began. "Specifically, the Saps are on the 6D plane, seeking to ascend to higher planes. The crystalline network is at 9D with close ties to consciousness at 10D. And we have access terminals in our spacetime, which provide a direct link to the hyperdimensional crystalline network. Now, the 9D crystalline network has a special relationship with the 11D Duzies, storing information about the configuration of our spacetime reality, which can then be rearranged according to instructions from the 'reset terminals' or by direct instruction from 10D consciousness."

"Right, but…" I faded out. "Stars, I don't even know if I should ask, but why are there only access terminals down on our plane?"

"That's the question we kept coming back to," Toran replied.

"The only place those links could be formed?" Kaiden speculated.

"But why are they needed at all?" I insisted. "Or resets, for that matter."

Toran cracked a smile. "All the right questions. After talking it through, and getting some hints from Hoofy, the only reasonable conclusion is that life wasn't always as it is now. Remember, there were Ancients… and they ascended."

I thought about it. "Colren did indicate that the crystalline network was *made*, not a natural formation."

"Exactly." Toran nodded. "I'd bet that way back when, the Ancients found a way to step outside of time, away from their bodies. Physical reality was no longer a constraining factor, but they wanted a record of what they once had been. They devised a means to preserve those states through a civilization-wide network, stored indefinitely in the highest dimensions possible, to allow for effectively infinite capacity. Their descendants forgot that anyone had ever come before, and eventually they stumbled across the crystal interface and devised their own use for it—the ability to get a second chance whenever it was needed. And so, the quest to ascend began again with no memory that others had already walked that path."

Kaiden let out a long breath. "You know, it wouldn't surprise me in the least if that's *exactly* what happened."

"So, the Saps," Toran continued, "maybe they're an offshoot of the Ancients who were never able to ascend completely, or perhaps they're something else entirely. But they clearly understand the power of the crystalline network, and they're sick of it being under our control."

"Whoever they are, they're hungry for power," Kaiden agreed.

Toran looked around the room at us. "Agreed. And now that we have an inkling about what they're trying to accomplish, what are we going to do about it?"

"IT'S TIME FOR answers," I said. "Hoofy, it's now or never." I agreed with Toran's assessment about the Saps potentially being a rogue branch of the Ancients, but I wanted more than just hints to go on. The unicorn had been giving bits and pieces of some grand master plan to take down the Saps for hours, and I wasn't interested in planning *anything* without getting a straight answer.

"Can we talk now?" Maris asked more gently.

"Yes, the context has been established. We may speak freely," Hoofy replied, appearing once again as a ghostly image in the room.

"All right, so what's this plan of yours?" I asked, folding my hands on the tabletop. "How do we trap the Saps?"

"In the same way I was trapped," he replied. *"You must create a dimensional anomaly and then seal the entry."*

Kaiden frowned. "You say that like it's an easy thing to do."

"It will not be, but it can be done."

"Then explain," I prompted.

"The pathways to enter 8D, which my kind use for migrations, are a natural form of these anomalies. In the anomaly, the division between the planes is... less distinct. In the locations where one of these anomalies exists, the affected planes behave as one."

"And which planes are those?" Toran asked.

"Everything up through 6D, as you would distinguish them, become unified, but only a few access points from 6D through 7D to 8D would

appear in specific locations. However, such shortcuts are only fleeting."

Toran leaned back in his chair, pensive. "If that's the case, would a spatial disruptor blast affect the higher planes?"

"It would, precisely. And, the energy grid linking the Overlords would carry that blast through everything under the influence of that central core."

My stomach knotted. "That would *kill* them, not trap them."

Hoofy shook his head. *"No, you are thinking in terms of your physical forms. This would only be a setback, not death."*

I raised an eyebrow. "I don't see how a 'setback' accomplishes our goal. We need to permanently disable them."

"It would. Think about the anomaly."

Kaiden held up his hands. *"What* anomaly? There isn't some dimensional pocket thing that spans all of the territory the Saps now control."

"Isn't there? Have you forgotten about the Darkness?"

I did a doubletake. "Wait, what?"

"The Darkness is evidence of the collapsed dimensional barriers. Only you four can set foot there, because only you are infused with the Duzies— as you call them— which enable you to be present in any plane. The Overlords were using the crystalline network to enable the merging of their reality with yours, granting them easier access to the terminals that would give them a connection to their ultimate goal."

"The Duzies themselves—to control everything." My jaw went slack.

"Yes."

Kaiden swore under his breath. "I thought the worlds themselves were transformed."

"They were… just not in the way we thought." My head swam. Had we really been looking at everything incorrectly the whole time?

Maris' eyebrows drew together. "Does that mean we were wrong before?"

Toran was silent, thinking through the new information from Hoofy. "The Saps *did* gain partial control of the crystalline network—we detected the signals through the crystals and on their ship. But, it would seem that the spread of the Darkness was actually the expansion of the anomaly— *not* the result of reprogramming the crystalline network's reset mechanism."

"Except, we saw hybrid creatures," I pointed out. "We've been to those worlds—it wasn't just some blurred line with 6D!"

"Yeah, a lot of other things were different," Kaiden agreed.

Toran nodded. "Knowing what we do now, though, I think our assumptions about the *mode* of transformation were incorrect. Perhaps the alien hybrids were the result of each planet's native life being exposed to the Sap's energy grid."

"Huh." Kaiden absorbed the words. "That makes sense. Some things were able to meld with the grid, and they morphed to survive in the dimensional anomaly. Anything that didn't adapt... I bet the vegetation and everything falling apart when we touched it—and the corrosion of ships—was just the physical bonds breaking down from the forced transition to a higher plane."

"Yeah." I felt like my entire sense of reality had been pulled out from under me. "Stars! Somehow, this is so much worse."

Maris looked ill. "What about the black particles we all saw in the crystals?"

"They must have been the leading edge of the anomaly," Toran replied. "Most of the alien energy grid didn't appear to be quite solid when we saw it in our plane. Think about the conduits we saw radiating from the crystal in the town square on Windau."

"That's true. Some things *were* solid—the transformed stuff, I guess—but all of those 'energy conduits' did have a distinct not-quite-there-ness. One, giant spatial anomaly," I murmured.

"That would explain why our comms didn't work right on the Darkness-infected worlds," Toran said. "Spacetime was... different."

Wonder spread across Kaiden's face. "Only your modification to the comms to use the crystalline network itself could bypass that."

"And Crystallis... it has some sort of dimensional-alternateness of its own," I realized.

Kaiden sat up straighter. "Hold on, the Archive wouldn't be hurt by the disruptor wave, right?"

"*No, it is not connected to the Overlord's network. Not yet, anyway. They are headed for it. It is a place of great power, which they have sought to control for a long time,*" Hoofy replied.

"Okay, so every place that we've seen the Darkness is connected to the energy core on the planet, and all of those places are within a broad-reaching spatial anomaly with blurry dimensional plane lines, right?" I summarized. "But on the Saps' home planet itself—there's only limited evidence of the Darkness around the viewing-sphere. Is there an anomaly, or...?"

"No, that is the issue," Hoofy said. *"They have been careful to prevent the anomaly from breaking down the dimensional membrane around their home planet, to protect the core of their civilization and energy grid which empowers them. A disruptor would need to be placed in their native plane, but then the echo would carry to the other worlds."*

Kaiden placed a hand on his chin. "Problem: how do we do that?"

"Yes, a serious concern, indeed," Toran concurred. "Analysis of the detonation at the anomaly site revealed that the spatial disruptor functions up to 5D on its own. So, the device would need to be deployed on a higher plane in order to affect the Saps in 6D. However, the disruptor would need to be Duzie super-saturated in order for us to bring it with us through the dimensional transition."

"I am aware of that, and I do have a potential solution," Hoofy said. *"I have spent my time with you on this ship studying your technology and capabilities. I believe I have devised a way to supercharge your disruptor by creating an anomalous cross-universe dimensional rift at the epicenter, which can then expand to take out everything within the rest of the network. This transitory bridge would essentially suck out everything linked to the Overlord's energy grid and force it into a pocket universe that is confined to the 6D plane. The Overlords could never return to our universe."*

Maris blinked. "How could we make this anomaly-universe-bridge thing?"

"By using the properties of your artifacts and the viewing-sphere from your ship."

I winced. "Oh, Colren would not be happy about that."

"That sphere is our only means to initiate a universal reset after the battle has been won," Toran said.

"Short of going to the Archive," Kaiden pointed out.

"No, there's still the other sphere on the planet," Maris interjected. "Couldn't we use that one instead?"

"That would require going back to that place," I replied. "And, they'd certainly be waiting for us."

Kaiden brightened. "Unless we took 7D pathways to get there, the same way as when we went to the core earlier today. We could use the *Evangiel*'s sphere to enter 7D, then travel to the sphere on the planet, pick it up, bring it to the core's spacetime location along with a spatial disruptor—"

"Nope," I cut him off. "Can't travel through 7D with the disruptor, remember? Not unless you want to hug it for a few days to get it all Duzie-saturated."

"Hard pass," he replied. "If we can't bring the disruptor with us, then instead we need a shortcut. We could still enter the chamber containing the viewing-sphere on the planet through 7D, but not exit that way."

"What's the alternative?" Maris asked.

"We pop in, plant a locator to pinpoint the chamber's location on the planet, blast a tunnel to the surface, then pick up the sphere with a shuttle," he stated.

I laughed. "Yeah. Right."

"I'm serious. It could work," he insisted.

"But, the energy core location," I continued. "We'd still have to get there to plant the disruptor, and how would we know where that is?"

He shrugged. "Same strategy."

Sex really *did* make people lose their minds. "It would never work," I said.

"Not in that order, but if we located the spacetime location of the core first, *then* go after the viewing-sphere and are able to take a direct path back to the core's position, maybe," Toran stated.

I stared agape at him. "You've both gone insane."

Maris shimmied her shoulders. "I dunno, sounds kind of daring and exciting."

"Hey, *I'm* supposed to be the one with the crazy ideas." I sighed.

Kaiden nudged me. "You know you love it."

"I think we're doomed."

He smiled. "But you kinda want to try it now, don't you?"

I rolled my eyes. He already knew me too well "Okay, yes, it's so crazy, I *do* want it to work." I paused. "How would we blast those holes, though? A shuttle doesn't have that kind of firepower."

"The *Sanctum* does though, right?" Maris suggested. "Richards and Kess were all about seeing us in action."

"They'd be even crazier than us to agree to this plan," Toran said.

Kaiden nodded. "Which is exactly why they will."

"But, will Colren authorize the use of a disruptor?" I pointed out. "I mean, he wants us to extract the core intact. The disruptor is, well, destructive in that 'obliterate everything' kind of way."

"That part we won't know without asking," Kaiden replied. "But, I think this plan is just unconventional enough that the Saps won't see it coming and we have a genuine chance of pulling it off."

"We'll only get one shot," I said.

Kaiden grinned. "The Dark Sentinels only need one."

Maris chuckled. "This is either going to be amazing or fail spectacularly."

"Come on, have a little faith!" Kaiden urged. "We've tackled way worse."

I cast him a skeptical glance. "Oh, really?"

He faltered. "Okay, so maybe this is the most 'out there' thing we've attempted. But, I believe in us."

"This is what we were called to do." Toran nodded solemnly.

I clapped my hands together. "All right, let's get the pieces moving."

We found Colren in his usual place on the bridge and pulled him aside into Central Command's conference room. After a brief summary of the information we'd pieced together regarding the true nature of the Darkness and the alien invasion, we laid out our plan. Not surprisingly, he didn't seem overjoyed.

"That's, um…" I hadn't often seen Colren at a loss for words, but I couldn't blame his reaction in this instance.

"I know it's crazy," I said. "I thought the same thing."

"But, I really think this has merit," Kaiden insisted.

"Frankly, I'm in no position to question it," the commander replied after a long pause. "I haven't seen what you've seen, and I simply must trust that your recommendations are informed and in the Hegemony's best interests. I've conveyed to you the wishes of my superiors, which is all my position allows for me to do with non-military citizens."

It didn't take much to read between the lines. "A disruptor is essential to our plan. Will we be able to have access to another one?" I asked.

He inclined his head. "I'll put in the request immediately."

"And the *Sanctum*?" Kaiden questioned.

"You'll have what you need for your mission," Colren assured us. "This is a time for decisive action. We can't hold back."

I nodded. "We're ready."

"I'll make the necessary preparations. Stand by." He dismissed us, and we returned to our lounge to wait for the go-ahead.

"This is it, team," Kaiden said as we settled around the table. "The final battle is nigh."

"Dramatic much?" I raised an eyebrow.

"I *hope* this is really the end. I want to get back home," Maris said.

"If all goes well, we'll never know we were gone," Toran replied. "Now that we're almost to the end, I'm saddened to think I may not remember this time we've spent together."

Another pang struck my heart as I was once again reminded of that reality. "We'll figure out a way to find each other."

"What an unusual sight that would be, seeing the four of us meet up in a bar." Maris laughed.

I smiled at the mental image. "A Dark Sentinels reunion."

"It'll happen," Kaiden said with assurance. He took my hand under the table and gave it a loving squeeze.

I hoped more than anything he was right.

"Aside from the disruptor, do we need anything else?" Maris asked.

"Not that I can think of," Toran replied.

"You know, by the time we got to this point, I figured we'd be getting all sorts of new, fancy equipment," I mused.

Kaiden smiled. "Yeah, like that powered armor we saw!"

"Exactly. But," I looked down at my clothes, "now I can't imagine replacing this Duzie-saturated set."

"I never thought I'd utter these words," Maris took a deep breath, "but I'm actually satisfied only having one outfit. I mean, I even had this one patched when it was ripped rather than getting a new shirt." She bit her lip. "Stars, I don't know what's happened to me!"

I laughed. "I think all of us have changed our thinking about what's really important."

Kaiden placed his hand on his abdomen. "With that said, we should probably eat before venturing out the save the universe."

"Very true," Maris agreed. "A hero shouldn't try to save the universe on an empty stomach."

I smiled. "Glad our priorities are in order."

23

"OKAY, ARE WE ready to do this?" Fed and with my sword in hand, I looked around at the members of my team gathered around the *Evangiel's* viewing-sphere.

Kaiden nodded. "We should probably go before we realize this is insane."

"For the record, I am *well* aware how crazy it is," Maris said. "But Hoofy agrees this will work, so I'm in."

"Whatever will get me back to my family," Toran stated.

"All right," I said. "On three."

At the end of the countdown, we simultaneously placed our hands on the viewing-sphere.

The plan was far from straightforward, but it was clear. We'd scout ahead via the 7D pathways to get back to the energy core chamber. Knowing now that the chamber was directly below the column we'd seen rising from the facility's roof, we could guesstimate the core's placement within a reasonable measure without having to return to the chamber itself. With any luck, Hoofy could help us drop in from 7D close enough to our destination that we wouldn't need to remain in 6D for long. As soon as we'd established that location in our relative spacetime, we could begin the next phase.

Reality unfolded around us, and the ethereal filament bridge resolved underfoot with the viewing-sphere floating between us.

Hoofy was waiting nearby. *"Come, we must move quickly."*

I sheathed my sword, and we raced after him as he loped along the bridge toward our destination. The pathway branched and turned several times along the route. A few of the intersections seemed familiar, but it was clear to me that we'd be lost without Hoofy as a guide. As skeptical as I'd been about the unicorn at times, he was now an integral member of our team.

Eventually, we neared the intersection of bridges I remembered from our previous extraction from the 6D plane. Seeing it now from a distance, the complex junctures reminded me somewhat of a tree.

"This is as close as you can get from here," Hoofy said.

"Is the center of that intersection the energy core?" I asked. Something about the formation drew me in—a sense of great power within it.

Hoofy shifted on his feet. *"The core's position is not a coincidence. Hurry, we don't have long before your ship moves out from alignment."*

Reality folded around us again, replaced by darkness. Slowly, my eyes began to adjust to our new surroundings. We were standing near the base of the power station wall in 6D, only four meters from one of the sentries.

"Quiet," I mouthed to my friends, hoping they could make out the instruction in the low light. I pointed upward toward the vine-cover wall.

No sooner had I moved than a series of alien vocal clicks broke through the darkness.

"Go!" I dashed to the wall with my friends, jumping as high as I could to get a head-start on the climb. A protective shell cast by Maris appeared around me, but I didn't trust it to hold back the attacker.

The Sap snapped at our heels as it started to climb the wall after us, far faster and nimbler than we were. All the same, I was happy we were in its plane so it couldn't jump ahead of us like we experienced in the engagement back in our spacetime.

I drew my sword and tried to swing at it, but it was too far away. Rather than waiting for it to catch up, I figured I should keep climbing and confront it on the level surface of the rooftop instead.

Kaiden shot a crackling lightning beam downward to buy us extra time. As thankful as I was for the help, the use of magic in combination with my sword being drawn would likely draw every Sap in the vicinity to our location. So much for a stealthy entrance and exit.

I reached the top of the wall and pulled myself over the lip. Leaping to my feet, I turned back to face the pursuing beast.

Rather than one head, ten cleared the ledge.

"Run!" I shouted to my friends. Toran's telepathic resistance wouldn't be enough to give us an edge against that many at once.

"Where did they come from?" Maris yelped while heading for the facility's central column up ahead.

"No clue," Kaiden replied while sprinting next to her. "Whose crazy plan was this?"

I groaned. "Yours!"

Toran jagged to the side two paces ahead of me. "Watch the hole."

We sidestepped the opening we'd ripped in the skylight on our last visit. I risked a glance over my shoulder and saw the ten Saps we fanning out into a semicircle to trap us. Their attention was fixed on us, and two were headed directly for the hole.

A surprised yelp sounded a moment later as one dropped inside. The second jumped at the last second to avoid falling, leaving us with nine pursuers. To get an accurate location for the core chamber, we'd need time to get situated near the column, and that would be impossible with the Saps after us. We needed to fight.

I came to an abrupt halt and dove sideways, positioning myself between the path of two Saps at the center of the pack. I angled the blade toward the creature on my right, the tip just grazing its chest as it reached me. The creature instantly began to dissolve, and I swung the sword to my left a moment before the other Sap could snap at me. The second creature turned to ash as my blade connected. Seven remained.

My friends had stopped running and were positioning themselves back-to-back five meters from me. Five of the remaining Saps ran to surround them and two headed for me.

"*It will be ours,*" a voice hissed in my mind.

"*You said that already.*" I swung at the one closest to me, but it leaped back. "*Not going so well for you.*"

"*Submit.*"

"*Nope.*" I kept my gaze averted, lest they try a telepathic assault. I wasn't sure eye contact was necessary, but it certainly seemed to make it easier for them to get control.

The other Sap made a strike toward my legs, whipping its barbed tail up to slash my face.

I leaned back to avoid the sharp point, and it missed me by mere centimeters. Recovering my balance from the sudden shift, I blindly thrust my sword toward where the creature's torso should be. The blade met resistance, and a moment later the tail turned to ash as it flitted by.

Letting out a growl, the remaining Sap backed out of my reach. *"You are nothing without your blade."*

"I'm not giving it up, so we won't have to find out either way," I replied in my mind.

My limbs started to feel heavy, making it difficult to move. I sensed the creature's control closing in around me. I tried to resist the telepathic influence as it beckoned me to turn my head and look at it. My sword was too heavy. I dropped my arm to my side, my grip loosening.

"Elle, fight back!" Toran called in the distance. He seemed so far away.

"This can all be over. Give in," the voice urged me.

It would be so easy to let go. I wouldn't have to fight anymore. I wouldn't have to be a hero. I was so tired from the stress and responsibility that had been weighing on me for weeks.

For a moment, I was tempted. But the Saps didn't understand that 'easy' wasn't our way. We were driven by a deeper commitment, and I wouldn't give up.

I shook off the attempted telepathic seduction, charging the Sap. I swung for its neck, slicing off its head at the base of its skull before rounding on the others that were going after my friends.

Kaiden and Maris were frozen in place while Toran desperately tried to protect them. I rushed to his aid.

The five remaining Saps jumped backward as soon as they saw me, but I gave them no opportunity to retreat. I slashed at them, leaping and spinning to avoid their counterattacks. Each disintegrated in turn as my blade made contact.

Moments later, it was over. Only small piles of black dust offered any indication there had been a fight.

"Wow," Kaiden murmured. "Remind me to never upset you."

I smiled sweetly. "I'm unlikely to go into a murderous rage if you don't pick up your laundry. Probably."

"No time for chit-chat!" Maris resumed running toward the central column.

I took off full speed after her. More of the Saps would no doubt be after us any moment. We needed to get in position before they arrived.

We ran the remaining distance to the column base, glancing over our shoulders occasionally to see if we were being pursued. By the time we reached the column base, a second wave of Saps was coming for us—at least three times the previous force.

"Shit, we have to do this now!" Kaiden said.

"Okay, let me make some estimates, hold on." Toran assessed the column, looking around its side to gauge thickness and checking our rise relative to the roofline.

The swarm of Saps was halfway across the open span. We had seconds before they'd be on us.

"We have to go!" I urged.

"*This way.*" Hoofy's voice called to me, and reality folded into nothingness.

With a flash, the view of a sandy plane resolved around me. I took an unsteady breath as I adjusted to being in my physical form again. The nausea was even more intense this time—possibly due to having a different exit point than where we transitioned into the higher plane—and I had to resist the urge to double over.

My friends were looking rather green themselves.

"Everyone okay?" I managed to ask.

"Yeah," Maris replied weakly. "That was too close."

Toran's brow was furrowed. "I wish I'd had time to take proper measurements."

"*It will be close enough,*" Hoofy assured in our minds.

"Yeah, based on that last disruptor explosion, this entire place will be ancient history," I said. "Let's just signal the *Evangiel* and get out of here."

"All right." Toran beckoned us to him. "I believe the power core location would be approximately twenty meters below us relative to this plane."

"Okay." Kaiden pressed behind his ear to open a shared comm channel. "We're in position," he said as soon as the connection chirped.

No reply came at first.

"We see you, Dark Sentinel team," the *Evangiel*'s communications tech acknowledged. "Position marked. Shuttle is on its way."

This was the part of the plan that left us the most exposed. We had no way to transition back to the higher plane from here, so we had to wait for a shuttle to bring us back to the *Evangiel.* At that point, we could reenter 7D through the ship's viewing-sphere and then use those pathways to navigate to the location of the other sphere on the planet.

I kept my sword drawn as a precaution. "Strange that the location is underground here."

"Not really. We can walk through walls as easily as stepping over a chalk line when we're on the higher planes," Kaiden said. "A lot more than that, actually."

"Still, knowing there are such different landscapes out of sight..." I wouldn't have believed it if I hadn't witnessed those other planes myself. To have my awareness opened to such a broader perspective, this plane and everything I'd taken for granted in life seemed so restrictive now.

"It's incredible." Maris traced the toe of her boot through the sand. She stopped and bent down. "Hey, this is more of that crushed crystal. A *lot* of it."

Now that she mentioned it, I realized the walls sloped upward slightly and we were actually at the bottom of a massive, shallow dish. Normal sand had blown in, but the presence of crystal was unmistakable upon closer inspection.

"What was this place?" I wondered aloud.

"*A location of great influence,*" Hoofy said, still nowhere to be seen. "*When the Ancients still ruled this world, it was their holiest of sites—the nexus of their power. Those pure of spirit could use places like this to ascend to the higher planes, to become beings of pure consciousness. But, the Overlords tried to force their ascension through twisted means. They destroyed the crystals in the process, and these ruins are all that remain.*"

"Must have been beautiful to see so many crystals here," Maris said.

"*I never saw it for myself, but the elders always spoke of the magnificent crystal tree that once stood here. Its branches still live on in the network of bridges. It is said that all planes could be accessed from this place.*"

My heart dropped. "Wait, *all* the planes?"

"*So it was said.*"

I shook my head. "No, no, no! If that's true, then the spatial disruptor might not behave how we planned—5D on its own, boosted to 6D from the anomaly. But, if this epicenter has different properties, is it possible that it would take out the higher planes, too?"

Toran paled. "I can't say with any certainly that it wouldn't."

"We have to call off this plan!" I cried. "The Saps aren't the only hyperdimensional beings here. The bridges, the unicorns, the window maze…" My stomach turned over. How could we have overlooked that possibility before?

"Eliminating this threat is more important than the preservation of one location. The hyperdimensional pathways can be rebuilt. Trapping the Overlords, however, is not an opportunity likely to come again."

I couldn't believe how dismissive Hoofy was being. No wonder the other unicorns were furious with him.

"Why didn't you tell us this place was special?" Maris asked, distraught.

"The others are content to turn a blind eye, but while I was trapped, I did nothing except watch the Overlords plot their dark designs. I have seen their evil spirits and know they will not stop until they achieve their goal. Temporarily relocating from our lands is a small price to pay, to make sure no other races suffer at the Overlords' hands."

"Stars, this isn't what I thought we were signing up for," I murmured.

"I did not mean to mislead you," Hoofy said. *"The sacredness of this place was spoiled long ago. Our actions now can finally begin to heal those past wrongs."*

I wasn't entirely convinced by his logic, but I did recognize the truth in the words. We held the power right now, and we'd vowed to do anything to save our worlds. Displacing the hyperdimensional beings on this planet wasn't right, but allowing billions of others to die was a greater injustice.

The roar of an approaching engine broke the silence, and I looked up to see our shuttle approaching on autopilot.

"We have to move forward," I said.

My teammates gave grim nods of agreement. We were in the fight to the end.

"ALL RIGHT, PHASE One: complete." I settled into my usual seat on the shuttle.

I still had misgivings about using the spatial disruptor in a place where it might result in collateral damage, but the more I thought about it, the more I found myself agreeing with Hoofy's viewpoint.

"Okay, so now we do it all over again?" Maris questioned.

"More or less," Kaiden replied.

The most difficult parts of our mission were still to come. As soon as we were back on the *Evangiel*, we needed to reenter 7D and make our way to the location of the viewing-sphere on the planet. We would then transition back to our normal spacetime so we could send the pickup signal to the *Sanctum*, which would blast a hole to the chamber to serve as an egress point for us to take the planet's viewing-sphere with us. At least, that was the plan. Given how not-swimmingly our first phase had gone with the unexpected attack, I had no illusions that accomplishing the next tasks would be any easier.

Our shuttle flew on autopilot to the *Evangiel's* main hangar. After completing the decontamination protocol, we quickly made our way to Central Command.

Colren met us in the corridor outside the lift. "Well done," he said as soon as he saw us. "We've run a geological survey of the site you identified, and we found a dense mass near the specified depth. We'll use that as the target for the spatial disruptor when the time comes."

"Just have to get the viewing-sphere," I said.

He nodded. "The *Sanctum* is standing by to meet you. The *Evangiel* will be waiting at the pickup point."

"All right, we'll see you again soon," Kaiden said while we headed for the viewing chamber. He paused, giving us the look of someone potentially saying goodbye for the last time. "Thank you," he murmured.

"Just doing what's needed." I turned my attention to the task at hand.

It felt like we were running in circles, but the viewing-spheres were the only way we could transition into the higher planes from our normal spacetime. Movement between the higher hyperdimensional planes after that initial transition seemed easy enough—at least with Hoofy's guidance—but we had to work within the constraints of the system.

Knowing the Saps would be going on the offensive and practically had eternity at their disposal compared to our present time passage, we hurriedly gathered around the viewing-sphere.

"Ready?" I drew my sword, and my friends nodded. "Okay, on three…"

As soon as I completed the countdown, we initiated the transition. The world unfolded around us and we returned to the filament bridge in 7D.

"*Welcome back,*" Hoofy greeted us, trotting forward. "*This way.*"

We ran down the bridge after him. I found my stomach settled faster this time, presumably because my body was getting used to the bizarre transitions. I still couldn't believe what I was doing, let alone that I'd done it enough to be getting accustomed to it.

Our path along the bridges took us further toward the right than our previous route. Based on how long we'd been running, I knew we must be getting close to our destination. I was just about to ask Hoofy how much longer it would be when the unicorn unexpectedly slowed his pace. Up ahead, a herd of two dozen unicorns blocked our path.

At the front of the herd, I recognized the female elder we'd met earlier. "*Do not do this, Huefneril,*" she cautioned telepathically.

Hoofy continued forward slowly, meeting her gaze. "*This is the only way, Maricaela. Leave now and let this play out as it may.*"

She turned her attention to the rest of us. "*It is just like your kind to think only of yourselves.*"

I stepped forward to stand abreast to Hoofy. "The future of the Hegemony is at stake. We're doing this for all of those worlds."

"Bringing your problems to us," Maricaela replied.

I didn't care that I was talking to an ancient, powerful being; I wouldn't stand by while I was belittled because I was trying to save my civilization. "No, *this* place is the origin, and those problems came to find *us*. I won't make excuses for my commitment to protecting my home and my people."

She tossed her mane. *"Such a young race. You believe your lives and homes are the only ones which matter."*

"Not at all," I softened my tone. "I'm sorry if it seems that way, but that isn't the case. In fact, I suggested that we call off our plan because I found out what damage it may cause to your realm. I feel awful about it, truly. If you know of another way for us to stop the Overlords, then please, tell us. But right now, this is the only way I know. I understand that the structures on this plane can be repaired, but our worlds can't. This is our chance to eliminate an evil that will keep coming back over and over again if we let them go now, and I can't allow that threat to be a shadow on my people's future. We want to seal the Overlords away and then reset our worlds back to how they were—to give people back their lives and futures. Maybe that's selfish, but we wouldn't be worthy of survival if we didn't fight for it."

Maricaela evaluated me in silence. *"I sense purity of intent in your heart. However, actions must be judged on the result, not the motivation."*

"Then let's look at the results," I said. "If you allow us to proceed, you'll need to leave this place and go somewhere safe. I don't know how long it will take, but the hyperdimensional bridges will mend, and eventually you can return here. The Hegemony and all of its worlds will be saved. However, if you insist on stopping us, all of the Hegemony will eventually fall to the Overlords, and stars know how many other civilizations. They will figure out how to ascend, and you won't be safe, either. When you look at it like that, I'm not sure you can call *us* the selfish ones."

Hoofy bowed his head. *"This is why I have aligned myself with them,"* he stated. *"I would gladly accept banishment for helping to save this young, promising race on the cusp of coming into their own."*

Maricaela looked to the other members of her herd, possibly in a private telepathic discussion. *"We will leave this place, as you ask, and make sure others follow. Sacrifice is needed for the greater good."*

Maris clasped her hands. "Thank you."

Kaiden and Toran murmured their thanks, as well, and I smiled. "If we meet again, I hope it will be to begin rebuilding the past friendship between our races."

"Yes. Perhaps when the Overlords are no longer a threat, we will one day walk among you again." She turned away from us. *"We will alert the others about the need to evacuate. May you succeed in your mission."* The herd bounded into the mist alongside the bridge and disappeared.

Kaiden placed a hand on the small of my back. "Amazing job, Elle. Well said."

"I wasn't sure they'd listen," I admitted.

"They were never truly against us," Hoofy said. *"Their desire to avoid interference can blind them, but they would never condemn billions to death."*

"It certainly *seemed* like they were ready to let that happen," Kaiden said.

"A test of your resolve, more than anything," Hoofy replied. *"To ensure the destruction of their home would not be in vain."*

I nodded. "Can't blame them for checking. I'd want to vet us, too, were the roles reversed."

"And now we must deliver," Toran said. "The others are waiting on us." He motioned down the bridge in the direction we'd been going.

"Let's go get that sphere." I resumed running after Hoofy.

Several bridges and intersections later, I spotted our target at the center of a six-way intersection: a translucent sphere identical to the one on the *Evangiel.* We'd reached the location of the underground chamber.

"Time to summon our ride," Kaiden said.

I drew my sword. "The Saps are going to be waiting for us—I know it."

He gave me an encouraging smile. "Then you'll slash them into oblivion like always."

"Standing by with a shield for as soon as we transition," Maris said.

"I will be watching," Hoofy said. *"Stars be with you."*

"Thanks, see you soon." In unison with my team, I reached out to touch the sphere.

Reality folded inward and new surroundings resolved with a flash. A protective shell appeared around me, and I raised my sword in anticipation of an attack, but the underground chamber was empty.

I lowered my weapon. "That's strange. I really thought they'd be waiting for us."

"Yeah, I did, too," Kaiden agreed. "Well, no complaints."

"We should summon the *Sanctum* before the Saps change their minds about an attack," Toran advised.

"On it." I tapped behind my ear to open a commlink. "*Sanctum*, this is the Dark Sentinel team. We're in position." Only static sounded. "Stars! Are the comm's working?"

Toran frowned. "Should be. They were working before."

"Could the rock be interfering?" Kaiden asked.

"Possibly, but—"

"We read you," Richards replied over the comm, cutting Toran off. "Sorry about that. We needed to clean up the signal."

"Great to hear your voice!" I breathed a sigh of relief. "We're in position in the cavern."

"We see you," Kess acknowledged. "Geological survey has us cutting through clay and then several meters of rock. The beam weapons on this ship weren't designed for precise excavation, so I suggest you clear the area."

"There's an adjacent chamber where we can go to," I told her.

"Perfect. Keep an eye on our progress and let us know when it's about to punch through," Richards stated. "We won't be able to see where we're going once everything starts to melt."

"Good thing we have shields," Maris said.

"Yours will be more reliable than the ones you cast for us. Mind being on watch duty?" I asked her.

She smiled. "Happy to."

"All right, give us a minute or two to get situated," I said while motioning Kaiden and Toran to deal with the sphere. We'd agreed during our planning session that it would be best to move it away from the drilling site so it didn't get coated in molten rock. While the crystals were supposed to be near-indestructible by most physical means, it wouldn't be easy for us to move if it was glued to the floor by a blob of rock.

Kaiden bent down to nudge the base supporting the crystal wrapped in the dark, alien tendrils, but it gave no sign of movement. "Argh, this thing is on here good."

Toran joined him, grimacing as he reached through the mass of vines to grip the inner support structure with both hands. It wouldn't budge. "I did not anticipate this problem."

"Hold off on the drilling," I instructed. "We haven't been able to clear the area."

"ETA?" Kess asked.

"Not sure. Hang on." I motioned for Kaiden and Toran to back away. "Let me try levitating it off."

I focused on the base, imagining the bonds within the stone and breaking them down. I held out my right hand, palm open, and shot a dark orb toward the center of the column. The vines recoiled, and the rock underneath condensed and crumbled at the impact site. When the structure began to tip over, I redirected my energy to catch the sphere and lift it up, then set it gently on the ground atop the bed of vines.

"You should really do that kind of stuff more often," Kaiden said.

I shrugged. "Too difficult to do in battle. I need a ton of concentration."

Toran jogged to where I'd set the sphere down. "We need to get it to the other chamber. Kaiden, your cloak."

Hesitantly, Kaiden removed the outer garment and handed it to the other man.

Toran draped the cloth over the crystal so he could grip it without touching it with his skin or gauntlets. He easily lifted the meter-wide sphere in his arms and strode toward the doorway to the adjacent chamber. "A little light?"

"Of course." Kaiden conjured a light orb in his palm and sent it floating ahead of Toran.

"Stars, no!" Toran almost dropped the sphere.

Red eyes reflected the light from the orb. Dozens of eyes.

Toran quickly stepped back. "Maris, shield. Now!"

Maris cast a shield over the passageway a moment before half a dozen of the Sap fighters lunged toward us.

"What are they doing in there?" Kaiden took a step back.

Maris cautiously approached the passageway so the silvery magical forcefield from her artifact sealed most of the opening, in case the cast one failed. "We might have to get cozy."

I looked between the Saps and the chamber that was about to turn into a lava tube. "They set us up."

Kaiden's face dropped. "Must have known we could use the sphere to go to back to 7D and get away from them. So, they tried to ambush us where we'd have nowhere to run."

I groaned. "And we *could* use the sphere to escape now, but there'd be no way to take it with us. Except, stars! The sphere is how they transition. We need to… block it somehow before more come through."

"Maybe, like, one hand on it?" Kaiden speculated.

"I dunno, worth a shot," I agreed. "Not sure if it's a one-activity-at-a-time thing, or it doesn't matter."

"I'll try," he said.

"Hey, what's going on down there?" Richards asked over the comm.

"Unexpected company," I replied.

"If we huddle together, maybe…" Maris sounded unsure.

"No choice," I said. "Come on."

Maris regulated her forcefield to allow us to pass inside while keeping the enemies at bay. The three of us had to crouch near the ground where the bubble was widest, but we managed to get within its boundaries along with the viewing-sphere, still wrapped in Kaiden's cloak except for the one bit he was touching.

"Okay, we're ready," I told Kess and Richards.

"All right, activating the beam," Kess stated.

The ground trembled and loose bits of rock and dust rained from the ceiling. On our other side, the Saps redoubled their efforts to break through Maris' special forcefield, though their clawing and biting bore no results.

I inched closer to Kaiden as the shaking intensified. "We were never supposed to be in the same room as this."

"Improvisation," Maris said.

"Three meters down so far," Richards informed us.

"Long way to go," Toran responded.

The Saps shifted in and out of our perception, but each time they tried to dimensional-jump to the other side of the bubble they immediate retreated because of the heat from the drilling.

Kaiden closed his eyes as one of the Saps snapped at him ten centimeters away on the other side of the forcefield. "These guys are getting antsy."

The mass of Saps pressed against the shield, unable to push through, but a force nonetheless. Maris slipped backward, unable to stand up to their combined strength. Snouts and limbs of some of the creatures began slipping through new gaps between the forcefield's dome and the passageway walls.

"Gah! I can't hold them." Maris leaned into her shield artifact, which formed the front of our defensive wall.

Toran braced himself behind her. "We're in this together."

As much as I loved the sentiment, that desire didn't change the physical realties of the situation. We needed to force the enemy back. I concentrated on my sword, trying to put myself in the mindset that had enabled me to augment our shield on the shuttle to stave off destruction from the spatial disruptor before. Energy surged through me, and I directed it toward the shell already around us.

"Kaiden, try to charge the shell," I instructed.

Confusion flitted across this face, then he nodded his understanding. A moment later, an electrical charge shot from his staff to the dome, which transitioned to the outer barrier.

The Saps cried out as electrical bolts shot toward them when they tried to touch the forcefield. The pressure sliding us backward began to dissipate enough that we could seal the gaps around its edges by pressing further into the passageway.

"How's it coming, Kess?" I asked over the comm.

"Getting close," she said. "You see anything yet?"

I checked the caver's roof but there were no signs of the drilling beam aside from the continued tremble and loose rocks falling. "Not yet."

The seconds dragged on as the Saps continued to snap at us. The electrical charge began to wear off.

"Recharging," Kaiden said, holding up his staff to pass the electrical current. However, with the sparks dancing on his staff, he suddenly froze.

"Hey, what are you—" It took me a moment to realize what had happened, but then I saw one of the Saps staring at him with its glowing, red eyes. Somehow, it had managed to ensnare him through the shield. "No, Kaiden, snap out of it!" I shook his shoulder.

The electrical charge arced inside the forcefield, unable to pass through without his coordinated direction with Maris. I bobbed to avoid being struck.

"This is going to fry us!" Maris cried. I saw her attempt to create smaller shields around each of us inside the dome, but her attention was already too directed on maintaining the larger protective dome for them to take hold.

I passed my hand in front of Kaiden's face with no response. The lightning continued to dance along his staff. If it kept up, we might fare better with the beam drill in the cavern.

"Stars, the rock on the roof is starting to glow!" Maris noticed.

Okay, so our chances in that chamber had just dropped significantly. I didn't think our odds against that many Saps was much better. We needed to do something. "Kaiden…" I pleaded.

"Let him go," Toran's voice boomed to my right. He was staring directly at the Sap who had telepathically linked with Kaiden.

The creature faltered.

"Let him go," Toran repeated even more forcefully.

To my surprise, the Sap ducked its head and turned to walk away.

"What the…" I faded out as Kaiden took a gasping breath.

"What happened?" he asked, his tone one of confusion and distress.

"One of the Saps got you," I replied. "But Toran here… he just gave it a treatment of its own."

"Do more of that!" Maris urged. "These guys are still pushing."

Toran locked in a staring contest with the Saps. "Leave us," he commanded. A couple of the Sap fighters hesitated, but there were too many of them for that to make a difference. It would seem one-on-one was the only effective strategy—at least where his abilities were now— and that would take more time than we had to address each of the creatures in turn.

"We're going to have to make a run for it," I realized. "As soon as the platform drops—" I cut off, noticing the roof of the cavern. "Stars, that's glowing a lot!"

"Dialing it back," Kess stated over the comm. "Almost through. We'll drop the charge." The bright point faded the slightest measure. "Detonating in three… two… one!"

I instinctively covered my head with my free arm as an explosive charge broke through the final section of the ceiling so the beam didn't cook us. Chunks of rock flew throughout the chamber, leaving a pile of super-heated rubble at the center, on top of the alien vines. As the dust cleared, I could see our three-meter-wide access shaft to safety now dominating the center of the ceiling.

"Get ready to run," I told my team.

"Lowering the evac platform," Richards said.

The deployment took nearly a minute, requiring Richards to hold the ship steady so the platform didn't touch the near-molten rock walls, which had yet to cool. It would be impossible for us to exit through the chamber if it wasn't for Maris' protective shields.

Finally, the platform came into view—a simple rectangle two meters by one with a railing around three sides.

"Okay, Maris, wall off this opening as best you can," I instructed. "Toran, get the sphere. It'll be a mad dash to get out of here."

"Ready," all members of the team confirmed.

I planned my running path to avoid the patches of hot rock. "Okay… go!"

We sprinted across the sweltering chamber and made a running leap for the platform hovering a meter above the ground. I landed first, lending my hand to Maris to help her aboard. Kaiden and Toran easily made the jump. To my relief, Maris' shield had managed to hold back the Saps.

"Get us out of here!" I shouted into my comm.

The *Sanctum* began to rise while the winch on the lift simultaneously engaged, pulling us toward the belly of the ship. Maris encased the platform in a new shield, diffusing the heat. The glow had faded from the rocks lining the shaft, but I could still see distortions in the air from the heat.

After a slow initial ascent, the platform finally cleared the shaft. A gust of wind rocked the platform, knocking me off-balance. I held onto the railing as the platform swung dangerously far to the side, pitching us toward the open side of the platform.

"The sphere," Kaiden warned, hugging the sphere still wrapped in his cloak.

Toran steadied it on the other side. "We won't let it go anywhere."

I looked between the sphere and my friends once we had safely entered the *Sanctum*'s cargo hold. "Let's go put those hyperdimensional bastards in their place."

THE PIECES WERE in place. All that we needed to do was detonate the spatial disruptor alongside the crystal sphere... and then somehow escape with our lives. True to form, the part of the plan where we didn't all die had been the most glossed over.

"Okay, how does this go, again?" I asked.

"We ride the detonation wave to 8D and seal the Saps inside," Toran replied.

"Right." I paused. "No, I still don't get it."

"It'll make sense in the moment," Maris said. "Hoofy will be there with us as a guide."

I took a deep breath. "All right."

The *Sanctum* was speeding toward the location we'd identified during the first phase of our plan, corresponding to the location of the energy core in the Saps' native 6D plane. If our assessments were correct, we'd be able to survive the detonation and then return through 8D to the *Evangiel*, which would be waiting for us, safely out of the blast range. And if we were wrong... well, we wouldn't be around to feel bad about it. Theoretically, it wouldn't matter, since anyone could subsequently initiate a universal reset to before the Darkness ever appeared. Still, I hoped I'd get to be a part of that special moment.

"ETA two minutes," Richards informed us over the ship's comm.

"All right, standing by," Kaiden confirmed.

One of his hands still rested on the sphere; thus far, no creatures had transitioned through it, so we didn't want to press our luck. It was only in retrospect we realized how lucky we'd been for no invasion force to enter through the sphere on the *Evangiel*; keeping the ship moving whenever it was within the Saps' territory had likely saved us from an unexpected attack.

Toran stood next to Kaiden with the spatial disruptor at his feet. "One more task."

"It's gonna be a wild ride," I said.

Kaiden nodded. "I have no doubt."

The *Sanctum* closed the remaining distance to our destination and dropped in altitude.

"You sure about this?" Richards asked over the comm.

"Not at all," I responded, "but we're doing it anyway."

"I like your attitude," the captain replied. "Blasting now."

A low rumble reverberated through the cargo hold as the *Sanctum*'s beam weapon charged. Through the viewport in lower deck hatch, I watched the beam lance toward the sand and crystal pit we'd identified during the first phase of the mission. The beam easily melted through the ground, too bright to look at, even with the auto-tint shading on the viewport. After seven seconds, the beam shut off.

"One entry shaft, made to order!" Kess declared.

I smiled. "Thanks."

The cargo hold hatch opened. We gripped the railing of the rescue platform as it began to lower toward the twenty-meter-deep pit. At the base, a dense boulder of dark rock now exposed, had survived the beam blast.

"That must be the manifestation of the energy core on this plane," Kaiden said.

"Then that's where we'll set the disruptor." Toran patted the device.

Kaiden continued to keep one hand on the viewing-sphere as we were lowered, knowing that the risk of Saps trying to transition through it increased as we got closer to the site.

A meter from the bottom of the blasted-out shaft, the platform stopped. I motioned my friends to jump off of it.

"All set," I told Richards as soon as we were clear. "Now, get back to the *Evangiel* and jump out of here."

"Don't worry about us," Richards replied. "It's been an honor."

"Happy hunting," Kess added.

The platform began retracting into the belly of the ship.

"Okay, Toran, get the sphere in place—remember to keep a hand on it. Kaiden, get the spatial disruptor set."

They got to work.

I turned to Maris. "We're going to have a major blast coming our way. The shield needs to hold. That'll be the only thing between us and…" I didn't want to complete the thought.

She nodded, determination in her eyes. "Everything up until now has been practice. We're ready."

"That's right." I drew my sword, savoring the power of it in my hand. Much of the plan would come down to me and my timing.

Above us, the *Sanctum* blasted away the moment its cargo hatch was closed.

Kaiden took a deep breath. "All right, we're committed now!"

I watched the ship disappear into the sky. "Ten minutes to go." The default timing had been set with Colren in advance, which should provide adequate time for the *Sanctum* to get on board the *Evangiel* and the ship to jump away. If we didn't hear from them, we were under standing orders to detonate no matter what. If they were ready to jump before then, they'd tell us.

Several uncomfortable minutes passed while Kaiden and Toran completed the equipment preparations.

"This rock thing is weird," Toran observed while he worked. "I've never seen a material like this."

"My pendant is glowing like crazy," Kaiden said.

"Must have some connection with the crystals," I suggested.

Kaiden stared at it pensively. "I wonder if this is some sort of ultra-dense crystal—like a diamond is to coal."

"I could see how that would be a significant energy source, assuming it maintains a direct connection to the crystalline network," Toran said.

My stomach twisted. "Too bad we have to blow it up."

"It will endure," Hoofy said, appearing before us for the first time on the world. *"But they are coming."*

The viewing-sphere turned black beneath Toran's hand. "How do we stop it?"

"You can't. They have been waiting, building their forces. You must detonate now."

"Kaiden, Toran, get back," I instructed. After a momentary hesitation, Toran removed his hand and ran to stand near me with Maris. "Shield!" I instructed.

Maris waved her hand, and a purple shell appeared around the spatial disruptor and viewing-sphere. "How are we supposed to get to them to do what we need to do with these shields up?" she asked.

"Still working on that." I assessed the scene. "Wait! I've got it. Shrink the shield."

Maris gave me a quizzical look.

"If it's tight enough against the sphere, we might be able to prevent them from transitioning completely," I explained.

"Ah, yes!" She made the necessary adjustment, positioning the outer boundaries of the shell just beyond the crystal sphere's surface.

"All right, if this can hold, we can drop it at the moment of detonation," I continued. "Stars, is the *Sanctum* back to the *Evangiel* yet?" With the way things were going, I didn't know if we'd be able to wait until the agreed upon detonation time.

"Something's coming through!" Kaiden gripped his staff, ready to act.

Dark forms pressed on the inside of the shield, flexing the shimmering purple outline.

I stepped closer, prepared to slash them if they broke through. "How long until our detonation time?"

"Three minutes twenty seconds," Toran replied.

There was no way we'd make it that long. The purple shield was already starting to stutter as the creatures pressed against it. I estimated less than a minute before Maris wouldn't be able to hold it any longer.

"Maybe I can force them back." Kaiden's staff electrified, and he shot a lightning charge toward the sphere. The energy danced along the surface.

"I can't loosen the field enough to allow it to pass through," Maris said. "I can barely hold it as it is."

"You're doing great," I encouraged her, my mind racing for another tactic. "Maybe—"

"Dark Sentinel team, you're clear to proceed," Colren said in our earpieces. "Jump commencing in fifteen seconds." The commlink cut before I had a chance to reply.

"Okay, set seventeen seconds on the detonator," I instructed Kaiden.

"Maris, on my mark, drop the shield and then we all make contact." I ran to the sphere and surrounded it with my friends. Kaiden finished setting the timer and joined us, each of us hovering one hand over the sphere and Hoofy alongside us with his horn poised.

With one second left on the detonator, I gave the order. "Now!"

The shield collapsed, freeing the beings waiting to emerge inside. Before they could fully materialize, we touched the sphere.

Reality unfolded around us, turning to blackness. With a flash, the eighth-dimensional window maze came into focus. Hundreds of window facets shined in the corridor, all displaying the energy core site spanning the dimensional planes. The viewing-sphere floated between us.

I immediately raised my sword, blade pointed down several centimeters above the sphere's surface. "Stay focused," I told my friends. They wrapped their hands around mine on the hilt, and Hoofy touched his horn to our hands.

The disruptor detonated.

Its wave of destruction spread throughout the innumerable window facets. It accelerated through the hyperdimensional energy connections to the farthest reaches of the Saps' domain, sucking everything it touched into a new dimensional pocket within the disruptor field.

The disruption around the new dimensional bubble continued to expand, pushing through to the higher planes. It was coming for us.

"Focus!" I shouted as the bubble broke through.

My sense of reality warped as the windows disappeared around me. They unfolded and expanded, each of the facets becoming a crystal. The crystals stacked on one another, forming endless fractals spanning as far as I could see. Somehow, we'd been pushed into the ninth dimension, the domain of the crystalline network itself.

I wanted to wonder at its beauty, overcome with pure joy. But, the dimensional pocket was collapsing beneath me. I was falling back to the lower planes.

The branching crystals collapsed into single facets and the windows returned to focus. The dimensional pocket we'd created was folding back, moving toward one of the windows. This was the moment we'd been waiting for.

I thrust my sword into the viewing-sphere while directing our combined magical energy toward the dimensional pocket. We focused our energy to force the pocket into that single window. I cried out with exertion as the energy channeled through me.

The sphere shattered, throwing my friends and me to the ground. I landed hard on my back, stunned.

I propped up on my elbows. "Did we do it?"

Inside our targeted window-facet, the disruptor wave dissipated, leaving only darkness. The other facets around it were now filled with light.

Kaiden grinned. "I think we did!"

Hoofy bowed his head. *"You have succeeded. The Overlords are now confined within the dimensional pocket, and this is the only exit."*

Toran rose to his feet and went to inspect the window. "Amazing."

I stood up and joined him next to the window. "A single exit point is one too many."

"Not sure we can do much about that," Kaiden said.

"There is," Hoofy stated. *"You can fold it so it will never be found."* He trotted to the facet's location and pointed his horn toward it. *"Elle, your sword is part of the crystalline network itself. It has the power to reform this plane of reality."*

"How do I—"

"Follow your instincts," he told me. *"The power is within you."*

I examined the area around the facet. I knew what I needed to do.

Trusting my gut, I traced the tip of my blade down the outer edges of the facets adjacent to the darkened section where the Saps were trapped. The two vertical lines glowed bright white. I then held my open right palm toward them, sending the same telekinetic energy commands I would to collapse matter. The two lines glowed brighter for a moment and then started to draw together, folding the dark facet backward and trapping it in a now-hidden fold between them. No one would ever find it unless they knew where to look.

"Wow," Kaiden murmured.

I let out a surprised laughed. "Did not know I could do that."

"Now that you have mastered your abilities, you can create a doorway to anywhere you wish," Hoofy revealed. *"This is a power to rival the Ancients."*

I stared at my sword. "Seriously?"

"You wield great power, I told you," Hoofy said. *"You have only*

scratched the surface of your potential. I would be honored to have the chance to join you in your future endeavors."

"Except, we're about to go back to our regular old selves," I muttered. At least, I assumed as much. I honestly had no idea what to expect from the upcoming universal reset.

"May I join you?" Hoofy asked, ignoring my comment.

"Of course!" Maris exclaimed. "I mean, five-year-old me would be furious if I turned down a unicorn companion."

I laughed. "Our families are going to have us committed if we breathe a word about what's happened."

"All the more reason to get the team back together as soon as possible," Kaiden said.

"Very true." I paused. "So, back to the *Evangiel?*"

"Actually, if you can make a doorway to anywhere, do we even need to go back to the *Evangiel* in order to get to Crystallis?" Maris asked.

"Everyone will be wondering where we are," Kaiden replied.

Maris shrugged. "But if we're about to do a universal reset, does it matter? They won't remember any of this, anyway."

Kaiden looked at me with longing. "That doesn't give us any time to celebrate our success."

My heart ached as I thought about the different ways the next several days we could go. One option was to return to the *Evangiel*—to celebrate, receive the thanks of the Hegemony, and share final moments of friendship and love, all the while knowing we were about to say goodbye. Or, we could return to the Master Archive now while the victory was fresh and get to our new futures that much sooner.

As much as I wanted more time with Kaiden, I couldn't bear the thought of growing even closer before it would all come to a sudden end. I wanted to save something for the reunion I had to believe was coming.

"I've never been one for long goodbyes," I said at last. My gaze met Kaiden's, and I saw the understanding in his eyes.

"Returning to my family is all I've ever wanted," Toran said. "The sooner, the better."

Maris frowned. "I wish I had something I was looking forward to back home. What I used to think was a pretty good life is now..." She faded out, shaking her head.

"We remembered before, we can remember again," I said. "We can find each other."

Kaiden took my hand. "We better."

Maris held up one finger. "Wait, what about the crystal shard? Don't we need that for a universal reset?"

"Not if we're in the Master Archive, I wouldn't think," Kaiden replied.

"What'll happen to that shard, then?" I asked.

Toran shrugged. "I'm not sure. But, that might not be a bad thing to have floating around somewhere. It's not like the average person would know how to use it or have access to a viewing-sphere."

"True, I guess you never know when something like that might be needed." I took a deep breath. "Okay, so we're decided?"

When my friends had nodded their assent, I took my sword in both hands and traced it through the air, picturing a doorway to the crystal cavern deep within the Master Archive. The air glowed bright white where the blade passed. After I had completed a full rectangle, the entire shape flashed white and then dissolved, leaving a gateway to our destination.

"I've gotta say, this is a *way* more convenient way to travel," I said.

Kaiden sighed. "Figures we'd learn about this trick *after* we complete our task."

Maris shrugged. "Who knows? Maybe we'll be called for future missions—or maybe even some adventures!"

"*I will find you then,*" Hoofy said. "*Your next stop is a place I cannot go.*" He faded from sight.

"Well, he seems confident enough," I said.

"Assuming we can ever find these artifacts again," Kaiden replied.

Toran flexed his hands in his gauntlets. "I imagine that if these items truly have become a part of us, and us of them, that reunion is inevitable."

"I hope so." I smiled, looking through the open doorway to the darkened Archive. "For now, let's put everything back how it should be."

IT WAS BITTERSWEET stepping through the passageway into the Master Archive on Crystallis. I hated the fact that our mission's success meant our time together was coming to an end—at least for now. We'd become a surrogate family in our weeks together, living through experiences no one else could possibly understand.

"I'm gonna miss you guys," I said, my heart heavy.

Toran nodded. "Likewise."

Maris started to tear up. "I'm not sure if I'm happy to be going home or sad this is over."

I gave her a hug and she squeezed me back. "Whatever future you want, go out and get it," I told her.

She nodded, pulling out of the embrace. "Same with you."

We walked slowly down the rock pathway leading to the crystal column for the Archive's interface. Having witnessed the crystalline network in our brief touch with the higher plane, I had even more reverence for this place.

"I have to admit, I wasn't sure this day would come," Kaiden said.

"Things were looking pretty bleak at a few points," I agreed. "There were times when I wasn't sure we'd make it through."

"Yeah, seriously." Maris shook her head. "The only thing that kept me from losing hope was Colren's assurance that there are future entries in the Archive, so I knew it would all work out."

"No," the mysterious voice in the Archive stated.

My heart skipped a beat, surprised by the sudden interjection. "Sorry, 'no' about what?"

"There are no records from the 'future'," the voice clarified.

Kaiden's brows drew together. "There aren't? Then what did the Hegemony observe to make them think they were seeing records of future events?"

"They misinterpreted the layered progression. No records exist beyond the furthest point of physical progression in spacetime." That didn't clear up matters in the least.

"I don't know what you mean," I admitted. "But why base everything around spacetime? There are so many other beings in the higher planes. Why is everything centered around us?"

"Because that is where we began, before we ascended," the voice replied.

"What did I tell you!" Toran looked rather pleased with himself.

"All right, that confirms it." I nodded. "And the 'Overlords'?"

"We encountered them when we first began to expand our consciousnesses. We sought to share with them, to stand as equals, but their spirits were too driven by greed for them to ascend."

"That explains the city ruins," I concluded. "Did everyone ascend?"

"Those who could did. Others ventured out from their home planet— you could consider them your ancestors who were brave enough to leave their oppressors behind. Much of the technology they brought with them was lost until recently," the voice explained.

"Stars..." Kaiden murmured.

"The ascended just let the Overlords take over their former world?" Maris asked.

"It wasn't ours or theirs. We resided in the same place on different planes. One could make no more claim to it than another. After ascension, many no longer cared about their roots. Others wished to maintain a connection to the corporeal realm, so we developed technology to allow our consciousness to take physical form when we desired."

Toran came to attention "The bioprinters! Those were originally used to enable the 10D pure-consciousness beings to take physical form?"

"That was their original purpose, yes," the voice confirmed. "You have found a... creative new use for them, which was needed in this time of crisis."

"No wonder we had so much influence over our attributes," Kaiden mused. "I guess the original design was quite literally to form a body based on the innermost desires of our consciousness, from the sound of it."

"Yeah, I guess so," I realized, absently running my fingers through my fuchsia hair.

"And what are *you*?" Maris asked. "Are you one of the ascended?"

"I am a… copy. A preservation of one of our leaders who has since moved on, just as those who guard the artifacts were created to endure beyond natural life."

"If you're already ascended, what's next?" Maris questioned.

The voice let out a musical laugh. "Words could never describe."

"Back to what you were saying before…" I said slowly. "Why do some of the records in the Archive look like they are future events, but you said they're not?"

"This place is the result of the physical cause and effect—the chain of the events—transpiring in your plane," the voice explained. "New records cannot be created until that path progresses, only previous states are overwritten."

"But there are records beyond the reset point," I protested. "How could those exist?"

The musical voice chuckled again. "These progressions don't have to happen at the same pace. The hours elapsed have not yet reached the point of a previous universal reset."

Suddenly, everything clicked for me. "Stars, that's it! We *did* win this battle against the Saps, but we hadn't lost yet after this amount of chronological time in another previous-future timeline."

"Ow, my head," Maris moaned.

Kaiden perked up. "Damn, you're right."

"There was never a 'bright future' ahead… it was only evidence of another reset loop where we waited longer before initiating a universal reset," Toran said.

Maris stared at him blankly. "I'm still lost."

Kaiden crouched down and traced his finger along the stone floor over the cavern, leaving a glowing, golden trail behind wherever he touched. "Okay, this is the timeline." He drew a narrow rectangle. "It goes on forever, but physical reality can be altered. Say some corn is growing and is almost ready for harvest." He filled in most of the box. "But then we reset back two weeks—that corn is now immature again." He drew a horizontal line through the shaded part of the box at the one-quarter mark. "Now, the corn needs to grow for two more weeks and then a little more until harvest," he traced his finger up the shaded area, "but it's only after it completes the growing cycle that it will be ready." He shaded in the remaining area of the box. "Up until that final stretch, it's just growing back to the growth point it achieved before the reset."

"And anything could happen to it after the reset," I chimed in. "There's no guarantee it will ever grow as well as it did that first time because the environmental conditions might change—or it might do better. But as far as any records in the Archive are concerned, everything up to the reset point already happened, and that same amount of time must elapse before new records are formed, versus adding a layer when looping over the same timeframe."

Maris thought for a few seconds. "Okay, so, if we were the corn, we grew faster than we did on one past loop leading up to the universal reset. The events from that old loop now *look* like the future only because we got to 'here' faster."

"Exactly," Toran said. "Just because we grew more efficiently, the overall rate that time passes isn't any different; planets will still orbit at their natural pace, cells will age. It's been, what, a little over a week since we sealed the Master Archive?"

Kaiden nodded. "Yeah, something like that."

"Well, a previous iteration may have taken two weeks, or a month. The future we thought the crystals showed was really just us being terrible on a previous loop."

I smiled. "Damn, this version of us is *good*."

Toran chuckled. "I suppose we are."

"After we catch up with that longest duration loop, it's back to etching untouched crystals, no more layering," Kaiden concluded.

I shook my head. "All this time when we thought the records showed a future of victory, but it was actually a record of failure."

Kaiden took a shaky breath. "But without that, we might not have believed we'd make it through."

"Maybe that's why we finally gave up and reset that first time," Maris said.

"Perhaps," I agreed. "And every time since, we've been trying to achieve the bright future we were convinced we must have—taking less and less time with each reset as our confidence grew, believing that victory was possible."

"That's pretty crazy when you look at it in those terms," Kaiden said.

"Yeah, it really is." I fell into quiet reflection. The hyperdimensional beings weren't beholden to the constant of time, but we still were—as strong as we had become. Despite all our abilities, hope remained one of the powerful most tools are our disposal.

"This next loop will be different," Maris said, breaking the silence. "No more Darkness."

"How long do we go back? Four months?" Kaiden questioned.

"Sounds about right." I shrugged, then groaned. "Ugh, I'll still be in school then."

"Hey, if our memories are as bad as they were on the other loops, you won't remember you've done it before," he pointed out.

"No, instead I might just have a frustrating case of déjà vu—as if senioritis isn't bad enough as it is." I chuckled. "Except, remembering all of the answers on my finals would be handy."

"Do you think we *will* remember anything?" Maris asked.

"We've never done a reset that far back, as far as we know," Toran replied. "I can only imagine that duration will exacerbate the recall issues we experienced with other universal resets. However, perhaps the Duzies in us will give us enough of a boost to retain some memories."

"Memories or not, our physical upgrades will be gone." I'd be going back to my injured self, but perhaps I could look into a corrective surgery on another world. The time for self-pity was far in my past.

"I would value the chance to reconnect, even if our magic is no longer present," Toran said.

"Yes, absolutely," I agreed.

We exchanged details about where each of us were residing before the Darkness came and how we could be reached on the Net. I didn't know how many details we'd retain after the universal reset, but it was worth a shot.

"What about the Hegemony?" Kaiden asked. "We saved civilization, and no one will ever know."

"Is it possible to leave a note somewhere?" I wondered.

"The Hegemony references the Archives' records," the mysterious voice offered. "This place will not be affected by the reset."

"Can you make some sort of entry about our team and what we did?" I asked it.

"Yes, but the Archive must be un-sealed for such modifications to be made."

Kaiden came to attention. "Oh, right! Almost forgot about that part."

"We'd like to unseal the Archive now. The threat has been neutralized." I grinned. "Always wanted to say that."

"Your intentions are pure," the voice replied. The crystal at the center of the platform flashed and then began to glow brightly. "The Archive is now active."

I nodded. "Please make a record that the four of us are the Dark Sentinels, and we—"

"Highlights from your memories will annotate the record," the voice replied. "It is done."

Maris looked taken aback. "Not sure I want everything in my mind, you know, hanging out there for anyone to look at."

"Yeah, I hope those 'highlights' are focused on the battle-y things and not… private stuff." I glanced at Kaiden and he gave me a knowing smile.

"The record will convey the necessary information," the voice stated.

"I guess that will have to do," Toran said.

Maris bit her lip. "Is that everything, then?"

I looked around at my friends. "Yeah, I guess it is. Everyone ready?"

"No. One more thing." Kaiden took me by the waist with one hand cupped the other around the back of my head, drawing me in for a kiss.

I felt awkward at first with Maris and Toran standing right there, but I blocked them out. Nothing could be allowed to ruin that moment, knowing this would be our last together in… I had no idea how long.

We parted, and he leaned his forehead against mine. "This isn't goodbye."

I fought back the lump my throat. "I know."

When we turned back to Toran and Maris, I saw they had wandered away to give us some privacy. "Okay, the grand romantic moment has passed," I said.

Maris turned around, flashing a smile. "I would have been disappointed if there wasn't one."

Toran chuckled. "Time to go home?"

Kaiden nodded. "Yeah, it is."

We gathered around the column at the center of the platform.

"We'll find each other," I emphasized, as much for myself as them.

Kaiden gave my hand one last squeeze. "We will."

Toran smiled. "We really did it. We stopped the Darkness and now everything will go back to how it was."

"Not everything," I replied. "We'll be different."

He nodded. "Yes, I suppose we will be."

"Well, it's been great," Maris said with a grin. "Terrifying and maddening, but great."

"Couldn't have had a better team." I smiled back. "See you around."

EPILOGUE

TWO MONTHS BEFORE the end of school, I started to remember.

It was just flashes at first, no more than fragments of a half-remembered dream. But, as the weeks passed, the images became vivid—previous-future memories of another life. I had been a warrior, a partner, and a leader. I had fulfilled my aspirations and become a hero in a way I never imagined was possible.

With the thrill of the discovery came the harsh realization that I couldn't tell anyone. Unless the Hegemony managed to uncover our message in the Master Archive, there would be no documentation for what the Dark Sentinels had done to save our worlds. My memories were of a reality that would never come to pass, at least not as it had unfolded before the universal reset. The only people who would believe me were my teammates. We'd vowed to reunite, in whatever bodies we now possessed, and I intended to keep that promise.

I was nervous about meeting them again—for them to see me in a damaged body, unable to move in the ways I had before. I knew they would be different, too, but I'd always taken comfort in the knowledge that they'd gotten to know me in a form that matched how I'd always viewed myself on the inside. Except, as I came to accept that there was nothing I could do about it, I started to transform.

The changes came slowly. First, my injured shoulder ached less in the morning, and I didn't get winded as easily during gym class at school. As time went on, I continued to feel more vibrant, stronger. By the time graduation rolled around, others had started to notice I was different.

I brushed off the observations for as long as I could, but when my hair began growing fuchsia at the roots, my parents insisted I visit our family doctor for a full physical. Scans revealed that my shoulder had completely healed, and I was as physically conditioned as a seasoned athlete. Defying all conventional medical explanation, the doctor justified it as a delayed 'growth spurt'. I played along, but I knew the truth: the Duzies were still inside me. They were a part of me, and I was forever changed.

The reset had rolled me back to a base state, but the zepto-exotic singularities had been gradually recharging my body, allowing me to return to the state that my higher dimensional consciousness longed for me to have. I had no way to be certain if my magic-casting abilities would also return, but I was compelled to find my friends like we'd agreed, to see if we still shared the kinship we'd developed during our time together.

Through some careful sleuthing on the Net, we made contact and set our rendezvous for Falstan II, where Kaiden was in the middle of a research study that required his presence.

I broached the topic with my parents in terms of a post-graduation trip, making the case that interstellar travel would broaden my horizons and help me decide on a career path. Adrianne and Jiro had asked to come, eager to get away from our remote world and see the rest of the Hegemony. I let them down as gently as I could, explaining that this was something I needed to do on my own. In the fashion of true friends, they wished me well and promised we'd get together as soon as I returned. I didn't tell them that I might not come back, at least not for a long time. As much as I loved my family and friends, my experience in the previous-future had fundamentally altered my life outlook. Erusan was no longer my home; I belonged among the stars.

Seasonal work for the month following graduation allowed me to scrape together enough money to fund a ticket off my homeworld. I wasn't sure what to expect on Falstan II when I arrived, but I promised myself to take everything in stride.

After a grueling slog aboard a budget civilian transport ship, I finally arrived at my destination. Falstan II was a small world, relatively barren in appearance from space, with only a handful of green patches where industrious settlers had set up agricultural operations. I boarded a shuttle headed for a port on the small northern continent.

I stepped off the shuttle into the quiet port, tended only by an elderly man who seemed content to read the news and nap while on his shift.

"Can you direct me toward Holloway Farms?" I asked him, hoisting my backpack onto my shoulders.

He cracked open an eye. "Holloway? It's up Route 7 to the northeast. Not much reason to head up to those parts."

"I think I'll find what I'm looking for." I smiled to myself. "Is there any public transport headed that way?"

"You can take the Number 2 bus as far as Independence. You can walk from there," the old man replied.

"Thank you."

I located a stop for the bus number he'd indicated and rode it to the town twenty kilometers away. Independence was little more than a fueling station and grocery store, but the locals were able to direct me toward the road that led the rest of the way to Holloway Farms.

I took a leisurely pace on the three-kilometer walk, enjoying the warm sun and the dirt road beneath my feet. The quiet was a welcome change from the tight quarters and constant mechanical hum during the previous part of my journey.

Eventually, I reached a sign marking the official facility entrance. My stomach fluttered, knowing I was only minutes from seeing my friends again.

Three structures—a large house, a cabin, and an industrial lab—were positioned along the access road. A man in his late-fifties emerged from the house as I approached.

"Can I help you?" he asked.

"Hi," I greeted. "I'm here for the reunion—a friend of Kaiden's."

"Yes, yes! Welcome. I'm Bill Holloway." The man extended his hand.

I shook it. "Happy to meet you, Bill. I'm Elle. Thank you for hosting us."

He smiled. "Our pleasure. The farm's been too empty and lonely since the kids moved out. Susie always loves to cook for a group."

"Sounds like we came to the right place." I looked around. "Where is—"

"Elle!" a high-pitched voice called out, followed by rapid footsteps on wooden stairs.

I turned to see Maris barreling toward me. "Hi!"

She wrapped her arms tightly around me as soon as she was close enough, almost knocking me off balance. "I can't believe we're finally back together!"

"I know, this is surreal." I pulled back so I could examine her at arm's length. She looked almost identical to the last time I saw her in my previous-future memories—same wavy, dark hair, curvy figure, and bright eyes, though it was strange to see her in normal street clothes.

Maris gently ran her fingers along a length of my hair. "You weren't kidding about the fuchsia hair coming back! That's wild."

I grinned. "I know! Freaked my parents out."

"How'd you explain it?"

"I didn't. Not well, anyway." I glanced at Bill, not wanting to say too much in front of him. "You know how it is."

"Yeah, I got off easy. Wait until you see Toran." Maris nodded toward the house.

The door opened a moment later, and a large man stepped outside— not quite the behemoth I'd traveled with, but formidable nonetheless. "Stars!" My jaw dropped.

"Hello, Elle," he greeted. "I'm glad you made it."

"Toran, wow!" I gave him a hug as soon as he jogged over, my arms barely wrapping around his torso. His muscular physique was a scaled-back version of how I remembered him, but seeing him with dark hair threw me off.

"How was your trip?" he asked, his voice still deep and warm.

I smiled. "I have to say, it was kind of nice being put under for the hyperspace jumps. Budget travel, but it wasn't all bad. The food was better than on the *Evangiel*!"

He laughed. "It doesn't take much to top that bar."

"I'll, uh, leave you to your pleasantries," Bill interjected. "Would you like me to take your pack to your room for you?"

"Oh, that would be great, thanks." I slid off my backpack and handed it to him. "Thank you again for having us."

He nodded. "Dinner will be in an hour."

"Great, see you then." I smiled.

We waited for Bill to enter the house.

"Talk about a transformation!" I said as soon as Bill was out of sight.

Toran chuckled. "Caught me by surprise when it first started to happen. Fortunately, the memories had started to surface, so at least I had some idea about what was going on."

"How'd your wife react?" I asked.

"Shocked and concerned, at first." Toran shook his head, his eyes sparkling. "I had no choice but to tell her what had happened. Took a little convincing, but," he gestured to himself with both hands, "I had some good physical evidence to back up my story. Once she got used to the idea, she wanted to come meet all of you, but she couldn't get time off from work. And then there's Leia's school, of course... But, we'd love to have the three of you come for a visit on Dunlore, if you're interested."

"That sounds great, Toran. I'd love to meet your family," I said.

"We'll need to decide if we should reveal ourselves to the Hegemony," Toran stated.

I shrugged. "Maybe they'll find that message we left. But, for now, I'm happy all of the worlds are safe."

Maris shook her head. "It's like it never happened—except, we know it did."

"Brought us together!" I said.

Toran smiled. "Whoever would have thought we'd all end up as friends?"

Maris laughed. "*Not* me! I still can't believe we're all here."

I looked around. "Speaking of which, where's Kaiden?"

"Ah, right!" Toran exclaimed. "I'm sure you're anxious to see him. He's still out in the fields."

Maris smirked. "We'll give you two some privacy."

"You should be able to find him out that way." Toran gestured to the west.

"Thanks." I took a slow breath. "I'll see you in a bit."

"Elle." Maris gave me another hug. "It's great to see you again."

I smiled. "You too."

"I'm looking forward to getting to know this other version of you," Toran said.

"Likewise. I knew we'd find our way back to each other."

He patted my shoulder. "Things are now as they should be."

With a renewed wave of nerves, I headed toward the western field. The crop was still young, barely reaching my knees. Despite the clear visibility across the flat field, I didn't see anyone at first. After a minute of fighting the glare from the afternoon sun, I finally spotted the back of a young man with medium-brown hair crouched down, collecting a sample.

"Hey," I called out, approaching him.

He straightened and turned around. Instant recognition filled his sky-blue eyes, and his lips spread in a warm smile. "Hey yourself."

I smiled back, trying to play it cool as I strolled toward Kaiden. He was just as handsome as I remembered in my previous-future memories. "Nice place you have here."

He surveyed the field. "It's been fine for the past few months."

"And now?"

He stepped forward to meet me. "Now, you're here."

We ran the last several paces and embraced. He scooped me up in his arms and held me close.

I buried my face in the crook of his neck. "I missed you."

"I missed you, too," he murmured into my hair.

Our lips met in a passionate kiss, as comfortable and familiar as two longtime lovers after a prolonged separation.

Breathlessly, we pulled apart, laughing with joy to be back with one another. I entwined my fingers in his, never wanting to let go again.

"What now?" I asked, looking into his eyes.

"Well, I'm not sure how long Toran and Maris intend to stay, but I'll need another month to finish this research study. After that…"

I nodded and squeezed his hands. "I have nowhere else I want to be."

Kaiden turned so his back was to the farmhouse. "Good, because things could get interesting." He pulled his right hand free from mine, and electricity danced across his fingertips.

I grinned. "Oh, this is going to be fun."

THE END

AUTHOR'S NOTES

Thank you for reading the Dark Stars trilogy!

I had the idea for this series floating around in my head for a long time, and it wasn't until this year that the timing worked out for me to finally write it.

I first started playing video games in my late-teens—well after many of my peers. For the longest time, I thought games were all Mario-style "platformers" or racing-style games, and I didn't know the genre of role playing games (RPGs) even existed. *Chrono Trigger* was the first RPG I played, and I found it to be like an interactive novel. After I played *Final Fantasy VII* next, I was hooked.

One play mechanic I always found interesting in these games was that when you got a "game over", you could reset and try again with some knowledge of what was coming. With boss battles, in particular, there was almost always a trick to beating them that you could apply from the get-go on subsequent attempts. The *characters* didn't know what was coming, but you as the player did.

I started thinking about how to mimic that precognizance in literary form where the characters were in control of their own destiny without an omniscient player to guide them. And thus, Dark Stars was born.

With that said, there are several assumptions about the story universe that are touched upon but didn't get fully explored in the book's narrative. If you're curious about the universal mechanics, read on :-).

Q: What is the dimensional hierarchy, and what's in each dimension?

3D – normal physical reality

4D – time

5D – telepathy/thought

6D – Toran's gauntlets artifact; Saps/Overlords

7D – Kaiden's circlet; Hoofy and other 'mythical' beings (unicorns, dragons, etc.)

8D – Maris' shield artifact; window maze; nimbuses (nimbuses also have a 7D component)

9D – Elle's sword artifact; crystalline network connections/storage
10D –Consciousness
11D –Duzies

Q: **How does the 'magic' work?**
A: The 11D dimensionally ubiquitous, zepto-elemental singularities
('Duzies') enable the apparent magic. The team's hyperdimensional
artifacts concentrated and intensify Duzie energy. Kaiden's circlet
functions like a magic antenna that allows his non-magical staff
weapon to become super-saturated with Duzies, making it a
concentrated director of magic. As the team's bodies become
saturated by Duzies, they are more readily able to cast their own
magic without their artifacts.

Q: **Why could only 'viewing-spheres' be used for dimensional
transitions and not normal crystals?**
A: Crystals only exist in 3D spacetime while viewing-spheres span all
dimensions. Crystals are Duzie-saturated normal matter. Viewing-
spheres are Duzies in pure solid form.

Q: **Do all planets that exist in spacetime also have extended existence
in higher dimensions in some form or another?**
A: The planets have a distinct physical presence in 6D, 7D, and 8D. In
5D, 9D, and 10D, all mass is amorphous 'dark matter' which supports
thought channeling and network storage. In 11D, all matter is pure
Duzie-plasma.

Q: **Why do Darkness planets have reduced-gravity in normal
spacetime?**
A: The anomaly-related, Duzie-powered Darkness draws power from
transmutation of planet's mass, reducing its density but not
disturbing its magnetic field or geologic underpinnings.

Q: **Why did the anomaly site in space where the aliens first appeared
have excess gravity but no apparent mass?**
A: The dimensional-rift anomaly channeled and concentrated normal

matter and dark matter gravity from nearby systems across extended dimensions into 3D spacetime at a central point. The 6D aliens used this unique site as a staging ground for their intended invasion from their home plane.

I hope you enjoyed this story and found it to be a satisfying blend of sci-fi and fantasy. I've loved both genres for as long as I can remember, and I'm excited to have been able to merge the two in what I hope was a fun, unique way.

I couldn't have brought this book to market without the amazing team helping me behind the scenes.

My fantastic team of beta readers helped craft this book into what it is today. Jim Dean, in particular, was instrumental in helping me articulate the hyperdimensional concepts. Special thanks to Kurt, Eric, Pam, Liz, Troy, John, and Randy, you have incredible insights and I love your honest feedback! I appreciate you saying the tough truths and pushing me to bring my writing to the next level.

I also owe huge thanks to my proofing team to add the final polish. Nick, Charlie, John, Diane, Leo, and Jim, thank you for your time and eagle eyes. You are fantastic, and I'm so happy you have my back! Thank you for your continued support and for donating your time to helping me turn dreams into reality.

On the personal side, my husband, Nick, has been my greatest cheerleader. He kept me fed and sane during the late nights of working, and I'm forever thankful to him for enabling me to pursue a career writing full-time. He is the best friend and life partner I could ever imagine.

Thank you again for reading the Dark Stars trilogy! Readers like you are who enable me to be a full-time author, and I'm so thankful to you for making that possible. If you'd like to see future stories in this universe, please let me know in your review or send me a message via the contact form on my website. In the meantime, look for other new books in the coming months :-). Happy reading!

ALSO BY A.K. DUBOFF

Dark Stars Trilogy
Book 1: Crystalline Space
Book 2: A Light in the Dark
Book 3: Masters of Fate

Cadicle Space Opera Series
Book 1: Rumors of War (Vol. 1-3)
Book 2: Web of Truth (Vol. 4)
Book 3: Crossroads of Fate (Vol. 5)
Book 4: Path of Justice (Vol. 6)
Book 5: Scions of Change (Vol. 7)

Mindspace Series
Book 1: Infiltration
Book 2: Conspiracy
Book 3: Offensive
Book 4: Endgame

Troubled Space
Vol. 1: Brewing Trouble
Vol. 2: Stealing Trouble
Vol. 3: Making Trouble

ABOUT THE AUTHOR

Nebula-nominated and *USA Today* bestselling author A.K. (Amy) DuBoff has always loved science fiction in all its forms—books, movies, shows and games. If it involves outer space, even better!

Now a full-time author, Amy can frequently be found traveling the world. When she's not writing, she enjoys wine tasting, binge-watching TV series, and playing epic strategy board games.

To learn more or connect, visit www.amyduboff.com.